I0591047

THE EPIMETHEUS TRIAL

BOOK THREE

BEYOND THE VEIL

E. A. SETSER

The Epimetheus Trial

Elder Blood

Into Antiquity

Beyond the Veil

.

To Celia

For putting up with my ramblings and stupid humor

Also for the blue rose iconography

Prologue

Truth is a matter of degrees

Perception one of layers

Within the folds of reality

Between the reaches of the senses

Do the broken lie

Tending their wounds

Mending their strength

Yet no matter how steadfast

None are immune to corruption

Toxicity infiltrates anything

Madness poisons anyone

For as beneath is buried hope

So beyond awaits despair

Chapter 1

Galo shifted in his hospital bed, bracing himself on a pair of leather-bound books by his side. His attention shifted between the cards in his hand and the heap on the over-bed table. With a gravelly cough, he laid a card face up and took another from the deck.

"Your cough is getting worse," Gabdur noted, "You ought to have that looked at."

"It's nothing," Galo insisted, scratching the bloody gauze on his inner elbow, "Just the weather. I'm unaccustomed to changing latitudes this fast."

"Sure, that might be it," Gabdur said from in the adjacent bed, "That or you donated too soon."

"They were low on blood supplies. Would you rather I'd left you needing?" Galo argued, "Besides, I got approval from the ship physician."

"Well, that's because he's stupid."

"And you wouldn't have cleared me?"

"No, I wouldn't," Gabdur said, "Not after all that mortar dust you inhaled. And especially not this soon after your coma. You shouldn't even have volunteered."

"I risked my health for you, and you can't thank me," Galo snipped as he slapped his next card down, "The least you could do is not chastise me, and you can't even manage that."

"I'm sorry. You were just trying to help. And with so much troubling you," Gabdur sighed, sitting up, "I expect you're not quite at terms with everything that happened."

"And you're not?" Galo challenged, "It was two nights ago. Get back to me in two years. Maybe I'll have a clear head about it by then."

"My work with The Coalition has me at an advantage here," Gabdur said, "Not to say I'm not troubled by it, but I've learned things that have made it easier to put these things in perspective."

"Maybe I should join them," Galo muttered, more musing than seriously considering.

"But all that work didn't prepare me for any of this," Gabdur confessed, "I put all this thought and effort into dealing with grandiose crises, but I'm clueless when it comes to being a father to you."

"I'm a grown man, Gabdur," Galo insisted, "Not a child in need of rearing."

"You can argue your age all you want," Gabdur dismissed, "The fact is, were I a better father, I would know what to say at a time like this."

Galo sighed and shifted in his seat. He rubbed the head of the Serpent Bracer, Leviathan's murmurings sending vibrations up his arm. He took his move and laid his hand out on the table.

"Remchuk," he said, "Care to go another round?"

"I think you've beaten me thoroughly enough," Gabdur said as he straightened the deck, "Are you ready to talk about the Heniokhos Disaster?"

"Not yet," Galo said, "I need to focus on my research for now."

"I understand," Gabdur nodded, "But are you positive you want to go through with this?"

"It isn't so much that I want to as that I have to."

"Yes, but have you considered the repercussions?"

"I thought the repercussions were what you were after," Galo challenged, "Wasn't this the whole reason The Coalition removed you from Berinin?"

"To an extent," Gabdur conceded, "But if they thought this sort of collateral damage was acceptable, they would have just had me do this myself."

"Collateral damage?" Galo scoffed, "Anyone who permits child abduction and slavery is in no place to talk about acceptable collateral damage."

"Fair criticism. So, consider this coming from me. Not as a member of The Coalition. But as an individual," Gabdur said, "Are you prepared for the consequences?"

"And what else would you have me do?" Galo asked, "The tradition you set out to undo is impeding us because you couldn't follow through on the revolution you started."

Conditions in Berinin had yet to favor an upheaval of the Chieftain Bloodline. But he knew Galo wouldn't accept that. Regardless of who was accountable, Gabdur knew he had failed Berinin.

"My alleged death created civil unrest," Gabdur explained, "To hear Mortvill tell it, Berinin should have been stable enough for me to conventionally sire a child within a decade."

"What stopped you, then?"

"The ancestor posing as my father refused any involvement with The Coalition. Berinin was in the hands of a man far out of his element, and we were helpless to stabilize it."

Galo scoffed. "Perhaps, The Omnimath should have thought of that before he sent NalSet to drag you away."

"Perhaps," Gabdur shrugged, "But nobody said his predictions are absolute. He deals in probabilities."

"I remember how you said NalSet explained it to you. The outcome is usually between the two most likely possibilities," Galo said, "But what do you do with unanticipated outcomes?"

Gabdur sighed. "… We improvise."

"Think of this," Galo said, gesturing first to his books, then to Gabdur, "as that."

A Northlander woman entered the infirmary, carrying a black kit under her arm. Gabdur signaled to her to wait and turned back to Galo.

"I suppose I'll have to make peace with your decision, but think about what I said."

"I'll keep it in mind."

Galo tucked the books under his arm and rose from his bed as Gabdur waved the woman over. Galo gave her a cordial nod and greeting as they passed one another. He stopped by the door, looking back as the visitor opened the makeup kit.

"It was nice catching up with you, Aleepo," he said.

Gabdur inclined his head to Galo, then faced the makeup artist. He sat stone-faced as she worked, masking his discomfort at what was to come and the role his decisions had placed him in.

The revolution would come to Berinin.

He who would have been Chieftain Sage would watch as a stranger.

And for his failures and hesitation, Masnethege would fall.

Later that afternoon, Galo and Gabdur disembarked at the Berinin annex island. They hung back at the recently built pier while other passengers headed inland or scattered along the beach.

"This is where you found the lab?" Gabdur asked, scanning the tropical landscape.

"We believe we have, yes," Galo said as he walked, "Some researchers uncovered a suspiciously modern-looking wall."

"Odd. Middle of nowhere. No front. No way to hide it within its environment," Gabdur said, "Not that I don't believe you, but this isn't how they usually operate."

"We think this is where they infected Sinkua," Galo said, "Perhaps, it was a matter of opportunity and necessity."

"Quite the trouble to get at one Hybrid."

"Seems reasonable after they built a prison over a mechanical maze just to get at me."

"You were a means to an end. They needed the Serpent Bracer and the Chieftain Bloodline. Once they knew about me, they weren't so concerned with you."

"A means to an end?" Galo considered, "Yes, I see what you're getting at. They meant to use me to kill Leviathan and collide a chunk of ArcNos with Tanelen. Nikasu, they used for experimentation and to keep Malia on a short leash."

"So, if they built a lab here to infect Sinkua, it must go beyond that," Gabdur said, "If all they wanted was to corrupt him, they would have dragged him into any of their labs in ArcNos."

"Perhaps, they had to wait until he tapped into his pyromancy," Galo grasped, leading Gabdur along a riverbank, "The microtumors might have stunted his development otherwise."

"Wouldn't have made a difference. Consider Nikasu. They doped her with psychotropics, and her gravimancy came along just fine," Gabdur argued, "It's not impossible, but history suggests his pyromancy wasn't a factor in their timing."

Knots twisted in Gabdur's abdomen as a distantly familiar face greeted them. Time hadn't been kind to his face, but his baritone cadence remained as it always had.

"So, the kids told the truth this time," Nenbard remarked, "It's been like a game for them, sending us off to fetch you. Much as I'd love to tell them to bug off, Sanus insists I humor them."

"Judge Nenbard," Galo smiled, "I hoped we'd find you here."

"Yes, until sundown," Nenbard said. He nodded toward Gabdur. "Giving him a tour?"

"Briefing him on our work," Galo explained, "We met in ArcNos after I was released from prison. He rehabilitates survivors of Avatar labs. I believe he may be of help to us here."

"Judge and Interim Chieftain Sage Nenbard. It's an honor to meet you," Gabdur beamed, taking in twenty-five years of aging as he offered a handshake, "My name is Aleepo. I hope I can be of service to all of you here."

"Ahh, Aleepo. I've heard of you. You're responsible for the blue roses in Ferya," Nenbard noted, "Never realized you were a fellow Berininite. Your name sounds more…"

"I was born in Poravit to Berininite parents."

"And they opted for a local name," Nenbard nodded. He turned to Galo, flicking occasional side-eye toward Aleepo. "So, did you bring him here expecting to find survivors?"

"No, I brought him because he's the closest we can safely get to a first-hand account of life inside," Galo said.

"Of course. Sorry for the indiscretion. I've been a touch on edge," Nenbard said, "By the way, what's become of your arm, Aleepo? Avatars catch word of your rehab program?"

"Something to that effect," Aleepo said, "Found myself in an incident on account of a certain patient."

"Quite the trouble over a single patient," Nenbard said, studying Aleepo's eyes.

"We're getting off topic here," Galo interjected, "What has you so troubled and on edge? It can't just be the children fibbing about my return."

"We're behind schedule, and there's no sign of it getting any better."

"Does everyone always leave by sundown?"

"Not by my orders, but yes," Nenbard said, "Between current affairs in the Northlands, your abduction, and the anniversaries of the Battle of Masnethege and the ArcNosian Civil War, your townspeople have mounted a convincing opposition to being away from the Sacred City past dusk."

"What about the workers not from Masnethege?" Aleepo asked, rubbing his stump.

"Somehow, this island is an extension of Masnethege," Nenbard said, eyeing Galo, "Excavation by torch and candle doesn't exactly fit the parameters of the Workplace Safety Act."

"I assume full responsibility for that," Galo said, ignoring Nenbard's glare, "I forget who saddled my proposal with that condition because I had thought nothing of it. But I've been researching the means to rectify the matter."

"See that you do," Nenbard demanded, "Will you request the minutes from that Assembly, or would you have me do it for you?"

"I'll deal with the matter personally," Galo insisted, "For now, return to your day's work. Aleepo and I will await you by the pier. See that any other site managers join us."

Galo turned and walked away, leaving Nenbard to quell his temper alone as Aleepo followed.

They returned the way they had come. Galo kept his eyes fixed forward as his thoughts diverged between his plan and Nenbard's embittered disposition.

The two sat on the end of the pier. Gabdur groaned as his joints creaked. Galo hocked a throatful of dark phlegm into the ocean. He darted a glance at Gabdur, hoping he hadn't noticed.

"Have you always known Nenbard to be that ornery?" Gabdur asked.

"I was thinking to ask you the same," Galo said as he drew his legs into a lotus position, "Was he that irritable when he was your student?"

"Never."

"Clearly, the stress is getting to him," Galo concluded, "Should he come to run for my office, I don't think I would endorse his campaign."

"I would advise you to remain silent on the entire affair. Otherwise, your unprecedented act will be mired by malcontents and conspiracy theorists," Gabdur said, "Though, should you choose to involve yourself, there's certainly merit to ArcNos's Ministries and Parliament. The Late Chairman aside."

"He did need to go to extraordinary lengths, at that," Galo nodded, "I'll take both thoughts into consideration. Thank you."

They passed the hours with increasingly idle conversation. Spans of silence stretched in correlation with their shadows.

Tiny sparks crested the horizon shortly after sunset, growing into torch flames as they approached. Galo and Gabdur stepped down from the pier while shiphands moored the ferry that had just arrived.

Nenbard and four others stopped before Galo and Aleepo and posted their torches in the sand. Their shared silence grew palpable as they waited for the workers to pass. The shiphands remained on the dock after the last of them boarded the ferry.

"Well, you two look to be enjoying the view," Nenbard snipped, "Having a nice little chat while we wait, are we?"

"Oh good, you're here," Galo said. He gestured to the pier. "Take a seat. We need to have a talk. Pleasure to see the rest of you, by the way. I'll address your concerns shortly."

"Yes, we certainly do," Nenbard sneered, "What do you plan to do about this fiasco you've created?"

"I'll address that momentarily, but first we need to speak of your handling matters in my absence," Galo said, "I accepted that you would serve as Interim Chieftain Sage because I thought I could trust you. But if I had known you'd be this troubled by technological limitations, I would have asked that the office be left to a Masnethegean child instead."

"Chieftain Sage Galo, sir, do you suppose you're being a mite harsh?" Aleepo asked.

"Excuse me, but who are you?" a middle-aged woman asked.

"Oh, where are my manners? My name is Aleepo," he said, "I run a rehab program for Avatar lab escapees."

"Nenbard may have mentioned that," she nodded, "I'm Sanus, Nenbard's wife. Do you like tea, Aleepo?"

"I happen to love…"

"Yes, run aboard and prepare the tea. Just as you always do," a man a few years her junior dismissed, "Before you ask, my name is Ocronn. I'm her brother."

"Excuse me?" Sanus asked, rubbing her wrist, "What are you implying?"

"Are they always like this when they work together?" Galo asked the last two crew managers.

"They're siblings," Borret said, "Of course they are."

"Well, that explains our problem," Nalygen added, "We're not incompatible. You just behave like a colossal ass because you think you're meant to."

"Both pairs are like this every night," Nenbard supplied, "Anything we've accomplished has been largely by happenstance."

"Have they long been like this?" Aleepo asked.

"Oh, damned if I know," Nenbard brushed off, "I've been far too busy trying to get anything done at all in our sparse hours."

"What a pathetic display of leadership," Galo derided, "You've grown entirely too spoiled with your modern conveniences."

"Exactly who are you calling spoiled?" Sanus asked.

"You, you, and you," Galo said, pointing to Sanus, Nenbard, and Ocronn, "Had either of these two been in charge, I wouldn't have come home to this mess."

"Sir, do you really think so?" Borret asked.

"Shut up, Borret. I'm still talking," Galo dismissed, "I came here prepared to set out on an act of revolution, but you sniveling tits have reduced it to a matter of pity with your incessant bickering and excuses."

"What are you getting on about?" Ocronn demanded, his patience depleted by the string of eloquent insults.

"Masnethege will abandon its tradition of technological stagnation," Galo announced, "As long as we hold on to this antiquated custom, we can never truly work with the rest of Ouristihra or even Berinin itself. Despite my belief that the people of Masnethege have thrived under this limitation, it has come to my attention how it endangers us."

"Chieftain Sage Galo, sir, think of the history you're discarding," Nalygen gasped, "Surely, you can't just cast off centuries of tradition with an announcement and a pen stroke."

"I thought the same, but it turns out that I can. That custom was only immune to the Chieftain Sage's authority until two hundred years ago. So, I only need the approval of our Chieftain Heir, which we don't have, and our Union Parliament Judge," Galo explained, "Judge Nenbard. Any objections?"

"None from me, sir," Nenbard said.

"In that case, I'll begin scouting excavation crews tomorrow. And at the next Ouristihran Union Assembly, I will enact the Reestablishment Protocol," Galo said, "Stay clear of the dig site in the meantime."

"Until then, I'd like to look over your safety equipment," Aleepo added, "I fear that prolonged exposure may have already been problematic."

Elemeno pulled a framed painting from the wall. She cleared her throat and sighed as she sat at the foot of the bed. A lump grew in her throat as she ran her thumb along the edges of the frame. Tears welled up, which was fitting as the scene was perceived through bleary eyes.

Edged with melted shades of black and gray, the painting showed a one-story stone building isolated by a dense forest. Those aged trees would later become a city. Elemeno now knew this vision to be a product of Nikasu's recurring nightmare.

She returned the picture to the wall and took another, more recent painting. A distorted image of Gabdur stood behind prison bars. Sinkua accompanied him, appearing as contrite as he did vicious. But the perspective was misleading, as closer inspection proved the vision to be from within the cell.

Elemeno fixated on Gabdur as she combed through memories of Eytea's last visit. She lifted her head, eyes drifting much of their own accord. She rose as her eyes settled on blue roses in oil paint.

Leaving the painting of Galo's nightmare on the bed, Elemeno took the one of Sinkua's dream of a memory. Eytea knelt in a patch of blue roses, her wings unmarred. Even in the deepest recesses of his mind, Sinkua could only see the best in her.

Elemeno searched the landscape, immersing herself in the scenery. Her eyes fell shut, the scent of blue roses seeming to waft from the canvas. She recalled Eytea's story of that place. Amber leaves drifted to the ground in her mind's eye. Cicadas chirped around her. A name appeared on a wooden sign.

Country Living Bed & Breakfast.

She had found the answer to her mourning. Not an end, but the means to make use of it. She didn't know how to find them, but now, she knew how to have them find her. Elemeno headed to the hall closet to fetch her suitcases. Her home had become unbearable with painful memories.

Chapter 2

Malia studied the gnarled street sign, its twisted post encased in thick frost. She twirled her finger as she mumbled to herself. Frustrated, she craned her neck and looked back down the ruinous boulevard for some other indication.

"We should have asked EshCal for landmarks," she sighed, "Do either of you remember what street we're on?"

"We're on East Springs," Nikasu said, "We turn left, go four blocks, then hang a right. The epicenter is just east of the intersection of Calatin and Sechoria."

"You memorized the directions?" Malia asked, rereading the last page of EshCal's convoluted directions.

Nikasu notched the ice with the tips of her scythes, jerking Malia from her notes. With a pair of scissoring backhand swings, she wedged the inner curve of each blade in the loosened ice.

Silverish violet light crackles from her scythes, amplifying the pull of gravity on the ice. Crystals buckled and collapsed into each other. Her arms trembled under her milystic effort as the icy encasement shattered under its own weight.

"I simplified them," Nikasu asserted, as though uncovering the twisted post made the matter perfectly clear, "See? East Springs."

Malia looked up and down the post, mentally uncoiling it. Her eyes, however, betrayed her concentration as they fixated somewhere beyond her task. She blinked hard, forcing herself back into the moment.

Nikasu rubbed the back of her neck, gritting her teeth as Malia mumbled to herself. Her hand swept around to her forehead, smearing sweat down her frost-reddened face. Her grinding teeth yielded to a shout of frustration, but Vielle cut her off at the first syllable.

"Hey!" Vielle called over, "Come on. I can see Calatin Street."

"She headed left," Malia pointed, "I guess you were right."

"Damn right, I was right," Nikasu muttered, "I don't know why you brought me here if you won't listen to me."

"I never said I'm not listening to you," Malia sighed, "I just... I need to see it for myself. I can't... Um... You understand."

"No. You know what I'm capable of. So why can't you trust me? Is it because you can't be trusted? I've heard liars have trust issues."

"What? I... No!" Malia protested, alarmed by the calmness of the accusation, "I've just learned better than to always take people's word at face value. Especially when someone important to me is at stake."

"You didn't think of that before you traded me for a seat at an Avatar dinner party to pick up loose gossip?" Nikasu seethed.

"Nikasu!"

Malia whipped around, staring dumbfounded.

"Is that why you brought me to get Phylus back?" Nikasu continued, "You gambled me once and came out okay, so what the heck?"

"Nikasu," Malia urged, "Where did you get that idea?"

"At least I'm better off than Vielle. Obviously, you brought her because she's expendable."

"Excuse me?"

"Was she always expendable since she's one more Hybrid than The Omnimath planned for?" Nikasu bombarded, "Or is it only now that she's planted Yggdrasil?"

"Is this about what happened in ArcNos?" Malia ventured.

"A lot happened in ArcNos," Nikasu grumbled, shouldering past her, "You're the last person I want to talk to about it."

"Hey, Nikasu!" Vielle called, perching atop a heap of wreckage, "Come up and look at this crater."

"You can see the epicenter?" Malia asked.

Vielle nodded with an almost childlike excitement, her eyes flicking toward Nikasu. She and Malia held a moment's eye contact, surreptitiously nodding aside. An ephemeral, anxious grin flickered across Malia's lips.

"I'll meet you on the other side. I can't climb like I used to," Malia insisted, "But I want to hear how the view is from up there."

Nikasu headed for the mound as Malia walked away. Her momentum carried her a short way up the slope until she crouched to brace herself. Her eyes glazed as she alternated her milystic influence between diminishing gravity as she stepped and intensifying as she settled.

Vielle grabbed her hand and hoisted her atop the heap of wreckage. They sat together for a silent moment. Vielle glanced aside to check on Malia.

"Do you want to talk about it with me?" she asked, "Don't worry. She can't hear us."

"Then how did you…?" Nikasu gaped, realizing what her sister had concocted.

Vielle pointed to a scattering of frostbitten plant detritus. "My hearing has been getting stronger since Yggdrasil," she explained, swallowing anxiously, "So, what's on your mind?"

"I think I regret coming along," Nikasu sighed, "No. That's not it. I regret letting her bring me."

"Are you worried we left at a bad time?"

"I'm worried I was wrong about Malia."

"Can you be more specific?"

"They conditioned me not to trust her. Eventually, I stopped trusting them, and I realized everything they said about her was wrong. But by then, I'd found my own reasons to distrust her," Nikasu explained, her voice grinding with her mounting frustration, "It was her fault that I was there. She sold me into captivity! My own mother!"

"Oh please, you think that's bad?" Vielle asked, "My own mother didn't even show up for my birth day."

Nikasu glared at her as Vielle's discontent dissolved into a mischievous smirk. That too dissolved into a look of contrition as Nikasu grumbled and shook her head.

"Sorry. It sounded better in my head," Vielle said, "When I was in a conundrum about our mother, Eytea tried to break the tension with cheeky humor."

"How did you take it?" Nikasu asked, straining against the catch in her throat.

"Offended. Just like you," Vielle nodded, "But I felt better about it later. I realized she was trying to help. And that I'd never find the answers I needed if I was worrying about whether they'd be the answers I wanted."

"I can't believe she's gone," Nikasu choked, pinching the bridge of her nose, "Just so much…. So, so much blood. I can't stop seeing it."

"The funeral was surreal," Vielle added, "Pahres's, too. Probably because there were no bodies to bury. I watched both of them die, but some part of me still tried to deny it. It was like I thought they might show up and tell me everything was okay."

"I couldn't have taken seeing her body again," Nikasu said, her voice trembling, "Not after what that thing did to her."

"I understand," Vielle said, "I'm sorry. I took us on a tangent. You were saying about Malia?"

"It's okay. This is still kinda relevant to what I was getting at," Nikasu excused, "I sometimes saw her when I was little. I didn't know how or why she came to the lab. But she would stop at my cell to say hello. Whisper nice things to me. The whole time, acting like she was conducting business."

"That was nice of her."

"I never spoke back. I always either couldn't trust her or couldn't forgive her," Nikasu continued, "Eventually, she stopped showing up. Somehow, I blamed her for that, too. I know it doesn't make sense, but it felt like she had abandoned me again."

"You don't need to justify what you felt back then," Vielle insisted, "Nobody can tell you how to feel. Or what to think. Nobody should have to go through what you went through. And even fewer could recover from it like you have."

"Thank you," Nikasu said, flashing a reserved smile, "When I heard she'd sent you guys to save me, I started thinking I might've been wrong about her. And that I should think about giving her another chance."

"Everyone was supposed to believe she was an Avatar of Fate," Vielle explained, "I'm sure she thought about what it would do to you, but she knew she had to do it. So, you weren't wrong to be wary of her. But try to understand that she struggled with her decisions."

"I know that now. Since I got out, I've been realizing that I was wrong to write her off."

"She has done a pretty good job of making up for lost time. All things considered."

"But then she talks us into coming to Tanelen only a week after the Heniokhos Disaster!" Nikasu exclaimed, flinging her hands above her head, "We shouldn't have come. It's too soon."

"From a tactical standpoint, I agree with her that we shouldn't have waited any longer," Vielle countered, "But it could be I'm just saying that because we're looking for my father."

"I know," Nikasu sighed, "I love Phylus. I hope he's safe."

"… But?" Vielle baited as Nikasu's voice and eyes trailed away.

"But I also love my brother. He's always looked out for me. He doesn't remember it, but in the lab he was held in, before we knew we were siblings, he fought to protect me. But now, I'm running off and leaving him to grieve his fiancée alone," Nikasu bemoaned, "Phylus would be no worse off if we'd waited. One week or two in their custody wouldn't make any difference."

"You would know that better than either of us," Vielle agreed, careful of unintended condescension, "But I have known Sinkua longer than you."

"Since the ArcNosian Civil War, right?"

"A few weeks before. We became fast friends despite his rough exterior," Vielle continued, "But no matter how close we've become, whenever he's in turmoil, he wants to be left alone. Not because he doesn't want to be bothered, though. He thinks he's protecting us."

"…Really?"

"Really."

"He did shut everyone out when Eytea went back to Ferya."

"And again when that book was stolen."

"Maybe you're on to something," Nikasu nodded, "Maybe he does just need some time alone."

"He does, but well…" Vielle began, trailing off as she steeled her nerves, "Nikasu, there's something you should know. There's more to this trip than you realize."

"What? What do you mean?" Nikasu asked, her pulse quickening, "Is it Malia? Was I wrong to trust her?"

"It isn't that," Vielle said, "Spril talked to me before we agreed to the trip. When Galo was in the hospital, Sinkua told him he thinks there might be a turncoat in The Coalition. Spril thinks there's some merit to it."

"That's why you agreed to do this right now," Nikasu gleaned, watching Malia as she spoke, "Spril wants us to investigate her."

"Yeah. And to protect Dad."

"But you don't think she is, do you?"

"No. If Sinkua is right, something tells me it isn't her."

"Why not?"

"I don't know. It's just…" Vielle pondered, "It's too obvious."

Malia knelt in the center of the asphalt crater. She drew a handheld device from the satchel hanging on her shoulder, and it hummed to life as she squeezed a trigger button on the side.

The screen flickered into focus, showing the crater in reddish hues. A green splotch in the middle indicated herself. She pulled her bottle of radiation sickness pills from her pocket and flicked one into her mouth.

She turned the first of two dials on the radiation radar, and her indicator shrank as the view expanded. She slowed as a ring of orange appeared and stopped as it faded to yellow. Except in one area.

Malia locked the first dial and twitched the second with her thumb. Distinction between colored regions shifted with the slightest motion. Eventually, she brought the anomaly into sharp focus.

Phylus had been taken in that direction.

The rocks shifting behind her drew her attention over her shoulder. Her daughters approached down the slope, the younger having clearly found comfort in the elder. For all she could never give them, they at least had each other.

She jerked around as another presence crossed the corner of her eye. In the opposite direction as her radar had indicated, a svelte woman with an olive complexion and dark blonde hair hunkered down just outside the crater. The stranger drove a nail into the pavement, its head anchored to an unfamiliar device.

"It isn't safe to be out here," Malia called to her, "You could get hurt. Or worse."

"I should say the same to you," the woman answered, "Standing around in that crater. Thing must be teeming with radiation."

"I brought pills for that, but..."

"I wouldn't count on those helping much."

"... But I meant politically," Malia said, "This is volatile territory."

"So, why do you get to hang around, but I have to pack up and leave?" the woman countered, "Do you have any idea who you're talking to?"

"Excuse me? And who exactly are you?"

"Nobody you know, but that isn't the point. I was hired to come here."

"And so was I."

"Fine, then. You pestered me," the stranger said, "You answer first. Who are you?"

"Farim!" Vielle called out.

Malia watched as Vielle loped down the rest of the hill, unsure if she was more surprised by her familiarity or disappointed by her friendliness. Nikasu moved in alongside her, tight-lipped and avoiding eye contact. She continued into the crater and quietly approached Malia while Vielle circled to Farim.

"Vielle?" Farim answered, "What are you doing out here?"

"We actually were hired to come here."

"Oh, you're with her? I'm sorry."

"No offense taken."

"No, I mean I'm sorry you're with her," Farim said, "Who is she, anyway? She seems to think she's too important to tell me."

"Malia."

"Ah, the mother I helped you find. You two are getting along, then?"

"Well enough to work together. Phylus went missing."

"I heard about that," Farim nodded, "Rumor is that he was abducted."

"I'm not at liberty to say one way or the other," Vielle said.

"Of course not," Farim said, "By the way, I heard about Eytea. How are you holding up?"

"Hurts too much to think about, if I can be totally honest," Vielle said, wincing at her own mention, "So, were you also hired to search for Phylus?"

"No, but I am here on a missing person case," Farim explained, "A lot of people are unaccounted for out here. Presumed fatalities without bodies outnumber unidentified bodies five to one."

"Vielle, are you going to introduce us to your friend?" Malia asked as she and Nikasu emerged from the crater, "Or should I just pretend she wasn't rude about my being here?"

"I don't have a problem with you being here, Malia," Farim corrected, "My problem is that you assume nobody else has any business here."

"You were about to tell me off yourself!"

"I was trying to warn you about the radiation."

Malia's expression flattened. "Fine, then. Farim. How do you know my daughter?"

Farim eyed Malia for a moment but eventually offered a stiff handshake, "I was part of the Subtransit Resistance."

"Ah. Right. You're the one Vielle hired to find me," Malia said. She cocked her head toward Nikasu. "Have you met Nikasu yet?"

"Once," Farim said, turning to Nikasu, "So, I won't be offended if you don't remember me."

"You showed up when we were leaving Laboratory 3891," Nikasu said.

"Right," Farim nodded, "Anyway, it looks like our investigations cross paths here. We might do well to stick close while we can."

"Is yours heading the same way as ours?" Malia asked, showing the radiation radar.

"Looks that way," Farim answered, showing her own tracking device, "Besides, I forgot to bring someone to watch my back."

Serpentine tracks of cerulean light played chaotic ceiling shadows with Mortvill as he paced the vast onyx-tiled floor. He took off one of his black leather gloves to find the once desiccating flesh had become taut. A smile shifted his mask as he watched his liver spots vanish.

"I regret to be empowered by such enormity," he sighed, "Though it would be an ingratitude to the dead to deny my ecstasy in this vigor."

"Better you than The Harvester," Chekov added, "Had he fed on their deaths, he would have become too strong to contend with."

"Of course, had we prevented those deaths, you and he would be equal footing," MalVek said, "Regardless of everything else, you must be the one to bring The Epimetheus Trial to its end."

"The arising prevented, yes," Mortvill nodded, "Their Goddess must remain banished. For all we have lost, we cannot fail in our prime endeavor."

"Our Native emissaries helped minimize the death toll in ArcNos," NalSet reminded, "Given the hopelessness of the task, they performed remarkably."

"Quite true. We can't discredit their efforts," Chekov agreed, "Thanks to them, we were able to evacuate the threatened areas here in Tanelen as well."

"I suppose that is true," MalVek sighed, "Too many have died despite our efforts though. I know we could do more. Or better."

"I understand, but this is not the time for regret," Mortvill insisted, "It is a disservice to the dead to stagnate in the past. We must move forward with this knowledge."

"Are you serious?" MalVek snipped, "Your regret is the whole reason we're here."

"Be that as it may, we cannot change what was. Only what might be," Mortvill said, "In that interest, it is prudent that we determine how best to exploit my new advantage over The Harvester."

"Strike before he regains his bearings," Chekov advised, "We have no time to waste on pretense. If The Harvester gets to Sinkua while The Veil stands, we could lose everything."

"Typically, I would readily agree with you," Mortvill said, "However, I have not sensed his presence for twelve hours."

"Sinkua has also died?" NalSet asked.

"He'd become too much of a liability," MalVek derided, "If we didn't need him on the other side of The Veil, he wouldn't have been worth half the trouble."

"That's rather heartless even for you," Chekov snipped, "He can't be blamed for what they did to him."

"No, but he can be blamed for spitting at rehabilitation," MalVek argued, "We don't blame the terminally ill for their afflictions, but mutually accepted euthanasia is regarded as an act of mercy."

"So, his death is a necessary mercy, then?" Chekov challenged, "Never mind the fact that this completely alters the parameters of our mission. Have you forgotten the good that's come of his efforts?"

"His efforts?!" MalVek scoffed, "His efforts have endangered thousands of lives."

"Never mind that I shall not tolerate any of you speaking ill of my kin," Mortvill snarled, silencing the tumult, "I cannot confirm what has become of Sinkua, but I worry for the possibilities. Death may be a tame reprieve from what he now endures."

"What do you mean?" NalSet pried.

"His soul vanished from this world entirely."

"Could The Harvester have gotten to it?"

"Impossible. This passing did not feel as his death would," Mortvill explained, "The ignorance pains me, but I otherwise know not what has become of him."

"Perhaps, it's the nature of your kin," NalSet suggested, "Is it possible that you forgot what their passing feels like?"

"I will never forget that feeling," Mortvill sighed. He gestured to the sword strapped to his throne. "Besides, I have felt no change since that moment. Logically, he must still be alive in some capacity."

"You've mentioned this feeling before," Chekov observed.

"Thrice prior. Once, three weeks ago. Once, six years ago. And once nine."

"Speaking of which, I think we're near a breakthrough on Phylus's disappearance," MalVek interjected, "The nature of the biomechs was suspect."

"Their behavior was erratic, just like the Civil War Sentinels before they broke down," NalSet added, "Somebody was interfering."

"Could their EMPs have caused it?" Chekov asked.

"Not in this case," NalSet refuted, "I'm certain there was a second host."

"I see," Mortvill pondered, "Well, this is a curious turn of events."

"I'm sorry, but I don't follow," Chekov said, "How does this get us closer to the other vanishings?"

"Consider the knowledge and resources necessary to accomplish this. Somebody overrode real time commands issued across an isolated channel through an EMP shield," NalSet coaxed, "Who could have done that?"

Chekov thought it over. NalSet and MalVek were capable, but they couldn't have done it. She cocked an inquisitive eyebrow at Mortvill, but he shook his head. Her eyes came alight as all other plausibilities yielded to one.

"Do you mean…?"

"Yes," NalSet nodded, "The First Native lives."

Phylus's legs trembled as he walked. A violet abyss of roiling liquid fractals surrounded him. He pawed at the air, feeling for walls. Fatigue and hunger provided his only sense of time, the two gauging minutes rather than hours since he left the old man.

Two aquamarine pinpoints of aquamarine appeared in the distance. Phylus ran. The floating gems lowered and narrowed, then rose again. Phylus narrowed his eyes as the gems cocked with an almost inquisitive nature.

He sprinted as the shape of a face poured around the luminous gemstones. Black goggles outlined the stones. Nondescript features filled an unremarkable face, proving nothing and suggesting even less beyond its presumed humanness.

The old man sat just beyond the androgynous visitor. He lifted his head to face it, only to look away as it turned toward him. Electrical components filled a chrysalis upon the rear of the goggles. The visitor raised a fist across its shoulder.

Phylus called out in protest, and the intruder turned to face him instead. The androgynous invader stared him down with arrogant stoicism. Phylus threw a haymaker, but the intruder stepped back and vanished through the liquid fractals.

Phylus looked about in bewilderment, hunched over with his dangling fist grazing the floor. A thrumming called his attention over his shoulder. The intruder reemerged, throwing a haymaker of its own. Phylus took it across the jaw and collapsed.

"Do not wander," it said, then pointed aside to a tray, "Eat."

The warden turned and once again departed through the jagged fluid. Phylus noticed two curiosities. One that gave him hope. And one that destroyed it. The mechanism in the chrysalis shimmered and hummed to life as the warden passed through the liquid fractals. But the device had been drilled into its head.

Even if he could endure that pain, their rations denied him the strength to disable the warden. He and the old man had each been allotted a stale biscuit, pale fruit cocktail, indeterminate salted meat, and tepid water. Just as they had for every second meal since Phylus arrived.

"Were those the Eyes of the Dragon?" Phylus asked. Until now, he had been asleep whenever the food had been delivered.

"Yes, but…" the old man said. Crumbs fell from his open mouth, and he scrambled to gather them. "But why do I know that? Eyes of the Dragon?"

"Swallow before you speak, friend," Phylus insisted, offering the old man a fragment of his biscuit, "Maybe it has to do with why they put you in here. What kind of work did you do?"

"Oh! It was, ah… Oh…. You, um… You know, with the…" the old man flustered. He pointed to his eyes, then out before him. He laid his hands flat, pumped his arms, and swirled his hands about. "Why?!"

"Shh, shh, shh, shh. It's okay," Phylus consoled, "You said the young lady worked with you. Do you remember where you two were from?"

"Ah! We lived in the, ah…. Oh geez, it was the, um…" the old man fumbled, tears welling at the failing words. In a fit of distorted epiphany, he thrust his finger at the meat on his tray. "That! There!"

"You're from the…?" Phylus puzzled, failing to connect this barely-food to any place in Ouristihra, "Never mind. We'll try again later."

"Do you know what this is like?" the old man choked, jabbing his finger against his temple. "The thoughts are there, but… But I can't make sense of them. The words just…. I just can't!"

"I'm sorry. I can't even imagine," Phylus said, "Would you like to talk about something else?"

"No. We can keep talking about the Eyes of the Dragon," the old man said, managing the briefest of eye contact, "Do you really think they put me here because I knew about them?"

"It was just a hunch, really," Phylus admitted.

"A hunch. I… I think I quite like the sound of that," the old man said, "But something doesn't add up. I had been alone until you came. If they weren't using the

Eyes of the Dragon, what did they stand to lose by my knowing about them? And why would they put me here in particular if I had special knowledge of how to escape?"

"You certainly enjoy a mystery," Phylus observed, "Maybe you knew too much about the origin of the name."

"Could you elaborate?"

"I know a couple of people whose eyes can glow like that. For a second, I thought one of them had found us."

"Could you tell me their names, Phylus? I realized when you introduced yourself how much I've missed learning a person's name."

"Sinkua and Nikasu."

"Sinkua… and… Nikasu?" the old man pondered, "Oh… Oh, those names sound dreadfully familiar."

Elemeno choked on a lump in her throat as she took one last look at her home of nearly thirty years. A voice through gelatin prickled her bubble of introspection. Her fingertips kneaded the envelope that she clutched. The voice spoke louder, though no more distinctly. Elemeno blinked slowly as she inhaled scents tied to countless memories. Painful as they had become, she couldn't bear to forget them.

As she opened her eyes, she noticed the urging face of her neighbor.

"Elemeno?" he beckoned, his voice still like molasses, "Are you sure you're okay?"

"I'm…" Elemeno began, her own voice sounding surreal, "… I'll have to be."

"Can I do anything else for you?" he offered, "Drive you to the docks, perhaps?"

"No… No, thank you," Elemeno refused, "I've already ordered a taxi."

"Nonsense! We've been neighbors for twenty years. Better I see you off than a stranger."

"I'm sorry, but being seen off by a stranger is exactly what I need. I have to leave this village behind. It would hurt too much if the last face I see in Ferya is one I know well."

"I can't pretend to understand what you're going through. If there are words to console you, I don't know them," he confessed, "But I'll make two promises. Nobody can replace you and Eytea, but we'll make whoever moves here feel just as welcome."

"Thank you," Elemeno choked as she stole a glimpse of eye contact, "And the second?"

"I'll take good care of Sestak."

Elemeno collapsed against him, burying her face in his shirt. Relentless tears welled up and overflowed her eyes. She hung there, trembling and staining his shirt with salty agony.

"The old boy has a lot of years on him," she said as she withdrew, "but he still has a lot of spark."

A bright red car with a thick yellow stripe pulled up with the windows down. The elderly driver called out to Elemeno. He popped the trunk as she bent down for her suitcases.

Her neighbor slipped his hands under hers, taking hold of the luggage in her stead. She gave him an uncomprehending stare until she huffed a self-deprecating laugh through her nose.

Elemeno slid into the back seat and buckled herself in, while her neighbor lay her suitcases in the trunk. He shut the trunk and came around to her window.

"I guess this is goodbye, huh?"

"Yeah. Tell everyone I'll miss them."

"We'll miss you, too. Take care."

Elemeno rolled up her window, and the driver pulled off the property. She watched the village she had called home for more than half her life pass for the last time, the pain of forgetting it overshadowed only by that of trying to remain here. As it faded in the mirrors, she pulled a folded sheet of paper from her pocket and a few bills from the envelope.

"Excuse me," she beckoned, "Could I trouble you for a detour before you take me to the docks?"

The driver took the note and unfolded it while he steered with one hand.

"Do you need to check in with Doctor Ophalin before your trip?" he asked.

"Oh, never mind the name," Elemeno said, "I just want to ride around that city for a while."

"Of course," the driver smiled, "Since we're going to be together for a few hours, can I ask why?"

"My daughter went there the first time she left the village."

"She fought in the ArcNosian Civil War, did she not?"

"She did," Elemeno said, "My Eytea grew up to be a hero. Just like Gijin said she would."

The driver pushed her hand back with the money still in it.

"Our side trip is on me, then."

"… Thank you."

"I saw her at last year's Tournament. Amazing young lady."

Elemeno smiled as she recalled the stories of Eytea's fight with EshCal.

"I'd love to hear more about her," the driver continued, "When you're ready."

Chapter 3

The crashing gavel echoed against the mahogany podium, and an uproar of applause rang out.

"By election of Parliament and by witness of the Prime and High Ministers of ArcNos under the moderation of Prime Minister of Domestic Affairs FerLyn," the High Minister of Domestic Affairs announced, "we hereby induct Representative TolRou as Chairwoman of Parliament."

"Thank you for your support," Chairwoman TolRou accepted, taking the stand between FerLyn and her High Minister, "Thank you, Prime Minister FerLyn. High Minister JeiRol."

The two shook TolRou's hand with a slight bow of the head and stepped down.

"I do not deserve to be here. Nor do the rest of us," TolRou began, stunning all into an uncomfortable silence, "LenSom took command of Parliament by force. By intimidation. And what did we do? We cowered. We capitulated. Yes, we could justify it at the time. At least to ourselves.

"Conspiracy, scandal, and sabotage ruined our predecessors. We thought the same would somehow befall us if we resisted LenSom. Once we knew The Avatars of Fate were still active, we knew he was a sympathizer. But we let him operate with impunity because we feared the ruin of our careers.

"Let that sink in for a moment. We let a man who aspired to the favor of megalomaniacs and terrorists control us out of fear for our jobs. Not our lives. Not our loved ones. Not the citizenry. Our jobs. Had he continued to have his way, we would have gone to war with Tanelen. We were willing to sacrifice ourselves and our neighbors just to keep our jobs.

"Only by the efforts of a few have we been granted this opportunity to prevent the unthinkable. And I do not regard myself among them. I did nothing until they came to me.

"Prime Minister of Defense Spril approached me with a plan to overthrow LenSom and cut off the Avatars of Fate. My role would be simple. All there was for me to do was fetch something in plain view. My partners would manage the rest. A Civil War spy and Prime Minister of Human Resources SenRas.

"Let me reiterate. I played third chair to a woman with zero affiliations to our administration and a man in his late seventies. Now, I'm scarcely a decade his junior, but if he can stand up to an Avatar of Fate on two occasions, surely, I can speak out against internal corruption. Surely, all of us can.

"Again, it has only been by the efforts of a few that war with Tanelen has been avoided for the time being. I would like to take a moment to commend those few.

"Prime and High Ministers of Defense Spril and EshCal infiltrated areas controlled by The Avatars of Fate on multiple occasions, including a rescue mission for Chieftain Sage Galo. Prime and High Ministers of Treasury Biroe and KalChi unraveled a financial scandal aimed to destabilize ArcNos's economy and vilify Tanelen. Prime Minister of Foreign Affairs Phylus reached out to Noble Doyen Joren with talks of peace despite the mounting scandals. Prime Minister of Human Resources SenRas worked with independent agents to undermine The Avatars of Fate.

"All of them risked themselves to disprove any association between the biomech outbreak and either of our administrations. Working in no official capacity, they and a handful of others tried to save us from corruption that we ignored. So, it is not with pride, but with shame, that I accept the title of Chairwoman of Parliament.

"We must no longer be crippled by our cowardice. Tens of thousands of lives have been lost. But without their efforts, the losses would have been orders of magnitude greater. If we are to truly recover, we must make peace with Tanelen and eradicate The Avatars of Fate once and for all."

A dull murmur washed over the crowd as the new Chairwoman concluded her inaugural speech. To hear her speak so negatively of nearly all of them, herself included, created an awkward enough silence. But knowing the truth of her accusations created a palpable discomfort.

"Can we afford to make peace negotiations with Tanelen a top priority right now? We're dealing with an unprecedented disaster. Tens of thousands of lives lost. Billions of iolas in damages," JeiRol challenged, breaking the silence, "Long-term medical care for the survivors and rescue workers. Frankly, I say we can't spare the resources on reaching out. We need to concentrate on mitigating the Heniokhos Disaster."

"How certain are you that Tanelen will stand aside and let us work on repairs?" High Minister of Foreign Affairs Calhosin asked, his microphone all but gratuitous alongside his Southlander basso, "We've received an ultimatum of war from Noble Doyen Joren. How would ignoring the tension between us make peace?"

"Not involving them during repairs will show that we don't hold them accountable," FerLyn supplied, "Even reaching out to tell them we don't blame them could be used against us, as it shows that the thought occurred to us."

"Who said they're free of blame?" Calhosin asked, "For that matter, who says they won't use the Heniokhos Disaster as a catalyst for war? Joren accused us of assassinating IlcBei and JalRov after they had outlived their usefulness as scapegoats."

"In no uncertain terms, mind you," EshCal added, "In fact, that's how the ultimatum came about."

"Further, LenSom was declared responsible for the scandals leading to the outbreak and said ultimatum," Calhosin reminded, "And he has been taken to task to the utmost extent. So, if Tanelen desires peace, why have they said nothing of returning our Prime Minister of Foreign Affairs?"

"Our current theory is that The Avatars of Fate captured him," EshCal explained, looking aside to Spril, "We were set upon by the same biomech technology that was used in the Heniokhos Disaster."

Spril sat with a notebook on his lap His eyes darted about the page in no particular progression. Now and then, he jotted something down. After a stretch without making a mark, his attention fixated on a single point on the page. His eyes glossed over.

EshCal cleared her throat, and Spril began absently drumming the notebook with his pen. EshCal glared and cleared her throat more loudly. Spril dropped his pen and shrank down into his own shoulders.

"I…" Spril choked out, "Yes. The Avatars controlled the biomechs."

He blinked hard as he returned his attention to his notebook

"I have to ask," KalChi said, "High Minister Calhosin, why have you not attempted to negotiate the release of Prime Minister Phylus?"

"I can see where you think your suspicions are valid, but I have been asked not to involve the Ministry of Foreign Affairs," Calhosin defended, "I was going to negotiate his release, just as you said. But when I sought High Minister EshCal's intel, she insisted I refrain."

"What he says is true," EshCal mediated, "We need more time to prepare in case negotiations go awry."

"So, my inactivity is not of my design," Calhosin concluded, brushing a strand of hair behind his ear, "I'm simply yielding to the needs of the Ministry of Defense."

"What is being done toward recovering our Prime Minister of Foreign Affairs, then?" TolRou asked, "If we are to avoid war with Tanelen, we need him leading negotiations."

"Third party contractors are currently on site, gathering intelligence," EshCal explained, "They have no documented ties to our government."

"Why can we not also have Calhosin reach out, though?" FerLyn asked, "I understand that The Avatars of Fate are responsible, but it happened in Tanelen."

"A recent addition to the Ministry of Human Resources has alerted us to probable Avatar sympathizers in Tanelen's federal government," SenRas said, "Thus if any of us meddles in either side of their joint affairs, it could result in war."

"Tanelen may be under Avatar control?" TolRou asked, "How did we not see this happening?"

"May is the operative word here. We're investigating the possibility," SenRas assured, "As to your second question, we may have been too distracted by our recent run of scandals to notice the seeds of corruption in our northern neighbors. Mind you, this is not an excuse. Merely an explanation."

"So, who is this source that you mentioned?" FerLyn asked.

"She's a former courier with Black Tie Delivery. When asked why she left that position, she asked for protection," SenRas explained, "I promised it, and she revealed she had unknowingly facilitated contact between The Avatars of Fate and their sympathizers. In fact, she helped to prove LenSom's ties to them."

"How did she know she was delivering missives for The Avatars of Fate?" Calhosin asked.

"She grew suspicious of certain deliveries. She sought the counsel of the Subtransit Resistance and learned that she was almost certainly aiding communications to and from known Avatars," SenRas recounted, "Several of them also involved Chairman LenSom."

"I assume at least as many involved offices of the Tanelenese government?" TolRou asked, to which SenRas nodded, "Do we have any leads on identities?"

"The Ministry of Treasury is looking into it," Biroe added, "If LenSom stood to profit from a war, someone in Tanelen does as well."

"Yes, we believe that if we can isolate the sympathizers, we can bring them to trial and clear both our nations of inciting a war," KalChi explained.

"Should we broker peace with Tanelen, we will then seek their help in uprooting The Avatars throughout Ouristihra," EshCal added.

"I would advise us not to presume their collaboration," TolRou said, "For the past two centuries, their idea of peace has been silent coexistence.

Ever since Kirts attempted to implicate them in the ArcNosian Kirtsian Trade Conflict, Tanelen has refused all forms of active alliance."

"It's a weighty undertaking, but it's one worth pursuing," Calhosin said, "Uprooting Avatar corruption in Tanelen will provide me with substantial leverage. In fact, should Phylus still be missing, I can use that to garner their aid in his recovery."

"Very well, then," TolRou nodded, "Would the Prime Minister of Defense like to add anything?"

Spril's hand went numb, dropping his pen. It rolled across the notepad with rumbling thunder. Gelatinous voices enveloped him and gurgled in his ears. His fingers twitched as the cacophony compounded.

Bloody images flashed through his mind. The lobby of 3891 manifested, the receptionist and her desk chair bathed in crimson. The staging area beneath 1341 flickered appeared, immaculate white walls pulsating with the rolling pen as blood trickled upward. Feathery plasmatic burst from Eytea's back as the biomech appendage gored her. Sinkua shattered as he collapsed upon the wreckage.

The gaping biomechanical maw closed around Spril, drawing tighter as the gelatinous voices grew louder. His limbs collapsed, bones caving in on themselves. Blood trickled from every orifice. His eyes glazed over as he stared into the crimson oculus.

He should have died.

His pen hit the floor with a terrible crash, ripping a panicked cry from his throat.

"What's come over you, sir?" TolRou asked.

Every word of the assembly rushed into Spril's ears at once.

"He's in shock, Madam Chairwoman," Calhosin said, "Post-traumatic, no doubt."

The words in Spril's thoughts rearranged themselves into a sense of order.

"Are you well enough to share your thoughts, Prime Minister?" Calhosin continued.

Spril nodded vigorously. "Yes," he choked out, "We need to prepare for war."

"You can't be serious!" FerLyn protested, "We can't afford to provoke Tanelen. Did you forget their connection to The Avatars? Have you forgotten they have our Prime Minister of Foreign Affairs? Did you forget what they did on Heniokhos?"

"I have forgotten none of this!" Spril roared, "Who the hell do you think you're talking to? I have been dealing with The Avatars of Fate since they sent CreSam after me at age fifteen. Since they sent The Hunter to assassinate me at age twenty-three. And every day in between and since. Always looking over my shoulder. Trying to anticipate their next move. I can't look anywhere without gauging the probability of their influence.

"And I know damn well they have Phylus. I have spent every spare thought since I heard about it obsessing over how to get him back. Never mind his benefit to ArcNos. That man has been my father since I was eight years old.

"And don't you dare presume that I could forget the Heniokhos Disaster! To everyone questioning my stability, where were you while I was in the thick of that? Where were you while people were dying in the streets? I saw good people slaughtered and broken out there. Where the fuck were you?

"As for Tanelen? Fuck Tanelen. They collected our tax money for months and never offered to rectify. Their Noble Doyen spat at diplomacy. So, any hand or fist they have for us now won't be a damn priority."

Spril's neck muscles twitched as his head jerked about. Bitter whispers and suspicious mumbles resonated. He ran his tongue over his gums, his mouth tasting oddly of iron.

He closed his eyes and breathed deeply. The cacophonous whispers, the thunderous shifting of pens and papers, the shredding of fingers over hair. It all quieted. He opened his eyes and exhaled.

"Spril?" EshCal ventured, "Do you need to step out for some air?"

"No..." Spril refused, pausing to consider, "No, I'll be fine now. I'm sorry."

"Nobody here means to downplay what you've been through. We understand if you need time to steady yourself," EshCal consoled, "Your health is important to us."

"Thank you," Spril mumbled, finding it difficult to hold eye contact.

"Now, what did you mean by preparing for war?" EshCal asked.

"War against The Avatars of Fate," Spril clarified, "We've spent years trailing behind them, only rooting them out when the damage is done. So, no more blind eyes to corruption. No more fearing the repercussions of confrontation. No more bandages on bullet wounds. We band together and take the war straight to them."

"Well, it's a noble vision, but it's at least just as ambitious," EshCal said, "Where do you propose we begin?"

"In the months leading up to the ArcNosian Civil War, Galo and Sinkua planted seeds of diplomacy throughout Ouristihra. Ivaria and Haprian had a brush with The Avatar's influence until those two helped. Calhosin can begin with them," Spril explained, "Prime Duke Norum is a pacifist, but even he can't deny the risk of another Olsa usurping his authority. And no Quarunite can forget the threat contained largely by one of our diplomats at Radial Axiom."

"Of course, but when Parliamentary ArcNos called them for aid, what came of it?" High Minister of Education SouSol asked.

"Oh, now surely, they can't be faulted for that," Prime Minister of Education NeiRos countered, "Scarcely anyone was in a position to get involved with our war."

"But even if they had, they would have been in danger long before they got here," SouSol argued, gesturing to EshCal, "We should neither expect nor ask their help."

"Let's not forget, however, that several immigrants were instrumental in both victory and recovery," NeiRos said, "We need a multinational effort to drive them out."

"Of course, but only after they settled here in peacetime," SouSol insisted, "In fact, one might find a link between that and the rise of conflict. The Avatars who corrupted our leadership were foreigners."

"If you're quite done," Calhosin scolded, glaring at SouSol. He turned to Spril. "You mean to build an international task force in order to suppress..."

"Not suppress," Spril interrupted, "Destroy."

"... destroy The Avatars of Fate, then?"

"Yes."

"Well, as reluctant as I am to defer to our esteemed High Minister of Education, that point in time may be too delicate to work from," Calhosin said, "I can set the groundwork though, but recovering Phylus is crucial."

"Fine. You're the diplomat here," Spril said, "Do it as it suits you, so long as you do it."

Yrlis trudged down the stairs, warming her hands around a mug of hot tea. A steady hum came from the room below. She groaned as she turned the corner at the bottom of the stairs, pausing to sip her tea.

Sleep had been a fleeting luxury these past few weeks. Since transcribing it into modern script, Yrlis had become obsessed with understanding the deeper potential of the genome. Her lab was wallpapered with diagrams and reports ripped from scientific journals.

Yrlis settled into her chair, panning the open books and notebooks scattered over her desk. Sipping from her mug, she plucked passages from the books in no perceivable order. She stopped frequently to highlight a passage, scrawl in the margins, or jot something in a notebook.

The front door unlocked and opened, and someone came inside. Gauging by how cold her tea had become, Yrlis figured she had been in her lab for at least an hour. She stopped and listened to Spril's after work routine, as comforting as it was disconcerting in its calculability.

He had been retracting since the Heniokhos Disaster, compounding Yrlis's restlessness. She considered that it could have been because of Eytea's death. Not out of any romantic interest, of course. Witnessing the growth of Yggdrasil, so soon after the emergence of Leviathan, may have put him into functional shock.

Neither of those sounded adequate, though. He had returned from the dead to turn rejects into revolutionaries. One death, even that of a Hybrid, shouldn't have broken him. The eldritch beings might have driven Spril into shock had they appeared at least a year earlier. Instead, they followed a murderous chimera, a Faux-Hybrid, and swarms of biomech spiders. His sense of reality had been primed to deal with a talking sea serpent and an unfathomably vast tree.

The lab fell into silence as the ambient humming faded. Yrlis drummed her pen on her desk, craving noise to fill the void. That sound had gone on for weeks, her preoccupation with the genome map driving so deep that she forgot why the humming had started.

Yrlis paced her lab, running her fingertips over all manner of machines. She stopped as she found one of them warm, and she turned on the monitor.

She furrowed her brow. Two of the samples matched each other but not the rest of the batch.

Somebody had tampered with her specimens.

The ferry ride and subsequent taxi ride from the docks of Quarun passed in a blur. Elemeno was preoccupied with her taxi ride through Ferya. The driver had been eager to regale her with the local history. She had kept quiet when he spoke of a neighborhood built atop a bulldozed military outpost. Such negativity ill suited memories of Eytea's stories.

In fact, it had been in that neighborhood when the tour turned sour. Motorists had become irate, hurling asinine accusations at no perceivable provocation. She had recalled that house, had even asked the driver to circle until she found it.

Eytea's picture had proven unnecessary though, as the front of the house bore a faint warped shadow where the last owner had been beaten against it. Streaks of rust riddled the top rail of the chain-link fence. As the driver had given no insights, Elemeno had avoided divulging any sensitive details.

In retrospect, she realized that the ubiquitous anger had centered around that house. She contemplated what it could portend, recalling Eytea's story about Sinkua's first outbreak. Part of her regretted having taken so long to notice the pattern. Doctor Ophalin may have had some insight or found that information useful.

Another part knew that if her scheme panned out, though, she might not need to consult him. Once she checked in at Country Living Bed & Breakfast, all she could do was wait.

Chapter 4

Backhoes and excavators rumbled along the dirt roads, crushing mutated floral detritus. The platoons of machines announced themselves with klaxon pulses, keeping time in a steady flow of work.

"I must confess," Galo said, "I feel a touch guilty for eschewing tradition as I did."

"I understand," Gabdur nodded, "Change is always difficult."

"True enough. But know that I'm telling this in the strictest confidence."

"What am I if not a master of keeping secrets?"

"I suppose you are," Galo snickered, "Still, I sometimes feel like I'm spitting on custom for profit, even though I know there are far more important things to be gained here."

"Well then, let's look at this from a broader perspective," Gabdur said, "What benefit did anti-technological culture bring to Masnethege? Or Berinin? Or Ouristihra?"

"Aside from your tragedy, we lived comfortably with it. It only recently became a wider problem."

"Galo, do you honestly believe my wife and father were isolated incidents? Given, they were especially macabre, but many Masnethegeans have died because custom put crucial treatments beyond timely reach."

"I… didn't realize. We create revolutionary medicines, but our own people die for lack of medical treatment?"

"Well, medical treatment goes far beyond pills and serums," Gabdur explained, "You should know this quite well."

"I do now," Galo agreed, scratching his phlebotomy scars, "Had I been left to Masnethegean medicine, I'm afraid I'd still be in a coma."

"At best," Gabdur said, "But second, you've never been in a position to know about the unnecessary deaths. I didn't know about it until after Zheal died."

"I'm the Chieftain Sage!" Galo exclaimed, "How have I not been in a position to know?"

"The trouble with the darker side is that it looks like nothing's there from the outside," Gabdur said, "Had your ascension been more customary, you would have learned about it from your aunt and uncle. Instead, you're finding out from a traveling therapist six years into your reign."

Galo's expression flattened at the abrupt loss of familiarity. Gabdur nodded ahead, pointing out someone hastily approaching.

"Sirs," Sanus gasped as she reached speaking distance, "You're…"

"Catch your breath first, Sanus," Galo insisted, "Are you okay?"

"Fine, sir. Quite fine," Sanus dismissed, waving him off, "Just need a moment."

She untucked a handkerchief from a wristband on her otherwise bare forearm and wiped her face. Aleepo furrowed his brow at the darkened area around her eyes and faint stripes of discoloration on her wrists.

"Sanus, have you…?" Aleepo began.

"You're needed at the excavation site, sirs," Sanus interrupted, her throat catching, "Nenbard's crew found something."

"What sort of something?" Galo asked.

"I couldn't see," Sanus excused, "He said to tell you it's a tunnel."

"Meaning you were unable or unallowed?" Aleepo asked.

"Unallowed. I've been having bad allergic reactions near the dig site."

Aleepo subtly observed Sanus's wrist as she wiped her nose, noting a ring of lateral banding. She had scars, and she was self-conscious about them.

She had also never been so withdrawn, not to his memory. Sure, it could have happened gradually. He had been away for over twenty years. But so radical and intrinsic a change must have had a catalyst.

Then there was Nenbard's temper.

"Is it only near the dig site?" Galo asked.

"Yes. It's clearing up now," Sanus insisted, snorting loose phlegm.

"That's good to know," Galo said, casting a knowing glance toward Aleepo, "Now then, shall we be going?"

"Yes, best not to keep Nenbard waiting," Aleepo muttered, scratching his leg until the fabric bunched around his fingers, "Sanus, do you suppose he'd have time to speak with me privately?"

"I can't say for certain," Sanus shrugged, "Work is still a mite hectic, you know."

"I can pull him aside if need be," Galo offered, "I'm not above throwing my weight around when he gets disrespectful."

"I'll wait nearby," Aleepo said, "Call me in if he asks for my input."

Nenbard walked along the top of the unearthed wall, his breathing labored through a filtration mask. Heavy machinery lined the perimeter, hollowing the subterranean chamber. Nenbard stopped at a corner, gazing out over the array of broken walls.

From his vantage point, he noted other tunnel-like structures scattered throughout the dig site. Curiously, all but the first they had found were filled to ground level. Nenbard pulled at his chin in contemplation.

New voices joined the tumult of machinery and conversation. He looked toward the edge of the forest to see his wife, the Chieftain Sage, and that traveling therapist whose face he couldn't quite place.

Nenbard hopped down from the stone upcropping and approached them, waving broadly. The therapist drifted aside toward a patch of shrubbery.

"Nenbard," Galo greeted, "I believe Aleepo advised us all to keep our distance from the dig site, did he not?"

"He did, sir," Nenbard nodded, "But surely you don't expect us to take his advice as orders. The man has no authority on our affairs."

"I do," Galo asserted, "Now then, why are you so near the dig site?"

"Scouting a discovery one of the backhoe operators made," Nenbard explained, "I know they're supposed to come to you or well, Aleepo with anything unusual. But you were both predisposed, so he came to me instead."

"Sanus says it's some manner of tunnel," Galo said.

"Column, more like. They found it while digging out the interior," Nenbard explained, "There are others, but this one wasn't filled in. Just covered."

Galo bounded onto the masonic upcropping and turned to offer Nenbard his hand. Nenbard brushed it off. As he hoisted himself up, his knees popped so loudly they might have echoed had he been any closer to the open column.

"See those squares?" Nenbard asked, catching his breath.

"Elevator shafts, I'd wager," Galo said, "None in Masnethege Proper, but not that baffling. Or were you all puzzled by it being left empty?"

"Not particularly," Nenbard defended, "I just thought it was worth calling you in for."

"Well, I have a theory, but I'll need to go inside to investigate."

"I'll accompany you. It wouldn't be smart for you to go alone."

"No, but I can't allow you to go down there. Not with your joints creaking like that," Galo refused, "Does Ocronn still leisure run?"

"He does. Should I send for him?"

"Yes. We'll also need two climbing harnesses with belay lines and somebody to operate them, as well as a pair of breathing masks with backup filters."

"Of course. Anything else?"

"Yes," Galo said, "Aleepo wants to speak with you."

Gabdur stood before a shrub, inspecting a blood-red flower. His lips curled into a pursed sneer as he rubbed a petal between his finger and thumb. The texture was wrong. Not abnormal. Wrong.

Overheard conversation pulled at his attention. He plucked and pocketed a sandpaper petal, then turned to face his old friend.

"Aleepo," Nenbard nodded, folding his arms, "The Chieftain Sage tells me you wish to speak with me."

Aleepo considered the mannerisms. His posture was guarded. He spoke with finality, more challenging than inviting. Aleepo knitted his eyebrows flat and tight.

"How long have you and Sanus been married?" he asked.

"Twenty-five years," Nenbard said.

"Twenty-five," Aleepo repeated, whistling faintly, "Tell me. What does Sanus do for a living?"

"What? I don't…" Nenbard trailed off, tightening the fold of his arms, "I don't see how that's any of your business."

"I need to get a feel for the people I work with," Aleepo explained, "But I can't get anything out of Sanus. She's always so distant, almost like she's uncomfortable speaking for herself."

"I don't know what to tell you," Nenbard said, shifting his feet to angle his shoulder more toward Aleepo.

"Of course, you don't," Aleepo droned, "Listen. I think I know what's going on here."

"I would think it should be clear to you," Nenbard flippantly agreed, "But it's no business of yours. I suggest you butt out."

"I…" Aleepo trailed off, thrown by Nenbard's ownership without a shred of contrition, "I've seen the bruises on her wrists. The ones she's always hiding."

"It's her choice to hide them," Nenbard defended, "Were it up to me, she wouldn't deny that part of her life. But there's no reasoning with that woman."

Everything else added up to spousal abuse, but this didn't fit at all. Now, the only way it worked was if Nenbard had gone beyond sociopathy. If he were abusing Sanus, he went beyond justification to take a measure of ownership.

"I've also noticed the redness around her eyes," Aleepo continued.

"Yes, from her allergies. I know she's told you as much."

"She looked like she had been crying," Aleepo said, "A lot, in fact."

"Yes. She gets emotional," Nenbard said, tightening his brow, "You of all people should understand that."

Now, that was a loaded statement. His familiarity almost sounded like he had seen through the facade. That couldn't have been true, though. He had no reason to believe Gabdur had lived long beyond that day.

He only knew Aleepo. Berininite by blood. Poravitian by birth. Feryan by immigration. Floral breeder by trade. Therapist by profession.

Epiphany blindsided Gabdur.

Nenbard wasn't guarded about Sanus's present. He was protective of her past. He didn't take ownership of abusing her. He accepted the burdens she couldn't endure. He didn't tell her what to say. She told him what not to say.

Sanus hadn't been abused.

She had been taken.

"Oh, my goodness," Aleepo sighed, "Listen. I know you said it's none of my business. But if Sanus was…"

"Because it isn't," Nenbard doubled down, "But… You are correct. That's all I can say."

"Right," Aleepo said, choking on the word, "It's best to honor her wishes."

Nenbard walked away. Aleepo swallowed anxiously. Push too hard, and he might never gain her insight. Too softly, and he might not get it soon enough to matter.

"How long ago?"

Nenbard paused, but he didn't turn around. "… Eight years."

"How long was she in?"

"… I've already said more than I promised."

"Would you like to know how I lost my arm?"

"No more than you've told me."

"It might do her well to know."

"…. That's enough, Aleepo."

Time had been unkind to the depths of the old laboratory. Nearly a decade of pressure from rich sediment drove fissures through the once immaculate walls. Mildew grew in stagnant water beneath cracked pipes.

"Where do we begin?" Ocronn asked as he adjusted his head lamp.

"From what I've seen of their other facilities, there will be a hidden elevator in a corner. I suspect it's in the unfilled shaft," Galo said, unclipping his climbing harness, "Make note of any other anomalies you find."

"What sort of anomalies?"

"Anything that looks suspicious."

"That's helpful," Ocronn grumbled.

"This is only the third of their facilities I've visited, and only one was operational," Galo snapped, "If you've experience to call upon, you've yet to speak of it."

"No, sir," Ocronn muttered, his voice trailing off, "None at all."

They drifted apart as they wandered the vast staging area, contemplating how it might have looked while operational. Bulges along the walls indicated derelict pipes. Their arrangement told a story about this place, but it was in a language neither of them could read.

"Chieftain Sage Galo, sir?" Ocronn beckoned, inspecting a bundle of frayed wires, "May I ask you something?"

"… Yes, what is it?" Galo asked as his mumblings trailed off.

"Why did you bring me down here?"

"It wouldn't be safe for anyone to explore this place alone."

"I know that. I mean, why did you choose me?" Ocronn specified, "I have no particular skills that would be of use down here."

Galo thrust himself to his feet with a throaty huff. "Do you want the truth?"

Ocronn spat on the frayed wires. No reaction, just as he expected. "I do, sir."

"It was between you and Nenbard. And if I may be candid, he's been a thorn in my ass since I returned."

"Is that all?" Ocronn asked, restraining a chortle, "What about Sanus?"

"Too timid," Galo said, "I couldn't trust her to explore unguided. She never struck me as assertive."

"And Nalygen and Borret?"

"We have… too much history," Galo dismissed.

"You're afraid to tell them," Ocronn deduced, "aren't you?"

"Afraid to tell them what?"

"Sir, I'm familiar with the repercussions of The Reestablishment Protocol," Ocronn explained, "I assume you are as well."

Galo sighed. "… I am."

"Are you prepared, then?" Ocronn asked.

"To take action, yes," Galo nodded, looking down at the Serpent Bracer, "To give the order…. I don't know."

"I hope you find the courage, sir," Ocronn professed, "You only have…"

"I know how much time I have," Galo interrupted, "Thank you."

Minutes progressed in uncomfortable silence as they continued searching. They both moved toward the same corner, drawn to it by suspicion of a crack running its height.

Ocronn stopped and crouched. "I found something," he announced.

"What is it?" Galo called, turning to join him.

"I smell copper," Leviathan spoke inside Galo's mind.

"Normal copper or…?" Galo thought, trailing off as the right words escaped him.

"The other kind," Leviathan said, "Infused copper. Organic."

"I'm not sure," Ocronn said, "It looks like blood, but it smells too metallic."

"Thank you," Galo thought. He then spoke aloud to Ocronn. "Well, let's have a look at it."

Galo crouched beside Ocronn, finding him scratching at a dark reddish circle with speckles of discoloration.

"It's the spots, isn't it?" Ocronn asked, "You're also wondering what they are."

"I am," Galo nodded, "They look like copper, but…"

"But how would someone end up with that much copper in their blood?"

"In these places, the question is never how," Galo said, "It's always a matter of why."

"There's a trail," Ocronn pointed out, "Looks like it ends here."

"But why here of all places?"

"I don't smell enough of it to suggest exsanguination," Leviathan said.

"Stanched the wound?" Ocronn suggested, shrugging.

"What?" Galo asked, "Oh sorry. I was more just thinking out loud when I said that."

"Ahh," Ocronn nodded, "So, do you have any ideas?"

"Well, unless we find a lot of blood behind that corner, it doesn't look like this person was exsanguinated," Galo said, "But we can backtrack to where they started bleeding once we break through the wall."

"And what do you suppose is behind that wall?"

"An elevator," Galo asserted, "And I don't suppose. I know."

Galo swaggered to the corner and stood before the elevator facade. The cracking of his knuckles echoed as he rolled his fingers into a fist. This had become typical since Malia accidentally doped him with the Hunter Formula.

Galo ignored Ocronn's protests to his methods, focusing on a single point in the facade. He plowed his fist into it, cracking the stone. His knuckles swelled and reddened though, pain shooting up his arm in screaming pulsations.

Leviathan suggested his body was rejecting the Hunter Formula, but Galo insisted he was still acclimating to it. Dropping the argument, they sent a joint effort of milystis down his forearm to erupt from his fist as a pressurized burst of water. The paltry cracks spiderwebbed as the milystic water surged throughout the facade.

Ocronn came to his side as Galo lowered his fist. Wet stone sheets sloughed away, uncovering a pair of elevator doors.

"Now, how do we get inside?" Ocronn asked, "For that matter, how do we operate it?"

"Well…" Galo began, lifting his filtration mask to hock a salvo of dark mucus, "Aleepo told me he once used the severed thumb of an Avatar agent. I don't see a scanner though."

"Or an agent," Ocronn added, his brow knitting tightly, "Didn't you and Sinkua find one of these places in Ferya?"

"We did," Galo nodded, "The two of us and Eytea pried it open with my glaive."

"Well, maybe the two of us can pull that off. What about riding?"

"That won't be an option."

"It won't be…?" Ocronn trailed off, his mouth agape, "How did you get down there, then? Or did you…?"

Galo cut him short with a stern seething glare, holding eye contact as he drew his glaive and whipped it down at his side. Ocronn's mouth fell shut as Galo turned away and, with a frightful bellow, plunged the head of his glaive between the doors.

"Oh!" Ocronn remarked, his eyes wide with realization, "Oh, I'm sorry, I didn't…"

"Yeah," Galo cut off, "Unless you can channel electricity with your bare hands, we won't be riding the elevator."

His head down, Ocronn sidled up to Galo and grabbed the end of the glaive. Galo and Leviathan forced a column of freezing water between the doors. He and Ocronn leaned back with the glaive, while Leviathan widened the milystic column. Eventually, the locking mechanisms snapped, and the doors slid freely on their tracks.

"We're going to cut through the floor, then?" Ocronn suggested, rolling his dominant shoulder.

Galo nodded as he leaned his glaive against the wall, pausing to stretch.

"I'll be working alone from here," Galo insisted, "I can't expect anyone else to withstand the drop."

"Sir, how do you suppose yourself better able than the rest of us?" Ocronn asked.

"Did you hear about how The Hunter jumped from the top of the Triad Titan without injury?"

"Seems one of the Masnethegeans may have mentioned it. Why?"

"During the Heniokhos Disaster, someone shot me with the stuff that made him that durable," Galo explained, "Accidentally. We call it the Hunter Formula."

Baffled silent, Ocronn watched as Galo hunkered down and ran his fingertips over the elevator floor. "I'll keep looking around up here," he said, "I'll tell you if I find anything interesting."

"Likewise," Galo absently muttered.

Unsure what he'd agreed to, Galo tried to dig up what should have been an immediate memory only to find gray beyond talking about Malia shooting him.

"He said he will remain on this level," Leviathan said, "You and he agreed to share any interesting discoveries with each other."

"Okay," Galo nodded, "But if you could hear him, why couldn't I?"

"Simple. You were ignoring him," Leviathan explained, "As for how I heard him, in this state, I am best understood as a sentient extension of your milystis. Another level of consciousness, conscious in and of itself."

"I see," he said. He reached under his Chieftain Robe to rip off his shirt sleeves. "Then, you already know what I'm about to do. I need the same help as before. Only more so."

Galo wrapped his knuckles and, over the next several minutes, pounded the elevator floor with a slow rhythm of fortified punches. Cracks spread as the fabric wore through. Those cracks became fractures as his skin began to abrade. Finally, his fists smeared with blood, the middle of the elevator floor fell through.

Galo swung his legs down, took a deep breath, and dropped three or four levels. The sound of his knees popping echoed as he braced to absorb the impact. He wedged his glaive between the doors and, with even more of Leviathan's help, forced them apart.

He came across some curious detritus just outside the elevator shaft. He bent to pick up a thin sheet of amber metal with faint ripples and ruddy edges. He pocketed it in his Chieftain Robe.

Another two steps, and he kicked up another piece, more curved but absent the reddened edges. He pocketed this one as well, but when he immediately found another three, he took just one more and stopped bothering to collect them.

"What are these things?" he asked, speaking aloud for the comfort of an external voice.

"Infused copper," Leviathan answered.

"Right," Galo said, hastening deeper into the disused testing area, "With what?"

"Cotton, mostly. The first also carries traces of hemoglobin."

Galo mulled over the possibilities. The simplest answer sounded too bizarre to be true. That, or he dreaded trying to comprehend what it implied. With no other choice but to confront his fear, he set the second sample on his shoulder. The curvature fit comfortably.

"These are from a shirt," he gasped.

Galo ran now, the red and amber in the blood stains gradually shifting to swap dominance. In the middle of the testing area, he found a pedestal with clods of soil and moss caking the base. Atop it was a pair of copper shoes split up the middle. A toppled suspension rack lay beside it.

"This pedestal," Galo swallowed, "It looks just like the one at home."

"Yes," Leviathan said, "You still have much to learn about the one you call Grandfather."

Chapter 5

Farim sat atop a pile of rubble with the sun setting behind her. She muttered under her breath as she slapped her tracker against her palm. She checked the screen yet again and shook her head as she turned it off.

"You and I need to talk," Vielle said, sitting beside her.

"Malia send you?" Farim asked, staring out at the snowy cityscape.

"She's asleep," Vielle said, "So's Nikasu."

"Okay. What's on your mind?"

"I think I should be asking you that," Vielle said, gesturing to the tracker, "I've seen how you look at that thing."

Farim turned on the display and fiddled with the controls, finding it still failing. She mumbled something and turned it off again.

"You're not here on business," Vielle continued.

"That depends on your definition," Farim dodged, "But I guess there's no point trying to hide it from you. Probably never was."

They shared a moment's silence together, observing the ironic serenity of snow on urban wreckage.

"Who is it?" Vielle asked.

"Have I told you about my mentor?" Farim asked.

"Sparingly."

"There's a reason for that."

"That reason being?"

"Mixed company."

"Right," Vielle nodded, "How long has he been missing?"

"He disappeared three years before the ArcNosian Civil War," Farim said, her voice catching, "So, nearly nine years now."

"That's why you joined the Subtransit Resistance," Vielle gleaned. Farim nodded. "You were looking for him."

"I was looking for answers," Farim corrected, "And revenge."

"And now?"

"Depends on the answers," Farim said. She turned to Vielle, making eye contact for the first time since Vielle sat down. "You promise Malia's asleep?"

"Snoring."

"His name is Dourias. He was a deep cover agent planted among The Avatars of Fate. Matter of fact, he was The Coalition's first recruit after their founding members," Farim said, "He was investigating developments in Tanelen during CreSam's rise to power in ArcNos. The last message I got from him was a hand-written note passed to me by a stranger. I don't know how it reached me, but I knew what it meant."

"What did it say?"

"My ears are wet."

"… He was getting in over his head?"

"Yeah," Farim sighed. She forced her shoulders and back to relax. Sharing her burden eased her tension, but she had to overstate it. She still held another burden and had yet to steel herself to confess. "I went to ArcNos to find out what happened to him."

"But you knew he was working in Tanelen."

"Going to Tanelen would have been too obvious," Farim explained, "The revolution in ArcNos gave me the opportunity to get close without arousing suspicion."

"You knew someone sold him out," Vielle asserted, "That's why you approached Spril and my dad for a seat on their Parliament. You knew that was your best chance to get your eyes on The Coalition."

"I take it you're finding it hard to trust them, too."

"Sinkua thinks there's a dissenter among them. I've started to see his point."

"He's a good judge of character," Farim said, "So, you're investigating Malia, then?"

"Auditing, more like. But yes. Spril asked me to as a matter of opportunity," Vielle said, "I don't think it's her though. What about you?"

"She's still a possibility," Farim said, "But she's among the least likely."

"Why are you still following us, then?" Vielle asked, "Don't take me wrong, I enjoy having you along. But three days is a long time to pretend we're on the same trail just so you can disprove your least likely lead. You must be pretty far off track by now."

"No. No, trust me, I'm still on track. We'll be on the same trail for a while," Farim said, lowering her head. She felt Vielle's hand on her shoulder. Firm. Clutching. Beckoning. "Vielle," she continued, swallowing hard, "I'm the reason your father is missing."

Vielle's brows tightened. "… Explain yourself."

"I got word of some new structural implants that could also have applications in remote robotics. I followed the paper trail and discovered The Avatars had a hand in it. I had a bug planted among them, which allowed me to take control of any robotic application," Farim recounted, "I targeted it to Dourias's genetic profile."

"How did taking my father factor into it?" Vielle asked.

"Dourias is either a captive or a corpse," Farim said, her voice catching, "I couldn't have one of their units just show up and break him out. I needed to bring another prisoner to them."

"To put more people on his trail?" Vielle pried, "Or to help him escape from the inside?"

"More the latter, but I appreciate the help I got. The bug left a distinct radiation signature," Farim said, "It was either Phylus or EshCal. Either came with more repercussions than I was comfortable with, but I would have sooner taken EshCal if my control over the biomechs was more secure. The fact is, your father was just in the wrong place at the wrong time. And for that, I'm… truly sorry."

Vielle didn't answer. Farim didn't press her. Silence stretched so long under the dead streetlamps that time grew vague.

"I…. can't hate you for that," Vielle choked out, "Not after what I've done."

"What you've done?" Farim puzzled.

"I killed thousands of people," Vielle confessed, "When I planted Yggdrasil, it leveled the high-rise district."

"But you saved the rest of ArcNos," Farim insisted, "A large part of Tanelen as well."

"I know, but saving those lives shouldn't have cost so many others. I was too willing to sacrifice them on a theory. My father and my sister are the only things holding me together right now. My girlfriend is too new to all of this to understand," Vielle poured out, "I can forgive you for taking my father, considering the circumstances. But if we find him dead, I'm holding you accountable. My last purpose in life will be to call you to task for it."

"… I would insist that you do."

The prisoner opened his coat with a wave of fermentation and body odor. He slipped a spoonful of fruit cocktail into a sock fastened under his arm.

"So anyway, SenRas came back a few days after we leveled the cavalry," Phylus recounted with a cheek full of biscuit, "That night, he came down and told Sinkua and Eytea that Kabehl was dead. We found out later that his ex-wife was a retired neuropsychiatrist…"

"Let me stop you there," the prisoner insisted, "SenRas went to Quarun to get out from under Kabehl and Amirione's noses. He and his ex-wife talked shop. He came back after the Imperialists took heavy casualties and used something his ex-wife gave him to kill Kabehl."

"Yes! Yes. How'd you know?"

"Oh, it was obvious enough that SenRas wanted no part in what was becoming of ArcNos. He was using his connection to CreSam to stay close until he knew enough to destroy them."

"Yeah, that's exactly what he was doing," Phylus said. He leaned in with a spoonful of his own fruit cocktail. The prisoner pushed the spoon away from his coat. "But what about EshCal?"

"Keep your strength, young man," the prisoner insisted, "What about her? She's a non-factor."

"You said SenRas was getting away from Kabehl and Amirione, but EshCal had ingratiated herself to Amirione," Phylus reminded, having deliberately excluded EshCal and her troops from the cavalry ambush story.

"No. They were good for her career, but she wouldn't have been loyal to them for long, if at all."

"How do you suppose?" Phylus asked.

"Her loyalty to ArcNos came first. All she would need is a glimpse beyond her own ambition to see how bad they were for her homeland."

"Again, that's exactly what happened. There was an incident at sea, and she and a few hundred of her soldiers defected."

"I knew your ambush fared too well with what you had," the prisoner said, "You had turncoat professionals and stolen armaments as well."

"Yes. Wow. You didn't even say anything about it at the time."

"A good mystery writer never points out a clue," the prisoner said, "And a great detective never mentions a hole until he knows how to fill it."

Phylus smiled as he took a bite of the grayish meat substance, finding it moderately palatable. All of it, in fact, had begun to taste more agreeable. Or at least less like shoe leather and wallpaper paste.

Trying to discuss the prisoner's past always came to no avail. Phylus had tried easing into it, but it always led to a nervous breakdown. Eventually, Phylus had promised not to bring up his past again.

Instead, Phylus started telling him about books and movies. Mysteries became the prisoner's therapy. At first, he would absorb the stories with the entirety of his attention. Eventually, he listened more passively, but the man who had insisted he was from the grayish meat substance would solve the mystery long before the protagonists had.

Clearly, this man had been a detective. That must have been what had landed him in this place, but Phylus couldn't risk pulling that string. Instead, he transitioned from works of fiction to recent history.

Phylus had been counting his meals since his encounter with the warden. Judging by that alone, Phylus had been inside for over six weeks. He forgot how many meals he had before that, but he ballparked his total time in the chaotic prison at two months.

As eager as he was to get out, he equally dreaded mitigating the damages of his absence. Calhosin lacked the finesse to talk Noble Doyen Joren down from declaring war, knowledgeable and skilled as the High Minister was. More than that, however, he feared ArcNos declaring war on Tanelen, particularly over his disappearance.

"Here, smell this," the prisoner blurted out, cutting into Phylus's reflection. He held out the sock full of fruit cocktail. "How do you think it's coming along?"

"Rancid," Phylus said, "I can't wait to drink it."

The prisoner chuckled and withdrew the sock, the trail of drippings assimilating into the churning liquid fractals. He began to drop in another spoonful, but Phylus reached over and pinched off the top of the sock.

"You need your strength, too," Phylus insisted, "It's almost time."

The search and rescue team stood at a strange and sudden border. Behind them, municipal wreckage stretched to the horizon. High-rises had toppled to gashes through their lower levels. Lamp posts had been sundered, their sparking live wires scorching rubble.

Ahead of them, however, the cityscape was unblemished. Every building in sight appeared unoccupied. In fact, by the total absence of shoe prints and tire tracks, nobody had been out there for a while.

Malia tweaked the dials on her radiation detector. She furrowed her brow, then angled the display to show it to Nikasu.

"You getting anything with yours, Farim?" Malia called out.

Vielle and Farim crouched beside each other. Farim held her radiation tracker while Vielle handled the wire and probe. The screen flickered with every motion, but it refused to give any sort of distinct reading.

Farim patted Vielle's forearm. Vielle pulled the probe out of asphalt, and Farim turned off the tracker.

"Dead end here as well," Farim said, "Have any suggestions, Malia?"

"Oh? The great detective Farim is stumped?" Malia goaded.

"I'm still thinking. But seeing as you know more than I do about what happened, I thought I'd ask for your input. I figured you might have planned for something like this," Farim snipped, "Besides, I am talking to The Investigator."

"Oh, don't you start with me," Malia said, "But no, I didn't anticipate this. And don't even start about The Coalition and predictive analysis."

"Call the base, then," Farim suggested, "I'm sure NalSet or MalVek could make sense of this."

Malia sighed. "Let me check if my comm works now," she said, pinching her earlobe.

"Malia," Mortvill greeted, "I expected I would hear from you."

"You have that little confidence in me?" Malia asked, putting her back to Farim.

"Nary the issue," Mortvill dismissed, "Should I have gleaned correctly, your once-lover diplomat is beyond your reach."

"You mean I'm incapable of finding him?"

"You mustn't be so insecure," he said, "I speak literally. It is humanly impossible to perceive, much less enter his prison without a particular manner of assistance."

"Wait. What are you saying?" Malia asked, lowering her voice, "He's what? In another world?"

"Not exactly," Mortvill said, "He has been displaced from three-dimensional space."

"How is that even possible?" Malia gasped, "Can we get him back?"

"Our universe has a fourth dimension not directly observable," he explained, "We have the means to retrieve him. As well, he may recover another asset long ago lost to us."

"Another prisoner?" she asked, "I haven't heard about anyone else being taken."

"That is because we have not spoken of his disappearance. Only recently could I confirm he may yet live," Mortvill said, "Does the term First Native hold any relevance to you?"

"I'm afraid not. Should it?"

"It ought to, though you should not have known a name or face to accompany it while you were undercover," he said, "It's the code designation given to our first recruit. He was a deep cover agent who served as a gatekeeper for others such as yourself. He invented tsora-magnetic ink."

"Color me impressed," Malia said, "So, he's the other prisoner?"

"I have every reason to believe so."

"Well, excuse any disrespect, but if you know what happened to Phylus, and this First Native is so…?"

"Why did I wait for you to contact me?" Mortvill interrupted.

"Um… Yeah. That's what I was getting at," Malia said, "This doesn't seem like a good time for forced personal growth or what have you."

"Nothing of the sort," he assured, "The fact of the matter is that I don't know from where each of them were displaced. I had no other choice but to wait for you to narrow the search band."

"You didn't think to tell me any of this ahead of time?"

"I maintain that it would not have made any positive impact," Mortvill insisted, "But while I have you, what's become of the message I gave you?"

"Um, Spril has it."

"Ah, so, you've made progress?"

"I don't see how that's progress," Malia muttered, "Look, not to get pushy, but when can we expect help?"

"I'm triangulating your position. The radiation is interfering with the database," Mortvill said, "That message applies to Spril."

"Then why didn't you give it to him?"

"It is for you to hear and deliver to The Subtransit Resistance. Were you not aware of Spril's relevance to us?"

"I was not," Malia said, "Have you found the nearest gate point?"

"I have," he sighed, "Remain where you are."

Mortvill disconnected, then called for the other three Originals. Chekov, MalVek, and NalSet came before him shortly.

"Malia and her daughters have nearly found their objective," Mortvill opened, pulling a small notepad from his pocket, "They are through the blackout zone, but now, they need our assistance. NalSet. Chekov. Take these supplies from the repository and gate to this location."

He tore off the top page and handed it to Chekov.

"Do you truly think he's still alive?" Chekov asked, passing the list to NalSet.

"He was always especially resilient," NalSet said, flashing her a reassuring smile as he read the list, "In fact, I would be more surprised if we don't find him alive."

NalSet pocketed the note and left with Chekov close behind. Once the door closed, Mortvill turned his attention to MalVek.

"For you, I have a different assignment," Mortvill said, "One to which you are specifically suited."

"What would you have me do, sir?" MalVek asked.

"Nikasu will soon return to an empty home, none to her knowledge," Mortvill explained, "As you and she have spoken, I've elected to send you to assist her."

"You want me to help her find Sinkua?"

"First, ease her into the knowledge of his disappearance. But yes, you are to assist her in recovering him."

"I'll see to it right away, sir," MalVek said, then left the chamber.

Mortvill swiped the side of his mask, shifting the display to a vast spreadsheet. With a small utterance, a printer in the corner of the room began to hum.

"Words are insufficient recompense for the burdens I foist upon you," he sighed, lifting his mask to pinch the bridge of his nose, "I only wish for you to know that I am sorry."

Phylus lay on the roiling ground with his eyes closed and jaw slack. The androgynous warden nudged him with its foot. He didn't stir. The warden set Phylus's tray down beside him. Phylus's feet shifted and shoulders twitched. The warden paused, but Phylus was still again. Stone-faced, the warden turned away, and luminous liquid fractals rippled around it.

Phylus opened his eyes and sprang upright, clutching the tray. The warden turned to see him with his meager ration raining around him. Phylus swiped at it, but the warden pulled the rippling fractals around itself and vanished.

Phylus closed his eyes and shallowed his breathing, listening to his surroundings. Back and a bit to the left, the air thrummed almost imperceptibly. Phylus spun around and snapped out his arm.

The warden appeared just in time to take Phylus's tray to the throat. Hacking and choking, it dropped to its hands and knees. Phylus kicked the warden in the throat, and a rivulet of blood fell from its mouth. Phylus struck a second time, bones cracking against his shoe. The warden's arms gave out.

Phylus snapped his tray in half, then a quarter, over his knee. He crouched beside the warden.

The prisoner came to Phylus's side and withdrew the festering sock. Phylus took it in exchange for the tray fragment. He untied the top, pulling a face at the odor, and threw back a long pull of dirty laundry prison wine.

"Hold it down," Phylus said, gesturing to the warden.

The prisoner dug a knee into the warden's upper back. He palmed the back of its head and pushed down.

Phylus took a second longer pull and grabbed the chrysalis affixed to the back of the warden's head. Phylus wrenched the crystal chamber, and the warden shrieked horribly. The prisoner lifted the warden's head and slammed its face against the liquid fractal floor. While the prisoner drove the warden's face into the floor, Phylus kept twisting until the chrysalis popped free.

No blood issued forth from the open wound. The inner surface was raw but seared over.

The prisoner held up the warden's head, and Phylus removed the goggles. Phylus took one more swig and returned the sock to the prisoner. The prisoner tied it off while Phylus donned the goggles and lay facedown.

The prisoner pinned Phylus with his knee and dripped fruit cocktail wine on the back of his head. He pressed the chrysalis's mounting screw under the base of Phylus's skull, but for all his grinding and twisting, he couldn't pierce flesh.

Muttering an apology, the prisoner pushed a corner of the broken tray into the spot until a thin rivulet of blood burbled forth. Phylus's body tensed and wrenched as the prisoner screwed in the chrysalis, quickening the bleeding with every turn. Phylus cried out in agony, and the prisoner stuffed the half-empty sock in his mouth.

After what felt like several minutes, the prisoner successfully mounted the chrysalis into the back of Phylus's head.

"Okay," the prisoner whispered as he dismounted, "Let's get you to your feet."

Phylus accepted the prisoner's hand and brought himself to standing. He braced against the prisoner as he pawed at the goggles, further disoriented by the distortion of the lenses. Eventually, he found the controls, and the crystals came alight as he turned them on.

The liquid fractals stopped churning. The roiling surfaces and rippling edges cohered into straight lines and smooth angles. The very nature of this prison suddenly made sense, looking as though reality had been rolled into itself along an imperceptible dimension.

More importantly, he could see an exit.

Scattered about were patches congruent to the world outside. They showed a room in utter disrepair, but that was of no particular concern. Anywhere outside of this strange pocket in space would have been easier to find their way home from.

The two hooked arms, and Phylus guided the prisoner toward the exit. Sensible light peeled outward as he staggered through, but he stopped as the prisoner cried out and collapsed.

Phylus fell to a crouch and looked back to find the warden clutching the prisoner's ankles and dragging him back. The prisoner swiped at the warden with the tray fragment, but he couldn't quite reach. Phylus's hooked his arm under the prisoner's shoulder and pulled him back to his feet.

He powered forth in clumsy and uneasy steps, guiding the prisoner and dragging the warden as it scrambled upright. Sensible light peeled all the way to the edges of his peripheral vision and beyond. They had returned to the outside world.

Standing just outside the portal, Phylus wrenched the warden's hands from the prisoner and grabbed its shoulder. The prisoner shuffled off to the corner, well clear of the portal.

Phylus plowed his fist into its abdomen, doubling the warden over. He drove his knee into its face, hooked its arm, and thrust-kicked its kneecaps. The warden's legs slid out from underneath itself. Phylus eased it to the ground, walking the warden halfway back into the liquid fractal prison.

Phylus turned off the Eyes of the Dragon. The portal vanished. And it took everything below the warden's abdomen with it.

The search party and Chekov stood in a small derelict lobby, watching as NalSet slowly swept a probe through the dusty air. Vielle's eyes wandered to the furniture, timeworn and largely overturned. In her periphery, she noticed Farim doing likewise, though with a greater measure of subtlety.

Vielle turned her focus to NalSet, wondering if he had just become a person of interest in Farim's search. After all, he had just happened to show up shortly after they freed Nikasu and her subversive cellmates. She tapped Nikasu's hand, and they entwined their fingers.

"What exactly is he doing?" Malia asked.

"Scanning for soft spots," Chekov said, "Basically."

"Soft spots?" Farim asked.

"Areas vulnerable to hyperspace crossover," Chekov explained, "It can potentially be done anywhere. But as I understand, each subsequent use is easier than the last, because crossing over, well, softens the area."

"Or weakens it," Malia said. Chekov nodded absently. "So, is he looking for any soft spot or the one where Phylus was taken through?"

"He's working toward the latter."

"If Phylus is alive, someone would need to bring him rations. So, we're looking at a very soft spot at the center of a huge displacement of some form of radiation," Farim reasoned, "He's following its wake to the source."

"It's more like he's backtracking it," Chekov corrected, "The finer details aren't my forte, but the meat-and-potatoes is that exiting hyperspace causes more pronounced displacement than entering it does."

"Hypertriangulation," Malia nodded, "Fascinating."

"I suppose you could call it that," Chekov agreed.

NalSet waved them over. "I've picked up a trail," he announced, "Follow me."

The prisoner and Phylus stumbled arm-in-arm along the rundown halls. The top half of the warden hung lifeless from Phylus's shoulder, bouncing against his back with each step.

Phylus struggled and largely failed to keep his focus against the combination of alcohol, blood loss, and impending food poisoning. The goggles periodically flickered on, none to his accord. He was acclimating to looking through gemstones, but those flickers nearly floored him.

The walls were riddled with the damages of neglect. If not for the frequent attendance to their displaced quarters, the building would have looked long ago abandoned and condemned.

Yet, voices echoed through holes in the walls. Though he couldn't pin down an exact direction, Phylus was sure that they came from nowhere near where he and the prisoner had been held. One of the only ways it made sense was if this building housed multiple such prisons.

The other was that somebody had come for them.

As they came around a corner, they came upon another androgynous warden. Phylus dropped the half-body, and the prisoner handed him the tray fragment before breaking away to brace on the wall. Phylus swaggered toward the warden with a glower that could have frosted the Southland Sea had they not been obstructed.

"Who are you?" the warden asked, stoic with its head askew, "How did you get here?"

"You can call me The Patriarch," Phylus said, "And I am sickened by what you're doing to my children."

The corner of the tray fragment ripped through the warden's throat, and it collapsed into a bloody heap. Phylus palmed its face and bashed the back of its head against the floor until the chrysalis shattered.

Phylus gathered up the bisected warden and offered the prisoner the tray fragment and his hand.

"Come on," he offered, "If we go back the way this one came, we ought to find an exit."

NalSet stopped in a breezeway office and cocked an ear. "I hear voices," he said.

As though to confirm his assertion, the opposite door opened, and in swaggered a grizzled man with blood speckling his salt and pepper beard. His unkempt hair was tamed only by a set of goggles with intricate gemstone lenses. A line of dry blood encircled his neck and traced down his sternum.

In one hand, he held a bloodied fragment of a cafeteria tray. With the other, he clutched the wrist of a bisected human body, which he had draped behind his back.

Vielle was first to step forward. "Dad?" she asked.

He dropped the shiv first, then the body. A smile strained through his pain as he nodded and held out his arms. Vielle ran to him, wrapping her arms around his midsection. The stench, the blood, the dead body, and the shiv, none of it mattered. All that mattered was that her father had escaped.

Nikasu and Malia moved in closer. Phylus lowered himself to sit on the floor.

"Come on, friend," Phylus called back over, "They're here to help."

A second man, frail with malnutrition and age, shuffled into the breezeway office. He moved without certainty, pawing at the air. Blood stained his right hand from the fingertips to halfway up his forearm.

Farim, Chekov, and NalSet all stood dumbstruck. After all these years, here he was. Alive. Even if he looked as though far more years had passed for him.

"Dourias!" Farim exclaimed.

"Y-young lady?" Dourias stammered, his eyes alight with returning lucidity, ".... Farim."

"Yeah," Farim nodded, her voice catching as she took his hands, "I'm so glad you're alive."

"And I you," Dourias professed, "I have to say, you've aged remarkably."

"Dourias?" Chekov asked, "Do you… remember us?"

"You two," Dourias pondered, "You're Chekov, yes? And… you're NalSet. Or MalVek? But…"

"I'm NalSet. MalVek is my younger brother. And this is Chekov," NalSet said, "Did you have any sense of time while you were gone?"

"It… became meaningless."

"So I would suppose, seeing as it doesn't exist in hyperspace," NalSet said, pacing off, "But how would that account for this?"

"I'm sorry, but I'm at a loss," Dourias said, "What is he talking about?"

"You disappeared nine years ago," Chekov said.

"Only nine?" Dourias puzzled, "No. No, that can't be right. By the looks of me, I must have been gone much longer than that. But you're all far too young."

"Dourias…" Farim beckoned.

"B-but you!" he cut off, "Your son must look like your older brother by now!"

"I don't have a son," Farim said, "I miscarried shortly after you disappeared. Nine years ago."

"Oh… Oh dear," Dourias muttered, hunkering down against the wall, "What's going on here? I feel like…"

"Somehow, the, um, nonexistence of time caused you to age faster," Farim said, crouching beside him. She placed her hand against the front of his shoulder in reassurance. "You look about twenty years older than you should be. I think Phylus experienced a similar phenomenon, judging by his beard."

"H-has it truly only been nine years?"

"I'm sorry, but it has."

"I see…" Dourias said, staring at the floor

"We'll figure it out," Farim promised. She turned and called to NalSet. "Hey! Any theories as to his accelerated aging?"

"You know damn well it's too soon for any of that," NalSet snapped, "Damn fool."

"Well, maybe you can answer something else for me," Farim said, guiding Dourias to his feet alongside her. She squeezed his hand as she drew a handgun from inside her coat, leveling it at Chekov and NalSet successively. "Which one of you sold him out?"

Chapter 6

SenRas paced through the array of conference tables, surveying the seamless workstations. Fingers chattered along keyboards as discussions bounced around the open-air office. He closed his eyes as he sipped his Ierodhesan dark roast.

The free exchange of intel within the Ministry of Covert Affairs made for more expedient processing. And the absolute irony was the perfect cover, it being more widely known as the Ministry of Human Resources. But it also made a terrible racket, the sort that most people in their seventies wouldn't willingly endure.

He stopped beside a svelte young woman and patted her shoulder. "Lights, please."

While MarLys made for the light switch, SenRas continued to the head of the room where he prepared the projector. MarLys turned off the lights, and the chattering ceased at once. SenRas smiled and sipped his coffee as all attention turned to him.

"I'd like to begin by apologizing," SenRas said, "Since its induction, this Ministry has been so inundated with work that we've had no time to discuss our overarching objective. Granted, the scandals we've been investigating have been part of it, but we're no more useful than everyone else if we're only chasing shadows. Let's leave that to the other Ministries. In here, our work boils down to two questions." He uncapped a pen and wrote on the projector. "Who are The Avatars of Fate? And what are they after?"

He paced for a moment, letting the questions linger. One young man raised his hand.

"MerSul?" SenRas said, gesturing with the pen.

"Mass destruction?" MerSul said, "They're trying to destroy the two Northland powerhouses."

"Yes, they appear to be," SenRas nodded, pacing the head of the room, "But if that's the extent of it, why do they go to such elaborate lengths?"

"Because it keeps people like us from catching up to them," MerSul argued, "What if all their machinations and manipulations only exist to keep us chasing our tails?"

"Chaos," MarLys chimed in, "They create madness all over Ouristihra until everyone else is panicking, and they're the only ones with a sense of control."

"I think you're both correct by a certain measure," SenRas said, "They assert dominance by engineering madness. However, they must have some design beyond that. But what of it is meant to keep us chasing our tails? And what of it serves their ends?"

"So, if we know what's relevant, we can figure out their ends," MarLys said, "But we need to know what they're after to figure out what's relevant."

"Truly a pickle," SenRas said, stopping at the projector, "Now, the good news is that we've deeply damaged their ranks since the ArcNosian Civil War. The bad news is that the remaining Named always become bolder and more cunning after every loss. Here's what we know and where we've come to.

"Kabehl. Code name: The Scout. From Ferya. In charge of recruiting. Carried a device that produced solid holograms of melee weapons. Equipped with an intravenous nanochip that repaired fatal injuries. He died at the end of the war. You're welcome.

"Amirione. Code name: The Hunter. From ArcNos with Kirtsian lineage. In charge of assassinations. Bone structure was chemically reinforced to be highly impact resilient. He also died at the end of the war.

"Malia. Code name: The Investigator. From Ivaria. In charge of intercepting messages and planting disinformation. No known enhancements. Is actually a mole from an opposing agency called The Coalition. The role has most likely been reassigned.

"Masfaru. Code name: The Criminal. From Quarun. In charge of keeping valuable commodities away from their enemies. Endowed with superhuman strength and a reinforced prosthetic hand. Killed shortly before the war.

"AinZun. Code name: The Engineer. Also from Quarun. In charge of developing electromechanical systems. Armed with self-accelerating alloy boots and gun barrel vision. She died shortly before the Heniokhos Disaster. Again, you're welcome.

"Ebralgi. Code name: The Geneticist. From Berinin. In charge of biological and genetic research and developments. Endowed with a shifting-state body structure which morphed around incoming physical threats. He died during the Heniokhos Disaster.

"Olsa. Code name: The Politician. Former Prime Duchess of Eprilen. In charge of directing political discord. We believe they removed her from The Avatars of Fate following her impeachment. We are currently investigating a theory that Noble Doyen Joren replaced her.

"The General. We know of this rank, but we've yet to put a name to it. We have theorized that CreSam was under consideration. Given what followed, the only safe assumption is that the role is held by someone outside of ArcNos.

"Pahres. Code name: The Prophet. Homeland unknown. In charge of cultural manipulation via cultish mysticism and manufactured prophecies and symbolism. Superhuman traits are unreported. A few years after the war, he developed a form of dissociative identity disorder with a second persona working for The Coalition. He died during the Heniokhos Disaster. Reassignment seems improbable.

"Last, The Harvester. Name and homeland unknown. In charge of developing and overseeing all operations as well as probabilistic outcome analysis. The meaning of his name and the extent of his abilities are unknown. Psychic foresight and telepathy are both highly suspected. He may be the only one who knows the true overall agenda of The Avatars of Fate.

"Any questions?"

"So," MerSul began, "We've got an unknown supreme leader and nine subordinates, six of whom are dead. Two with your help."

"And of the three remaining," a second man added, "we only have one name."

"Are we sure that's all The Named agents?" MarLys asked.

"Our intel is inconclusive," SenRas said, "The data we collected from Black Tie should provide an answer though. For now, we'll focus on filling the gaps in what we already know. We can expect The Politician to collude with

The Investigator and The General in manufacturing a war between Tanelen and ArcNos."

"The General could be a senior officer in Tanelen's military," MarLys suggested, "But maybe that's too obvious."

"That could be why they do it," MerSul countered, "They know we'd ignore it because it's too obvious."

"We'll investigate the Tanelenese military for evidence of Avatar indoctrination," SenRas said, sipping his coffee, "In the meantime, however, consider where else they might gain a tactical advantage."

"What about The Investigator?" an older woman asked.

"I think they meant for LenSom to assume that role," a younger man said, "He actively suppressed the influence of the Ministries and obstructed anybody connected to the Subtransit Resistance."

"That makes sense," MarLys said, "But what about Eprilen?"

"Elaborate?" SenRas beckoned.

"What if instead of discharging Olsa, they reassigned her to replace Malia?"

"It's feasible," SenRas nodded, "Probable, even. Look into it."

The door to Biroe's office flew open, the knob bouncing hard against the bumper. A tall, portly man crossed the floor with his gaze fixated on Biroe. He pulled up a chair and sat, wiping a sweaty strand of thinning flaxen hair from his forehead.

"Would you mind explaining this last message?" he demanded.

"Prime Minister OshMar!" Biroe beamed, extending his arms, "Welcome to the Ministry of Treasury. Come in. Have a seat. Would you like a cup of coffee? A nip of something harder, perhaps?"

"That's quite enough," OshMar grumbled.

"Yes, and quite enough of your attitude as well," Biroe countered, "Let's start over."

"Fine," OshMar sighed, slouching back, "Why has there been no change in your budget?"

"The number is set in stone, I'm afraid," Biroe said, "But why hasn't yours changed either?"

"The contractors can't budge on their estimate," OshMar said, "Things cost what they cost. Repairing the high-rise district is no exception. So, you need to do what Infrastructure can't and move money around."

"Well, I can't," Biroe said, "Everything is choked at the moment. My estimate is the sum of what we can spare from every sub-budget for the next thirteen months."

"I'm not sure which disgusts me more," OshMar sneered, wiping that same strand from his forehead, "Your miserliness or your presumption of the entire Ministry's stupidity."

"Pardon?"

"You expect me to believe we can only afford forty percent of the cleanup cost for the Heniokhos Disaster because, in your own words, everything is choked? I know how these things work."

"Oh, now if that were true, you'd work in Treasury. But speaking of presumptions of stupidity," Biroe said. He wheeled over to a file cabinet and pulled a stack of papers, then returned and laid them out before OshMar. "I did some research and drew up my own estimate. How do you explain the vast discrepancy against their numbers?"

OshMar skimmed the papers, hoping to find a mistake as he compared Biroe's figures to the contractors' from rough memory. But, as he ought to have expected, the last three pages were Biroe's research into market norms for raw costs and markups. OshMar dropped the papers on the desk and slid them back to Biroe.

"I've asked them to come down on the estimate," he sighed, "They won't budge."

"And I'm the miserly one," Biroe laughed, "Would they change their minds if you showed them this research?"

"No, I don't think that's not the problem," OshMar said, "This seems to be a political matter for them."

"What the hell?" Biroe snarled, "Tens of thousands of people have died, that being among the better potential outcomes, and they'd rather bitch about politics and choke even more money out of us?"

"I'm afraid we're at an impasse with them," OshMar said, "You're sure there's no way to come up with the money."

"We'd run a considerable deficit if we did," Biroe said, quickly continuing as OshMar poised himself to interrupt, "Meaning we would need to borrow from abroad."

"I'll assume you've already tried that."

"And you'll assume correctly. Nobody will loan us anything."

"Unwilling?" OshMar asked, to which Biroe nodded, "Not just unable?"

"The general reasoning is how we've treated Berinin lately," Biroe explained, "Everyone knows how we involved Chieftain Sage Galo in the Heniokhos Disaster. Frankly, with everything he went through here, just after we fulfilled our compensatory contract, nobody wants to enter a fiscal arrangement with us."

"Damn. More of this," OshMar muttered, "We're both stymied by protests over the very thing we're trying to fix."

"Who are the contractors protesting?"

"Insider involvement. Prime Minister of Defense Spril was seen in the area with a Junior Consultant and a former but recent employee of the Ministry of Foreign Affairs."

"Vielle and Sinkua. Right. One moment," Biroe said. He turned his back to OshMar to make a phone call. "EshCal? Contact Calhosin and FerLyn. Lunch Break Protocol."

"Lunch Break Protocol?" OshMar asked as Biroe hung up and turned back around

"Yes," Biroe said, wheeling around his desk, "I assume you're hungry."

Sanus sat on the ottoman, resting her elbows on her knees. Aromatic steam billowed from the mug of tea beside her. A sense of calm drifted through her as she breathed it in, feeling all too artificial. Too routine.

Nenbard knelt before her and patted her forearm. She held out her hand, more on ingrained reaction than awareness. Nenbard kissed her palm heel and pushed her wristband down, revealing a splotchy bruise spanning the width of her wrist.

At its center was a slightly darker circular indention. Next to it was a scar tissue divot.

He opened a bottle of some pungently floral substance. Sanus sipped her tea as Nenbard soaked a cotton pad with the fluid, staining it scorched blue. He pressed the pad over the discolored indentation, and the burnt blue substance soaked into it until it overflowed and spread across her wrist.

Nenbard picked up a second bottle, its perimeter lined with tiny syringes. He detached one, stuck it through a hole in the cap, and filled the chamber.

Sanus finished her tea and returned the mug to the saucer at her side. The discoloration had already begun to fade. She grazed his cheek with her fingertips and laid her hand back in his. She closed her eyes, and a glimmer of a moment later, he pressed the needle into her skin.

The sensation of cold, sterile metal under her skin subsided. Sanus opened her eyes and watched the discoloration vanish. She kissed Nenbard on the cheek.

"I think…" she whispered, "… it's getting weaker."

"We'll run a blood test tomorrow," Nenbard said, "Maybe the infection is finally…"

Sanus shook her head and put her finger to his lips.

"The treatment," she said, gesturing to the bottles, "It's not doing as much."

Nenbard stared at the bottles in a moment of contemplation. Down the hall, the phone rang once and most of a second time. He looked back to Sanus.

"Actually," he exhaled, "Your brother and I discovered something that might advance our research."

"What is it?" Sanus asked, her eyes drifting shut.

"There might be more to that flower than we thought," he said, "But you need to rest. I'll tell you more later. I already let our associates know."

Nenbard stood and gathered everything up. As he headed out of the living room, Ocronn emerged from the hall with the cordless phone in his hand. They hesitated awkwardly at their near collision.

"Sorry," Ocronn said, "Call for you."

"Who is it?" Nenbard asked, twisting past him and continuing to the kitchen.

"Yrlis."

"Probably just calling me as a relay to Galo. Take a message."

"That won't do," Ocronn said, following him, "She's insisting on speaking with you."

"I can't fathom why, but let's have it," Nenbard conceded. He set everything on the counter and took the phone from Ocronn. "Hello? Nenbard speaking."

Spril winced as the light pierced his squinting eyelids. Shielding his eyes with his forearm, he groped along the wall until he found the light switch.

He moved up the hall until he found the thermostat, and he turned off the heater. A distorted voice reverberated from beyond the hall.

Spril ambled on until he came to the dining and living areas. Ignoring Yrlis in the kitchen, he switched off the lights and continued to the living room.

He lay facedown on the couch, unfolded the paper he had left on the arm last night, and stared at it. Just as he had every morning.

Spril winced at the light from the refrigerator as Yrlis swiped an iced coffee. She grabbed a second bottle from a case on the counter. Wrapping them in her shirt, she uncapped the bottles. Yrlis put on her slippers and joined Spril in the living room.

She sat in front of the couch and laid her upturned hand near his shoulder. Spril wriggled his arm out from under himself and set his hand in hers.

"Morning," he choked out, testing his voice and his ears. Both hurt less than yesterday. He accepted the coffee and took a sip. "Thanks for the drink."

"Any time, love," Yrlis said, "Are you up for letting me check you out?"

"No," Spril grumbled, "It's nothing that… I don't know what it is, but it's nothing you can do anything about."

"You think staring at that note all day is helping?"

"It keeps everything from hurting too much."

"You know, at first I thought it might be a migraine. The way the light hurts you. But then I realized all your senses were easily overwhelmed," she said, "I don't know what the point of that note is. But somehow, it's calming your senses, isn't it?"

"Yeah. It's, um… shit," Spril trailed off, wincing as his thoughts prodded his senses, "It gives me something else to focus on."

"Something else?" Yrlis pondered, "What exactly happened at Heniokhos?"

Spril choked out a rueful chuckle. "Am I that transparent to you?"

"You seemed different when you came home," Yrlis said, "And you're not getting any better. So, either I'm not seeing something, or you're not showing me the whole picture."

"Well, it's…" Spril hesitated, "I guess I haven't told you everything."

"Sweetie?" she beckoned, "You know I'm here to help. You won't get any judgment from me. So, why are you still holding out on me?"

"Because," he sighed, "I'm not ready to admit to myself that it's real."

"Not talking about it won't keep it from being real. Now, I've got a whole case of Popken Lime in the fridge. And you've got a pack of Schauzen's Deluxe beside it. We can sit here all day while you tell me what happened."

Spril took another pull of his room temperature coffee as he let her assertion marinate, bolstering his vocal faculties to speak through his trepidation.

"I guess you're right," he choked out, "It started a few weeks before Heniokhos. I was investigating Laboratory 1341 with EshCal. I had a strange experience in the subbasements."

"What was it?"

"I was checking the walls for defects. Anything to denote a hidden passage. The constant whiteness was dizzying. I could feel my pupils dilating and contracting. Then, everything was too loud, and I was hearing things I shouldn't have been able to hear," Spril recounted, "EshCal noticed it, too, but she didn't say anything. I think she thinks I didn't notice her noticing."

"This is good," Yrlis smiled, "I mean, not that this happened. But letting it out will be good for you."

"Thank you. Anyway," Spril continued, "I had a few more moments like that in the following weeks. But what happened during the first biomech outbreak really worried me."

"What was it?"

"I approached the first one to enter Epsilon Burger. It was just looking around, mostly fixating on Vielle, Galo, and Nikasu. Probably just a scout," Spril said, "It pounced at me, and I put my hand out like a jackass."

"That's where those scars came from," Yrlis said.

"Yeah," Spril said, "Anyway, I caught it by its beacon light, but it went out before it hit my hand."

"Did anyone else notice?"

"SenRas joked about it, but I denied it ever happened. Denied it more to myself, now that I think about it."

"Has it happened since then?"

"Yeah," Spril muttered, his voice weakening, "One more time. At Heniokhos."

"Spril," Yrlis urged, "Are you sure you're ready to talk about that?"

"Can't turn back now," Spril insisted, downing the last of his tepid coffee, "Ozzera had been creating biomechs from the wreckage, and we'd been busting them up pretty well. So, she gathered the scraps we'd piled up and built them into a single mass. Obvious act of desperation, but it didn't matter. She put all of us on our asses.

"Well, all of us except Eytea. Ozzera used that enormous biomech to corner her in the sky. Drove her into an absolute panic. Now, I've seen a lot of shit, but seeing someone like her in a state like that is pretty damn unsettling.

"Sinkua was first on his feet. Love like theirs wouldn't let him stay down. I swear, for all his talk of failing people, he'd be the last to quit trying."

Yrlis looked at him solemnly.

"Sorry… I'm digressing," Spril sighed, "Sinkua scaled the biomech. Easily ten meters up, and he leapt off to pull Eytea away from it. Probably would have worked if Ozzera hadn't figured it out.

"The biomech swatted him away. Would've knocked most people out cold, but well…

"Anyway, as he was falling, Ozzera impaled Eytea. Drilled the biomech through her. I've seen a lot of deaths, but that was particularly gruesome."

"Spril?" Yrlis beckoned, reaching for his shoulder.

At the touch of her hand, he realized his entire body was trembling. His knuckles popped with the force with which he ground his fingertips into the arm of the couch.

"Y-yeah?"

"I'm glad you're getting this out. But what does it have to do with what happened at Epsilon Burger?"

"I'm getting to that," he insisted, "Ozzera went after Sinkua next. The tip opened like a mouth made of tentacles. It had a massive red beacon light inside. The thing surrounded him. Started closing like it was going to eat him.

"Then… Well… I don't know how it happened. I just blinked and… suddenly, I was shielding him. Once again, I put my hand out like a jackass. Nothing happened at first, but I couldn't make myself move.

"The beacon light shattered so hard that the tentacles whipped back and broke off. Set off a chain reaction all along Heniokhos. Blew out Ozzera's chamber."

"And that's when Vielle planted that huge tree," Yrlis nodded.

"Yggdrasil, yes."

"I think I understand," Yrlis said, presenting two sheets of paper from her pocket, "Do you know what these are?"

"Genome maps?" he guessed, "From the samples I gave you?"

"Yes, but these two don't match each other. I only asked for samples from Sinkua," she said, "You gave me your own blood, didn't you?"

"Just two were mine," Spril confessed, "The rest were his."

"You were hoping I'd find an explanation for what's been happening to you."

"… Did you?"

"Well, I found something to work from," she said, "I can't account for your sensory fits. Not yet anyway."

"Can you explain it in a way I'll understand?" Spril asked.

"See these sequences?" Yrlis invited, pointing to a string of highlighted letters, "It's nearly impossible for these to occur in nature."

"How close to impossible? I mean, there are a few dozen million people in the world. That has to make some difference here."

"The population could be a few dozen billion, and the odds would still be against more than a few popping up once apiece. And the odds of two or more in one person would be astronomical."

"So, if it's virtually impossible for me have these genes naturally," Spril pondered, "Do you think I was... tampered with? The way Sinkua was?"

"It's a possibility. A very distinct one, actually," Yrlis said, sipping the last of her iced coffee, "But the sequences themselves are actually quite mundane. The most remarkable thing about them is their rarity."

"But how else would I have these abilities?"

"I'm still..."

"Hold on," Spril cut in, "What would it take to, um, reconcile these sequences?"

"What do you mean?"

"What would you have to change in them to make them, well..."

"Something more reasonably probable?"

"Yes. That."

"Well..." Yrlis said, trailing off as she studied the genome map, "Actually, for this one, you'd only need to swap out two letters."

"Not much, then," Spril said, "But what would happen to the letters they swapped out?"

"Well, it's..." Yrlis said, trailing off once more, "You know what? I think I might be on to something."

Spril's phone rang. He answered, spoke briefly, then offered it to Yrlis.

"Who is it?" she asked.

"EshCal," he said, "She didn't say what it's about."

"Hmm. Give it here."

Spril's attention returned to the note before the phone was out of his hand. He rose from the couch and shuffled out of the living room.

"I'll be in the garage," he said, "I might be on to something, too."

EshCal waved OshMar over as he walked into Epsilon Burger. He moved through the crowded dining room to join her and the others, sitting at the end of the booth seat where a tray of food awaited him.

"Hey! Good to see you, OshMar," FerLyn greeted, "I got you a patty melt and barbecue chips."

"How did you...?"

"You had it in the cafeteria last week," FerLyn reminded, "When we had lunch together."

"Ah. Right," OshMar nodded, "So. Where are we?"

"I was just asking these two," Calhosin said, gesturing to Biroe and EshCal, "why we would have our offsite meeting here of all places."

"It's because we have history here," Biroe cut in.

"No, we don't," Calhosin refused, "You have history here. None of us were part of the Subtransit Resistance. And EshCal went turncoat much later in the war."

"We get discounts," EshCal said, "Half off for everyone who fended off the biomechs. Thirty percent off for their guests. Forty and twenty for anyone else who was here for it."

"Oh," Calhosin said, rubbing his chin, "Well, that's nice of them."

"It is," EshCal said, "Can we get to business now?"

"Now that the Prime Minister of Infrastructure has joined us," Calhosin said, "We most certainly may. OshMar?"

"Well, the only contractor capable of reconstructing the high-rise district is charging more than double our budget," OshMar said, "Biroe may have already filled you in, but they're inflating their estimate out of political protest."

"Biroe told us about the impasse," FerLyn said, "The contractor is protesting domestic involvement in the Heniokhos Disaster. And we can't get an international loan because of what happened with Chieftain Sage Galo after we completed our recompensatory contract."

"That's the size of it," OshMar nodded, "Do you have some insight as to how to address the contractor's protests?"

"No, just more bad news," FerLyn replied, "Active protesters are gathering in the high-rise district. The fact that they're willing to enter that environment without protective equipment should be a testament to how serious they are."

"Or testament to their ignorance," Calhosin said, "Never discount the power of mass delusion."

"In any case," FerLyn continued, "whether it's ignorance or persistence, the movement is gaining momentum."

"Have they resorted to violence or threats?" EshCal asked.

"No, but it's not impossible," FerLyn said, "And their growth is nearly self-sustaining. The last time an organized protest hit that point, we ended up with communities down here."

"Meaning we're about to be on the wrong side of a revolution," EshCal sighed, rubbing her temples.

"So. The only capable hands have tied themselves. Nobody abroad will help us unbind them. And the site is overrun with protestors because we're not restoring the area," Calhosin summarized, "I assume you brought me here hoping I could negotiate a loan from one of our neighbors."

"Something to that effect, yes," Biroe said, "Infrastructure, Treasury, and Domestic Affairs are all stymied."

"Well, I've been reaching out to other leaders and diplomats as a precursor for Spril's Anti-Avatar task force," Calhosin said, "Everyone's keeping their distance for fear of being implicated in our difficulties with Tanelen."

"Well, this isn't going well," Biroe sighed, rubbing his chin, "Four Ministries at an impasse."

"So, I suppose you invited me here as some kind of failsafe," EshCal said, raising an eyebrow, "Sorry, but the news from Domestic and Foreign Affairs bodes poorly for Defense."

"I understand," Biroe said, "What about The Coalition?"

EshCal panned the table. FerLyn. OshMar. Calhosin. She scarcely spoke with any of them until recently. FerLyn had all but taken up residence on the line between shrewd and suspicious. OshMar was constantly burdened by anxiety. And Calhosin thrived on contradiction. Any of them could have been spies.

She would need to choose her words carefully and be inconspicuous about it. Offer enough to not appear distrusting, but not so much as to appear too trusting. Enough to be useful. Not enough to use against her.

Or just enough to lure them to action. Surely, Biroe had exactly that in mind.

"I'm not aware of any Avatar involvement in the aftermath of the Heniokhos Disaster," EshCal said, "But I'll report what we've discussed and request a more thorough investigation."

"In the meantime, is there anything we can do to rein in the situation?" OshMar asked.

"Are there any contractors we could hire for partial restorations?" Biroe asked.

"Not that I've found, but I doubt I've exhausted my options."

"It could help if we knew how the Heniokhos Disaster was orchestrated," FerLyn suggested, "How were so many beacons installed without anyone getting suspicious?"

"Likely by hiding them in plain sight," OshMar said, "They probably gave them to utility workers with a mundane cover story."

"Makes sense, I suppose," FerLyn said, fidgeting with her bangs, "Sorry. Sorry. I'm sure I'm just worrying over nothing."

"Dealing with The Avatars takes a healthy dose of paranoia," EshCal assured, "By the way, isn't what these contractors are doing illegal? I'm quite sure that anti-discriminatory business practice laws extend to political discrimination."

"You're right, but it isn't a matter of simply taking them to court," FerLyn explained, "There's a conflict of interest at play."

"Right. Right," EshCal said, tapping her finger on the table, "Would it be a matter to bring before the Ouristihran Union or Union Parliament?"

"Not that simple," Calhosin said, "If one of our own brings it up, we risk being prematurely halted. We, having an arguable direct line to the Ouristihran Union, would be pressing charges against civilians for our own gain. That's what FerLyn meant by a conflict of interest. And clearly, nobody abroad will take up the charge on our behalf."

"If another civilian brought the case to them, that could work," OshMar considered, "But anyone we found to do it could be traced back to us."

"Well, it sounds like our best option is to take the problem into our own hands," Biroe suggested, "We'll start a volunteer service committee and clean out some of the wreckage."

"Fix the high-rise district while we fix our public image," FerLyn added, "Eventually, the contractor will have no choice but to cooperate."

"Speaking of public relations," Calhosin said, "Won't the protestors insist we're only doing this to save face?"

"And?" Biroe challenged, "If they want to bitch about ulterior motives while we're cleaning things up, that's their problem, and they're the problem."

"We?"

"Yes, when I said we should start a committee, I meant we and volunteers from our Ministries drive up there and shovel garbage."

"Oh, I understood that much. But how much," Calhosin said, gesturing to Biroe's wheelchair, "cleaning up do you expect to do in your condition?"

"I intend to manage the budget," Biroe said, "I believe I can keep tools and protective equipment well enough within our means that we can furnish the protestors with safety gear as well."

"And coerce them into helping us?" Calhosin asked.

"That's up to them," Biroe shrugged, flashing a smirk, "But no matter their decision, it's our responsibility to see to their safety."

"Pardon me," EshCal cut in, rising from her seat, "I need to make a phone call."

Chapter 7

Galo sat on the beach, propped back on his elbows with his feet in the breakers. The afternoon sun skewed across his back, casting an oblique shadow into the Southland Sea.

Galo closed his eyes, basking in the quiet of human solitude. The distant caws of seagulls. The muted warmth of the Frigid sun. The breakers rolling along his feet and shins.

The sand drying under his legs.

He grumbled as he opened his eyes. The surf now bent around his legs.

"You've not spoken to me in several days."

Leviathan had been prodding at him for so long that her voice had faded into his passive thoughts. But now she spoke more urgently. He hadn't learned to ignore her after all. It had been her choice to respect his space.

"I've had a lot on my mind," Galo thought.

"I know. I am bound to your thoughts after all."

"Then what does it matter if I speak to you?"

"It is not strictly necessary," Leviathan said, "But I have always enjoyed speaking with my Hybrid. Passive telepathy is impersonal. It's easy to forget you're dealing with another sentient life."

"Well, you know what's been bothering me," Galo answered, "What would you like to talk about?"

"Where would you like to begin?"

Galo contemplated for a moment. His troubles fell into two categories. The Reestablishment Protocol and his grandfather. The former branched into the aftermath and his ulterior motives. The latter was an issue of accepting the truth. That one seemed a more apt place to begin.

"I suppose I'm still in shock," he opened, "over what happened to my grandfather. Or the man who raised me as him."

"Is your trouble with the betrayal?" Leviathan asked.

"That's part of it," Galo nodded, "How could he have been fooled to the last? And how can I expect to fare any better?"

"Pahres was a master manipulator. It was how he chose to use his gift as the child of an Yggdrasil Hybrid," she explained, "Takmet was none too foolish. Pahres merely exploited his kind nature. Everyone was taken in, but he and I were among those to suffer most directly. That Pahres sacrificed himself for his deception was but shallow reprieve."

"I should say you suffered immensely," he said, stroking the Serpent Bracer, "A mind trapped in an undying and immobile body. Death would seem a welcome reprieve."

"Takmet was afforded the privilege of hearing his surroundings. He loved listening to his descendants go about their lives," Leviathan said, "I had only my telepathic connection to the Chieftain Sage. Though the bond atrophied with each generation since my last Hybrid."

"That's how he destroyed the defense system on the Triad Titan."

"As the son of my last Hybrid before you, communing his intentions to me was a simple matter," she confirmed, "As for your next concern, I'm of the mind that you're taking the correct action."

"Gijin and Takmet were both deceived," Galo lamented, "And both were smarter than me. I'd be stupid to think I'll fare any better."

"You come from a long line of pacifism and benevolence. There will always be those who seek to exploit it. Your burden is to hold fast and preserve it for prosperity," Leviathan said, "You are correct that Gijin and Takmet were both wiser than you, but only for their decades of experience beyond your own. But wisdom is meaningless without useful knowledge, nor vice versa. You have had experiences beyond their own, particularly your amicable dealings with those versed in deception and clandestinity."

"The Coalition?"

"Indeed. They were wiser for their years, but you are better resourced for your experiences."

"So, you think things will work out for the best?"

"I am hopeful."

Galo tipped his head back at the susurrus of footsteps through the sand. Gabdur nodded to him. He had a suitcase in his hand and a satchel hanging from his shoulder. Galo got to his feet, dusted himself off, and moved up the beach. Closing in, he noticed Gabdur's eyes appeared focused yet distant, as though he was intensely aware of some far-off elsewhere.

"You look upset," Galo said, "What's on your mind?"

"I... have business to tend to," Gabdur managed, "Coalition business. I... don't know how long I'm going to be."

"You don't need to worry that I'll think you're running off on me," Galo insisted, "What's happening in Tanelen?"

"Well, they found Phylus," Gabdur began, "He had Dourias with him. He was the first recruit after the founders of The Coalition."

"Sounds like fine enough news. Both alive and well?"

"Alive. Not particularly well, but alive."

"So, they need your help with medical treatment, then?" Galo asked.

"Yes, but it isn't just about that," Gabdur said, "There's been... ah... someone's been shot. Non-fatally, but..."

"What? Who?" Galo asked, "And by who?"

"I don't have any details. But the why concerns me more than the who," Gabdur explained, "There's talk of a traitor within The Coalition. Unconfirmed, but it's a very real possibility."

"Are you going to join the investigation or to be subjected to it?"

"Both. After everyone gets the necessary medical attention," Gabdur said, "So, after a quick stop in Quarun to return the weapons I, um, borrowed, I'm off to Tanelen. I'll do my best to keep in touch."

"Very well," Galo nodded, "Good luck, Dad."

Gabdur smiled weakly and pulled Galo into a hug, bumping his suitcase against the small of his back. Galo put his arm around his shoulder as Gabdur muttered his gratitude. They pulled apart, and Gabdur nodded and turned away.

As Gabdur walked up the beach and out of sight, Galo lay on the sand and stared up at the clouds.

"What the hell do you mean by that?!" NalSet barked as he moved in.

Farim cocked her gun. "One more step toward him, and I'll put one between your eyes," she said, "There's a traitor among you."

"So I gathered," he snarked, "And you think it's one of us after we helped you rescue both of them?"

"Your insistence that that proves your innocence says more about your guilt," Farim cautioned, "Now, you can cooperate, and we'll leave together peacefully. But if you get in my way, I'll assume you're at least protecting the traitor, and you can assume the worst will come of that."

NalSet stared her down, unflinching. The barrel stayed trained on him, directly between his eyes. He tilted ever so slightly, and the gun followed him as though it was tethered to the bridge of his nose.

Chekov grabbed his shoulder and beckoned him back. "Farim. Please," she urged, "Lower the gun, and we'll talk."

Farim's eyes darted about, assessing the circumstances in split-second glimpses. Dourias stood as well as could be expected, still bracing on her but enduring most of his own weight. Vielle watched her expectantly. Malia's eyes shifted between her with Dourias and NalSet with Chekov. She couldn't see Phylus's eyes through his crystal lenses, but he looked to be losing lucidity. Nikasu watched Chekov and NalSet fearfully, the trust they had cultivated in her fading.

Farim lowered her pistol. "Talk."

"I know you don't value my word, but it's all I can give you. This is the first I've heard about a traitor in The Coalition," Chekov insisted, "Likewise for NalSet, I should say. But regardless of if you believe me, do you really think this is the right time for a standoff?"

"I've waited too long for this," Farim grumbled.

"And I respect that," Chekov nodded, "If you're right, I can see why Dourias took you on as his apprentice. But right now, he and Phylus both need medical attention."

"Butter me up all you want, but I trust the two of you about half as far as I can throw you. Now, I've got connections who can see to them. So, give me one good reason I should let you leave with either of them."

"I'll go with them," Malia offered, "Do you trust me?"

"More than these two, but not entirely," Farim said, "But you need to take Vielle and Nikasu home."

"Of course. We'll gate back to…"

"Gabdur," NalSet interrupted, "If it's anybody, it has to be him."

"What?" Farim said, "Explain yourself."

"The Mechanical Crypt," he said, "Only a member of the Chieftain Bloodline could get them into the central chamber to reconfigure it."

This gave Farim pause. Somehow, she hadn't considered that angle. After all, at the time of Dourias's disappearance, Gabdur had been lying low in Ferya as a botanist named Aleepo. But NalSet was right about the Mechanical Crypt and the Chieftain Bloodline.

"Malia," Farim urged, "Take Nikasu and Vielle home. Don't return."

"What about Phylus?"

"He needs medical attention. From Chekov."

"But what about…?"

"I was bluffing. Go."

At Malia's beckoning, Vielle and Nikasu withdrew from Phylus. She led them to the door and applied her portal strip. With the push of a few buttons, a liquefied image of a more southerly landscape manifested in the doorway. The image fizzled out shortly after they stepped through it.

Farim whispered to Dourias, pressing her index finger against his collarbone. He nodded and shuffled away to sit beside Phylus.

"Farim, would you like to join us?" Chekov offered, "Given the circumstances, I'm sure…"

Farim cut her off with a gunshot, the bullet finding its mark on NalSet's kneecap. The bone shattered, and he toppled, clutching his leg and roaring with infuriated agony.

"Exactly how stupid do you think I am?" Farim derided.

"What the hell are you doing?" Chekov shouted, "I was going to have my hands full just with Dourias and Phylus."

"I know. But if NalSet wants to lie to me again, I'd be glad to unburden you of him," Farim offered, her eyes on Chekov as she leveled the gun at NalSet again, "Or you can call Gabdur to help you, and you can all leave as you are now."

"He wasn't lying to you. He was just…" Chekov said, "I told you we didn't know about the traitor."

"Well, either way, my job just got real simple," Farim said, "But regardless, I need both of you out of my way. Especially him."

An array of blue light blended crooked fractals of a snowy Northland lawn with a distant Southland beach. Gabdur crossed the lobby and set down his suitcase. He flung his satchel onto the counter.

"Ah, Master Gabdur," the innkeeper greeted, "How might I help you today?"

"Good day, Jex," Gabdur said, "I'm just passing through to return some provisions I… borrowed."

He opened the satchel to reveal an assortment of pressure bombs, smoke balls, and resonant disruptors with a photonic emission weapon on top.

"I was wondering if you'd decided to keep them for yourself," Jex said, "Or if you thought I hadn't noticed."

"I considered it," Gabdur admitted, "The former, that is."

"Of course," Jex said, "Far be it for even you to think you could slip my notice."

"The way these were all but packed for me, how could I?" Gabdur asked, laughing under his breath. He gestured to a shelved box with an electrical wire peeking out of it. A single canoe paddle leaned against the wall beneath it. "Speaking of which, looks like you've been keeping busy."

Jex glanced back at the box. "I got some ideas after I heard about the Mechanical Crypt," he said, "Nothing's come of it but a way to keep occupied so far."

"Well, keep me posted if it comes to be more," Gabdur said. He noticed a single empty peg on the key rack. "Are they already here?"

"No, I have an honest to goodness guest. Strange, I know," Jex said, "But now, who were you asking after?"

"Oh, I thought Chekov may have brought NalSet and some others here."

"For what purpose?"

"NalSet was shot in the knee by Farim," Gabdur said, "The rest is, well, complicated."

"Master Dourias's old apprentice?" Jex asked, "I hadn't realized she was still involved. Has she joined The Coalition?"

"Well, she shot NalSet in the knee. So, I doubt it," Gabdur said, "She insists there's a traitor among us."

"And that it may be Master NalSet?"

"More that he's getting in her way."

The tip of a kitchen knife pressed against the small of Gabdur's back, the one carrying it having gone unnoticed. Gabdur stiffened up, his back arching.

"Good afternoon, Picuarus," Jex said, "I would ask that you not threaten my other visitors. Now then, are any of your amenities in need of refreshing?"

"I knew one of you would come here eventually," Picuarus said, "Now, I could say I'm formally asking for an audience with your commander, but let's be honest. I'm not giving you any choice in the matter."

"Madam. If you could draw back your knife, I'd be glad to discuss this with you as civilized people," Gabdur urged, "What's your business with my commander?"

"I'm sorry I've had to be so brash with you, Aleepo," Picuarus said, withdrawing the blade, "This isn't how I ever imagined we'd first meet."

Gabdur turned around to face her. She was short and stocky. Calluses covered her palms. A scar adorned her collarbone. A spark of indirect familiarity flashed through his mind.

"Are you… Elemeno?" he asked, to which she nodded, "Oh. Oh dear. This is about your daughter, of course."

"My Eytea died at war with The Avatars of Fate as the destined hero Gijin said she'd become," Elemeno said, "But she was all I had left."

"And now, you want revenge through The Coalition."

"That's a crude way to put it, but I suppose you're not wrong."

"As much as I admire your passion, I can't just bring in everyone who starts craving Avatar blood. No matter the trauma they've suffered," Gabdur said, "What skills can you offer? I need some kind of leverage to get you an audience with The Omnimath."

"Leverage? What if I turned you in as the traitor?" Elemeno suggested, raising the knife to his abdomen, "Would he see me, then?"

"An audience for a ludicrous accusation? Of course not," Gabdur argued, "By what logic would I be the traitor?"

"The Mechanical Crypt was linked to the Chieftain Bloodline. Could be you got them inside. Taught them how to use it," Elemeno suggested. She indicated his stump. "And when you'd reached the extent of your usefulness, they tried to throw you away. But the damage had already been done."

"Elemeno," Gabdur gasped, "You don't honestly think that, do you?"

"Honestly? No," Elemeno said, lowering the knife to her side, "But if you won't cooperate, I can pretend that I do."

Gabdur lowered his head and sighed. "In that case, shall we be going now?"

"We shall," Elemeno nodded. She turned to Jex. "I'll come back for my bags."

Vielle parked across the street from Nikasu and Sinkua's house and booted the kickstand down. Nikasu dismounted and swept her hair from her eyes, lamenting how long overdue she was for a haircut.

"Hold up a sec," Vielle said. She flicked her wrist, manifesting a braided length of vine. "Put your hair up with this."

"Oh. Thanks," Nikasu said as she pulled her hair into a ponytail, "So, how do you think they're doing in Tanelen?"

"I'm trying not to think about it," Vielle sighed, "I just want to believe that Dad is safe and leave it at that."

"Farim seemed to have things under control," Nikasu said, "But I'm finding it hard to believe that Gabdur is the traitor. Hell, this whole traitor business is hard for me to swallow."

"Yeah, the thought of it sort of nauseates me," Vielle said, "But I don't think it's Gabdur either."

"NalSet was just covering his ass, wasn't he?"

"Probably," Vielle said. She and Nikasu slipped into a moment of silent reflection. "Anyway, say hi to Sinkua for me. Tell him to call me soon, okay?"

"I will. Be safe."

Nikasu stood by the curb, watching as Vielle drove away. Alone for the first time since the Heniokhos Disaster, the weight of it all dropped upon her all at once. She sat down on the snowy grass, trembling as the stress and trauma washed over her.

She hadn't realized it, but since that day in the high-rise district, she had been running from her troubles. Or perhaps not running away so much as hiding. For the days and weeks since, she had kept herself busy and in the company of friends.

But now, she and her brother could lean on each other.

Nikasu got to her feet, dusted the snow off her backside, and headed for the front door. She stopped halfway up the lawn, given sudden pause by a rattling from the back gate. A figure emerged from behind the house.

"MalVek!" Nikasu called out, "What are you doing here?"

"I need to talk to you," MalVek said as he closed the distance between them.

"What about?" she asked, stuffing her hands in her pockets.

"Too much to discuss in this frosty bullshit," he insisted, "Mind if we go inside?"

"Um… sure," she nodded, uprooting the key from her pocket as she continued to the front door, "So, should I be worried?"

"Possibly," he said, "Hopefully not."

As Nikasu looked back over her shoulder, MalVek cracked her across the temple with an iron ball wrapped in leather. She dropped upon the front step as her peripheral vision collapsed upon itself.

Tangled roots with dense greenery rushed up around him. Wan sunlight faded behind him. Darkness washed over him. Gnarled and spindly roots buffeted the thrumming air. Mounting momentum and his upturned position atrophied his consciousness.

A percussive rhythm permeated the wooded cacophony in an eight quarters signature. The last remnants of his consciousness homed in on it, anchoring him to a paltry wakefulness.

The rhythm grew tighter. Faster. Nearer. Something gripped the back of his shirt. His momentum slowed. The eight-pulse rhythm calmed.

His body turned upright, and his collar tightened against his throat, the jerking causing a slight weight to drop from his hands. He fell a while more, growing dizzy from his strangulation. On the brink of fainting, it released him, and he crashed upon the ground. Hard. But endurable.

He stirred at the sound of heavy boots thumping beside him. He rolled onto his back and pulled the fabric off his eyes. A towering figure garbed in glimmering armor stood over him.

Snowy hair flowed over his shoulders. A beard swallowed half his face. A silvery eyepatch concealed one of his eyes, his singular oculus radiating eldritch authority. Upon his back, he carried a familiar halberd, and on his hip, a broadsword in an elaborately adorned scabbard. At any greater an angle to his back, the tip might have routed the floor.

The old man spoke in a throaty tongue, thick with angular consonants. He sounded urging.

"What… What is this?" he managed, his own voice sounding distant.

The elderly giant spoke again. Angrier. Frustrated.

"Who are you?" he demanded, pushing himself upright and struggling to his feet.

The old man spoke on despite the language barrier, effortlessly maintaining his posture of grandiosity. He drew the halberd from his back, even the simplest movements emanating regality.

"What the hell are you doing with that?" he shouted, lunging at the towering figure.

The regal elder barred him with an outstretched hand. His answer was succinct but, yet again, unintelligible. He gripped the axe blade, the fine edge not so much as scuffing his leathery palm, and pried it from the shaft, pitching it aside. The spearhead glimmered as though it had been shadowed by the axe blade.

"How did…? Are you…?" he fumbled, staggering back from the display of strength and resilience, "Who are you?"

The old giant didn't speak. Instead, he unclipped the scabbard and kneeled as he presented it to him.

Silenced as much by awe as confusion, he accepted the broadsword. He unsheathed a few centimeters. The blade gleamed as though freshly polished.

The elderly titan mounted his horse, a bizarre equine possessed of an extra set of legs. He spoke once more. Counting off with his fingertips, he gestured with a sweep of his arm over his head.

Only vaguely noticing the counterintuitive weight of the sheathed sword, he nodded his comprehension. Whoever this grandiose elder was, he would return in ten days.

The eight-legged horse climbed the air as though it tread upon the ubiquitous wisps of viridian smoke. The regal titan held fast to the reins as the beast mounted the tips of the roots hanging into the thrumming, roiling chamber. As they rode upward into darkness, he pitched a silvery and crimson charm into the chasm.

He set down the scabbarded broadsword and nudged it aside with his foot. It settled beside a severed hand adorned with a ring. The appendage had begun to sink into the ground, as though to be consumed by it. He could do nothing about it.

He crouched to pick up the charm. It was a four-pointed ruby star in the middle of a medallion which hung from a chain. Warmth swept through him as he put the chain around his neck.

Sinkua stood alone below the roots of Yggdrasil.

Chapter 8

Dual shadow pairs scissored across each other under the lines of blue sconces along the walls. One long and lean. The other short and stocky. The corridor stretched well beyond the last light, abandoning the two in darkness.

The taller one stopped and grabbed the other's shoulder. He pressed his hand against the wall that the other hadn't seen, still couldn't see. Nor did he, only knowing of it from memory. Blue light traced his hand and branched out in serpentine patterns.

A door opened, welcoming Gabdur and Elemeno into the assembly chamber of The Coalition.

"We're in the infirmary," came Chekov's voice over an intercom.

Gabdur pushed a button under a speaker by the door. "We'll be right up."

"We?"

"I've come across a refugee."

They crossed the room and continued through a door in the back. Gabdur led her to an elevator. Once the doors shut, Elemeno broke the silence.

"Why did the lights end so long before the door?" she asked, "Is The Omnimath sensitive to light?"

"He is, but that's not the reason," Gabdur said, "It's a security feature."

"I don't follow."

"Psychological security. Cheapest stuff, but sometimes the most effective. Most people assume there's nothing for them, nothing worth the risk, or nothing at all past the last sconce."

The elevator doors opened, and Elemeno followed Gabdur out. Rounding a corner brought them to the infirmary.

They stood in dumbfounderment in the open doorway. A wiry old man lay on a hospital bed, looking emaciated and sallow. On a second bed lay a roughened and disheveled middle-aged man. He wore a pair of goggles with large blue crystals for lenses. NalSet sat in a wheelchair with his leg propped up and bandages around his knee.

Chekov pushed him toward the door to greet Gabdur and Elemeno. The four of them looked each other over pensively.

"Where should we start?" Gabdur asked.

"What happened to you?" Chekov asked, gesturing to his stump.

"Who the hell is this?" NalSet demanded, almost in unison with Chekov.

"Hm? Oh, I haven't checked in since the Heniokhos Disaster, have I?" Gabdur realized, "Incident at 1341. They sought to use me to activate the Mechanical Crypt."

"Like we knew they would," NalSet said, "Now, who the hell is this?"

"NalSet!" Chekov scolded, "The man had his arm pried off by a machine. Have some patience."

"And I got my knee shot off by a psycho bitch," NalSet barked, "We're on even ground."

"My name is Elemeno. I'm…"

"I did not ask you. Last time we let someone barge into our business, this happened."

"She's Eytea's mother," Gabdur said, "Also The Scout's wife, as I'm sure you've surmised."

"Well, I'm sorry for all you've been through," NalSet said, his civility laced with impatience, "But we're in a crisis here. I don't know if you're here for a job or protection, but we've got neither to spare."

"Well, you're clearly in immense turmoil, sir," Elemeno said, "So, I won't push the issue with you."

"So, fill me in on… all of this," Gabdur said to Chekov, "What happened to these two?"

"They were trapped in hyperspace. Beyond human perception."

"What we know as time doesn't exist there," NalSet added, "But somehow, they experienced accelerated aging. And before you ask, don't."

"That explains why Dourias looks twenty years out of place," Gabdur said, "This is my first time meeting Phylus, but he looks months overdue for a haircut."

"I hadn't seen him in over twenty years, but I'd say you're right," Chekov said.

"How are you taking it?" Gabdur asked, "Finding Dourias like this, I mean."

"Honestly?" Chekov asked, "I'm struggling more with the fact that I gave up on him than I am with his looking old enough to be my father."

"You never got over your feelings for him," Gabdur observed, "Even despite your arrangement."

"No. I didn't. Can we change the subject now? Please?"

"Of course," Gabdur said, "Now, why is Phylus wearing those goggles?"

"They're screwed into the back of his head."

"That's… horrifying. But I was asking why he put them on, not why you haven't taken them off."

"Ahh. Right. We think they allowed him to see their way out of hyperspace," Chekov said, "Judging by the blood and the broken lunch tray he was carrying, he killed their way out."

Gabdur stood at Dourias's bedside. His eyes were sunken. His breathing was shallow and gravelly. Somehow, his arms were both wiry and baggy. An IV bag was connected to his arm in the middle of a cluster of red dots.

He looked to Elemeno, who stood at Phylus's bedside. Gabdur didn't know if the two had met, but she watched over him with deep and genuine concern. It was as though she had known him for years. As though she understood his pain.

"NalSet," Gabdur beckoned, his voice low and soft, "No theories at all on their aging?"

NalSet shook his head. "Told you not to ask."

"I know, but…" Gabdur said, trailing off as he watched Elemeno brush the hair from Phylus's closed eyes, "… It's not like you to be at a total loss for hypotheses."

"Been too preoccupied with all this traitor business."

"He's worried it might be MalVek," Chekov supplied.

"Farim thinks it might be MalVek," NalSet argued, "I'm worried about what might happen if she finds him."

"You haven't considered the possibility?" Gabdur challenged.

"It isn't him," NalSet scolded, "He's my brother. I know him too well."

"Fine. So, this Farim. Dourias's apprentice?" Gabdur asked, to which Chekov nodded, "If she's so sure there's a turncoat in our ranks, why would she let you bring him here without her?"

"See that bump on his collarbone?" Chekov indicated, "It's a subdermal biometric tracking chip. She tagged him before we left."

"Where did she get that?"

"I assume she inherited Dourias's cache of pilfered Avatar tech."

"But those were all broken," Gabdur puzzled, "And even if they were repaired, it would be impossible to isolate them from the network."

"Not according to MalVek," Chekov said.

"With talents like that, why did we never try to recruit her?"

"Aside from the fact that she hates us?" NalSet challenged. He turned to Chekov. "Have you paged Mortvill yet?"

Chekov pinched her earlobe, activating her comm implant. After a brief quiet conversation, she pinched it again, ending the call.

"All three of them will need to go into curative hibernation. NalSet for two days. Phylus and Dourias for at least three, possibly as long as five," Chekov said to Gabdur, "I'll need you here to assist, particularly when it's my turn to go under investigation."

"As I assumed," Gabdur said, "I can't see how you would be the traitor though."

"We all have reasons why it shouldn't be us," Chekov said, "But Mortvill thinks it's worth investigating, nonetheless."

A few minutes later, Mortvill stood in the doorway of the infirmary. All conscious turned to face him as he surveyed the state of things. He approached Elemeno.

"Pardon me, but what business have you here, madam?" he asked.

"My name is Elemeno, sir. I'm Eytea's mother," she introduced, "I asked Gabdur to bring me here to see if I can be of service. On behalf of my daughter."

"I understand," Mortvill nodded, "Wait in the hall. We'll speak later."

Elemeno nodded and exhaled her gratitude. Mortvill waved his hand, and NalSet, Chekov, and Gabdur gathered. He hung his head and breathed deeply before he spoke.

"Farim's suspicions of a traitor came not as a surprise to me. I, too, have harbored the same for many years," he began, "Ever since Nikasu was first taken from Masnethege, I have been investigating this theory with my every decision as to your deployments and assignments.

"Earlier today, I struck my final gambit in this pursuit."

"Sir," NalSet urged, "Are you getting at what I think?"

"While you and Chekov were assisting Malia and her daughters, I sent MalVek to ArcNos to accompany Nikasu when she learned of Sinkua's disappearance. And to help her search for him once she was ready," Mortvill recounted, "His comm implant is no longer active, and his portal strip has vanished from the network. Nikasu's safety is suspect."

Within half a blink's time of the words leaving his mouth, a meaty fist crashed into his mask. He stumbled back and dropped onto his buttocks.

"Gabdur!" NalSet shouted.

"No. It's quite alright," Mortvill insisted as he returned to his feet, "I deserved as much at the very least."

Mortvill straightened his mask, wincing as the dent scraped the bridge of his nose.

"And what, pray tell," Gabdur snarled, his every word oozing contempt, "do you intend to do about this?"

"This mess is mine. I shall take it upon myself to ensure Nikasu's safety and apprehend MalVek," Mortvill said, "In that respect, I ask that this information not leave this room and that none of you involve yourselves unless I ask it of you."

"Why?" Gabdur spat back, "So we'll be out of your way while you play puppet show with the Hybrids?"

"Gabdur, I admire your passion, but I feel I should remind you that I permitted you to land that punch," Mortvill asserted with no trace of malice, "MalVek is likely to notice any other pursuit of him than my own. I only wish to be cautious enough to not endanger Nikasu or any of you any further."

Gabdur set a piercing gaze upon Mortvill, as though to see through the mask and into the eyes behind. Eyes he had never seen. His fingers twitched as he fought the desire to clench another fist.

But Mortvill gave him nothing. His face remained unseen and thus unreadable. His body language betrayed no ill intentions.

"Gabdur," Chekov beckoned, setting her hand upon his shoulder, "Come on. We have work to do."

Gabdur lowered his eyes and relaxed his arm, apologizing. As he followed Chekov to the beds, Mortvill called to him.

"One last thing, Gabdur," he said, "After you've put those three under, bring Elemeno to my inner sanctum. I would speak with her further."

Gabdur nodded to him, and the two turned to their respective business.

"He said Sinkua disappeared," Gabdur said as the door fell shut, "What's that about?"

"That's about all we know," Chekov sighed.

"Son of a bitch," he muttered, "Abducted or…?"

"He's alive," she said, perking up somewhat, "So, we know that much."

"Hyperspace?"

"Possibly. Mortvill said it felt the same as when Phylus and Dourias disappeared."

"But wait… No. That doesn't add up."

"What doesn't?"

"MalVek just abducted Nikasu. Bastard though he is, he's smart enough to know she and Sinkua together would tear him to shreds," he said, "So, either he really is stupid enough to take both of them. But why? Or Sinkua put himself into hyperspace. But how and, again, why? Or MalVek didn't abduct Nikasu. But why else would he secede from the network?"

"I hadn't thought of that, but you make a good point," Chekov said, "We'll talk it over when you get back from Mortvill's room."

KalChi popped the trunk on her car amid metropolitan ruins and the chants of protesters. Her clothes were visibly older than some Ministry interns, with waterproof boots completing the ensemble.

She first put an air filtration mask around her neck, then wriggled her hands through another pair. Then another. And another. And so on until she had seven or eight on each arm. KalChi closed her trunk with her outstretched arm and walked toward a line of protesters.

The sound of snow crunching under her flat-footed steps drew their attention, and they turned toward her. One broke away and approached her.

"You with the Ministries?" he asked.

"Yeah," KalChi said, "How'd you know?"

"Heard rumors about you Ministry folks bringing those masks. They say you're trying to coerce us into doing the work for you."

"Well, it's more that we want you to work with us. But we need you to be safe, regardless."

"Figured as much," he assured, "I mean, a lot of you folks were part of the Subtransit Resistance. You guys built an entire community to protest. Course you wouldn't make someone else fix this mess for you."

"I'm glad someone here understands us," KalChi smiled, extending her arm, "Now, here. Take one for yourself and a few for your friends."

"And if we want to help clean up?" he asked as he relieved her of half of her haul.

KalChi's phone rang. As she unpocketed it, she pointed to a truck beyond her car. "Go see JeiRol, the High Minister of Domestic Affairs."

She moved on to the next cluster of protestors, bouncing her attention between them and her phone call. Unloading the rest of the masks coincided with wrapping up the call, and she moved on to join FerLyn and OshMar.

"KalChi!" FerLyn called out, propping her shovel in the rubble, "OshMar just told me he could stay late with me. You up for joining us?"

"What? Oh, um…" KalChi fumbled, "You don't want it to just be the two of you?"

"Well, no. It's…" OshMar muttered, "It's nothing like that."

FerLyn laughed and shook her head, "MelDas is taking the kids out for gyros. So, it's either this or an empty house."

"Oh! You're married!" KalChi exclaimed, "I thought you two were, you know, a thing."

"Nope. Just friends."

"Okay, then. Well…" KalChi said, trailing off into mounting awkwardness, "I'm going home at the usual time. You might see Biroe later, though. He's been coming out to survey the area as part of his job costing research."

"We'll say hello if we see him," OshMar said.

"So, you looked like you were in a hurry," FerLyn asked, "What was that about?"

"SenRas just called me," KalChi said, "He had some great news."

Elemeno watched as Gabdur pressed his hand against a curved wall panel of no particular remark. Just as with the entrance to the assembly chamber, blue light outlined his hand and spread into serpentine patterns. This time, however, the light faded and vanished once he removed his hand, the panel standing as silent and unassuming as ever. After a moment, it shifted back and slid behind an adjacent panel.

"Thank you," Elemeno said as he waved her in, "I'm sorry for all that business in Quarun."

"Quarun is behind us," Gabdur excused, "Though I think you made quite the impression on Jex. He's seen more than enough to be quite proficient at feeling people out."

"Well, that's exactly my strength," Elemeno grinned, "Nobody suspects me."

"Indeed, they don't," Gabdur smiled, "Picuarus."

The panel slid back into place shortly after she entered the room. Looking back, she found it to be of no particular remark from this side either.

The ceiling sloped into a perfect dome. The floor was circular and adorned with round and crescent-shaped throw rugs. Arcs of blue light filled the gaps and ran up the walls. She suspected a pattern, some kind of relevance, but it was too much to follow.

But the strangest thing was in the middle of the sanctum. The Omnimath, Mortvill, paced about with his mask slightly upturned, chewing on pieces of lamb jerky. He appeared as Elemeno had never imagined him.

Unnerved.

"Ah. You have come," Mortvill remarked, straightening his mask, "Excellent. I have need of you, you see. Your timing is, in a word, impeccable."

"I don't understand. You need me?" Elemeno asked.

"Well, yes. You heard our conversation in the infirmary," he said, "I cannot ask for their help in this matter."

"Because he would expect them?" she guessed, "Or is it because you're not sure you can trust them to side with you?"

"The latter has crossed my mind, but I assure you it is all but entirely the former."

"So, you need me because I'm unfamiliar?" Elemeno asked, "I'm only asking because I need to know how disposable I am to you. After all, I heard your conversation in the infirmary."

Mortvill signaled her to give him a moment. He slipped a piece of lamb jerky under his mask, chewing it as he continued pacing. As he finished, he wiped his mouth with his thumb and cleared his throat.

"Elemeno," he began, "Do you know the two most powerful forces at humankind's employ?"

"Um…" Elemeno stalled, "… Venture capitalism?"

Mortvill snickered. "I said powerful, not predatory," he said, "No, I speak of things innate, not those devised."

"Oh! You mean emotions and thoughts," she realized, reddening a smidge in the face, "Well. Hatred is powerful, but it can also be self-destructive. Is love one of them, then? Or is that too passive?"

"Love is quite anything but passive, and it is indeed one of the answers," Mortvill said, "The other is fear. Mismanaged or unbalanced, they can destroy us from within. Handled properly, however, they can make playthings of the implausible. This makes humans remarkably dangerous, beyond even your own comprehension.

"I have looked into your eyes, Elemeno, and I have found that you may be among the most dangerous people I have met in many centuries."

"What…" Elemeno stumbled, the weight of his compliment overpowered only by the revelation of his longevity, "What do you need from me?"

"On my desk," he began, gesturing to it, "are two records of portal strip activity for the past three years. One I printed shortly before sending MalVek to ArcNos. The other, after his secession. I ask that you join me in isolating his unique destinations."

"To figure out where he took Nikasu?"

"That is our eventual goal, yes. From that list, we will deduce, by my analysis and your instinct, where he has most likely taken her."

"And from there?"

"You will gain us entry by seeking employment there or nearby," Mortvill said, "You will, however, need another alias. MalVek would most certainly find Picuarus familiar."

Sinkua scaled the walls of his roiling green sanctuary, dredging up skills left dormant since his last isolation. The substance bent to his fingertips like putty, adopting a more solid quality as he squeezed it.

The gnarled ends of roots, solid and sure, hung from the pitch blackness above. Pieces of fruit would occasionally sprout from these. He knew these to have been illusions, of course. No edible fruits sprouted that quickly. Not that he knew of. Besides, fruits certainly never grew on roots.

What he was most likely eating was some exotic form of carrot or potato. Which was quite astounding enough on its own, casting such an in-depth illusion as passing a root vegetable off as a piece of citrus. But he couldn't help but wish the outcome could, now and again, be something savory. If it could convince him that oranges grew this far underground, it could pass off lamb chops as growing on trees.

He plucked today's offering, a red grapefruit, held it in his teeth by the stem, and descended the wall. Then again, calling it specifically today's offering was perhaps the biggest assumption of all.

Honestly, he wasn't sure how long he had been down here. As far as he could tell, he slept just as sparsely as ever. So, he couldn't count the days by that. And without the sun, he had no sense of the time of day. The offerings may have been regularly intervaled, but he had nothing certain to base it on.

He hadn't worn a watch the day he left his house, having seen no point in it. His only appointment was with his own death, and that was more of a destination. If it didn't wait for him to reach Yggdrasil, it would meet him along the way. Either would have been fine with him.

Not anymore though, Sinkua realized as he sat and tore into the illusory grapefruit with his fingernails. He wished that old man had also had time to bring him his dagger. But he realized that expecting even more from someone who had chased him down a chasm and caught him in freefall could only appear greedy.

Whoever that old man was, he must have had some connection to Eytea. Most likely, it was the same connection as Galo shared with Leviathan and Vielle had with Yggdrasil. But that he appeared to be human, even with his impressive stature, didn't follow the pattern. He postulated that her bond was with the horse, and the old man was an intermediary serving as its voice.

Sinkua got to his feet, leaving the grapefruit peels to be absorbed into the roiling floor. He had agreed to wait the ten days for that man's return. But so far, he had idled away the time in passive contemplation.

Now, having seen the significance of that old man, Sinkua realized that piddling away this time was a dishonor to Eytea. He approached the broadsword, still sheathed since he glimpsed the base of the blade.

The ground had consumed Eytea's hand. Only her engagement ring remained. Sinkua fixated on it a moment before deciding to leave it there. Best that what he found of her be buried there.

Returning his attention to the sword, he picked it up with one hand at the middle of the scabbard, finding it nary a burden. Given how loudly it had first hit the ground, he doubted that even his deceptive strength could account for that discrepancy. Had he had any power over gravity or even metals, it could have been a milystic reaction.

He pulled the sheath and sword apart, casting the scabbard aside. The blade was double-edged and looked sharp enough to cleave his eyelashes if he stared at it too long. Engraved along both sides was a string of unfamiliar characters, the same on each side.

Sinkua ran his fingertip along the flat of the blade, feeling the concaves and ridges of the runic etchings. His touch drew out an ephemeral crimson glow from each letter, again as though it might have been a milystic reaction.

He squared himself, assuming an offensive posture. With the broadsword angled forth, he closed his eyes and inhaled deeply. Raging thoughts coalesced into a singular focus as he called upon the one thing he still had to fight for. To live for.

Eytea's honor.

Sinkua's eyes opened, radiating a brilliant green glow. The runes flickered red. Wherever this sword came from, it had somehow been designed around his milystis.

As he exhaled, he swung the massive blade in a sweeping arc. Again and again, he sliced the air in shimmering streaks, its movements feeling remarkably natural for his first time with a sword.

He would live to honor her. He would take up her fight to resume his own. And when the time came, he would take vengeance on her behalf with the most spectacular of bloodshed.

Chapter 9

The door alarm buzzed. SenRas raised a finger to his guest, pausing their conversation.

"MarLys," he called as it buzzed a second time, "Answer that, would you?"

MarLys kicked her rolling chair away from her workstation, turning it about with a twist of her legs. She sprang to her feet and bumped the chair back under the table with her hip. Good news had come that morning, and she walked to the door with a spring in her step.

She threw the door open to find her standing there with a weak smile.

"Hi," Vielle exhaled.

"Get your perky butt in here," MarLys said. She grabbed Vielle by the front of her shirt and pulled her into the office. "And bring the rest of you with it."

MarLys spun Vielle around, kicking the door shut along the way, and pushed her against the wall. She pulled the diminutive Hybrid into an open-mouthed kiss, forgetting the professional environment around her for a lingering moment.

The clearing of throats brought them out of it. MarLys pulled back and looked behind herself. Several of her male colleagues, as well as a handful of female ones, shifted in their seats. MarLys flashed a devious smile.

"You're just jealous that you didn't get to answer the door," she teased, "But I saw her first."

"Vielle, what are you doing here?" SenRas's guest asked.

"Malia?" Vielle asked, "I wasn't expecting you either. Coalition business?"

"Yes, I still have that despite your investigation in Tanelen," Malia said, "Frankly, I'm offended that you thought I could be the traitor."

"Well, it's not like I could prioritize your feelings," Vielle said, "But since you've been cleared, I can tell you I didn't think it was you. Short version, Sinkua suspected a turncoat, and Spril agreed. We had no leads. You were the most opportune to audit. Okay?"

"Well, it's nice to know that you didn't flat out distrust me," Malia said, "But I thought we were at the point where you could be forthcoming with me about this sort of thing."

"You do know that that would've defeated the whole purpose, right?" Vielle countered, "Besides, I didn't come here to talk about that. Did you tell SenRas what happened with my dad?"

"She did," SenRas said, "We've actually been discussing this turncoat situation. Am I correct to understand that NalSet outed Gabdur?"

"Yes, but he was either wrong or lying," Vielle said, "It's MalVek."

"You were right. NalSet was bluffing," SenRas said to Malia, "Of course, that beckons the question of whether he was deliberately covering for MalVek."

"Right. Was he aware of his brother's treachery?" Malia asked.

"And if so, is he also involved?" SenRas added, "Or was he protecting him out of kinship?"

"Or was he trying to save him?" Malia considered. She turned to Vielle. "How did you figure it out?"

"He took Nikasu," Vielle spat.

"He did what!?" Malia shouted.

"Knocked her out and took her through a portal just after I dropped her off."

"Does Sinkua know about this?" SenRas asked, his heightened emotion betrayed only by a vein on the side of his neck.

"I don't know. I can't get him on the phone," Vielle said, "Either he already went after them or MalVek got both of them."

"Can I ask how you know what happened to Nikasu?" Malia asked.

"I gave her a vine hair tie when I dropped her off. Like this one," Vielle said. With a flick of her wrist, she produced another, which she gave to MarLys. "When I was driving home, I started hearing her voice. So, I pulled over and listened to the last bit of their conversation through Yggdrasil's roots. Enough to know."

"Fuck," Malia muttered, "So there's some reconnaissant property between Yggdrasil and your arbormancy?"

"Yeah. And as long as she has the hair tie, I think I can find her."

"And what can I do to help you accomplish this?" SenRas asked.

"I need you to send me to Berinin with your portal strip, please," Vielle beckoned, "As close to Masnethege as possible."

"You're going to ask Galo to help you meditate?" MarLys speculated.

Vielle nodded. "It's the best idea I've got."

"Well, I can oblige that," SenRas said, producing the portal strip from a desk drawer, "You ought to find Gabdur with him as well. He can send the two of you back this way."

"I was counting on it," Vielle said, "Thank you for this. It means more than you realize."

"I'm more than glad to help," SenRas said, "In fact, take MarLys with you." He turned toward MarLys. "Once she finds Galo, I need you to coordinate with Judge Nenbard regarding our research into Avatar sympathizers."

"Of course, sir," MarLys nodded, "I'll alert you to any new intel when I return."

SenRas thanked her as he applied the portal strip to the door to a small private office in the corner.

"Let either of us know if you need anything else," Malia said, "This is bigger than any bad blood between us."

"I will," Vielle said, crossing the room with MarLys, "Sorry for being brash with you."

"It's fine," Malia shrugged, "Now that we know about MalVek, we'll need to bring EshCal into this meeting. All three of us were recruited by or because of him."

"What do you think it might mean?" MarLys asked.

"We'll trouble ourselves with figuring that out. You have your assignment," SenRas insisted. He activated the strip, manifesting an electrified vision of Masnethege in the doorway. "And Vielle, if you don't mind, I'd like to spread the news of your father's impending return."

"Go right ahead," she said, clasping MarLys's hand, "It'll be nice to know there's happy news going about."

Nikasu became aware before her eyes opened. She kept them shut, listening to her surroundings. Her last memories were of unlocking the front door and talking to MalVek.

He was the turncoat. But that couldn't have been. NalSet had implicated Gabdur, and his reasoning with the Mechanical Crypt was air tight. To her knowledge, NalSet had no reason to sabotage Gabdur.

Unless, of course, he was protecting MalVek. But that only brought on more questions, the least of which was how The Avatars accessed the Mechanical Crypt without a Chieftain.

People spoke nearby, three of them, arguing as far as she could tell. But she couldn't tell any farther than that.

Nikasu shifted her weight, gauging the responsiveness of her body. She had experienced some strange drugs before, and if the turncoat was willing to out himself to bring her back to The Avatars of Fate, they promised to get worse. Her body felt sluggish, but it was hard to tell, as they had strapped her down.

Exploring her mouth with her tongue, she found they had gagged her as well. Between the fact that she couldn't taste the gag and how muffled yet near the voices sounded, she realized the drugs hadn't worn off. Even if she could use her gravimancy to break out, she couldn't be sure that she could fight.

But it also meant MalVek had had a long way to transport her. If she could get him talking, perhaps she could get an idea of her whereabouts. The likelihood that she would need to escape on her own hung heavily around her thoughts.

Two of the three voices faded as the last one came closer. Nikasu opened her eyes. MalVek stood over her.

"Why?" she choked out through the gag.

MalVek spoke, but his words were still incomprehensible. He picked up a syringe from a nearby table. Bound and helpless, Nikasu could only cringe as he inserted the needle just below her jugular.

The fluid was warm but somehow chilling. MalVek kept talking, saying the same thing over and over, judging by his face. What she actually heard kept changing, slowly becoming clearer over the next several seconds. Or minutes. She couldn't be sure.

"Can you understand me now?" MalVek asked.

Nikasu nodded, and MalVek removed the gag. Nikasu took her first deep breath in she knew not how long.

"Why are you doing this?" she asked.

"Don't misunderstand my intentions, Nikasu," MalVek said, "I'm doing this to keep you relevant."

"I... I don't follow."

"I'm saving your life. You should be thanking me."

"I'd thank you to let me go," Nikasu grumbled, "Explain yourself."

"I'll be brief, seeing as the drugs haven't worn off. I apologize if the dose was higher than necessary," MalVek said, "Anyway, they're going to have you killed. You've caused a lot of trouble."

"They deserved it."

"Yes, but you took it too far," he continued, "As far as they're concerned, you're only worth keeping alive along with Sinkua. I promised to help them find a use for you without him."

"Without him?" Nikasu gasped, her voice catching, "You mean my brother is…?"

"I know this a terrible way to find out, but yes, I'm afraid so," MalVek said with a tinge of sorrow in his eyes.

"Why?" she whimpered, tears rolling down her temples, "Why did he have to die?"

"Play along as my hostage, and we both get to stay alive," he said, "We'll make his death mean something."

"What… What do I need to do?"

"Whenever we're not alone, keep acting like I betrayed you. Pretend we never had this conversation," MalVek explained, "And if you're going to use your powers to break anything, don't try too hard. I told them the drugs would weaken your powers."

"They won't?"

"Not to that extent."

His story at least sounded reasonable enough. She couldn't focus on picking it apart, though. Not after learning Sinkua had died while she was in Tanelen.

She tried to focus on what he would do in this situation. He would look for a weakness, a flaw in the design. An anomaly. And he would grab it and pull it until the whole thing fell apart and pick the truth out of the remains.

"Can… I ask you something?" she asked.

"Sorry, I don't know how he died."

"Not that," she said, clenching her eyes, "How did you find out?"

"About Sinkua?"

"That they were going to kill me."

"Here, look at this."

He turned his head and pulled his hair back. He pressed his palm heel to the exposed area, and an emblem like Pahres's manifested behind his ear.

"All of us in The Coalition have these," he explained, "Mine lets me see and interact with over the air communications. If I'm in the path of, say, a wireless call, I can see the waves and listen in if I concentrate hard enough."

It wasn't enough. She had her doubts, but so far, his story was sound. She held her tongue and nodded. For now, she would have to play along. Walk into a trap to catch a hunter.

Just like her sister had said her brother would have done.

Galo rose from his desk and crossed the living space of his hut. The bell by the door rang a second time. Leviathan warned him that the voices outside sounded distressed.

He pulled back the flap to find Vielle and MarLys standing on his doorstep.

"Vielle. MarLys," Galo greeted, "Come in. What can I do for you two?"

"Has anyone told you there might be a turncoat in The Coalition?" Vielle asked as she slunk past him and into the living space.

"I just heard a few hours ago. Gabdur went to Tanelen for the investigation," Galo said, "Well, partially that. As I understand, your father and someone named Dourias were in dire need of medical attention."

"Farim asked Malia to take Nikasu and me home," Vielle recounted, "That was right after NalSet outed Gabdur as the traitor."

"Well, I don't think it's him," Galo cut off, "Someone there was shot, apparently after you left. He wouldn't say or maybe didn't know who."

"Farim must have shot NalSet for lying. Either that or he shot her because he's in on it," MarLys said, "She sent you away to keep from implicating you."

"Why would NalSet have lied?" Galo asked, "Or been in on the treachery?"

"MalVek is the real turncoat," Vielle said, "And I need your help to catch him."

"Protecting his brother," Galo sighed, sitting at his desk, "What's your plan?"

"He took Nikasu," Vielle choked out. Galo shoved his chair out from under himself, jostling the unoccupied aquarium on the corner of his desk. "I have a way to track her down, but I need to meditate with you."

"Meditate?" Galo puzzled, pacing the living space, "How is that supposed to help?"

"MarLys, show him what I gave you," Vielle said. MarLys took her hair down and handed Galo the vine hair tie. "I made that from my arbormancy. Nikasu also has one. When I'm near Yggdrasil's roots, I can hear her and her surroundings."

"Just like the tree relay system," Galo said, "You suppose that, through meditation, you could pinpoint her location."

"Down to a narrow radius, at least."

"MarLys?" Galo beckoned, "Did you need also something, or are you here for emotional support?"

"A little of both," MarLys said, "I'm here to meet with Judge Nenbard to coordinate our intel on Avatar sympathizers."

"Searching for potential agents?" Galo asked.

"Yes, mainly The General, The Investigator, and The Politician. The General is the only Named that we've never had a face or, well, a name to go with. And I had a candidate for The Investigator, but it's just a hunch," MarLys recalled, "We're looking into the likelihood that Joren is The Politician. All other Named, SenRas thinks it's too soon for them to have been reassigned."

"Who were you looking into as the new Investigator?"

"Olsa. I suspect she was reassigned instead of being flat out dismissed."

"Well, it's a sensible hunch," Galo said, "But as it were, I'm in the process of trapping some Avatar sympathizers. The Investigator may be among them."

"Who is it?" MarLys asked.

"I don't know," Galo said, "But I know they exist, and I know how to manipulate their next move."

He returned to his desk and waved them over. As they came, he removed his Serpent Bracer and dropped it in the unoccupied aquarium. The copper scales became flesh, and Leviathan wriggled in renewed freedom.

"A pleasure to see you again, Vielle," Leviathan said, peering over the edge of the tank. MarLys leaned in slowly. "You must be MarLys. Galo has mentioned you. I know I am odd to witness, but I assure you I am harmless to you. What Yggdrasil is to Vielle, I am to Galo. Though Yggdrasil's existence still puzzles me, but that is a matter for another time."

"I'm surprised you'd say that," Vielle said, "I assumed you were around when Yggdrasil was destroyed. So, I figured if anyone knew how it returned, you would."

"I was, but I'm afraid I'm as much at a loss as everyone else," Leviathan apologized, "But returning to the more pressing matter, we suspect Ebralgi retained contact with somebody in Masnethege after he left with Nikasu. Our efforts to lure them into the open comes in two parts. Are either of you familiar with The Reestablishment Protocol?"

Vielle shook her head.

"I've heard of it," MarLys said, "But I don't know what it is."

"It ends the Chieftain Bloodline's patrilineal authority and dissolves Masnethege," Galo explained, "But it opens Berinin up to a new, hopefully more democratic, government. And more to our immediate goals, it eliminates the anti-technological tradition."

"You're serious?" Vielle gaped, "I mean, I know you've thought this through, but... Wow. This is a big deal."

"Truly, but it must be done. Never was that lifestyle the intention of Fentak the First Chieftain Sage," Leviathan said, "Now, as to the second part. The statue in this home is one of three."

"Is the one here of Fentak?" MarLys asked.

"No, it is of his son Takmet," Leviathan said, "As I was saying, the second statue was of Pahres. Son of the Last Yggdrasil Hybrid, or so we thought his mother had been."

"Was the Pahres that we met the old one in a new body, or...?" Vielle asked.

"That was just him," Galo said, "Same spirit. Same body. The Avatars broke him out by, from what I could tell, torturing Sinkua or Nikasu until their milystis wore through the seal."

"That is... just horrifying," Vielle winced, "I assume your plan hinges on the third statue, then?"

"Yes, the third was of Arestor, son of Vuserah, Hybrid of Gavaevodata," Leviathan said.

"Since they released Pahres and tried to cut off the Chieftain Bloodline," Galo said, "It stands to reason that they would go after Arestor."

"Had we a map of Ouristihra as it was then, I could perhaps find him first," Leviathan lamented, "But the sea has changed much in those millennia, and with it so too has the land. Many small islands have eroded to nothing, including the one on which Arestor stood."

"But since they found Pahres, they should also know where Arestor is," Galo explained, "By my abdicating my power and dissolving Masnethege, they'll be free to act on this knowledge."

"Thus drawing The Geneticist's contacts out in the open," MarLys deduced, "And you two will swoop in and take Arestor out from under them."

"Of course," Galo said, "And it's more of a hope than a working theory, but I have a feeling that his contacts were the ones who knew where to find Pahres."

"If this all works out, do you plan on releasing Arestor?" Vielle asked.

"Well, it stands to reason that four Hybrids plus Leviathan and Yggdrasil could manage it without any of us needing to be tortured," Galo said.

"Well, I only ask because technically, we're one for two on these statue people siding with us," Vielle argued, "Pahres only came around because of the Platinum Orchid, and he was like a different person than who The Avatars pulled out."

"I know beyond any doubt that Arestor would fight The Avatars of Fate," Leviathan assured, "But I cannot speculate on whether he would actively ally with any of us."

"How did they end up like that, anyway?" Vielle asked, "You know, spirits trapped in statues."

"Give her the abridged version," Galo said, "We need to get to work."

"This world had long been ravaged by two icons of chaos, an Etherworlder such as myself and her Omphaloworlder counterpart. Her Hybrid," Leviathan explained, "Those three, known as The Trifecta, attempted to seal them beyond the reach of existence. Though such a veil was eventually erected, The Trifecta's power backfired, and they became those undying statues. I, unfortunately, was trapped in my copper form. Otherwise, I could have protected Takmet."

"I'm sorry," Vielle said, running her fingertip along Leviathan's snoot, "That's a long time to carry around that kind of regret."

"Well, now that we're all caught up, are you ready to get started?" Galo asked, coughing into the crook of his elbow, "There are a few roots around town. We can begin at any one you'd like."

"Actually, I need to be at the trunk," Vielle said, "I tried a few spots, and even though I didn't get enough details to work with, I got more the further north or west I went."

Galo gave her a moment's level stare. If he went with her now, he'd miss out on his chance to bait Ebralgi's conspirators. As well as to validate the modern technology he'd already begun using on the satellite island. But if he hesitated, Nikasu's life could be forfeit.

"I assume you brought a portal strip?" he asked, "Because otherwise, it's just not feasible for us to make it there and for me to make it back in time for the Ouristihran Union Assembly."

"No, SenRas sent us down here with his, but he kept it there," Vielle explained, "We all thought Gabdur was still with you."

"Well, I don't know what to do then," Galo sighed, "Are you sure you can't..."

"I'll call SenRas," MarLys offered, "He should be with Malia and EshCal right now. I'm sure one of them could spare a minute to pick you two up."

"Of course," Galo said, rubbing his forehead and chuckling at his own oversight, "First, let me write down Nenbard's address for you. Would you like us to walk there with you?"

"How far is it?"

"About an hour on foot."

"I'll be fine, then. You two go find Nikasu," MarLys insisted, "And when you find MalVek, kick the bastard in the berries for me. Twice."

EshCal paused in the doorway to the Ministry of Covert Affairs, panning the collective open-air office. She made eye contact with SenRas and gave him a skeptical look. He glanced out over his staff, then nodded to her.

She wasn't ready to trust this many people being privy to their business with The Coalition. But SenRas found them trustworthy enough, and that would have to be good enough for her. After all, she had decided he was worth staking her name on with The Omnimath.

"So then," she said, walking to his desk, "What's going on?"

"I won't mince words," SenRas began, "MalVek went turncoat."

"Spril told me he was looking into a potential traitor in The Coalition," EshCal said as she pulled up a chair, "How long has he been working against us?"

"Well, Vielle found out because he kidnapped Nikasu," Malia said, wincing at her own words, "So, we suspect he was with The Avatars when they first took her. He may have influenced The Omnimath's decision to let them have her when she ended up with The Geneticist."

"Which would mean he was working for The Avatars when he recruited me," EshCal realized, "Did he also recruit you?"

"He did," Malia confirmed, "All three of us are in The Coalition because of him."

"Which puts everything he told us under scrutiny," SenRas added.

"And everything he gave us," EshCal said, "He gave me a photonic weapon. An epee, I assume. I haven't used it, but…"

"Submit it to R&D."

"That's what I was thinking. The photonic shotgun he gave to Phylus worked, but that could have just been a matter of maintaining his cover."

"That's possible," Malia said, "But I think it was also part of the plot to have Phylus abducted."

"Sorry, but you told me Farim had Phylus captured."

"This is the first I'm hearing about this," EshCal puzzled, "Has Farim also turned against us?"

"The Avatars took him," Malia argued, "Farim hijacked the abduction and had him taken to where they were keeping her mentor, a man named Dourias. He was The Coalition's first recruit, code-designated as the First Native."

"Strange code name," EshCal mumbled, more thinking aloud than bringing it under scrutiny, "So, Farim is still our ally?"

"She's not with The Avatars, at least."

"And I assume, since you're back, that Phylus is safe," EshCal said, "Dourias, too?"

"Yes, they were both taken into curative hibernation. I'd say Phylus will be out in time for the Ouristihran Union Assembly," Malia said, "but it's not my place to promise."

"Malia, am I right to deduce that you only recently learned of Dourias and his code name?" SenRas asked, to which Malia shook her head.

"Obviously, this is the first I'm hearing about him," EshCal added, "You as well?"

SenRas nodded. "MalVek must have withheld it from both of you. And myself by extension."

"He must have been responsible for his disappearance," Malia said, "So, he had something to gain from developing hyperspace tech with The Avatars." She turned to EshCal. "They were in a fourth-dimensional prison. That's why it took Farim so long to find Dourias."

"Fourth-dimensional," EshCal contemplated, "Could he have derived it from portal strip technology?"

"That sounds plausible," SenRas said.

"I'll see about arranging a meeting with The Omnimath for the three of us," Malia said, "We have more to discuss than we can safely speculate on."

The door alarm buzzed. SenRas skimmed his itinerary. "Are we expecting anyone else?"

"Spril asked to speak with Malia," EshCal said, rising from her seat, "I asked him to wait ten minutes before he followed me."

EshCal opened the door to find Spril as she expected. He hesitated, his jaw tightening as he looked over to open-air office. She set her hand on his shoulder with the slightest pressure. He focused on her, and she gave him an assuring nod.

"Prime Minister SenRas," Spril said, swallowing hard as he approached the desk, "How does the day find you?"

"Prime Minister Spril," SenRas reciprocated, "It finds me neck-deep in intrigue. And how does it find you?"

"Quite the same," Spril said, staying on his feet, "Malia?"

"Yes?"

"I've figured out that note," he said, offering her the folded crinkled paper.

Malia unfolded the note and read it, her face screwing up in bewilderment. She ran her finger along the paper as though trying to follow his thought processes. Shaking her head, she refolded the paper.

"No. No, that's not possible," Malia argued, handing the note back to him, "It doesn't make any sense."

"And everything else in my life has been sensible?" Spril challenged, dropping the note on SenRas's desk, "These two can both tell you there's something strange going on with me."

"It's true," SenRas said, "He deactivated a biomech just by putting his hand near it."

"Which I did again on a larger scale against Ozzera," Spril added.

"When we were investigating Laboratory 1341, he could hear things that should have been beyond human hearing," EshCal said.

"Hell, the fact that I survived getting shot in the head long enough for Yrlis to heal me is suspect."

"Spril, I don't doubt that there's something special about you," Malia said, "The Omnimath told me you're important to The Coalition. He said the note was about you, but..."

"Then why is this so hard to believe?" Spril argued.

"Because Phylus met you the day you were born," Malia said, "So, how would this even work?"

"I don't know, but that's hardly a counterpoint," Spril said, "Besides, what else could the note mean?"

"Well, I don't know, but... this?" Malia challenged, "How could I have been in The Coalition for this long and not known about any of this?"

"Because of MalVek," EshCal said.

"MalVek is the traitor," SenRas supplied.

"Son of a fuck," Spril muttered, "Do you have any other ideas, Malia?"

"I guess not, but I still can't believe this," Malia admitted, "I'll ask The Omnimath about it."

"Good. If I'm right, I'd like to meet with him," Spril said, "Yrlis wants a word with him, too. And her mother."

"You've told her, then?" Malia asked, to which Spril nodded. "Good. Whatever's happening with you, she should know. How did she take it?"

"Fairly well," Spril said, "She wasn't all that surprised, really. So, can you arrange a meeting for us?"

"The three of us need to meet with him, too," Malia said, "I'll call ahead and see if you and Yrlis can join us."

"It will be some time before either of us can break away to visit headquarters," SenRas said, gesturing between himself and EshCal, "Take them at your leisure."

"Thank you. We both appreciate it."

"But I'll be honest, I still have my doubts about your interpretation," Malia said.

"Well then, we'll just have to wait and see," Spril said as he walked to the door. He paused, holding the doorknob. "But for his sake, I had better be wrong," he continued, "If I'm correct, he won't like my answer."

Malia, SenRas, and EshCal watched as Spril exited the Ministry of Covert Affairs. Once the door closed, SenRas unfolded the note and quietly read it aloud.

"Spril came from another time."

A low hum reverberated throughout the roiling green chamber. The sound had surrounded Sinkua for what he assumed to have been hours. Had it been consistent, he could have tuned it out.

But it fluctuated in volume and pitch. Occasionally, it would stop entirely. The first two times, he hoped it it was over. Both times, though, it resumed within moments, and the third time, he didn't bother hoping.

Sinkua stood in an offensive stance with his sword angled forward. In an effort to distract himself from the noise, he focused on keeping the tip of the blade in the exact center of his vision as he moved about.

The irregular thrumming dulled to a pulsating hum. Everything faded beyond black into the imperceptible color of obscurity, his temple throbbing all the while. His breathing grew ragged, and he hurled his sword aside.

It landed with a crash indicative of its actual weight. Sinkua collapsed to his hands and knees, shouting at himself, everyone else, and nobody in particular.

"Everybody… left me… behind," he growled, "Why? Why?!"

Flames erupted from his fists as he hammered the churning fractals.

"Why…. didn't they lose me sooner?" he continued as tears welled up, "Everyone… gets hurt around me. Every… body…. dies!"

He rolled onto his back. Blood welled in his palms as he ground his fingernails into the soft flesh. His necklace thumped his sternum with the irregular bouncing of his chest.

"You," he snarled at it, "You worthless piece of shit. What good are you?"

This thing, this relic from Grandpa Gijin, was supposed to protect him. To help him protect others. But it never did. His mark of greatness was nothing more than an instrument of vengeance.

His mother. Grandpa Gijin. Half of Masnethege. Most of the Haprianite Coastal Patrol. RoeZal. The children of Parliamentary ArcNos. CreSam. Pahres. Eytea.

Eytea. He relived her death every time he closed his eyes to grasp at sleep.

Every one of them, a death he witnessed. Every one of them, a death he could have stopped. Should have been able to stop. But this gem, this supposed source of his power, failed him, and so he failed them.

He could never save anyone. Only avenge them. But that path always led to more deaths for him to fail to prevent. And so the cycle continued. Endlessly.

His ragged breathing turned to screaming, brimming with hatred and agony. Then, overwhelmed with self-loathing and spite, it became laughter.

"I am no hero," he grumbled, his laughter growing louder, "I am the harbinger of death!"

Staring at the ceiling of thrashing roots, his palms stained with blood, Sinkua lay on his back laughing maniacally. Darkness closed in from his periphery. Just before everything turned black, an image flashed and scorched itself into his subconscience.

Himself. Morningstar in hand. Blood in his toothy smile.

Chapter 10

Off-road trucks and people with wheelbarrows navigated the upturned urban terrain. A layer of trampled muddy snow coated the landscape. Vielle and Galo caught a few sidelong glances as they walked deeper into the high-rise district, empty-handed all the while.

"Looks like things are well under control here," Galo noted.

"I wasn't aware there was an issue," Vielle said.

"Nenbard picked up some gossip," he said, "Apparently, the only construction crew capable of restoring the district was trying to price gouge the Ministry of Infrastructure."

"This doesn't look like a single crew," she said, "Or professionals."

"Do you think they're volunteers?"

"Looks that way."

"Well, for what became of this place two weeks ago, I'd say they're in a good place," Galo said, "All things considered."

The throngs of people grew thinner as the roots grew thicker. The ground darkened as the foliage reduced the daylight to scattered gray pinhole beams. False rain came down as snow melted and trickled from the leaves.

Vielle halted.

"Are you okay?" Galo asked.

Vielle swallowed hard and took a couple of shaky steps toward the trunk. She narrowed her eyes, scrutinizing the anomaly from a safe distance. Her eyes widened as it became clear.

She straightened up and ran toward Yggdrasil's trunk, scrambling over roots and under low limbs. She exhaled her denial with each rapid footfall, crescendoing into cries of refusal. Galo followed, stopping several steps behind her as she reached the trunk.

Sinkua and Eytea's bedroom door leaned against Yggdrasil's trunk. Plunged into it, just below the carved word, was Sinkua's dagger.

Vielle leaned against the door, pounding her fist against it and sobbing. Tears ran down her cheeks as she sputtered incoherently. Someone she barely knew died to save her. Eytea was murdered before her eyes. Sinkua had taken his own life.

And Yggdrasil did nothing to help any of them.

She cursed the ancient tree, exhausting and expanding her knowledge of expletives. Thorny sprouts curled out of her skin as she expelled her anger and disillusion.

She turned and ran to Galo, throwing herself into his chest. He put an arm around her but offered no words. He knew there was nothing he could say that would comfort her.

She looked up at him. "You're... not crying," she said, "Why?"

"I don't know," Galo lied, "I guess... maybe I'm in denial?"

"I wish I could do that. Just pretend it isn't true."

He cleared his throat and winced as he swallowed. Gabdur had been right about his cough. That much had been clear since his mucus began going dark. Now, there was the matter of finding time to undergo testing. This wasn't the time to bring up any such concerns, though.

"Do you want to try somewhere else?" he asked.

She shook her head. "I can't do it anywhere else," she refused, "I have to be next to the trunk."

"But can you concentrate here?" Galo asked, "We could go to the other side of the trunk."

"Won't work," Vielle insisted, "I'll know it's there. And I don't want to move it."

"Neither do I," he said, "We'll just camp out here until you can focus."

"But… what about the Assembly?"

"I'll figure something out."

"… Thank you."

"Besides, when was the last time you rested? Or ate something?" Galo asked, "Weren't you in Tanelen just this morning? You're going to burn yourself out."

"Um… Yesterday. I think. Or maybe the day before that," Vielle said, "Maybe I am trying to do too much."

"Definitely," Galo said, clearing his throat, "Come on. I saw a food truck about a block before the leaves started dripping on us. I'll buy you some, well, whatever meal this would be."

"Brunchner?" Vielle suggested with a tinge of laughter in her voice.

"Brunchnerssert, if you'd like."

Before they left, Galo walked over to the trunk to pay his last respects to Sinkua. Standing before the door, something odd about the handle of the dagger caught his eye.

It was shoulder level to Sinkua, but it was angled slightly downward. He tapped the underside of the handle. It moved with relative ease.

The hole was wider than the blade. Either someone had pulled on it, or something had been hanging from it.

Galo swallowed his suspicions and returned to Vielle's side. Together, they walked to the food truck for a long-needed meal. He would wait with her however long she needed.

MalVek looked aside as Nikasu stirred on her gurney. Her eyes flickered open a sliver, revealing dilated pupils. He nudged the operative to his left, drawing her attention to Nikasu's waking.

The operative injected Nikasu just below her jugular. She followed with shots to several pressure points and one to the chest. Nikasu's eyes closed again, and her body went slack.

"Subject is prepared for attempted activation," the operative said, "Commencing first test on your ready, sirs."

"Very well, then," MalVek said. He turned to the operative to his right. "Come with me."

MalVek led him into the next room. Once inside, MalVek activated a console at the back of the room. The wall came alight with a map of Ouristihra drawn with glowing green lines, speckled with perhaps thousands of tiny dots.

"How sure are you of this plan?" the operative asked.

"That's for you to worry about," MalVek said.

Mechanical humming from beyond the door indicated that the testing had begun. They both kept their eyes on the map as they continued to talk.

"This is your plan, sir," the operative argued, "Your credibility is on the line."

"I devised this plan to help you," MalVek insisted, "Do you understand the hierarchy here?"

"Sir, don't insult me by trying to frame this as an act of altruism. If this succeeds, it'll only further ingratiate you to Lord Harvester. In what way does this help me?"

"It's quite simple, actually. The Politician formulates our war. I direct our troops into battle. You, in the absence of The Geneticist, create those troops. Hence, I am helping you."

Flashing lights outlined the door within the frame. The hum of machines swelled to a grinding roar. Slurred screams soaked through the walls.

"You think I'm worthy of taking his place, then?" the operative asked.

"You have the intellect of a parsnip compared to Ebralgi," MalVek scolded, "But you are of the greatest aptitude among your colleagues. Simply put, we're settling for you for the time being."

"In that case, what investment do I have in this working?" the operative challenged.

"If we get results, I can endorse you for a promotion. Perhaps have you Named," MalVek said, "But if this fails, The Politician may find it necessary to have you executed."

The console beeped, faintly heard over the screams and mechanical growls from the next room. A single light in the southwest turned red and blipped rapidly.

"We have an activation," the operative said, "Berinin. Northeast coast."

"So we do," MalVek said, "Hope for your sake that we can yield better results before The Politician comes."

MarLys stopped by the curb, given pause by the ambulance in the driveway. SenRas had briefed her on Nenbard and his family, and nothing of an ongoing medical condition had come up. Galo hadn't alerted her to any such thing either.

She closed her eyes, forcing herself to ignore any theories about the implications. The stress would help nothing. Once she heard the ambulance leave, she opened her eyes and, steeling her nerves, walked up the driveway.

She knocked once, and a middle-aged man handling a wet washcloth answered before she brought her arm down to her side. She paused, not nearly as steel-nerved as she hoped, with her fist half-cocked. Blinking hard and shaking her head, she collected a moment's composure.

"Good afternoon, sir," MarLys said, realizing the poor choice of greeting as it left her mouth, "Would you be Judge Nenbard?"

"Who are you?" he asked.

She swallowed hard as she noticed the red stains on the washcloth. "My name is MarLys, sir. I…"

"But who," he reiterated, pausing for emphasis, "are you?"

"I'm with ArcNos's Ministry of Human Resources," MarLys explained, "Prime Minister SenRas sent me here to speak with Judge Nenbard."

"… Nobody here sent for you."

"I know, sir. This was a matter of opportunity."

"Do you have credentials?"

MarLys pulled her wallet from her back pocket and presented her Ministry ID. The man held her wrist as he scrutinized the card, still in its wallet pocket.

"Okay," he said, releasing her wrist, "What's your business here?"

"We're tracking down the remaining Avatars of Fate," MarLys said, "I'm..."

"Why is Human Resources in charge of that?"

"We have the most comprehensive and unrestricted access to citizen records," MarLys said, "It helps us vet applicants."

"Fine," he said, his jaw tightening, "You're tracking down The Avatars, and...?"

"And I'm here to coordinate intel with Judge Nenbard," she said, "We're already up to speed with Chieftain Sage Galo."

"I see," the man sighed, "Come in, then."

MarLys crossed the threshold, and the man shut and locked the door behind her. He walked deeper into the house, waving her along.

"I'm afraid," he continued, "that your timing couldn't have been any worse."

"He was in that ambulance," she said, "wasn't he?"

"He was. So was his wife," he nodded, swallowing audibly, "I'm his brother-in-law and political advisor. My name is Ocronn."

"Ocronn, sir?" MarLys managed, keeping her voice steady, "If you need me to come back later, I will. I don't want to impose while you're grieving."

"No. No, you came for intel, and intel you will have," Ocronn insisted, "Now, have a seat, and write this down."

MarLys sat on the ottoman, but Ocronn shooed her off of it. She moved to the couch, leaning hard against the arm. Ocronn set aside a rolled-up paper and sat in the armchair.

"Because ultimately," Ocronn continued, "They are responsible for the deaths of Sanus and Nenbard."

Thunderous poundings reverberated between her skull and brain, throwing her to the floor. Tension squeezed her bones in rapid pulses. Darkness consumed her vision and released it into stabbing brilliance so rapidly as to feel like strobing sunlight. Sanus writhed in anguish, driving her fingernails against her scalp hard enough to draw blood.

Her mouth stretched open, straining out a strangled scream. Her throat became raw, tainting her weakened cries with the gurgling of bloody mucus. Her jaw locked as she tried to close her mouth.

Sanus's lips curled back. Her mandibles extended past the tip of her nose. Her nostrils widened and flattened as her protruding jaws crushed her nose from behind. The spaces between her teeth widened as her gums stretched.

Insurmountable pressure bore down from within her gums. Her cry of desperation crescendoed into a shriek as new jagged teeth stabbed through with dozens of spurts of blood.

The muscles in her hands swelled. Her knuckles cracked as the bones stretched. Her fingertip bones broke away, and the skin stretched, pulling them further away. New bones and an extra set of knuckles grew in the empty space. Her fingernails extended and hardened into rough claws.

Nenbard ran into the living room and scrambled to her side. He opened the kit and dumped the medication bottle into his hand. He stabbed one of the syringes through the hole in the cap, withdrew, and plunged it into the side of Sanus's neck.

Her hand ripped out of her hair with five ribbons of crimson and swatted his hand and the needle away. Several bones in his hand chipped, and the syringe cracked as it struck the wall.

With tears on his cheeks, Nenbard jammed the next needle against the cap, missing the hole. She was upon him before he could try again.

Sanus, now a creature with no clear memory of humanity, wrapped her arms around him and plunged her fingernails between his ribs. Her stony claws notched his bones. Her teeth plunged into his neck, ripping through both jugular veins, and crushed his throat as she clamped her jaws.

A thunderous blast stopped her assault. Her head snapped back, ripping her from his neck. Tarry blood burbled from a hole in her temple. Her arms clutching Nenbard's dead body, what had become of Sanus collapsed lifelessly atop him, resting her head in the crook of his tattered neck.

"That's what the medical examiners were able to piece together," Ocronn said, his voice trembling, "I only saw the end of it. When she bit his neck. I… had no choice."

"You…" MarLys choked out, "You brought your gun into the room with you?"

"As a precaution," Ocronn insisted, "I keep it in my study."

"So, you were in your study when this started?" MarLys asked, keeping her head down. She couldn't look at his face, knowing the horror on it would feed her own and haunt her with visions of his story.

"I'm usually in my study if I'm home," Ocronn said, "When I heard her having an attack, I grabbed my gun and ran to the living room. As I always do. None of us liked it, but we all knew I might need to use it."

"These were a regular occurrence?"

"Somewhat. But it was always screaming, writhing, sometimes incoherent babbling. Then, she'd black out. Sometimes, she'd complain about pain in her hands and mouth when she woke up. But they never looked any different, except for some bruising sometimes."

MarLys stared at the floor, letting everything settle into her mind. As his story and the events that had brought her here shifted into place, the answer became undeniable. She looked up, focusing just beyond him as she couldn't look him in the eye yet.

"I think," she managed, fixating on the blue wax seal of the rolled-up paper, "I have some idea how this happened."

"The Avatars of Fate did something to accelerate the attack," he said, "They're amping up for something major."

"Yeah," she nodded, emotionally distancing herself with the floral shape of the wax seal, "They just recovered a prisoner they'd lost a few months ago. A Hybrid. I think that's connected to this."

Chapter 11

Vielle sat upon an Yggdrasil root thicker than her hips, watching the eastern horizon. She breathed deeply of the cleanest air in the ruins, rich with oxygen. Steam rose from her cup of hot cider. For the first time since they arrived, she felt some sense of calm.

She had come to accept the inevitable. She couldn't get Eytea back. Or Sinkua. But she had gotten her father back, and she could get her sister back as well. She still had MarLys and Galo as well.

The sky began to turn pink. She glanced over at Galo, asleep in a crevice in the roots. His snoring reminded her of cicadas, a sort of ubiquitous background noise.

As the sun crept over the horizon, Vielle scooted closer to the trunk and turned to face it. She pressed her hand against the bark and closed her eyes.

Narrow, stony sounds echoed throughout her thoughts. Voices from all over Ouristihra swirled around and shifted over and under each other. She focused on Nikasu, on her vine hair tie.

Several voices faded in rapid succession. But of the few that remained, though still incoherent, Nikasu wasn't among them. Someone had taken the hair tie off of her, but they hadn't destroyed it.

Vielle concentrated on the direction of the voices. Almost directly behind her. Slightly to the left. They were southeast of her current position.

MalVek had taken Nikasu to Poravit. But that wasn't enough.

Vielle blocked out everything else. Galo's snoring. The buzzing of bugs. The dawn songs of birds. The morning light. Even the curve and texture of the root beneath her. All of it faded from notice.

Visions of an examination room filled her mind's eye. Her eyes shifted, exploring the remote vision. The hair tie was on an instrument tray.

Vielle concentrated on the voices again, letting them slip into her thoughts. They came through slowly at first, one or two here and there. Eventually, phrases entered her mind, soon followed by full sentences.

Vielle relaxed. The voices faded into incomprehensibility. The blurred edges of her remote vision pushed deeper toward the center. The ambient details of her surroundings returned, aside from Galo's snoring. The other voices and sounds reemerged, blending with the bleary remnants of her remote vision. As she removed her hand from the trunk, those vanished, returning her to her physical surroundings.

She opened her eyes and turned her head. Galo was sitting nearby, clear of the filtered sunbeams that dappled her back. He gave her an inquisitive look. She smiled softly and nodded.

"I know where she is."

Voices and footsteps cropped up around him, sounding as though they came through churning water. The muffling faded, leaving the voices clear but only somewhat coherent. He became aware of uneven pressure against his back and a deep itch over the bottom half of his face. His hand, heavy and rubbery, drifted toward his face.

A voice cried out, seemingly happy. His eyelids parted a bit. His vision was cloudy. This place was dimmer than any hospital he'd ever seen. The ceiling was black with pale cool toned lights. A figure appeared over him, just to the side.

"Are you back with us, sir?" he beckoned, "Don't rush. Take your time."

"What…" Phylus managed, "What's… going on?"

"This is The Coalition's headquarters," he explained, "You were badly injured escaping…"

"I…" he interrupted, only to trail off, "… remember. Goggles. And blood."

"That's right. NalSet and Chekov brought you here. You've been in curative hibernation for five days," he continued, "We were finally able to remove the goggles last night."

"The other guy?"

"Dourias came out of hibernation about an hour ago. He's resting."

"Good," Phylus choked out. He rubbed his beard. "I need a shave. And some water."

"I don't know," a female voice chimed in, "I think salty sea captain looks good on you."

Phylus chuckled and propped himself up on his elbows. The clouds fading from his eyes, he looked around to find Chekov.

"Feels more like mangy hobo," Phylus said, "Had enough of that during the occupation."

"I suppose that's unbecoming of a top diplomat," Chekov agreed, "ArcNos does need you at your best."

"With Tanelen still threatening war," the man said, "at least the entire Northlands needs you at your best."

"They're still…?" Phylus puzzled, "The ultimatum was months ago."

"You were only imprisoned for about two weeks," NalSet said, his voice accompanied by the squeaking of wheels, "despite your beard's apparent disagreement. The ultimatum has been in place just short of a month."

"Oh, right. I… vaguely remember you talking about that," Phylus said. He looked him over, his jaw slack with confusion. "Your knee?"

"Healed up. I also underwent curative hibernation," NalSet said, "Just spending some time in this wheelchair while the muscles reacclimate. Feels like gelatin as it is."

Phylus nodded, then turned to the other man. "I take it you're Gabdur. You have Galo's cheek bones and jawline."

"I am," Gabdur nodded, "All things considered, it's good to finally meet you."

"Likewise," Phylus said, managing a grin, "Your arm. Is that a recent development?"

"It is," Gabdur said, "The Avatars of Fate tried to use me to activate the Mechanical Crypt."

"Did they succeed?" Phylus fretted, sitting upright.

"Only temporarily."

"I'll bring you up to speed while I escort you back to ArcNos," Chekov promised, "I'm sure you have a lot of questions. Best to answer them one on one."

"I remember hearing about a possible turncoat," Phylus said, "Have you figured that out yet?"

NalSet grunted as he turned and wheeled himself away from Phylus's bedside.

"It's MalVek," Chekov said, "Mortvill is developing a plan to apprehend him."

"I'll need time to know what to do with this information."

"I understand. The Ouristihran Union Assembly is next week. Just focus on that for the time being."

"Assuming I even have the authority to attend," Phylus said, "But nonetheless, I'd like to speak with Dourias before I go."

Chekov smiled and nodded. She moved to Dourias's bedside and shook him by the shoulder. They spoke in hushed tones, beyond the reach of Phylus's ears.

Dourias nodded and rose from his bed, groaning along with the audible creaking of his joints. Phylus pushed himself out of his bed as well, only vaguely noticing that he was in different clothes than he had escaped in. They hobbled toward each other, looking as though they were both learning to walk all over again.

"It might take some time for you to get your coordination back," Chekov warned, "Your sense of time as well."

The two eventually met in the middle of the room.

"Thank you for everything, young man," Dourias said.

"I'm glad you're well, Dourias," Phylus said, "I wasn't sure you'd be able to make it out, but..."

"But I tried anyway, thanks to you. And here we are."

"Yeah. First time I saw you, I thought all your fight had burnt out."

"I had nobody to fight with me," Dourias said, pressing his fingertip against Phylus's forehead, "For that matter, I thought everyone I had to fight for was long gone or assumed me to be dead."

"Well, I'm glad you got your spark back," Phylus said, "What's your plan from here?"

"Chekov and Gabdur are going to help me recall the intel I siphoned from The Avatars," Dourias said, "She's also going to arrange for me to meet Yrlis. To say I haven't been a model father would be an understatement, I'd say. And once we have a secure line of communication, I also intend to reconnect with Farim."

"Well, that's... I don't know what to say but to wish you luck," Phylus said, having only just learned of his parentage to Yrlis.

"Thank you. For that and everything else," Dourias said, "Now then, isn't it about time you returned to ArcNos?"

Phylus nodded, then called to Chekov. "Where's the restroom?" he asked, "I need to get this beard under control before I go home."

Chekov led him out of the infirmary. His orientation seemed to be getting back to normal. His legs felt sturdier after some time under his own weight, as well. Having spoken with Dourias had proven therapeutic, it seemed. At the very least, he gave his mind time to recalibrate.

They crossed paths with a masked man, Mortvill presumably, and Elemeno in the hall. Mortvill took Chekov aside and gave her a folded sheet of paper. She opened it partway, her eyebrows tightening as her eyes bounced across the page.

"Keep it to yourself," he implored, "It is only a last resort."

Mortvill stopped in the doorway to the infirmary. He glared at NalSet, seething yet pitying. "Why have you come out of treatment early?"

"All I skipped was tissue recuperation," NalSet argued, "Besides, I couldn't expect Gabdur to guard the place on his own."

"Does this mean you're finally accepting that MalVek went rogue?" Gabdur asked, "Or do you think you'll recover him after they extract our location from him?"

"I suspect he thinks to fight alongside him when he returns with the remaining Named," Mortvill said, folding his arms, "You suspect he is setting a trap for them, do you not?"

"That's enough out of both of you!" NalSet boomed, "Be on your way. My leg will recover in its own time."

"Of course, it will," Mortvill sighed, "In any case, Elemeno and I have determined with great confidence where MalVek has taken Nikasu. They are in an unnumbered facility in Poravit."

Mortvill asked Elemeno to step outside, reasoning that there were some matters to which she was not yet privy. She exchanged handshakes with NalSet and Dourias, then a hug with Gabdur, and exited to the hall.

"Words cannot express my relief at your return, Dourias," Mortvill continued, "Alas however, I expect this parting to be our last farewell."

"You mean to confront him," Dourias gleaned, "don't you, sir?"

Mortvill nodded. "For too long have we failed to subdue them. Though we now understand why, rectification mandates my direct intervention."

"Spril and Yrlis will be visiting shortly," Gabdur announced, "Malia is escorting them. Spril says he figured out your note. Do you wish to meet with him?"

"Let them come. Greet them on my behalf," Mortvill said, "I had hoped to see him through this, but hope and priority rarely coincide."

"What are you going to do about MalVek?" NalSet asked.

"I will do whatever I find to be necessary."

"Let me deal with him."

"I will leave him to you if it is at all possible. But for now, just know that, should I return," Mortvill said, "you are to kill me without question."

Phylus sat in the lobby of the Parliamentary offices, thumbing through an issue of an archery magazine. This one had been published the month following the last issue he seen. Unless whoever stocked the lobby had been slacking in their duties, he had indeed only been gone as long as Chekov said.

He reflected on everything she had told him during the cab ride from the gate point to the capitol building. It was a lot to take in at once, but if nothing else, it proved a necessary and appreciated priming for the sight of enormous tree roots all over town. He looked to the clock, finding that he had been in ArcNos several hours fewer than it felt like. Whether that was a residual effect of hyperspace or the weight of all he'd learned, he couldn't be sure.

Chekov had begun by further detailing how Gabdur had lost his arm. When she told of Galo's coma, she skipped ahead to assure him that he was well again. Phylus felt relieved at Yahsek's and Ozzera's deaths, knowing the threat their existence posed to everyone he regarded as his children. Pahres's sacrifice, however, left him with bittersweet mixed feelings.

She had recounted the assassinations of LenSom, The Engineer, and The Geneticist from SenRas's and Malia's reports. Their deaths had been thorough and brutal, and as little a fan of capital punishment as Phylus was, he felt that anything less would have been insufficient. He had spent the years since the war trying and failing to convince himself of the necessity of all his own killings.

But for those three, there was no grief. No particular exuberance either. The necessity of their deaths took no convincing. But that's all they were. Necessary.

Cold as he felt toward them, he knew all three were replaceable. Thus, their deaths were only small temporary victories. Someone like Yahsek couldn't be so easily replaced, though. Nor could Ozzera. The threat they posed, between their powers and their positions to destabilize the relationships among the Hybrids, was over.

An assistant popped out of the largest set of office doors. He cleared his throat, and Phylus turned to him.

"Madame Chairwoman will see you now," he announced.

Phylus crossed the floor, still somewhat disoriented in three dimensions but hiding it better, while the assistant held the door open. The two shook hands as he passed, the assistant welcoming him back. Phylus thanked him and closed the door behind himself.

"Phylus!" an elderly voice simmering with authority called out, "You truly are back."

"Yes, I have my daughters and Malia to thank for that," Phylus said, crossing the vast distance to her desk, "I suppose I'm to call you Chairwoman TolRou now?"

"It would be quite proper of you," TolRou said, "I apologize that we had to hold the election before we were even sure of your condition."

"It's fine, really. I would have voted for you anyway," Phylus said, "Besides, I guess it's all the more fitting that the one who cleared up this position would set out to find me. Knowing her, she probably hoped to find me before the election, just in case it came down to one vote."

"Ah, I did hear you correctly, then," TolRou said, "High Minister EshCal would only say that third party contractors were on the case."

"Yes, that would be Malia and her two biological daughters, both Hybrids. A couple of comrades from the Subtransit Resistance and an old acquaintance from Poravit converged with them along the way," Phylus recounted, "Now, I've been briefed on the highlights of the past month. And honestly, I'd normally be loath to return to such a fiasco, but after what I've been through, I'm actually looking forward to it. But if we can't get better coffee in Foreign Affairs by the time I return, I'll be forced to raid SenRas's stash, and we know that can't end well."

"I'll see what I can do," TolRou said with a small laugh, "Have you met with High Minister Calhosin yet?"

"No, I thought that would be overstepping my bounds," Phylus reasoned, "I still have about five weeks left on my suspension, do I not?"

"Ah, so that's what you meant," TolRou realized, "You can actually return any time you'd like. The sooner the better."

"Wait. I'm un-suspended?"

"You are. Parliament's first order after LenSom's death was to rescind his recent terminations and suspensions. I assumed you knew."

"This is the first I've heard about it, but that's great news. I'll go get a crate of better coffee and catch Calhosin after his lunch break," Phylus beamed, "By the way, would that rescinding have included Sinkua?"

"It only covered Ministry executives. Whether to rehire any of your own staff is left to the discretion of you and your High Minister."

Phylus nodded and thanked the Chairwoman as he shook her hand. On his way out, he gave her assistant a hearty pat on the shoulder.

After a walk around downtown, first to the supermarket for a couple dozen kilograms of imported coffee, then to AlsRim's Deli for the biggest sandwich he'd ever eaten in one sitting, Phylus returned in the late afternoon. He worked his way toward the center of the Ministry of Foreign Affairs, exchanging greetings with his associates as he passed. Whether it was being back in his element or just a matter of time, he realized that his sense of space and time had recalibrated by the time he reached his destination.

He turned just before the vestibule in front of his office doors and headed down a small perpendicular offshoot. At the end stood a pair of double doors. Phylus pushed one of two buttons on the wall, and a voice came through a speaker a moment later.

"State your name and business."

Phylus pushed the second button. "Oh, you know damn well who I am, buddy."

There was no answer. Instead, he heard a chair roll in a short burst, and a series of thick clapping footfalls followed. One of the doors flew open, and there stood the fellow immigrant that he called his second in command.

"Hello, Calhosin," Phylus smiled, "I'm back."

"I… see that," Calhosin sputtered, his mouth agape, "I guess the third party contractors came through."

"Yeah, Vielle, Nikasu, and Malia found me and saw to my safety."

"Well, I assume you're here to catch up," Calhosin said, stepping aside, "Come in. Leave a bag of coffee on the counter. Take a seat."

"You assume right," Phylus said as he lobbed a kilo bag next to Calhosin's brewer, "I've gotten a few highlights, but I need specifics."

"What do you already know?" Calhosin asked as he opened the bag of Eprilenese grounds.

"I know how the capitol building was locked down and retaken, including LenSom's assassination, and about the Heniokhos Disaster and Yggdrasil."

"Do you know about the quagmire concerning the damages?"

"Are we being blamed for it?"

"Only by one side," Calhosin said with backhanded reassurance, "There's one contractor in ArcNos capable of restoring the high-rise district, but they're price gouging to as much as triple market norms, according to Biroe. OshMar says they say it's a political matter."

"How so?"

"Insider involvement. With Spril, your daughter, and that employee with glowing eyes having been in the area, they're insisting the Ministries had a hand in it."

"Has FerLyn spoken with them?"

"I'm under the impression that she has."

"What sort of magic has Biroe worked on the budget?"

"As much as mathematically possible," Calhosin said, handing him a mug of coffee, "He's willing to pay if that's what it takes. Get the job done now, take them to task on the gouging later. But the money isn't there, so his convictions are moot."

"What about foreign aid?"

"Not an option. After everything that happened to the Chieftain Sage under our watch, nobody else wants to draw up a contract with us."

"So, what is being done about the high-rise district?" Phylus asked as he sipped his coffee, "And what steps have you taken to repair our international reputation?"

"Volunteer crews led by a few Ministry executives have been picking away at the mess. Several protesters who were rallying against our inaction have even gotten involved," Calhosin said, "As for our image, that leads us on a tangent. Spril has made a rather groundbreaking proposition. But our tools have been dulled, and the ground is unrelenting."

"Something about going on the offensive against The Avatars, I'm sure."

"Yes, an international Anti-Avatar Task Force. Covert Affairs has begun coordinating intel with Judge Nenbard, but that's the only headway we've made so far."

"Is that also because of what's transpired with Chieftain Sage Galo?"

"No, it seems the consensus is that nobody is willing to risk implication in our affairs with Tanelen."

"Okay, let's make sure we're up to speed," Phylus sighed, "We can't get a fair price or foreign aid to repair the high-rise district, but we do have untrained volunteers picking away at the mess. Tanelen is still out for blood. Everyone else is keeping their distance, except Berinin. Their Judge is sharing Avatar intel with us, and that's our only appreciable progress toward Spril's Anti-Avatar Task Force. That about the size of it?"

"That about covers it."

"Has Sinkua called to ask for his job back?"

"The guy with the glowing eyes?" Calhosin asked. Phylus nodded. "Not that I'm aware of. Why?"

"This is a bitch of a situation, and he has a talent for formulating plans at times like this. Be good if he was here to brainstorm with us."

"If you want to redact his termination, we can call him."

"No, I don't think that's an option at this point," Phylus insisted, "We're too close to the Ouristihran Union Assembly. It wouldn't do to call him in at half past the eleventh hour."

"Do you have an initial proposition?"

"Working on it," Phylus said, drumming out a fingertip beat on the desk. He rose from his seat. "I'll be in my office, drawing up forecasts. Come see me if you think of anything."

Awash in darkness, Malia pressed her palm against the wall panel. An array of lights emerged from the outline of her hand and zigzagged into the walls. The panel shifted and opened, and Spril, with Yrlis at his side, followed her into The Coalition's assembly chamber.

The Omnimath's hovering throne sat empty. In four of the other seats, all grounded, sat Chekov, Gabdur, NalSet, and Dourias. NalSet had a wheelchair folded and propped against his seat, but he wasn't in a cast. Trails of light from around the bases of their seats converged in the center as pieces of a massive glowing insignia.

"Where's the top shit?" Spril asked.

"The Omnimath is on a mission," NalSet said, his rolling basso resonating under the domed ceiling, "Malia. You've deciphered his message, correct?"

"Well, it was Spril who figured it out, but…" Malia said, trailing off as she checked the note and solution yet again, "I… I don't… see how…"

"Let's have it," NalSet ordered, reaching forth and beckoning her.

Malia crossed the floor and handed him the note. NalSet read it, nodded, and waved Chekov over. She exhaled with relief as she read it.

"You are correct," NalSet said as Chekov returned to her seat.

"How the hell?" Spril barked, "Phylus has infant pictures of me."

"As we would expect…" Chekov said.

"So, what was it?" Spril raged on without the slightest acknowledgement, "Is my childhood all phony memories? The Avatars can cut off memories. So, why not?"

"Spril, you need to…" NalSet said.

"Or maybe you stole me from my real parents," Spril theorized, "Yeah. That must be it. You snatched me right out of the maternity ward as part of a half-hatched, half-cocked, all-fucked plan. That's your style, right? Steal babies and emotionally ass-rape families as some vague means to even more vague ends that you never fucking accomplish."

"Young man," came a voice from the periphery, weary yet deep and gravelly. Spril looked aside for the source. The voice continued before he could speak further. "You have spoken your piece. Permit them to speak theirs."

"Malia told me about you," Spril sighed, lowering his head, "I suppose I may have gotten carried away." He raised his head. "By no means am I content with the prospects here. But NalSet, Chekov, what do you have to say on the matter?"

"Would somebody fill me in on the matter?" Gabdur asked.

"The note was an anagram of 'Spril came from another time,'" Malia said, "The core members of The Coalition are time travelers, probably from the future."

"Oh, I already knew that about them," Gabdur said, "Not about Spril though. I knew he was of interest, but I didn't have details."

"We thought MalVek had…" NalSet offered.

"Don't," Malia cut off, gritting her teeth.

NalSet turned his attention to Spril. "We are from the future, as Malia says, but our circumstances date back into the distant past," he began, "Several millennia ago, Omphaloworlders, those being humans and Hybrids, and Etherworlders such as Leviathan and Yggdrasil coexisted reasonably well."

"But this harmony wouldn't last," Chekov stepped in, "War broke out among the Etherworlders. It began in their world, but eventually, it spilled over into ours."

"Leading the charge for unraveling our world was an Etherworlder with the power of chaos. A Goddess, as her acolytes came to call her, obsessed with attaining absolute power," NalSet said, "The Etherworlders and Hybrids were nearly destroyed protecting the Omphaloworld. Their numbers fell from thousands to fewer than twenty."

"Aside from herself, only three Etherworlders were known to have survived, with a fourth missing and thus of unknown status. There's no reliable record of how many Hybrids were left," Chekov said, "The surviving Etherworlders secured themselves such that she could not acquire their powers."

"The Trifecta, a team of three sons of Hybrids, sealed her on an island in the Southland Sea, cutting the island and everything on it off from reality," NalSet said, "She and her Hybrid have been there ever since."

"The Hybrids' return portends two possibilities," Chekov said, "Either the remaining Etherworlders figured out how to destroy her, or she's figuring out how to break down The Veil from within."

"In our history, The Veil fell this year," NalSet said, "The Goddess of Chaos emerged into a world that was ill-equipped to weather her wrath. But absolute power was still beyond her grasp. So, unable to dismantle the laws of physics which bind our reality, she conquered and enslaved this world instead, thus beginning The Era of Chaos."

"We come from five hundred years later," Chekov said, leaning forward, "Spril. We genetically engineered you to be our most powerful resource, colloquially referring to you as The Weapon. But it was too dangerous to raise you in that period.

"We brought you here as an embryo and implanted you into a woman who would ultimately fail to conceive with her husband. We even took care that you would show as their own on any modern genetic tests. You were to grow up here in a safer environment, where you could develop leadership and tactical abilities. Eventually, you would undergo treatments which would allow you to use the abilities that we built into your DNA.

"But now, certain abilities are manifesting on their own, meaning we waited too long to begin your treatment regimen. For that, I apologize. We feared the possibility of dire, even fatal, complications if we began prematurely."

"Once the regimen is complete, we'll return to our time, Mortvill, Chekov, you, and myself," NalSet said, "As The Weapon, you'll lead the final charge against The Goddess and destroy her once and for all."

A stinging pain flashed behind Spril's eyes. He pinched the bridge of his nose and gritted his teeth. His very skull seemed to tighten as he fought to either rationalize or reject their story. As much as it explained these recent episodes, it destroyed what he knew about himself, his place in the world, and the world itself.

The more he tried to focus, however, the more pronounced his senses became. Thus, the more every stimulus, from the snaking cerulean lights to the dull hum of The Omnimath's levitating throne, aggravated him.

"This treatment regimen?" Yrlis opened, reaching into her portfolio as she approached Chekov with decidedly soft steps, "Does it have…?"

"I have a question," Malia cut in, raising her head abruptly. She lowered her voice as she caught sight of Spril. "Sorry. But where is The Omnimath for this? I know you said he's on a mission, but… What kind of mission could supersede this?"

"He wanted to be here, but one of the only things that could take precedence came up," NalSet explained, "He went after MalVek. Whether to hunt or recover him ultimately depends on what MalVek does when Mortvill finds him."

"Right," Malia scoffed. She gestured to Yrlis and Chekov. "As you were."

"Does the treatment regimen have anything to do with this?" Yrlis asked, handing her mother a stack of papers.

"What exactly am I looking at here?" Chekov asked, "Beyond a genome map, obviously."

"I mapped Spril's genome, and I found several extremely improbable gene sequences," Yrlis explained, "He suggested that I see what genes would need to be changed to reconcile the sequences into something more probable."

"And what did you find?"

"I haven't completed it, but so far, it looks like the replaced genes will comprise an active pair of Hybrid Chromosomes."

"That is essentially correct. Once the regimen is complete, his Hybrid Chromosomes will appear on modern genetic mapping programs," Chekov said. She turned her head to address Spril. "But you would be so much more than that. Not quite human. Not quite Hybrid. Not quite Etherworlder. And yet, beyond all three. Something not yet defined and perhaps undefinable."

"I didn't ask for any of this," Spril grumbled, "And nobody asked me if I wanted to go fight your war."

"You're not exactly special in that regard, kid," NalSet said, "Nobody has a say in the genes they got. Destiny doesn't need permission either. You're made of whatever made you."

"Destiny is bullshit, and talking like that makes you sound like an Avatar," Spril pushed back, "But no, you're right otherwise. Except nobody else was engineered to be a living weapon. And nobody else is being cornered into throwing their life away to fix someone else's failures."

"There have, admittedly, been complications in getting to this point," Chekov said, "Unforeseen circumstances, you might say."

"What sort of complications?" Spril demanded, "You mean other than your waiting until I'm thirty to tell me any of this and being surprised that I'd have the audacity to be reluctant?"

"You weren't supposed to have the capacity for emotional bonds beyond necessary camaraderie," Chekov explained, "But Phylus and Vielle reached you in ways we thought were impossible. As a result, you've grown too attached to this place and time. The treatment regimen should remedy that."

"Listen to me good, the only thing keeping my hand off your throat is the fact that you're basically my mother-in-law," Spril said, "But if either of them hears you blaming them for the consequences you wrought, they will not be as merciful, and I will not restrain them. Do you understand me?"

Chekov nodded, her eyes wide.

"I could go with you," Yrlis offered.

"Yrlis," Spril gasped, turning to her, "Are you sure? I mean, you have your own life here."

"I know, but," Yrlis said, a smile spreading across her face, "I could have my own life anywhere. Besides, it'd be a pretty bleak life without you around."

"If I can bring you along, then…"

"Can't happen," NalSet interrupted.

"Exactly how do you expect to stop me?" Yrlis challenged.

"By following the laws of temporal physics," NalSet said, "My or anyone's permission doesn't factor into it."

"I would be going just as far into the future as the rest of you. What's the problem?"

"When we arrived thirty-five years ago, a second timeline sprang into existence as a preventative measure against temporal paradoxes. That's why Spril can't just kill The Goddess now and be done with it," NalSet explained, "We are guests in this timeline, and so, when we return to the future, we will return to our own timeline. You, on the other hand, were conceived and thus would remain in this timeline."

"But doesn't it make a difference that my mother is from your timeline?"

"It might, but…"

"But your father," Dourias cut in, leaning forward, "is from the new timeline."

"You mean…?"

"Yes. I'm your father. And I'm sorry I..."

"No. There's no need to apologize. Your absence finally makes sense," Yrlis said, "I just wish my mother hadn't led me to believe you were neglecting us."

"Yrlis, you need to understand that..." Chekov implored, but NalSet cut her off.

"Before we digress any further," he pressed, "Had both of your parents been from the first timeline, it would be possible to bring you forward into the first timeline. But it would be extraordinarily unlikely. In fact, tampering with the temporal shift process would be more likely to land you in neither timeline, and none of us wants to speculate what that would mean for you."

"You knew this would happen," Yrlis said, turning to Chekov, "But you introduced us. Why?"

"That was before we knew Spril had developed the capacity for emotional bonds," Chekov said, "You were to study and learn from him. And in some ways, that has turned out how we wanted.

"The best thing we can leave behind is knowledge and technology from our time. Not by handing it to the people of this period, but by guiding them toward it. Your work with his genome, his surgery, and his rehabilitation were all at least two hundred years ahead of their time."

"Suppose I don't go and fix your future," Spril said, "What would become of me?"

"Without the treatment regimen, your current symptoms will worsen at an exponential rate," Chekov said, "Psychosis would be inevitable and untreatable."

"Right. So, hey. Tell me something. Can you actually not cure Sinkua's condition? Or are you holding out because his self-destruction factors into your agenda?" Spril challenged, "Or is it because he won't march to your stupidass drums?"

"Spril!" NalSet boomed, "You would be wise to..."

"You would be wise to suck my dick," Spril snapped, "Chekov gets a gram of mercy, but I have no love to spare on you.

"Now, the way I see it, I can go with you and become something that can't function in society. Or I can stay here and go mad. Either way, I'm losing my sense of self, and I'll be dead by thirty-three. Well, if it's up to me, then I'm choosing to fall apart and die among the people I love."

"What are you saying?" Chekov asked.

"I'm saying that I'm going to stay here and fight The Goddess of Chaos with my people on our terms," Spril said, "Now, I wish you the best of luck with your war, but you need to understand that it's just that. Your war. Not mine."

"You need us at least as much as we need you," NalSet argued.

"You human trafficking thunder cunts have fucked up countless lives with your incessant meddling. There's not a damn person who needs you unless they buy into the bullshit idea that you're the only ones who can fix the problems you created. You know, when it comes down to it, Sinkua was right about you all along. And I am embarrassed that I'm just now seeing it," Spril spitfired, "Now, I'm going to go on my hunt and leave you to yours. Stay out of my way."

Spril turned and walked away before any of them could level an argument. Yrlis followed close behind. Malia remained in the middle of the assembly chamber just long enough to speak her piece.

"Gabdur. Follow us to the front door. Take my portal strip after we leave," she insisted, "This is my official resignation."

Chapter 12

Light flashed and flickered through the doorframe, illuminating the white walls of the short branching hall in erratic brilliance. The new employee stopped as it caught the corner of her eye, falling back from her supervisor.

"Excuse me!" she called forth.

"Yeah, what is it?" her supervisor answered, his face tightening as he found her several steps behind, "Teyaku! What are you doing? Come on. We're on a tight schedule here."

"There's a light acting up in that room," Teyaku said, her eyes darting between her guide and the flickering doorframe.

"What of it?"

"Should we do something about it?"

The guide sighed and rolled his eyes. "After your tour, yeah, I'll deal with it," he said, "Come on."

"I'll just go turn off the light then," Teyaku insisted, "I'd hate to find out later that it shorted out."

"Don't go back there!" he shouted.

Before the words were out of his mouth, Teyaku had already disappeared down the short corridor. He scrambled after her, fumbling with his earpiece.

"Bypass actuation chamber security! Disable Flush Protocol!" he shouted, "Full system shutdown! Full system shutdown!"

A hair-thin beam of light swept down Teyaku's face as she opened the door.

Galo approached the reception desk while Vielle waited next to a potted tree near the door. Galo put on his most cordial smile, and the receptionist straightened up and cleared her throat.

"What can I do for you today, sir?" she asked.

"I have a meeting at, ah…" Galo said, drawing back his sleeve, only to chuckle at himself as he recalled that he doesn't wear a watch. He looked to the clock on the wall. "Oh! Sixteen-thirty. Looks like I'm quite early. My apologies."

"The Chieftain Sage has an appointment that I didn't know about?" the receptionist asked, arching an eyebrow.

"He may have listed me under an alias," Galo suggested.

"Well, let me see what I can find," the receptionist said, setting to work on her keyboard, "Some days, I swear these people give me nothing to work with in the morning and expect miracles by the afternoon."

Galo glanced back at Vielle. She cocked her head toward the potted tree and shook her head. Galo turned back around.

"That's no way to treat people," Galo sighed, "I'm sure they'll come to regret it when you find the decency you deserve elsewhere."

The receptionist looked up at him, a tired smile gracing her face. Galo smiled back as she set back into her work. As much as it was supposed to have been an act, he understood.

A buzzing and a familiar voice from the overhead speaker sundered the moment.

"Send them back," MalVek ordered, "We will see them now."

Galo thanked the receptionist for her effort and straightened up. He turned to Vielle and waved for her to come along, cocking his head toward the hall beyond the receptionist's desk.

At his behest, Vielle waited just inside the hall. Galo hunkered down beside the receptionist. She turned to him as he cleared his throat, her posture relaxing.

"Excuse me. Could I ask one more favor of you?"

"Of course," she said, swallowing hard, "Anything within my abilities."

They had a brief exchange, Galo having a simple enough request. The only caveat was that she couldn't use any company lines. She complied easily enough, but the fact that she didn't understand his insistence told Galo that she didn't know what went on below.

"Thank you," he said, kissing the back of her hand. A vague tingle ran through his hand and mouth, coalescing in this chest. A hollow feminine shape flashed through his mind's eye. "Be safe."

The receptionist nodded vigorously, tucking her bottom lip between her teeth as Galo got back to his feet. She scooted her chair into the reception desk and setting into his request.

Galo found Vielle with a quizzical expression and her hands on her hips.

"Laying it on a little thick there?" she asked, her voice low.

"I was giving you time to work," he argued, "Besides, she needs to feel appreciated."

"Oh, I don't think that was only about her needs."

"… Perhaps not."

MalVek and Joren emerged from the elevator at the end of the hall. Galo had become aware of the well-founded suspicions that Joren was The Politician, but he still was taken aback to see him with MalVek. Through some effort, though, Galo looked unsurprised enough that the faintest scowl flickered across the Noble Doyen's face.

"Before either of you say anything," The Politician began, "let me just say that I know why you're here, and your grievances will be addressed shortly."

"Do the Tanelenese know you're involved in human trafficking, Joren?" Galo asked.

The Noble Doyen flinched. "Is that what you think has been happening?" he asked, "I won't deny the impurity of my methods, but I stand by the assertion that my motives are for the greater good."

"Your partner," Vielle said, her voice dripping with contempt, "bludgeoned and kidnapped my sister. Did you know about that?"

"How did you know about that?" MalVek asked.

"Oh, I'm just full of surprises, you fat fuck."

"Vielle, that was uncalled for," Galo scolded, "There's enough wrong with him without bringing his weight into it."

"Come now," Joren cut in, raising his hands in a capitulatory gesture, "Let's not be sour when there's air to clear and deals to execute. Now, about this sister of yours. She has bright purple eyes, yes?"

"Yeah. And now, she knows how to fight back," Vielle warned, "So, don't count on keeping her locked up for long, with or without our help."

"Well, you'll find we're quite glad you showed up. You see, she's reached the extent of her utility," The Politician explained, "She is quite alive. That much I promise. But though we have no policy on the matter, I always endeavor to release our patients to loved ones. I pride myself, you see, on being a unifier."

Vielle folded her arms and looked him over. "Sure," she nodded, her mouth flattening, "Take me to her."

"Of course. Wait by the elevator, please," The Politician said, "I need to speak with these two first."

He turned and directed MalVek and Galo toward a door nearer to the lobby. Galo followed more mechanically than consciously as he directed his thoughts toward Leviathan.

"I'm going to give you an out," he thought, "Ensure their safety, then return to me."

"On the front steps in thirty minutes, I suppose?" Leviathan confirmed.

"That'll do just fine."

"Shall I also see that the facility is decommissioned?"

"Time permitting," Galo thought, "But don't risk collapsing the building."

"Flood damage, then."

Galo blinked and rolled his neck as his thoughts returned to his surroundings. He and MalVek followed The Politician into an unoccupied break room. While The Politician set to work at the coffee brewer, at his behest, Galo and MalVek sat at a round table.

"Now, Galo, I realize you have many grievances and questions, as is your right. So, I thought it best to have MalVek address them while I take Vielle to fetch her sister," Joren explained, "MalVek, no matter how uncomfortable it makes you, I implore you to answer his questions to the best of your abilities."

Galo and MalVek glared at each other. Galo with an expression cold and flat. MalVek with one indifferent. Even as The Politician set two mugs of coffee between them, neither blinked nor budged.

"Now, I'll leave the two of you to your discussion," The Politician said, "I should think to return soon."

He crouched beside MalVek, grasping him by the shoulder. Though he angled his face toward MalVek, his eyes were fixed on Galo. Galo watched for some secret within their exchange. Leviathan growled within Galo's mind as the air thrummed before The Politician's voice.

"Kill him."

The flickering lights went black. Mechanical whirs stretched to groans as machines slowed to a halt. Teyaku braced herself in the doorframe.

Red beacons flashed on, spinning in rhythm with blaring klaxons. Streams of smoke poured from nozzles in the ceiling. Operatives doubled over and collapsed, coughing up bile and blood.

Teyaku found Nikasu unconscious and strapped to a gurney. Puncture wounds and bruises riddled her limbs and speckled her neck. Teyaku ripped a sleeve off her shirt and tied it around the bottom half of her own face. Ignoring the obscured shouts of her supervisor, Teyaku rushed to Nikasu's side.

Nikasu spasmed and yanked against the straps. Her eyelids flickered as she groaned and babbled incoherently. Teyaku stood over her, choking back her panic as she considered how best to wake this tortured girl.

"Nikasu!" she whisper-shouted, shaking the gurney, "Wake up! We're going home!"

Nikasu's eyes shot open, her pupils so dilated that her eyes were all but consumed with the darkest purple. Her eyes darted about, taking in everything and focusing on nothing. Teyaku placed a hand on her shoulder, only to snap back as Nikasu jolted.

Nikasu's body arched against her binding straps until only the top of her head and the balls of her feet touched the mattress. A primal scream exploded from the depths of her lungs. Her bent body quaked and rattled the gurney.

Stung by the streaming smoke, Teyaku's eyes began to water. Her nostrils burned and throat constricted despite her improvised mask. Teyaku pulled at the binding straps. They needed a special tool to unlock. Instead, she leaned under the gurney and stomped out the wheel locks.

Nikasu collapsed back onto the mattress. Her eyes were glazed over, and her chest bounced in rapid irregular rhythms. Teyaku ripped off her other sleeve and laid it over Nikasu's face. As the groans of collapsed operatives swelled around them, Teyaku threw her weight at the gurney and rushed for the door.

The hall offered no sanctuary as she found it just as flooded with smoke and groans. Teyaku pulled the utility knife from her tool belt and cut through the binding straps. As the groans swelled into animalistic snarls, Teyaku tied the cutoff sleeve behind Nikasu's head and slung the girl across her shoulders.

With her eyes forward and expression neutral, Vielle felt Joren's eyes searching her.

"You're imagining how you might kill me, aren't you?" he said.

Vielle shot him a dry glare. "What are you…?"

"Oh, I'm not psychic. No, given the circumstances, it's common sense," Joren continued, "But I feel it's only fair to warn you that my death would…"

"Diplomatic fallout. Political discord. I know," Vielle cut back in, "I want you dead or incarcerated, but it isn't my place to do either. I'm only here for my sister."

"As long as you understand that," Joren said, pulling a card from his breast pocket as they stepped into the elevator.

"But isn't that what you want?" she challenged, "Volatility between ArcNos and Tanelen? Justification for war?"

"I suppose it could be interpreted that way. I, for one, do not," he said, swiping his card and pushing a button, "Regardless of the semantics about my intentions though, I am neither eager nor even willing to die for any of them. I wish to live to see the fruits of my labor. So, as much as others here might wish you dead, it is neither my place nor in my best interest to attack you. I know enough about you to foresee the consequences of such an altercation."

"Mutually assured destruction," Vielle said, shoving her hands in her pockets, "I'm familiar with the concept."

The elevator stopped, and the doors opened to a surprisingly orderly staging area. Technicians rushed about from gurney to gurney, from console to console. The entire room emitted a dull grumbling murmur of activity. Vielle couldn't say if anyone was there by will or coercion, but from the elevator, nobody looked to be suffering.

She stepped forward, but Joren barred her.

"I'll need to go first," he insisted, "We've installed additional security measures due to some, well, recent infiltrations."

Joren pushed the door open button until it locked, then stepped out of the elevator. He rubbed his chin as he inspected the wall next to the doors. He poked at something, a keypad presumably, and shook his head.

Vielle suppressed the urge to poke her head out for a closer look. She wasn't sure if she was more afraid of the new security measures or the consequences of her discovering they were a ruse.

Joren stepped back and stood front and center before the open elevator doors. He pulled a small remote control from his pocket, looked it over, then pointed it at the top of the doorframe and pushed a button.

The room crackled and fragmented. Flashing red light seeped through the cracks. Anguished and bloodlusting screams spilled over as the shards of the orderly staging area melted over the fury of the one behind. People and monstrous abominations scrambled about with no discernible order as to who hunted whom.

Sprouting a vegetal cat-o'-nine-tails from her forearm, Vielle stepped into the madness that this facility had held all along.

Galo leaned back in his chair, one foot propped on the opposite knee, and watched MalVek. The man had his head down and had been clutching his stomach since Joren whispered to him. Galo withheld the urge to show sympathy, whether as an estranged friend or a student of medicine.

"Why did you do it, MalVek?" Galo asked.

"Wh… Which part?" MalVek grumbled, snickering to himself, "You'll have to be more specific, boy."

"Well, for one, why did you take Nikasu?"

"They weren't done with her. Still plenty of work to be done."

"They wanted to make another Yahsek and Ozzera?"

MalVek looked up at him, grinning with bloodshot eyes and raw lips. "If that's what you believe," he said, casting his eyes back down, "you're not entirely wrong."

Galo took a sip of his coffee and set the mostly full mug down on the table. He scooted his chair closer, folding his arms on his lap.

"Well, pushing that matter isn't going to get me anywhere," Galo conceded, "Now then, why did you defect from The Coalition? Why are you sharing tech with The Avatars of Fate?"

"To restore order," MalVek said, his voice strained, "You, of all people, I thought would understand."

"Well, I'm afraid I don't," Galo said, scratching at his sleeves, "How does defecting to a terrorist organization factor into restoring order?"

"This world has grown complacent under the watch of people like us. The Coalition. Hybrids."

"And you think that your working for The Avatars will pull Ouristihra out of this slump of complacency."

"Precisely. Our thankless suffering has so illuminated this world that they've forgotten what shadows look like," MalVek waxed, "Hey, you talk to fish, right? Do they know they're wet? Or is the idea beyond their ken because they don't know otherwise?"

"You must have me confused with someone else. I don't speak with fish," Galo corrected, "But while I comprehend your philosophy, I can't stand aside and let you punish Ouristihra because you think they're too soft or don't appreciate you enough."

"I was afraid you'd say that. Trouble is, I need to keep you alive," MalVek said, clutching the table. His arms trembled, shaking the table hard enough to slosh coffee from their mugs. "When Ouristihra is dark enough to appreciate the light, they'll need people like you. Not to save and shelter them, but to guide their restoration."

"So then," Galo began, "you have a quota? You'll relent once you've advanced The Avatars' agenda far enough?"

"When these people will fight for themselves, I'll stand down," MalVek promised, "I only ask the same of you now. Leave with your friends, and I won't pursue you. Refuse or resist, and I can't promise your life or safety."

Galo took his foot down from his knee and continued fidgeting with his sleeves. Silent and stoic, he watched as MalVek trembled with the mounting impatience of his unacknowledged demand.

This was his opportunity. MalVek's anger had reached a threshold. But nudging him over the edge wouldn't be enough. Galo needed to say something so provoking, so offensive, that MalVek would be forced, despite all platitudes to the contrary, to act upon his rage.

He needed to say the sort of thing that Sinkua would have already said in this situation.

"Well then, you're going to have to kill me here and now," Galo said, standing to lean over the table, "Because I'm going to rage-fuck your agenda until it's nothing but a list of ways to curse my name, you feculent son of a whore."

MalVek sprang to his feet, mule-kicking his chair away, and flipped the table with a bestial roar. Galo bounced and spun back as the opposite end of the table and a full mug of hot coffee flew toward his face. He whipped off his Chieftain Robe off of his body with the Serpent Bracer tangled in the sleeve. He landed in a Tide Dancer stance as the two heirlooms hit the floor.

The table crashed down flat on its top. Snarling with blood between his teeth, MalVek flung the table aside and charged at Galo.

The Harvester stood in an otherwise dark room before a vast wall of security monitors, many of which flashed red. Now and again, his attention jumped to the green map of Ouristihra with one red dot in Berinin, cyclically overlaid with such data as magnetic fields and topography. In passing glances, he checked a facial recognition program as it analyzed the new employee who had breached the actuation chamber.

The door opened behind him, none to his surprise. Traversing beyond his eyes was impossible here, and his eyes had long since locked onto that familiar mask. The Harvester turned around.

"The Imposter has come," he said, "Precisely as The General foretold."

"Imposter? Is that what he called me?" The Omnimath chided, "I would dare say that man has taken us both for fools in our hubris."

"You have the audacity to don this vulgar facsimile of my mask. So marred, no less," The Harvester boomed, "And you deign to assume yourself my brother? You are as garbage before his name!"

"My claim is not entirely untrue. Better a harmless reframing of truth than absolute disclosure, should it preserve public sanity," The Omnimath said. He curled his fingertips around the edges of the mask. "Your sanity, however, I have no other choice but to strip you of."

The Omnimath removed his mask, and The Harvester became pale and rigid at the all too familiar face behind it. His skin bore traces of reversed aging, faded liver spots and retightened wrinkles and such. His deep black eyes brimmed with the wisdom of centuries.

"What is this madness?" The Harvester shouted, staggering back, "You mean to unnerve me with this ruse. I know not your true identity, but I will strip you of this uncanny mimicry when I consume your soul."

"This is no ruse," The Omnimath said as he walked toward him, "I am the man you ought to have become."

"Man?" The Harvester scoffed, regaining a modicum of conviction, "You cannot be I, for I am far beyond the likes of Man. I am an Etherworlder, you flagrant knave. One worthy of being called a God."

"Just as you, I ought sooner to have shed such hubris and realized my place among them," The Omnimath said, "But no matter the semantics and philosophies, I have brought the means by which to end this."

With one hand over his shoulder and the other around the small of his back, he unhooked and brought a massive sheathed sword before himself. He grasped the hilt in one hand, the scabbard in the other, and pulled them apart with no more strain on one arm than the other. He revealed a broad blade, easily a meter and a half long, with runic inscriptions running its length. But despite its bulk, The Omnimath swung it about like a rapier.

"Impossible!" The Harvester bellowed.

The Omnimath pitched the broadsword in a low and long arc. It glided smoothly at first, but the instant it began to descend, it plummeted. The Harvester jumped back as the sword crashed before his feet.

"Pick it up," The Omnimath ordered.

The Harvester swallowed hard as he bent down to grab the hilt. A surge of energy cohered with his own milystis to ease much of the burden of the sword. He felt it become as light as water, and yet it still felt sturdier than any metal born of the Omphaloworld. The Harvester erected himself with the sword in his hand.

"Why are you here?" he demanded.

"Broadly speaking, to prevent the arising. I had thought to appeal to the fact that your methods will fail irrevocably. But being that MalVek, or rather The General, has been in your employ for no less than sixteen years, I should presume that he has told you at least as much. Your path has diverged too far from my own not to think it," The Omnimath explained as he paced the room, snatching glimpses of the monitors and map, "Be that as it is, I have no other choice but to destroy you."

"And yet," The Harvester taunted, spinning the nigh weightless sword around his hand, "I find myself at the grandest of advantages."

A blunt impact at his side jolted Sinkua from his sleep. Churning, somehow clashing, shades of green flooded his eyes as they snapped open. The tastes of bile and blood burbled in the back of his throat. His palms throbbed with the sting of open wounds.

Memories of the panic attack leading to his blackout dropped into place. He stayed on his back, staring up into the void as though the gnashing, ephemeral vines held the answers.

With an instinctual urge to defend himself, he pawed about in search of his sword. In the instant his hand found the hilt, the blunt impact repeated, this time unmistakable for a sudden cramp. Another memory crashed into place.

Sinkua turned his head, and his stomach churned as he once again saw the last thing he had seen before blacking out. There was another of him here, and this second one seethed with bloodlust. His other self kicked him a third time, his face twisting up in fury but never making a sound.

The doppelganger unclipped the bindings on the morningstar. Sinkua rolled toward the sword, and the ball dropped where his face would have been. He came up onto his feet with the runic broadsword in a single-handed grasp. Crimson glow crept up the inscription as he squared himself.

Despite the circumstances, Sinkua struggled to comprehend what stood before him. Not only was there another of himself, consumed with anger and apparently mute, it also had his morningstar. Judging by the throbbing pain in his side, it was impossible to write the doppelganger off as a hallucination.

But where this doppelganger had come from and whether it was real or Sinkua had truly gone mad would all have to wait. He forced the questions aside, focusing instead on defending himself against this embodiment of his rage. Because at the very least, if it was real enough to injure him, it was real enough to kill him.

As the doppelganger charged with the morningstar flailing, the flare in his eyes said that he would stop at nothing less.

Chapter 13

Hairy fingers with bones too long for their skin curled around the doorframe. Bending the structure in their clutches, they launched forth some foul amalgam of human and badger in a lab coat. Its neck was so swollen that the stretch marks had worn down to the endodermis.

Tightening her grip on Nikasu, Teyaku kicked the gurney into the malformed beast. It struck the creature in the abdomen and rolled back into the actuation chamber with it. But more creatures of similar form vomited from the door as it swallowed the first.

Teyaku scrambled back as she retrieved the utility knife from her tool belt. Nikasu stirred on her shoulders as Teyaku thrust the knife at the beasts. Her nostrils and throat raw, she backed toward the main hall with no plan beyond fading optimism and improvisation.

"Teyaku!" her supervisor shouted, his voice muffled, "What are you doing with that patient?"

"Mitigating the damage!" Teyaku called back, "This one's too valuable."

She looked back to find him donning a gas mask. Chalking that up to the reason he hadn't transformed, she returned her attention to those who had. She swerved into the main hall in the direction she had come from, nearly colliding with the supervisor.

"Dammit! Get out of my shot!" he shouted, brandishing a strange pistol loaded with syringe darts.

As the mob of beasts turned to pursue, Teyaku shifted in the opposite direction. With her arms curled over Nikasu, she swooped low to duck their grasping hands. She whipped the utility knife at one of the beasts, splitting the back of its neck, though the blade didn't stick.

With a pop and a sickly stabbing sound, that creature's limbs went limp, and it collapsed among the mob. Teyaku stared back at the supervisor through the gap in the crowd. He flicked the chamber, loading the next dart.

He pulled the trigger, and another creature slumped and collapsed. "Get out of here!" he ordered, "Alert the other floors!"

Teyaku drew the longest wrench from her tool belt and ran as best as her aching joints and the teenage burden on her shoulders would allow. Bestial snarls swelled around them. Claws swiped through the thick smoke, glowing red under the light of the alarm klaxons.

Her memory failing her in her panic, Teyaku found herself and Nikasu backed into a dead end. She kicked the locked utility closet door but to no avail. A gnashing beast decorated in fresh blood emerged into her visibility range. Teyaku crouched to lower her center of gravity and brandished the wrench. Blood trickled over her upper lip, staining the makeshift mask.

The air cleared as the smoke condensed toward the floor. The creature slowed, apparently pained by the effort to walk. As the toxic smoke tightened to a roiling sheet, the beast could no longer so much as lift its feet. It cried out with its strain to resist, but its body pulled down into a crouch.

The condensed smoke billowed upward. Nikasu's hand thrust into Teyaku's peripheral vision, and the creature scrunched down with an audible cracking of multiple bones. As the creature shrieked in agony, Nikasu rolled off Teyaku's shoulders.

Hunkered down and panting, Nikasu put her hand in the smoke and coaxed it back down to a churning layer on the floor. With the air clear, she untied her makeshift mask and draped it over her neck. She turned to face Teyaku.

"Thank…" she began, trailing off with confusion apparent in her skewed features.

"Just doing what needs done, dear," Teyaku said.

Nikasu pulled down Teyaku's mask and gasped. "Elemeno?" she asked, "How did you end up here?"

"By wanting to prove The Omnimath right," Elemeno said with a conspiratorial grin, "Now, let's be going."

With a guttural bellow, MalVek threw a haymaker with ferocious force. Galo pivoted out of the way, bouncing on the balls of his feet. For all his momentum, MalVek stopped just short of pounding his fist against the tile floor.

Galo danced just beyond his reach as MalVek erected himself. They circled each other with Galo leading MalVek almost imperceptibly. MalVek's pupils had become so dilated that they had reduced his irises to hair-thin rings.

Galo staggered as he stepped across the overturned table. MalVek pounced, closing the distance in the split second Galo was off balance. Galo spun off of the table and yanked it out from under him.

MalVek stumbled back and dropped to a crouch, his throat burbling with a guttural snarl. Galo, now a few steps behind the table, stood still and just watched. MalVek spat blood and mucus.

"Why aren't you fighting back?" he grumbled, stomping away the space between them.

He hurled a powerful hook, but Galo scarcely broke his stillness, leaning back only enough to let MalVek's fist breeze past his nose. MalVek swung again, his eyes now bloodshot and veins bulging in his neck and forehead. Galo bobbed just as slightly to dodge this second blow.

"Fight back!" MalVek snarled.

This pattern continued with little variation for several minutes. MalVek grew more infuriated with every failed strike, blood trickling from the corners of his mouth as he ground his teeth. Galo conserved his energy, his selective movements perpetuating MalVek's ire.

"Fight!" MalVek bellowed.

Backwash in the sink drain burbled. Galo smirked as he bounded out of MalVek's immediate reach.

MalVek stopped and stood straight, rubbing the side of his neck. He paused with his fingers between his jugular and the back of his ear. He ran his tongue across his gums as he stared off inquisitively. His eyes stayed fixed on Galo, but he appeared distant.

"I tire of this," he grumbled.

He backed away from Galo, keeping him locked in eye contact, as he moved toward the overturned table. He grabbed it by two of the legs and reared back.

"I don't know why you won't fight back," he muttered, his voice escalating to a shout, "But I'm done with you!"

MalVek lifted the table and swung it at Galo. As it obstructed their view of each other, Galo devoured most of the distance between them in loping strides. He leapt and twisted onto his side to put his feet forward.

The table left MalVek's hands with lethal force, only for Galo to catch it on the momentum of his dropkick. Galo broke the table between his feet and MalVek's chest and knocked MalVek onto his back. Galo bounced off and stuck the landing.

"Because I only came here," Galo said as he fetched his Chieftain Robe, "to waste your time."

Galo walked away, and a faint trail of water followed.

Some wolf-snouted abomination with too many limbs charged at Vielle almost as soon as she stepped out of the elevator. The creature scrambled across the floor in erratic zigzags. Vielle bound her milystic cat-o'-nine-tails to her palm and closed her fist around it.

The creature pounced at her, legs flailing in disagreement. Vielle cracked her thorny whip, catching it across the throat and binding both arms and one leg. The seven-limbed creature dropped onto its side and thrashed about. Vielle sprouted a wooden spike along the back of her fist and drove it through the creature's neck.

She pulled the stake out and ventured deeper into the staging area. Abominations of diminishing humanity closed in from the darkness. Flashing klaxons gave her crimson glimpses of their approach. Figuring that they could see her no better than she saw them, Vielle invoked her last two advantages. Her rationality and her petite frame.

From flashing glimpses, she simultaneously pieced together multiple trajectories. She evaded when she could, waiting until they struck to leave them lashing at shadows. Those she couldn't escape, she bound with her cat-o'-nine-tails and skewered with her wooden stake.

Their fury escalated the deeper Vielle moved into the subbasement. The structural integrity of the room suffered against their feral rage. In a single klaxon flash, Vielle glimpsed a hole through the floor.

She saw an opening and broke for the hole. Dehumanized beasts scrambled after her, but she kept running. Another klaxon flash showed her what was beneath the hole, or more relevantly, what it wasn't.

Her forays into Facilities 3891 and 1341 had taught her to expect a staging area with a hidden elevator connected to a testing area. This was a level between the two where she had assumed there would be nothing but infrastructure.

Vielle wrapped a vine around a piece of rebar and swung down into the secret chamber. The creatures stopped short of diving after her, held back by survival instinct.

Vielle rushed about with her head swiveling. She scarcely engaged the abominations now, focusing more of her energy on finding Nikasu. Or, for that matter, anyone still within their human faculties. Besides, their minds were so far gone that they were more likely to hurt her by happenstance than deliberately.

Between blares of the alarms, Vielle shouted her sister's name. Her eyes panned busted medical equipment and dead bodies, human and abomination alike. If Nikasu had escaped, whether because of or causing this destructive security sweep, dead abominations meant Vielle was closing in on her. But dead humans meant she could have found her sister among the deceased.

After what could just as easily have been a few seconds as several minutes, Nikasu emerged from a hall. Blood spatters adorned her tattered clothes, and her exposed skin was riddled with punctures and bruises. In her tow came a middle-aged woman gripping a long wrench with fresh blood on the head.

The older woman followed at a jogging pace as Vielle and Nikasu ran at each other. They crashed into a tight hug while the middle-aged woman paced about, watching both their backs.

"You're alive!" Vielle remarked as she pulled back.

"Yeah, I woke up in the middle of all of this," Nikasu said. She nodded toward the woman. "She was carrying me and fighting off some man monster thing."

"There's more upstairs. Ground level is okay though," Vielle said, "So, who's your friend?"

"Oh, right! You never got to meet her," Nikasu realized, waving the woman over, "This is Elemeno. Elemeno, Vielle."

"Right," Vielle nodded, "It's… an honor to meet you, madam."

"Same to you, Vielle," Elemeno said, her voice distant as her eyes panned the room, "Now, let's be going."

The Harvester held the beastly broadsword aloft, parallel to the floor, and dragged his fingertips along the flat of the blade. The runes illuminated in black and purple. Smoky tendrils of milystis flowed from his hand and enveloped the blade. He pulled the sword back under his arm and slashed the air, launching the stored energy in a wide arc.

The Omnimath charged just after the blade came forth and side flipped over the shadow arc. His chest tightened, slowing him as he passed within a hand's breadth of The Harvester's milystis. He brought his foot down on the slope of The Harvester's neck, pulling him down to a crouch.

They crossed forearms as they came up together. The Omnimath rolled his wrist around The Harvester's and wrenched the sword from his hand. With the sword drawn back, he kicked him in the sternum, pushing him out of arm's reach.

"It's quite ironic, is it not?" The Omnimath pondered. He glimpsed the monitor running facial recognition. "I am possessed of five centuries more wisdom as well as the vigor of youth,"

"It was you," The Harvester spat, also stealing a glance at the monitor, "You stole those souls from me."

"Is it stealing if they weren't yours?" The Omnimath chided, circling him, "But yes, I skimmed ambient tsora to my needs and sent the rest to their second life. As is my charge. As is your charge."

"My charge? Pah!" The Harvester snapped, taking one last glance at the monitor before it slipped out of his periphery, "Their lives are too fleeting to hold sway over one of so grand an origin and destiny as myself."

"That their lives are fleeting is why we are so obligated," The Omnimath said, slowly spinning the broadsword, "They suffer much in their too-short lives, often cursed for much of it by single mistakes that we would find innocuous. We were to live as them, had we not abused our power."

"And what of you?" The Harvester goaded, "You speak of abuse, and yet you still feed."

"I live only long enough to undo the damage you have done, the mistakes I made when I was you," The Omnimath reasoned, "I owe at least as much to them."

"We owe them nothing. They betrayed us!"

The Harvester rushed The Omnimath, pivoted behind his back, and struck the base of his spine. The Omnimath spun and slashed at The Harvester, but The Harvester ducked the blade and stepped back as he righted himself.

"We betrayed them!" The Omnimath bellowed. He lowered the sword as he took forcible strides toward The Harvester. "Omphaloworlders and Etherworlders nearly went extinct because we let The Goddess rise to power despite our brother's sacrifice."

"Don't you dare speak of him!" The Harvester roared, "I seek to appease The Goddess for his salvation, you treacherous swine."

"If The Goddess returns, it will be the end of the Omphaloworld!"

"A necessary sacrifice, for rise, she must," The Harvester said, spreading his arms, "And I shall at last be in her service. All must come to pass for the arising."

The Omnimath backhanded him, knocking away his mask and sending it clattering across the floor. The Harvester winced against the red light from the security monitors. The Omnimath hurled the sword at the control station, taking out the security feeds.

"Inaction! Failure! Betrayal!" he bellowed, punctuating each word with a black-streaked jab, "These have been our legacy. I'll not have you giving this world to her!"

The Omnimath kicked The Harvester in the abdomen, black and purple plumes erupting from the impact point. The Harvester stumbled back and collapsed near the monitors. Fists coursing with violet shadows, The Omnimath closed the gap with slow deliberate strides.

He stopped as The Harvester looked aside. Both their eyes fell to the sword. It lay nearer to The Harvester, but being in repose put him at a disadvantage.

The two instances of Mortvill locked eyes with each other.

Sinkua caught the morningstar with his sword. His doppelganger snarled as he twisted and pulled the morningstar from over his shoulder. Sinkua squared his stance and choked up on the hilt.

He dug his heels into the roiling green floor as he and his doppelganger pulled back on each other. The doppelganger wrenched the morningstar around, twisting Sinkua's arm. Sinkua pulled in the opposite direction and kicked at the doppelganger.

As the doppelganger reared back, Sinkua released his sword. His alternate self staggered back on his heels. Sinkua charged and grabbed the broadsword out of the air. He knocked the doppelganger onto his back and skewered him to the roiling green floor.

Sinkua chuckled under his breath as he pulled out his broadsword, but he paused as he noticed the blade was clean of blood. Stranger still, the blade left a translucent spot rather than a wound. Sinkua spat an expletive as his other self returned to its feet, its abdomen regaining opacity.

The doppelganger stared Sinkua down, looking perpetually infuriated by its inability to articulate its anger. He lunged a palm heel at Sinkua's sternum, but Sinkua knocked it aside with his forearm. Sinkua struck him in the kidney, pulling the punch as the doppelganger's skin hardened upon collision.

Sinkua clutched the doppelganger's shoulders. The skin softened. Sinkua reared back with his brow tightening. The skin hardened. With a warrior's bellow, his head barreled forth. Just before impact, his own face screaming toward him flashed across his eyes.

Disoriented, his attack stopped short. The doppelganger freed himself and buried his fist in Sinkua's stomach. The sight of himself doubled over flickered in Sinkua's eyes.

Sinkua righted himself. Sighing, he lowered the broadsword and let it fall from his hand. It struck the ground with a clang that echoed throughout the chamber.

The doppelganger swung the morningstar from overhead. Sinkua ducked and spun out of the way. He swung from the side, and Sinkua stepped back.

The cycle went on and on, the doppelganger swinging furiously while Sinkua dodged with comfortable disinterest. The doppelganger grew clumsier as his rage and Sinkua's calm pulled against each other. His presence, Sinkua noticed, diminished in opacity.

Sinkua took several steps back as the spiked ball screamed at his head. The doppelganger charged, morningstar whirling erratically. Sinkua spread his arms.

For a split second, his perspective flickered into the doppelganger. The cocktail of epinephrine and endorphins danced on the edge of orgasmic. His perspective returned as the weapon made contact. It didn't break skin as far as he could tell, but the impact knocked him around and dropped him to his elbows and knees. The sudden withdrawals of those hormones set him dry heaving.

The doppelganger bashed his booted foot into his side over and over. Tears welled up in Sinkua's eyes as he muttered under his breath, trying to force the doppelganger into incorporeality by telling himself that it was just an illusion.

His every failure flashed to the surface. Every plan gone wrong. Every life he failed to save. Every death he brought upon those who were only on the wrong side at the wrong time.

He was the common denominator. Perhaps, he thought, it was better to give in and let this hallucination overtake him.

That thought, however, dissipated as he noticed something. The closer his memories came to the present, the more failures he recalled, the stronger the doppelganger became.

Anger, he realized, wasn't the tool he thought it was. Sure, he had often used it for noble means, but at its core, anger was a weapon. It was indiscriminate and essentially only good for one destruction.

Passion, on the other hand, was an instrument of change. Used ignobly, it could indeed bring ruin. But with honor, it could mend, could bring positive change. For far too long, he had mistaken anger for passion.

Sinkua tamped down his obsession over his failures, forcing his thoughts to congregate around his intentions and acknowledging circumstances beyond his control. He wanted to protect people, to empower them, and he had done what he could within his knowledge and means.

The doppelganger's kicks weakened. Sinkua got back to his feet. The doppelganger moved as though he was swimming in tar as he wound back the morningstar. Sinkua extended his hand forth with his fingers spread.

The doppelganger and morningstar became translucent. The morningstar passed through Sinkua harmlessly. The doppelganger's faded body stretched and warped into a howling vortex, spiraling into Sinkua's palm.

Anger gnawed on Sinkua's thoughts as the doppelganger vanished into him. His necklace flickered and trembled as he tamped down the rage. Focused it. Gave it purpose. Fiery arcs surged from the necklace and wrapped around his body, flickering into the shape of dragonfly wings.

Sinkua recovered his broadsword while the flames dissipated. Every inscribed rune illuminated when he picked it up. He reflected on it a moment before returning it to its scabbard.

Sinkua stared up the side of the chamber, his gleaming eyes just making out the shapes of static roots high above. The rage he had felt at having been forgotten and left behind subsided into a sense of responsibility.

The Beast did not give way to The Warrior. Rather, The Beast and The Warrior stood together as one.

Galo stopped and crouched beside the reception desk. "Excuse me?" he beckoned.

"Hey, yeah. Excuse yourself," she chided, "The hell's going on back there?"

"I can't get into details, but you need to look for another job."

"What? Why?"

"I'm flooding the basement," Galo said, "Also, you've been working for The Avatars of Fate."

"Son of a fuck," she grumbled, "Seriously? I thought I had a good thing going, and I'm working for terrorists?"

"Afraid so," Galo sympathized, "Hey, how long would it take to put the files on this computer onto something portable?"

"Like a flash drive?"

"Sure, I guess."

"I don't know right off hand," she said, "Maybe a couple hours. Why?"

"We don't have that long," he said, scratching his leg.

"Most of the files are encrypted, though."

"I know people who can deal with that. Probably," he said, "Tell you what. Start with the files with the strongest encryption. Get as much as you can and meet me out front when the water comes up through the floor."

"I can do that," the receptionist nodded. She swallowed hard as she fished a flash drive out of one of the desk drawers, "But first, what kind of protection can you give me?"

"I'll ask Magnate Supreme Naletas to fast-track you into witness protection," Galo said, swiping a business card, "I also know someone in the area who might have work for you. No promises there."

"That's all I needed to hear."

She downed more than half a cup of lukewarm coffee in a single gulp and tossed the mug over her shoulder. She took the coaster, a metallic disc riddled with hasty punctures, and stuffed it in her shirt pocket.

"Alrighty then," she said, cracking her knuckles and licking off her coffee mustache, "Wait outside while I fuck this bitch up."

Galo nodded and walked out the front door. The trail of water snaked up his pants leg and along his back, then circled down his arm. It gathered around his forearm and reverted into the Serpent Bracer.

The Harvester pulled up to his hands and knees and scrambled across the floor. The Omnimath lunged and dropped into a diving roll.

The two instances of Mortvill each came up with a hand on the broadsword. They wrestled for control as its blade thrummed and pulsated chaotically.

Pushing his forearm against the other one's throat, he pried the sword from his grip. He plunged the sword through the other one's sternum, blood erupting as he split the spinal column.

Plumes of black and violet milystis poured from the wound and enveloped his body. His skin became pockmarked and saggy. Muscle and fat deteriorated. Hydration dissipated through gaping pores, pulling his leathery skin against his bones. His flesh grayed and cracked, falling from his bones like busted papier mâché. Cartilage dissolved, and his skeleton collapsed into a heap of bones. A fog of milystis faded into ripples in the air.

Mortvill picked up both masks. One, he tossed onto the pile of bones. The unmarred one, he donned upon himself.

Vines emerged between the elevator doors, branching into an elaborate latticework as it pushed them apart. Rising water lapped at their feet as Vielle and Nikasu pulled the doors the rest of the way open. Elemeno shuffled along the ledge and pivoted out into the already wet hall with brackish water rushing around her ankles.

The three of them, drenched and bloodied, waded hurriedly up the hall. Nikasu and Vielle flanked the lead spot with Elemeno bringing up the rear, white-knuckling her bloodstained wrench. From the end of the hall, Galo called to them, urging them to hurry.

Vielle looked to the receptionist with impatient disdain as they emerged into the lobby. "Why are you still in here?" she demanded, "For shit's sake, the place is flooding."

"I asked her to steal company files for me," Galo answered.

"And seeing as I've been working for The Avatars of Fate," the receptionist said, pounding her fist against a desk drawer, "I'm jumping at the chance to fuck things up."

"I also told her to leave when the water comes up through the floor," Galo grumbled, "But she didn't, so I came back to check on her."

"Oh, what about us?" Vielle asked.

"Leviathan saw to your safety."

The receptionist stood up, yanked out the flash drive, and stuffed it in her pocket. She pushed the computer tower off the desk and into the shin-deep water.

"I have one more obligation," she said to Galo, slapping the flash drive into his hand. She turned to Nikasu. "Some masked man told me to give this to a girl with purple eyes, and I'm thinking he meant you. I don't know what the deal is with, well, any of this, but he seemed like the kind of person I shouldn't argue with. Or question."

She produced the mangled coaster from her shirt pocket and handed it to Nikasu.

"What…?" Nikasu began to ask.

"I. Know. Nothing."

Nikasu shrugged and pocketed the metal disc before heading outside with everyone else. While the other three women followed Galo, the receptionist headed in the opposite direction with no further acknowledgement. Galo stopped at the corner to wait for his cab.

"Well, Joren got away," Vielle bemoaned, "What about MalVek?"

"I knocked him out and went back to the lobby," Galo said, "I needed to give her time to get these files."

"So, we don't know if he's alive or dead?"

"I'm assuming he's alive."

"You had the opportunity to off him, and you let it pass?"

"He's of more use to us alive," Galo insisted, "Besides, I kept him out of your way long enough for you to rescue Nikasu."

"I just don't see how this puts us at an advantage."

The cab pulled up, and Galo opened the door. "I'll tell your father you're safe," he assured, "Both of you."

"Hold on," Nikasu said.

She strode up to Galo, who stood with one foot in the waiting cab. She cupped his chin, pulled him down with fleeting traces of milystis, and kissed the corner of his mouth. He closed his eyes as his lips pursed toward hers.

A warm sensation tingled along his flesh, enveloping his head and running down his torso and into his fingertips. Paradoxical essences of every aspect of her being flashed through his mind. Her voice in silence. Her scent in odorlessness. Her shape in formlessness. Her texture in numbness. Her face in sightlessness. Unbound, unfettered essences.

"What was…?"

"Thank you," Nikasu interrupted, "For, you know, coming for me."

"Yes. Of course," Galo nodded. He lowered himself into the cab. "Vielle, I hope you understand my reasoning by the time we see each other again. Elemeno, thank you for your help. My deepest apologies for your loss."

Chapter 14

Patches of moonlight dappled his head and shoulders as Sinkua pulled himself up between a pair of roots. Churning green light flickered against the underside of the canopy, perhaps only visible because he was aware of it. He had come within reach of the surface.

He emerged into the sounds of crickets and nocturnal mammals chittering about, their proximity impossible to gauge for all the echoes and distortion. The sounds of mechanical humming and crunching bark joined in, but Sinkua thought nothing of them, reveling as he was in his safe return from his own suicide. He threw back his arms and stretched his back.

His throat burned, filling with the taste of hot metal. He doubled over, coughing violently. Tension pulled at his skull hard enough that he swiped at the back of his head in a panic that he might find blood.

"What's with you, man?" a nearby voice called.

The pain faded, as did any other sensation. In a matter of seconds, he went from debilitated by pain to disconcertingly numb, save for the taste in the back of his throat.

"I… Ah…" he managed, grasping for sensation, "Biroe?"

"Yeah," Biroe said, "You okay?"

"Um…" Sinkua pondered, smacking his lips, "Do you taste smoke?"

"Ah… no. Why? Do you?"

"Yeah, but… it's going away."

"Count it as a good thing," Biroe said, "Can you walk?"

"I think so," Sinkua said. He gestured to the off-road tires and spring-loaded chassis on Biroe's wheelchair. "Nice upgrades. When'd you get them?"

"Ever since we started relief work out here," Biroe said, "Come on. Let me help you get home."

Biroe turned around and began riding away. Sinkua walked alongside him, finding he needed Biroe's backrest for his own balance. At Sinkua's behest, Biroe made their way around to the old door. Sinkua recovered his dagger and suspended it in two of his belt loops.

"Are you sure you want me in your car after…" Sinkua began to protest.

"Buddy. Shut up. I know you have an abusive relationship with my car. But today, I don't care. You're a two hour drive from your house, and I'm not going to let you walk it," Biroe deflected, driving faster to pull Sinkua along, "Besides, it doesn't matter what I want. I'm sort of obligated."

"Why's that?"

"It worries me that this doesn't sound crazy, but an old man told me I'd find you here one day soon and that you'd need my help. No idea how he knew, but he didn't strike me as the sort of bloke I should argue with."

"Tall and burly with an eyepatch and a spiderhorse?"

"Spiderhorse is new to me," Biroe chuckled, "But the rest fits. Who is he?"

"Never told me his name," Sinkua said, "But I think he's to Eytea what Leviathan is to Galo."

"Interesting. Did he give you that sword?"

"Yeah. I don't know where he got it, but I think it was made for me. It becomes almost weightless when I hold it," Sinkua said, "Well, it sounds like he learned our language after he left."

"That explains his diction. It was a bit, well, off," Biroe said, "He still managed to be pretty damn convincing though. Had this certain regal air about him."

Sinkua nodded absently as Biroe opened his car door. He helped him into the driver's seat, this model of wheelchair being too wide to fit in the car. As he folded down the wheelchair, he broke the silence.

"What, um…" he hesitated, "What day is it?"

"Second of Arus. Why?"

"Got here on the eighteenth of Piscus. Twelve days," Sinkua muttered to himself, "Of course he did."

"What's that?"

"I just feel like I understand that old man a little better."

"That makes one of us," Biroe smirked.

Sinkua put the wheelchair in the trunk and closed the hatch. As Sinkua got into the car, Biroe was putting his phone in his pocket. Sinkua shut the passenger's side door, and Biroe began driving away from the trunk of Yggdrasil and across the ruins of the high-rise district.

"So," Sinkua said, breaking a long silence without turning away from his window, "I guess this means you know what I did."

"… Yeah."

"Have you told anyone else?"

"No," Biroe said, "It's not my business to."

"… Thank you."

Farim's phone rang. She shot it a quick glance. Unfamiliar number. She reached into the center console where it sat, hit the ignore button, and kept driving.

It immediately rang again. She sighed, then pulled over, shut off the car, and answered her phone.

"Hello?"

"Good afternoon. This is a courtesy call from Southwest Quarunite Hillside Oncology to inform you…"

Farim's stomach folded and tightened. Nobody there should have had her contact information. She considered destroying the phone, albeit briefly.

"How did you get my number?" Farim cut in.

"I'm sorry, madam," the caller said, "I can only take questions once I've completed the script."

"Of course," Farim sighed, "Go ahead."

She mouthed a string of increasingly creative expletive phrases as he droned through his script.

"Good afternoon. This is a courtesy call from Southwest Quarunite Hillside Oncology to inform you of a recent quarantine which may affect you. Our records show that you may have been in our osteosarcoma ward between the second week of Saggitus and the first week of Capricus," he recited, "At this time, it is not mandatory that you return to our facility. However, for your health and the public good, we implore you to submit for screening at your earliest convenience. We will inform you if compliance becomes mandatory."

Silence dragged on for a minute.

"Is that it?" Farim asked.

"Yes. Sorry," he said, "Do you have any questions?"

"What's the reason for this quarantine?"

"Viral outbreak."

"I see," she nodded, "And it began between the second week of Saggitus and the first week of Capricus?"

"That's what we've narrowed it down to."

Her stomach tightened. Her consultation over Uulan's death fell within that time frame, "How contagious is it?"

"Still being determined," he reported, "But the more affected people who report back, the better informed we can be."

"Thank you. I'll keep that in mind," Farim said, "Now, where did you get my number?"

"Visitors log."

"And my name?"

"Come again?"

"What name was next to my number?" she reiterated, "I'm pretty sure you have the wrong number."

"The name is illegible, but…" he trailed off, "Oh! You're right. I'm sorry. I should have noticed this sooner."

"Noticed what?"

"Your voice. It says this number belongs to a fifty-year-old man. You're clearly neither of those things."

"Clearly not."

"Sorry for the trouble. Enjoy the rest of your day."

"Likewise."

Farim hung up the phone. She turned it over in her hand as she considered the implications. Her car wobbled with each vehicle that zipped past.

She dialed and waited. Someone answered on the second ring.

"Hi there," she greeted, "Could I get a ticket to Quarun, departing as soon as possible? I'm one hour out."

Spril's eyes darted about the whiteboard as he twirled a dry erase marker in his left hand. The rest of the multicolor pack lay strewn about the tool tray and the floor. He scratched his salt-speckled goatee, the unkempt thing tickling his collarbone.

The stairs creaked, and he cocked his head in acknowledgement.

"Well, I didn't expect to find you here," Yrlis mused, "How are you taking the news?"

"Working," Spril said, "Probably just like you thought I would."

"That does sound just like you," Yrlis said, panning the whiteboard, "So, what am I looking at?"

"These are all the interactions I've had with MalVek or that I've received a first-hand account of," Spril explained, "This spans from developing the Subtransit community to the night of the Heniokhos Disaster."

"Honey?" Yrlis beckoned, "You're not… you know?"

"Blaming myself?" he asked, "No. That's not what this is about."

"Determining when he turned on us?"

"Not exactly. It's possible that he's been working for The Avatars longer than we've known him," Spril explained, "If that's the case, he's playing the long game. If I reconsider his past behavior with what we now know in mind, I might get an idea of his larger agenda."

"Get in his head and cut him off," Yrlis nodded, "I like the way you think. It's like you're some kind of hotshot general."

"Some kind of hotshot general," Spril laughed, "Thanks. I needed that."

"Hey, my stuff goes over your head. Your stuff goes over mine," she shrugged, "Humor's all I've got here."

Spril chuckled. "So, what are you doing down here?"

"What am I doing down here?" Yrlis asked, "What am I doing in my lab?"

"Okay, that was a bad way to phrase it," he said, "Were you working or looking for me?"

"I was looking for you, but I came down here to work until you turned up," she said, "But since you're here, I can tell you I've decided to develop a regimen to manage your genetic condition. One that won't risk your humanity."

"Are you sure about this?"

"Am I sure I want to help the man I intend to marry?"

"No, I mean…" Spril trailed off, "I don't know what I mean. Hell, I just don't know how much confidence I can put in you to pull this off. No offense."

"None taken," Yrlis said, holding his shoulder as she looked over his work, "Honestly, I don't know how much I can do. That's why I have to devote my full attention to it."

Spril wrapped his arm around her and pulled her against him, kissing her above her ear.

"What about Sinkua?" he asked after a moment's reflection.

"I built rapport with Ophalin during Galo's case," she said, "I forwarded Sinkua's genome map and my notes to him."

"Good. I don't want you to give up on his case for my sake," he said, "And your research into the Sisyphus Fir?"

"I can't do anything with it while we're in this situation with Tanelen," she said, "But right now, I need to call Sinkua and bring him up to date. Do you have his number?"

"In my phone," Spril said, pointing to it on the table, "Matter of fact, invite him over for dinner. We've left him alone to mourn for long enough. I'd also like him to look at this if he's up for it. It might be good for him."

Yrlis pecked him on the cheek before crossing the room to retrieve his phone. She dialed, then drummed her fingers on the table while she waited for an answer. But her brow tightened and mouth twisted into a puzzled sneer when it came.

"I'm… sorry," she said, walking toward Spril, "I must have the wrong number."

"What happened?" he asked as she handed his phone to him.

"Some woman answered."

Spril checked his phone. She had dialed the right number.

"You didn't recognize her?"

Yrlis shook her head. Spril considered the possibilities. None of them were favorable, some less so than others.

The epiphany was so obvious when it struck that he felt embarrassed at having taken so long to see it. He had been so wrapped up in that note that he hadn't noticed what should have been perfectly plain. The Omnimath's absence. NalSet's explanation. Malia's disillusion. The fact that he hadn't spoken with Vielle or Nikasu since they returned from Tanelen. Or from Sinkua since the Heniokhos Disaster. He shouted an expletive.

"I need to go."

"Why? What happened?" Yrlis asked.

"MalVek's partnered up," Spril said, rushing up the stairs with Yrlis trailing him, "They got the drop on Sinkua. Nikasu and Vielle may have also been compromised."

MarLys stared at her phone as it rang in her hand. She set it down, favoring her lowball glass instead as she downed the last of her rum. She checked her facedown card and looked up at the dealer as she tapped the table.

Then, on the fifth ring, give or take two or three, she answered her phone.

"What's shaking, you sexy bitch?" she slurred, tipping up her chin at the man at the other end of the table.

"MarLys?" Vielle asked.

"Yes?" MarLys answered, stretching the word to uncomfortable lengths.

"Are you drunk?"

"… Yes."

"Are… Are you okay?"

MarLys groaned. "No."

"Shit. What happened?"

"I don't wanna…" MarLys said, choking back a wet belch, "What's going on with you, sweet thing?"

"Nikasu is safe," Vielle said, "We're on our way home."

"Well, fuck yeah for that!" MarLys blurted, "At least one of us had a good time."

"Where are you?"

"I in a… um… I'm in a casino."

"I didn't know you gambled."

"I only gamble when I drink."

"Yeah, that's another thing. I didn't know you drank either."

"I… think I only… drink when I'm… gambling."

Vielle sighed. "MarLys. I love you," she said, "But I need you to get to the point. What happened after we dropped you off?"

"He was…" MarLys hiccupped, her throat tightening, "And she. They both… He said… Fuck!"

"Who said what?" Vielle urged.

"Ocronn said…"

"Okay. So, what happened to Sanus and Nenbard?"

"They're both… you know," MarLys choked, "… dead."

At this point, MarLys had the attention of most of the table, but she didn't have the capacity to think anything of it.

"What?!" Vielle exclaimed. MarLys cringed back from her phone. "How did that happen? Are you okay?"

"She killed him, so he killed her," MarLys muddled, "You're gonna think I'm crazy, but he said she was a monster."

"That's actually not crazy at all. We saw monsters in clothes where they were holding Nikasu."

"Hey!" MarLys urged, calling out as though she was just entering the conversation, "You need to tell Galo."

"He already left for Eprilen," Vielle said, "I'll corroborate that you tried to get the message to him in time. Are you okay?"

"I'm not hurt, but…" MarLys trailed off, "SenRas told me to take a slow boat home. Give me time to cope. Turns out I suck at it."

"When we get home, let's get back to looking for an apartment," Vielle insisted, "We'll start our own lives together. Get away from all this death."

"I like how that sounds."

They shared silence for a while. MarLys played a few more hands of blackjack with wavering and waning attention. She sipped what might have been her third drink. Could have been her seventh.

"MarLys?" Vielle beckoned. MarLys chirped back wordlessly. "Do you need me to stay on the phone?"

MarLys set her phone down on the table. She laid her head beside it, her cards sticking to her cheek. She blinked hard and swallowed a lump in her throat.

"Uh-huh."

Chekov stood in the doorway, watching Dourias work. He tapped feverishly at his typewriter, the clacking of keys filling the otherwise silent room. The silence was so deep that the grumbling of his stomach sounded like distant thunder. Chekov snickered as she rattled the tray in her hands.

Dourias sighed as he ripped the page out of his typewriter. He slapped the paper down and gave Chekov a beckoning wave.

"Come in, dear," he insisted, "It won't do to have you standing there all day."

Chekov crossed the room and placed the tray on the table. She glanced over his work, finding it amounted to a heap of half-used paper. Several stopped in the middle of a paragraph, even more in the middle of a sentence. Dourias was struggling to follow through on his thoughts.

He chomped a piece of toast in half as he looked over the spread of crackers, toast, and cheeses. Dourias brought the mug of tea to his lips, a slow blissful smile taking shape as he took the first sip.

"Lemon mint tea," he said, "You remembered."

"Of course, I did," Chekov said, leaning on the corner of the table, "Remembering people's quirks is a strength of mine, after all."

"Correspondence mimicry. I could tell you about someone after spending a day with them, and you could write a letter that would fool their own mother."

"It isn't always a point of pride, but it's necessary work," she said, "But I have my own reasons for remembering your quirks."

"Such as my being unparticular about crackers and cheeses?"

"Wouldn't do for a deep cover agent to have too particular of tastes."

"Truly not," Dourias said, "But who worth their mug doesn't have a favorite tea?"

Chekov helped herself to a slice of cheese. "So, how's it going?" she asked.

"As well as it appears," he said, gesturing over the papers, "Perhaps worse."

"What's the trouble?" she asked.

"I'm not sure," he sighed, "I'll be articulating a memory or an observation, but the thread of it just fades." His stomach grumbled again.

"Maybe you've been too hungry to focus," Chekov said, "You always were bad about forgetting to eat when you're working."

"This isn't hunger," Dourias corrected, "I've been having indigestion. And it's always preceded by stress."

"That shouldn't come as a surprise, after what you've been through," she said, "But then again, this is unfamiliar territory. So perhaps, we shouldn't presume anything."

"Yes, I'm afraid our only data point is my own observations."

"Well," Chekov pondered, "does your indigestion coincide with your losing your train of thought?"

"Not consistently," he said, "I'm sorry I can't be of more help."

"Don't overextend yourself, dear."

"It's just…" Dourias sighed, shaking his head, "What happened to us? To The Coalition?"

"What do you mean?" Chekov asked, "Sure, we've had a few setbacks, but none of us accounted for a turncoat. Especially not an Original."

"We failed to protect BeiLou and CreSam. Malia resigned of her own accord. MalVek has betrayed us. Mortvill disconnected himself to mitigate the damage. And Spril hates us collectively," Dourias rattled off, "And what of NalSet and Gabdur?"

"Gabdur went to Berinin. He said he needs to make peace with his past before he moves forward, which I realize could end with his resignation," Chekov said, "NalSet, on the other hand, has locked himself in his room with a month's provisions."

"And The Keepers?"

"We still have Jex and Murdega."

"I'm sorry. Who?"

"Murdega joined us after you disappeared," Chekov clarified, "It was a matter of opportunity."

"Well, I'm glad something of my work continued in my absence," Dourias said, "But what happened to everyone else?"

"A few got killed," she recalled, "The rest got scared and quit. I helped them rebuild their old lives. Or fabricate new ones."

"So, our ranks have been reduced to the two of us, a wanderer who may not come back, a recluse who may not come out, and an eager newcomer of no particular talent," Dourias recounted, "To top it off, we've lost nearly all The Keepers and with them the safe-houses."

"We built The Coalition from even less," Chekov said, "And that was a small fraction of what we set out to start from."

"Yes, but none of us are in any shape to rebuild it," he said, "It's time we accepted the truth. The Coalition, as we know it, has failed."

"No. No. We haven't," Chekov refused, tightening her lips and shaking her head. "We have to do this. We have to."

"We may have done enough for The Hybrids to destroy The Goddess in my timeline," Dourias said, "But as for your timeline and your mission…"

"Shut up and listen to me," Chekov insisted. She pushed off the corner of the table and cupped his cheeks in her hands as she stared into his eyes. "I don't care if it's down to you and me. Somewhere in that beautiful brain of yours is the key to stopping The Avatars of Fate from freeing The Goddess."

"Chekov. I…"

"We're going to get those answers. I won't give up on you," she continued, running her hands down the sides of his neck and across his shoulders, "And as long as Spril is still alive…"

Chekov trailed off into a bewildered silence. Her forehead tightened as she tilted her head to look down either side of Dourias's neck.

"What is it?" he asked.

"Your neck, it's…"

At a loss for explanations, she unfastened the top button of his shirt. As she traced the underside of his collarbone, her index finger left a trail of irregular black line segments, hooks, and arcs.

"Tsora-magnetic ink!" Dourias exclaimed, "I tattooed myself with the intel I collected."

"I knew it!" Chekov exclaimed, planting a firm kiss on his lips, "I knew it. I knew it. I knew we still had a chance."

"The key isn't in here," Dourias snickered, tapping his temple. He grabbed Chekov's hands. "It's in here."

"But how did you make that ink while you were in deep cover?" Chekov asked, "I suppose it doesn't matter at this point, but I am worried that you might have left that technology in The Avatars' hands."

"After all that elation, you doubt my rigor? I either skimmed from your batch or made note of your tsora data before I left," he suggested, "The important thing is that now we stand a chance, provided we can make sense of my diagrams."

"Oh, if that's our biggest obstacle, then I would dare say we're unstoppable," Chekov said, "Spril's contempt for The Coalition will do more to hinder us than any Avatar or traitor ever could."

"You may need to become amicable with Farim. Do you think…"

Dourias fell silent mid-sentence, and Chekov yelped as he collapsed against her legs. She dropped to a crouch and checked his pulse, finding it too strong and too fast. His eyes wide, he convulsed and gasped with shallow gaping yawns.

His heartbeats strengthened as they spread further apart. Chekov laid him on his back and pulled his shirt open. Black streaks blossomed over his bare skin as she pressed on his chest in a resting pulse rhythm.

Despite her persistence, however, Dourias's heart stopped. The strokes of black ink vanished. Chekov crumpled atop him, her face red and streaked with tears. Her hand trembling, she squeezed her earlobe.

"NalSet?" she beckoned into the silent line, "I don't know if you can hear me, but I need to talk to you. Dourias has…"

"What happened?" came NalSet's somber reply.

"Dourias just died," Chekov choked out.

"Damn," he grumbled, "This is too much. How did he go?"

"Heart attack. But something was off about it."

"Off how?"

"Asphyxiation was too abrupt. We were just talking, and suddenly, it was as though he forgot how to breathe."

"Start the holoautopsy at your discretion," he said, "But first, bring me his biometric tracker. I'd like to run diagnostics on it."

"There's one more thing," Chekov said, "We just learned that he gave himself encrypted tsora-magnetic tattoos of the intel he collected from The Avatars. They're activated by my touch."

"Clever," NalSet said, "But that ink doesn't react on a dead body, does it?"

"No, it doesn't. And even if I figure out the underlying cause of death, I can't do anything about it," Chekov bemoaned, "We need Dourias back, but…"

"I know. I'll go find him."

"Even if you do, and even if he's tapped into that power, can we still count on him to help us?"

"I'll get through to him," NalSet promised, "I have an angle to gain his empathy."

Silvery fog hugged the contours of the landscape, set aglow by city lights and the nearly full moons. A slight streak of pink tinged the eastern horizon. Sinkua contemplated how he would tell his sister about his suicide attempt. Or if he would at all. He had to have some explanation for his extended absence.

He came out of his contemplation as Biroe pulled into a parking lot. Sinkua looked through the fog with glowing eyes and found the sign for NieRie's Bakery.

"What are we doing here?" Sinkua asked. He was in no position to turn down a free breakfast, assuming Biroe figured he hadn't brought his wallet, but the place wouldn't open for at least four hours.

"That old man said to bring you here," Biroe said with his face forward and eyes darting scrutinously, "He didn't say why."

"Are you going to wait out here?"

"Open the glovebox."

Sinkua did as he was told and pulled out a cheap portable phone. "What's this for?"

"I can't impose myself on whatever business you have with this guy. But if I wait out here, it'll look like neither of us trust him. But I don't trust him enough to leave you here with him," Biroe elaborated, "That's a burner phone. It's untraceable. My number is in the contacts list. Call me if you need anything."

"Got it. Thank you," Sinkua said, stuffing the phone in his pocket, "You know, all that tactical talk is making you sound like me."

"I'll try not to let it go to my head," Biroe chuckled, "Anyway, good luck."

Sinkua strapped his sword and scabbard to his back and got out of the car. He headed up the front walk as Biroe drove away. He could only see one light on inside. A bulky figure sat with his back to him under that light.

Sinkua pulled on the door. It was locked. He knocked on the glass, and the bulky figure cocked its head. A moment later, a beam of light fanned over the dining room as a much smaller silhouette emerged from the kitchen. The second figure approached the foyer as the dining room flickered back to dimness with the swinging door settling shut.

NieRie turned on the foyer light and opened the door. She held a paper bag with a fruity and savory aroma wafting from it.

"Hello, Sinkua," she said.

"Good evening, NieRie," he said, his eyes cast down, "I, um… I'm sorry for what I said before. I was, well…"

"Hey. Sweetie," NieRie beckoned, "It's alright. Folks say things what they don't mean when they're in a bad way. But now, you owned up to it, so it's all down river, 'kay."

"Thank you," he nodded, "So, how has that man been treating you?"

"You know, I honestly cannot get a handle on him," she huffed, "He's demanding as all get out. Bit sexist at times. But danged if he isn't polite to a fault. Almost painful how chivalrous he acts. And his diction is so... You know."

"Weird?" Sinkua offered, "Yeah, he's not from around here. Did he say why he wanted to meet with me here?"

"Just that you needed to stop feeling sorry for yourself. Figured I'd be a good place to start. Don't know how he knew, seeing as you're not the type to gossip even about your own business," NieRie said, "Anyway, I heard you tried to take things too far. So, I whipped something up to tell you there's no hard feelings."

She reached into the bag and pulled out a muffin a third of the size of his head. He accepted it graciously.

"Is there bacon in this?" he asked, turning it in his hands, "Because I smell bacon, but I don't see any."

"Only one way to find out."

Sinkua bit into it, and his face lit up as it flooded his mouth with savory tartness. The whole thing tasted like bacon.

"That's my standard pomegranate muffin. Scaled up for what I figured as your current appetite," NieRie said as Sinkua took another bite, "But I swapped out half the butter for bacon grease."

"Mm. Yeah," Sinkua remarked, cheeking his third bite, "Can I get half a dozen to take home?"

"Of course, you can," NieRie laughed, "Anyway, best not keep that man waiting any longer. Mosey over, and I'll bring you two some coffee and orange juice."

Sinkua walked to the one illuminated booth. The old man straightened up as he came around to the opposite bench. His monocular glare was as piercing as ever, yet tinged with a vague sense of warmth.

"Ah. Sinkua," he said, drawing out each syllable, "At last, have you come."

"Yeah. I'm here," Sinkua said. He unhooked the sword and sheath and leaned it against the side of the backrest. "Biroe brought me. Just like you ordered."

"Be so kind to have a chair," the old man said, gesturing to the bench, "I have certainty that you have many questions you will to ask of me."

"You've learned a lot of our language in just twelve days," Sinkua commented as he sat down, "I guess your diction makes sense in your native language. Whatever it was."

"Whatever it...?" the old man puzzled, "Remember you not Fjarthursk?"

"Feeyarth Hersk?" Sinkua asked, now dragging out his pronunciation, "Is that one of the ancient languages?"

"From the perspective of yours, yes. Now, be so kind to ask your questions."

"Am I right to think that you and Eytea share the same bond as Leviathan and Galo?"

"Yes, we have the same connection. She called me here when she had death," the old man explained, "Many of her memories were given upon me. Those memories mostly were of you and the mother of hers. That is how I have knowledge of the coffee wench."

"Her name is NieRie," Sinkua seethed, "You would do well to respect her at least that much."

As though on cue, NieRie emerged from the kitchen with a drink tray. On it was a carafe of coffee, a pitcher of orange juice, two mugs, and two glasses.

"Ah, so returns the coffee wench!" the old man boomed. Sinkua corrected him, only to be spoken over. "How glorious it is to see you again. A thousand thanks for your service."

"Thank you, NieRie," Sinkua said, bowing his head slightly.

She returned the gesture as she placed the tray in the middle of the table and set a mug and a glass before each of them. The old man cocked his head as he tilted the orange juice pitcher.

"What curious…"

"Anything else, sirs?" NieRie interrupted, ignoring the old man's glare, "Good. Now, if you need anything else, just know that my name is NieRie." She turned to look at him. "You would do well to remember it."

As she returned to the kitchen, the old man burst into hearty laughter.

"The women of your world grow bolder with every passing century," he exclaimed, "Believe you this one plays at being lord of this establishment in the absence of the husband of hers?"

"She isn't playing. Her husband is a dental assistant or file clerk," Sinkua corrected, "She is, as you put it, lord of this establishment. She always has been."

"Eh? Became it common for women to own businesses?"

"It wasn't always?" Sinkua deflected, "Look, you didn't invite me here to discuss gender relations. Can we get back on topic?"

"Yes, of course. Be so kind to continue with your questions."

"Well, as a start, what's your name?"

"What? Remember you not me?"

"I don't know why you keep asking that, but no."

"It is because… No. We will return to that," the old man said, "I am called Odin."

"Okay then. Odin. Where is your horse?"

"Sleipnir is away. He attracted much undesirable attention. Your world is accustomed not to such sights."

"We've had a bad time with strange creatures lately," Sinkua explained, "Anyway, if Eytea called you when she died, why did you wait so long to get involved?"

"Her greatest wish was that you be protected," Odin said, "I am bound by honor to carry out her wishes to the extent which I deem to be of necessity."

"So, you waited until I needed to be saved from myself and left me under Yggdrasil?" Sinkua asked. Odin nodded and took a swig of black coffee. "But why didn't you come back in ten days like you said you would?"

"At last! You ask a pertinent question," Odin remarked, "I did that to teach a lesson upon you. That which others speak are not of consequence. The life of a man proceeds when a man has himself action, not when he awaits others to act. After all, a man is in command of his own fate."

"Roll up your sleeves," Sinkua ordered. Odin's face screwed up into a puzzled expression. Sinkua repeated, "Odin. Roll up your sleeves."

Odin pulled his sleeves up to his shoulders. Sinkua looked at both his biceps, finding them bare.

"Are satisfied you?" Odin asked as he rolled his sleeves down.

"Yes," Sinkua said, "I don't have to kill you."

"Kill me you?" Odin exclaimed, laughing robustly, "By what manner would be necessary that? Or possible?"

"I had to make sure you're not an Avatar of Fate," Sinkua explained, "You all but preached The Epimetheus Trial."

"Speak not that name in my association!" Odin boomed, pounding the table, "Epimetheus is a coward and a traitor! As have you been! Protect you? Pah! Always my Hybrid asks that of me."

"First of all, this is the first I'm hearing that Epimetheus is a person," Sinkua scolded, "Second, in what way am I a traitor?"

"Remember you not…?" Odin began, trailing off as Sinkua shot him an urging glare, "Ah. Right. Epimetheus gave rise to the Goddess of Chaos who rent both of our worlds asunder. He swore to her fealty when he followed her from my Etherworld to your Omphaloworld. And you so spoiled the gift of yours from his brother in her service."

"Look, Odin, I know my memory is flawed," Sinkua began, pausing to bite a muffin and wash it down with orange juice, "but I don't even have the slightest memory of this stuff. Besides, didn't all of this happen long before I was even born?"

"Of course, it happened long before you were born," Odin scoffed, "Know you nothing of reincarnation?"

"Past lives and stuff like that?"

"Yes, past lives and stuff like that. Truly, you are a beacon of eloquence," Odin grumbled, "When humans and Hybrids have death, they go to a second life beyond the Omphaloworld. There, they are regarded as they regarded others in life. When have passed seven of their lifetimes, they return in a new body."

"So, Eytea will be reborn in about one hundred sixty years?"

"Approximately, yes."

"Well, I don't know what it was like last time you were in the Omphaloworld, but nowadays, we don't remember our past lives," Sinkua explained, "And obviously, The Avatars of Fate are my enemy. Which means I'm opposed to The Epimetheus Trial. Ergo, if I was a traitor back then because I followed Epimetheus, I must not be one now. Right?"

"Well. I suppose that is so," Odin conceded, "Very well, then. I will protect you as ordered with greater respect than I had intended. But understand you should that still I like you particularly not."

"Seriously? What's your problem with me now?"

"I approve not of your always bonding with the Hybrid of mine. Always the two of you find each other, and always by you is the Hybrid of mine hurt."

"Odin, if you have Eytea's memories, there's something you should already know about me," Sinkua said, his voice lowering to a thunderous grumble, "People I love have been dying near me since I was ten years old, and I have been struggling to convince myself that it isn't my fault. So, I don't need you blaming me for my fiancée's death. I damn near broke my back trying to save her."

"Be so kind to calm yourself, boy," Odin said, "I speak of what comes after death."

"Seven lifetimes in the second life," Sinkua pondered, "Is it that she always dies several years before me, so we're apart seven times as long in the second life?"

"No. You are exempt from this cycle by the Hybrid power of yours," Odin said, "When next does an unborn of the family of yours grow a mind, upon it are you reborn. Scores of generations have spread wide the blood. Often have you been reborn before was discarded the previous body of yours."

"So, that means," Sinkua choked, wrapping his mind around this information as it took a stranglehold on his sense of the world, "that Eytea will spend her entire time there without me. If I had killed myself at Yggdrasil, I would've just ended up right back here as a newborn."

"Yes. The Hybrid of mine has awaited you upward of six centuries at a time," Odin explained, "You die and are soon reborn. You have yourself vague memories of the life of yours. You know only that something is missing. The Hybrid of mine holds vivid memories of life, knowing of you very particularly. Always wanting. Never fulfilled."

"There has to be something I can do about this."

"Naught there is which you can do. Always I ask that you distance yourself. Always do you heed not my warning, or I arrive too late, such as now," Odin insisted, "Once made is the bond, suffering of the Hybrid of mine is inevitable."

"No. No, no, no. There must be…" Sinkua trailed off, "Hold on. How does controlling fire exempt me from the seven lifetimes rule?"

"It is not controlling fire which exempts you. I speak of the greater Hybrid power of yours."

"My greater Hybrid power?"

"Yes," Odin nodded, pressing his index finger against Sinkua's star-cross ruby. "The power to turn back death."

Nikasu trudged through the snow toward the front of her house. Vielle walked alongside her with her motorcycle parked in the driveway. Nikasu's eyes panned the hedge lining the face of the house while Vielle scanned the lawn.

Though their anxiousness was justified, they reached the front door without incident. But at that point, Nikasu realized another problem that she hadn't accounted for.

"Small problem," she said, "I, um, think we're locked out."

"Do you have a hide-a-key?" Vielle asked. Nikasu shrugged. "Well, probably not. Now that I think about it, it would be a bad idea for any of us to have one."

"I had put the key in the lock when MalVek bashed me over the head," Nikasu said, "Obviously, it's not there anymore."

"Obviously," Vielle nodded, her voice distant as she panned the lawn again. There were several lines of shoe prints through the snow, as though people had been cutting across their lawn. She couldn't tell how fresh they were, but the fact that some circled toward the back of the house caught her attention. "Hey, I think we…"

"Maybe Sinkua is home!" Nikasu realized, "I mean, MalVek lied about pretty much everything else. Makes sense that he'd lie about my brother dying, right?"

Her enthusiasm snapped Vielle into the realization that she still hadn't told Nikasu what Sinkua had done. Time to ease her into it was running out.

"Nikasu, there's something I need to tell you," Vielle blurted out.

Nikasu turned to Vielle with her fist hovering a few centimeters from the door. Vielle cleared her throat as she ordered her words.

They both jumped as the door flew open. In the foyer stood a woman who looked to be in her early thirties, save for her eyes. Those were heavy with wisdom, thick with burden. She had a pale Northlander complexion and thick black hair running halfway down her back.

A spark gleamed in her eyes as they fell upon Nikasu.

"Oh!" she gasped, "Oh, I think you and I need to have a long talk."

A rough shuffling from above, a dusting of snow, and a dull thud within the space of a second placed someone behind Vielle and Nikasu. A quarterstaff extended between them, the tip landing against the woman's clavicle.

"Where is Sinkua?" Spril demanded.

"He's alive. That's all I can be sure of," she said, "This is still his home, isn't it?"

Nikasu nodded.

"In that case, we're all in the right place," the woman continued, "You're welcome to wait for him with me."

"We're welcome to?" Nikasu scoffed, "Bitch, I live here."

"Well, then that means I was right about you," the woman said, "And I think I know who your bodyguard is as well."

"Who are you?" Spril asked, lowering his quarterstaff ever so slightly.

"Oh, there's a perfectly useless question. If you've never heard of me, the answer won't mean anything. But if you have heard of me," the woman said, "you won't believe me."

Chapter 15

Gabdur paused at the edge of the yard. Standing in the shade of an evergreen, he ran his thumb along the edge of a strip of police tape. It had been shorn off and, from what he could tell, largely gathered up. Whatever business the police had had here, they were done with it.

There was a suspiciously fresh sheet of paper pinned to the front door, likely masquerading as a notice from the local police. He double checked his belt for his photonic fauchard, retrieved from Jex. He panned the yard as he approached the house, cursing the cold grass for disrupting an otherwise stealthy approach.

After far more anxiety than ado, Gabdur reached the porch steps. As he crossed the porch, he realized that the unassuming paper on the door bore his alias. He plucked it off the pin and unfolded it.

"Gabdur,

"Just to be out with it, yes, I know who you really are. I'm sure Nenbard did as well, though neither of us talked about it.

"He came to peace with your disappearance and your reported death rather quickly. He believed you and Zheal both died that night in the hospital, and he thought it was a mercy. When the official story dated your deaths two years later, he thought it best not to meddle in the Chieftain Sage's business.

"But it was also an opportunity to separate himself from the budding conflict between your family and The Avatars of Fate. He didn't know about it at the time, but he suspected there was something more to Zheal's illness.

"That was why none of us confronted you about your identity. It's also why he was defensive about Sanus's discomfort around the dig site. You clearly hadn't come back for a reunion, and they were already more involved than any of us ever wanted to be.

"You see, The Avatars infected Sanus when they took her. Nenbard had been coordinating with some doctors in the Northlands to develop a suppressant serum. However, the infection recently crossed a threshold, although there was no apparent trigger. Sanus slaughtered Nenbard while he was administering her daily treatment.

"I had no choice but to execute what was left of her. She had become inhuman. Please understand that I did not kill my sister. The disease killed her. I merely discarded the husk that was left behind.

"I've gone to the assembly of the Ouristihran Union Parliament in Nenbard's stead. There, I will give Galo all of Nenbard's notes and my observations on Sanus's illness. I have also shared all relevant intel with MarLys of ArcNos's Ministry of Covert Affairs.

"Once he has this information, I wish to disappear.

"As I've said, none of us wanted to be involved in the war with The Avatars. When you disappeared, Nenbard saw it as an opportunity to break away before the conflict escalated. But it followed us, and because of that, I have lost everything.

"So now, I'm asking you explicitly. Let me walk away. Whether the world ends in five days or five million years, I can do nothing to change it. Of course, I wish you the best of luck in your war and lament the fact that you never had a choice. But I do.

"Whatever time I have left, let me spend it in relative peace.

"Conclusively,

"Ocronn"

Gabdur folded the note, stuffed it in his pocket, and walked away.

Farim collected snow on her shoulders as she hustled across the salted parking lot. She shook the snow out of her coat over the front step before continuing into the vestibule. As she crossed into the lobby, the nursing assistant behind the reception desk called her over.

"Can I help you with something, miss?"

"Yes, I'm here about the quarantine."

"Okie-doke. And your name?"

"My name isn't on the list. It was..."

"Are you checking in for testing or following up on a loved one?"

"Someone here called me about it, but..."

"You just said you're not on the list."

"My number was on the visitors log, but..."

"So, you were on the list?"

"Would it be too much to ask for you to not interrupt me?" Farim asked. She paused. The receptionist tightened her lips and glared as she gestured for Farim to continue. "I need to speak with Nurse Jevana."

"Have a seat. I'll see if she's available."

No sooner had Farim finished pouring a cup of coffee than Jevana entered the lobby. Her shoulders relaxed at the sight of Farim, though her face was still tight with apprehension. She waved Farim over and led her back into the hospital.

"I wasn't sure if you'd actually come," Jevana said as the door closed behind them, "Sorry we had to call you back here like this."

"We'll talk about how you got ahold of me later," Farim said, "I told those two guys in forensics to erase any evidence of my visit."

"Sorry about that. Uro's bad about not following orders. So far, Caylence is the only department head who can keep him in line."

"I'll talk to Caylence then. Older guy?" Farim asked. Jevana nodded. "Okay. So, what happened in the osteosarcoma ward?"

"The substance from Uulan's IV bag has gone missing," Jevana said, "We suspect foul play, but we've hit a dead end after getting basically nowhere."

"Son of a bitch," Farim muttered, "Have you seen any other cases like his?"

"We've seen a few flare-ups that could have been caused by the substance. Fortunately, we've been able to sort them all out with steroids," Jevana explained, "Unfortunately, that's kept us from definitively linking them to the substance."

"Well, I can't exactly ask you to let one run its course," Farim pondered, "Who has authorized access to the storage area?"

"I'll get you a list."

Shimmering blue light filled the space between the door and its frame at the end of the hall. As the light receded, the door opened to a break room with overturned furniture. MalVek, bruised and disheveled, shambled out into the hall. The break room vanished in a flash of light, leaving the surgery access hall in its place.

MalVek set a foreboding stare on Farim. He stormed at them in long stomping strides.

Farim shoved Jevana out of his path and into the wall. She squared herself, shielding her face with white-knuckle fists. Somehow, he had found her and knew she had figured him out. She twisted her body and slid her foot back, poising to intercept his charge.

MalVek drew a photonic emission weapon from his belt. A luminous warhammer manifested as he consumed the last of the distance. Farim dropped her posture to slide in under the hammer.

MalVek crouched lower, catching her with an upward swing. The photonic hammer bashed her sternum and clavicle, scorching her skin as it snapped her upright. A second blow to her abdomen knocked her prostrate.

Farim heard MalVek's footsteps heading away from her. Short of breath and with her muscles locked, she strained to tilt her head upright. He headed back toward the surgery access hall. And she was helpless to do anything about it. Her neck gave out, and the back of her head clapped against the tiles.

Jevana scrambled to her side and propped her head up. She pressed her thumb against the side of Farim's neck, checking for a pulse. Keeping Farim's head cradled, she pulled her walkie-talkie from her belt. Her voice rang out over the loudspeaker.

"I need a crash cart in Osteo!" she announced, "East end of Surgical Access A!"

Alone in the dark, Elemeno pressed her hand against the wall panel. Hair-thin beams of blue light outlined her hand, only to scatter into wisps that fizzled back to blackness.

After a few minutes and a lot of pacing, however, the wall opened. Chekov stood on the other side, her expression quickly turning from anxious to puzzled.

"Elemeno," she said, "Hello."

"Hello, Chekov," Elemeno nodded, "Has Mortvill returned?"

"No, he hasn't. I thought you were him."

"Oh! I'm sorry. I waited all night, but he never showed up. Should I go look for him?"

"There's no need," Chekov said, waving her inside, "Honestly, I'm surprised to see you."

"Why is that?" Elemeno pried, "Did you expect me to have second thoughts and back out?"

"No, I know you wouldn't scare off easily," Chekov said, "It's more that I'm surprised that Mortvill took measures to ensure your safety. NalSet and I thought it might not be much of a priority for him."

"What are you saying?" Elemeno asked, "You thought he was taking me on a suicide mission?"

Though she posed it as a question, it was more of a proclamation. She knew the answer. She just needed to get Chekov to say it.

"The fact that he gave you a portal strip, his own no less, means we were wrong," Chekov refuted, "Storage unit logs show he only took the one."

"Well, I suppose I can see that," Elemeno said, "But why would it be surprising that he looked out for my safety?"

"Ah… Let me think how to explain Mortvill. He's, well, been around for a long time. A very long time."

"Yes, he told me he's several centuries old."

"Oh! That makes this a lot easier," Chekov remarked, "Yes, we've lost track of his exact age, but he's well into the second half of his sixth millennium. He's at least fifty-seven hundred years old. And all that time has given him unusual and sometimes contradicting philosophies on life and death."

"He sees human life as fleeting and disposable?"

"Fleeting, yes, but he often laments how much shorter our lives are than his. Not only has he watched countless friends grow old and die, he's seen even more struggle for years or even decades over a single mistake. It isn't uncommon for a person to be outlived by one bad decision," Chekov explained, "Mortvill has experienced so much death that sometimes the thought of one more devastates him. Other times, witnessing a dozen more is no bother, as long as he thinks they serve a purpose."

Elemeno nodded in comprehension, taking it all in. "That's what this is about for him, isn't it?" she said, "Digging his way out from under a mistake."

"His entire life, yes. Longer life. Bigger mistakes," Chekov sighed, "This was a small but important victory for him. Just thirty years ago, he wouldn't have taken these sorts of precautions. But it wouldn't have been that he didn't care if you died. More that he would have thought it was a mercy to let you die. Have you go out in a blaze of glory."

"I'll have to thank him when I see him again. Perhaps I can get my hands of a leg of lamb," Elemeno pondered, "For now, do you have anything I can help with?"

"I'm taking you to NalSet's chamber," Chekov said, "As much as he'll deny it, he could use an extra set of hands."

"Is he still having trouble walking?" Elemeno asked. Chekov nodded. "What is he working on?"

"Diagnostics," she said, knocking twice just before she opened the door. "I'm sorry to shove you off like this. It's been a good talk, but I need to get back to work. He'll explain."

Elemeno entered, and Chekov shut the door behind her as she panned her surroundings. The far end of the room was done up as a living area with basic comforts. This end was riddled with overloaded steel shelves, storage units both refrigerated and not, machines in varying states of completion, and countless miscellany and apparati.

"Elemeno," NalSet called out, "Chekov brought you to help me, didn't she?"

"Yes, sir," Elemeno said, braving further into his chamber, "She said you could use an extra set of hands."

"Well, I'm doing fine on my own," he protested, "But I wouldn't object to the company. Take a seat. I'll say if I need your help."

Elemeno looked around, hesitating longer than she liked. There were plenty of chairs, but all of them looked like they could have put her in the way of his work. Finally, she settled on the farthest one from anything that looked fragile or dangerous. NalSet, to her relief, had long since resumed his work.

"So, what are you working on?" she asked.

"How much did she tell you?"

"Diagnostics."

"Hah! Of course, she did," NalSet chuckled, "Well, there's no easy way to say it, so I'll just be out with it. Dourias passed on while you were gone."

"Oh goodness!" Elemeno gasped, "That's why Chekov rushed me off."

"Yeah. She's performing a holoautopsy on him," he said, "It's an autopsy using holographic x-ray projection. Keeps from damaging the body."

"Have you heard from Farim?"

"No, and I doubt we're going to," NalSet said, "See, he died very abruptly. I'm running diagnostics on a subdermal chip that she planted on him. It's a location tracker, but it also alerts her to any significant changes to his vitals."

"You think that had something to do with it," Elemeno said, "Like a reversed version of Kabehl's nanochip."

"Yeah," NalSet said, turning to face her, "You worked that out that quickly?"

"I listen. I absorb," Elemeno shrugged, "I know I haven't had the most active role in these things, but I try to be up on the latest."

NalSet nodded and returned to his work. He moved a few displays around on the screen. With a few more taps, a progress tracker appeared, and a nearby machine began to whir.

"That reminds me. I've... been meaning to apologize to you."

"Oh, if it's about my Eytea, I know everyone did as much as they could," Elemeno assured, "It's Ozzera's fault and nobody else's. And as I understand, she was killed as thoroughly as anything could be."

"I meant... Well, it's more than that. I've taken people like you for granted," NalSet explained, turning toward her again, "Lot of folks have been dragged into this conflict with no warning or say in the matter. I never really gave any thought to the harm we were causing, getting people involved without their consent. But now, I'm having to come to terms with losing my brother."

"I would never gloat about that," Elemeno assured, "I can tell we come from very different backgrounds."

"It used to be I could hear people die by the handful without so much as a flinch," NalSet said, "See, in my homeland, death is so familiar that it killed empathy itself. We mourn deeply for the few we let get close to us. But we feel nothing for everyone else, not even our nearest neighbor.

"I brought that callousness with me. And for a while, I convinced myself that it served a purpose. But not anymore. I'm sorry, to everyone we've gotten involved, that I've been so cold. You have my respect."

"Thank you, NalSet," Elemeno said, "So, where is your homeland?"

"The where isn't so much the issue as the when," he said, "Mortvill, Chekov, MalVek, and I all come from five hundred years in the future."

Elemeno trembled and shook her head as though to expel what he had just told her. Somehow, all her exposure to Hybrids, enhancement tech, unidentifiable illnesses, chaos drones, and eldritch beings had failed to prime her for the possibility of time travel. Much less that time travelers lived among them.

"Why have you come back here?" she managed at last.

"To stop The Avatars of Fate, of course," he said, "Nearly four hundred seventy years after their overall objective had come to pass, we came back five hundred years. Things haven't transpired quite how Mortvill remembers, but in the first timeline, my timeline, it happened later this year."

"Of course, he would have lived through it the first time around," Elemeno nodded. She straightened up as an epiphany struck. "He and The Harvester aren't brothers, are they? The Harvester is himself from now."

"Clever. Yes, physiologically, they're the same person. Ethically, not so much. As should be obvious, Mortvill has dissociated from his past ways," NalSet explained,

"The fact that he's lost the thread of his past self's methods is why we can't lose Dourias."

"But is there even anything you can do about it at this point?" Elemeno asked.

"It depends on how the diagnostics pan out, but we'll stand a chance if we can find Sinkua," he said, "Nobody's heard from him since the Heniokhos Disaster, but he has the potential to resurrect the dead. It's in his…"

"Do you mean he…?"

"I'm sorry, but Hybrids are off limits."

"What? Why?"

"I've never understood it. I've just had to accept that it works that way because it just does. And as a scientist and an engineer, I hate that," NalSet empathized, "Now, he can't just run about waking the dead with no particular care. He experiences any pain that they felt as they died. So, he can only resurrect people he sympathizes with enough to endure that pain."

"And he's never even heard of Dourias," Elemeno observed, "Not that he ever mentioned."

The console beeped, pulling NalSet's attention back to it. He opened what Elemeno figured to be the diagnostics readout.

"No, but he's friends with Farim," NalSet said, "If she still has her chip in her, reviving her should revive Dourias. Just as killing her appears to have killed him."

"So, that's what the chip had to do with it," she sighed, "Instead of his chip informing her that something had happened to him, her chip killed him when she died."

"That appears to be the case," he said, "The implants have the potential to work both ways, but running in reverse malfunctioned and, to put it simply, flatlined his vitals to match hers."

"Sounds like it didn't so much malfunction as function differently than advertised."

"Yes, I also suspect sabotage," he nodded, "But for now, fetch me the map from that cabinet, please."

"So, what exactly was that program doing?" Elemeno asked as she searched the cabinet, "In lay terms, of course."

"Before you got here, I determined that his and Farim's chips were still linked and still communicating. But then, his time of death according to his chip is a ways off from that according to Chekov."

"Human error?" Elemeno asked, closing the cabinet with the map under her arm.

"Not to this extent. Not with Chekov, at least," NalSet insisted, "Now, that program was calculating data transmission speed. That is, how quickly the chip could send and receive information, given the conditions at the time."

"Oh, I think I get it," Elemeno said as she set the map on the table, "Now, you know how far apart they were?"

"Will in a moment, yeah."

NalSet produced a compass with a small digital interface at the base and punched the anchor into northern Tanelen. Mumbling to himself and scribbling out calculations, he punched a number into the interface. The draw arm stretched out about halfway across the Northlands. NalSet drew a circle at that radius, running well off the western edge, then repeated with a second number.

"Farim died within this ring," he said, "Now, we need to figure out how best to search it."

"I overheard Galo say he might contact her as a favor to someone," Elemeno said, "We could find her the same way my Eytea found her Sinkua. Well, similar."

"Followed a tracking pigeon to him?" he asked, to which she nodded, "It's a solid start. If Galo has the means to contact her, we can reach out to him for help. And in the meantime, we'll locate Sinkua and help him realize his power."

Farim's body lay upon a cold metal slab. Electrical burns and bruises covered the top half of her torso, riddling her chest with pustules and pock marks.

Seirakh stood over her with a utility cart at his side. He continued working as the door opened, dabbing a pustule and sliding the specimen swab into a culture tube.

"Well, if this is the sort of thing you're into, then it's no wonder you're single."

"I certainly am glad you can find humor in this, Jevana," Seirakh bit back as he capped the tube, "Now then, are you here to be useful or just to make baseless necrophilia jokes?"

"Checking up," Jevana said, "She died on my watch after all."

"I'm quite aware," he said, continuing to take samples, "As for your checking up, I've yet to determine the cause of death."

"I thought that was obvious," she said, "She was beaten with a big glowing hammer."

Seirakh capped the last culture tube. He passed an ultraviolet flashlight to Jevana, ordering her to shine it over Farim's wounds. On a clipboard, he scribbled notes with furious speed and dubious legibility.

"It's improbable that these injuries alone would have killed her, especially with medical attention readily available," Seirakh reasoned, "I'm checking for potential complications in her health."

"And if you don't get anything from the samples?"

"Exploratory surgery. Which reminds me."

Seirakh walked to the wall and pushed a button next to an intercom. "Uro," he called out, "Status on next of kin for Farim?"

"Still nothing," Uro called back over the speaker, "Her records are minimal."

"Can you check her phone?" Jevana suggested.

"Thank you, Jevana," Uro snarked, "Maybe next you can come show me how to turn on my computer?"

"Watch your ass, boy," Caylence warned, his voice distant, "Check her coat."

"Yes, sir."

Seirakh cut the line and returned to the slab. As he looked down to pick up his clipboard, something caught the corner of his eye. It was the tiniest of anomalies, just a speck of red. He took a magnifying lens from the cart as he leaned in for a closer look.

"What is it?" Jevana asked.

"There's a prick mark here," Seirakh said, "It looks fresh."

"Oh, Seirakh. Seirakh. Seirakh," Jevana said, "You always were too observant for your own good."

Sinkua stood on his doorstep with Odin a few steps back and aside. He hadn't brought his house key, but shoe prints in the snow and Vielle's motorcycle in the driveway told him someone was there. He knocked on the door.

Spril popped his head out a moment later, looking just as startled as he did thrilled. He slipped out onto the front step and shut the door.

"Hey, you're back," he said, "Where have you been?"

"What are you doing here?" Sinkua asked, "And how long have you been here?"

"Couple hours. I called you, but some strange woman answered. I thought The Avatars had gotten you, so I came to look for you," Spril said, "Nikasu and Vielle are making sure she stays upstairs."

"Who is she?" Sinkua asked.

"She won't say, but she insists that she knows you. We decided to hold her here until you came home," Spril said, "Now, where have you been? Vielle's been acting weird whenever anyone mentions you."

"I, ah... I ran off and tried to kill myself."

"Oh, shit. I am so sorry," Spril stammered, "We all just... You know."

"Everyone thought I wanted to be left alone. I get it," Sinkua said. He gestured over his shoulder. "But he saved me and gave me time to reflect. I realized I should've spoken up instead of expecting people to come looking for me."

"I'll try to be better about reaching out in the future," Spril promised, "So, who's your friend? Seems like he doesn't talk much."

"He's still getting the hang of Ouristihran," Sinkua explained, "The last language he spoke was Fjarthursk."

"I am called Odin," Odin greeted, "I am an Etherworlder, just as Leviathan and Yggdrasil."

"Odin. Nice to meet you. My name is Spril," Spril greeted, offering his hand. Nodding to the spear, he asked, "I take it you're Eytea's Etherworlder?"

"Yes. Eytea is the Hybrid of mine," Odin said, "Told you anyone that have you a strange sense about you?"

"Yeah, more than once. But now, I have an explanation for it," Spril said, then gestured to Sinkua's sword, "Did you give him that blade?"

"Yes, I delivered it to him," Odin said, "Epesol. The Sword of the Sun. It is an inheritance of his."

"Looks heavy," Spril said, addressing Sinkua, "But you always have been stronger than you look."

"Well, it also reacts to me," Sinkua added, "When I hold it, it becomes a lot lighter than it actually is."

"Huh. Interesting," Spril said, "Anyway, come inside. Not all of us are self heating, you know."

"It is pretty convenient," Sinkua snickered.

"By the way," Spril said, "it turns out you were right."

"Could you sound less surprised when you say that? I feel like it happens often enough that you shouldn't sound that surprised," Sinkua said, "But if you don't mind, what was I right about this time?"

"There was a traitor in The Coalition," Spril said through waning laughter, "MalVek kidnapped Nikasu after she helped rescue Phylus. He took her to Poravit."

"Well, at least she's safe now. I'll deal with him later."

"Vielle and Galo went in after her. They said Elemeno also showed up. Nikasu even said she's the one who broke her out. I don't know Elemeno that well, but I find it hard to believe."

"I don't," Sinkua said, "She's helped Eytea fight two different Avatars, and she tried to blow Kabehl's cover."

"Well when you put it that way," Spril conceded.

He opened the door, and Sinkua and Odin followed him into the house. Sinkua looked to the couch where he saw the backs of two familiar heads.

"Hey girls," he said. Vielle and Nikasu turned sharply. "I'm home."

"Sinkua!" Nikasu squealed, vaulting over the couch.

Sinkua unstrapped Epesol and propped it beside the door. Footsteps clapped across the floor behind him. While he was leaned over, Nikasu sprang and slammed onto his back.

"Nice to see you, too," Sinkua laughed as he came upright.

"Yep. Hey! What's in the bag?" Nikasu asked, dangling over his back, "It smells like bacon. And fruit."

"Just something NieRie whipped up," Sinkua said, opening the bag, "Bacon grease pomegranate muffins."

"Oooh! Can I try one?"

"Well, this is my last one."

"Aww. I don't wanna be rude."

"Tell you what," Sinkua said, "I'll trade it to you for, let's see, a kiss on the cheek from the world's asskickingest little sister."

Nikasu tightened her arms around his shoulders and smooshed her lips against his cheek, tickling her nose and chin on his unmanaged scruff. Sinkua laughed as Nikasu snatched the bag and hopped off of his back.

"Hey, Eyepatch!" she called out. Odin cocked an eyebrow at her. "Wanna go splitsies on this thing?"

While Nikasu and Odin became acquainted over the last muffin, Vielle rounded the couch and approached Sinkua with far less enthusiasm. Her chin trembled as she drew her lips back between her teeth. He smiled sympathetically and held out his arms.

"I was so worried," Vielle choked out as she collapsed into him and threw her arms around his midsection, "I saw the door and your dagger, and I just..."

"I'm sorry," Sinkua said, rubbing the back of her head, "I got in a bad way, but I'm better now."

"Well, you're back now. And Nikasu is pretty damn happy about that muffin. So, I'll forgive you this time," Vielle said, grinning up at him. She pushed up on her toes and pecked his other cheek. "Did Spril tell you who else is here?"

"All he said was that it's someone who says she knows me."

"That's all she'll tell us," Vielle said, "Wait here, okay?"

Vielle walked over to the stairs and knocked on the wall.

"Sinkua's home!" she called up, "Come down here!"

A few lingering moments later, the guest came around from the bottom of the stairs. Sinkua's mouth fell open. She was just as he recalled her, albeit shorter now. Or rather, he was taller. They stood at opposite ends of the dining area, taking in the sight of each other.

Thick jet black hair hung to the small of her back. Her green eyes were both soft and piercing, heavy with experience beyond her apparent years. A small smile graced her lips as she crossed to the living room. She stopped before him, looking up at his eyes.

"Even brighter than I remembered them," she said, her ArcNosian accent peppered with Quarunite.

"M... Mom?" he choked out, "Is it really you?"

"Yes!" BeiLou exclaimed, throwing her arms around him. "It's me, MeiLom."

"I.... I don't know what to say," Sinkua stammered, "I'm just..."

"Well, I'd offer you my shoulder," BeiLou said, pulling back to face him, "but I looked away for a few years, and suddenly you're so much taller than me."

"I have been eating my pomegranates," Sinkua snickered as they pulled out of the hug, "By the way, my name is Sinkua now."

"Yes, Takmet told me," BeiLou said, "You knew him as Grandpa Gijin. You see, he…"

"I've heard the story," Sinkua cut off, "This is just my first time hearing his real name."

"Well anyway, I guess I'm still used to calling you MeiLom."

"You can call me either one."

"So, she really is your mother?" Spril asked.

"She is."

"How?" Spril asked, "I came back from apparently being dead, but that was a special case and much shorter than this. And I would say she hasn't aged at all."

"It's my necklace. It doesn't just give me power over fire. It also lets me resurrect the dead," Sinkua explained, "But Odin says Hybrids and Etherworlders are exempt. Also, it means that when I die, I'm reborn as the next person in my family tree, while everyone else spends seven lifetimes in the afterlife."

"Incidentally," Odin interjected, "if I may ask, Lady BeiLou, how long ago had you death?"

"Sixteen years."

"Preserved was your body?" he continued. BeiLou shrugged, and Sinkua shook his head. "How could have this itself occurred? Your body should have itself been too decayed."

"Sinkua was under Yggdrasil," Vielle offered, "Could that have had something to do with it?"

"Why were you…" Nikasu cut in.

"Investigating," Sinkua interrupted.

"That is another matter," Odin said, "Yggdrasil cannot be. It was destroyed long ago."

"My mother is impossible. Yggdrasil is impossible. You're obsessed with calling things impossible, and yet, there they are," Sinkua confronted, "Do you expect everyone here to agree with you just because you can't stand being wrong?"

"Yes, I think it's time you fit your perspective around reality," BeiLou complemented, "Rather than trying to force reality to fit your perspective."

Odin folded his arms and glared down at them. After a moment, he lowered his head and sighed. "You are correct. I am, most of all, a scholar," Odin said, "I will seek to learn to understand these strange occurrences."

"I've actually come into some intel that might explain how Yggdrasil came back," Spril said, "It's more of an informed hunch than a solid theory."

"Does it have anything to do with your teleportation act?" Sinkua asked.

Vielle's phone rang, and she excused herself upstairs.

"It might, but…" Spril pondered, "Did I actually teleport?"

"Hard to say," Sinkua shrugged, "I was looking down. But one second, you were a ways off, the next, you were in front of me. And I don't remember hearing you running."

"Hmm. I don't remember anything in between either," Spril said, "In any case, I'd like to wait until Galo is with us to discuss what I know."

"Well, in the meantime, I have some books that I need to translate," BeiLou said, "But first, I need to get the supplies to open them from the hardware store. A case of Raspberry Popken would be good, too. And a bag of whatever Nikasu's been eating, because it smells amazing, and I haven't eaten since I got back. Oh, and someone more fluent in Harkzanian than I am. Odin?"

"Did Takmet teach you Harkzanian?" Sinkua asked.

"Sort of," BeiLou said, "He taught me Mberhali. Then, he taught me Harkzanian in relation to that. So, I have to go through Mberhali to translate Harkzanian into Ouristihran."

"I have learned Ouristihran through my native language of Fjarthursk," Odin said, "Thus, I too must translate Harkzanian through another language, but I can be of assistance."

"That'll help. Thanks," BeiLou said. She turned to Sinkua. "By the way, I met Eytea before I came back. She told me you two had just gotten engaged."

"Yeah," he said, swallowing hard, "I proposed the night before she died."

"Well, this may be at least a couple of kinds of inappropriate, but I have to say, hot damn!" BeiLou remarked, "You got yourself a bombshell!"

Sinkua laughed at her brazenness.

"Clever, strong, and sweet, too," BeiLou added, "She told me what happened with the missing book. I'm glad they're important to you, but I'm even happier that you're important to her."

"Yeah… Yeah, so am I," Sinkua said, "I'm done with all that. Shutting people out. Losing my cool. Storming off. It's not me anymore."

"Good. Oh, and she and Takmet said to tell you not to blame yourself."

"That's good to hear. By the way, um…" Sinkua trailed off. He wanted to apologize for everything at once. For what happened to her. To her husband. To her mother. To her estranged half sister and her son. To her old professor. He wanted to tell her the father she never knew had spent nearly fifty years becoming the man he had always wanted to be. But none of it would come. "How's Dad doing? Did he come back with you?"

"What are you talking about?" BeiLou asked, "I was going to ask you that."

"Why would you…?" Sinkua puzzled, "Dad died six years ago."

"I never saw him."

Vielle came back downstairs with heavy eyes and a sunken face.

"Is everything okay?" Spril asked.

"That was Hillside Oncology. In Quarun," she choked out, "Farim just… passed away in their care."

"What had she been checked in for?" BeiLou asked, "Maybe it's something The Coalition could help with."

"She was on a call list about a quarantine," Vielle said, "She came in for an examination, and she was… They're calling it a random act of violence. But they need someone who knows her to confirm her identity. And fill in the gaps in her medical history."

"Oh shit," Nikasu blurted out, "Brother! Could you…?"

"It's worth a shot," Sinkua said, "Spril, could you drive me to the docks in a few hours? If it's all the same, I'd like to get some sleep before I set off."

"You'll need to prove you know her," Vielle said, "My dad should still have both your papers from your time with Parliamentary ArcNos."

"I'll come pick you up at sundown," Spril said, "Nikasu, why don't you come stay with Yrlis and me until he gets back? We'll leave BeiLou and Odin here to work."

"Then I will escort the Lady BeiLou in the errands of hers," Odin offered.

Chapter 16

A knock came at the door, and OshMar jumped hard enough to bang his knees against the underside of his desk. He snarled an expletive as he pushed his chair out. The visitor knocked again. OshMar pressed a button under his desk, and the lock clicked open.

"Come in."

"Hey, OshMar," FerLyn said, slipping around the partially open door, "Do you have any plans for the weekend?"

"Not particularly," OshMar said, putting his nose back in his work, "I'll just watch movies and keep my distance from this damn weather."

"Sounds like a blast," FerLyn snarked, crossing the office to take a seat across from him, "Well, I just wanted to tell you that MelDas got the billiards table refelted, and he's itching for another rematch."

"FerLyn, I don't think this is a good idea."

"Oh, he doesn't take it as personally as he lets on. Besides, even the kids sometimes ask when you're coming over again."

"No, not beating your husband at billiards again. Well, not just that," OshMar floundered, "Look. We need to stop spending so much time together."

"OshMar, we're colleagues. Same position in different Ministries," FerLyn argued, "Spending time together is to be expected."

"At work, yes, but personal time, not so much," he countered, "People are going to talk."

"Well, it can't be that you're worried about a sex scandal."

"Yes, I'm attracted to you, and it's obvious to everyone. But I wouldn't do that to MelDas, and certainly not to Tulira."

"I know. I'm just messing with you," FerLyn assured, "Is this about the Heniokhos Disaster?"

"It is."

"Neither of us signed those papers!"

"Yes, but think about the timeline," OshMar said, running his palm over his thinning hair, "They came to me. I refused to sign. They had no leverage. They moved in on you. You asked me for advice. Suddenly, there're active beacons all over the damn place. Think about how that looks to everyone else."

"What it should look like is that The Avatars planted them without authorization," FerLyn insisted, "Either that or LenSom went behind our backs like he always did."

"It should, but that doesn't mean it will," he refused, "Especially not with how much time we've been spending together since then."

"Harrowing times tend to be bonding."

"FerLyn."

"Nobody suspects anything," she continued, "Look, I understand that you're scared. I can't and don't want to imagine how it feels to go through what you've been through. But this is going to turn out okay."

"FerLyn," OshMar doubled down, "Until the investigation is over, we need to keep our contact professional. Otherwise, we're both going to get hurt."

"OshMar, I..." FerLyn began to protest, trailing off into a sigh, "Okay. I'll go along, but it's not because I agree with you. Honestly, I think you're paranoid. But if it means that much to you, I'll distance myself."

"Thank you."

"Sure thing," she said, rising from her seat, "See you around the building."

Scores of fingers clattered along dozens of keyboards. Printers spat out documents almost as quickly as the paper trays were reloaded. Workers moved hastily yet smoothly around each other, never halting but never colliding.

SenRas looked up from his desk as something grabbed his attention. One of his workers had a sudden uncertainty in his step. SenRas watched him approach the printer with tensed shoulders, leaf through the papers, then deflate with relief as he found his document.

SenRas put his attention back in his work, feigning nonchalance. A moment later, a shadow stretched over his desk.

"Prime Minister SenRas, sir?" MerSul muttered, "There's something you need to see."

"You are free to speak up," SenRas said, "We don't keep secrets from each other."

"I think this qualifies as an exception, sir," MerSul said, thrusting the document onto SenRas's desk.

As SenRas read it over, a grim somberness that even he couldn't subdue cracked his practiced image of calm and control. There was no sense by which it should have been possible, and yet, here it was. Nothing appeared to betray it as a forgery. If it was, he might have sought to hire its creator, had they not implicated a Prime Minister in a terrorist attack.

The most immediate concern was that this did, in fact, need to be kept under wraps. He had to play it off as something not quite so serious as MerSul clearly thought.

"Tell you what," SenRas said, "Make a second copy. I'll take one and look into it personally. And we'll leave the other here for our records."

As MerSul went off to his task, SenRas's phone rang.

"Ministry of Human Resources. Prime Minister SenRas speaking."

"It's Malia."

"Ah, hello! And what would this be concerning?"

"I've left The Coalition."

"That does sound serious. Fax me the details. I'll contact you once I've looked them over."

"Okay. I'll keep my schedule open. Thank you. And would you tell EshCal?"

"Of course. Thank you as well."

Two copies of the document on his desk told that MerSul had come and gone in the space of the phone call. SenRas folded and pocketed one and pushed the other aside into a pile of papers that he still needed to look over.

MarLys walked in soon after, clutching a manila folder. She looked disheveled and artificially focused, as though she was putting too much effort into looking mentally present. SenRas waved her over.

"Here's my report from my assignment in Berinin, sir," she said, offering the folder, "What would you like me to do now?"

"Honestly, I'd like you to go home for the rest of the day," SenRas insisted, "Come back fresh in the morning."

"Sir, could you not treat me like a porcelain doll?" MarLys asked, "I'm ready to work today."

"Oh, come off it, young lady. This is no sort of special treatment," he dismissed, "Besides, I heard Vielle was here today. If you hurry, you might still catch her."

"Well, when you put it that way," she said, rubbing her jaw. She straightened up abruptly. "Hold on. Vielle doesn't work here anymore. You're just trying to get me to leave, aren't you?"

"Yes," he smiled, "She was here though. She came to see her father."

"Probably some Avatar-hunting business," MarLys said.

"Most likely," SenRas agreed, "Tell you what. Run my outgoing papers to Chairwoman TolRou while I go on lunch. Whether you're here when I return, I'll leave to your judgment."

"Hmm. Well, I suppose I could go for that."

"Fantastic," SenRas said, groaning as he hefted himself out of his seat, "Welcome back, young lady."

The desk nurse didn't look up as he reached the front of the queue. He scratched the side of his leg, bunching the fabric of his pants in his fingertips.

"Name?" she asked.

He cleared his throat and began to speak. The nurse looked up, suddenly taken aback.

"Ah, Chieftain Sage Galo," she said, "Pardon me."

Galo shrugged off her impoliteness, his mind being too otherwise absorbed to give it any concern. She had been just as indifferent with everyone else.

She produced a manila envelope with his name and handed it to him with her usual platitude of luck and plastic pitying smile. Galo accepted it with a mumbling of gratitude and a solemn nod.

He took the envelope outside and sat on a bench. Hunched over, he opened it and pulled the paper out just far enough to find what he needed.

Galo grumbled an expletive and stuffed the paper back in the envelope. He thrust himself back to his feet and shoved the whole thing into one of the pockets of his Chieftain Robe.

Leviathan prodded from the depths of his subconscience. Galo sent a single word her way as he headed down the sidewalk to hail a cab.

"Yeah."

Blue light traced his hand, and the wall panel shifted back and aside. Gabdur walked through to find Chekov, NalSet, and Elemeno waiting in the assembly chamber. Mortvill's throne sat unilluminated and nestled in its base, a once scarce sight becoming uncomfortably familiar.

As Gabdur completed the circle, standing across from NalSet, Elemeno turned to him.

"How are you holding up?" she asked.

"Horribly," he sighed, "But I suppose things are as they need to be."

"Well, as Chekov likely told you, Dourias has passed away," NalSet said, "Chekov has also told us about Nenbard and Sanus. We're sorry to have called you back at such a time, but your assistance is, well, indispensable."

"You don't need to defend your decision," Gabdur said, holding eye contact with NalSet, "Dourias's passing is reason enough. Besides, I never resigned."

"Good, because we have a plan to bring him back, but it requires your specific skill set."

"I'm not sure what impression I've given you, but if it was beyond Chekov, I won't fare any better."

"It isn't your medical knowledge," Chekov said, "It's your work in animal genetics. We need to send a message that we can follow."

"But that MalVek cannot," NalSet added.

"I see. I may be able to help, then," Gabdur nodded, "What exactly are we doing?"

"To the best of our knowledge, Dourias was killed by a sympathetic response between his and Farim's biometric trackers," Chekov explained, "We want to use an enhanced tracking pigeon to locate her."

"When we recovered Nikasu, Galo told the receptionist that he might contact Farim on her behalf," Elemeno said, "We can have him use this new pigeon to send the letter. If you can have it ready in time for the Union Assembly, we'll know where to find him. I'll bring it to him and ask for his help."

"Well, that's too short of notice for genetic engineering, but I'll see what else I can come up with," Gabdur said, "So, what happens after we find Farim?"

"While you're working on the pigeon, I'll be locating Sinkua," NalSet said, "I'll help him awaken his latent power and bring him to Farim once she's been located."

"We agreed we would let him discover that on his own."

"Yes, well circumstances dictate otherwise."

"So, here's the plan," Chekov said, "Gabdur, first thing, NalSet needs to complete curative hibernation. Once he's in, begin work on the tracker. It's urgent that you finish before the Union Assembly.

"Elemeno, you'll monitor NalSet while he's in hibernation. Page Gabdur or myself if anything is amiss. If he isn't out before the Union Assembly, delivering the tracker to Galo takes priority. Gabdur and I will take over on monitoring. Once we've sent the letter, you and Gabdur will go to its destination to find Farim."

"NalSet, once you're out, go find Sinkua. Regain his trust or, at the very least, his empathy. Help him understand his latent power. Whether we bring him to Farim or Farim to him will depend on the circumstances we find her in.

"When I'm not assisting elsewhere, I'll be mitigating Dourias's decomposition to ensure that this plan remains feasible."

"I'm sorry," Gabdur said, "What do you mean by mitigating his decomp?"

"Left to its own devices, the process is greatly accelerated," Chekov explained, "I think it's a side effect of his prolonged hyperspace exposure."

"That's why you're in such a hurry to get this done in time for the Union Assembly," Gabdur realized, "It isn't just a matter of convenience."

"More one of necessity," Chekov said, "If we let Galo get back in the wind, we may not find him in time to save Dourias."

Streaks of fuchsia zipped between the evergreens. The three moons, all nearing their third quarter, clustered just above the treetops. Sinkua realized he had never thought about the moons' phases. Now though, he wondered if he had ever seen all three full or new at once.

"So, this woman," Spril said, interrupting his pondering, "You're sure she's the real deal?"

"As far as I can tell," Sinkua said, "My father had her death covered up as a disappearance, so she wasn't declared dead until ten or eleven years ago. Only a few people knew I proposed to Eytea. Or that I'd have any reason to feel like her and Grandpa Gijin's deaths were my fault. Or that I called him Grandpa Gijin."

"Sounds like you've thought this over," Spril conceded, "I'll take your word on it, then."

"Plus, Raspberry is a bold guess for anyone's favorite Popken flavor," Sinkua added, largely as an aside, "Right guess in her case."

Spril let out a small chuckle. "True. I don't know anyone else who'd say it's their favorite."

Silence stretched through a long gap in the evergreen forest. Spril broke that silence with an audible swallow and a clearing of his throat.

"So," he said, lingering a moment, "Is it weird that I think she's hot?"

Sinkua belted out a loud guttural laugh. "No, but don't expect me to ever call you Dad," he said, "Yrlis would kick your ass if you made a move on another woman, anyway."

"Yeah, she would," Spril chuckled, "By the way, she wanted to talk to you."

"What about?"

"She finished mapping your genome, but she had to drop your case. Too busy," Spril explained, "She forwarded her notes to Ophalin though."

"That's okay," Sinkua shrugged off, "There's no rush for a cure anymore."

"What do you mean?"

"I've, well… been cured. It happened while I was under Yggdrasil."

"How?" Spril asked.

"Yggdrasil pulled my blackout rage out of me as a separate person," Sinkua said, "I literally fought my darker nature, and I won. My mind has never been clearer."

"Can… Can it do that?"

"Apparently," Sinkua shrugged, "I mean, Odin would say otherwise, but…"

"That guy says a lot of stuff is impossible," Spril cut in, "You said it yourself. It's kind of an obsession with him."

"It is, and it's really getting on my nerves," Sinkua said, "So, was that why you called me?"

"That was part of it. I also wanted your insight on something."

"Yeah?"

"I've been going over our history with MalVek. I'm trying to get a handle on what his goal or even his next move might be," Spril said, "If I couldn't do it, I figured you or EshCal would be my next best shot. And she was at work."

"Well, if I'm runner up to the High Minister of Defense, I guess I'm cool with that," Sinkua said, chuckling, "So, what have you come up with so far?"

"Don't worry about it right now. It's all written down in Yrlis's lab," Spril insisted, "But I may have a job for you soon, depending on how the Ouristihran Union Assembly pans out."

"Tactical Avatar Hunter?"

"Basically. Phylus is going to propose an International Anti-Avatar Task Force. I'd like you to assume a tactical leadership role," Spril explained, "If you can bring Farim back, we'll try to bring her on as an investigative specialist."

"We should gather up the Subtransit Resistance and build on that," Sinkua suggested, "We built it from all over Ouristihra. If we're taking the fight abroad, it makes sense to bring that full circle."

"Whatever's left of us outside the Ministries and the Hybrids, but I appreciate the idea," Spril said, "So, I guess I don't have to tell you that this whole situation is probably a trap."

"No, I've thought that for a while now," Sinkua said, "I'm sure everyone of significance in The Avatars and The Coalition knows about this power. And I've been unreachable for the past two weeks. Doesn't take someone in a tactical leadership role to figure it out."

"Well, when you put it that way, I guess not. As long as you realize MalVek might try to get the drop on you."

"I wish that motherfucker would."

Now, it was Spril's turn for a loud guttural laugh. It tapered off as they crested a hill, and the docks came into view. Spril pulled into the first available parking space.

"Well, I'd wish you luck, but you've got foresight on your side," Spril said, "One more thing though. Nikasu told me that MalVek said he can intercept transmissions. We don't know if it's true, but just in case, try not to call any of us until you're back in ArcNos."

"I'll keep that in mind, thanks," Sinkua said.

He climbed out and opened the door to the back seat where Epesol lay waiting. As he grabbed it, another layer to MalVek's plot occurred to him.

"Hold on," he said with only his top half in the car, "MalVek wants us to believe that he intercepted Hillside's call to Farim?"

"Right," Spril said, looking over his shoulder, "Where are you going with this?"

"They were both probably in Poravit. MalVek just happened to be between Farim and Hillside when they called her?" Sinkua challenged, "Depending on where she was, there could be a serious shortage of dry land between her and them."

"That is a bit of a stretch. A lot of a stretch, actually," Spril said, "In that case, it's possible that he has a contact at Hillside."

"Which means Farim was both bait and a mark. And we can be damn sure they've got a contingency plan in case we both come out of the morgue alive," Sinkua concluded, strapping Epesol to his back. "And I'm realizing now that Phylus might have anticipated this."

Chapter 17

As the double doors settled shut behind Phylus, the set to his immediate right groaned open. Chieftain Sage Galo emerged, and the two of them converged to the mahogany divider for an enthusiastic handshake. Phylus pulled Galo close enough for a hearty pat on the back of his shoulder, all the while keeping an eye on Noble Doyen Joren.

"Thank you," Phylus said as they drew back, "for saving Nikasu. It means, well, everything to the three of us. Vielle and Malia and me."

"I only did what needed to be done," Galo insisted, "Did Vielle tell you about Sinkua?"

Phylus looked past him as two more sets of double doors opened. Galo looked back, and they watched as Grand Sultan Zelphius of Ferya and the Magnate Supreme Naletas of Poravit filed into the Assembly Hall in even closer unison than they had. Phylus made a quick note of their lingering eye contact with Joren, then returned his focus to their conversation. He tapped the divider to rein in Galo's attention or at least pull it away from Naletas.

"She told me about the door at Yggdrasil. The one he had carved into," Phylus said, "But she also assured me he's alive and well after all."

"You're... sure about this?" Galo asked.

"She talked to him this morning," Phylus insisted, "She said he's different now. He's calmer for the most part."

"How? How is that possible?" Galo stammered, "Don't take me wrong. I'm thrilled. But... How?"

"She just said it was a long story, and I left it alone," Phylus excused, "But she also assured me that Nikasu doesn't know that you two thought he had committed suicide. As far as she knows, he was just out investigating beneath the trunk of Yggdrasil."

"That's good," Galo nodded, "She doesn't need that stress."

Prime Duke Norum and the High Magistrate Orthean of Haprian filed in next, flanking Zelphius. Galo and Phylus gave them both a respectful nod. Orthean exchanged lingering glances with Joren and Zelphius, with Norum watching sidelong.

Beginning with Governess Premier Subralis of Lenguardia, four of the remaining five double doors opened in short succession. The double doors to the Kirtsian Hall, now absent a flag, had not moved since the ArcNosian Civil War. Phylus lingered on that long empty seat as the last double doors settled shut. He pondered what impact their titleless representative might have made, had he been more than a scarcely necessary tiebreaker.

Once everyone else had taken their seats, High Magistrate Orthean descended the steps onto the Assembly Hall floor. He crossed to the podium where, as officiator, he made his opening statements.

Sinkua paused just beyond the vestibule to survey the waiting room. Nothing seemed to be amiss. The sense of discord was no worse than he'd seen in other hospital waiting rooms. If MalVek had baited a trap, either he was keeping a low cover or the staff was in on it.

The desk nurse whistled to him and waved him over. Epesol shifted along his back as he weaved through the crowd, taking quick stock of everyone he passed. As he reached the desk, he produced a folded paper from his coat pocket, surreptitiously palming the card he had slipped inside of it.

"Whaddya need, hon?" the nurse asked.

"I'm here to check on a friend," Sinkua said.

"Uh huh," she said, looking to the computer monitor. Sinkua glanced at her nametag. "Room number?"

"Um… Morgue. Mortuary," Sinkua fumbled. He checked the card in his palm. Her name was on it. "Whatever you call it here."

"Ah. Confirming the deceased. Name and nationality?"

"Farim. Poravitian."

"Just a sec," she urged, letting her last word linger while she tapped at the keyboard, "Okay. Got her right here. Connection to the deceased?"

"Colleagues," he said, presenting the paper.

"I don't need to see that, hon," she said, pushing it away, "Give it to Caylence when you get downstairs. Take that hall back there to the second elevator hub. Can't miss it once you're in there."

"Thank you."

"And be sure to check your sword in with the security guard over there."

Sinkua nodded and walked away. The guard looked to him just long enough to make acknowledging eye contact. Sinkua glimpsed his nametag and checked the card again. Phylus hadn't listed any security guards. But he also hadn't listed Caylence as a medical examiner, only that he should ask about Seirakh if he didn't come up.

Sinkua unstrapped Epesol as he came within arm's reach. He held it out with his biceps and shoulders tensed, emulating its apparent burden.

"You'll get this back on your way out," the guard said, "Provided you don't cause any trouble."

"Thanks, Khirsan, but I can't promise there won't be trouble," Sinkua said. Khirsan cocked an eyebrow. "I mean, I think someone might have followed me. Or lured me here. If I describe him, can you tell me if you've seen him?"

"I'll see what I can do."

"Well, he's short and stocky. About sixty. Wide jaw. Wide nose, hooked at the tip. Rough skin with calluses all over his hands," Sinkua rattled off, "Sound familiar?"

"Eh, let me think," Khirsan said, rubbing his chin, "Sorry, doesn't ring any bells."

"Okay, well if he shows up and starts causing trouble, I'll need you to get that sword to me," Sinkua urged, "Can I ask that of you?"

"I'll do what I can," he said, "You're a Hybrid, aren't you?"

"You got me," Sinkua said, igniting his own fingertip.

"I don't suppose you're here about the woman who was attacked over in Osteo, are you?"

"I am, actually. Why do you ask?"

"It seems like the sort of thing a Hybrid might follow up on," Khirsan said, "Especially one with his head on the pivot for someone trying to catch him off guard."

"I have a hunch that she was attacked by the man I'm watching for," Sinkua said, "Were there any witnesses? Security tapes?"

"No good shots of his face. No witnesses either," Khirsan said, "Well, Jevana was escorting her, but she was too shocked to remember his face. If you'd like, I can page her to accompany you."

"Somebody say my name?" came an urgent voice.

"Ah. Jevana," Khirsan called back. Jevana kept her distance. "This man is here about Farim. I was just telling him you might escort him to the mortuary."

"Sure thing," Jevana nodded, "What's your name, Scruffles?"

"Sinkua."

"Right. Come with me."

Ocronn drew all heads his way as he entered the Ouristihran Union Parliament Hall. Most of them rolled their eyes and returned their attention to their notes. Upon seeing the flag-draped doors behind the table, he realized why they were so perturbed with him.

Ocronn made his way around the semicircular table and filed into his seat. As he set his briefcase on the table, he turned the nameplate around to find it no longer bore Nenbard's name. He checked his watch as he unlocked his briefcase and realized he had arrived ten minutes late.

He reviewed his notes for some indeterminate while. At some point, he lost track of when he had sat down and even how late he had arrived. Puzzled, he called to the ArcNosian Judge in a sharp whisper.

"What's your problem, mate?" she asked.

"Wasn't this supposed to have started already?" Ocronn asked, "I thought everyone was angry that I walked in late. And through the wrong door."

"Catching on a bit, are you?" she said, "Not much though. The problem wasn't that. It's just who you're not."

"What? Are they mad that I'm here instead of Nenbard?" Ocronn recoiled, "Believe me, I am far less thrilled about this than any of you."

"No, you wank," she scolded, rolling her eyes, "You're not Zelphius. Union Assembly's running long, so we don't have a Moderator."

Ocronn nodded and returned to his notes, masking his embarrassment. "So…" he said, braving to speak but keeping his head down, "How long do we…"

"One hour," she said, "Then one of us steps in as Interim Moderator. It's Ferya's turn this year."

BeiLou sat at the glass and black metal desk, poring over the first ancient tome. An amalgam of lemon juice, rubbing alcohol, and generic household cleaner scratched at her nostrils. Her focus shifted between the book and Sinkua's computer, where she typed the Mberhali translation of the Harkzanian text, followed by Ouristihran at the end of each page.

Behind her, Odin sat at the foot of the bed with the second book on his lap. He didn't seem at all put off by the smell of the substances needed to open them, but whether it was supernatural resilience or obstinate machismo, she couldn't tell. He had a notebook at each side. On the left, he wrote the Fjarthursk translation as he read, while on the right, he translated the previous page into Ouristihran.

BeiLou leaned back in the seat, her shoulders popping as she stretched. The illusory body in the afterlife was incredibly convincing, but one of the most enjoyable flaws was the absence of stiff joints. Her head lolled back until she was looking at Odin upside down.

"Hey, Odin?" she called, her voice lilting.

"Yes, BeiLou?" he answered, not looking up from his work.

"What's your deal, anyway?"

"What means you?" Odin asked, "I offered not a bargain or contract. I am helping you by choice of my own."

"What?" BeiLou puzzled, sitting up and spinning to face him, "No, not that sort of deal. I mean…"

"Ah. You speak in colloquialism. What else means this word, deal?"

"I want to know what makes you the way you are. Something doesn't add up, and I'm trying to make sense of it," BeiLou explained, "Takmet told me the Etherworlders nearly went extinct back when the last of these books was written."

"We were diminished to fewer than thirty," Odin said, "Down to a single digit after I disappeared. What of it?"

"Even when the Etherworlders were numerous, you were hailed as this great hero," BeiLou said, "So, how did someone like you just vanish? And how did you return? And why now?"

"My heroics were nothing without Yggdrasil. Hope was a thing decaying when dying was the World Tree," Odin recalled, "I cast myself into its roots, seeking the means to restore it. Alas, the roots became void and closed before I could make good my escape."

"Once Vielle had replanted Yggdrasil, could you have come back at any time?" BeiLou asked, "Or did you have to be, I don't know… summoned?"

"Upon Sleipnir, I could traverse the arboreal leylines via the roots of Yggdrasil. Thus, we could have navigated our escape of our own will," Odin explained, "Eytea's emotional and milystic expulsion, however, anchored us to her."

"She gave you your bearings?"

"One might say it was more that she compelled and hastened us to her."

"Well either way, if Vielle had planted Yggdrasil sooner, do you think you could have helped Sinkua save Eytea?"

"I can say for certain only that it is possible," Odin said, "And I know enough of Omphaloworlders not to discuss such matters with Vielle."

"Yeah, this conversation never leaves this room," BeiLou insisted, "But either way, at least you got Yggdrasil back."

"That is but a bitter reminder of my failure," Odin lamented, "It does not call for celebration so long as I do not comprehend how one might recover it from naught."

"Whatever," BeiLou shrugged. She thrust herself up out of her seat. "Hey, let's take a lunch break. This woman from my university runs a pretty bitchin' deli."

"The deli… complains too much?"

"Colloquialism. As an adjective, it means something is really good," she explained, "So, do you want to go? Pretty much every food in the world is new to you again, and I want to see the look on your face when you try it."

"I suppose it is to be expected that you would be of considerable appetite," Odin reasoned as he closed the book, "Very well. However, neither of us owns an automobile, and Sleipnir is what some call an eyesore. Should we use this public transit I have seen about or have Sleipnir take us across the sky?"

"Oh, let me think about that," BeiLou snarked, "Squeeze onto a city bus with you or ride a flying horse."

As she stepped into the hall, crackling blue light seeped out around the linen closet door. Faint and hollow hums drifted out as the door opened, sounding like they came from the end of a kilometers-long flask. An aging man with an awkward gait emerged through the sheet of electric blue light.

He stopped just beyond the threshold, transfixed on BeiLou. He reached back and recovered his portal strip, and the sheet of light dissolved. The two stared at each other for a moment, their mouths agape, until Odin broke the silence.

"You two are familiar?" Odin asked.

"BeiLou?" the man asked.

"I will leave you to reacquaint," Odin said, returning to the room.

She nodded. "NalSet?"

He nodded back. "How did you come back?" NalSet stammered, "I'm aware of Sinkua's power, but…"

"I know. I should have been beyond it by now," BeiLou said, "So, I suppose neither of us knows just what he's capable of."

"I guess not," NalSet conceded, chuckling under his breath, "Would it be too much to ask if he brought CreSam back as well?"

"Yes, but only because CreSam might not be dead," BeiLou said, "I never saw him in the afterlife."

"Well, that corroborates it," NalSet said, "When Sinkua disappeared, Mortvill said he felt a similar sensation ten years ago and again six years ago. He never found out for certain what happened to them or who they were, since they were tsoran. But when it happened to Sinkua, he could sense that he hadn't died."

"Which would suggest the other two had also survived."

"Precisely. A recent rescue mission led us to Dourias, the First Native," he said, "We've concluded that he was the one from ten years ago."

"And you think CreSam is the one from six years ago."

"Yes, but of course, we can't say for sure until someone recovers whoever vanished. But the strongest case by far is for CreSam."

"It's an equally pleasant and unsettling thought," BeiLou said, "Well now, I suppose you came here to ask Sinkua for help."

"I did. Remember how I said we got Dourias back?"

"Fifteen seconds ago? Yes."

"Well, now he actually has died," NalSet said, "And he has crucial intel on The Avatars' master plan. It's absolutely imperative that we recover him."

"Well, Sinkua's off reviving someone else right now, but I'll get the message to him. Does he know how to reach you?"

"Wait. Only a few people know about his resurrection power. Who is it?"

"Uh, they said her name is Farim," BeiLou recalled, "I don't know who she is, but she sounded important."

"Son of a bitch. That's perfect," NalSet grinned, "Where are they?"

"Hillside Oncology in Quarun. What do you mean it's perfect?"

"Farim and Dourias are… Well, their vital signs appear to have become quantum entangled, so to speak. By all reasoning, he died because she died, which suggests that reviving one will revive the other," he explained, "I came here to ask Sinkua to resurrect Farim, being that he'd have a much easier time with her than with Dourias."

"He didn't know about any of this," BeiLou said, "He just went because they're friends."

"I know. When did he leave?"

"Three days ago. He should get there today."

"Then, I'll go straight there," NalSet said, "You and I will catch up more soon, I promise."

"Just watch Sinkua's back," BeiLou insisted, "We can trade stories after he comes home."

BeiLou and NalSet exchanged a one-armed hug and a pat on the back. NalSet returned to the linen closet where he reapplied his portal strip and keyed in his next destination. He stepped through the sheet of blue light, vanishing into a distorted image of a vacant security shed.

Odin emerged from the bedroom. "Shall we ourselves be off now?"

"We shall," BeiLou said, "First, let's see if Nikasu wants to join us. We should also invite Spril and this Yrlis woman."

"I cannot ask Sleipnir to carry such a burden."

"So, we'd have to take the bus, huh? Shit."

"Besides, it is for the best that Nikasu does not join us," Odin insisted, "She has herself grievances best resolved before she will be comfortable with you."

"Grievances? What sort of grievances?"

"Come. We will discuss this over some bitching sandwiches."

Chapter 18

"I'd like to begin by introducing myself to those of you whom I've yet to meet in person," Phylus said, his otherwise panning eyes settling on Joren for a scarcely perceptible moment, "My name is Phylus, Ivarian-born ArcNosian immigrant and Prime Minister of Foreign Affairs. Though we no longer have a singular federal authority figure, the Ministries and Parliament have decided that this role will represent ArcNos the Ouristihran Union.

"Our strength, you see, is built from the collaboration of numerous individuals. Such as it was for Parliamentary ArcNos during our civil war, so has it been for the new establishment since then. We built both as much by natural citizens as by willing immigrants, not on the backs of forced servitude nor isolationism.

"But that jingoism was not a product of Imperial ArcNos's leadership, but rather of its top advisors. CreSam ensconced himself within his inner circle. The survivors have since redefined themselves by helping develop and integrating into the new power structure. The others were the driving force behind the fascist plague. They were the very catalysts for the war itself.

"These people were key members of an extra-national organization known as The Avatars of Fate. Although their activity has largely been focused on The Northlands, we have felt their influence throughout Ouristihra. By reaching across the seas, however, we have been able to overcome their influence time and again.

"But now, the time has come to push back. No longer are we to be satisfied with recuperated losses as spoils of victory. No longer are we to make sacrifices on the chance that we might draw their hand. No longer are we to react. No longer are we to strike back.

"We are simply to strike."

His words lingered, enforcing silence as though to speak would disrupt their shadows.

Joren got to his feet, squaring his shoulders as he faced Phylus from the other end of the semicircle. The weight of Phylus's words dissipated as palpable tension grasped him instead. Joren raised his hands to shoulder level.

And his hands came together in a clap that resonated throughout the Assembly Hall.

Another followed. And another and another, establishing a steady rhythm. One by one, the rest of Ouristihran Union, federal authorities of the sea-scattered nations, joined in. Most took part out of passion. Others, though few, joined out of courtesy.

But no matter their reasons, they all joined in. The entire Ouristihran Union gave Phylus a standing ovation for his delivery of Spril's vision.

Oddly, it had all begun with the one he thought to be the most likely contrarian among them. Phylus nodded to Joren ever so slightly, as much a sign that he had taken notice as one of respect. Joren tapered off his applause, and the rest of the Ouristihran Union followed.

"I implore you to elaborate," Joren insisted, "By what means do you intend we, as you said, strike at them?"

"An international task force. As they are an organization without a country, our greatest hope is as an organization with every country."

"We understand as much," Grand Sultan Zelphius said, "But how is this going to work? We need details."

"Come now, friend," Joren said, the expression sounding unsettlingly genuine, "Don't lose your momentum."

"We're proposing the free exchange of all intelligence pertaining to The Avatars, within both the Ouristihran Union and the Union Parliament," Phylus said, "How we act upon it will be decided on a contextual case-by-case basis."

"Well, you're as articulate as you are ambitious, but it's not much of a plan," Magnate Supreme Naletas derided, leaning forward on her elbows, "Share intel. Then what? Arrest them on the spot? Better than half of them could break out by brute force alone."

"Given the circumstances, we can't..."

"And much of them mightn't even be on the straight and narrow with The Avatars, if you catch my meaning," Naletas continued, "Back when Olsa was sitting where Norum's at now, Eprilen's Judge Malia would've been found out as one of them."

"Further investigation proved her circumstances were more complicated than they appeared," Phylus said, "She was protecting her daughter while she tried to create an opportunity to..."

"Fine, yes. But what evidence did you or anyone have to merit a deeper investigation?" Naletas probed, "Besides, everyone saw how you ogled her tits. And how she encouraged it. You two have history, most of it the sweaty and horizontal sort. Without extraordinary evidence that maybe she had an ulterior motive, any call you made for a deeper investigation would've been refused as a purely emotional appeal."

"The free exchange of intelligence is a necessary paradigm shift in how we deal with The Avatars," Galo cut in, asserting himself with his basso cadence, "Every suspected operative, supporter, and enthusiast will be investigated with the same level of scrutiny. No matter who stares at whose breasts."

"In the event of moles and saboteurs..." High Magistrate Orthean said.

"We will hold investigations and trials under the utmost privacy and security," Prime Duke Norum asserted, "Verdicts and responses will be kept even more so."

"Intelligence will only be shared freely among the Ouristihran Union and the Union Parliament," Phylus reminded, "Not with the public."

"I, for one, stand in favor of Prime Minister Phylus's proposal," Galo said, "Several thousand lives might have been saved had he been able to make such a proposal during his tenure as Negotiator under Brigadier General Elite HarEin."

"The ArcNosian Civil War might have been averted," Orthean agreed, his voice laced with derision, as though he was doing Galo a favor, "But don't hold any delusions that Masnethege's fate would have been any different. Or your grandfather's."

"As a matter of fact, it would have. Especially for Chieftain Sage Gijin, since you've found it necessary to invoke him," Galo asserted, "Because SenRas…"

"Exactly. SenRas," Orthean cut off. Galo folded his hands atop his length of table. "He, a member of Lord CreSam's inner circle unaffiliated with The Avatars of Fate, co-captained the fleet with Amirione, also part of the inner circle and a Named Avatar under the alias The Hunter. This… task force… would only have removed one head from a two-headed beast. It would be slower, sure, but at that size, scarcely less of a threat than what you actually faced."

"SenRas provided me with a copy of the original mission directives, signed by CreSam," Galo said, "The primary objective was to have been excessive property damage with minimal casualties. My grandfather was to have been spared. Not wounded. Not taken prisoner. Spared."

"It's a bit off topic, but this could significantly alter CreSam's legacy," Prime Duke Norum said, "Would you be able to furnish the rest of us with copies of this mission directive?"

"Upon request, yes."

"What about the one they actually used?" Zelphius asked, "The one that said to firebomb the village and assassinate the Chieftain Sage."

"Yes, CreSam signed off on that one as well, did he not?" Naletas asked.

"SenRas provided our esteemed Chieftain Sage with a copy of that as well, but I've seen the original," Phylus said, "Multiple independent analyses bore out that the changes, besides being forgeries, were made after the contract had been signed. Brigadier General Elite CreSam neither ordered nor endorsed Chieftain Sage Gijin's assassination."

"Colleagues. Friends. We've strayed from the matter at hand," Joren beckoned, "Come now. Back to this Anti-Avatar Task Force."

"Yes, I believe it's time to bring this to a vote," Orthean said, raising the gavel. He paused, then began twirling it as he narrowed his eyes at Phylus. "But before we do, tell me something, Prime Minister Phylus. Is there anyone in our midst whom you believe to be a cause for concern?"

Phylus considered the circumstances with far greater deliberation than the question, keeping his watch in the corner of his eye. Truthfully, there was. Joren was The Politician, and there was no other way about it. But he had stood in clear support of the Task Force throughout the debate. He had even started the standing ovation.

It all could have been a ruse, though. In fact, his enthusiasm struck Phylus as overcompensating, quite to the point that it should have been obvious to everyone. But that ruse could have gone two ways. Either he was deflecting suspicion, or he wanted to unite The Avatars' most influential opponents so they'd be easier to hunt down. Guns, fish, and barrels.

Or, a third and far more distant possibility, he was trying to succeed where CreSam had failed. Work for The Avatars and use his influence to put them in shooting distance of the unified might of Ouristihra.

"No," Phylus said, knowing he might appear to be stalling if he thought it over any longer, "To the best of my knowledge, nobody here is associated with The Avatars of Fate."

"… Very well, then," Orthean conceded, "Voting will now begin for the free exchange of intelligence within the Ouristihran Union and Union Parliament concerning The Avatars of Fate. Establishing further details will be contingent upon the motion passing."

The motion moved across the table rather quickly, each aye coming with little hesitation. Even Zelphius and Naletas, despite their contrarian behavior, voted in favor with barely more than a hint of hostility and condescension. Orthean eyed Joren sidelong as he completed the unanimity of the vote and kept hold of the floor a moment longer.

"… and in the interest of unity," the Noble Doyen appended, "I am hereby calling off the ultimatum of war between Tanelen and ArcNos. I will notify General Sbaglien straight away."

"Doctor Caylence. Nice to meet you," the aging medical examiner greeted, "I understand you're here to identify a body."

"I am, yes," Sinkua said, offering the paper, "But I was told I'd be meeting with Doctor Seirakh."

"He went on leave," Caylence's younger assistant offered, shooting a disconcerted look past Sinkua, "Family emergency."

Sinkua nodded and watched Caylence look over his paper, stealing glimpses of the assistant. Something about Jevana put him off. Sinkua shoved his hands in his pockets, feigning nonchalance.

"Thank you, Sinkua. Everything checks out," Caylence said, "Uro. Pull the slab."

Sinkua noted the assistant's name. Though he dared not turn to check on her, he heard a faint swishing as Jevana shifted her weight. He couldn't risk tipping her off to his suspicion of her. Family emergency, indeed.

At Caylence's beckoning, Sinkua stood across from him over a blanketed body on a steel slab. Caylence folded the blanket back to Farim's collarbone.

With her face sunken and frozen in pain, she looked so much like Eytea. He grazed her cheek with his fingertips.

What shot through his mind wasn't so much a voice as thoughts and emotions taking shape. This manifestation, he realized, was emanating from his necklace.

"It is nice to convene with you once again," she said, "You may recall that I am known as Phoenix."

"My parents in this lifetime named me MeiLom," Sinkua thought back, "Takmet called me Sinkua as a mark of my Hybrid power."

"An appropriate name, coming from him. The Mberhali last knew you as Tsenukoa," Phoenix said, "This woman. She is important to you."

It wasn't a question. Sinkua nodded internally.

"Do you wish to know how she died?" Phoenix continued.

"These look like electrical burns," Sinkua thought.

"Sir, please don't touch the deceased without gloves," came Jevana's voice as though from the bottom of a well.

Sinkua realized his internal exchange was transpiring far more quickly than it would as a spoken conversation. Complete thoughts formed all at once, rather than stringing words together.

"Jevana, if you wish to give orders here, you're welcome to file for my job with HR," Caylence scolded with the same trilling and hollow affectation.

"She was poisoned," The Phoenix said, "Directly to the carotid artery."

"The burns are a scapegoat?"

"Yes. Her death was quick but painful."

"How do we do this?"

"You feel strongly enough about her to endure her pain," Phoenix affirmed, "Place your hand upon the left side of her neck."

"Sir? What are you doing?" Uro asked as Sinkua cupped Farim's jugular.

A stinging burn shot through Sinkua's neck, sharper than any blade he'd felt and hotter than any flame he'd manifested. It radiated from his own carotid artery toward his brain and heart. His breathing grew labored.

"By the ether…" Caylence gasped.

Sinkua opened his eyes, gritting his teeth as his circulatory system all but came to a boil. In the bottom of his peripheral vision, he saw intricate wings of fiery crimson milystis sprout from his necklace. Farim's face filled out, her skin regaining its usual olive tone.

Her eyes opened, and she inhaled deeply, arching her back. As she settled, her eyes fell to Sinkua, standing over her and cupping her neck. She gasped and threw her arms around his neck.

"Sweetums!" she exclaimed, pulling him down.

Sinkua leaned over Farim with his arms hanging deadweight. He became acutely aware of Caylence, Jevana, and Uro staring at them. It also didn't escape his notice that she had bared her chest and was now pressing her naked breasts against him. Quite to his chagrin with himself, his body didn't reflect his moral discomfort.

Farim nibbled on his earlobe and exhaled words barely above a whisper. "Play along, you big idiot."

Tamping down his remorse, he wrapped his arms around her and pulled her slightly upright. He planted a kiss on her jawline.

"I missed you so much," he choked out, "I just… I couldn't. I had to…"

"I know," Farim said, "Thank you. Thank you so much."

"What happened here?" Sinkua exhaled.

"Jevana," she whispered, "She poisoned me."

"I… suppose I should go pull her records," Jevana said, "Sorry, this is just… This is new territory."

"Do you want me to go with you?" Uro offered, "To corroborate, I mean."

"Stay here," Caylence ordered, "Let's wait in the office. Give these two a minute."

Farim and Sinkua kept their embrace until the room cleared out. After the last door closed, they pulled back. Still holding his shoulders, Farim smiled up at Sinkua. She leaned up and kissed him on the corner of his mouth, then pulled the sheet up to the point of modesty.

"That was just to thank you," she insisted, "Don't read anything else into it."

"I figured," he said, "I'm not sure I'll ever be in a place to take it as anything else."

"I know. You and Eytea were something else," Farim empathized, "You've always been hers, even before you realized it."

"That's a lot truer than you realize," Sinkua said, "I assume these burns on your chest are MalVek's handiwork."

"So, you know he's the turncoat that you suspected," Farim noted, "Yeah, he had this bigass hammer made of solid light. Laid me out, but it didn't quite kill me."

"He was covering for Jevana," he said, "But he could have just killed you himself. He must have plans for her."

"So keeping her here is just as important to him as getting rid of me."

"I have a hunch that Seirakh's absence has something to do with his noticing too much."

"I met him once. You're probably right," Farim said, "Okay. Go see about Jevana. I need to talk to Uro and Caylence. I think Uro is in cahoots with her."

At Orthean's beckoning, Galo stood to address the Assembly.

"Excavation on the annex island has uncovered the remnants of an old Avatar facility. Being near this facility has caused several people to fall ill," Galo began, "Bearing this in mind, we will withdraw from both inhabitation and research until further notice."

"Do you not have the means to protect your people from this illness?" Lenguardia's Governess Premier Subralis asked, "Whether it's medicine or protective equipment you need, I suspect it should be a relatively simple matter."

"The effort would be uneconomical. The spillage has contaminated the ground water, perhaps irreparably so."

"Perhaps, my people should be the judge of that," Orthean cut in, almost under his breath.

"In any case," Galo continued, "This has resulted in floral mutations far in excess of Berinin's Imported Species Regulatory Doctrines. Thus, we can't incorporate any of it into our medical research."

"You've clearly given this considerable thought, but if I might suggest something," Subralis said, "If you withdraw your governance of the annex, we could perhaps use it as a base of operations for this new Anti-Avatar Task Force."

"Tell me something, Governess Premier," Galo beckoned, "What's the going rate for sixty-two and a half cubic kilometers of concrete, twenty-five by twenty-five by zero-point-one?"

Subralis cocked her head as she took her phone from her pocket.

"In any case, in one year, that decision will no longer be mine," Galo continued. All eyes but Subralis's turned to him in greater earnest. "I've been weighing my options since I ascended to my position of Chieftain Sage. The time has come to withdraw. Not just for me as Chieftain Sage. But for my bloodline to withdraw as the political authority of Berinin. It has only been by blood that any of us have been inducted into this position, and genetics alone do not a leader make.

"The people deserve a voice in their federal government, just as they've long had in their district and city governments. In point of fact, the Chieftain Bloodline has been little more than a centerpiece. A sentimental decoration that serves no real function and sometimes gets in the way.

"Thus, I will reach out to Berinin's district and city governments to collaborate on developing a new form of federal government. If we have not reached a consensus in thirteen months, I will resign nonetheless and pass my authority to Berinin's Judge on an interim basis.

"I will be the last Chieftain Sage."

A deep hush fell over the Assembly. He suspected that those who had served when he placed Nenbard as Interim Chieftain Sage had expected that he might do this. But to hear it from his mouth was surreal. He was bringing several centuries of tradition to an end.

"You'd be looking at about nine trillion iolas," Subralis said, breaking through the pensive silence, "Of course, that's not accounting for a possible bulk discount."

Galo stared at the Governess Premier with an unreadable expression. He sighed, pinching the bridge of his nose.

"Naletas? Could you," he said, waving his hand urgingly, "bring our esteemed Governess Premier up to speed?"

"Of course," Naletas said, sounding respectable enough if not for the clicking of her tongue.

"Now, while they're doing that," Galo continued. He scratched the back of his ear as he made passing eye contact with Norum. "I think we can all agree that nine trillion iolas exceeds our combined budgets. Therefore, I propose we write the island off as a loss, rather than try to pave the whole damn thing. There are plenty of better qualified islands out there. Uninhabited, uncontaminated, and more geographically convenient."

"That much is obvious," Joren said, "What I would like to know is if anything of use has come of Berinin's occupation? You were quite firm on the notion that your people could extract the most utility out of it."

"As a matter of fact, there has been," Galo said, panning the Assembly again, "While searching the ruins with one of the research team leaders, we found the base and fragments of a statue in a subbasement. Soil analysis showed that it had not come from the annex or from the Berininite mainland. However, chemical analysis showed that the fragments share ninety-nine percent of their composition with the statue in Masnethege. Radiocarbon dating put them at roughly the same age as well."

"So, whoever created that statue of your ancestor made a statue of someone else, then?" Phylus asked, "Makes sense that they would have made more than one piece. But what would The Avatars want with it?"

"I'm getting to that," Galo said, "Now, we didn't find the entire face. But what we did find and reassemble had an uncanny resemblance to a particular recently deceased ex-Avatar."

"How could there be an antique statue of someone current?" Orthean argued, "You must be mistaken."

"Who did it look like?" Naletas asked, returning from her conversation with Subralis, "And what do you mean by ex-Avatar?"

"The Avatars don't take well to traitors," Norum said, "Could they have coated one in old molten copper?"

Everyone looked in bewilderment at the typically pacifistic Prime Duke.

"That would be like them, but that isn't the case," Galo said, "I met this one personally. He abducted and brainwashed me after they took me prisoner in ArcNos. Code name, The Prophet. Birth name, Pahres. After the Heniokhos Disaster, I learned he sacrificed himself to save three of my fellow Hybrids.

"That being said, I've put out some feelers for information on any other such statues."

Of course, much of what Galo had said was untrue. Everything about the tests, at least. All of his information had come from Leviathan, but he couldn't exactly say he had heard it from the quasi-magical talking serpent who lived on his arm. He just needed them to think he was searching for data and closing in on a breakthrough.

"Well, getting back to the matter of your resignation," Naletas said, "You can't just announce it, and that's the end of it."

"Actually, I…" Galo began.

"No. Not actually," she scolded, "Any federal overhaul must first be approved by the Ouristihran Union and the Union Parliament. Spril went through it, and so did CreSam before him."

"Actually!" Galo said, "I don't need your approval. My ancestors saw to that. Specifically, Chieftain Sage Fentak, I believe."

"He's talking about the Reestablishment Protocol," Norum said, "Chieftain Bloodline surrenders its authority, and the Sacred City of Masnethege is disbanded. That being said, Galo, the statue of your ancestor will be protected under the Historical Preservation Act."

"I'm familiar with the Reestablishment Protocol," Subralis scolded, "But there's the problem of local approval. Without that, he'll need special permission from us to proceed."

"Well, I'm not having a Chieftain Heir any time soon," Galo said, "But if that means I need additional clearance from the Ouristihran Union, then let's be on with it."

"And your Judge?"

"What about him?"

"Judge Nenbard was recently murdered," Subralis said, "His advisor is attending today's Union Parliament Assembly in his place."

"Wait. You're serious?" Galo gasped. Naletas nodded. "This is the first I'm hearing about this. Do we… Do we have any idea who was responsible?"

"His wife, Sanus," Orthean provided, "According to Ocronn, she had become some kind of monster."

Galo muttered a long-winded expletive.

"I'm sorry, but how were you not aware of this?" Zelphius asked, his voice far less contrite than he claimed, "All three of them were involved in your annex research, were they not?"

"I've been out of the country for personal diplomatic reasons," Galo said, shooting a pensive glare at Joren, "Phylus's daughter asked for my help rescuing her half sister. Both of them being Hybrids."

"We're all familiar with the Hybrids' capabilities to some extent," Zelphius said, "Was that really the most necessary place for you to be? It would seem to me, to all of us, that one Hybrid would be sufficient to rescue another."

"As a matter of fact, it was necessary," Galo insisted, "Only five Hybrids have been born in the past twenty-six years, the last having been sixteen years ago. We thought we found another, an older one, but he turned out to be a willing genetic experiment from The Avatars of Fate. Do you know what came of our trusting him? The Heniokhos Disaster.

"One of us was killed in the process. Twenty percent of the Hybrid population, gone in an instant that I still see too fucking vividly damn near every night. So, no. If one of us is taken, the only sufficient response is for as many of us as possible to rain vengeance upon their captors."

"Very well, then," Zelphius conceded, "The issue of the Chieftain Heir notwithstanding, would you be willing to wait until a new Judge has been elected?"

"No."

"Okay, so we're voting on whether Chieftain Sage Galo can proceed with the Reestablishment Protocol with neither a Chieftain Heir nor a Judge," High Magistrate Orthean announced, "Let's begin."

"Somebody…" Farim shouted, throwing the door open with enough force to crack the drywall, "… needs to explain what the hell is going on here."

"Your guess is as good as ours, Farim," Caylence said, rising to approach her, "By all sensibilities, it's impossible, but…"

"Not that. Not you," Farim cut off. She held her bedsheet shut with one hand as she thrust her finger at Uro. "You!"

"Look, what you need to understand about Uro…"

"That's enough, Uncle," Uro interrupted, "I'm done hiding. What do you need to know, Farim?"

"You're the one who called about the outbreak," she observed, "That's why you barely spoke last time I was here. So I wouldn't recognize your voice later."

"Yes, that was me on the phone. But that wasn't why I was so quiet," Uro confessed, "My mouth tends to get me in trouble. So, I try to keep it shut."

"Did you know what you were getting involved in?" Farim demanded, "Answer honestly, or I'll shove a straw in your ear and drink your brain. Remember, I'm a zombie now. Don't put it past me."

"No. Well, sort of. Um…" Uro stammered, "Look, I've had a sort of on-again, off-again thing with Jevana. But I realized it's like an addiction. She tempts me to do things that I know I shouldn't. But I do them anyway. I get in trouble. She gets out untouched. But I always convince myself that it was my idea. Because sex. So yeah, I knew nothing good would come of it. But this? It never occurred to me that she might kill you."

Farim sighed as she sat down at an unoccupied workstation. She scanned the office as she let Uro's story settle in her thoughts. On the coat rack, she noticed two jackets with the same unfamiliar logo of a swan silhouette wearing some kind of belt. Tucked in the back of Caylence's workstation was a curled hand-written letter. That much was unremarkable, but it looked to have been closed with a wax seal. Those had fallen out of favor years ago.

"So, you did know that she's the one who killed me?" she asked, tucking the curiosities in the back of her mind.

"Seirakh figured it out. Jevana doesn't know I overheard him."

"And she killed him over it?"

"I think so," Uro said, his voice breaking.

"Shit," Farim spat, "How long has she been in contact with The Avatars of Fate?"

"I don't know. I think it started after what happened to Uulan," he said, "But ever since I realized it, I've been trying to cut myself off from her. Without her noticing I'm trying, of course."

"Of course," she said.

"I've been telling you to break off that cunt for years," Caylence snarked. Farim glared at him as she snatched a pen and unscrewed the tip. Caylence turned his palms forward. "Sorry. Sorry. See, she got him in deep shit with every supervisor he had upstairs. So, I asked the administrators to put him down here. Told them the fewer living people he was around, the less trouble he could get in. Which is true. I love my nephew, but the boy's got a mouth with or without her. But it was more about getting him away from her."

Farim reassembled the pen and set it down, her face softening. As much as she resented Caylence's disrupting the rapport she was building with Uro, she had to respect his devotion to his nephew.

"Well, at least one of you has done something," she said, "So, how did you figure out she'd gotten involved with The Avatars?"

"Shortly before she had me call you, she was talking about breaking a designer drug into the black market," Uro said, "I suspect it has something to do with the substance from Uulan's IV bag. I thought maybe I could slip you some info on the sly and maybe you could figure it out."

"Son of a bitch," Farim muttered, smearing her hands down her face, "So, the outbreak is real?"

"It's isolated for now, but yes," Uro said, "Incidentally, why did you still come after I told you I had the wrong number?"

"I thought it was a cry for help," Farim said, "I've seen what The Avatars are capable of. Your only chance of living to see outside help could have been through plausible deniability."

"No, that was just me chickening out," Uro said, "Lucky for me, I guess. Not so much for you, but I mean…"

"Well, I'm alive now, and I don't think you were in on it anyway," she reasoned as she got to her feet, "So, you need to come with me."

"Where are we going?" Uro asked.

"I sent Sinkua upstairs to find Jevana. We're going to catch up with them," Farim explained, "and we're going to expose that bitch."

"And then what? I mean…"

"Stick with me, and I can offer you protection in exchange for information."

"So… Does this mean you're not going to eat my brain?"

Farim laughed. "Uro. Please," she said, "Stop being so gullible with women."

Galo tapped Phylus's coffee cup with his own as the Prime Minister eased down beside him on the steps. Beyond a tilt of the chin, he offered no other acknowledgment. His eyes fixated on a large upcropping of Yggdrasil's roots, but his mind was scattered in a few elsewheres. The gentle chill rain bent to fall around, but never on them.

"Convenient," Phylus said, gesturing to the dome of raindrops. Galo grunted and sipped his coffee. "Hey, I just wanted to thank you again for helping Nikasu and Vielle."

"Like I said, I was just doing what needed to be done."

"Doesn't mean I don't appreciate it," Phylus argued. Silence lingered for a moment. "Hell of a meeting, hey?"

"Certainly more eventful than usual," Galo said, sipping his coffee. He drank more for the warmth on his throat than for the caffeine and even more than for the taste. "Before you ask, I have thought it through, and I am serious."

"It's not my place to question your judgment."

"As long as we're clear on that," he said. His eyes cast down between his feet. "Speaking of Nikasu," he continued, turning to face Phylus, "I think it's only fair to tell you that, as we were leaving the facility, she kissed me. Mostly on the mouth."

Phylus gave him a level look. Galo returned the expression, maintaining it only briefly before he swallowed hard. The corners of Phylus's mouth twitched up.

"Why did you think you needed to tell me that?"

"Well, for all intents and purposes, you've become her father."

"Sure, but it's obvious that you two have been falling for each other," Phylus said, "I'm not going to interfere with that. I'm aware of the age difference, but I'm also aware that you're both special cases. You won't hurt her. In fact, she wouldn't be as safe with anyone else as she'll be with you."

"That's nice of you to say, but I still can't be with her," Galo insisted, "No matter how much I might want her."

"Might?" Phylus chuckled, "Why not? If it's because Vielle disapproves, don't let that stop you. She means well, but understanding boundaries has never been her strong suit."

"No, not that. It's…" Galo trailed off, hesitating as his eyes cast along an encroaching shadow. Joren approached, clutching a black umbrella. Galo's words slipped out as his focus shifted to the Noble Doyen. "I'm dying."

Phylus turned to face Galo. "Hold that thought," he ordered. He rose to meet Joren with a stiff handshake. "Noble Doyen."

"Prime Minister," Joren said, "I thought it best to clear the air in less mixed company. Ask me whatever you'd like."

"Great. For starters, what brought about your decision to call off the ultimatum?"

"Phylus…?" Galo cut in. Phylus gripped his shoulder.

"Would you like the official story or the truth?" Joren asked.

"Both," Phylus insisted, "Official first."

"Our intelligence found that the catalyst who had brought us to the brink of war had been brought to justice," Joren explained, "We've also noticed a growing volunteer restoration effort at the site of the Heniokhos Disaster, led by multiple Prime and High Ministers."

"Right," Phylus nodded, "And the truth?"

"War with ArcNos no longer suits my agenda," Joren said, "Nor did having LenSom as my apprentice."

"Care to elaborate?" Phylus implored, "EshCal suspects you're The Politician, but I'm getting mixed signals."

"I am, but it isn't what you think," Joren said, "Being so culturally and economically isolated, Tanelen will be lucky to sustain itself beyond another century. I enlisted with The Avatars for the betterment of my people's way of life."

"I knew a man who got neck-deep with them to strengthen his country," Phylus mused, "He ended up burying more than half his citizens and drowned in his own hubris. What makes you think you'll end up any different?"

"Because I've learned from CreSam's mistakes," Joren said, "I have no delusions of destroying The Avatars of Fate."

"Then why have you elected to join the Task Force?" Galo scolded.

"I envy your idealism, but I'm not so naïve as to think it's possible to destroy them," Joren answered, "They're too vast, too ubiquitous, and too pervasive. I seek to redefine them as a positive force for Ouristihra."

"That's at least as lofty a goal as destroying them," Phylus argued, "Despite several setbacks, we've made considerable progress these past few years."

"Oh, you've cut through The Named quite handily. Eliminating The Scout and The Hunter crippled their recruitment and assassination capacities. And now, you've gutted their capacity for building new armies by taking down The Engineer and The Geneticist," Joren explained, "But there are thousands of operatives available to take their place. Besides, even with The Prophet gone, there are still two other populous influencers, The General and myself. I do still need to operate within their parameters after all."

"What about The Investigator?" Phylus asked.

"Not a matter for the open," Joren excused, his eyes darting about the parking lot, "Now, from the outside, it's easy to think this means they're on the ropes. And I say that with no disrespect. But in reality, it makes it easier for any one of The Named to change the direction of the organization. Hell, we've had about a dozen interpretations of The Epimetheus Trial in the past ten years alone."

"Which means The General has just as much pull with The Harvester as you," Phylus reasoned, "And you don't like what he's doing with it."

"Not in the slightest. He embodies their worst aspects taken to unspeakable extremes," Joren spat, "If I need to turn on him to protect my interests and my people, then so be it. Once that living carbuncle has been taken care of, I'll be able to redefine The Avatars' agenda."

"The General," Phylus acknowledged, "You're talking about MalVek, are you not?"

"Yes. And I'm aware enough of his history with you and yours to know we have a mutual enemy in him."

"Excuse me," Galo cut in, "How do you expect either of us to trust you when you just recently ordered MalVek to kill me?"

Joren gave him a puzzled look. "That... order was for both of you."

"Oh, well, in that case, how naïve of me," Galo scathed, his voice dripping with sarcasm, "You and I are not colleagues inside those facilities."

"No. No. No. That doesn't matter," Joren grunted, pinching the bridge of his nose, "I can manipulate people with the sound of my voice."

"As in mind control?" Galo asked.

"It's more like a faster and more reliable form of hypnosis," Joren explained, "I can't make anyone do anything they absolutely don't want to do. But if there's the slightest desire or even the slightest doubt to their aversion, I can compound it. The easiest things are neutral orders. I suppose the best way to explain it is show me your thumbs."

So abruptly did his cadence shift that Galo became aware of it as he noticed he was giving Joren a double thumbs-up. Phylus had done the same, and they looked at each other as though agreeing to keep a dirty secret. They both shoved their hands in their pockets.

"What the hell was that?" Galo asked. He directed his thoughts toward Leviathan. "Where were you on that one?"

"He caught me by surprise," Leviathan answered, "Better you know the extent of his power though."

"A test," Joren said, "I had to be sure you weren't immune to my powers. Then, how did you both leave there alive? It couldn't be that you're purely disinclined to kill him. I believe I overheard Phylus saying you've fallen for the girl you had come to rescue from him."

"You overheard correctly," Galo nodded, "I had stood too near the bells and horns back at the docks. Sleep deprived stupor. My ears were still ringing."

"Ahh. I suppose that would explain it," Joren said, "Well, I trust that the next time you're alone with him, I won't need to compel you."

"Depends on whether I think he's useful to us alive anymore."

"In that case, give me some time to compile what I have on him," Joren pleaded, his voice even, "I'll try to have it to you by the end of next week. Meanwhile, keep looking into those ancient statues."

Without waiting for confirmation, Joren turned and walked away from Galo and Phylus. He took out his phone, dialing as he walked, and a car rounded the corner and pulled up to the curb moments after he reached it.

"So, the mutations on the annex," Phylus said, "Is that what's killing you?"

"No," Galo said, his attention returning to the upcropping of roots, "I'll explain when more of us are together. Easier that way."

"Okay then."

"So, do you trust him?"

"I don't see that we have any other choice," Phylus said, "But I'll keep him at arm's length for the time being."

"Likewise," Galo said, "What about that business about The Scout and The Hunter?"

"What about it?"

"If his logic adds up, The Harvester's decision to deploy them so early doesn't. Why would someone with a supernatural capacity for forecasting and manipulating the future risk agents whose deaths would cripple his enterprise?"

"Excuse me, sirs," a third voice interjected.

Galo and Phylus had been so wrapped up in their conversation that they hadn't noticed the strange woman approaching them. She was hunched over and draped in bulky shawls and blankets. She clutched a birdcage, draped with a blanket of its own.

Galo leaned for a better view of her face. "Elemeno?" Galo asked, "What are you doing here? And why the disguise?"

"I'll give you the short version, dear," Elemeno said, straightening up as Galo extended the rain barrier to encompass her, "Farim was killed. This bird will lead us to her body. NalSet is looking for Sinkua. He has the power to resurrect her. The disguise is because I can't trust everyone here."

"Well, you can tell NalSet to call off the search," Phylus said, "Sinkua has already gone to Hillside Oncology to bring Farim back."

"Really?" Elemeno asked, "How did he find out?"

"Hillside called Vielle to ask her to confirm Farim's identity. She offered to send Sinkua in her place. She asked me for his and Farim's Parliamentary ArcNos papers to prove their connection," Phylus explained, "He should have met with Doctor Seirakh this morning."

Elemeno's phone rang. She turned her back as she answered. The conversation was brief, and her voice stayed low. She faced them again as she pocketed her phone.

"That was NalSet," she said, "You were right."

Chapter 19

Sinkua rifled through Farim's mortuary folder as the elevator climbed to the ground floor. As he worked backward, he learned she had already been dead by the time someone got to her with a crash cart. Jevana had ordered said crash cart. And the attack had taken place in the bone cancer ward at the east end of Surgical Access A.

He muttered under his breath as he walked, trying to commune with Phoenix the way he figured Galo did with Leviathan. His necklace had nothing to say to him.

Sinkua stopped at a directory only long enough to locate the bone cancer ward. A couple of turns and an elevator ride put him at the west end. He paused at a fire escape floor plan, where he found a route to the east end of Surgical Access A.

Nobody was around. The entire bone cancer ward, he had found, was sparsely populated.

He pulled a chair under a security camera. By no stretch was he an expert on the things, but he had read up on them since he stole that one from the abandoned lab. This was another closed-circuit system. No tape to steal. He needed a backup plan.

Sinkua snatched the notepad and pen from beside a wall-mounted phone and scrawled a message in the thickest lettering he could fit on the page. He pulled the chair in front of the camera, stood on it, and covered the lens with his hand. Figuring the black screen had gotten the security guard's attention, he hopped down and held up the notepad with a simple message.

"Back up cams for this hall. Past week. Sabotage probable."

Blind to any possibility of closure, he lowered the notepad after about a minute. He ripped off the page he'd written on and stuffed it in his pocket. He returned the notepad to its spot on the wall and, finding a directory, located the records office.

Sinkua focused on his ire as he made his way there. Thanks to Yggdrasil, he no longer had any risk of slipping into an episode. But he still needed part of that package. He still needed that fury to shake a confession out of Jevana. Were he having an episode, he would scarcely have been lucid enough to manage it. Not to any legally admissible extent. However, at any other time, he could only exert such aggression toward clear and immediate threats.

He couldn't count on that with Jevana. She had waited to strike until Farim was too vulnerable to fight back. She may have only been MalVek's pawn, but she was clever enough to only engage when she had the upper hand. Or the only hand.

His stint with the Ministry of Foreign Affairs was of no use here either. This had gone beyond the point of diplomacy. So, his only tool was to recall the pain, Farim's dying pain, that he had endured through Phoenix, knowing that Jevana had inflicted it upon her.

The door to the records office had a key card scanner and no doorknob. But regardless of the electromagnetic lock, the rest of it was an ordinary door and thus little match for brute force and intense heat.

Sinkua slammed the bottom of his boot against the strike plate, erupting a split-second plume of flames. The door broke the frame, scattering wood splinters, and pried the hinge screws out of the frame.

The entire room, all but one, turned to face him. He grabbed the top of the door, boring his red-hot fingers into the wood, and ripped it the rest of the way off the frame.

"Jevana!" he bellowed, the last person turning to him, "I need to have a word with you."

Ocronn kept his nose in his papers while the ArcNosian Judge presented her case. He had no authority to speak or vote on anyone else's matters. Besides, he was there to deliver Nenbard's final message. Nothing more.

He did pick up fragments of her case on the edge of his awareness. No details, only enough to catch the gist of the subject. She spoke at length about ownership and control of the Subtransit.

Ocronn knew the previous owner had been killed in an Avatar terrorist attack. He also knew that she may have been targeted. This added up to his knowing just enough to know it was unsafe to learn more.

He lost himself deeply enough in his work to not catch the outcome of the vote. Or even who they were voting on for ownership and control. He felt Grand Sultan Zelphius's eyes upon him and came to attention.

"Standing in for the recently deceased Judge Nenbard, we have…?"

"Ocronn, sir. Advisor and brother-in-law to the Late Judge."

"Very well, Ocronn," Zelphius said, "I suppose by these documents that you have missives from Nenbard?"

"I do," Ocronn said, swallowing hard.

"Very well, then. When you're ready."

Ocronn jogged his papers straight. "As many of us are aware, ArcNos has been in perpetual turmoil since the Heniokhos Disaster," he began, "Ground zero has gone unaddressed beyond a minimally resourced group of volunteers gathered around various Ministries authorities. This has put many, both domestically and abroad, under the impression that the government is neglecting its people.

"The truth, as usual, is more complicated. Due to ongoing circumstances, the Ministry of Infrastructure lacks the resources to carry out the restoration. Their only option is to outsource to the private sector. However, the one company which can take on this project has exploited the situation. The estimate they have given is three times the calculated market standard, and they refuse to negotiate.

"This being a legal conflict between Entities of the People and Entities of the State, this must be brought to the Union Parliament. Therefore, Judge Nenbard's final order was to vote for the organization in question to lower its estimate to within ten percent of market standard or, failing that, to be more open to negotiations."

Silence swept the room. Settling such conflicts was a quagmire of an affair, what with all the conflicts of interest and the generous definition of that concept. The last time it happened had been with Imperial ArcNos forcing people out of their jobs and homes. Just enough of just the right people had been bribed, threatened, or otherwise coerced to force a verdict in favor of the State. They had been rare before, but since then, nobody had dared bring such a conflict before the Union Parliament.

"Suppose the Ministries try to take more than they deserve," the ArcNosian Judge began, "exploiting tragedy to get labor at a markdown. Will Chieftain Sage Galo offer this same courtesy? Would he speak against a fellow Entity of the State in the interest of a foreign Entity of the People?"

"I'm not at liberty to speak on his behalf," Ocronn said, "But he's a man of enough honor and decency that I would be surprised if he didn't."

"Unfortunately, you are not at liberty to put matters up to a vote," Zelphius interjected.

"Then why ask if I had missives from Nenbard?" Ocronn scolded.

"Out of respect," the Grand Sultan said, "Allowing you to bring these matters before us was a personal choice. However, the Union Parliament can only vote on issues presented by a democratically elected Judge. I'm sorry, but it is not within my authority to change that."

"... Understood, Grand Sultan Zelphius, sir."

Ocronn sat down and pried a rolled-up paperback out of his coat pocket. By sometime between the Haprianite Judge and Ivarian Judge, he managed to tune out anything that any of them were saying.

Soon, though, the feeling of eyes upon him pulled at his attention. As he looked up, he found the Tanelenese Judge standing to speak, facing him with her arm extended toward him. One by one, the rest of them looked his way. And when all eyes were on him, the Tanelenese Judge spoke just three words.

"What he said."

"You'll need a disguise," Uro said as they walked out of the research office.

"Already on it," Farim said as she wound her hair into a tight bun.

She rifled through the staff wardrobe and came up with a set of basic scrubs as well as a surgical cap and mask. Farim hid behind the wardrobe door as she changed out of the clutched bedsheet. With the mask hanging under her chin, she borrowed a makeup kit from someone's personal effects. She lightened her complexion with foundation, recalling a scarcity of Midlanders when she had arrived. She then applied a touch of eyeliner and let her eyelids droop a bit.

She pulled up the mask and shut the wardrobe door. "Would you recognize me?" she asked.

"Not for a while, no," Uro said, "By the way, I think your friend stole your folder."

"What makes you say that?"

"It isn't here."

"Right. Obviously," Farim sighed, "Okay. Change of plans."

Inside the elevator, Farim stared up at the numerical floor display with her hands locked behind her back. She could feel Uro watching her, as though he was hoping she would break the silence.

"So, the new plan?" he asked.

"I told Sinkua to go see about Jevana. I meant for him to draw out her connection to MalVek," Farim explained, "But if I know him half as well as I think I do, he took it to mean I wanted her to confess to killing me. And for him to do something about it."

"And we're going to help?" Uro asked, "I mean with the confession. Not with the... um... doing something about it."

"We'll sit it out unless he needs us or he risks us losing the trail between her and MalVek. Things will get messy if we rush to intervene. She could play our cases against each other or use the confusion as a diversion."

Uro took the lead when they reached the ground floor. Farim noticed he used the wall-mounted directories to find his way to the records office. But he observed them and moved on so fluidly that Farim kept quiet about it.

A security guard looked them over as they came into an administrative hall. He gave the incognito Farim a passing glance, then set his eyes on Uro. He walked slightly bow-legged, as though he'd sprung from his seat with sleeping legs.

"Uro! What are you doing here?" the guard called out as they came together, stopping just beyond arm's reach, "Eh, nevermind that. Is Seirakh… sorry… I mean… Is Caylence downstairs?"

"Yeah, he's…" Uro hesitated, "What's going on? Didn't he answer the phone?"

"I need to tell him in person. It's ah…" the guard said, turning to Farim as he trailed off, "Sorry. Do you mind?"

"Sorry. I'll be over there," Farim said, the mask muffling her fake Feryan accent and compensating for how unconvincing it was.

She stepped away and turned her back, shallowing her breathing so she could just make out their conversation.

"You know that Midlander what got assaulted in Osteo?" the guard asked, "The one with Jevana?"

"Farim. Yeah," Uro nodded, "We've got her downstairs. What about her?"

"Well, some scruffy bloke popped up on the feed in that hall. Said to back up the files in case of sabotage," the guard explained, "Now, I've looked them over a dozen times, yeah. But I think, might as well make it a baker's. So I give it a real close one and get this. When Jevana crouched next to her? She stuck her in the neck with something. That some shit or what?"

"Yeah, that's… weird," Uro muddled, "I don't know what to make of that. I mean… Shit."

"Right? I know you two are… whatever, but…" the guard fumbled, "You need to keep your distance. I mean, she might've killed somebody."

"No, I get it. It's just a lot to process is all," Uro said, "Well anyway, go tell Caylence. And thank you for telling me."

Farim returned to Uro's side as the guard walked past her, and they resumed their search, finding the straightaway to the records office only moments later.

"How do you want to do this?" Uro asked.

Farim bared her wrist and pulled the surgical mask off her nose. She smelled the soft side of her wrist and let the scent linger deep in her olfactory. She then covered her wrist and breathed deeply of the surrounding air.

"He hasn't been here yet," Farim asserted, "We'll wait nearby. Inconspicuous, but not obviously so."

"Did you just scent track your friend?" Uro asked.

"Pyromancy and a love of pomegranates and fried meats give him a very distinct odor," Farim explained, "I got some on me when I hugged him."

"Hold on. Have you been planning for this since you, well, came back?"

Farim's wolfish smile stretched the borrowed surgical mask. Uro shifted his weight.

"No, that was just lucky," she chuckled, "Anyway, let's…"

She trailed off and paused as a stout older man stopped before them, sizing her up with his beady eyes. He stood close enough that she could count the age lines in his craggy features. As much as she hoped he wouldn't recognize her, his disrespect for personal space didn't bode well.

"Farim?" he asked.

"NalSet," Farim nodded, keeping the mask on, "You're looking rather… bipedal. What are you doing here?"

"I originally came here to find Sinkua. Got word he had headed this way," NalSet said, "But, he's already done what I needed him to do. So now, I just need to send you to headquarters."

"And you think you're in a position to give me orders?"

"We need your help," he insisted, "Dourias needs your help."

"What happened to him?"

"Nothing anymore. It's…" he trailed off as his eyes darted to Uro, "Son, if you're not already neck-deep with The Avatars of Fate, you need to walk away before you hear too much."

"He's already neck-deep."

"Son of a bitch. What's his story?" NalSet asked. He pivoted to Uro. "What's your story, son?"

"Well, sir, there's this drug, and ah…" Uro fumbled.

"The stuff from Uulan's bag is still a problem," Farim said, "Someone dropped the trout on the disposal. Uro's a key witness."

"There's a black market release in progress," Uro said, "Possible staged outbreak."

NalSet muttered an elaborate string of expletives.

"Okay, so what happened to Dourias?" Farim demanded, "Or no longer happened?"

"When you died, a sympathetic reaction from the tracker implant killed him," NalSet recounted, "But he's alive again. Chekov called and told me a few minutes ago. Said his heart started as abruptly as it'd stopped. He's sleeping it off."

"That explains why it never made it beyond the prototype phase."

"We think it's how MalVek exposed him. Tempted him with some erroneous tech intel."

"It's a sound theory," Farim said, "No way that level of entanglement happened by accident."

"I thought the same. So did Elemeno, matter of fact," NalSet said, "Now, as for what we need from you, Dourias tattooed himself with diagrams of all the intel he picked up. Tsora-magnetic. Reacts to Chekov."

"Clever."

"Incredibly. Trouble is, he can't decipher it."

"And you want me to try?" Farim gleaned.

"You and Chekov have the best shot."

"I'll be ready to go as soon as Sinkua comes back."

"Where is he now?"

"He's looking for Jevana. The nurse who killed me," Farim said, "I sent him to draw out her connection to MalVek. But I don't think he took it that way."

"She's in the records office," Uro added, "It's around the corner. The only way inside is with a key card."

"I'll wait nearby. Here," NalSet said, slapping something into Farim's outstretched hand, "You two wait in the parking lot. I'll tell Sinkua where to find you."

Farim looked down at the portal strip. "What about you?"

"MalVek will come back once he knows you're alive," NalSet said, "I'm going to have a word with him."

"No. No way," Farim argued, "If MalVek's coming, I'm not going to…"

"I know. You're not going to walk away. Not after what he's done. I get it. But you? You don't," NalSet scolded, "I know what he's done. I know better than anybody. Everybody wants a piece of him, but do not forget that he is my brother. The line starts far behind me."

"… Fine," Farim accepted, looking over the portal strip, "So, how do…?"

"I'll tell Sinkua," NalSet interrupted, "Can't risk you leaving without him."

"I wouldn't…"

"Uro," he cut off again, "When you get where they're taking you, tell Chekov and Aleepo everything you know about this black market outbreak. Are we clear?"

"Crystal, sir," Uro said.

NalSet nodded to him and walked away, taking his phone out of his pocket. Farim rolled up the portal strip and stuffed it in the borrowed scrubs.

"Well," she sighed, "Let's go."

"You two have history?" Uro pried.

"We were in the Subtransit Resistance," Farim said, "And I recently shot his kneecap off."

Uro's mouth hung open.

"Strictly business," she added.

"How is he…?" he stammered.

"Uro, you've just opened your world to all kinds of weird shit."

Galo and Elemeno sat in idle banter under the late afternoon sun. Phylus had left some time ago, reasoning that he couldn't keep his driver waiting any longer.

Galo didn't have the luxury of a personal driver. Nor had any of his predecessors, not since the automobile had risen to prevalence. Masnethegean tradition dictated as much, custom being that a federal authority's personal driver be a native and resident of their capital. This left him not just at the mercy of taxi services but at the leisure of departing no sooner than he was ready.

At Elemeno's behest, NalSet had promised to send Farim and Sinkua to see her. Some new acquaintance would be tagging along as well. They were taking longer than either of them expected, though. Which was no trouble because Galo had meant to give his condolences to Ocronn, and the Union Parliament Assembly was running quite long.

Through all the waiting, the birdcage had remained draped in a blanket. Beyond Elemeno's word, only the occasional squeaking of its perch assured Galo that there actually was a bird inside.

The sun was just beginning to consider setting when the Judges emerged from the Union Parliament Assembly Hall. Galo got to his feet and offered Elemeno his hand. As he helped her upright, he reached for the birdcage. As soon as she saw this, though, she slapped his hand away, taking the cage as her own burden.

As they approached the bottom of the stairs, Galo found himself in uncomfortable eye contact with Ocronn. He looked as somber and forlorn as Galo had expected.

"Ocronn," Galo nodded as they came within conversational distance, "You have my deepest condolences. I apologize for not speaking with you sooner. There is no excuse for my neglect."

"Thank you," Ocronn said, "But I'm not interested in explanations. The less I know, the better."

"As you wish it," Galo conceded, "Well, you might be glad to know that the Reestablishment Protocol has passed."

"As overdue as we are for a democratic government, I suspect it won't matter much longer," Ocronn lamented.

Galo sighed and nodded, more in comprehension than agreement. They stood in awkward silence for a moment until Ocronn turned to Elemeno.

"Do you mind, Northlander?" he insisted, "We have business to discuss before I go. The sort that civilians shouldn't be present for."

"Any Avatar business that I need to know about, Elemeno can know as well," Galo said, "That is what this is about, isn't it?"

"It is, but..." Ocronn said, trailing off as he looked Elemeno over, "... She's really involved? Can't think what they'd want with her."

"Young man, I've been involved since before you got your first inopportune erection," Elemeno scolded, "I'm the mother of a Hybrid."

"I'm sorry to hear that," Ocronn said.

Elemeno's open palm clapped across Ocronn's face, hardly disturbing the blankets draped over her shoulders. Ocronn opened his mouth in protest.

"Her daughter just died. So, whatever you think you need to say to her, no, you don't," Galo admonished, "Now, what business did you wish to discuss with me?"

"Fine then," Ocronn sighed, turning away from Elemeno, "First off, I know who Aleepo really is. But don't worry. I have no interest in profiting from this information. Nor in knowing how it happened."

"The less you know, the better?" Galo asked.

"Exactly as much," Ocronn continued, "I just thought it polite to inform you. I left him a note at my house, so I'd estimate he knows by now as well."

"Thank you for that. I'm glad he's had such good friends," Galo said, "Will that be all then?"

"Not quite," Ocronn said, thrusting the satchel into Galo's hands, "These are all of Nenbard's notes on Sanus's infection. Whatever you learn from them, I insist you don't connect any of it to me. Can I ask that much of you?"

"Of course, Ocronn," Galo said, "And thank you. This might help me save a lot of people. Sanus and Nenbard's sacrifice won't have been in vain."

"Don't call it that," Ocronn said, "They didn't die preserving this knowledge. They were killed by how they came into it. Because your father and his father involved them in matters they had no need to be a part of."

"Be that as it may," Galo dismissed, "I'm sure I can put this information to good use. There are others like Sanus, and..."

"Stop," Ocronn cut in, "Don't tell me anything that might keep me involved any longer. After this, you and I are parting ways for the last time."

"Where are you going?"

"Away."

"You're not...?"

"No, just living afar."

"Well, good luck with that," Galo said, "You'll truly be missed."

"I need you to listen to me, Galo. I understand that some people, people like yourselves, never had a choice. And you have my sympathy for that. But for those of us who do have a choice, you have to respect that right,"

Ocronn scolded, "It doesn't matter if you agree with our decisions. You must respect that they are ours to make. So, stop plying me with your platitudes."

"I'm not trying to guilt you into staying. I would never try to stop anyone who could walk away from all of this from doing just that," Galo explained, choking back his doubt that he had never done so, "Not intentionally anyway. So, go. And may you find peace."

Ocronn turned and walked away, apparently satisfied with getting his point across. Once he was out of earshot, Elemeno straightened up to her usual posture and discarded the blankets.

"Well, he was a proper ass," she snarked, "Had a bit of a point, yeah, but still rather an ass."

"No. He's not," Galo said, "He was disconnecting himself."

Sinkua closed the distance between himself and Jevana in slow, swaggering strides. Everyone else scrambled out of the room, keeping their distance as dodging his eyes. He swiped at one who came too close, snagging him by the collar and pulling him to his side.

"You're going to call security, aren't you?" Sinkua asked.

"N... No. No! I..."

"It's cool. I want you to."

"You... want me to call security?"

"Yes. Khirsan has my belongings."

Sinkua crossed the rest of the records office, stopping so near to Jevana that she had to crane her neck to see his face. She glared up at him.

"Well?" she demanded, "That was all rather uncalled for. Especially if you've got nothing to say."

"Why did you kill Farim?"

She stepped back, her face screwing up with incredulity. "What? I would never..." she stammered, "It was that older bloke with the hammer. You saw the bruises. Do I look I could swing a hammer hard enough to do that?"

His temple throbbed at her insolence. Tension ran down his neck and along his shoulders, spreading down his arms.

"What about the poison in her neck?"

Her face hardened and paled. "What are you talking about?"

"We'll just say a little bird told me," Sinkua said, "It was also in her death records."

"That's impossible!" Jevana cried, "I..."

"Silenced Seirakh? I know. But that didn't keep what you did off of Farim's records," Sinkua scolded, his breath heating, "Either you're not as clever as you think, or Caylence isn't as foolish as you think. And your scraggly boyfriend won't cover your ass this time."

"Uro's not my boyfriend."

"Fine! The guy whose dick you suck so you can get away with your bullshit," he snarled, "Thanks for confirming everything I suspected, by the way."

Jevana swiped at his face with the back of her hand, but he tilted just out of her reach and grabbed her wrist.

"Now, I'm sure MalVek told you plenty about me. Probably that I'm unstable when I'm angry. But what he probably didn't tell you," Sinkua said, "is that I'm quite particular about the well-beings of the women in my life. And I've got a penchant for vigilantism."

"What…" Jevana rasped, struggling against his grasp, "What's your point? You're going to kill me for killing Farim?"

"Maybe. Maybe not. She is alive again, after all," Sinkua reasoned, "Besides, I left all my poison needles with my other pants. And my photon hammer is out for repairs. So, I'll have to settle for the next best thing."

In a single motion, he clenched his fist, set it ablaze, and plowed it into her chest. The impact and momentum lifted her a few centimeters and drove her back, sending her staggering into a file cabinet.

Jevana clutched her chest, her breathing labored and ragged. She lifted one trembling finger, never taking her eyes off him, and settled it behind her earlobe. She muttered under her breath, then let her hand fall to her side.

"Oh," she choked, "Oh, you are in for it now."

A moment later, a blue flash grabbed Sinkua's attention. He looked to the door just as a shimmering war hammer spun toward his face, pounding the air.

Sinkua took one step to the side and wrapped his hand around the handle, stopping the hammer dead. But as he lowered it to his side, a gloved hand emerged from the blue light, and the hammer lurched toward it.

"Do you want this back?" Sinkua chided, "Fine. Take it!"

Sinkua hurled the hammer with well more force than it had flown at him with. The doorframe bowed and cracked through, causing the portal to dissolve. To Sinkua's chagrin, however, MalVek emerged in the split second between the hammer taking flight and finding its mark.

"Well, that was quite rude of you," MalVek said. The hammer leapt into his open hand, and he deactivated the photonic emission weapon. "I was only trying to get your attention. And you tried to split me in half."

"Okay. You have my attention," Sinkua said, consuming the space in long strides, "What do you want?"

"For you to stand down," MalVek demanded, "Or look the other way. Just stay out of my way. You're interfering with my work."

The back of Sinkua's hand clapped across MalVek's temple. "If your work involves killing off the Subtransit Resistance, you can bet your stumpy ass I'm gonna get in your way."

"Clearly, you don't understand," MalVek grumbled, "Look. I shouldn't be telling you this, but I'm using them to get information."

"… What sort of information?"

"I thought that might pique your interest," MalVek grinned, "If I can learn enough about how they created Yahsek and Ozzera, Chekov and Gabdur may be able to reverse engineer an antidote. Same with your condition. And anyone else similarly afflicted. Surely, you know that you're not the only one."

"You mean to tell me," Sinkua said, "that all the double-crossing, kidnapping, and murdering has been to build defenses against The Avatars of Fate? Why do I find that hard to believe?"

"I play the role well. Sometimes too well. That's the trouble with mole work."

"And I suppose that's why you were chosen for this?" Sinkua asked, "Because you're the most skilled at deception?"

"I wasn't chosen so much as self-appointed," MalVek explained, "Too dangerous for the others to know what I'm up to."

"Then why tell me?"

"Because I need someone to know, both for the catharsis of it and in case I need to be fished out someday. I weighed my options and realized it ought to be you."

"You should have chosen Nikasu," Sinkua insisted, "The serums were derived from her blood. Don't you think she feels some responsibility for it?"

"Too risky," MalVek brushed off, "Their work with you has concluded. We can't assume the same with her."

"Don't listen to him," came a third voice from the ruined doorway.

The corner of MalVek's mouth flicked upward. "How nice of you to join us, NalSet," he greeted as he turned around, "I was just bringing our curmudgeonly friend up to speed."

NalSet passed MalVek without acknowledgment. He came to Sinkua's side and put a hand on his shoulder.

"Sorry for all the trouble. Glad you're well," NalSet greeted, "But I need you to get out of here."

"What the hell is going on?" Sinkua asked.

"This is for me to deal with," NalSet assured, pulling a folded paper from his shirt pocket, "Farim and her new friend are waiting for you outside. Find them and follow these instructions."

"I'm not leaving without answers," Sinkua argued, snatching the paper.

"Yes, you are," NalSet said, "I'll answer your questions when I catch up with you later. But for now, let me deal with this."

"Yes, let him deal with this," MalVek called, "Clearly there's bad blood between us. What with my being outed as a traitor and a saboteur."

Sinkua looked back and forth between them. Their faces betrayed only a mutual urgency that he leave. Sighing, he shoved his hands in his pockets and walked out of the records office.

As he rounded into the hall, he snapped into eye contact with Khirsan. The guard, carrying Epesol in its holster, froze at the sight of him. Sinkua closed the distance with an impatient gait and swiped the sword without stopping.

"You're late," he scolded.

Galo and Elemeno sat on a bench just beyond the Ouristihran Union parking lot. A pair of flanking streetlamps bathed them in pale orange light. A mostly empty pizza box open sat between them, delivered to a bench thanks to a promised tip that bordered on bribery.

As they always did, they craned their necks as a pair of headlights crested a nearby hill. Many had slowed, but this time, the vehicle stopped.

Elemeno and Galo stood as the cab door opened and Sinkua climbed out, followed by a Northlander man a few years his senior, and Farim. They split to either side as Galo moved in on Sinkua and put his arms around him.

The warm electrical sensation that Nikasu had once given him washed over him again. For a moment, he reconsidered what he had thought this meant. Perhaps it wasn't a sign that he had fallen for her. Or perhaps it was, and his tastes were more varied than he'd realized.

"Sinkua," Galo choked out, "Brother. I… haven't been sure what to believe."

"Galo. Hey," Sinkua smiled, patting his shoulder as they separated, "You were with Vielle when she found the door, weren't you?"

"Yeah. I'm sorry I wasn't there for you."

"And I'm sorry I didn't reach out."

Galo flashed a grin and nodded, casting his eyes down. He looked aside at Farim.

"I heard you had been killed," he said, "I'm glad to see that's no longer the case."

"Just as NalSet told me," Elemeno added, "It's good to see you again, Farim."

"Likewise," Farim nodded.

Galo gestured to the stranger who had been standing aside in pensive silence. "So, who's the new guy?"

"This is Uro," Farim said, "He's an assistant medical examiner from Hillside."

"You're sure we can trust him?" Galo asked.

"Well…" Farim pondered, "He did call me into MalVek's trap. But he insists he didn't know. Plus, it forced MalVek to out himself. And I'm alive again, thanks to Sinkua. So, I suppose I'll give him a pass." She flashed a wry grin at Uro. "For now."

Galo and Elemeno introduced themselves to Uro.

"So, what do you know about MalVek?" Galo asked.

"I'd never heard of him before today," Uro said, "Jevana put me up to calling Farim and fabricating the quarantine. I knew it was a trap, but I didn't know to what extent. But she was also plotting some black market release, and I thought Farim could crack the case if I got her inside."

"Black market release?" Galo pried.

"She's trying to get a designer drug into the black market," Uro clarified, "I think it's connected to the stuff from Professor Uulan's IV bag."

"Well, I had a run-in with MalVek before we came here," Sinkua said, "He has a glove that attracts his photonic emission weapon. It looked like proximity affects it."

"Did he feed you a line about why he's gone rogue?" Galo asked.

"Yeah. He told me he's getting intel so Chekov and Gabdur can develop a way to prevent another Yahsek and Ozzera," Sinkua explained, "And possibly a cure for my condition."

"He told me he's lashing out until ordinary people appreciate how good they've had it and learn to stand up for themselves," Galo said.

"Sounds like bullshit," Uro piped up, "He's giving everyone a different story."

"Right, the question is which one is true."

"None of them," Farim said, "Pathological inconsistency is a diversion tactic. He's trying to confuse us."

"Well, be that as it may, is NalSet going to be joining us?" Elemeno asked.

"I should think so," Sinkua said, "His instructions said he would follow, just not what to do if he fell behind."

"He gave me his portal strip," Farim added, "We waited for him for over two hours before we decided that leaving you two waiting would be worse than stranding him."

"He probably went back to that headquarters that he mentioned," Uro suggested, "Do you have coordinates for it?"

"I do," Elemeno said, "And they did send me here without a portal strip of my own. The plan was for NalSet to pick me up after Galo sent the letter that would lead us to Farim."

"NalSet must have been delayed after confronting MalVek," Farim said, "Hopefully, he's safe, and if he is, he must have figured we would go ahead without him and called Chekov to pick him up."

"Well, now that we're all caught up," Galo said, "Sinkua, there's something I'd like your help with in the Southland Sea."

"Name it."

"Leviathan has informed me there's a third statue like Grandpa Gijin's. Or Takmet's, rather."

"Where was a second one?"

"Pahres," Galo said, "His statue had been moved to your refuge island. But the third one is at the bottom of the sea."

"Well, you're better suited than anyone else to retrieve it," Sinkua said, "Do you need someone to cover you while you dive?"

"Sort of, but not exactly," Galo said, "I'm almost certain that someone was feeding intel to Ebralgi after he left Masnethege."

"And you're using this as bait to draw them out."

"I've missed this," Elemeno smiled, "Seeing how in-tune you boys are with each other."

"All things considered, it's probably our strongest weapon," Galo nodded, "But yes. Also, Leviathan can't remember exactly where it sank... Oh! Wait a moment."

He pulled off the Serpent Bracer and lobbed it into the wet grass. The surface turned fleshy, and a flexing of its rejuvenated muscles rolled it to wet the rest of itself. Leviathan, still at her Serpent Bracer size, sat upright.

"Hello, Sinkua. It's good to see you," she began, "And that you've made your bond with Phoenix. I wish to ask you something."

"Shoot."

"Odin has returned, yes? I believe I sensed him recently."

"He did. He saved me and gave me Epesol."

"Splendid!" Leviathan exclaimed, "Galo, we change our plans. Sail to ArcNos with Sinkua. Tell Odin of our ordeal. We will use the delay in your return to our advantage."

"You make it sound like you're not coming with me," Galo observed.

"I'm not. Drop me in the sea along the way. I'll monitor the Southland Sea for suspicious ships."

"But how will you alert me?"

"You and I can communicate across any distance connected by water."

"My house is several kilometers inland," Sinkua said.

"A tap will suffice," Leviathan said, "Provided the pipes lead in from the sea or a river."

"Okay, so how is this Odin supposed to help us here?" Galo asked.

"He might remember where Arestor was positioned."

"He's been translating those books, by the way," Sinkua said, "Is it possible that there's a record of it in one of those?"

"You tell me," Leviathan said, wriggling in a limbless emulation of shrugging, "We should suppose so. And hope that we suppose correctly."

"Okay. Sinkua, you, and I will take a cab to the northwest docks," Galo said. Leviathan slithered to him and reverted to her copper state. "The rest of you are going to The Coalition's headquarters, correct?"

"Actually, if it's all the same to all of you, I'd like to go to ArcNos with you boys," Elemeno said, "I can't imagine my return is urgent. I'll write the coordinates down for you, Farim. I should assume they're expecting you."

"Thank you," Farim said, "I'll tell them you're safe when we get there."

"Well, before you go," Galo said, producing a flash drive and a business card from his pocket, "the receptionist at the lab where we found Nikasu stole some computer files. They're encrypted, but they might have information about some of their other captives. Maybe about the experiments that were done on them."

"Sounds like it's worth looking into. I'll do what I can," Farim said, taking the flash drive, "And the business card?"

"I told her I'd ask the Magnate Supreme to fast-track her into wit pro, but I don't know how much I can trust Naletas anymore," Galo explained, "I thought you might help her instead."

"I'll see what I can do," Farim said, "But I won't make any promises."

"Sinkua," Elemeno beckoned, pulling him aside, "Before we set off, I just wanted to tell you that I don't blame you for what happened."

"Th... Thank you, Elemeno."

"So, stop blaming yourself, okay?"

"Okay," Sinkua nodded, "And... I'm sorry I didn't reach out to you. I didn't consider what Eytea's death had done to you."

"Nor I you," Elemeno confessed, "There's just one more thing."

"Name it."

"If it's okay with you, I'd like to keep calling you my son-in-law."

"Of course," Sinkua smiled.

MalVek and NalSet stared at each other with near perfect stoicism. After what could easily have been several minutes, MalVek sighed and rolled his eyes.

"Well?" he demanded, "Out with it!"

"I'm giving you a chance to explain yourself," NalSet muttered, nothing moving beyond his mouth.

"Explain myself?" MalVek scoffed, "Like you could understand my motives."

"Try me. Deception or not, nobody understands you better than me," NalSet insisted, "How long has it been?"

"Years. I've lost track," MalVek confessed, his voice cracking, "Playing both sides has become so normal for me that, well..."

"You've forgotten any other way," NalSet sighed, "You've lost sight of the mission."

"Oh, now I wouldn't say that," MalVek refuted, fidgeting with his dormant photonic weapon, "If anything, you've lost sight of what we're sacrificing."

"I know damn well what we've lost!" NalSet snapped, "But look at where we are. Have you forgotten the world we left behind? We've spent the past thirty-some years away from all of that. Out of the dozens who set out for this era, the four of us were lucky enough to make it."

"Three decades in the shadow of a decaying paradise. How wonderful," MalVek chided, "And what do we get for it? We go right back to the shithole that we've all forgotten how to cope with. Three days back, and we'll start a crafting circle to make entrail nooses."

"We get to go back with the means to fight back," NalSet corrected, "Spril will become The Weapon, and we'll bring The Era of Chaos to an end."

"And then what? The world will be healed overnight? Bullshit!"

"And you've turned against us for that?! Because there's no instant gratification? You selfish little…"

"I would rather die than go back to that shithole!" MalVek shouted. He took a deep breath and leveled himself. "Understand this. I want you to win. But I can't go back. I refuse to spend the rest of my life there."

"Then disappear," NalSet grumbled, "Don't fight us. Don't help The Avatars of Fate. They're the very fuckforsaken people we came here to stop."

"I'm not helping them," MalVek chuckled, shaking his head, "I'm using them, you myopic pud stain. In case I get dragged back to our home time."

"Using them for what?"

"To find a way back to this timeline, of course."

"You know that isn't possible," NalSet sighed.

"When we were growing up, time travel was impossible," MalVek proclaimed, "And yet, here we are. Four hundred seventy years before we were born, and we're both pushing sixty.

NalSet paced the room, rubbing the back of his neck. "Look, if you'll…" he stammered, "If you'll come home… stay home… we can work on a way to come back when we're done."

"You… Do you mean it?" MalVek gasped, his body tensing with anticipation, "Are you… really willing to forgive everything I've done?"

"I did not say that. We'll all have a long talk about that and how far we're willing to trust you," NalSet corrected, "But I can't say I haven't thought about looking for a way to come back here after we've saved our home time and timeline."

"I can't believe it," MalVek choked out, tears welling up as he swallowed his laughter, "After all this, I get to… to…"

"Come home, little brother," NalSet said, putting his arm around his shoulder.

"You know what's the funniest thing about all this?" MalVek asked. NalSet shook his head. MalVek's expression turned grave. "You still think I'm your brother."

MalVek slammed the butt of his weapon against the base of NalSet's skull, embedding it in his brainstem. NalSet's body stiffened. His eyes widened.

"Wh… What are you…?"

"I've been asked to get you out of the way."

MalVek struck a sequence of buttons on the weapon, and NalSet began jolting violently. The hole in the back of his head spewed electrical arcs, enveloping his body in a sparking cocoon. Flames of the bloodiest crimson, deepest sapphire, and numerous shades of purple spouted from the forks in the current. They pulled against his body, shrink-wrapping him in liquid fire. The churning mass absorbed the electric cocoon, reducing it to sporadic spitting of the brightest emerald sparks.

NalSet's body lifted off the floor, his back arched and arms limp. Flames and sparks surged along his body faster and faster. When it had all become smears and blurs of color, all of it just stopped.

The silent shape of NalSet hung in the air for a moment. A sphere of light erupted from the center of his body, thundering to a two-meter diameter in the space of a heartbeat. In the space of another, it stretched and flattened with an ear-splitting shriek. When it vanished, so too had NalSet.

MalVek helped Jevana to her feet. She looked him over with mind-reeling reverence.

"My Lord," she gasped, "You're… hurt."

"Ah. So I am."

The disc of light had carved into his abdomen. The edges had mostly been cauterized, but blood still trickled through. He gestured to Jevana's midsection.

Jevana bared her midriff and gazed at him in anticipation. He pressed his hand against her abdomen, and she closed her eyes, panting.

Strands of sinew and flesh wove around each other in MalVek's wound, while one just like his opened on Jevana's midsection. She clutched his forearm to brace herself. He pushed her upright and against the wall.

"Right then. We have work to do," MalVek said. The scattered workers filed back into the office and began straightening up. "Where do we stand on the noncompliant?"

"Mostly weeded out, My Lord," Jevana said, "Uro has escaped. I offer my deepest apologies."

"He is too small a fish to trouble ourselves with," MalVek dismissed, "The Politician will help us deal with the others. You there!"

Khirsan straightened up. "Sir?... Er, My Lord?"

"Did you get your hands on Epesol?"

"Yes, My Lord. He took it back though. My deepest apologies."

"Again, nothing to trouble ourselves with," MalVek assured, "I expect a full write-up of your findings by morning."

"... Yes, My Lord."

Chapter 20

Sleipnir galloped skyward as BeiLou and Odin walked through the glass door. Chiming bells announced their entrance, and they stepped aside from the foyer as BeiLou looked around.

Nothing was as she remembered it, and this offended her more than she knew it should have. She knew that it was unreasonable to expect the world to resume where she had left it off. But she couldn't help but feel slighted at how much had changed.

For one, her favorite deli had come under new ownership, the founder's sister's if her memory served. Why the place had changed hands, though, she was loath to contemplate.

BeiLou queued up while Odin found a table for them. The entire menu was approximations of classic sandwiches and salads with one or two ingredients changed. Trouble was, she couldn't recall whether those were further changes beyond the founder's personal twists.

By the time she reached the front of the queue, she still had no idea what to order. She stalled.

"Hi, um…" she began, trailing off to look for a name tag on the cashier's shirt, "… Sorry. This used to be SalMei's, didn't it?"

"I'm sorry, could you excuse me for one moment?"

The cashier stepped back to the swinging door and poked his head into the kitchen.

"AlsRim!" he called back, "One of them."

He returned to the counter and muttered for her to wait a moment. As AlsRim came to the counter, he moved aside and busied himself cleaning the drink station.

"What can I do for you?" she asked with a plastically hospitable smile.

"Sorry to impose," BeiLou said, "But didn't this used to be SalMei's?"

"Yes. Twelve years ago," AlsRim said, folding her arms, "Why do you ask?"

"I haven't been in the area in a while, and well," BeiLou faltered, "SalMei's was my favorite deli. The owner and I were…"

"Uh huh," AlsRim cut in, looking her over, "Let me guess. She was your babysitter? Badminton coach? Cello teacher?"

"What? No, we…" BeiLou said, "I guess I shouldn't expect you to remember me."

"Not if you were always like this," AlsRim said, "Look, I don't know what your deal is, but if you don't stop, I'm going to have to ask you to leave."

"Oh, no no no. You're right. I'm sorry," BeiLou backpedaled, "It's just… Nevermind. Can I still place an order?"

"Money's money," AlsRim shrugged, tipping her chin at the long queue, "Be quick, and I'll pretend this conversation never happened."

"Please and thank you," BeiLou sighed as AlsRim looked down at the register, "Let's put this behind us. I never should have pried about your sister."

AlsRim looked up sharply, her eyes simultaneously cold and fiery.

"No," she proclaimed, "I am not doing this with you. You and your grandfather need to leave. And don't come back."

"What?!" BeiLou cried, "What did I say?"

"You have known damn well this whole time exactly what you're saying," AlsRim snapped, "I can smell a media vulture from a kilometer away. So, I'm gonna tell you what I told all your colleagues. My story isn't for sale."

"AlsRim!" BeiLou accosted, "I honestly have no idea what you're talking about."

"Of course, you don't," AlsRim chided. She tipped her chin up at Odin, who approached from the table he'd found. "Oh, and the disabled veteran angle is a new low. Real classy."

"I don't..."

"Leave before I call the authorities."

Gritting her teeth, BeiLou slapped a ten-iola note on the counter and took a couple of bags of chips, well aware that she had paid nearly double for them. She whipped about and walked at Odin, turning him around as they nearly collided. With her head down and dodging eye contact, she went back outside with him.

"What has occurred?" Odin asked.

"The new owner is my friend's baby sister," BeiLou explained, "She thinks I'm trying to capitalize on her story. Whatever it is."

"Yes, some fellow patrons were of willingness to share what has become of this SalMei," Odin said. BeiLou looked to him with pleading confusion. "I am elderly and foreign. They find me endearing when I do not impose myself.

"As I was speaking, SalMei died when the imperials seized for themselves control. It took place near to twelve years ago."

"And AlsRim took over in her sister's honor," BeiLou sighed, "with her own twist on the recipes. Dammit."

BeiLou sat on the curb with her head in her hands. Odin settled in beside her.

"You must not trouble yourself over one misunderstanding," he said, "She will soon forget this encounter."

"No, not that. It's just..." BeiLou grasped, "I finally realized what my place is in the world."

"And what suppose you that would be?"

"There isn't one."

"I might speak that I can relate, but I at least am not surrounded by faces that I recall yet have forgotten mine own."

BeiLou scoffed a breathy chuckle.

"Hey, didn't you say Nikasu had some grievances with me?"

"Yes. She fears that you have hatred for her, because she is the child of the husband of yours and another woman."

"That's absurd," BeiLou remarked, "I'll talk with her when we all get back together. Hell, if I'd been around last time they took her, I would have gone and taken her back myself. She needs to know that."

"And you should know that I would have escorted you, even if only for the sake of urgency."

"Could Sleipnir really do that?"

"What means you?"

"Could your magical spider-horse get us there faster than a boat? Or at all?" BeiLou clarified. Odin's face screwed up in bewilderment, "I mean, he can apparently run on anything, but that's at least a thousand kilometers of open sea."

"What speak you of this open sea?" Odin demanded, "A pair of rivers separates this land from the neighboring kingdom."

"Look, I don't know what the world looked like before you got locked out," BeiLou said, "But right now, we're an hour's drive from the beach, and from there, it's saltwater well beyond the horizon."

"This warrants deeper investigation," Odin proclaimed, "Given she yet lives, I will speak with Leviathan."

"For now, let's go home," BeiLou said, "We have work to do. I'll show you the beach later."

Sinkua sat in a modest wooden aft cabin, reading a last-decade paperback under a hovering fireball. Being Masnethegean, Galo's ship lacked any electrical amenities, and Sinkua had chosen what he suspected to be the only cabin without lamp oil.

He had thought to ask a crew member for some oil, but the idea didn't sit well with him. At Elemeno's behest, he was trying not to blame himself for the extension to their assignment. Also, Galo had promised to significantly compensate them. But he was still uncomfortable asking them for favors, and so, he floated a fireball just below the defunct ceiling lamp instead.

The fireball flickered out when a knock at the door jostled his concentration. He set the book down and, with a flick of his fingers, conjured a new fireball. Joints creaking, he pushed out of the rocking chair and crossed the cabin.

Elemeno stood outside the door, holding that bird cage from earlier that evening. Sinkua had meant to ask about it and realized that, in all the other conversations, he had forgotten.

"Hey, mother-in-law," he said, "You wanna come in?"

"Yes, but I'll only be a moment," Elemeno said, "Son-in-law."

"What's going on?"

"Well, if I know you like I think I do, you were wondering why I had a bird cage."

"I assumed it had something to do with finding me or Farim," Sinkua guessed, "But it did seem strange that you kept it."

"We were going to use her to find where Farim had died while NalSet looked for you in ArcNos. Gabdur gave the bird something that would let us follow her," she explained, "Something about a radiation trail. I don't fully understand it."

"Reminds me of how Eytea found me."

"That was the inspiration for it, yes," Elemeno said, "But now there's the matter of what to do with her."

"Right, you can't just release her into the wild, can you?" Sinkua said, "She's too valuable, and there are probably some ecological issues, I'm sure."

"Sweetie, I thought you had more a mind for sentimentalities than that."

Sinkua cocked an eyebrow as Elemeno set the birdcage on the table. She drew back the blanket, and the bird stirred and opened her eyes. Sinkua sat down and drew back a sharp breath.

The feathers along the bottoms of her wings had been dyed the same shade of deep purple as Eytea's wings had been.

"I think she's meant to be with you," Elemeno said.

"I've never had a pet bird before," Sinkua said, whistling at the pigeon, "Or any pet really, unless you count animals sleeping near my camp for scraps."

"Well, there's a first time for everything."

"Yeah. No. I mean..." Sinkua stumbled, "I'm not saying I don't want her. It's just..."

"It's okay," Elemeno insisted, "I think Gabdur meant for me to give her to you when we were done."

"What makes you think that?"

"He had me bring a sample of your tracking scent."

"In case NalSet couldn't find me, I'm sure."

"Well yes, that's what he said," Elemeno argued, "But my intuition said it was more than that."

"Look, you don't have to..."

Elemeno kissed her palm and slapped it on his cheek, looking him square in the eyes as she cupped his face. "Keep the bird, you big doofus," she said, "She'll be happy with you."

Nikasu leaned back against the wall with her hands stuffed in her pockets. She swayed forward on the balls of her feet, then rocked back to settle gently, all the while staring at the plain wooden door across from her.

Spril walked by, talking on his phone. He swerved toward the opposite wall to stay clear of her pensive swaying. As he passed, he cupped his hand over the mouthpiece and looked her way.

"There's Popken Lime in the fridge."

"What? Oh, I don't..."

"Not offering," he said, cocking his head toward the door.

It took until Spril turned the corner for Nikasu to notice she had stopped swaying. She grabbed a cold Popken Lime from the refrigerator and opened the plain wooden door. Now, she had a purpose that her anxiety had no bearing on.

"Hey babe," Yrlis said, not looking up from her work, "What's going on?"

"Not much, sweetie," Nikasu said, "Just thought you could use a drink."

Yrlis turned sharply. "Spril put you up to this, didn't he?" she asked, crossing her lab, "That man. I tell you."

"He's on the phone, so he had me bring you this," Nikasu said, handing her the drink, "But I think he was trying to get me to come down here."

"What gave you that idea?"

"I've been staring at the basement door a lot."

"Why would you..." Yrlis stammered. She popped the can, took a sip, and cleared her throat. "Why?"

"I was trying to work up the courage to come see what you're doing."

"Why would it be so hard for you..." Yrlis trailed off, "Oh. Right. Sinkua's condition. They, ah... probably derived it from your blood."

"Maybe let's don't pussyfoot around it. We know they did," Nikasu said, "So, there it is. I've wanted to come see your work, but just thinking about seeing anything to do with that part of my life makes me really damn nervous. You know? It's like, I know it's not my fault. I can tell myself that. I can tell you that. I know it's true. But I also had a pretty damn strong sense of self-loathing and self-fearing pounded into me my whole life up until a few months ago. And. Well. You know. That part of me still thinks it is my fault. Even if I tell it to shut the fuck up. And. You know."

"Nikasu. Nikasu?" Yrlis beckoned, "Nikasu!"

"…What?"

"I'm not working on your brother's condition anymore."

"…What?"

"I'm. Not. Working…"

"No. I got that," Nikasu said, "Why didn't I know about this?"

"I thought Spril or Sinkua had told you."

"Guess they never had a chance," Nikasu shrugged, "So, what are you working on now?"

"I… Well…" Yrlis trailed off, "… Have you talked to anyone from The Coalition lately?"

Nikasu shook her head.

"Okay so, Spril's got something genetic going on," Yrlis continued, "I'm trying to work it out, but it's proving even more difficult than I suspected."

"I guess his parents not being around would be a problem," Nikasu guessed, "So, what's going on with him? And what does The Coalition have to do with it?"

"Actually, his parents not being around is the least of my obstacles," Yrlis said, "Have you noticed anything weird about him lately?"

"Well, there was one thing," Nikasu recalled, "Right after that thing killed Eytea, it was about to eat Sinkua, and Spril sort of but not really teleported in front of it and broke it without touching it."

"Well, that's the sort of thing that I'm trying to figure out," Yrlis said, "And The Coalition wants him to fully realize those abilities."

Nikasu paced before the array of dry erase boards, looking at vaguely familiar calculations and diagrams. Her understanding of the stuff was tenuous at best, rarely going beyond identification. She could glean a general idea of how Yrlis was approaching the issue, but comprehending the interactions and emergent properties escaped her.

"What's going on with Sinkua's condition, though?" she asked, "I mean, if you're not working on it."

"I sent my notes to Ophalin."

Nikasu nodded and kept looking over the boards, unsure what she was looking for. She knew she wasn't expecting any sort of epiphany. Far be it from her to be so arrogant.

She realized that what she sought was acclimation. This sort of thing had long been the root of her torment and dehumanization. But disconnected from that trauma, it was actually rather fascinating. Her tenuous understanding was a seed of curiosity awaiting, at a minimum, neutral grounds to germinate in.

She abruptly excused herself and rushed upstairs. She dug something out of her bag and hurried back to the basement lab with it.

"Any idea what this might be?" she asked, handing the coaster to Yrlis.

Yrlis looked it over for a moment, rubbing the edge and the holes.

"A coaster with holes punched in it?" Yrlis puzzled, "Weird hobby. Why do you have it?"

"The receptionist at the lab MalVek took me to gave it to me," Nikasu said, "She said a masked man asked her to give it to me. Obviously, she meant Mortvill."

"Which means the holes actually mean something," Yrlis said, "Well, I don't recognize any patterns here. But if you want, I can take a picture and tell you if I come up with anything."

"Sure, thanks," Nikasu said, "Actually, I was wondering if you have any astronomy books."

"Not my thing. But I guess it could be a constellation."

"When does Spril go back to work? Do you think he could take me to the library tomorrow?"

"Next week," Yrlis said, "But you know, sailors used to use constellations to navigate. Star charts are obsolete these days, but you can probably find someone who still has them if you know where to look."

"So, I should ask around at the docks?"

Yrlis looked at her flatly. Nikasu held eye contact until, unsure what Yrlis meant by that look, she shrugged urgingly. Yrlis sighed and rolled her eyes.

"Masnethegeans shun modern technology," Yrlis spelled out, "And the Chieftains are very comfortable at sea."

"You think Galo has star charts?"

"Yes!"

"Ooh! That gives me an excuse to be alone with him," Nikasu said, smiling wolfishly.

Yrlis laughed. "You have a crush on him, don't you?"

"I'm not familiar with that phrase," Nikasu confessed, "Does it mean I want to do dirty things with, to, and for him?"

"That's, ah… one way to put it."

"In that case, yes," Nikasu said, "I have such a crush. So many crushes on him."

"But aren't you a bit young for him? You're, what, seven years apart?"

"We're both adults."

"So you'd like to think."

"I'm sixteen!"

"Yes, and age of consent is eighteen now," Yrlis said, "They bumped it up from fifteen a couple of years ago."

"Seriously?" Nikasu asked. Yrlis nodded. Nikasu swiped the disc and shoved it in her pocket. "Dammit!"

MarLys sat on the edge of the couch, looking over a newspaper fanned across the coffee table. She dragged her finger along the page, mumbling to herself, until she found something worth mentioning.

"What about this one?" she asked, tapping the apartment listing.

Vielle, hunched over on the arm of the armchair, stared vacantly at the newspaper. MarLys called her name, and she shut her eyes and shook her head.

"Sorry," she said, "I um…"

"This apartment," MarLys said, "Does it look good to you?"

Vielle clutched the edge of the paper as she stared at the entry. She furrowed her brow, struggling to comprehend despite her intense concentration. She blinked slowly and breathed deeply.

"It ah, it looks good," Vielle said, "Sorry, I'm just… Are you okay with it?"

"Hey, I'm sure you'll get another job soon," MarLys said, "And yes, I'm okay with it. I can afford it for us in the meantime."

"Okay. Okay," Vielle said, nodding emphatically, "Let's do it. Let's go check it out."

"Honey," MarLys beckoned, "Is something wrong?"

"What makes you say that?"

"It's all over your face. I mean, it's not like everything's ever right, but I know how you are when it's stuff you're used to," MarLys said, "This is different."

"I've been… hearing voices," Vielle confessed, "Not in a psychotic way."

"Like how you heard Nikasu when you gave her that hair tie?"

"I think so, but I don't recognize any of them," Vielle said, "It's hard to sort them out and even harder to shut them up."

"Well, that sounds awful," MarLys empathized, "Look, I mean, I've never known anyone who's had a problem like this. But if you ever want to talk about it, just to get it out there, I'll sit and listen."

Vielle said nothing. She just smiled and kissed MarLys on the cheek.

A knock came at the door as MarLys wrote down the address to the apartment complex. Vielle answered the door, and MarLys saw Malia on the front step through a well placed mirror on the living room wall.

"Dad's at work," Vielle said, "Want me to tell him you stopped by?"

"Actually, I came to talk to you," Malia said, "Can I come in?"

"Figured I'd be here since I got fired?"

"Yes, but it's not like it's a slight against you, Vielle."

"I know. I know. I'm just… bitter," Vielle sighed, stepping aside, "Come in, then. What did you want to talk about?"

"I need to pick your brain about something," Malia said as she crossed the threshold, "I've left The Coalition, but I'm having second thoughts."

"Well, I can see why you'd want to bail on them," Vielle said, "But what does that have to do with talking to me?"

"Why would you have second thoughts?" MarLys chimed in, "Weren't you recruited by MalVek?"

"I was, and that's a big part of why I left. There's more, but I'm not in a position to talk about it," Malia said aside. She returned her attention to Vielle. "You've made it clear that you don't particularly like me."

"You've grown on me, but I'll admit, it's taken some time."

"Well, even when we were at our worst, you never flat out pushed me away," Malia continued, "I mean, you've kept your emotional distance, but you've never tried to keep me out of whatever you and your friends are going through with The Avatars. You know? You've never kept me away from the Subtransit Resistance or whoever else has gotten involved since then."

"It's not my place to say who other people can talk to," Vielle shrugged, "Besides, Dad seems to enjoy having you around."

"Is that all it is?" Malia pried, "Because I'm feeling exposed without The Coalition. But it's not like I can go back just because my ex's adopted son's girlfriend's mom is part of them, and it helps them keep in touch."

"No, I guess that is a stretch of a reason," Vielle chuckled, "But if you want to go back, just talk to them."

"It isn't quite that simple," Malia said, "I need them, but I don't know how far I can trust them. How did you keep working with me when you weren't sure I could be trusted?"

"Benefit of the doubt. Maybe," Vielle pondered, "I don't know what it was. I guess maybe I figured we had common goals, so I should get over my distrust. Or maybe, some part of me wanted to trust you and was willing to overlook what you did to Nikasu and everything else with The Avatars. Or maybe, I thought the best way to prove you couldn't be trusted was to trust you long enough for you to exploit that trust."

Malia settled on the arm of the couch. "You're a complicated young woman," she said, "But I think I see your point. The Coalition and I still have common goals. And a big part of my distrust has to do with MalVek."

"Yeah, you can't blame them for that," MarLys said, "He had everyone fooled."

"Back in Tanelen, when we were looking for Dad," Vielle said, "I told Nikasu that everyone was supposed to believe you were an Avatar during the war. This is sort of like that. You can't blame anyone for having trusted MalVek, just like I couldn't blame her for hating you."

"I think I'll talk to them about working together again," Malia said, "We want the same things, and we were both deceived by MalVek. Us splintering is exactly what he wants."

"What about your other reasons?" MarLys asked.

"MalVek was the main issue. But I think I'll keep them at arm's length for a while," Malia said, "Thank you both. So, what are you two up to today?"

"Apartment hunting," MarLys said, "We were about to go look at one."

"Oh, how cool," Malia remarked, "Would you like a ride?"

"I've got my bike," Vielle said, "But thank you."

"It's been raining off and on all day," Malia said, "Is it safe for you to ride in that?"

"We'll be fine," Vielle said, "I drive in the rain all the time."

"Hey, safe or not, riding in the rain sucks," MarLys said, "Let's take her up on it."

"Okay. Okay," Vielle said, "Sure. Thanks."

"No problem," Malia said, "I'll talk to Chekov once I figure out what to say."

Galo turned the journal over on his lap and gazed out over the Midland Sea. He breathed deeply, mingling the tastes of salt, marine life, and seafaring birds in his throat.

A shift in the air set his brow askew. Suddenly, it smelled like they were nearing land. He closed his eyes and cupped an ear. A vibrato coo drifted through the air.

Galo turned the journal back over and looked over his shoulder. Sinkua approached, looking rather like a storybook pirate. He leaned one hand on the back of the seat, and Galo's eyes traced up his arm to settle on the bird on his shoulder.

He extended his finger, and the violet-winged pigeon nuzzled against it.

"Hey there, Luvros," he cooed, "How are you doing? You being good? You keeping my brother out of the wrong kind of trouble?"

"I don't think I can get into much of that out here," Sinkua said, "MalVek can't gate to a moving location."

"You haven't noticed?"

"Noticed what?"

"We're adrift, biding our time," Galo clarified, "I'm giving Leviathan time to explore before we land in ArcNos."

"So, that's why it's not getting colder," Sinkua said.

"You're not in any hurry, are you?" he asked.

"I suppose not," Sinkua said, offering his finger to Luvros, "Nikasu might worry, but she's staying with Spril and Yrlis. She hit it off pretty well with Odin, too. Better than I did, anyway."

"Well, I'm sorry we don't have a way for you to contact her," Galo said, "Until the Reestablishment Protocol goes through, I'm…"

"Hold on," Sinkua interrupted.

Sinkua turned around and headed back toward the cabins. Luvros hopped off his shoulder and fluttered down to Galo's armrest.

"What is it?"

"Biroe gave me a burner phone."

Galo returned to his journal as Sinkua vanished into the cabins. The frustration he had diverted his attention from returned almost immediately. Nothing even close to a pattern was emerging from this patient's attacks. As far as he could tell, whatever drove the severity and frequency of them hadn't been documented, even though her records appeared to be exceedingly thorough.

When Sinkua returned, Galo had become so absorbed in his work that he had no reliable metric for how much time had passed.

"Were you able to reach her?"

"I think so," Sinkua said, "I only have Biroe's number, so I asked him to tell Phylus. But he sounded distracted."

"Trouble in the Ministries?" Galo asked.

"Probably, but he couldn't tell me anything," Sinkua said, "So, what's in the journal?"

"These are medical records from other people who The Avatars of Fate may have experimented on," Galo explained, "I petitioned several doctors in Berinin shortly after I'd returned home."

"MalVek might have been telling the truth, then," Sinkua said, "He told me I'm not an isolated case. But what about confidentiality?"

"They're anonymized," Galo assured, "I thought if I could find a pattern, maybe I could leverage it into a more effective treatment."

"But so far?"

"Nothing but frustration."

"Would it help if you had my records?"

"I've considered that," Galo said, "It might, but I'm not hopeful."

"What about my genome map?"

Galo shrugged. "Possibly. Ask me again when I'm feeling less cynical."

"I'll ask her for it when I get home," Sinkua offered, "While I'm at it, I'll see if she can generate maps for the other patients in your journal."

"That could take several months," Galo pointed out, "Which I suppose doesn't mean we shouldn't do it."

"Hey wait," Sinkua urged, pointing to a line in the journal, "That's the same day as The Tournament of Duelers?"

"Huh?" Galo wondered, "Yeah, it was."

Sinkua flipped the page back. "And this one happened two days before that."

"Right? Not much time to recover," Galo sighed, "There's a very small list of people I'd wish that upon."

"Galo!" Sinkua beckoned.

Galo looked up, giving Sinkua a puzzled stare. Sinkua looked down at him urgingly, his brow flat and eyes wide.

"Do you really think…?"

"It's worth checking on," Sinkua insisted, "You have medical release forms on board, right?"

"Yes and our own tracker pigeons. So, we don't have to send Luvros out," Galo said, "Thank you, brother. This can't be easy for you to think about."

"It's just what needs doing," Sinkua said, "If we're quick, Ophalin can have my records ready for you by the time you get to Ferya."

"And I'm glad to..." Galo trailed off as his thoughts shifted into speculation and scrutiny. "... It just might be possible."

"What might be possible?"

"It would be asking a lot though," Galo exhaled, "Even for her."

"What would be..."

"I need to know if Vielle can map Yggdrasil's roots."

Biroe pushed a button on the underside of his desk, and his office doors groaned open.

"Ah, good morning, Madam Chairwoman," he greeted, "How does the day find you so far?"

"Prime Minister," TolRou nodded, "You may want to withhold any further pleasantries."

"What makes you say that?"

"I have a missive that I am, well, remiss to deliver," she explained as she sat across from him, "You might not think so nicely of me in a moment."

"I'll judge for myself. You are only the messenger after all," he insisted, "Let's have it."

She handed him the paper and sat back with her jaw clenched and shoulders tense. Biroe read it, thought it over for a moment, then read it again. He mulled it over and read it a third time.

"You're sure about this?" he grasped.

"The investigation has been inconclusive. I've been informing the Ministries for the better part of the afternoon," TolRou said, "Besides, I have to remain neutral in this."

"Right. Right," Biroe nodded, slapping the paper against his hand as he grasped at contradictions, "It may come down to your judgment."

"Yes, and given the highly classified nature of this, it is forbidden from discussion via the Lunch Break Protocol."

"How do you know about the Lunch Break Protocol?"

"I'm privy to a lot of things in my position."

"Well, who else have you...?"

Biroe halted as his phone rang in his pocket. He checked it, then excused himself to answer it.

"Sinkua," he greeted, turning his wheelchair to put his back to TolRou, "Is everything okay?"

"Yes, sorry if I worried you," Sinkua said, "I need to get a message to Nikasu."

"I'm sorry. Who?"

"My sister," Sinkua clarified, "She's..."

"Okay, but how am I supposed to get this message to her?"

"Sorry. She's staying with Spril, but I don't have his number."

"Neither do I, and he's on psych leave."

"Did I call at a bad time?" Sinkua asked, "You can..."

"It's fine," Biroe cut off, "Nothing for you to concern yourself with."

"Is there something going on with the Ministries again?"

"You don't work here, so it's not your business," Biroe said, "Besides, the Chairwoman of Parliament is sitting behind me."

"Shit."

"Right. So, what do you need to tell your sister?"

"I ran into Galo," Sinkua said, "We're staying at sea for a while. I'll tell her the rest when I get home."

"Got it. And how should I get this to her?"

"Just tell Phylus."

"Okay," Biroe said, "I'll get it to him. So long."

Biroe disconnected and pocketed his phone. As he turned around, he found TolRou with her arms folded and a quizzical glare.

"You don't suppose you said too much?" she asked.

"Not enough to glean particulars."

"If you say so."

"Well, anyway," Biroe said, skimming the paper again, "Who else have you told about this?"

"Healthcare, Education, R&D," TolRou rattled off, "and Foreign Affairs. I just came from there."

"Foreign Affairs?" Biroe asked. TolRou nodded. "I thought Phylus wasn't due back until later today."

"I spoke with High Minister Calhosin. He'll inform the Prime Minister upon his return from Eprilen."

"So, this is open for discussion between Prime and High Ministers?"

"Only on an intra-Ministry basis," TolRou said, "Each pair of Prime and High Ministers is to come to a shared consensus to represent their Ministry, should this matter go to court. Parliamentary Representatives and Senior Executive Advisors have been thusly isolated."

"Well, if you're up to anything dirty," Biroe said, narrowing his eyes at the bottom of the paper, "you're doing a bang-up job of masking it."

"Nothing of the sort."

"In that case, it's only right that I inform you that I have been recording this conversation."

"Come again?" TolRou asked, "In what manner?"

"Audio," Biroe said, "After that business with your predecessor, I've taken certain precautions."

TolRou sighed and leaned back. "I can't say I blame you," she said, "Just see that you don't share the recording."

"Not unless you come under investigation yourself."

"Of course. So, what are your initial thoughts?"

"It seems infeasible," he said, "FerLyn wouldn't have agreed to this."

"So, yours is a character witness defense?"

"I thought you were supposed to be neutral, but yes," Biroe said, "My individual off-the-record hypothesis is that it's illegitimate."

"Noted," TolRou said, "Off the record."

Chapter 21

Salty humidity tinged with dead fish filled Odin's nostrils. His eye watered, he was so unaccustomed to such pungency. He swept his beard over his nose and mouth as he grasped Sleipnir's reins in his other hand. Odin swung his legs over the side of the oversized equine and dropped to the ground.

He turned and offered BeiLou his hand. Finding her unbothered by the stench, he uncovered his face. She took it as she dismounted, and he brought her to the ground.

"Thank you," BeiLou nodded, dusting herself off, "Now, if you look to your left, you'll see the Northland Sea. You might notice that it is not, in fact, a pair of rivers and nothing more."

"Yes, that much is quite clear."

At his urging, Sleipnir settled on the frosted sand and dune grass, curling his legs under his torso. With BeiLou never more than a step behind, Odin walked down to the end of the pier.

He and Sleipnir caught several odd glances, no longer to his surprise. When he had entered the root system, his fellow Etherworlders had fallen to low double digits. He knew at the time that their numbers could, and likely would, continue to fall. It also didn't escape him that, should his kin have fallen to their last, the Omphaloworld might eventually forget them. Still, both realities had proven more difficult to come to terms with than he had anticipated.

Odin knelt at the end of the pier. He closed his eye and grazed his hand along the surface of the water. Chills ran along his torso in every humanly perceivable direction. He shook his head as he rose to his feet.

"What's wrong?" BeiLou asked.

"This water," Odin said, "It is threaded with the essence of Leviathan."

"Meaning what? That she's still alive?"

"It means that this rising of the seas was her doing. This water is formed of her milystis."

"Well, can you tell if she's alive?"

"Under other circumstances, certainly, but these waters obscure my ability to sense her," Odin said, glaring out over the vast sea, "Though I certainly hope she yet lives."

"So she can do something about this excess water?"

"No," Odin asserted. At the other end of the pier, Sleipnir lifted his head and huffed. "Better she have the opportunity to explain herself that I might bring her to justice."

Odin turned and walked back toward the land end of the pier. BeiLou scrambled to keep up, calling to him with every step, but he continued until he came to Sleipnir. The horse stood up with as much ado as could be expected from an octopedal mammal.

"What are you talking about?" BeiLou demanded, "Do you honestly think…"

"I revel not in the thought of it, but yes," Odin said, hoisting her onto Sleipnir's back. He vaulted onto the saddle in front of her. "It would appear that Leviathan has defected into the services of chaos."

"Well, if she can flood the world, what can we even do to fight her?"

"There are yet mechanisms beyond your awareness."

"Such as?"

"Your home," Odin said, "Beneath it sleeps the power of your ancestors."

EshCal sat at her mahogany desk, surrounded by the most highly ranked officers of the Ministry of Defense. The smells of sweat, shoe polish, and about twenty varieties of coffee fought to dominate the space. Her office was far from cramped, but it certainly hadn't been built with standing room for some hundred people in mind.

EshCal panned the room, counting raised hands. She reached a majority long before she'd come back around to where she started.

"The motion passes," EshCal sighed. Everyone lowered their hands. "I'll speak with him when he returns. You're all dismissed."

No sooner had EshCal lifted her pen from the paper than an incoming visitor grabbed the door and navigated through the crowd of officers. EshCal shoved the papers in the top drawer of her desk and composed herself as she tried to recall the purpose of this next visit.

"Chairwoman TolRou," she greeted, feigning confidence, "Sorry for the overlap. My previous meeting ran long."

"Quite a meeting it looks to have been," the Chairwoman remarked, "Looks to have been all your top brass, yes?"

"Approximately," EshCal said, "Now, what did you say the nature of this meeting would be?"

"We didn't have a meeting scheduled, Madam High Minister," TolRou said, "I apologize for the intrusion. I had been looking for your Prime Minister, but I recalled that he's still on psych leave."

"For two more days, yes."

"Well, my business is with you as well," TolRou said, producing papers from her satchel, "This is strictly confidential. Not to be discussed with anyone except Prime Minister Spril."

EshCal rubbed her jawline as she examined the top sheet. She held it up to the light, studying the signature. It looked real enough, and it wasn't implausible. But something about it, something she couldn't place, just didn't quite seem right.

"What do you make of it?" TolRou beckoned.

"Well, I'm not an expert on forgeries," EshCal said, biding her time, "but if this is one, it looks exactly like her signature."

"So, your initial impression is that it's genuine?"

"That or a masterwork forgery. Possibly by someone close to her."

"As an act, though," TolRou specified, "what's your initial impression?"

"Well…" EshCal trailed off, "I never thought much about it, but she never showed much concern for the protesters' message. Just that they were in the way."

"I understand," TolRou nodded, writing in a notepad, "Anything else?"

"Her concern with the aftermath was laid on thick," EshCal added, thoughts reeling behind calm eyes at the sound of herself, "It seemed like she was overcompensating."

"Well," TolRou exhaled as she clapped the notepad shut, "I've made note of your thoughts."

"I don't necessarily think…"

"I know," TolRou cut off, "This is all off the record. Talk it over with your Prime Minister and prepare your statement in the event that this goes to trial."

"I'll see that we do," EshCal said, "If there's nothing else, you may see yourself out."

Chairwoman TolRou left High Minister EshCal's office with no further word or gesture. EshCal slumped in her seat and stared at the ceiling, still clutching the papers from TolRou.

After some time, she sat up and opened the top drawer of her desk. She winced at the papers from her meeting with her top brass, harder still when she added the ones from the Chairwoman. She threw the drawer shut and made a call on her mobile phone.

"Thank you for calling Dapper Rabbit. What can we do to serve you today?"

"Hi. This is EshCal."

"Ah, nice to hear from you. How have you been finding our services?"

"Quite pleasing. I'm actually calling to request additional services this week."

"Oh! Well, we're happy to accommodate you. What would you like?"

"Double my usual bookings."

"Would that be double your single sessions or the same number, but double sessions?"

"I hadn't considered doubles."

"It's up to you."

"Come to think of it, I don't think I have it in me for a double. Not this week."

"Okay, so twice your single bookings. Would you like one of them tonight?"

"If it's possible, yes."

"I'll see what I can drum up. Do you have any preferences for this one?"

"You're familiar with my tastes. Take that knowledge and surprise me."

"As you like. Can I note on your account that you're considering a double?"

"Yes. Please do."

"Great. Thank you for your continued patronage."

Calhosin leaned forward, warming his hands on his coffee mug. "We both know this will come down to us versus them," he insisted, casting a level look at Phylus.

"I'm afraid you're right," Phylus sighed, "Sometimes, I hate when you're right."

"And yet, that's exactly why you brought me and keep me around," Calhosin said, "So. Ministries versus Parliament. What's our angle? And what's theirs?"

"Well, obviously this is a fabrication."

"Why?"

"She's not the sort," Phylus insisted, "She doesn't fit any of the profiles, and she has nothing to gain that she would think was worth the cost."

"But she does have a lot to lose," Calhosin argued, "Enough to be worth the cost?"

Phylus sighed and took a long swig of his coffee. "So, we have to prove that she couldn't or wouldn't have done it."

"But you can't prove a negative," Calhosin said, "It falls to Parliament to prove that it's real, which ought to be easy, seeing as how feasible it looks."

"So our best defense is to prove that someone else did it," Phylus said.

"Which we don't have the resources for," Calhosin pointed out, "Certainly not the time."

"Covert Affairs is probably already working on that anyway," Phylus considered, "It could look suspicious if we both take the same angle."

"The papers came from Covert."

"Shit. Well, the only active Avatar we know of is MalVek."

"And Joren," Calhosin insisted, "If we suppose, as we should, that he's full of it."

"Right. Right," Phylus nodded, gazing into his mug, "Neither of them has the means to get to her directly though."

"Which means she did it," Calhosin asserted, "Now, it's a matter of her sentencing."

"Not necessarily," Phylus said, "Let's compile a list of all suspicious individuals that have come through the Task Force lines."

"You're trying to catch plankton with a tuna net," Calhosin said, shaking his head.

"What do you suggest we do, then? You don't actually think she did it, do you?"

"Instinctively, no."

"Then why are you rolling over?"

"I'm not," Calhosin said, "I'm just preparing for the possibility that the defense won't win this case."

"Well," Phylus exhaled, "if you're right about this coming down to Ministries versus Parliament, we should look at who has the most to gain from such a schism."

"Well, you're up to krill now."

"Actually, come to think of it, the case would end in a stalemate."

"And would then be settled by Chairwoman TolRou."

"Exactly. Which means we only need to bring her around to our way of thinking."

"Which at least half of Parliament has surely already thought of," Calhosin argued, "But it's about our only hope of a workable defense. At the very least, it might buy us some more time to investigate."

OshMar ground his teeth and swallowed hard. His pulse quickened and pupils dilated. He pushed the papers and TolRou's outstretched arm away.

"I'm sorry," he stammered, "I can't testify in this case."

"I apologize if this comes as a shock," TolRou said, "Why will you be unable to testify?"

"She and I have history," OshMar said, "Any testimony I give will... It's just that..."

"You believe your objectivity will be under scrutiny?"

OshMar nodded vigorously. He ran a hand through his sweaty hair.

"Well, we need every Ministry to testify," TolRou continued, "Are you willing to grant your High Minister sole representation of the Ministry of Infrastructure in this case?"

"Yes," OshMar asserted, squaring his jaw, "I concede my authority in this matter."

"Very well, then," TolRou said, "You'll need to file a Dissent to Testify form. Bring it to my office by the end of the day tomorrow."

SenRas leaned against the doorframe, exchanging idle banter with the delivery worker and shifting his weight with the youth's shifting gaze. SenRas didn't read any sort of malice from him. They made their exchange, a takeout bag and about ten iolas, and SenRas sent the curious young man on his way.

SenRas backed into the room and let the door fall shut. Once the lock engaged, he took a deep breath from the bag. This was the closest thing to authentic Quarunite cuisine that could be delivered to the capitol building, and for a place owned by a native Ierodhesan, their recipes were remarkably passable. The scent reminded him of the joys of his youth, the same way cheap pork stew and cheaper cigarettes reminded him of the struggles.

He looked up from the bag as he turned around and found himself rather surprised. He had assumed he was alone, the whole staff having gone to lunch, but he found a single straggler.

"MarLys?" he asked, "Are you not going to lunch?"

"I needed to talk with you about something," MarLys said, squaring her shoulders in a transparent bolstering of confidence, "It's... private."

"I see," SenRas nodded, "I assume you spoke with Malia during your time off."

"Why would you...?"

"You're dating her daughter," he cut off, "What did she tell you?"

"She wants to make amends with The Coalition," MarLys said, "Which I can understand, but you and EshCal never came up in our discussion."

"And what conclusion have you drawn from this?" SenRas asked.

"You and EshCal are working on something that she can't be involved in," she said, "She said she feels exposed without them, and that would only happen if she and you two were no longer looking out for each other."

"Quite astute of you," SenRas said, offering MarLys one of his side dishes, "I knew I hired you for more than your material connections. It's rare anymore that I'm wrong about people."

"So, is this... You know?," MarLys said, sampling the heavily spiced rice dish, "Is LenSom's influence still a problem?"

"You tell me."

"Come again?"

"I've been meaning to talk with you about it, but this was your doing."

"What?!" she recoiled, "What are you talking about?"

"We have a lead as to how the activators were planted in the high-rise district," SenRas said, "You brought that information to Chairwoman TolRou."

"I don't... I couldn't..." MarLys stammered. She shoved a forkful of rice into her mouth, wincing at the spices. "When? How?"

"When you returned from Berinin, I asked you to take the papers in my outbox to the Chairwoman," SenRas recounted, "You took more than that, and now a federal official has been implicated in the Heniokhos Disaster."

"Oh, son of a bitch," MarLys whimpered, "Who was it? Who's being framed?"

"I'm not at liberty to discuss that with you if you didn't know prior," SenRas asserted, "But why do you assume someone is being framed?"

"You and EshCal wouldn't be working together on this if you didn't think something was amiss," she said, "It's my understanding that cross-Ministry collaboration is forbidden on cases like this."

"A sound conclusion," he said, "But what of Malia?"

"Obviously, she would draw undue attention," she said, pausing to chew on the deeper implications, "But maybe her returning to The Coalition circles back to this. She could have figured you two might need access to their resources."

"You may be on to something there," SenRas agreed, "The three of us had considered forming a splinter cell of Coalition defectors, but circumstances have proven that to be unwise."

"Factions only make it easier for The Avatars to work us against each other," MarLys asserted, "The Task Force lines are already proving the value of unity."

"Quite true," SenRas nodded, taking a spoonful of his stew, "But even if our splinter group was a nonstarter, there are still certain precautions that I can take."

"What do you mean?"

"Although I'm rarely wrong about people, I can't get a clear read on you."

"You... You think I did this on purpose?" MarLys stammered, "You think I tried to frame someone in the Heniokhos Disaster?"

"The possibility occurred to me and has yet to pass," SenRas said, "As I said, I can't get a clear read on you. But as long as there's a possibility, you need to be dealt with."

MarLys's eyes widened and jaw tightened. The rigidness swept down her torso until her fingers dug into her armrests. Her eyes crept down, and she swatted the bowl off the desk. It landed facedown with a spluttering of saucy rice. She threw the chair out from under herself and scrambled to the bathroom.

SenRas sighed. "I didn't poison you!"

He pushed himself to his feet and made his way to the bathroom, shaking his head and muttering to himself. He was in no shape for haste, and it sounded like there was no use for it anyhow. He paused at the water cooler and filled a cup.

Sure enough, he found her huddled over the toilet with the contents of her stomach spilling from her gaping mouth. SenRas approached to offer his hand and set the cup atop the vanity.

"I said I didn't poison you," he repeated.

"How can I be sure?" she defied, refusing his hand, "I know what you did to Kabehl and AinZun."

"Curious that you would call them by their birth names, but I did what I did because I was absolutely certain. With you, I'm not," SenRas explained, "Besides, you can't honestly think I'd do something so amateur as hiding an ingestible in spicy food. Especially one that can be counteracted by vomiting."

"Then what did you mean by needing to deal with me?"

"Until I clear your name, I can't trust you with the sort of information that we handle here," he said, "I'm relieving you of your position."

"Oh. Oh shit," MarLys groaned, "If I hadn't just thrown up, I would be right now."

"Don't be so quick to assume," SenRas insisted, "After all, look where that just got you."

"You just said you're relieving me of my position," she reiterated, "What else am I supposed to assume from that?"

"Well, I just as well can't send you out into the world with what you already know."

"I'm sorry, I… I don't know where you're going with this."

"I need to keep a closer eye on you," SenRas said, "You will no longer work as an investigator in this Ministry. Instead, you are to be my personal assistant."

"Your… So, I still have a job?"

"It comes with a considerable pay cut, but yes."

"Oh. Oh wow. No. No, that's fine. A pay cut is fine," MarLys stammered, "I'll take the job."

"Well, I'm glad to hear that," SenRas smiled, giving her a sandwiching handshake, "You'll start right away, and it's a good thing, too. A former investigator thought to paint her frustrations on the carpet with Quarunite spices. See that the team knows nothing of it, yes?"

"Right," MarLys sighed, cracking a smile as she took the cup of water, "I'd better go deal with that."

Sinkua sat on the port railing with the southeastern coast of Ivaria faintly visible on the horizon. He passed a stream of flame between his index fingers, coiling it down the receiving finger and the rest of his fist, then back up to his fingertip.

A fish crested the surface, and he shot the stream of flame at it. Luvros swooped down and plucked the scorched and stunned fish. She returned to Sinkua's side and dropped it with the others.

At some point during their hunting, Galo sidled up and nudged the small mound of fish with his foot.

"You know the mess hall has plenty of food, right?" he asked "We restocked before we left Eprilen. In excess."

"I know," Sinkua said, "I'm just training Luvros. Besides, these are too small to eat."

"That was going to be my next point," Galo added, hopping up on the railing beside him, "So, what's on your mind, brother?"

Sinkua thought it over for a moment, organizing his thoughts.

"Did I ever tell you about the giant that Eytea and I fought at Radial Axiom?" he asked. "I overheard MalVek say it shouldn't exist."

"And you're taking that at face value?"

"This was before he was ready to out himself."

"Fair point," Galo said, "So, I suppose it's worth considering who it actually was."

"Right?" Sinkua said, "The Avatars didn't just make up that giant when they created that device. It was somebody."

"Well, we don't have much to go on," Galo said, skewering a fish with a finger-sized ice spear, "It might be an Etherworlder, but where's its Hybrid?"

"Maybe that's what he meant by how it shouldn't exist. An Etherworlder who came to the Omphaloworld without a Hybrid."

"Well, if you'd like," came a third voice from behind, "I could reach out to The Coalition about him."

"That would help, thanks," Sinkua said, turning to face Elemeno, "I had been scheduled to face Mortvill there, after all."

"Yes, well, I also have my own reasons," Elemeno said, taking her phone from her pocket.

While she made her call, the water alongside the ship swelled into a rippling column. It curled at the top and took the shape of a draconic serpent head in modest detail.

"Sinkua," a voice burbled from the serpentine water column, "A word?"

"What's up, Leviathan?" Sinkua asked. Luvros swooped up and picked at the liquid scales. Sinkua scolded, "Luvros! You know better!"

"The little one is no bother," Leviathan excused, "I've sensed Odin more strongly. Can you think why he might be so ireful?"

"If I had to guess, I'd say someone disagreed with him. Maybe corrected him."

"Hah! He does have a bit of an ego on him."

"All this time out of touch with the world hasn't been good for him either."

"I should suppose not," Leviathan said, "But I digress. No, I meant he seemed angry toward me in particular. Any thoughts?"

"Hard to say."

"Maybe he found out about what happened with the Mechanical Crypt," Galo suggested, "and he thinks you activated it willingly."

"That's... possible," Leviathan said, her liquid proxy churning, "Look into it in ArcNos, please. Try to smooth things over enough that I might speak with him. Nothing good can come of a fight between us."

"I'll do what I can," Galo promised.

"Sinkua," Elemeno beckoned as Leviathan's proxy collapsed into gentle waves, "Chekov wants to speak with you."

Puzzled but agreeable, Sinkua accepted Elemeno's phone.

"This is Sinkua."

"Elemeno tells me you were asking about the giant at the Radial Axiom Arena."

"Yeah," Sinkua said, "Does Mortvill know anything about it?"

"Well, nobody's seen him since he left with her to find Nikasu," Chekov said, "I'm not sure what to make of it, but I think it's as he intended."

"Shit. What about NalSet?"

"I... was about to ask you that."

"Wait," Sinkua urged, "He's not with you?"

"No!" Chekov cried, "Farim told me you all had to leave Hillside without him last week. I assumed he had caught up with you."

"I thought he found his way back to the base."

Chekov muttered to herself. Sinkua couldn't pick out any specific words, just that it was rapid and agitated.

"What happened last time you saw him?" she asked.

"I had a run-in with MalVek," he said, "NalSet stepped in and sent me to find Farim and Uro."

"Did MalVek have anything unusual with him?" she asked, "Any tech you didn't recognize?"

"Actually, yes," he said, "He had these gloves that pulled his photon weapon back to him."

"Like a magnet?"

"More like a tether. It felt like a direct line when he was trying to take it out of my hand. And it only affected his weapon."

"Hmm. Well, now we have proof that he's been developing derelict tech."

"What does that mean?"

"He's finishing projects that he and NalSet agreed were dead ends," Chekov explained, "Elemeno said you're still out at sea. How far are you from ArcNos?"

Sinkua mouthed the question to Galo, who held up three fingers. "Three days," Sinkua relayed, "Where do you want to meet?"

"At your house," she said, "I'm sure this is a long shot, but are you familiar with Epesol?"

"The Sword of the Sun?" he said, "It's in my cabin."

"Really?" she asked, a trace of hope in her voice, "How did you find it?"

"Odin brought it to me," he said, "How do you know about it?"

"Not important right now," Chekov dismissed, "What is important is that I know where to find another one. Epelun. The Sword of the Moons. Is Nikasu still okay?"

"She went to stay with Spril and Yrlis before I left," he said, "She should still be there."

"Great," she said with a trace of wincing, "Well, make sure she's there for our meeting."

"She'd be back at our house anyway," Sinkua said, "But what is this about?"

"Epelun belongs with her."

"So I gathered."

"Then, the rest will be discussed later," Chekov said, "I'll see you in…"

"No," Sinkua cut off, "I need you to tell me what's going on."

"This isn't the best time to go into it."

"Nikasu already worries that you guys are just using her. And I am up to the fucks with your cloak and dagger routine and tell-you-later lip service," Sinkua scolded, "So either tell me where to find Epelun so we can get it ourselves…"

"Or what?" Chekov challenged, "I am quickly running out of things to lose, and I know you won't hurt what I have left or attack me outright. Neither one is in your nature."

"You don't know a damn thing about my nature," Sinkua snipped, "Case in point, I wasn't going to threaten you."

"Then, what were…?"

"Or tell me what The Coalition is plotting for my sister and me."

"Haven't you realized?" she sighed, "We're dissolving The Coalition."

Chapter 22

Spril navigated the halls of the Ministry of Defense, receiving bland well-wishes and generic niceties. His colleagues regarded him like some distant relative or long estranged friend, speaking and posturing themselves as though they thought he was fragile. Or perhaps volatile.

He wanted to be offended, could even feel his ire rising against his composure. But it made sense, what with his having been on psych leave. Still, their delicate distant regard of him struck him as suspicious.

In the hall for the highest-ranked officers, he found all the office doors shut with every light but his own turned on. The sounds of people working inside swarmed him. Someone pushed their seat out and thrust to their feet. He closed his eyes to focus on that particular office, fading all other sounds into a murky burbling sigh.

A door opened behind him. He opened his eyes, and all the sounds normalized.

"Spril," EshCal greeted, sounding less cautious than everyone else, "How are you feeling?"

"I'll let you know after I get to my office," he said with a plastic smile, "How bad is it? Should I be worried?"

"I've kept your workload under control," EshCal assured, "Could you come to my office? I need to speak with you before you start your day."

"Sure," Spril said, tamping down his suspicions as he followed her. She closed the door behind them. "What do you need?"

"Well, there's no easy way to go about this," EshCal hesitated, her eyes casting down, "We had a meeting."

"Who had a meeting?" Spril said, his voice even and firm.

"The officers and I," she said, forcing her eyes up to his, "Everyone in this hall."

"And should I assume it was about me?" he asked, his breathing becoming uneven.

"Yes," she said, "We want you to consider resigning."

Six words confirmed his suspicions. He rubbed his temples with his thumb and forefinger, grinding his teeth. The sounds from every office grew louder and more distinct, though they sort of echoed with a two-second delay.

"Resign…" he stammered, "Resigning?! Do you know what it took to get to this point? Can you… Can you even comprehend what I've been through?"

"Yes. Yes. And no," EshCal said, folding her arms, "Look. We're not forcing you out. We just think that…"

"I'm fine," Spril insisted, "Your concern has been noted."

"I don't think you're taking this seriously."

"Of course, I'm not! I went on psych leave, and I can't even get to my office before you want me gone for what I assume is the reason I went on psych leave."

"You're right. That is why we want you to step down."

"We?" Spril challenged, "No, no, no. It's you, isn't it? This was your idea, and you flexed your authority because you want my position."

"That is absurd!" EshCal recoiled, "How dare you suggest…"

"What happens if I don't step down?"

"… It's more an issue of…"

"Or if I don't give it the consideration you think it deserves."

"In that case, we would…"

"You would drag Parliament into this… this… nonissue with everything else that's going on?" Spril asked, rubbing the space between his jaw and his earlobes. "Do you have any idea how much of a scandal that's going to look like?"

"I know exactly what it'll look like. And I know what this would do to our professional relationship," EshCal said, "You need to understand that I don't want to do this. But if it comes to it, I will."

Spril rubbed his jaw and earlobes harder. His breathing grew ragged. All the other sounds faded into a murky stew and eventually into a wavering distant wind. EshCal's voice was the only thing he could pick out now. That and the two-second echo. And there was no distinguishing between them. No fading or hollowness or loss of integrity.

"How long do I have?" he managed through gritting teeth.

"Well, that depends."

"…. On?"

"Are you willing to speak with…"

"The therapist doesn't need a coalition!" Spril shouted.

He immediately realized what he had said, that his argument had become muddled between his mind and his mouth. But what especially alarmed him was when he had said it.

The echo hesitated and diverged from her voice. Worse, to call them voice and echo was a mistake, as EshCal's mouth moved in perfect unison with the echo. All along, she had been speaking the second words he heard, and this time, they didn't match what he heard first.

"How did you know I was going to say that?" she asked.

"Reasonable assumptions," he lied. He rubbed the back of his neck, wincing as his every touch felt like scalding needles. "Of course, you'd send me to a therapist. Or back to the… The Coal… ition."

"No. No," EshCal refused, daring to settle her hand on his shirt fabric atop his shoulder. "I was about to recommend The Coalition, but I had second thoughts. You see, I…"

"You left The Coalition," Spril announced, catching flashes of his last encounter with them. He could hear Malia's exchange with the panel as he and Yrlis left more clearly in memory than he had in the moment. Amplified memories and pre-echoes compounded on one another. He stumbled through preemptive reactions, giving up on distinguishing pre-echoes from spoken words. "No, you didn't tell me. Neither had SenRas or Malia. I know. I don't trust them either. But maybe we…"

"But they might be the only people who can help you," EshCal said, "As much as I'd…"

"The Task Force isn't ready," Spril said, his expression shifting into pleasant surprise, "Phylus pulled it off?"

"He did."

"Great! What have we…?"

His vision crumbled into darkness from the periphery inward. His voice sounding garbled, he gave up on speaking. But EshCal's voice rang clearly as she called out his name. The floor betrayed his legs, and he hit the floor in a ragdoll mess, the last of his vision blackening on the way down.

A hand pawed at his thigh, relieving him of a dense isolated weight. The last thing he heard was EshCal conversing with some distant woman. Yrlis, he was rather sure, but his senses were fading.

The floor pulled away from him. The last thing he felt was his body folding over a shoulder as an arm wrapped around his waist.

"Am I correct to understand," MalVek said, his hands linked behind his back, "that you've called off the war between Tanelen and ArcNos?"

"Yes, General," Joren said, bowing slightly.

"Despite the fact that it counteracts our objectives?" MalVek said, facing The Politician squarely.

"Quite to the contrary, my colleague," Joren said, "What is our primary objective, General?"

"Who are you to…"

"Answer his question," The Harvester cut in, emerging from a corner of the room, "What, above all else, is the purpose of The Avatars of Fate?"

"Of course, my lord," MalVek capitulated, smiling plastically, "Our purpose is the arising. So must it all come to pass and such."

"And begetting the arising all comes down to one thing. Sowing discord," The Politician insisted, "That is what I have done."

"What you have done is make them complacent," The General snarled, "We have decreed this to be their time for action."

"Their brass is tarnished with the unspilled blood of the Subtransit Resistance. They would have realized this to be one of our plots long before we could realize our ambitions," The Politician said, "Besides, we ought to change our heading on the fly every now and again. We'd be fools not to assume we always have another Malia, EshCal, or even Pahres among our sympathizers."

"Do not speak as though they could outsmart me," The General snarled, "Nor that I wouldn't keep such things in mind."

"Let it stand," The Harvester ordered, "We can work with this."

"I refuse to be so condescended to."

"Or perhaps another CreSam," The Politician said, leveling his eyes at MalVek with an expression that betrayed nothing.

MalVek snarled something incomprehensible. It sounded like an indignation layered with an insult coated in an accusation, all spoken at once. He drew back his fist and barreled it forth in punctuation.

"Stop!" The Politician asserted.

The General's fist halted mid-flight. His muscles strained to push the blow onward, but nothing came of it.

"I realize how powerful you are, General," The Politician said, guiding MalVek's fist to his side, "But should you think to challenge me, realize that I am more so."

"That's quite enough, Politician," The Harvester said, "I dismiss you to fulfill your duties."

"Of course, my lord," The Politician said, bowing more deeply than he had to MalVek, "Before I go, however, the two of you may delight to learn that the Prime Minister of Foreign Affairs and the Last Chieftain Sage believe my powers to be so limited as common hypnosis."

"This is an interesting development indeed."

"The fools think me their allies."

"I don't trust him," The General said shortly after the door closed.

"You have made as much quite clear," The Harvester said, "Act not upon that distrust."

"You're not thinking to abandon our arrangement, are you?" The General pried, "I delivered The Impostor as promised."

"A proving of your loyalty. Not a call for such privilege as assassinating your fellow Named on suspicions alone," The Harvester asserted, "You also failed to tell me The Impostor possessed Epemort."

"You denied the truth of my origins," The General said, "Had I told you he wielded Epemort, you would have killed me for trying to make a fool of you."

"In that case," The Harvester said, "I suppose you know every failing of my original designs for the arising."

"I do indeed. Corrective machinations have been integrated into your policies for years."

"And my brother?"

"We will see him home."

Sinkua climbed out of the cab behind Galo and Elemeno. As he raised his head, he saw eleven people waiting for him on his lawn. With the two he knew were waiting inside, that put attendance at sixteen.

Chekov had brought everyone from The Coalition, which at this point was just Dourias and Gabdur. Farim and Uro, having been guests at headquarters since they left Hillside Oncology, also came along.

Galo had contacted Phylus through the emergency telegraph. Phylus was to have told Vielle and Nikasu as well as Spril and Yrlis. The latter hadn't made it. Sinkua had asked that Nikasu be told to wait to let everyone inside. MarLys, Malia, and SenRas were also there, apparently having been told by Vielle.

Greetings and introductions were exchanged all around, though it quickly became clear that everyone else had become acquainted while they waited. While Galo spoke with Farim, Dourias took Sinkua aside.

"I don't know if you know who I am, young man," Dourias began, cupping both his hands around one of Sinkua's, "but I knew your father."

"Before or after he went mad?" Sinkua asked. As he saw Dourias was taken aback, he patted the back of his hand and shook his head. "Sorry. Am I right to assume you're Dourias?"

"I must be the only person here you don't recognize," Dourias said, "Yes. I am Yrlis's biological father and the one they call The First Native."

"I didn't know Chekov was into older men," Sinkua said, "Never thought about it, honestly."

"Oh! No, no, young man, I'm actually about thirty years younger than I appear. It's a rather unsettling side effect of spending the better and worse part of a decade in a hyperspace prison. Phylus grew a six-month beard in a few weeks," Dourias explained, "In any case, I knew your father before he went mad. Your mother as well, though not as directly."

"Well, it's nice to meet you, Dourias. Let's head inside."

"Of course. I just wanted to say that I'm glad to have found your sister and yourself well."

The two of them followed everyone else as Nikasu unlocked the front door and waved the crowd inside. They entered the foyer to find everyone else either taken aback or bewildered at those taken aback.

An elderly one-eyed man standing in the middle of his kitchen looked odd enough, to be sure. But Sinkua knew he wasn't drawing this reaction, what with most of them not knowing who he was. That, and there was the considerably younger woman by his side.

Sinkua pushed to the front, exchanging acknowledging nods with Odin. BeiLou smiled up at him, and he turned to face the others with his hand on her shoulder.

"Everybody!" he announced, "I'd like you all to meet BeiLou. My mother."

SenRas looked to her pensively. She gave him a puzzled glance and continued panning the crowd. SenRas let his look drift away.

"BeiLou?" Chekov said, approaching her slowly, "I didn't know you had come back. I knew Sinkua had convened with Phoenix, what with Farim, but…"

"I as well am still coming to terms with this matter," Odin interjected, "We think his proximity to Yggdrasil was a factor."

"Yes, I'm surprised NalSet didn't tell you," BeiLou said, "He came here when he was looking for Sinkua."

"He… hasn't returned," Chekov said, her eyes casting down, "Look, if I could just address the room, we could all get on the same page. Sinkua?"

Sinkua turned to the crowd to find that numerous side conversations had broken out.

"Everybody!" he called out again. Attention gradually came his way. "A lot has happened since the Heniokhos Disaster. I'm still alive. BeiLou is back. This one-eyed bloke is Odin. He's Eytea's Etherworlder, same thing as Leviathan with Galo. Now, Chekov has some announcements."

Chekov waited with her hands folded before herself while everyone else, save for Dourias, found seats in the dining room, kitchen, and living room. Galo leaned on the kitchen counter and turned on the tap to a slow drip, opening a line for Leviathan. Once everyone had sat down and had their last exchanges, Chekov addressed the gathering.

"The Coalition has long been in the business of secrets. Simply put, having you aware of how much we know and what we're doing with it interferes with predictive analyses. But that has become both virtually impossible and quite impractical," Chekov opened, "The fact is, the founding members, NalSet, MalVek, Mortvill, and I, are from five hundred years in the future."

Silence swept the congregation as quizzical glances shot between the few who knew and the several who didn't.

"Am I to understand that Bahamut is to return?" Odin asked, "Or have humans replicated his power in the future?"

"He's still dead in our time," Chekov said, "We've managed a very rudimentary and very limited replication of his power."

"And you've come back to do what?" Galo asked, "To save us from The Avatars of Fate?"

"In part, but it isn't our primary objective. That would be to cultivate a weapon for a war in our own time," Chekov explained, "The ultimate goal of The Avatars of Fate is the return of Pandora. They call it the arising. She is an Etherworlder of unfathomable power. The embodiment of chaos."

"In my time," Odin interjected, "what I have gathered to be a bit over five thousand years ago, she drove the Etherworlders and our Hybrids near to extinction. When we perish, we forcibly surrender our powers unto her."

"Yes, thank you," Chekov nodded, "In my time, she's gained the power of nearly every Etherworlder, making her virtually indestructible."

"I'm sorry," SenRas cut in, "But could you not just help us destroy this Pandora in our present, your past, and be rid of her in our future, your present?"

"Good question, but sadly no," Chekov said, "The nature of time travel protects against paradoxes. The moment we interacted with this time period, a second timeline branched off from that point. When we return to our home time, we will arrive back in the first timeline. If any of you try to go with us, you would remain on the second timeline, being that you're native to it."

"Hence the term First Native?" SenRas asked.

"Precisely."

"Does that have something to do with how Yggdrasil came back?" Vielle asked, "Or why Pahres had shifting identities?"

"Possibly," Chekov said, "We've theorized that Yggdrasil has the power to bridge timelines. Someone else could have gone back and saved Yggdrasil in a third timeline, which created the Platinum Orchid. We suspect there's another in the first timeline."

"And Pahres?"

"Pahres was the son of the Last Yggdrasil Hybrid and a member of a counter-chaos activist group called The Trifecta. Near the end of the original war, their souls were sealed inside of copper statues."

"Pahres, Takmet, and Arestor, correct?" Galo asked.

"Yes. As you may know, Takmet posed as your grandfather when the real Gijin died before you were born," Chekov said, "Now, in the first timeline, Pahres became and remained The Prophet. According to our theory, saving Yggdrasil changed this. Vielle, when you planted Yggdrasil, it facilitated a connection to the third timeline, allowing the new persona to take over."

"Hence why his changes were contingent on how likely I was to plant it," Vielle nodded, "But could that happen to anyone whose past was changed by time travel?"

"Not that we're aware of," Chekov said, "As children of early generations of Hybrids, the Trifecta had unique mutations. Pahres's was that he was preternaturally charismatic. Between this and his connection to Yggdrasil, we speculate that this enables his most recently incarnated persona to overwrite the others, with the Yggdrasil Hybrid acting as a bridge guide."

"While we're on the subject of The Trifecta," Galo said, "Odin, do you know where we can find Arestor's statue? Or Chekov, do you?"

"This took place, as might you say, after my time," Odin said.

"There might be something about it in those books," BeiLou offered, "We've translated the first four."

"I asked Leviathan, and all she said was, 'You tell me,'" Sinkua said, "I don't know what she meant by that."

"She means you wrote those books," Odin said, his expression stern and hard.

"You mean my previous incarnations?"

"Yes. The war spanned thirteen Omphaloworlder generations. The Phoenix Hybrid chronicled one in each of those books."

A pop rang out from the kitchen tap, and water flowed freely. The splash radius shrank as the water receded and flowed back on itself. Soon, it stopped short of the sink, the end of the stream rounded and rippling. A liquid proxy of Leviathan took shape in the halted flow.

"I'm searching the Southland Sea for Arestor's statue," she announced, "Odin, BeiLou, if there's a diagram of…"

Black sparks exploded from Odin's torso as he crossed the living room and half the kitchen within half a blink, his milystic discharge killing the lights. His body swelled until his frame threatened to destroy the kitchen ceiling if he stood at his full height. He grabbed the liquid proxy just under the head and stretched it up to eye level.

"What have you done to the Omphaloworld!?" he roared.

"What are you talking about, you arrogant fool?" Leviathan demanded, "I have done nothing in malice. Release me!"

"The seas have risen to consume the land," Odin growled, "Do not deny this, serpent wench. It reeks of your milystis."

"Don't you dare judge me for my efforts to save Yggdrasil when yours also ended so catastrophically."

"… What speak you of?"

"A machine they now call the Mechanical Crypt," Leviathan said, wriggling free. Odin shrank to his usual size, still formidable but now looking like the smallest person in the room. "After you entered the root system, we repurposed it that I might give of my own power to save Yggdrasil."

"You were to… water Yggdrasil?"

"Yes, as a counteraction to Nidhogg's consumption."

"And when Yggdrasil fell to the two-headed serpent…"

"My power was irrevocably released upon the Omphaloworld," Leviathan confessed, "It's how this world came to be so flooded. And how I came into my copper state a generation after I joined the war. The catastrophe of the Trifecta stripped me of the ability to transform at will."

"I…" Odin began, "… apologize for judging you, Leviathan. This is a time for unity among our kind. I ought to have known you would not betray this world or our cause with intent."

"Yes, you should have, but I won't dwell on it. The fact that I speak their language far better than you is my consolation," Leviathan said, "Now then, check the thirteenth book. Get back to me if you find out where Arestor stood."

The column of water collapsed to a steady flow, which receded to the slow drip that Galo had turned it on to. Sinkua found an empty candelabra in the cabinet and placed it on the dining room table. He filled it with candles he found stashed in a kitchen drawer.

"Odin," he said as he lit the candles with his fingertip, "Could all humanoid Etherworlders do what you just did?"

"Within limitations, all Etherworlders can alter our size within the Omphaloworld," Odin said, "What is your intent with this question?"

"Do you know if anyone from here has ever been able to do that?" Sinkua asked, "Maybe one of the mutated children of the early Hybrids?"

"No, but there existed giants among them."

"If I give you a picture of a certain giant, could you tell me who it was?"

"Unfortunately, the arena giant emitted a strong EMP," Chekov said, "There's no video or pictures of it."

"I may be able to make a composite sketch from audience descriptions," Malia offered.

"That could work," Sinkua said, "How long would that take?"

"Couple of weeks."

"What was the nature of its presence?" Odin asked, "Physical or proxy?"

"Um... not really either, but... not neither. Kinda both, kinda not," Sinkua grasped, "It was an artificial projection that, uh..."

"It was a remote controlled hard light construct," Malia provided.

"Wielded it a weapon?" Odin asked.

"A big fuckoff hammer," Sinkua said.

"That most likely was Seriamus," Odin said, his voice tinged with unmistakable fear, "Last I knew, he was Pandora's Hybrid. Appeared he to you as a titan, then they presented him in his true form. Means this that The Avatars of Fate are intimately familiar with the bygone era of this war."

"Their leader was alive during it," Chekov said, "During all thirteen generations, in fact."

"What is named their leader?"

"He goes by The Harvester," she said, "But his common name is Mortvill."

"I recall nobody by that name," Odin pointed out.

"That's The Omnimath's name," Nikasu said, "I thought they were brothers. Unless..."

"They're the same person," Chekov said, ignoring Odin.

"He's been playing both sides?" Nikasu cried out, "He's been using us, and you just let him?"

"No! Listen to me," Chekov demanded, "In the first timeline, after Pandora betrayed Mortvill, he held himself accountable for the inexorable slow death of our world."

"Okay," Nikasu said, taking a deep breath, "And that's when he became The Omnimath?"

"Yes," Chekov said, "He pledged himself to coming up with a way to destroy her. Five hundred years later, he assembled us, and we came back to just over thirty years before Pandora's return to set the last phase of his plan into motion."

"Four people is a small team for a job like that," Sinkua pointed out, "Tech limits or trying to keep it clandestine?"

"Neither," she said, "There were to be dozens of Coalition Originals, but only the four of us made it. I had assumed they died in transit or arrived at different times. But knowing what we now know about MalVek, I suspect they were, well, pushed."

"Son of a bitch..."

"Well now," Dourias announced, "As necessary as this has been, we have digressed from the original purpose of this meeting."

"Yes, we have. Thank you," Chekov sighed, "When The Omnimath went with Elemeno to rescue Nikasu, he never returned. When NalSet went to find Sinkua so he could resurrect Farim, he also never returned. Dourias, Gabdur, and I suspect the worst in both cases.

"As I told Sinkua, The Coalition is in the process of dissolution. Those of us who remain will integrate into the Anti-Avatar Task Force. Odin was right. This is a time for unity."

A disconcerted hush swept the room. Minutes ago, she had spoken of The Coalition as spearheading the fight against Pandora and The Avatars of

Fate. Now, its foundation had crumbled, and she was resigning to a startup as the next best thing.

"What about the weapon you came here to cultivate?" Sinkua asked, breaking the silence, "The one for the war in your time."

"It's Spril," Malia said, "Spril is The Weapon."

"That's impossible," Phylus protested, "I met him the day he was born. I knew his mother when she was pregnant with him."

"Our colleagues created his embryo in the future. In the first timeline," Chekov said, "We planted him with suitable host parents. In our history, they never conceived a child."

"So, it's not just sentient beings that are restricted to the timeline we're born in?" MarLys observed, "It's anything with DNA?"

"Yes, but none of that matters," Chekov sighed, "Spril has made it abundantly clear that he has no intention of leaving. And I wouldn't be of much use returning alone. So, as it is, I'll be staying here to help clean up and rebuild after we stop the arising."

"You know," Galo said, "You could have spared us the headache of all that time travel and branching timelines talk and just said you genetically engineered Spril as an Anti-Avatar weapon. Nobody would have wondered anything when you stuck around after he stopped the arising or killed Pandora."

"No, I couldn't," Chekov said, "Keeping secrets got us in this mess."

"Besides, Spril could change his mind," Sinkua said, "But for now, how do Epesol and Epelun figure into all of this?"

"I'll take this one," Dourias said, holding Chekov's shoulder, "During my infiltration into The Avatars of Fate, I collected a wealth of intel, but I had no secure way to transmit it to The Coalition. I was also direly limited in how I might keep this information. So, I used tsora-magnetic ink to tattoo myself with encoded diagrams."

"Meet my mentor!" Farim announced.

"Yes, well, let's hold off on any applause," Dourias said, chuckling nervously, "Unfortunately, during my imprisonment in hyperspace, I forgot I had these tattoos, not to mention what any of them meant. The only thing I remember is that they involved you and you."

He pointed at Sinkua and Nikasu, the Hybrid siblings standing within each other's arm's reach. Nikasu tensed, and Sinkua pulled her closer.

"What are you getting at?" Nikasu spat.

"Somehow, the two of you are pivotal in unraveling their designs on the arising," Dourias said, "Sinkua carries Epesol. The Sword of the Sun. It resonates only with his milystis, allowing him to wield it as though it weighs as much as a rapier and channel his powers as a perfect conduit."

"And Epelun…" Nikasu trailed off, "… resonates only with mine?"

"Yes," Dourias nodded, "The Sword of the Moons."

"Clearly, this concerns Drakougeneospa," Odin asserted.

"Drakougeneospa. That's, ah…" BeiLou pondered aloud, "… Famujokoumba in Mberhali. Roughly, House of the Dragon Family in Ouristihran?"

"In Fjarthursk, we called it Husefamidraget. Sinkua and Nikasu are the only people left who could raise it from its burial site, but doing so mandates they have Epesol and Epelun," Odin said, "That must be the foundation of their role in this encoded master plan."

"We reached the same conclusion," Dourias said, "Unfortunately, that's as far as we've gotten so far."

"Well, I know where to find Epelun," Chekov announced, "It's in the Nemesis Ion Cloud."

"Would that be to where Nemesis has fled," Odin asked, "or what which he has become?"

"Fled," Chekov said. She turned to Nikasu. "There's an ion cloud a few million kilometers beyond our moons' orbits. Nemesis is inside of it. He has Epelun."

"Great!" Nikasu remarked, "Who's Nemesis, what's an ion cloud, and why is he inside of one?"

"And why have none of us heard of the Nemesis Ion Cloud?" Galo added.

"Nemesis is the Etherworlder dragon icon of gravity," Odin said, "Nikasu, you of course, are his Hybrid. As for why he is in an ion cloud, I should presume he ensconced himself there when only he and Phoenix remained of the Dragon Family's Etherworlders."

"And few laypeople have heard of the Nemesis Ion Cloud. It's actually come to be a taboo topic in the astronomy community," Chekov explained, "It's only visible once every twenty-eight years, and that's if the sky is clear enough. So, there's debate as to whether it's even real."

"Why does it appear so infrequently?" Galo asked as Nikasu walked to the coat rack.

"The slightest moonlight flushes it out," Chekov said, "It can only be seen when all three new phases coincide."

"And that happens once every twenty-eight years," Galo said, nodding, "I never knew that. Do you know the next time it'll happen?"

"In about three weeks," Chekov said, "Nineteen days from now."

Nikasu took something from her coat pocket and came to Chekov's side. "Does it look like this?" she asked, holding out the coaster.

"Well, let me see," Chekov said, taking it and holding it up to the light, "Where did you get this?"

"The receptionist at that lab gave it to me. I think The Omnimath left it with her," Nikasu said, "So, is that the Nemesis Ion Cloud?"

"Yes, as far as I can tell," Chekov said, "When it appears, line up these holes with the bright spots and focus your milystis through them. You should form a bond with Nemesis and draw him down to you."

"Do I need this to do it?" Nikasu asked, "Yrlis said it was just a coaster with holes punched in it."

"She's not wrong. It's just that she doesn't know about the Nemesis Ion Cloud," Chekov said, "This is just to help you focus."

"It'll also help you find it," Gabdur offered, "In any case, Nikasu, we'll contact you that day to remind you."

"We'll all stay in ArcNos until then," Chekov said, "We'll be in touch once we've found a place."

Those who weren't staying at the house began gathering their coats and hats from the backs of seats, corners of tables, and in rare instances, the coat rack.

"Before you go," Galo spoke up, "Vielle, I need to ask you something."

"Sure, what is it?" she said, pulling her skull cap down over the curled tops of her ears.

"Since you used Yggdrasil to locate Nikasu," he began, "is there any chance you could map its main roots?"

"I, ah…" Vielle trailed off, rubbing the back of her neck, "I don't think I could. I'm sorry. What are you hoping to find?"

"I have medical records from people who have had episodes similar to Sinkua's," Galo said, "Several dates on one of them match his, but there's no apparent catalyst."

"We think my episodes are triggering them in other people," Sinkua offered.

"And you think Yggdrasil is facilitating the connection?" Vielle asked.

"Yes," Galo nodded, "She had an especially violent episode at roughly the time when Sinkua came out from under Yggdrasil. She had to be euthanized."

"I'm sure you're trying to keep it a secret," MarLys interjected, "But are you talking about Sanus?"

"… We are," Galo admitted, "I'm sorry. Ocronn asked me to keep this from being traced back to him. But I'm in trustworthy company."

"It's okay," MarLys said, "There was a visible Yggdrasil root on their lawn."

"Which means it might be connecting me to other afflicted people," Sinkua said, "Son of a fucker."

"Son of a fucker, indeed," Galo sighed, "Also, it's only fair that I tell you that these are actually only Sanus's records. I'm sorry to have lied to you."

"It's fine, honestly," Sinkua said, "I get why you did it."

"I have reached out to some doctors in Berinin for other cases," Galo said, "I expect to be able to collect on those upon my return."

"Well, should it still be intact," Odin said, "There is an apparatus in Husefamidraget which ought to help map the roots of Yggdrasil."

"When I found Nikasu, I overheard the supervisor call the room she was in an actuation chamber," Elemeno offered, "People started turning into monsters after I tripped the security system."

"Which means I might be triggering episodes, too," Nikasu concluded.

"Unfortunately, it looks that way," Elemeno said, "But more to my point, many of the staff were afflicted. Farim, you still have that flash drive, yes?"

"The one Galo gave me? Yeah," Farim said, "It's been touch and go getting anything off of it. Or even making time for it. But knowing what to look for should make things easier."

"Okay, let's make sure we're all on the same page," Chekov announced, "BeiLou and Odin will check the thirteenth book for clues Arestor's whereabouts while Leviathan continues searching the Southland Sea. Once they locate him, Galo and any reasonable company will set out to recover him and to collect whatever medical records have been furnished for his request. In nineteen days, Gabdur will call Nikasu to remind her about the Nemesis Ion Cloud. Once she has Epelun, Odin and I will instruct her and Sinkua on how to raise the House of Dragons. If the apparatus is intact, Vielle will map Yggdrasil's roots. In the meantime, we'll continue deciphering Dourias's tattoos. Farim and Uro will also research any lab captives they find on that flash drive."

"We'll be looking for biological commonalities," Uro said, "Whatever made them susceptible to this condition might be enabling a sympathetic reaction."

"We'll also look at where they live and their travel habits," Farim added, "Depending on how precise the root map is, we could be able to determine if relocating would help them."

Chapter 23

Two processions of people with wheelbarrows lined up behind a pair of trucks, one with crushed rocks and the other with wood scrap and rebar. As each one wheeled away their freshly emptied barrow, the next pulled up, waiting to unload.

"Hey! KalChi!" Biroe called from the cabin of his rented truck, "I'm winning."

KalChi looked back at the truck beds. Hers, the one bound for the quarry, was filling much slower than his. She rolled her eyes.

"It's not a contest," she called back, "you one-legged buttmunch."

"Temper, temper, crab dumpling," Biroe teased, "Only reason it's not a contest is because you're losing."

KalChi laughed. "What am I going to do with you?" she remarked, "Nevermind. I already know. By the way, is your wheelchair still under warranty?"

"Yeah, but it wouldn't be a problem if it wasn't," Biroe said, "These shocks can take a lot more than you think."

"Oh? Was that a challenge?"

"Only if you're winning, apparently."

KalChi leaned her head back and let out a rolling alto laugh. She shook her head and closed her eyes, smiling as she bit her lip.

As he watched her, Biroe's mind wandered to places best not ventured at a worksite. Fortunately for his dignity, a knock at his door pulled his thoughts back to his work. Unfortunately for his composure, he jumped so hard that he punched the horn. The volunteer behind his truck spilled her wood and rebar off the ramp.

"Sorry," OshMar said, slicking his hand through his hair, "I thought you saw me."

"Not as little as I'd like," Biroe snarked, "Sorry. What are you doing out here?"

"I have some papers you'll want to see," he said, holding up the packet.

"It's after office hours," Biroe bemoaned, "Can't it wait until morning?"

"Yes, but I thought you'd like some good news."

"I don't know how much you heard, but there's not much you could tell me that'll top what we've got planned for later."

"I'm not interested in topping anything between the two of you," OshMar said. Biroe stared at him expectantly, but OshMar either missed or ignored a perfectly good lewd joke. "Just take the damn packet."

"What are you guy talking about?" KalChi called over.

"I'll tell you once I know," Biroe said, taking the packet.

The first page outlined everything with the subsequent pages spelling out the terms in the finest of details. Biroe's mouth fell open and spread into a smile.

"Hot damn," he gasped, "She pulled it off."

"Who?" OshMar asked.

"What is it?" KalChi called over.

"They came down on the estimate," Biroe answered, "They're taking on seventy percent of the work at ten percent over market standard."

"Nice!" she exclaimed, "What are we doing about the other thirty? More of this?"

"Don't know. Maybe. But it's going to take a while to get everything lined up. Lot of paperwork to…"

"Hold on," OshMar cut back in, "Who pulled it off?"

"Sorry," Biroe said, "EshCal."

"How do you figure it was her?"

"Lunch Break Protocol, when she excused herself to make a call," he recounted, "I overheard enough to tell she was talking about this situation. Word must have reached a Judge so it could be brought up at the Union Parliament Assembly without it connecting to any of us. Probably Nenbard. Or, well, whoever attended in his place."

"Well, what matters is that we got a better contract," OshMar said, "But it wasn't Berinin. Turns out Tanelen backed us. Not sure how the Noble Doyen feels about that."

"Really?" Biroe asked. OshMar nodded. "Hm. Hey, by the way, can we expect you at the trial?"

"We're not supposed to discuss that," KalChi called over the rumble of dumping debris.

"I filed a Dissent to Testify," OshMar said, "I'm too personally involved."

"Personally involved? Are you and FerLyn, you know," Biroe asked, making a thrusting motion, "making four-legged monsters?"

"What? No!" OshMar recoiled, "She's a married woman."

"Hey, I'm not here to judge," Biroe said, "How are you personally involved, then?"

"They approached me first," OshMar explained, shifting his weight, "They moved on because they didn't have any leverage."

"That doesn't mean you're…"

"I offered FerLyn my counsel when I learned they were leveraging her," OshMar continued, "That's how we became friends."

EshCal sat watching Spril's wakeless body on the adjustable bed in the center of the room. His chest faintly rose and dropped under the sterile sheets. Never taking her eyes off him, she obliquely watched Yrlis pace and tend to the complicated equipment surrounding him.

Yrlis settled down in the chair across from EshCal. She stroked Spril's cheek and kissed his forehead. She reached for the IV pole and fiddled with the drip settings.

"These doctors know what they're doing," EshCal assured her, "You can relax."

"I'm sure they do," Yrlis said, "for other people. Not for him."

"He's stable. That's all anyone can do," EshCal said, "Even you."

"I should be able to do more," Yrlis insisted, "I know things about him that they don't."

"Such as…?" EshCal pried, "I already told them about his sensory spikes and psychic glimpses."

"But do you know why he has those?" Yrlis challenged, "Or where he came from?"

"I suppose you mean other than Ivaria," EshCal said, "I remember he thought that note said he was from another time. I never heard if that was true."

"It is," Yrlis said, "The Coalition… engineered him in the future. He's a living weapon."

"That explains a lot," EshCal sighed.

Though she kept her eyes on Spril, EshCal could feel Yrlis glaring across his body at her. His eyes didn't stir. His breathing didn't deepen. But the pulse on the side of his neck quickened. He could hear them, perhaps even smell Yrlis.

"How did you get him here?" Yrlis asked, "You were alone with him when I got here, and nobody had seen him yet."

"I carried him," EshCal said, "I put him over my shoulder and walked here."

"You…?" Yrlis puzzled, trailing off. She sighed and smeared her hands over her eyes and down her cheeks. "Level with me, EshCal. Are you in love with him?"

"What? Why would you…?"

"I wouldn't hate you for it. I know nothing has happened, even though you've been alone with him several times," Yrlis clarified, "But to go to those lengths?"

"I would have done it for anyone in the Ministry of Defense. Or the Subtransit Resistance," EshCal insisted, "Even you. This was an act of camaraderie."

"I can't see it that way," Yrlis said, "He's at least fifty kilos heavier than you. That kind of adrenaline doesn't come from camaraderie. There's only…"

Yrlis stopped as EshCal nearly toppled her seat pushing herself out of it. EshCal moved to the foot of Spril's bed. She grabbed the frame in both hands and hoisted it to her chin with only the faintest trace of strain. Yrlis stared agape as EshCal curled the bed nine more times before she put it down.

"What…? How did…?" Yrlis stammered, "How the fuck!?"

"I'm, well, stronger than I look," EshCal said, dodging eye contact as she sat down, "Don't be weird about it. Everyone's weird about it. Except for Spril."

"How did this happen?" Yrlis asked, "Wait. Did The Avatars experiment on you?"

"No, I did this myself," EshCal said, "Now please, stop being weird about it."

"I'm not! I'm not," Yrlis insisted, "It's just surprising."

"If I tell you how I got to this point, will you stop being weird?" EshCal asked. Yrlis shut her mouth and nodded, "Weight training was always part of my workout routine. But I got more serious about it when I got involved with The Hunter. I needed to be sure I could overpower him when I had my chance."

"And then you found out he was bulletproof?"

"Yes, that was a problem in and of itself," EshCal said, "But CreSam's encroaching psychosis was what really worried me. Bulletproof bones would've been nothing next to him turning on me."

"Do you think you could have…?"

"Yes," EshCal cut off, "If CreSam had attacked me when I betrayed him, I would have taken him down."

"Ten minutes ago, I would have thought you were deluding yourself," Yrlis said, "Have you gotten stronger since then?"

"Slightly. I plateaued shortly after the war ended. I'm happy with my body as it is."

"I used to think that if CreSam had chosen you instead of The Hunter, Spril wouldn't have ended up like he did," Yrlis said, "Now, I'm not sure I could have saved him."

EshCal shook her head. "He would have been better off. It's never been my way to hide in the rafters."

"I already knew that about you," Yrlis said, "I just didn't think about the fact that you weren't this strong back then."

"No, but I've always been stronger and faster than Spril," EshCal said, "But he's always had sharper reflexes and been more skilled with polearms. It would've come down to timing and reach."

Silence lingered while Yrlis watched Spril, seeming to take it all in. EshCal's phone rang in her pocket. She checked it and excused herself. Yrlis nodded and waved her off as EshCal walked to the corner.

"Hello?"

"Madam High Minister?" her assistant rasped, his evident nicotine habit adding a decade to the age in his voice, "High Minister of Foreign Affairs Calhosin just delivered a letter for you."

"What does it say?"

"Your Eyes Only."

"I mean, what does the letter say?"

"Madam?"

"PavRal," EshCal said, "If I didn't want you reading my messages, I would have stopped you the first time."

PavRal's breath became heavy in her ear as he clamped the phone between his cheek and shoulder. EshCal kept quiet while he worked at the envelope. After some ripping, shuffling, and mumbling, he spoke again.

"It's from Noble Doyen Joren," he said, "The ultimatum has been called off."

"Phylus mentioned that, but we were both skeptical," EshCal remarked, "So it's been made official, then?"

"Appears so," PavRal said, "Should I ready something suited to the occasion from your secret cabinet?"

"Not just yet. Come up with something, but hold off until I say."

"As you ask, Madam High Minister."

"I do have something else to ask of you in the meantime," EshCal said, "The Ministry of Infrastructure just finalized a deal to clean up the high-rise district."

"Seventy-thirty split, as I understand."

"Correct," she said, "There's a list of names in the second left-hand drawer of my desk. Make sure everyone on it resigns from Biroe's volunteer crew when he offers."

"Should I ask him to dismiss them directly?" PavRal asked.

"I need you to be more subtle than that. Coordinate with Prime Minister SenRas's personal assistant. Her name is MarLys."

"My Lord!"

MalVek lifted his head in slight acknowledgment and kept working without slowing his pace. Electrical hardware covered the table, scattered in what lesser minds would have found to be a haphazard manner. His portal strip sat in the center with several other devices wired into it and other peripherals connected to those. A deep grumble rolled in his throat.

"Speak, boy!" he shouted, turning his head sharply.

"My Lord," Khirsan repeated, tightening his grip on the canvas satchel, "I've completed the replica."

"Very well," MalVek said, facing him, "Let's have it."

Khirsan kept his eyes cast down as he approached, stopping just beyond arm's reach. He withdrew a dagger and laid it across his palms. Lowering his head further, he presented the dagger to MalVek.

"Rather smaller than I hoped for," MalVek said, taking the dagger and spinning it in his hand.

"My apologies, My Lord. That was as much material as we could synthesize," Khirsan said, raising his head but still not daring to make eye contact, "The specifications from the analysis were very demanding."

"Yes, those damnable Quircois were a clever lot," MalVek grumbled, "Too proficient for their own good, perhaps."

"I followed the analysis to the letter," Khirsan insisted, "Despite it's size, it should serve as a functional replica of Epesol."

"Should?" MalVek questioned, stopping with the blade angled toward the guard.

"We... won't know for sure until you... um... test it, My Lord."

"Yes. We must test it," MalVek mused, his voice trailing off. In a couple of moseying steps, he closed the space between himself and Khirsan. He leaned the tip of the dagger against the man's chest. "Fetch me one of the non-compliant. The one from downstairs."

"Right away, sir!"

MalVek returned to his work as Khirsan left. He made more connections between peripherals and uncoupled others. He linked stripped components in secondary and tertiary connections. Eventually, he had everything on the table wired together with his portal strip at the core.

MalVek opened the top drawer, revealing it to be bottomless. Leaving the peripherals atop the table, he mounted his portal strip to the inside of the bottomless drawer. He dialed in a set of coordinates and activated the strip.

Electric blue fractals flickered within the wooden frame. He adjusted a few of the peripherals until the images became consistent. He cocked his head and narrowed his eyes. But the images never took on any manner of sense.

"Goddamn Eyes of the Dragon," he muttered. He looked over his shoulder. "Mortvill!" No answer. MalVek grumbled and shook his head. "Lord Harvester!"

He returned his attention to the jagged fractals. A moment later, the sound of footfalls filled the doorframe.

"What manner of interruption is this?" The Harvester demanded with a voice firm enough to all but shake the room. "First, I hear your... henchmen... have attempted to replicate Epesol as a dagger? And now you bark my name as though I am their peer? I am well aware of our arrangement, but forget you not that you are my subordinate. Now, tell me why you have interrupted…"

"What's become of the homunculi?" MalVek asked, "The ones in Tanelen."

"They have been on standby since the prisoners escaped," The Harvester grumbled, "Two of them were decommissioned a man calling himself The Patriarch. His real name is Phylus."

"Yes, our… rogue captive," MalVek said, "Have The Politician bring here. All of them. I have need of the Eyes of the Dragon."

"Does the prison serve any further purpose for you?"

"Yes, but the structure is inconsequential."

"Very well. I'll pass your orders to The Politician," The Harvester said, "I will resume my search for the other Epemort."

"Ought to have asked The Impostor where he found his."

The Harvester's mask shifted with his sneer. For all the tension in his shoulders, he appeared to glide as he walked to the door and out of the room.

MalVek turned off his portal strip and ripped it out of the bottomless drawer. He tossed it to the back of the table, piled the peripherals on it, and pushed the whole mess against the wall.

Knuckles rapped on the doorframe. Gurney wheels rattled as they bumped over the threshold. Khirsan crossed the room with a bedded figure writhing against leather restraints. The noncompliant screamed, but all that came through his gag was muffled squeals. MalVek rose from his seat to stand over the gurney.

"Well, hello there, Doctor Caylence," he said, smiling in a way that touched his eyes with a measure of wrongness, "How are you feeling today?"

MalVek nodded along as Caylence shouted incoherently. He looked across the bed and extended his hand toward Khirsan. "Dagger."

Khirsan complied, handing it over with the flat of the blade between his thumb and index finger. MalVek took it and angled the tip against Caylence's clavicle. Caylence writhed against his restraints.

"I hope you know how much of a pain in my ass you've been. I actually wanted to do worse to you," MalVek said, "I wanted The Politician to make you think you had resisted his hypnosis. That you had the rare gift of being beyond his control. Give you a sense of hope along with a fear of futility. Such a decadent pairing, you know, especially when the hope turns out to be false. But he insisted that that was too cruel. Can you believe that? The nerve of some people!

"Well anyway," he continued, tapping the blade on bony flesh, "It would seem I've caught a bit of his humanity. I'm giving you a chance to appeal for your life. Granted, it will be a life of constant enthrallment. You have been one of the most troublesome of the noncompliant, after all. But who knows? Maybe you can earn back some of your self awareness. Perhaps even a measure of free will?"

MalVek reached under the gurney and unlocked the gag.

"You shit-shaped cross-eyed piranha!" Caylence shouted, "How dare you come in here and…"

MalVek folded Caylence's tongue back and skewered it to his uvula. The dagger blade punctured his esophagus, split his brain stem, and pushed through the base of his skull to pierce the gurney mat. Blood ran from the corners of his mouth and out of the back of his head.

"As I suspected," MalVek said, looking into Caylence's wildly dilating and contracting eyes, "This is the extent of your utility after all."

As Caylence's life extinguished, MalVek watched the blade expectantly. He tapped the pommel. Nothing happened.

As a tool of Phoenix and her Hybrid, Epesol could return the tsora of the deceased to their body. But it could take lives like any other sword, perhaps even better. It was an instrument of ultimate healing which could become one of ultimate torment, locking its victim in a cycle of death and resurrection.

This facsimile did no such thing. Minutes passed, and Caylence still lay just as dead. MalVek ripped the dagger from Caylence's mouth and whipped it across the room. The blade sank to the hilt, striking hard enough to leave an armspan crater of spiderweb cracks.

"Give me some good news, or so help me, I'll do the same to you," MalVek grumbled, "Damned Quircois, thinking they can outsmart me."

"Um… the… the Heniokhos Disaster," Khirsan stammered, "The contractors have agreed to… a… contract."

"Really now?" MalVek said, folding his arms, "That is good news. Thank you."

"Thank you for your mercy, My Lord," the guard exhaled, bowing.

"It is nothing," MalVek said, "Tell Jevana I said to make ready for ArcNos."

SenRas nudged the door further open as he tapped it with the back of his fist.

"Need something, MeiLom?" a voice from the other side asked.

SenRas's throat tightened and stomach folded over. They had only met the one time, but her voice already had that the power to remind him of everything he should have done differently.

"Sorry to interrupt," SenRas said, crossing the threshold, "Sinkua said I could find you here."

BeiLou turned around in her seat, her eyes narrowing on the cusp of recognition. Odin ignored them both and kept translating.

"It's cool. Is he still downstairs?" she asked.

"He is," SenRas said, "Were you expecting him?"

BeiLou shook her head. "Just checking. You were at that meeting, right?"

"Ahh… Yes," he fumbled, "But I don't believe we were properly introduced."

"Yeah, not much time for that with everything else going on," she excused, "Crazy stuff, but I think you get used to it, eventually."

"Yes… Crazy indeed," he sighed, "Listen, um… This isn't easy for me to say."

"Well, why don't we start with proper introductions?" she suggested, "I'm BeiLou, as you may remember. Sinkua's late mom. Or MeiLom's if he's okay with you calling him that. Anyway. Back from the dead. Struggling to adjust. And you?"

"Well, I…" SenRas fumbled, "I'm sorry. Did your mother ever tell you about me?"

"Ah… Sorry. Can't say she did," BeiLou said, "Can I ask why she might've mentioned you?"

SenRas lowered his head as he composed his thoughts. At least he tried, but nothing useful coalesced. He cleared his throat several times and scratched the back of his shoulder.

"What do you know about your immediate family?" he asked at last.

"Well, my son is a Hybrid with power over fire and resurrection…"

"Not that family," SenRas interrupted, "The one you were born into."

"I grew up with my mother. It was just me and her. She never talked about my father," BeiLou reflected, "I did see her on the other side though."

"And what did you two talk about?"

"She told me about my half sister AinZun, her daughter from her first marriage," BeiLou said, "She said that AinZun had killed her."

"Anything else?" he asked, shifting his weight.

"Yeah, she, ah… told me about how she helped save CreSam from The Avatars of Fate," she said. She rose from her seat and crossed the room. Stopping a step short of him, she angled her index and middle fingers on his chin, "Tell me something, old guy."

"… Anything."

"Is your name SenRas?"

"… Yes," he exhaled.

"What the fuck!?" BeiLou exclaimed, "I mean… Fuck! I don't even know where to start. What happened?"

"Could you… maybe…" SenRas stammered, almost stealing glimpses of eye contact, "… be more specific?"

"Where did you go? Why did we never see you?" BeiLou said, shouting loud enough to drown out any conversations happening downstairs, "She said you didn't come home from work one night, and the next thing she knew, she got an envelope full of money and a letter saying you'd died in an accident. Then you just show up forty years later with this business about CreSam and The Avatars and just… What the fuck!?"

"Well," SenRas said, locking his hands behind his back, "Did she tell you what happened to AinZun when she was little?"

"She told me she lost all custody and visitation. Irrevocably," BeiLou said, "AinZun was orphaned soon after. Did you have something to do with that?"

SenRas swallowed hard. "Did she say how AinZun's father died?"

"Suicide. Burned a hole through his own trachea."

"Well, the truth is," SenRas said, "I was the one who killed him."

"Dude! I know I keep saying this, but what the fuck!?" BeiLou recoiled, "Why did you kill her ex-husband? Was it the custody thing?"

"I didn't know it was him until after the fact," SenRas said, breathing deeply to compose himself, "I never told your mother about this. She thought I worked in a factory, but I was actually a hitman. He was my mark."

"And you had to run when you realized you'd killed your wife's ex-husband?"

"I wish I could say I would've run if that's all it was, but I don't know," he said, "No, the hit was issued on false pretenses. I was worried that someone was setting me up."

"You think The Avatars were after you?" BeiLou suggested, "Can't have been The Coalition. This was before their time. So to speak."

"I've considered it. The whole debacle could have been arranged to recruit The Hunter," SenRas said, "But that's no longer an avenue worth pursuing. It wouldn't do enough good to know what designs they had on me back then."

"Okay. So, you're a hitman. You get an assignment. You off the target. Same as always," BeiLou recounted, pacing as she did, "Then you realize you killed your wife's ex-husband. Then what?"

"Well, orphaning AinZun was bad enough. All the worse knowing that XalRut would surely find out," SenRas said, pacing and gesticulating, "But what put me on the run was the nature of the order. As I said, false pretenses. He was a minimally skilled assembly line worker, but the hit had been issued over investment fraud. Something was going belly up, and I couldn't be in the middle of it, as that might drag you and your mother into it as well."

"So, you faked your own death and fled to ArcNos," BeiLou said, her voice finally calming, "Not the most honorable decision, but I get your reasoning."

"Well, not so much faking my death," SenRas said, "Obviously, witness protection was out of the question. But I knew a few tricks to dust over my tracks. I erased any ties I had to XalRut and any prior jobs or accounts. Or to Quarun at all. Easy enough with an ArcNosian name."

"What about the envelope full of money?" she asked, "And the letter?"

"The money was my cut from the hit," he explained, "So, I suppose I did fake my death to her. But that was to keep her from looking for me. It was for her protection."

"Yeah. No, I get that," BeiLou said, "Then, I guess it wasn't a coincidence that you became CreSam's commanding officer."

"Not at all."

"Why didn't you say anything?" she choked out.

"I... didn't think you would accept me after so long," he said, his voice gravelly, "It was easier to keep my secret and wonder what you'd think than to tell you and risk knowing that you hate me. Instead, I did what I was best suited to do for you. I protected your husband's career."

BeiLou plopped back into her chair and buried her head in her hands. She ran her hands down her face, smearing her pinked cheeks with tears.

"This is just... Fuck," she managed, "What was CreSam like? After I died."

"Angry. Spiteful. Calculating," SenRas said, "I did everything I could to keep him on track to turn the rest of Ouristihra against The Avatars."

"Yes, I remember the plan," BeiLou said, "We were faking my death so I could translate the books in peace. He was going to become Named. And when everything caved in on them, he was going to have a change of conscience and flee. The Coalition would help him rehabilitate. All for show."

"I never knew about his ties to The Coalition. We had our own plan though, but it all began to go belly up when The Hunter went against orders and assassinated Chieftain Sage Gijin," SenRas recounted, "After that, CreSam started losing sight of himself. He became obsessed with hunting people in the Subtransit, especially the two vagabonds who pushed back the raid on Masnethege. Sinkua and Galo."

"No. No," BeiLou sobbed, shaking her head, "It was supposed to be an act."

"I'm sorry. They did something to him. It occluded his memories," SenRas said, "But when it looked like CreSam was beyond saving, I realized who Sinkua really is. So, I choked down my pride and went back to XalRut, and we devised a plan to restore CreSam's memories and take down The Scout."

"How did you do that?"

"The Scout had this nanochip that could repair virtually any fatal physical damage, keeping him suspended in near death hibernation all the while. I shorted out the chip by injecting him with magnetized iron suspended in dopamine," SenRas explained, "From there, the plan was to have CreSam execute him using the same gunpowder he had used with you, but when I got back, his mind was so far gone that he thought the world was ending. He even thought I was a ghost who had come to take him into the ether. Fortunately, your mother planned for something like that. I helped him remind himself that The Scout had set every wrong thing into motion."

"Smell is strongly tied to memory. Sounds like something Mom would come up with," she said, wiping away tears with the back of her hand and exhaling an awkward chuckle, "Did he realize Sinkua was MeiLom?"

"He remembered MeiLom, but MeiLom was legally dead," he explained, "I told him that Sinkua could help him end the war and find MeiLom. He misunderstood and had him brought before a firing squad."

"Shit!"

"Quite. But, obviously Sinkua escaped. Unfortunately, he burned the building down in the process. With CreSam still inside," he continued, "Which you probably already knew. Plenty of time for the two of you to catch up on the other side."

"I… never saw him over there," BeiLou said, "Sinkua watched his father die, but I never saw him in the afterlife."

"Odd. I wonder what became of him, then," SenRas said, "He said he remembered you. He ought to have sought you out in the six years hence."

BeiLou turned toward Odin and nudged him with her foot. "Hey, what do you think about all this?"

"There are places and circumstances where a person could end up and be mistaken by those here as dead," he offered, "Though with complications so bountiful as they are, it may be wise to cease further speculation. Lest we complicate matters perhaps beyond even my comprehension."

Galo sat in the middle of the couch with an open binder on his lap and papers strewn to both armrests. He pored over the pages in the binder, occasionally checking against the ones at his sides. Every confirmation, every match, had him shifting uneasily.

The papers at one side shifted as a weight plopped down on an armrest. He looked up to find Nikasu perched there. She crossed her legs and folded her hands on her knee.

"Are those the records from Farim and Uro?" she asked.

"The first batch," Galo sighed, "It's looking more and more certain that Sinkua is causing these episodes. Unintentionally, of course."

"Of course," Nikasu agreed, "I guess we can't know if Yggdrasil is involved until we get into Drakougeneospa though."

"No, but it seems likely."

"Yeah," she nodded, trailing off, "Anyway, I need to talk to you about something. Can I bother you for a minute?"

"Of course not," Galo said, closing the binder, "It doesn't bother me to talk with you."

Nikasu looked up at him flatly. She closed her eyes and sighed, shaking her head.

"It's about that kiss," she said, "What did you take from it?"

"That you were thanking me?" Galo replied, asking as much as answering, "And that you might have feelings for me."

"You're right on both counts," Nikasu said, casting her eyes down as she sandwiched her hands between her knees, "Yrlis told me it's called a crush."

"Crush. Infatuation. Lust. Love," Galo said, "It goes by several names."

"Yeah," she sighed, "But I can't be with you."

"I..." he trailed off, "I've actually... been thinking the same thing."

"I can't believe I'm saying this, but I'm glad to hear that," Nikasu said, biting her lip as she choked back uncomfortable laughter, "Yrlis also told me I'm too young to be with you. If you've already realized that and..."

"Not that," he corrected, "After everything you've been through, age of consent be damned. Up until about two years ago, you would've been an adult by now."

"Then what..."

A knock at the door cut her off. A shout from the top of the stairs announced Sinkua's approach before a rapid cascading of bare feet. He held a folded paper.

"This actually concerns him, too," Galo said to Nikasu. He turned his attention to Sinkua, who was now reaching for the door. "Sinkua! I need to talk to you."

"Sure thing, brother," Sinkua said, "Just a sec."

Galo and Nikasu sat in pensive silence while Sinkua answered the door and invited SenRas inside. Galo didn't pick up any details of their conversation, but he could guess why SenRas had come when Sinkua sent him upstairs alone.

Meanwhile, Nikasu read one of the pages that Galo had pushed aside. Galo couldn't tell if she comprehended it, but if she didn't, she faked it well.

"Okay," Sinkua said, sitting across from them on the ottoman, "What's up?"

"Nikasu and I were just discussing our feelings for each other..."

"About damn time."

"... and why we can't be together," Galo continued, "It concerns you."

He regaled them with his internal experience when Nikasu had kissed him that day. The shape without sight. The scent without smell. The texture without feeling. The sound without hearing. Nikasu bit her lip and blushed.

"Shit," Sinkua choked out, his eyes wide, "That was beautiful."

"But the same thing happened when I hugged you," Galo said, looking at him.

"Okay," Nikasu said, "Feeling a little less special."

"And with a nurse I met on the way to the Eprilen."

"Lot less, now."

"What's your point?" Sinkua asked.

"I don't think I've fallen for Nikasu. Not exclusively," Galo said, forcing himself to maintain eye contact with both of them, "I think I've fallen for both of you."

Nikasu and Sinkua looked at him blankly. Seconds dragged on.

"Either that, or I'm just so pent up that any physical interaction gets to me," Galo continued, shifting in his seat, "Either way, I'm almost certain that I'm bisexual."

In an eerie sibling unison, Nikasu's and Sinkua's chins drew up. Their lips receded as they tried to hold back smiles. Then, all at once, they burst out into laughter.

"Brother. I love you. Not like that. I mean. Platonically," Sinkua said, chuckling, "But anyway. No. You're not bisexual."

"Definitely not," Nikasu laughed.

"Look, I know it sounds weird," Galo said, "but it makes sense to me."

"Galo," Sinkua said, grabbing his shoulder. Galo noted that he didn't get the sensation this time. "If you were bi, I would've picked up on it by now. Probably before you did. That's how it works."

"Well… I don't know what else could be causing this," Galo said, "But there's something more to this. Particularly, why I can't sire a child with you, Nikasu."

"What?" Nikasu remarked, blushing again, "I want to do unspeakably dirty things with, to, and for you, but I don't want to get pregnant. You know we can have it both ways, right?"

"Not that. It's… Okay, yes, I want that, too," Galo said, choking on his words as he imagined it too vividly for mixed company. He turned to Sinkua, and the sensation waned. "Can we get Vielle on the phone for this?"

Sinkua excused himself to the kitchen. He returned with the cordless phone ringing. He hit the speaker button as an answer came.

"-llo?" came Vielle's interrupted voice.

"Hey Vielle. It's Sinkua."

"Oh, hey! What's going on?"

"You're on speaker. Nikasu and Galo are with me," Sinkua said, "Galo needs to tell us something."

"Okay, let me just, um… Hold on," Vielle said. There was some shifting on her end, followed by a barely audible side conversation. A door opened and closed. "Sorry. I had to step outside. What's up, Galo?"

"I was just telling these two why I can't be with Nikasu," Galo explained.

"He thinks he's bisexual," Sinkua laughed, "And that he's as infatuated with me as he is with our sister."

"I don't see it," Vielle said, "Galo, did you just have Sinkua call me for another opinion on your sexuality?"

"That's not what this is about!" Galo protested, "By the way, where are you?"

"MarLys and I are looking at apartments," she said, "We found one in her new budget, but the area's a tad seedy."

"Why?" Sinkua asked, "Just stay with your dad until we raise Drakougeneospa."

"But I'm not part of the Dragon Family," Vielle lamented, "I can't live there."

"Says who?" Sinkua challenged, "Nikasu and I are the only living Hybrids of the Dragon Family. Anyone we want to invite here, we've only got each other to answer to. So, do you want to be a permanent guest of Drakougeneospa?"

"I…" Vielle stammered, "I should've seen this coming. But yes! Yes of course. Thank you."

"Same goes for you, brother," Sinkua said, bumping fists with Galo, "So, are you ready to share your news?"

"Yes, I think we've hesitated long enough," Galo said. He breathed deeply, composing himself, "Something's happened to me since the Heniokhos Disaster. I don't know if it was the Hunter Formula or all the detritus in the air, but whatever the case, the damage is done.

"I've been diagnosed with stage three lung cancer. It is currently inoperable. If that doesn't change, I'll be lucky to live three more years."

Silence settled so deeply that BeiLou and SenRas could faintly be heard talking upstairs,. The creaking of Luvros's perch kept time with the grandfather clock.

"Brother, I…" Sinkua choked, his mouth agape.

Nikasu wrapped her arms around herself and huddled over, casting her face down as she rocked herself.

"So, that's what you meant," Vielle said, her voice weak, "when you said you were dying."

"Phylus told you, huh?" Galo said. He turned to Sinkua. "Sorry. I let it slip when we were talking after the Assembly."

"It's okay," Sinkua mouthed, unable to project words. He ran his hand up and down Nikasu's back.

"Actually, no," Vielle said, "I heard you through Yggdrasil."

"I thought that only worked with people you've tagged," Galo said, "Like with that hair tie you gave Nikasu."

"So did I, but lately, I've been hearing voices from all over," she said, "I can't make sense of most of it. Just people I'm close with."

"Sounds like it could be useful," Sinkua said, "But also frustrating."

"Mostly frustrating so far. But I'm learning to cope with it," Vielle said, "I didn't want to burden you guys with it. We've all got our own problems."

"That's why we've got each other's backs. So we don't have to cope with all of our problems on our own," Galo said, "Everyone has their limits."

"Thank you. I appreciate it," Vielle said, "Sorry, with all the voices, cutting myself off seemed like the best solution."

"I get it," Galo said, "But in the interest of not dwelling on our problems, Sinkua, what's that paper you're holding?"

Sinkua offered him the paper. "It's our bearings."

"To Arestor?" Galo asked, unfolding the paper. Sinkua nodded. "Why didn't you mention it sooner?"

"We had more important things to discuss," Sinkua shrugged, "He's been a statue for thousands of years. A few more minutes is no big deal."

"You don't understand. Time is very crucial here," Galo protested, "Someone in Masnethege was relaying intel to Ebralgi. This whole plan doubles as a trap. Eventually, they're going to take my extended absence as an opportunity and go after Arestor."

"Shit! That didn't even occur to me," Sinkua remarked, "Clever plan though. Marks to you for it."

"Thank you. I'll relay the heading to Leviathan and call my crew at the hotel," Galo said, "How soon can you be ready to leave?"

"Hold off on that call," Sinkua said, "SenRas might be able to get us a portal strip. I'll ask him when he's done talking with my mom."

"Good idea," Galo said, "Ask if it's possible to fit a boat through one."

"I'll ask Malia, too," Vielle said, "See you guys later. Good luck!"

Galo hung up the phone as Sinkua went upstairs. He and Nikasu were alone once again. She straightened herself up and inhaled deeply, releasing it slowly. She stood up and turned to face him.

"What is it?" he asked.

She cupped her hands on the side of his face, bent down, and pressed her lips against his. Puzzled at first, he fell into rhythm with her movements, letting his eyes drift shut. After several seconds, she pulled back and leaned her forehead against his.

"What was..." he exhaled, "Wow.... But... What was that for?"

"Go find Arestor. Catch the informant," she said, "On your way back here, buy a box of condoms."

"Nikasu," Galo gasped, "We just…"

"I know," Nikasu cut off, "But for whatever time you have left, I want us to be together. It's the only way I can say goodbye without regrets."

Galo stroked her cheek and kissed her again, this time more briefly. "I feel the same."

Chapter 24

Horns and bells resounded throughout the docks, announcing the departures and arrivals of numerous ships. Members of Galo's crew flanked his ship on opposite docks, guiding it into the covered marina with mooring ropes. Sinkua and Galo assisted on opposite sides, while Vielle and MarLys directed from atop pier posts. Gabdur and Chekov waited aside with a pair of small duffle bags. Aboard the ship, the rest of the crew completed preparations.

"And you're sure you know where Arestor is?" Chekov asked.

"We have a heading," Sinkua said, "Odin could only determine his general whereabouts."

"Fair enough," Chekov said, "What's your plan for when you find him?"

"Restore him if possible," Galo said, "Try to recruit him into the Task Force."

"And if you can't restore him?"

"Keep him away from MalVek."

"Not exactly the ambition I was hoping for when I put aside my work on Dourias's diagrams," Chekov lamented, "But I suppose your realism is refreshing."

The crew moored the ship and boarded. Vielle and MarLys hopped down from their posts.

"By the way, Aleepo," Vielle said, "what are your plans?"

"Regarding what?" Gabdur asked as he and Chekov opened their bags.

"The Task Force."

"Medical and therapy work, mostly," Gabdur said as he and Chekov fastened their devices to the entrance to the marina, "Granted, my direct dealings with the taken and their families may need to be sparse."

Vielle's eyes went distant as she watched them work, veterans of the newly dissolved Coalition. The once estranged and still publicly incognito father of her longtime friend. The mother of the girlfriend of her adoptive brother, whom she used to call uncle. It all came down to connections, and sometimes the most tenuous circled back to the closest. She turned to MarLys as her eyes returned to focus.

"Hey babe," she called over, "What would you think about fronting me the money for my therapist's license?"

"Can't squeeze her for rent, so you're going after her for tuition?" Sinkua asked, the corner of his mouth flicking up, "Just lost your job, and you're already iolite-digging."

"Hey, you're unemployed, too, you big fuzzy dork," Vielle shot back, "Don't you come at me with that business."

"I think I can manage that," MarLys said, her words threaded with laughter, "We'll look into it when we get back to your dad's place. I bet it won't take you long with your sociology degree."

"Okay, listen up, everyone!" Galo called out. His crew gathered along the rails. "You're about to witness to technology well beyond anything you've ever seen. And yes, I know that many of you witnessed the Triad Titan. But let me assure you that this technology and these people are safe. Trust them as I trust them."

At his signal, Chekov and Gabdur activated the pair of devices. Arcs of blue light lashed out from the vehicle portal strips. The luminous strands met halfway between the framing posts and latched to each other. More arcs branched from each contact point, cascading into an elaborate webbing of crackling cerulean light. The gaps filled in, and water's surface churned as warm light spread across it. Within the sheet of light, a fractalized vision of the Midland Sea crackled into view.

"All clear!" Galo shouted, "Moving out!"

He and Sinkua unmoored the ship and guided it toward the sheet of light. As the aft neared the portal, crew members pulled them up the sides and over the rails by their ropes.

"I should go," came a voice like boiling jam. EshCal's, he guessed. "Call me when he wakes up."

"Actually, he looks to be coming around now," came another. Undoubtedly Yrlis's.

Brilliant white light raked his lashes as his eyelids cracked open. Flakes of crust crashed against his eyes, and tears flushed them away like crashing waves. Pulling his lips apart sounded like ripping sandpaper, the chapped flesh burning like a branding iron. He gritted his teeth to the tune of gravel and mud under spinning tires.

His eyes fell shut again, and he let everything fall out of focus.

"I, um…" came the first voice, still churning but clearer and less distant, "It looks like he's slipping back out again."

"Just stay," Yrlis said, her voice crisp, "You need to get it off your chest."

"I have an appointment, but…"

Spril tried opening his eyes again. The light was tolerable. The crust was only a nuisance. And his chapped lips stung only in a way that chapped lips would.

"Your appointment can wait, EshCal," he choked, "They always have."

"You know about them?" she asked, cracking a small smile.

"Always have," Spril said, nudging her chin with his fist, "What did you need to say?"

"Just that I'm sorry," she said, "You know. For putting you in this situation."

"It's not your fault," he said, his voice clearing, "This whole thing is, well, complicated. But I think I'll schedule an appointment with a therapist."

"Thank you. And in the meantime?"

He opened his eyes and looked her way. "I'll return to work once I've been cleared," he said, "I think it's best that you prepare to assume my duties in a more permanent capacity."

"Okay," EshCal said, "I'll leave you two alone, then. I have… work to do."

Spril chuckled under his breath as EshCal walked out of his hospital room. He turned to face Yrlis, a smile spreading as his eyes aligned with hers.

"What was that about?" she asked, "Her appointments, I mean."

"Private matter," Spril insisted, "How long have I been here?"

"Four days. I've been with you the whole time," Yrlis said, "EshCal's been keeping me company when she can."

"Any developments I should know about?"

"Aside from the fact that we're suppressing our emotions now?"

"I'm sorry. I just… I need to take it easy," Spril sighed, "I think we need to talk to your mother."

"Are you…" Yrlis hesitated, "Are you saying you want to submit?"

"I think I have to," Spril said, "That's the only way this is going to stop."

"But you'll lose yourself. Your sense of self," she protested, "Everything that makes you who you are."

"We don't know that for sure. But if these attacks keep up…"

"Babe, I…" Yrlis fumbled, "I can't. I just can't. I refuse to lose you."

"Yrlis…"

"Listen. I think I'm close to a breakthrough."

"… Really?"

"Yes. When you were waking up just now," Yrlis said, "It looked like you dampened your senses. Am I right?"

"Well… yes," Spril pondered, "Come to think of it, it's never been that easy. You made that happen?"

"Who else could?" she teased, "I've been treating you on the sly. These quacks could hardly maintain your vitals."

"Interesting," he said, his eyes drifting to the ceiling. They coasted back to her after a moment. "They'll probably get worse. You're sure you can keep up?" It was more of an assurance than a question, but a question, nonetheless.

"I've got a better chance than anyone else, don't I?"

"Okay. But my health comes before your pride. If you get in over your head, we need to consult with Chekov."

"But I…" she stammered, "If you do that, she'll take you away."

"I know. I'm… still working on that," Spril sighed, "But for now, I need to find a therapist."

"Well, in the meantime," Yrlis said, kissing him on the cheek, "how about I get you some breakfast and a lot of it?"

Odin stared at the Fjarthursk translation lying atop the ancient book on his lap. After he and BeiLou had skipped ahead to the thirteenth book to locate Arestor, his unslakable thirst for knowledge drove him to keep reading. The Trifecta had erected The Veil after Yggdrasil was destroyed, and he felt compelled to learn what had become of the Omphaloworld between his disappearance and their copper imprisonment.

"Has already departed your father?" he asked without looking up from the translated page.

"Yeah, about two hours ago," BeiLou said, "You okay, Odin?"

"I apologize. I suppose my perception of time is… off kilter?" he said, looking her way, "Is that something people say?"

BeiLou nodded. "It is, but I'm guessing this isn't because you're an Etherworlder," she insisted, "Something's troubling you."

"I suppose could you say as such," Odin sighed, "I am trying to accept a stark change in my understanding of this world. I believe this is what you might call an awkward moment."

BeiLou rolled her chair to his side and looked at the book on his lap. Her attention shifted up to his face. Remembering that she hadn't learned Fjarthursk, Odin cracked a small smile.

"I believe I owe your son an apology."

"If you're not careful, this might become a habit," BeiLou teased, "What happened?"

"When I first met Sinkua, I accused Tsenukoa, his last incarnation that I knew, of having been a traitor. It also now occurs to me that Nemesis believed this to be the case as well," Odin explained, "According to this, however, that accusation was misguided."

"How so?"

"He sought not to surrender Phoenix nor himself to Pandora as I perceived," he continued, "He sought to negotiate an end to hostilities."

"He... Single-handedly?"

Odin nodded. "Absent further bloodshed."

Burnt flesh, stale blood, and mildew amalgamated into some anti-synergy of stench, far worse than the sum of its parts. Joren covered his nose and mouth with his shirt, cursing himself for having forgotten a respirator mask. The stench was so dizzying, so consuming of his attention, that he hardly noticed when his phone rang.

Joren answered with his official greeting as Noble Doyen. After a few seconds of dead air, someone responded.

"System test?"

"Cluck like a chicken."

"No thank you, sir."

"Anti-compulsion measures check out," Joren said, "What's the nature of your call, General Sbaglien?"

"I see you've returned to Tanelen," Sbaglien said, "Have you finished your business with your foreign consultants?"

"No, that's still in progress," Joren answered, "Carry on as you were."

"Very well, sir," Sbaglien said, "You should also know that ArcNos has received your finalization of the cease fire."

"Thank you. See that you follow it to the letter," Joren insisted, "We should expect residual signs of hostility. Do not react unless they explicitly break the cease fire."

"Understood, sir. Nothing else on my end. Any further business, sir?"

"Not at this time. Thank you for your call."

Joren disconnected and continued searching the old office building. He moved toward the smell of burnt flesh, much to his chagrin at its necessity. Those things had to sustain themselves, regardless of how sentient they may not have been.

Joren halted as the door at the end of the hall opened. An androgynous figure emerged, wearing goggles with gemstone lenses.

"We were told to expect you," it said, "Follow me."

Joren glowered at the homunculus as it turned and walked back through the door. He followed at his own pace, perturbed at being ordered about by The Geneticist's leftovers that MalVek had claimed for himself. The door two flights up fell shut as he entered the stairwell.

With no particular urgency, he caught up to the homunculus in a sparsely appointed room. Between a dozen and a score of homunculi stood scattered about, all facing the door. A series of coolers lined one wall. On a countertop opposite that wall was a line of microwaves and toaster ovens. The smell of burnt flesh emanated from that side of the room.

"How many of us does The General require?" the one who had led him there asked.

"All of you," Joren said, "But you look to be short by two. How are you accounting for this?"

"The Patriarch ended them. The General is aware of this," the spokeshomunculus said, "Would you like to sample what remains of them before we depart?"

"No thank you," Joren said, his lips flickering up in a sneer, "So you... things... are people?"

"In a sense. Did you think we were automata?"

"Something of that sort."

"The Geneticist created us rudimentary neuro-programmable lifeforms," the homunculus said, "The General has since expanded on our capabilities."

Joren looked it over, pulling at his chin. He panned the room, noting plates dirty with flecks of meat. The homunculi had eaten their deceased. Whether they had been programmed to do this or given the survival instincts to come to that choice, he couldn't be sure.

"Is there any connection between your neuro-programmability and my powers of compulsion?"

"There is a rather tenuous relation," the representative homunculus said, "I do not have the capacity to explain it."

"But you can be programmed," Joren asserted, pausing as he tried still in vain to see their eyes, "Just as I can program."

"Both of those statements are true."

"In that case," Joren continued, his cadence shifting, "Kill each other."

They all looked at him as blankly as ever, their body language betraying nothing.

"The cortices on which your powers work is structured differently in our kind," the representative said, "I must apologize to inform you that The General implemented countermeasures in the event of this circumstance."

With unnerving synchronicity, the horde of homunculi each turned a switch on the back of their goggles. The gemstone lenses came alight in an aurora of shades of blue. They moved with coordinated swiftness, boxing Joren in before he could so much as backpedal toward the door.

A ripple appeared in the air as one homunculus grabbed his shoulder. His struggles proved useless as the homunculus walked him toward the anomaly with no greater effort when he pushed back. As it directed his head through the spatial abrasion, his eyes became conflicted with the left seeing the room and the right seeing an endless sea of liquid fractals.

Another placed its hand in the middle of his back, and a second soft spot appeared around his knee. He couldn't see the bottom half of that leg in the churning fractals of hyperspace. His breathing ragged and pulse frenetic, Joren wrenched toward the liquid fractals. Better to give himself room to outmaneuver them now and mount his escape later.

But a third hand on the back of his neck held his head in place. Another spatial abrasion appeared, slashing through his left eye. Now, it saw the room with the homunculi melded with a utility closet that looked like it smelled like fermented cat urine.

One by one, the remaining homunculi each placed a hand on him. Ripples in the air, soft spots, interrupted his body with each touch. Soon, he had no sense of where any part of himself began or ended. His right eye saw segments of himself floating among the fractals, not all in their proper relative place.

"Your destruction is inevitable," they said in that same alarming synchronicity, "By the mercy of The General and The Goddess, we offer you a swift execution."

"In the name of the Task Force," Joren snarled, his own voice sounding disembodied and scattered, "I offer you to go fuck yourselves."

Their grasp tightened, so compressing his bones that he could have sworn he felt his marrow tightening. He let out an anguished scream, shattering his efforts to deny them the privilege of seeing him hurt.

"Should you resist further," they continued, "we must oblige you with a more painful death."

His resilience devoured, Joren's eyes rolled back, and his head slumped. His body went limp, held upright only by the homunculi. In his last glimmer of consciousness, he felt their hands withdraw. The abrasions vanished, and, scattered throughout hyperspace and the abandoned building, Noble Doyen Joren fell to pieces.

EshCal's boots clapped against the polished concrete, the echoes of her footfalls filling the mostly vacated parking garage. As she came around into the next level down, EshCal found an androgynous figure sitting on her car. They wore a black tailcoat tuxedo with a matching skimmer hat and leaned back on their hands. The corner of EshCal's mouth flicked up as they made eye contact.

The figure stood to welcome her, crossing one arm across the small of their back and extending the other toward her. As she came within arm's reach, EshCal put out her hand. The nattily attired figure cupped her fingers and kissed the back of her hand.

Even at such proximity, their androgynous self-styling was all but impeccable. In fact, had EshCal not already known them, their only tell was a strategically unfastened button which bared a bit of cleavage at a certain angle.

"Lady," she greeted.

She released EshCal's hand, and EshCal reciprocated the gesture and greeting.

"It's been a while since you came to me like this," EshCal continued.

"Well, I understand you've been under duress," the other woman said, "I thought you could do with a classic touch."

"I appreciate it. Truly."

"Though I apologize that none of your regulars were available for your extra booking."

"I didn't expect to see any of you on such short notice."

"Well then," the escort said, "how did you find him?"

"He was quite…" EshCal trailed off, the tip of her tongue tracing her lips, "…sturdy."

The woman laughed richly. "Mmm. He certainly is," she said, "Did he find you intimidating?"

"Not in the slightest," EshCal said as she unlocked her car and opened the door for her escort, "If he tried to overcompensate, I didn't notice. He tended to my pleasure all the same."

"Sounds like you might have a new regular."

"Perhaps."

"And I understand you're considering a double appointment?"

"Again, perhaps."

EshCal closed the passenger door and circled around to the driver's side.

"After that greeting," she continued as she settled into her seat, "I may have to insist that you be included in it."

"Well then," the escort said as EshCal started the car, "I'll have to see what I can do to make that happen."

Weighted ropes flew up the sides of the ship as it came through the sheet of fractalized light. Crew members hustled to the rails to secure the ropes while workers on the docks guided the ship into the port. Galo signaled to his crew to stay aboard, and he and Sinkua climbed down to the dock. An older portsman with a slight hunch and dense gray brows hobbled through the crowd of workers to welcome them.

"Thought I might see you scrappers today," he said, "Heard me a bit of word from Chekov what told she'd be sending a ship our way. Plumb near forgot it might come through one of these sheets of light."

"I'm sorry," Galo said, "You look familiar, but..."

"Name's Murdega. Quite alright you don't recall however, it having been a time and all," Murdega said, "Come to be thinking, I don't believe we ever swapped proper greetings."

"You're the guy who thought we were a gay couple," Sinkua said, pausing as he realized that didn't narrow it down much, "Right after we chased the Triad Titan out of Masnethege."

"Afraid that's a common mistake on my part. Always jumping to conclusions and such," Murdega said, shrugging in a halfhearted apologetic gesture, "You recall right, however, scrapper. I loaned you that boat what housed that new engine. Thanks a might for helping us get that license from Haprian, by the by."

"It's nice to know some good came of Judge Mikalan's sacrifice," Galo added, "That man risked his life to keep Imperial ArcNos from crashing your economy."

"Lot of folks gambled their lives on such fights then and since," Murdega nodded, "Missus and I have been running a bed-and-breakfast what Chekov and them set up for us. Comforts and such for weary travelers. Not much next to giving transport to vagabond Hybrids, but it's what I can do as of now."

"How long have you been in touch with Chekov?" Sinkua asked, "More to the point, did she tell you we were coming after we left Berinin?"

"I'm more for faces than voices," Murdega said, "Was a phone call I got that morning. Sure wasn't her, though. Was some bloke who told me to expect a couple of boys who looked just like you two."

"Well, we've got a heading to get on," Galo said, "If you could just get us the tide table, we'll be on our way."

"Bit out of sorts, teleporting across the sea like that?" Murdega asked. Galo nodded, waving him along. "Understandable. Bit ungainly reading the tides when one's just blinked off a thousand and some kilometers. I'll get you those charts, boy."

"How long do you think this'll take?" Sinkua asked as Murdega hobbled off.

"Day and a half, probably," Galo said, "Depends on the currents and winds."

"Any thoughts on how to restore Arestor?" Sinkua followed up, "I think it would help if we knew how they got Pahres back."

"Actually, I've um… been meaning to talk to you about that," Galo said, "Ocronn and I were exploring that lab on the satellite island."

"Was that where you found the pieces of Pahres's statue?"

"Yes, and I have a theory as to how they restored him," Galo said, "but I don't think you'll like the sound of it." His lips tightened, and he forced himself to maintain eye contact. "There was a pedestal with a suspension rack next to it. I think they tortured you to restore Pahres."

"Traumatically induced milystic outburst," Sinkua said, furrowing his brow, "You're right. I don't like the sound of that. I wonder if it has to be mine."

"I'm more hoping the 'traumatically induced' bit isn't necessary," Galo said, "Though I've been thinking. If we can't restore him and can't secure him in… ah… Famujokoumba… Drakougeneospa, we need to destroy the statue."

"I hate the thought of it, but with how long he's been in there," Sinkua said, "that might be the best thing for him."

Chapter 25

Yrlis held Spril's jacket up as he worked his arms through the sleeves. He split the blinds to look out the window and, finding it cloudy out, buttoned the jacket halfway.

"By the way," Spril said as he gathered his belongings, "Have you heard from Ophalin?"

"About Sinkua's case?" Yrlis asked, "No, but I assume he's got it under control."

"Sinkua told me he's been cured," he said, "He said that Yggdrasil, ah... Well basically, he fought the person that he becomes during his episodes. He told me his mind is clearer than it's ever been."

"Well, that sounds absurd."

"She said to her prenatally time traveling boyfriend."

Yrlis guffawed. "Okay, I have had to become more open-minded," she said, "But what happened to Sinkua is completely symbolic. There's nothing scientific about it."

"So, you don't think we should tell Ophalin?"

"I don't think he should be off his medication."

"Well, even on the off chance that he's right," Spril said as he put on his shoes, "it's not like everyone has that option."

"We don't even know how many people they infected," Yrlis qualified, "But I guess it's a safe bet to assume Sanus wasn't an isolated incident."

"With how many gurneys I saw in just the two labs, we should figure they've cast a pretty wide net."

An unanticipated knock pulled both their attention to the door.

"Come in," Spril beckoned.

The door opened. A lone woman in business attire peeked inside.

"Prime Minister Spril?" she asked, "Could I... have a word with you?"

"It's just Spril," he corrected, "And yes, of course. Come in, Prime Minister FerLyn."

Sinkua sat on the port rail, watching the opposite horizon. He held his dagger in one hand and half a pomegranate in the other, scooping bits out and rolling them into his mouth along the flat of the blade. Rivulets of juice ran down the dagger and over his clenched fist. Clenched, he realized as the juices drew his attention to it, all too tightly.

He looked down at his dagger hand to find his knuckles were snow pale. His fist and forearm trembled, knuckles and wrist popping in anything but a steady rhythm. In his other hand, his fingers bore into the pomegranate, threatening to puncture the rind.

He closed his eyes and steadied his breathing. Gradually, his hands relaxed, and the messy threat subsided. He opened his eyes and looked toward the horizon again. His lips curled at the line of trees cresting the horizon just beyond a distant beach.

"Motherfuckers," he grumbled, "Come for me again." He turned and spat mucus and seeds over the rail, igniting it in midair with a snap of his fingers. "I fucking dare you."

The sea doused the clump of burning seedy snot. Another snap from behind his shoulder crystallized the mass. Sinkua turned back around to find Galo standing before him. Whether by the quietude of bare feet on wood or his own introspection, he hadn't heard him approach.

"I'm sorry we had to sail so close," Galo said, "But are you sure that's a good idea? Getting yourself worked up like this?"

"It's therapeutic. Cathartic. Whatever you want to call it," Sinkua said, "The way I figure, it'll help me revitalize Arestor."

"Just don't push yourself too far," Galo said, "Don't give yourself an episode trying to pull this off."

At that moment, Sinkua realized he hadn't told Galo about his encounter under Yggdrasil. In fact, the only person he had told was Spril. He had had plenty of opportunities with Galo, though admittedly, some were far less opportune than others. Among that plethora of mixed company at his house would have been far from ideal, but Galo had been his guest for a few days since.

He told himself that the timing was never right, or other issues took precedence. But this nagging itch at the back of his mind insisted that it had been out of doubt. Although, even after everything he'd experienced, a world-hugging mystical tree turning him into two people to cure his indecipherable disease was more than a tad odd. But if it could grow treetop fruits from its roots, whether real or illusory, then maybe.

"You okay, brother?" Galo asked.

Sinkua shook himself out of his introspection. "Yeah. Sorry. I was just thinking," he said, "I've been so wrapped up in my own problems, I haven't asked how you're doing."

"Well, these currents are more than a tad odd," Galo said, "But unless Leviathan finds something, I'm chalking it up to The Veil."

"I was talking about closing in on your uncle's informant, but I'll keep that in mind."

"I'm trying not to dwell on that. I've got enough problems without obsessing over things that I can't anticipate."

"Well then," Sinkua said, pushing off the rail, "I'm going to sit in my bunk for a while. Come get me when we're near the drop spot."

"Will do," Galo said, patting him on the shoulder.

Ambient noises and a single voice brushed across FerLyn's range of hearing. She panned the courtroom, counting heads and podiums. Two people were missing, and the implications nagged at her while Chairwoman TolRou prattled on with a marmalade voice.

EshCal stood alone at Defense, despite the fact that Spril had returned from his psych leave. And OshMar's High Minister, whose name escaped her, stood alone at Infrastructure.

"Thus, it comes to me," TolRou said, her voice sliding between FerLyn's introspections, "However, considering the evidence, I am not ready to pass a definitive ruling."

Spril could have filed a Dissent to Testify. He had been off duty for much of the deliberation period. That would have been reasonable. He could also, FerLyn considered, have had his leave extended.

"Therefore," TolRou continued, "I motion to dismiss and reconvene at a later date."

If he was on leave, he would be no help here. Had he chosen not to testify, he might change his mind when they reconvened. But she couldn't approach him directly. And EshCal had voted guilty, though she seemed reluctant about it. Regardless, it would be too risky to coax her toward talking Spril into participating.

She shifted her attention to Infrastructure. The High Minister had voted not guilty. She could get him to talk to OshMar once she remembered his name.

"I open the voting at three weeks."

Three weeks was plenty of time. Rather, it would have been if it mattered. At that moment, the reason for OshMar's absence began to coalesce. The real reason. Not her inflated view of his attraction to her. It wasn't about other people seeing him as unobjective. He couldn't see himself as objective, and her ego had blinded her to the depths of the problem.

"Very well, then," TolRou said, raising her gavel, "We will reconvene in three weeks." She hesitated as her eyes settled on FerLyn. "Unless…"

FerLyn sifted through potential outcomes even faster than she had ever thought possible. There had to be a way to keep anyone from getting hurt. Or failing that, to minimize the damage, ideally limiting it to only herself.

"Prime Minister FerLyn," TolRou said, her voice ringing clear but distant in FerLyn's ears, "how do you plea at this time?"

She wasn't getting out unscathed, but if she was to take the worst of it, she would need help. Spril would be of more use to her on psych leave. As much as she loathed herself for hoping it, he would actually be of the most help if he had been dismissed from duty. Just as in the time leading up to the ArcNosian Civil War, he was at his most influential beyond the fetters of the government.

"Madam FerLyn!" TolRou shouted. FerLyn's head snapped up in acknowledgment. "How do you plea at this time?"

She would need to find out what had become of Spril. It wasn't in her nature to wish illness upon anyone. But if she found he hadn't returned to duty, that was her best chance of pulling this off. Perhaps her only chance.

"Madam Fer…"

"I plead no contest."

A strong current circled the ship, holding it in place. Galo watched the churning waters from the bow. They coalesced and swelled into a burbling mound, then smoothed into a liquid dome, spilling upon itself. Both breaking through and shaping out of the dome, a serpent's head manifested and ascended. A water proxy of Leviathan rose to address him.

"We're near the drop site," she told him, "He's embedded in sediment, but I see Arestor just ahead."

"Excellent," Galo remarked, "I trust you can bring him to the surface."

"In the strictest sense, yes, but I fear I won't be able to bring him to the surface intact," Leviathan clarified, "This islet sank not long after he came to be this way."

"I see," Galo said, casting his eyes down. After a moment's thought, he looked up at Leviathan's proxy. "I don't want to wake Sinkua up only for him to learn that Arestor can't be restored. Being out here already puts his mind in a bad enough place."

"I understand," Leviathan said, "Be that the case, I would wager that Arestor is too long deceased for Phoenix to resurrect him, even with Yggdra... sil..." The seawater proxy straightened up as she trailed off. "Someone is here."

"Here? Here as in...?" Galo stammered.

"Where you are," Leviathan said, her eyes becoming steely with confidence, "A ship approaches you from the east."

"We've found our informant."

"Shall I divert them while you prepare?"

"Subtly," he insisted, "I'll go wake Sinkua."

"So, I've come to you for help," FerLyn said, shoving her hands into her pockets and leaning back against the door, "I can't see any other way through this."

Spril stared at her flatly. After a lingering moment, he turned to Yrlis.

"Could you give us a minute alone?"

"Sure thing." Yrlis kissed him on the cheek and, excusing herself past FerLyn, stepped out into the hall.

"I don't know how much I can help you," Spril said once the door latched, "I'm still on psych leave. And if EshCal voted guilty, I can't change her mind just because you pleaded with me behind her back."

"It isn't..." FerLyn stammered, shaking her head, "That's not why I'm here. I have to go down for this."

".... Explain," Spril demanded after a long steel-eyed silence.

"When they first came to me with the contract, they threatened my family," FerLyn said, "They said if I betrayed them or refused to comply, they'd kill them one by one, starting with our youngest son. Officially, I did, but..."

"You did what!?" Spril shouted, "You sentenced thousands of people to death to... because a few people would be in danger if you didn't?" He tremored as he staggered across the short distance between them, knuckles whitening as his fists tightened. "Can you even comprehend the damage you caused? How many people died because of you? Do you have any damn capacity for how fucking selfish you...?" He trailed off, glaring and huffing down at her. He shook his head and grumbled, punctuating with a shouted "Fuck!" He plowed his fist through the door a hand's width from her head. "I can't stay here!"

Spril threw the door open, heaving FerLyn off of it, and stormed out into the hall.

FerLyn took a few steadying breaths and, ghostfaced and still trembling, stepped out into the hall after him. Only, he had already vanished around the end of the hall. She looked to Yrlis.

"What did you say to him?" Yrlis demanded.

"Not enough," FerLyn insisted, squaring herself and storming after him, "And I can't let him walk away from me like that."

Yrlis promptly followed.

Sinkua stood in the crow's nest, eyes glowing and facing eastward. He held Epesol forward, aligning the flat of the blade with the bow of the ship. The approaching ship changed course, bearing southward. He trailed its movements with the tip of his sword.

"Alter heading!" he called down as the other ship kept true, "Due south, twenty-five degrees!"

Galo relayed the order to his pilot, then called back his confirmation. Sinkua followed the other ship with the tip of Epesol as Galo's pilot followed the order. As the two ships aligned, Sinkua relayed an order to the pilot to keep true.

The other ship turned slightly northward. Sinkua narrowed his eyes, running mental calculations on their course. He relayed an order to bear six degrees northward. The other ship was close enough to count the planks.

As soon as Galo's ship began to bear northward, the other one pulled hard to the south, leaning hard enough to drag its port side through the water. The salty wind carried the shouts of their crew to the deck of Galo's ship.

"Forty-five degrees south!" Sinkua called down. As the pilot complied, the ship tilted toward starboard. "All hands port side!"

The ship straightened up as the crew congregated on the port rail, hauling whatever they could carry. The two ships sprayed each other's hulls with Galo's more upright vessel looming over the other. Sinkua sheathed Epesol and stepped onto the brim of the crow's nest, bellowing one last order.

"Brace for impact!"

Sinkua stepped off the brim, freefalling. He dropped into a crouch as he landed, his combat boots rumbling the deck. The port side of Galo's ship slammed into the starboard of the other.

FerLyn grabbed Spril's shoulder, spun him around, and slammed him against the wall. Despite their considerable difference in height, she seemed to look down her nose as she glowered at him.

"I don't know what your problem is, but you are not walking away from me," she snarled, "Now, you shut up and listen to me. Do you understand?"

Spril stared down at her, his eyes twitching. He ground his teeth and tensed his shoulders. His eyes darted between FerLyn's hand and her face. As Yrlis caught up, he looked aside to her.

"Answer me!" FerLyn demanded.

Spril looked to Yrlis urgingly. She stopped and stepped back. Spril looked back to FerLyn, swallowing hard as he nodded.

"Good," FerLyn hissed. She craned her neck, trying to see around the corner at the end of the hall. As she turned back to Spril, she spoke low and through her teeth. "I didn't do it. Okay?"

Spril's entire body relaxed, and he pushed FerLyn away with almost humiliating ease, enough that she suspected he had been humoring her.

"But you just told me..." he began, trailing off as his eyes narrowed, "Ahh. I think I understand."

"Good," FerLyn exhaled, "So, you'll help me?"

"You were set up, and you're worried that they'll come after your family if you don't take the fall," Spril recapped, somewhere between asking and stating. FerLyn nodded. "And you need me to find who did it?"

"No, not that. I..."

"Wait," he cut in, "Do you know who did it?"

"No."

"You're lying."

"You're quick."

"You're not going to tell me, are you?"

"No," she asserted, "Let's just say that I can't, okay?"

"Fine," he accepted, "Is this a matter of fear?"

"Not how you're thinking," FerLyn said, "Just know that it wasn't done out of malice."

Silence dragged on as Spril looked down at her dryly. After some stretch of time, he closed his eyes and exhaled, nodding. FerLyn couldn't brave to ask, but she was pretty sure he had seen into the depth of the circumstances.

"Got it," was all he said.

"Thank you."

"So, what do you need from me?"

"I'm worried they'll still come after my family, even if I go to jail," she said. He opened his mouth as though to speak, but she stopped him cold with a glare and a raised finger. "I need you to help them disappear for a while. Just long enough for The Avatars to lose interest."

"Why do you assume I'm the right person for this job?"

"Look, in the strictest sense, I wasn't part of the Subtransit Resistance," FerLyn said, "But I was in the community, and we all knew you'd been assassinated, only to pop up on Epsilon a year later."

"Fine, but…" Spril argued, shaking his head, "Those were unusual circumstances. I had no control over any of it. It all just… happened to me."

"Look," she sighed, "You're the only person I know of who has any experience with dropping off the map. Deliberate or not. And you garnered a lot more public interest than my family ever has. So, I can't say it shouldn't be hard, but it seems to me like you should be able to help."

"I'll see what I can do," Spril said, "but I won't promise anything just yet."

"I guess that's all I can ask, really," FerLyn said. "Just… If you can't help them disappear, can you at least protect them?"

"To the best of my resources," he said, "That's more in my wheelhouse than vanishing acts."

"Thanks," she said, straightening his shirt where she had roughed it up, "See you around."

A dozen portholes dropped open, and just as many gun barrels emerged. Harpoons with hooks on the backs of their heads exploded forth in rapid succession. They crashed through the port side of Galo's ship, snagging the hull as their ropes went taut, and pulled the marauders' ship upright.

A clamoring of rapid footfalls announced the first wave. They charged with no sense of order, clearly intended to disorient and intimidate.

The first one sprang off the starboard rail, soaring across the fistful of meters between the ships. As he cleared the gap, an outstretched foot whipped across his chest, sending him tumbling over a harpoon rope. The defending crew member bounced on the balls of his feet as that attempted invader hit the water. More came right behind him.

"Oh, I may have forgotten to mention" Galo said, grinning at Sinkua's bewilderment, "I staffed the ship with Tide Dancers." They hung back and watched as the entire first wave was held back with acrobatic kicks and sweeping punches. "Martial Tide Dancers," he added, "It's a, ah, thing I've been working on."

"It, ah, seems to be working," Sinkua nodded, an awe-stricken smile spreading. The second wave approached the rail with grappling hooks on thick ropes. By throwing them in a tight pattern, they formed a bridge between the ships. "Well shit," he sighed, unsheathing Epesol, "I'd say that's our call to step in."

Sinkua charged through a gap between Martial Tide Dancers, the deck rumbling under his every footfall. Fear struck the eyes of an incoming marauder, unable to stop for the momentum he needed to cross the rope bridge.

Within two strides of the rail, Sinkua rolled down to his hands and knees, revealing Galo barreling forth just behind him. Galo bounded and sprang off of Sinkua's back.

The marauder scrambled the last of the distance, ducking under Galo's airborne body. Sinkua lunged upright and plunged Epesol through the invader's abdomen.

Galo drew his glaive back as he landed on the rail, coursing icy blue milystis down the handle. He carved the air with his weapon, manifesting a curved icy blade. It sliced into the bridge, breaking against the thickest part of the ropes.

Out of the corner of his eye, he saw Sinkua bound back a few steps, giving himself more space to square off with the still incoming invaders. His fracturing the bridge had slowed them less than he had thought it would, but he had to leave it to his crew and his brother. His business was on the other ship, and that business was his alone.

Galo bounded off the rail, dropping past the rope bridge to light upon a harpoon rope. His toes curled around it as he crouched to brace himself, holding his glaive aside. He sheathed his weapon and, down on all fours, shuffled across the rope. Freezing and unfreezing his hands to the wood, he scrambled up the hull of the marauders' ship.

He crested the rail to find the main deck of the other ship was empty. As long as he could keep his crew and Sinkua out of mind, his task would be fairly straightforward. Find the captain. Find the informant. Deal with them as needed.

A clamoring below deck, however, killed any such hope of a straightforward task. He looked back to find his deck swarming with at least four marauders for every crew hand. At that moment, in struck Galo that, in their hubris, he and Sinkua had been manipulated.

Yrlis hooked her hand around the crook of Spril's elbow. She smiled up at him as he faced her, drawing a sorrowful smile out of him. He lowered his head and sighed. She held his chin in her thumb and forefinger and kissed him gingerly.

"Are you okay?" she asked, her voice low and breathy. Spril took a deep breath and nodded as he exhaled. Yrlis smiled and stroked his cheek, and they began walking. "So, what did she want?"

"I'll explain in the car," he said, his voice uneven and trembling, "I hate this. I can suppress my flare-ups or whatever you want to call them. But it's so taxing that I can't think straight."

"I'm sorry about that," Yrlis said, "We'll work on it together."

"Thank you. It's just that…" he said, trailing off into a frustrated sigh, "I should have known what she was getting at, but I kept guessing like a damn idiot."

"Well, I don't think she'll hold any of it against you," she assured, "She looked a lot more amicable when she left, so I assume you were able to help her."

"Yeah. I think I can."

They walked in silence with Yrlis's hand in the crook of Spril's elbow. Brisk late Frigid air swept over them as they exited into the parking structure.

"So," Yrlis said, her voice fragile, "What did you mean when you said you can't stay here?"

"Here as in, well… now," Spril said, his eyes cast down. He pulled her aside to lean against the cold concrete wall. "I need to reconcile with your mother. I need to submit to the treatments. And when we're done here, I need to return to the future with her."

"I was afraid of that," Yrlis exhaled. She squeezed her eyes shut as a tear coalesced in each one. She looked up at him, laying her hand against his cheek. "I want you to make me two promises."

"Name them."

"I want to be with you through every stage of your gene replacement treatments," she insisted, "I want to be one of the last people you see when you lose who you are now and one of the first you see when you become who you'll be then."

"I'll insist upon it," Spril said, "And I think I know what the other promise is."

Yrlis looked up at him expectantly. Spril cupped his hands under her butt and lifted her to eye level. She wrapped one leg around his waist and planted her other foot against the wall. Her pulse quickened as they looked into each other's eyes. And at last, he spoke the four words that were, well, close enough to the ones she had been so eager to hear.

"Let's go get married."

Chapter 26

Vielle watched as the interviewer mumbled over her records. Her eye twitched enough to make her self-conscious, despite her telling herself that he wouldn't have noticed if he looked up from the papers. Hands folded on her lap, she bunched denim in her clawing fingers.

From deep within her ears came the faintest ringing, so high-pitched that it was on the inner edge of audibility. Quiet. Distant. And absolutely annoying.

"Well," the interviewer said, drawing out the word. As he turned to his computer, Vielle jammed her pinkie in her ear and wiggled it vigorously, suppressing a sigh that could have made things awkward. The interviewer tapped away at his keyboard. "We have a fast-track program that I may be able to put you on. Let me see if we have any openings."

The ringing only became louder. Vielle opened her mouth wide, popping her ears. That didn't rid her of it either. Somehow, hearing it more clearly did make it less of a nuisance, but outside sounds were beginning to yield to it.

"Okay, so we have an eight-week program. Classes are at night. Does that fit with your schedule?" the interviewer said. Vielle winced and closed her eyes as though thinking it over and nodded. The interviewer turned back to his monitor and ticked a box. "Great. They're every weekday from twenty-thirty to two o'clock. And, as with all of our programs, this is fully accredited."

Vielle nodded along, straining not to wince hard enough for the interviewer to notice. Which, as far as she was concerned, would have been wincing at all.

"One of the things that enables us to keep this one so short," he continued, "is that the class sizes are small. Each cycle only has ten slots. We have one starting in two weeks that currently has eight students enrolled."

Vielle nodded, afraid to speak for the pain grinding into her inner ear. Her stomach shifted, and she with it.

"Should I put you down for that one, or would you prefer to wait six weeks for the next one?" the interviewer asked, "Just know that we will need a twenty percent down payment or a promissory note from your aid agency no less than a week before classes start. So, what would you like to do?"

"Umm," Vielle managed, "My girlfriend is paying my tuition. She's in the lobby."

"Okay. Would you like me to call her in here?"

"I'll go get her."

Her vision paled as she braced herself on the armrests to push out of her seat.

Galo stood firm as the clamoring swelled below the vacant deck. Before he'd received his diagnosis, he hadn't thought about the details of when or how he would die. Doing so on his own terms had been increasingly appealing, even if so far that only meant not surrendering to cancer. But at the hands of a traitor's cronies while adrift was far from his shortlist of alternatives. Never mind that he hadn't even identified the traitor yet.

The battle on his ship raged to the tune of flesh and metal colliding. The sightless vision of Sinkua coalesced in his mind's eye, outlined in calm flames and threaded with pinstripe-thin green scribblings. He may have been wrong about what those visions implied of his sexuality, but he couldn't place their real meaning. More pressing matters stood at hand.

A wave of marauders emerged onto the deck, armed with scimitars and bladed deck boots. Galo bounced on the balls of his feet, bobbing from side to side. Three of them spread out to flank him.

Galo spun, slashing at the nearest one. The marauder jumped out of reach, then lunged as the blade passed to deliver a sweeping kick to the head.

Galo grabbed the man's ankle, his boot blades a few hairs' breadths off his wrists. Redirecting his momentum, he spun around and sent the marauder tumbling into the second closest one. Blood spurted as the two tangled with each other. The third, Galo pivoted around with a diagonal slash from shoulder to hip.

The sightless vision flickered, darkening slightly.

The next handful swarmed Galo. Fortunately for him, their weapons only allowed a few to attack at a time. He also had a longer reach than all of them with his glaive and most of them with his legs.

But they could still challenge him four at a time, and each new set was fresh and ready when the previous one fell. The traitor's plan was clear. He meant to throw cronies at him and wear him down with sheer numbers.

Galo bobbed and weaved more erratically. Scimitars and boot blades swiped at him from belly to crown. He returned every deadly gesture with blurred sweeping kicks and glaive slashes.

All the while, he worked the brawl toward the captain's quarters. But they seemed to notice this as, for every two or three he progressed, they drew him two steps away.

The sightless vision flared more violently, fading darker as it calmed. Galo forced contemplations of it into the back of his mind.

He coated his feet and glaive in razor-edged ice. Wisps of frost trailed his every sweeping attack, coalescing into ice caltrops. These melted as they punctured his enemies, thinning the blood to drip more freely.

Their numbers ran low at last. Ten remained by Galo's rough estimate. But in their dwindling numbers, they became more reckless and thus more dangerous, both to Galo and themselves.

They swarmed him all at once, fighting through the wounds of overcrowding. Galo crouched and charged at the nearest two marauders. Bearing his weight into his forward shoulder, their ribs crunched as he barreled into them and bowled them over.

As he pushed through the swarm, he spun around to face them from outside. He raised his fist, his hand and forearm aglow with blue pulsations.

"Leviathan!" he bellowed, the ship trembling as the sea shifted in response.

A serpentine coil of seawater rocked the ship as it burst from the ocean. It arced over the deck, centering its head over Galo's fist. The semi-ethereal shape of Leviathan focused into a smaller form as it spiraled around Galo's milystically fortified forearm.

The sightless vision crackled and flared.

The marauders charged at him in a frantic mass. Driven by a combination of Leviathan's will and his own adrenalized strength, Galo launched his fist at them with such incredible momentum that it dragged the rest of his body forward.

Galo struck in the center of the foremost marauder's sternum, shattering it and fragmenting his entire ribcage. A cloud of ice caltrops exploded from the point of impact, spreading beyond the width of the deck. The pressure of the blast scattered the remaining marauders from port to starboard. Empowered by an Etherworlder and fortified by the Hunter Formula, the strike and the blast launched the recipient clear over the bowsprit.

Galo dropped to his hands and knees, panting and coated in a sheen of sweat. The sightless vision flared, then faded to black. It hadn't been doused. Rather, the flames themselves turned black. Galo's eyes widened. He looked toward his ship, only to have his attention brought sharply behind himself by a booming voice.

"That position suits you," it said, "Stay your weapons. All of them."

Sinkua ripped Epesol from the marauder's midsection, slinging blood over the rail. He bounded a few steps back as more of them poured in. It was only after several years of familiarity that he could fight alongside Galo in such tight proximity. This crew, proficient as they were, was all but strangers to him in combat.

The last wave flooded onto the deck, where they were greeted by flurries of sweeping kicks. But they overwhelmed the crew with greater numbers and blades in hand and on their boots. They knocked a quarter of the marauders overboard, but at least half of Galo's crew fell into their own fresh blood stains. And the further they moved from the rail, the less they could do against the marauders.

Sinkua charged into the fray, slashing at a marauder with Epesol ablaze. The marauder's abdomen split open, the edges of the wound cauterized by the intense heat. He whirled on another at his flank, cleaving head from body.

The remaining crew pulled back, their flesh reddening from his radiant heat. The marauders focused on him now, seeming to forget the Martial Tide Dancers with their singular intent. He cut them down as they came, but with their numbers, it didn't take long for them to close in faster than he could strike back.

A scimitar deflected Epesol. As his arm came up, a bladed boot came from the furthest edge of his peripheral vision and struck the side of his ribcage. He staggered, clutching his side with one hand and slashing haphazardously with the other. Another scimitar swiped across his forearm, laying it open.

Sinkua released his side to switch Epesol to his non-dominant hand. His wound pulsated, blood running down his hand and crusting between his fingers. To his chagrin, his own fire offered little more than warmth, failing to seal his wounds as it had never been able to burn him.

A sickly epiphany struck. If these marauders had connections to The Avatars, they might have known about his condition. And if they knew about his condition, they saw his blood as a contagion. He dragged the flat of his blade along the wound on his forearm, lining Epesol with his own blood. His vision blurred.

His surroundings turning milky, Sinkua slashed clumsily at the marauders. They reared back and stumbled over each other as droplets of his blood spattered over them. But as effective a deterrent as that tactic was, it couldn't last, and it was only a deterrent.

Sinkua closed the distance and struck two down despite the clouds in his eyes. A few others came close enough to the rail that the Martial Tide Dancers separated them and vaulted them overboard. But by then, Epesol was clean of Sinkua's blood, and the marauders were too tightly upon him for him to have time to wet it again.

A series of scimitar swipes took Epesol from his grasp. A boot blade across the back of his knee laid into his hamstring. Sinkua fell to his knees. A mess of hands grabbed his arms and pulled them back. He set them ablaze, but the marauders holding him endured the burns.

All but the few needed to hold back the Martial Tide Dancers gathered around him. They threw down their scimitars and kicked off their bladed boots. Sinkua looked up at them, their bodies looking like featureless masses through his milky vision.

Fists struck his chest in rapid and chaotic succession. Sinkua winced at each one, his throat growing raw as he choked on every attempted breath. His skin became riddled with bruises and welts, ribs buckling and welts splitting to give way to blood.

He writhed against them, but they tightened their collective grasp, those holding his injured arm grinding the heels of their palms into the wound. His temple throbbed. Blood pooled in his throat.

At that moment, another epiphany struck. A fearful one this time. Yggdrasil hadn't cured him. Not because it couldn't. But because it was in his nature to let himself be deceived by a comfortable lie. It was in his nature to be betrayed. It was in his nature to be exploited. And it was in his nature to allow it.

His vision flickered into painfully sharp focus. He spat a mouthful of mucus and blood at a marauder who crouched before him. The assailant recoiled, and Sinkua wrenched one arm free to spearhand him, splitting a rib and puncturing a lung in two places.

Sinkua's vision blurred once again, so starkly this time as to render him sick. A burbling shout erupted from his throat, punctuated by his vomiting bile and blood. The marauders released his other arm as his eyes rolled back in his head.

Sinkua collapsed facedown on the deck of Galo's ship.

Darkness swept over Nikasu's vision, washing everything in the deepest grays tinged with streaks of violet. Her periphery shrank with garbled lines. Her knees buckled, and her legs failed her, collapsing her into a heap of herself.

A far-off door slammed with a warbling thud. Urgent footsteps trod toward her, never seeming to come any closer as they always sounded both distant and near.

"Nikasu!" a directionless voice shouted, "Nikasu! What happened?"

Her throat burbled as she tried to speak, though from a faint corner of her mind, she felt she'd have no control over her words. She pushed herself upright, then to her feet. Her surroundings swayed as she wobbled.

The voice spoke again, distant, loud, and reverberant. Nikasu turned to face the apparent source. It was a woman, familiar from that one lucid corner, yet just as much an absolute stranger.

Nikasu's eyes rolled back in her head as the woman called out to her again. And that shred of awareness, that faint corner of her mind, fell silent.

Everything went milky, and Vielle's knees locked. Her forearms gave out, and she slumped onto the floor. The interviewer nearly toppled his chair as he sprang from it.

"What's wrong?" he asked, "Do you need a doctor?"

"I..." Vielle choked out, wincing and shaking her head, "Augh! This feels like the worst migraine I've ever had."

"Hold on. I think I have something for that," the interviewer rasped. Vielle heard him rummage through his desk drawers while she pushed herself back into the chair. She rubbed her eyes clear to find him holding a pair of imitation designer sunglasses across the desk. "No dimmer switch, but you can borrow these. Do you need painkillers?"

Vielle shook her head and put on the sunglasses. "I need to..." she trailed off, forcing herself to her feet in an awkwardly wide stance. Her mind cloudy, she realized she forgot where she'd left off. She gestured to the door. "...lobby."

"Your girlfriend, right?" the interviewer said, guiding her back to her seat, "Wait here. I'll call for her. What's her name?"

"MarLys," Vielle exhaled, a smile spreading at the sound of it.

The interviewer disappeared and reappeared some unknowable stretch of time later. She was on the floor now, slumped against the back of the chair, with no recollection of when or how she ended up there. She remembered shouting though, muffled yet urgent. Pain enveloped her head, save for a sliver of contentedness buried in the middle of it all.

MarLys appeared before her, distinct through all the clouds.

"Vielle," she urged, "What happened?"

"I'm not sure," Vielle said as MarLys helped her to her feet, "I just know that I hate it."

"Tell me what you need, sweetie."

Vielle clutched MarLys's forearm and looked at her urgingly. "Take me to a root."

Sinkua had no sense of anything between the time he collapsed upon the deck and when he slunk back to his feet. He stood slumped over and rolled his torso upright. He opened his eyes as he exhaled, luminous red smoke billowing from his throat.

The last few moments before he had collapsed had become cloudy. He recalled dropping Epesol and realized his hands were open. He looked down to find them empty, but somehow, it didn't worry him.

In fact, nothing worried him. Patches of a fine roiling layer of brick red flames swept along his skin. It gave him a dark glowing quality, his lower Northlander complexion becoming heavy with shadows and shallow luminescence.

He looked around at the dead and dying surrounding him. Exhaling a cloud of red smoke, he extended his arm toward one of them. The dead man rolled up to his feet, wounds closing as he opened his eyes.

And though his body was whole again, those eyes were vacant. He staggered along the deck, making for the fore.

More of the dead rose around Sinkua. Every one of them awoke with empty eyes. And every one of them staggered to the fore. They congregated behind the bow, shuffling and grunting.

Someone else pushed himself to his feet with throaty groans. Sinkua craned his head to watch this one. His wounds stayed open. And his eyes sparked with life, with a sense of purpose. It wasn't one of his.

The wounded man snatched one of many abandoned scimitars and scrambled toward the fore of the ship. The zombies kept shuffling in frustration, unaware of the approaching threat.

Sinkua walked after him and grabbed his wrist as he drew back the scimitar. He pulled the man's arm back as he pivoted to stand back to back with him. Sinkua pushed his shoulder between the man's shoulder blades and yanked his shoulder out of the socket as he flipped him over his back. As the man came over him, Sinkua planted his hand in the middle of his back, slamming him hard enough to splinter the deck.

"Pilot…" Sinkua choked out, "… the ship."

The man didn't answer. Sinkua grunted and shook him.

"Pi… lot…" he repeated. A brilliant light and a trilling shriek ripped through his mind. "… the…" He winced, clenching his eyes and grinding his teeth. "… shi…"

Choking on his own breath, Sinkua hunkered down on his elbows and knees.

Nikasu's hand snapped forth, clutching the woman's throat. Screams of protest burbled through the wall of noise in Nikasu's mind.

Her vision had been reduced to shapes and shadows. Negative space was darkness. Objects were clouds of luminous smoke and approximate shapes. People were scarcely different, just brighter than the nonliving. Plants were somewhere between.

The woman struggled and writhed in Nikasu's grasp. The burbling protests grew more strained as Nikasu clamped down and lifted.

The luminous smoke thinned, the effort Nikasu needed to lift this woman reducing as it did. A masculine shouting thundered from afar.

Her entire vision went blue. Thrumming light and thunderous vibrations squeezed and shook her head. The smoky form reconstituted as it dropped from Nikasu's grip. Blue faded to black, and Nikasu collapsed into a deep sleep, vaguely aware of the grass under her body.

Galo looked toward the cabin, still on his hands and knees. He couldn't quite place the voice, but he was in no place to rise to face him. Not in his current condition, and not with Sinkua apparently incapacitated. This was the culmination of a string of mistakes that had started with letting Sinkua fixate on that island.

The man's footfalls resonated through the deck as he approached.

"Stand and face me, boy."

"I'm… in no shape to fight you," Galo pleaded.

"I'm not concerned with fighting you," the man said, "On your feet, nephew."

Galo looked up and scrambled to his feet. Before him stood Borret. One of his two political advisors. Brother to his late mother. And, perhaps most importantly at the moment, brother to Ebralgi.

Yet, there was something unfamiliar, even uncharacteristic, about him. He looked, in a word, bold.

"I was told to expect you here," Borret said, "You and your friend both."

"Borret? I… What…" Galo stammered, "Wh-why?"

"You have many questions," Borret noted, "So many that you don't know where to start." He clucked his teeth. "Well, I'll begin by confirming the obvious. The Borret you've always known was a ruse."

"You've been manipulating me," Galo grumbled, "To what end?"

"Obviously, to safeguard against suspicion," Borret derided, "I needed to work without interference."

"What were you working on?" Galo demanded, "Why are you looking for Arestor? How deeply are you involved with The Avatars?"

"Whoa there, nephew. Let's not get ahead of ourselves," Borret said, patting Galo's shoulder, "We were orchestrating the downfall of the Chieftain Bloodline. Things snowballed from there. And, well, you know how poorly we Southlanders handle snow."

"You plotted with Ebralgi to kill my father and grandfather," Galo seethed through gritted teeth, "You plotted to kill your own sister. Don't you fucking dare tell me things snowballed!"

"My motivations were strictly political," Borret argued, unmoved by Galo's rage, "As were Zheal's." He chuckled as Galo's eyes went blank with bewilderment. "I knew that would get your attention. Zheal, Ebralgi, and I all endeavored to remove the Chieftain Bloodline from power. So, Zheal tempted Chieftain Heir Gabdur to court her."

"And what was the plan from there?" Galo rasped, "Assassination?"

"Any means necessary," Borret said, "We knew assassination was a possibility, but only as a distant last resort."

"Then why the poisoning?" Galo puzzled, "What could your own sister, much less any of them, have done to deserve that?"

"Ebralgi judged that she had become a liability. She genuinely loved the Chieftain Heir and believed in what he stood for," Borret said, "He poisoned her, knowing she would infect both the Chieftain Heir and the Chieftain Sage."

"But Gijin survived and created me."

"Obviously."

"When did you start acting like an idiot?"

"Just before Zheal began seducing Gabdur," Borret said, "It was for Nalygen's sake. Ebralgi was quite vocal about his desire to overthrow the Chieftains, but she had no interest in revolution. Better she think I at least had no part in it."

"Which shielded Zheal from suspicion as well," Galo realized, "If Nalygen ever doubted Zheal's love for Gabdur, it was just that she was securing her invalid brother's future."

"You're a quicker study than your father. I'll grant you that," Borret said, "Since then, I've been working as an informant for The Avatars of Fate. As long as The Chieftain Bloodline was in power, I was still indebted to them."

"Their failure didn't negate the contract?" Galo asked. Borret glowered as though it was the sort of thing he would have said under his ruse. "Of course, it didn't," Galo sighed, "Does that mean you're The Investigator?"

"The?" Borret asked, "There's no The. We're a network of passive data collectors. If anyone was told they're The Investigator, I would assume it was a means of counterintelligence."

"Why are you coming clean now?" Galo pried, "Do you need help getting out?"

"Don't be so eager to help everyone. It'll be the death of you," Borret said, "No, I'm on borrowed time, now, and frankly, you're to blame. Not that you could have known."

"Because I scheduled my resignation," Galo realized, "The contract is up. You've become disposable to them."

"Indeed," Borret nodded, "They sent me to these coordinates for my final mission."

"And yet you've been careful to survive so far," Galo said, "Why else but to escape and repent for the excess debt you paid to them?"

"I saw to my own survival so I could educate you, boy," Borret scolded, "You've fought them for years, yet you still don't have the slightest understanding of what you're up against. There's no stopping them. Only adapting. And only that for those they deem useful."

"Borret. I'm pleading with you," Galo urged, "I know people who can help you."

"Oh, come off your savior complex, you damn fool!" Borret chided, "You're the one who told us to save ourselves when you left for ArcNos."

"And you've done that by exposing them. I'm offering my hand for leverage."

"Get it through your skull, boy. Put the pieces together."

Galo's eyes twitched as he studied his uncle's face. His uncle he had known all his life but was only just now truly seeing. He had been consigned to a life collecting intel for The Avatars. He thought them incontestable. He had outlived his utility to them.

"You're wired, aren't you?" Galo choked out.

"Wired and on a short leash," Borret nodded. He drew a six-shooter from the back of his belt. "If I don't die here, I'll be lucky if they see it to shortly. Most likely, they'll force me into service on that damn island until I die of exhaustion." Borret flipped the chamber out, showing that the pistol was loaded. "Better I warn you first, even though you're too stubborn or stupid to knuckle under."

Galo's mouth trembled as Borret raised the gun to his own head. Borret stepped back, beyond his reach.

"Stay healthy, nephew," Borret said, pressing the barrel to his temple, "I'm sorry it took so much bloodshed for our politics to align."

But he faltered as a voice called out from starboard.

Vielle stood on a mulch island in the middle of the parking lot with a surfaced length of an Yggdrasil root between her feet. People from the lobby of the registrar's office had gathered at a distance. She squared herself and rubbed MarLys's hand where she held her shoulder, signaling her aside. Vielle watched sidelong as MarLys backed into the fore of the crowd, beside the registrar.

Vielle laid her hands out, palm down with her fingers spread. She closed her eyes and focused on the root between her feet. It shimmered in every conceivable shade of green and then some, coursing with what she could only comprehend as something beyond yet just short of life.

Tendrils of duller green created the vague shape of her hands in her mind's eye. They flickered and pulsated in rhythm with certain flows within the threads of light that formed the root. Yggdrasil was communicating with her.

Those certain flows snapped away from the root and snaked up toward the threads of her hands. Vielle felt them wrap around her fingers and hands with a sensation so distant as to border on foreign.

Yggdrasil circulated its milystis with her own. Her vision pulled back so swiftly as to render her nauseous.

A vast network of woven emerald strands filled the expanse of her mind's eye. Scattered humanoid smudges of light speckled the negative space. This, she realized, was the extent of Yggdrasil's root system.

The vision was too vast and the smudges too numerous to count them all. But as she focused, she picked up a glimmer of an anomaly. A nigh invisible yet worrying presence.

Somewhere in the Southland Sea, one smudge, in close proximity to another, had gone all but black. It glowed as much as any other, yet it shimmered with darkness. It had been so steeped in shadow that it all but sank into the negative space.

As Vielle got a handle on his particular shade of glowing black, she found a strand of the same color threaded through the nearest root. Vielle followed it through the Midlands and into the lower Northlands. At the end, she found another darkly glowing smudge, circulating with a strand of its own.

Sinkua and Nikasu were trapped in a negativity feedback loop via Yggdrasil.

Vielle fixated on the loop, guiding her own milystic threads into it. The root threads which circulated through her hands fed into it as well. The darkness of the smudges and the binding strand faded into light.

The mental image returned to her immediate surroundings. The root threads detached and retracted. Vielle lowered her hands and opened her eyes.

A small chuckle popped out of her mouth. She dropped to her knees and rolled onto her back, staring up at the sky with a distant smile.

BeiLou's foot twisted as her feet hit the sloped ground. Her ankle popped, and she collapsed into a heap. She scrambled forth on her belly.

She cupped her hand over Nikasu's neck, but she was too flustered and panicked to take proper stock of her pulse. She looked up and across the lawn. Odin approached from the patio.

"What did you do to her!?" she demanded, "What did you do?!"

"She lives," Odin asserted, "I took only her consciousness."

"Why? She wasn't doing anything wrong!"

"She tried to kill you. I cannot allow that."

"She didn't want to," BeiLou argued, shaking her head, "She was fighting it. She would have stopped." She pressed her hand more firmly against Nikasu's neck. The girl had a pulse, after all. "Besides, she's a Hybrid. Surely she can do more against Pandora than I could."

"Lost she her mind, she would be useless at best and detrimental at worst. I struck her down lest she became an enemy," Odin said, "You are one of the only humans with knowledge of the ancient languages."

BeiLou ran her hand down Nikasu's elongated arm, tracing patches of chitin that had sliced her sleeves. Blackish purple shards of exoskeleton, their edges were wet and sticky with waxy ooze.

"What are these?" she asked. She pried one of Nikasu's eyes open. Her pupils contracted. All twenty-odd of them. "TakMet never said Hybrids could do anything like this."

"As was he right not to," Odin said, "This is no Hybrid power."

"What do you suppose it is, then?" BeiLou asked, "I mean, we can assume The Avatars of Fate are responsible. But...?"

"Their intentions elude me. I would need to research the matter further," Odin said, "Though given that there is an exposed root nearby, Galo may have been right that they are using Yggdrasil as a manner of conduit. This may pertain to their talk of actuation chambers and the afflicted."

"What could they want with something like this?" she wondered. She rolled up into a sitting position, her injured leg out straight. "I need to tell Chekov. Maybe there's something in Dourias's tattoos."

"That would be the most logical answer," Odin said, "Though it may thus be the least likely." BeiLou looked up at him, confused. "I suspect The Avatars of Fate are a modern incarnation of Vuordevaltene. It translates to The Stewards of Disarray. It is thus plausible that they mean only to cause havoc with her."

"Useless at best. Detrimental at worst."

"Indeed. How fares your ankle?"

"I think it's sprained," BeiLou said, looking down at it. Out of the corner of her eye, she saw a patch of chitin fall off of Nikasu's arm. Her head snapped up. The chitin and waxy ooze dissolved with a smoky hiss, leaving unblemished skin behind. "Odin!" BeiLou remarked, "Look at that!"

"Yes, it is quite fascinating," Odin said. He poked at another patch of chitin, and the whole thing flaked off. "It would appear her transformation is reversing. A positive development indeed."

Sinkua was on his elbows and knees when he came to, abruptly lucid from a deep dreamless sleep. He sat up, puzzled, and looked around.

A pile of bodies lay near the bow, tugging at his memories with unplaceable familiarity. He thought he probably had something to do with it, but he had no recollection of the circumstances.

He winced all over as muscle cramps flooded his torso. His hamstring pulsated with a sense of wetness. He recalled being assaulted. Beaten. Slashed. He scrambled to his feet and inspected himself. The bruises had faded. The wounds had closed.

Therein lay the worrisome part. He had no sense of how much time had passed, but if he had healed that much, it must have been days.

But there was nothing in his memory of the time between collapsing and right now. It wasn't like the gaps in his memory from his time on the lam. Nor was it like sleeping or even passing out after an episode. There were no blackouts in his memory. No blurs. No fading dreams. Between falling and now, there was simply nothing. He collapsed, beaten and bloodied, and then he sat up, sore but healed.

He made his way to the bow with an uncertain gait, his hamstring feeling like it still bled. The way the bodies lay, they looked as though they had walked there as they were dying. One of them, his eyes still open, had frozen upon them a look of singular determination.

A scraping sound called his attention aside. Ropes at port still bound Galo's ship to the marauders'.

Galo.

Sinkua looked around, finding him unaccounted for. He hobbled over to the ropes, slowly regaining confidence in his gait.

Galo stood on the deck of the other ship, speaking with another Berininite considerably older than himself. Sinkua recognized him but couldn't quite place the name. But it felt more like he had been of little more than peripheral significance to him, rather than a blemish in his memory.

Sinkua crossed the rope bridge, bracing himself on the air as though that was possible. Though he could hear the cadence and pitch of his voice, he couldn't make out anything in particular that the older Southlander said. He didn't sound like anyone that Sinkua could put a name to.

His face was familiar, though. Watching him in profile as he raised a pistol to his own head, fragments of recollection bubbled to the surface. A piecemeal moment took shape.

A younger version of him entered Grandpa Gijin's home. A conversation, blurred by inattentiveness and time, took place between him and Gijin. Sinkua, standing below Gijin's eye level, was told that he needed to go home early.

His name fell into place.

"Borret!" Sinkua called out. The man wavered. Sinkua rushed across the deck. "Put the gun down!"

"S-... S-... Sinkua?" Borret stammered, "How are you...?"

"Give me the gun, Borret," Sinkua coaxed, standing between him and Galo. Borret lowered the gun slightly. "Come on!"

"I don't..." Borret said. He brought the gun down to his side, still clutching it but with his finger outside the trigger housing. "I was... We were..." Sinkua motioned for him to hand him the gun. "You can't save me. But... if you..."

"The gun, Borret!" Sinkua demanded. Shaken, Borret thrust his hand out, offering the six-shooter. Sinkua took it, opened the chamber, and dumped the bullets into his hand. "Thank you. I couldn't let you do that to yourself."

"Wh-... Why?" Borret managed, "Why do you two...?"

"I should've known you were a piece of shit."

Sinkua dropped five bullets on the deck and fired the sixth through Borret's mouth.

Chapter 27

"What just happened?" the registrar asked.

MarLys knelt beside Vielle and put her ear near her mouth. She was still breathing, just exhausted from whatever she had just done.

"I'm... not sure," MarLys said, "But well, she's the Yggdrasil Hybrid."

"Yes, I recognized her from the news reports about the Heniokhos Disaster," the registrar nodded, "But what did she just do?"

"If I had to guess," MarLys said, "And honestly, that's all I can do." She stopped to laugh at herself, hesitating as she coalesced her thoughts. "Anyway. Yggdrasil is sort of a communication system. I think someone hijacked it."

"And that caused her migraine?"

"Yes. Probably."

"And just now?" the registrar asked, "She... restored the lines?"

Vielle opened her eyes and thrust her fist skyward. "Suck my strap-on, chaos cunts!" Her eyes closed, and her arm went limp.

"Safe to say," MarLys said, stifling a laugh as she squeezed Vielle's shoulder.

"Is this a regular occurrence?" the registrar asked, sitting on the edge of the mulch island.

"That outburst? Not so much," she said, "This business with the roots? Not so far."

"Well, what I'm getting at," the registrar said, stretching his legs, "is that I need to know if this will hinder her from attending classes or hosting therapy sessions."

"I don't think it will."

"Okay. I'll take you at your word," he said, "Do you have a way to get her home?"

MarLys's head snapped up. She looked out across the parking lot. She'd been so wrapped up in Vielle's wellbeing that this particular complication hadn't occurred to her until just now.

"Shit," she remarked, "We came here on her motorcycle."

"Why don't you come wait in the lobby?" the registrar offered, "She needs to discuss enrollment options with you, and if she wakes up soon, I can be available to answer any questions you may have."

"Thank you, but I couldn't impose like that," MarLys insisted, "We'll call if we have any questions." She fished her phone out of her pocket. "I'll see if her dad can help," she said, "Otherwise, I'll call us a cab."

"Okay," the registrar nodded, "Just come tell my receptionist if you need anything else."

Phylus held his phone between his ear and his shoulder as he waved Calhosin into his office.

"Hello?"

"Phylus?"

"Speaking," he said, pouring himself a cup of coffee, "Who am I speaking with?"

"It's MarLys."

"Oh, hey," Phylus said, half-absently. He gestured the coffee pot toward Calhosin, who accepted the offer. "I guess I should save your number, huh?"

"I'm not in your phonebook?" MarLys asked with mock appall, "Well, I never!"

Phylus snickered. "What did you need, kiddo?" he asked, "Are you two still at Vielle's interview?"

"Just wrapped up."

"Cool. How did it go?"

"It went well from what I understand," she said, "But I was wondering if you could come pick us up."

"Sorry, I can't get out of the office," Phylus said, "Did something happen to her bike?"

"Not exactly, no," she said, "Um... remember the other day at Sinkua's place? They were saying Yggdrasil might be connecting him to other people and making his episodes contagious?"

"Yes," Phylus said, both hands trembling around his mug as he sipped his coffee, "Did she... catch one?"

"I don't think so," MarLys said, "I'll ask her when she wakes up, but I think she intercepted it."

"How do you mean?" he asked. Calhosin tapped his wrist at him. Phylus waved him off and gestured to a chair.

"She pulled up pieces of a root. I don't mean she grabbed them. She put her hands out and they just came to her," Phylus nodded along as he listened. In the edge of his periphery, he caught of a curious glint of light. "I mean, I guess that's normal for her. But then her eyes rolled back, and she looked, um... I think catatonic is the word." Phylus turned toward to anomalous light. A sliver of discoloration, its light and shadow were, in a word, wrong. "She was like that for maybe a minute or two. Trembled most of the time." Phylus approached the anomaly. As Calhosin shifted his weight, a bit of shadow swept through it. "Then the roots went back, and she just chuckled and collapsed."

"... Shit," Phylus muttered, unsure which matter he was reacting to. He poked the strange sliver, and his finger vanished into it. He jerked it back. "How is she now?"

"Sleeping on the grass. I think she just needs to go home and rest," MarLys said, "But we came here on her bike, so..."

"Are you okay with taking a cab?"

"I was gonna call for one if I didn't catch you on your lunch break."

"You did, but I'm working through it," Phylus said, "Sit tight. I'll send a cab and cover the fare."

"Oh! Are you sure?"

"That depends."

"... On?"

"Did Vielle get accepted?"

"She did! She just needs to decide on her schedule."

"And you're paying her tuition?"

"Of course," MarLys proclaimed, "If nothing else, I'm at least a lady of my word."

"Then I'm paying your cab fare."

"Cool! Thank you so much!"

"No sweat. See you two at home. I'll take her to pick up her bike after dinner."

Phylus cut the line and pocketed his phone. He returned his attention to the anomalous glint. In the corner of his eye, he saw Calhosin trying to hide his growing impatience. He stuck his finger into the anomaly, narrowing his eyes to try to see through it. Not to the space in his office across from it, but to the hyperspace he supposed was beyond it.

"What the bloody hell, man!?" Calhosin blurted, snapping Phylus out of his bewilderment, "Is that your finger?!"

Phylus straightened up, keeping his finger in the anomaly. He watched Calhosin as he pushed his hand deeper into the blemish of light and shadow. Sure enough, his hand emerged from another previously unnoticed anomaly in front of Calhosin.

Calhosin stared at him with fearful eyes as Phylus grabbed his coffee mug. Phylus nodded to him, and he let go of the mug. Phylus pulled it through the anomaly, taking his High Minister's coffee from clear across the office.

"What…" Calhosin choked out, scrambling to his feet and backing away, "…the bloody… hell?!"

"I told you how I escaped from that prison, right?" Phylus asked. He thrust Calhosin's mug back through the anomaly. Calhosin nodded as he hesitantly accepted it. "I think I'm getting side effects from wearing the goggles. I'm seeing soft spots. Spatial abrasions. Whatever you want to call them. They're holes in space."

"You're surprisingly calm about this," Calhosin said, swigging his coffee, "This is fucking bizarre!"

Phylus shrugged. "Panicking over every weird thing that comes my way would be a waste of time," he said, "My kid grows plants out of her arms. I've learned to just take it as it comes." He paused, contemplating the spatial abrasion. "Hey, come over here."

"Will I…" Calhosin trailed off, gesturing toward the general area of the soft spot, "…you know?"

Phylus shook his head, assuring him that it wouldn't put a hole in his chest. Calhosin, still reluctant, eventually stood and crossed the room to Phylus's side.

"Ready?" Phylus asked.

"For what?"

"I'm going to show you what I see. I think."

"Will it make me go crazy?" Calhosin asked, "I haven't seen the shit that you've seen."

"I'll be personally accountable for your therapy bills if it does."

He grabbed Calhosin's shoulder. The High Minister just stared at him as though nothing had happened. Phylus gestured to the spatial abrasion. Calhosin turned his head slowly, then jolted so hard he almost pulled out of Phylus's grasp.

"You see it, don't you?"

"Yeah…" Calhosin gasped, bending for a closer look. "Is this what they looked like where they kept you? Outside the prison but still in the building, I mean."

"I don't know," Phylus said, "The gems in the goggles distorted everything. Why?"

"Those led to some kind of fourth dimension hyperspace, right?" Calhosin said, "Well, this one is skipping across normal space. I thought they might look different."

"They might. One kind that goes through and one that goes in and stops," Phylus pondered, "Good to see you're learning to take the weirdness as it comes."

"Well, you made a good point."

Phylus snickered.

"Hey. Stick your pen in it."

"… I'm sorry. What?"

"Trust me. Just take your pen and put it in the portal."

Calhosin took his pen from his shirt pocket and eased the end into the spatial abrasion. Phylus pulled his shoulder, stopping him before he put any part of his hand through.

"Okay. Now what?"

"Just watch."

Phylus released Calhosin's shoulder. At the other end of the room, half a pen hit the floor. Calhosin brought the back half up to eye level, examining it with equal parts bewilderment and disappointment.

"What just happened?"

"You can only see the abrasions when you and I are touching," Phylus explained, "And you can only use them if you can see them."

"Ah! So, when we separate, anything I was holding through it gets cut off," Calhosin deduced, "That's why you stopped me before I put my hand in. Thanks for that, then."

"I cut the warden in half like that," Phylus said, grinning behind his coffee mug, "just after I ripped its goggles off of it."

"… Shit."

"What can I say? I'm a force to be not-fucked-with."

"Okay, Sir Badass," Calhosin laughed, "Are you going to be okay, seeing those things all over the place?"

Phylus blinked a few times. The abrasion was fading.

"Yeah. I'll be fine," he said, "I don't think it's permanent. Probably has to do with stress."

"Stress?" Calhosin asked, "You just said you don't let things bother you."

"I said I don't let weird shit get to me solely on account of its weirdness," Phylus clarified, "But I'm still a father, a father figure, a diplomat, and, well, a person. Hell, you've seen how much coffee and nicotine I go through in a week."

"Well, you've got a point there," Calhosin chuckled, taking a pen from the cup on Phylus's desk, "Okay. Let's get going."

"What the hell!?" Galo bellowed, whipping Sinkua around by his shoulder. Leviathan slithered off his arm and over the side of the ship. "Why did you do that?"

"He wanted to die," Sinkua said, "But he didn't deserve to do it on his terms."

"He didn't…" Galo stammered, tangling his hair around his fingers, "He didn't deserve to die in the first place. He got…"

"Yes, he did," Sinkua asserted, cutting him off.

"And who decides that?" Galo barked, "Me? You?"

"Yes!"

"S-Sinkua..." Galo exhaled, his eyes wide, "Do you... understand how that sounds?"

"Of course," Sinkua said, "It means I'm done pussyfooting. We're the ones The Avatars of Fate are trying to control and overpower. We're the ones with the power to stop them. We're the ones who decide what to do about their agents, activists, and sympathizers."

"So then... if someone gets dragged into their business," Galo said, his voice low, "the consequences are their own fault. Is that what you're saying?"

"Don't you dare put The Epimetheus Trial in my mouth," Sinkua snarled, "You know damn well what I mean. Our hesitation is what's given them so much ground."

"Our hesitation got us EshCal, Malia, and SenRas as allies."

"They're all liabilities because of MalVek. And speaking of MalVek..."

"None of us knew what he was up to!" Galo snapped, "Don't throw that in my face."

"No, we didn't," Sinkua shrugged, "But we both thought he was shifty as fuck. Think what we could have done if we'd kept pushing."

"Fine. We should've followed our instincts about MalVek," Galo conceded, "But the other three?"

"Might not have been an issue if not for him."

"Might have been though, but..." Galo trailed off, shaking his head. "Fine. We can't know either way. But what about Borret? One sabotage mission is enough to kill him over?"

"You know his record runs deeper than that."

"... Enlighten me."

"He killed my mother," Sinkua said, folding his arms.

Galo's face screwed up with bewilderment, worry, and fear. "No... He didn't," he managed, "CreSam killed your mother. You walked in on it. We talked about it after our blood transfusion."

"I know who pulled the damn trigger," Sinkua snarked, "Borret was the reason I went home early and ruined their facade."

"He couldn't have known it would lead to that!"

"But he knew he was working for someone who did."

"You can't..." Galo stammered, shaking his head, "You can't spend your whole life killing everyone connected to your mother's death."

"Of course not. Eventually, I'll run out of people."

Galo glowered at him. "That isn't what I meant. And besides, you got her back."

"I had to lose Eytea to get the power to bring her back," Sinkua snarled, "You were given your father back, and you still hunted Ebralgi down. You still avenged your father's death." Galo opened his mouth, but Sinkua jabbed his finger against his chest, unbothered by his reinforced bones, and cut him off. "Yes, he'd done a lot more. But you would've hunted him down, regardless. Do you know why?" Sinkua paused as though to let him answer, but continued before he could. "Because it doesn't matter that you got him back. You can't get the time back."

Galo glared at him, holding his ground. Slowly, his shoulders relaxed. His face softened. He grabbed Sinkua's wrist and pulled him into a one-armed hug.

"You're not okay, brother," he said, "You need to get help."

"No, I don't," Sinkua said, pulling back, "I know damn well I'm dragging a whole mess of dirty baggage. But it's mine to deal with, and I know what I have to do."

Galo shook his head. "You can't get time back by taking it from other people."

"Maybe not," Sinkua shrugged, "But it's a start. And with The Avatars, we can keep them from taking it from anyone else."

"We could be at this all day," Galo sighed, "But if you decide who deserves to die, I decide if you need to be institutionalized."

"... Fine."

"How are things on my ship?"

"There's a pile of dead bodies behind the bow," Sinkua said, stepping back, "I... don't know how they got there."

"You don't... They..." Galo stammered, "Mine or his?" Sinkua's mouth opened, but Galo interrupted him. "It doesn't matter. They all need a proper burial." He looked sidelong at Sinkua. "You had an episode, didn't you?"

"I... think so," Sinkua sighed, "I'll help with the burials."

"I need to report to their families. Alone," Galo insisted. He regarded Sinkua thoughtfully. "You need to go see Doctor Ophalin."

"And how would I do that?" Sinkua challenged.

"Do you still have your burner phone?"

"Yeah... Why?"

"Hand it over."

Sinkua complied, surprised it had survived whatever had happened to him, and watched Galo take it behind the cabin. He considered what his plan might have been. The most obvious solution was to have Biroe ask EshCal or SenRas to send a boat. But even if they used a vehicle portal strip and Murdega's marina, it would take a day and a half. A day and a half adrift, a person of interest on a boat of interest at a point of interest.

A rolling burst of water announced Leviathan's return. She crested the port rail with foremost three meters of her body coiled. She lowered herself and deposited a statue of a large bull-headed man with hooves for feet. Bits of wet rubble rattled loose despite her delicate handling.

"Galo's behind the cabin," Sinkua said, "This must be Arestor."

"I know. Thank you," Leviathan said, "And yes. People like this were once called minotaurs."

"I've seen them in stories," Sinkua said, inspecting the barnacle-riddled pockmarked statue, "Nothing that alleged they were real, of course." He rubbed his jaw, considering the dismal state of him. "Is he still alive?"

"I don't know," Leviathan said, "But assuming I'm reading your expression correctly, I agree that this does not bode well."

"Let me see," Phoenix spoke inside Sinkua's mind, "Hold his hands."

EshCal ascended the stairs to the courthouse with her androgynous escort on her arm, matching her stride all but perfectly.

"Sorry to interrupt your date," Spril greeted, "It was urgent."

"Yes, thank you for coming on such short notice," Yrlis added, her hands linked before herself.

"It's no sweat. I'm honored you thought of me," EshCal said. She shook their hands and pulled each into a one-armed hug. "Even if it's only because you just saw me this morning."

"Well, Phylus was busy," Spril teased, "So we had to settle for you."

EshCal sighed and shook her head. "Don't make me kick your ass, zombie boy."

Spril laughed with his entire body, while Yrlis beamed at his health and liveliness.

"So, when are you going to introduce us to your lady friend?" he asked through fading laughter.

"Soon as you ask," the escort said, leaning it to offer a handshake, "You can..." She stopped and pulled back. "Hold up. How'd you know?"

"Know what?"

"That I'm a woman," she clarified, looking herself over, "Nobody guesses right that fast and that confidently."

"Well, I figured either you're a woman or you're wearing copper underwear," Spril said, "And I don't think that's a thing even in your line of work."

"No, that's... too strong a conductor," she said. She smeared her hands over her face. "No. No. No! Hold up. I'm not even... I'm like five days off from my next period. How did you...? Just... How?!"

"You've heard of the Hybrids?"

"Those people with the crazy powers?" she asked. Spril nodded. "You're one of them?"

"No," Spril said with a viciously playful smile. The escort's mouth fell agape, and she slapped his chest. "But they're my friends. And The Avatars of Fate certainly haven't isolated their efforts to them," he continued, "So I decided I had to become the best version of myself."

"That's actually pretty cool," the escort said, "Anyway, you two can call me Hibiscus."

"Oh, sweetie," Yrlis said, holding EshCal's shoulder, "You know better than to date people who don't go by their real name."

"Okay, first of all," EshCal admonished, glaring as she muscled out of Yrlis's grasp, "Your fiancé and his second-in-command in the Subtransit both used aliases. Second, it's because of her profession."

"That doesn't make it any better!" Yrlis argued, "Amirione... Oh sorry. The Hunter... used an alias because of his profession, too."

EshCal pinched the bridge of her nose. Hibiscus and Spril exchanged quizzical and apologetic glances.

"Yrlis," Spril beckoned, "Hibiscus is an escort."

"Aliases protect us from stalkers. Weirdo clients who bypass the screening process," Hibiscus said. She looked Yrlis over. "And their weirdo friends, in some cases." Spril shot her a sharp glance, but she just shrugged. "I just mean that it's nothing like with The Avatars."

"I guess that makes sense," Yrlis sighed. She turned to Spril. "So, this is EshCal's big secret? She's dating an escort?"

"Only by the hour," Hibiscus said, "Today, she went for a more wholesome take on the girlfriend experience. For now, anyway."

"That's my big secret," EshCal asserted, "I use an escort service to get laid."

"But... why?" Yrlis puzzled, "I mean, nothing against your line of work, Hibiscus. It's just, if you don't mind my saying, EshCal, you'd be a hell of a catch. It's not as hard as you think to balance work and romance, if that's the issue."

"Not that," EshCal insisted, "My last relationship was with Amirione. It created trust issues running both ways in my love life. So, I just meet with Hibiscus or one of her colleagues once a week instead. I get laid. They get paid. Everyone's happy. No politics."

"Our consensual hedonism isn't gonna cramp your matrimony, is it?" Hibiscus asked, "I mean, Spril's obviously fine with it. But, Yrlis, are you good?"

"Better than I'm probably letting on," Yrlis insisted, "Honestly."

"Good. Good. This is your moment. I'm just here to watch," Hibiscus said, "Now, let's get inside so you two can go get married."

Yrlis hooked Spril's arm with hers and looked up to kiss him. They leaned on each other's foreheads.

"I like the sound of that," Spril exhaled, "'Go get married.' Has a nice... ring to it."

"You're horrible, and I love you for it," Yrlis sighed, "Not exactly the pre-ceremony anyone hopes for, is it? Discussing your partner's colleague's sex life."

"I don't think crosses anyone's mind," Spril shrugged, "But how often does life go as planned?"

"Well, one thing's been working out pretty well."

"For now."

"Best we make the most of it, then."

Strands of earthen brown and stony gray light wove their way around one another, in and out of the roiling black murk. These braids of light branched and coiled, jagged stretches of tar-like muddy copper filling the enclosed spaces. Gradually, they amassed into a humanoid bulk with tapering braids of light sprouting from its head. The ends frayed and faded into the roiling darkness.

"He seems dead," Sinkua thought, "But then, why is he still in his body?"

"You are correct," Phoenix said inside his mind, "It seems Arestor died quite some time ago."

"Can you tell how long ago?"

"Unfortunately, no," she lamented, "These circumstances are without precedent."

"Shit," Sinkua internally muttered, "Well, do you know why he's still in there?"

"He is trapped," Phoenix said, "This copper flesh is a barrier to both tsora and milystis."

"But only from the inside, I suppose. Seeing as they tortured me to release Pahres," he pondered, shuddering, "I'm glad I don't remember that."

"You suppose correctly. And yes, your forgetting is for the best."

"So, these breaks," Sinkua said, reaching for the tar-like strands, "Is his tsora decaying?"

"Neither tsora nor milystis decays as you understand it," Phoenix explained, "It may unravel in extreme circumstances."

"Such as now?"

"Such as now," she affirmed, "His tsora appears to be leaking through these cracks in the copper flesh."

"Can we revive him?"

"No."

"That was quick," Sinkua said, "Can you explain why?"

"You haven't the capacity to draw back his tsora, and even if you did, you could not simultaneously break the copper flesh," Phoenix explained, "Were you to break him out first, he would die before you recuperated. Quite painfully, at that."

"Can you revive him on your own, so I can focus on breaking the copper flesh?"

"Not so long as I am within this gem, and you do not yet have the means to break me out."

"I assume the same goes for you breaking yourself out?"

"Yes, but it would also be extremely harmful to me, possibly deadly," Phoenix said, "Only pure milystis can break the barrier, but it does so by extinguishing against it."

"What if I figure out how to break you out of this gem?" Sinkua asked, "I've broken copper flesh before."

"Only in the throes of great torture," Phoenix clarified, "You are grasping, my friend. We are at an impasse."

Sinkua sighed aloud. "So, why can't I revive him?" he asked, "Is it because he's been dead for too long?"

"No, his body is intact enough," Phoenix said, "It is because he and your incarnation of the time were quite spiteful toward each other."

"We were enemies?"

"More of disagreeable allies. Your commonality began and ended with ridding the world of Pandora."

"Not enough of a bond," Sinkua realized, "I couldn't endure the pain."

"I'm afraid not."

"Well, could you tell me about him so maybe I can empathize?"

"Yes, but the barrier is still an issue."

"I've given up on resurrecting him," Sinkua said, "I want to call back the tsora he's lost to draw the rest out more quickly."

"That is quite the more unconventional use of your powers than your past selves may have considered," Phoenix said, "I should say it's feasible, but it could just as likely backfire."

"How so?"

"His tsora may not reconstitute once it has all unraveled and escaped."

"You don't sound certain."

"I am certain enough to say that it is unadvisable."

"Dammit," he muttered, "Is there anything we can do for him?"

"You care much for this person you once despised."

"I have no memory of that life. So? Anything?"

"Take him to Odin," Phoenix asserted, "Now wake up. Your friends are waiting."

An afterimage of the frayed figure lingered as Sinkua opened his eyes. He blinked a few times, and it faded from his sight.

"What did you find out?" came a voice from behind his shoulder.

"In short, he's dead," Sinkua said, turning to face Galo, "I'm sorry."

"I take it you can't do it anything for him?"

Sinkua shook his head. "His soul is trapped in his body and unraveling as it leaks out. Phoenix and I can't do anything about it. It's complicated and confusing, even though we just talked about it," he explained, "She said to take him to Odin."

"I'll bring him to ArcNos after the burials have been arranged," Galo agreed. He gestured aside. "Now, Malia is here to take you to Country Living. I've arranged for you to wait there until your appointment."

Malia gave a small wave as Sinkua turned to face her. He hadn't noticed her until Galo pointed her out. At that, he realized just how much his time convening with Phoenix over Arestor's tsora had impacted his peripheral vision. Hopefully not permanently.

"How did you get here?" he puzzled.

"With a portal strip, of course," Malia said, "Lucky for you, Chekov is willing to trust me with them."

"No, I mean..." Sinkua said, trailing off as he sorted his thoughts, "I thought you could only go to doors you've traveled through before."

"Normally," she said, "But we can also work from coordinates." She nodded back toward the cabin door. "Now then. Ready to go?"

Sinkua cast one last look over the barnacle-riddled statue. He let out a long sigh of exasperated capitulation.

"Might as well."

Malia turned and walked toward the cabin. Sinkua dragged his feet as he followed.

"Sinkua!" Galo called out. Sinkua stopped and turned to face him. Galo stammered, "I just... I still respect you, okay? I don't... I don't want there to be any bad blood between us."

"It's cool. I get it," Sinkua said, "We're still friends." His mouth flicked up into a small grin. "And brothers."

Chapter 28

Nikasu tipped her book down and perked up at the sound of footsteps coming up the front walk. As someone knocked, she sprang from the armchair, spilling her book, and bolted for the door. She reached it by the third knock and threw it open as she heard movement upstairs.

Vielle stood at the other side with an outstretched fist and startled eyes. Phylus stood close by. Nikasu's shoulders slumped.

"Were you expecting someone else?" Vielle asked.

"Yeah. I mean… well…" Nikasu fumbled, "I'm not disappointed to see you. It's just… I thought you were Sinkua and Galo." Nikasu drummed her fingernails on the back of her other hand. "Sorry. Come in."

"I thought you'd never ask," Vielle remarked, flashing a smile.

"They're fine, by the way," Phylus said as Nikasu shut the door behind them, "Just delayed."

"What happened?"

"Galo is staying in Berinin to tend to some burials. Things went sideways on their search for Arestor."

Nikasu swallowed hard. "And Sinkua?"

"Malia went to take him to his doctor," Phylus said, "He had an episode. A pretty bad one, from what I understand."

"Shit…"

"Actually, I wanted to talk to you about," Vielle said, "Mind if we go sit down?"

"Hm? No. No, not at all," Nikasu said, still gripped by introspection, "Sitting sounds great."

Nikasu reflected on the darkness she had fallen into as she followed them to the living room. She remembered muffled shouting and screaming. She remembered an overwhelming sense of power. And she remembered sinking into it all.

"So," Vielle began as she sat down. Nikasu gathered up her book and put it on the coffee table. "Did anything strange happen to you the day before yesterday?"

"Um…" Nikasu choked out, "Why do you ask?"

"Remember how we thought Yggdrasil might be, well, spreading Sinkua's episodes?" Vielle asked. Nikasu nodded sheepishly. "Well, the day before yesterday, I got this feeling like the worst migraine imaginable. And then it got worse. I… consulted the roots, and well…" Vielle trailed off, rubbing the back of her neck as she ordered her next words. "I think I was sensing you and Sinkua. It was like you were in this… negativity feedback loop. Like you were both having an episode and feeding off of each other's."

"I, um…" Nikasu exhaled, "Yeah. I had an episode."

"I thought so," Vielle said, "Well anyway, I broke the loop, but…"

"She passed out," Phylus said, patting Vielle's shoulder, "She just woke up two hours ago."

"You slept for a day and a half?" Nikasu remarked. Vielle nodded, grinning sheepishly. "Well, thank you for stopping it. I'm afraid to think what might have happened if you didn't."

"So am I," Vielle said, "But I wanted to ask you, what happened just before your episode started?"

"Um… You're familiar with… um… snowmen, right?" Nikasu said, fiddling with her knuckles again. Vielle nodded. "Well, I realized I've never built one, and the snow has almost melted. So, I was in the back yard, about to make my first snowman."

The sweetest smile spread across Vielle's face, consuming every bit of her expression. Nikasu had no idea what Vielle had expected to hear, but she doubted that building a snowman was even up for consideration.

"That's nothing to be embarrassed about," Vielle assured her, "Hell, Galo was older than you the first time he even saw snow."

"Yeah, but… A snowman?" Nikasu said, "That's just childish."

"Says who?" Vielle shot back, "You didn't have a childhood, and even if you did, you don't owe anyone an explanation."

"… Thank you," Nikasu said, "So anyway, I suddenly felt like I was being swallowed by darkness. I heard yelling, but I couldn't make it out. I could see shapes of people, but I couldn't tell who they were." She shifted in her seat. "I… I felt like I was getting stronger. But it was also like it wasn't me. Does that make sense? It's like there was another stronger me that wasn't me, and I was trapped inside of it and getting smaller. Or maybe it was getting bigger."

"What happened after it was over?"

"I woke up in my bed some time later," Nikasu said, reflecting on her first waking moments, "There's a crater in the back yard, from where I caved the ground in."

"You're not telling them the worst part," came a voice from behind them.

BeiLou stood at the bottom of the stairs. Nikasu kept her head down as she approached the living room.

"I was gonna get to it," Nikasu said, shrinking into her seat, "I, um… attacked BeiLou. I lifted her over my head by her throat. Odin had to knock me out."

"Not that," BeiLou said, "The other thing." She turned to Vielle and Phylus. "Her body was changing," she explained, "She had compound eyes. She was growing chitin. And her arms and legs got longer. It was like she was turning into some sort of mantis creature."

"Oh shit," Vielle muttered.

BeiLou had only been two observations in by the time Nikasu had curled up in a ball and begun rocking on her buttocks. Vielle tugged her arm, and Nikasu leaned toward her. Vielle wrapped her arms around her little sister, whispering comforting nothings-in-particular.

"We never told you about Yahsek, did we?" Vielle asked. BeiLou shook her head. "He was a Hybrid who shared a cell with Nikasu. Except it turned out he was working for The Avatars all along. They planted him as her cellmate to keep her under control and discourage her from developing her powers." BeiLou's mouth fell open, but Vielle pressed on. "When we rescued her, he used that bond to get in good with the rest of us. That's why one of your books is missing. It also turned out that he wasn't even a real Hybrid."

"They used my blood to make a Faux-Hybrid," Nikasu grumbled, her voice muffled between her knees, "And to make Sinkua and a bunch of other people sick. Fucking jerks."

"Oh…" BeiLou managed, "Oh that… I'm so sorry." She watched Nikasu for a moment. "But… What does this Yahsek have to do with your transformation?"

"He was an animal shifter," Vielle said, "He could change like that at will."

"And now I'm doing it, too!" Nikasu cried out, facing BeiLou squarely, "I tried to tell you, but you wouldn't listen! You bitch!"

"It's not that I wouldn't listen," BeiLou defended, "It's just that whenever we talk about it, you get flustered and incoherent, and I can't follow what you're saying."

"Because you won't shut up long enough for me to figure out how to say what I need to say," Nikasu shot back.

"Sweetie…"

"Call me sweetie again, and I'll throw you on the roof."

"Nikasu!" Phylus bellowed. Nikasu turned sharply, her eyes wide with a new sort of fear. The fear of punishment. But not like she got in her cell. The domestic kind. "That was uncalled for."

"But… Dad…"

"No," Phylus said, "I don't care what's transpired between you two since your episode. You need to apologize."

"I'm sorry I threatened to throw you on the roof," Nikasu muttered in BeiLou's general direction, "And that I called you a bitch."

"Apology accepted," BeiLou said, "Now then…"

"As for you," Phylus cut off, "Nikasu has suffered in ways you might never comprehend. Yes, even considering what happened to you. So, treat her with the consideration she needs. When she needs to say something, shut up and let her figure out how to say it."

"Excuse me, are you…" BeiLou stammered, "… Are you trying to father me?"

"Yes," Phylus asserted, "I'm an actual father to one Hybrid and a father figure to the other three. And you're the same age as my adopted son. So, if you bicker with any of them, I'm going to step in and 'father you.'"

"Dude!" BeiLou shot back, "One of those Hybrids is my son."

"You'd sooner pass for his sister at your biological age," Phylus reminded, "You may have been fighting The Avatars before the rest of us, but you were out of the game for sixteen years. Now, you're a guest in my house. Do not condescend to my children."

Vielle and Nikasu looked at him with astounded admiration. BeiLou shrank back.

"That was uncalled for," she muttered.

"That's your opinion," Phylus said, "You're entitled to it, but I disagree. You need to remember your place."

"Yeah… I guess you're right," BeiLou sighed, "I've been reminded of that a lot lately."

"What do you mean?"

"You been to AlsRim's Deli?" she asked. Phylus nodded. "Do you remember when it was SalMei's?" Phylus shook his head. "SalMei was AlsRim's big sister and a close friend of mine. AlsRim took over the deli after she died."

"Huh…" Phylus said, "I never knew about that."

"Neither did I until I came back," BeiLou said, "Anyway, Odin and I went there for lunch. I tried to talk to AlsRim, but she shouted me out of her shop. She thought I was trying to cash in on her story. She didn't recognize me at all."

"Oh damn," Phylus sighed, "That sort of thing never even occurred to me. I'm sorry."

"It's okay," BeiLou said, "I was going to end up isolated if the plan had panned out, anyway."

"Sure, but not like this," Phylus said, "Look, I once called myself The Patriarch because of that whole father figure thing. And you're not exempt from it. But I'll try to do better about considering what you've been through." He turned to Nikasu. "You do the same, okay?"

"I'll try," Nikasu managed, "Sorry again, BeiLou."

"Well, no matter what, we need to talk to Dourias and the others when Sinkua gets back," Vielle said, "I'm sure the feedback loop and transformation factor into the diagrams."

Sinkua set a card in the discard pile and pinched one from the top of the deck. He eyed his opponent across the table, trying to discern the man's thoughts toward his next move.

"So, I was wondering," he said, "How much do you actually know about The Coalition?"

"As much as they need me to know," Jex said, "What brings you to ask all of a sudden?"

"I was just thinking about when Malia told you what's become of them," Sinkua explained as Jex took his move, "You didn't flinch at the thought of The Coalition disbanding or assimilating into a startup."

"Why would I?" Jex asked, "Three quarters of their founders are gone. The Weapon is noncompliant. Nothing much they can do on their own. Better they join up with something bigger and more stable with the same goals. Especially something with as fine a leadership as Spril will provide."

Sinkua glared at him as he slapped a card onto the discard pile. Surely, he was being facetious. Someone so trusted by The Coalition couldn't have been so uninformed. Then again, Jex's composure was unaffected by Sinkua's glaring. So maybe not.

"Dude," Sinkua said as he took a card, "Spril is The Weapon."

"…Truly?" Jex asked, his composure finally shaken as he chuckled to himself, "Oh goodness. That is ironic, isn't it?"

"Right? Their pet project won't fall in line, so they're lining up behind him instead."

"Well, I'm sure the irony isn't lost on Chekov," Jex insisted. He swapped a card from his hand for one of Sinkua's. "Oh! There's something I've been meaning to tell you," he said, laying out his cards, "Remchuk."

"Son of a mother!"

"There's a reason The Coalition only tells me as much as they need me to know."

"Hired you for your powers of deduction?"

"Observation," Jex specified, "Only way anything escapes my notice is if it seems irrelevant." He crossed the room to the vending machine. "Speaking of which, I met your girlfriend's mother. Did she tell you about that?"

"Fiancée," Sinkua corrected, "And we're calling each other in-laws." He thought back on seeing Elemeno in Eprilen. "But um…" He trailed off as he realized he couldn't recall one way or another. Better to play it off, he figured. "I think she said something about it, but it was just in passing."

"I didn't recognize her," Jex said as he opened a bag of chips, "I know Elemeno by name and reputation. She checked in as Picuarus, and I'm honestly embarrassed for not picking up on the alias."

"No reason to be," Sinkua shrugged, "People who don't know her well never suspect her. She shared a bed with an Avatar for twenty years and still snuck up on him and snapped his neck."

"Yes, and I prefer to think of myself as quite a bit smarter than those despicable bags of fuck," Jex insisted, "As should you."

"Well, I've known she was a secret badass for a while now," Sinkua said, "Eytea certainly didn't get that from Kabehl."

Sinkua walked to the vending machine to mull over the selections. He'd been at Country Living for four days, and he was no less indecisive about his snack purchases. Drinks were simple. Cherry Popken or anything with pomegranate.

"By the way," he said, finally settling on lamb jerky, "Do you know Murdega?"

"Ivarian dockworker?"

Sinkua nodded. "Kinda… weird?"

"Yeah. I know him," Jex said, "He and I are the last two Keepers. Why? He got some ironic story sitting in my blind spot, too?"

"No, it's not that," Sinkua said, washing down a pill with pomegranate grapefruit juice, "I ran into him recently, for the first time since I met him. That was just after the attack on Masnethege." He pulled a pamphlet from the tourism board on the wall, recognizing the patch of blue roses from the front lawn. "I got the impression that he'd gotten involved, but I wasn't sure he knew what he was actually involved in."

"Weird as he is," Jex said, popping a chip into his mouth, "He knows exactly what he's doing."

"Well," Sinkua exhaled. The pamphlet spoke of the blue roses' healing potential in marketable hyperbole, leaning into their developer being versed in classical Berininite techniques. "That is as disturbing as it is reassuring."

Jex chuckled. "Well, in any case," he said, "a cab will be here after breakfast tomorrow to take you to the docks."

"Oh, thank you," Sinkua remarked, "How much do I owe you?"

"Don't worry about it. I'll just add it to your bill."

"Are you sure? I feel like I should run that past Galo first."

"No need," Jex assured, "There's enough in the fund he set up for you."

Galo stood nodding on the front step, almost thankful that this was his last stop. He put on a believable facade of sympathy and understanding, but with so many holding him personally to blame, he was running short on both.

"When you ran off to ArcNos, you doomed everyone who'd following you," the elderly woman in the door shouted, "Then, now, and any time between. Should've stayed gone."

"I realize this is a difficult time for you," Galo said, "Your son was a great man. It was an honor to have him in my service."

"Better if you just owned up to being a deserter," she continued, "Never should've come back. Rebuilding was going just fine without you. Then you go dragging all that Northland fighting down here."

"I know nothing can replace your son," Galo continued, fully aware that they were having two different conversations, "but I'm holding myself accountable for compensating you, his wife, and his children as his next of kin."

"Arrogant fools, every last one of you Chieftains," she ranted on, "Should've died off with your father."

"As this was not official state business," Galo said, "this will not be expensed to taxpayers. He will, however, be honored as having fallen in service of the state."

"Sooner you get your hands off the state, the better off we'll all be."

Before Galo could say another word, she slammed the door in his face, looking quite satisfied with herself. Galo shrugged, having said all he needed to.

This was something that his grandfather had never prepared him for. All day, people had been blaming him for unforeseeable circumstances and throwing conflicting accusations at him.

He never should have gone to ArcNos. He should have stayed there. He never should have ended his suspension. He should have stayed in office. He never should have claimed that annex. He should have claimed it sooner. He never should have trusted his in-laws. He should have made peace with them.

Neither he nor Leviathan could comprehend how his in-laws' plottings were his responsibility. The worst of it took place before he was born. But he heard it more than a couple of times, nonetheless. Everyone knew what he should or never should have done, and as far as he was concerned, everyone could walk off.

His last stop was within walking distance of the beach. The smell of salty air had perhaps been the only thing keeping his patience even somewhat intact. Walking while he reflected on the day's reports, he stepped onto sand as he came to his conclusion about Berinin as a whole and politics in general.

Soon, it would no longer so intimately be his problem.

"Your great-great-grandfather committed travesties that would take generations to reconcile," Leviathan assured, "despite having had the best intentions." Galo sighed raspily, black phlegm rumbling in his throat. "Your grandfather died before he could quite put Berinin back on the inexorable path to recovery."

"This is a complicated issue," he thought back as he ascended the steps to the dock, "None of us could have foreseen the disasters that came of our decisions. We all acted on what we knew with Berinin's best interest in mind." He scouted the docks, pausing in his directed reflections. "Nobody can be held to blame, but I still need to take responsibility for making things right."

"Oh, but you're wrong about the matter of blame," Leviathan insisted, "You and I agree that MalVek knew what he wrought when he disrupted the Bloodline."

"That doesn't matter," Galo argued, "The best I can do for Berinin is to yield to democracy. All that's left for me is to walk away."

"And to destroy MalVek."

"I agree that he needs to die," Galo thought, "but your obsession with vengeance is unsettling. It reminds me of the path Sinkua is going down."

"You baffle me, child," Leviathan chided, "You speak so ill of killing out of vengeance, yet you kill strangers out of self-defense."

"You didn't stop me," Galo deflected, "In fact, you helped."

"I am honor-bound to see to your wellbeing. Had I not helped, they could have killed you," Leviathan explained, "But I meant none of it as an accusation. It was merely an observation."

"Noted," Galo conceded, "But you can't deny that Sinkua is taking things too far with his vengeance over his mother."

"Killing Borret as he did may have been excessive," Leviathan agreed, "But my opinion is inconsequential. Your dispute is with Sinkua."

"I'll talk to him about it after he sees Doctor Ophalin," Galo thought. He made eye contact with a man selling a modest dinghy. "But we've gotten off topic. I just want to get to the root of the conflict between the Chieftain Bloodline and my mother's family."

"As you ought," Leviathan said, "But do not assume that any of you would have fared better had that conflict been settled sooner. I believe The Avatars of Fate are the successors of Pandora's acolytes. The Mberhali called them Mawakouteza. Stewards of Disarray."

"Could you tell me more about Mawakouteza on the trip to ArcNos?"

"It would be more conducive that I bring them up at Famujokoumba."

"Fair enough," he said, his internal conversation blurring into the sales associate's greeting, "Teach me some more Mberhali, then?"

"Of course."

After a brief exchange with the man on the dock, Galo bought the modest dinghy. He had commandeered Borret's ship and sold it and his own the day after his encounter. That money had gone to compensating the families of the deceased and the survivors from both crews. The rest and much of his remaining wealth, he had pledged to various charities and research groups.

He couldn't realize Grandpa's vision for Berinin. But he could put the money he'd earned by trying into the hands of those who might.

MarLys unbuttoned her coat and hung it off her shoulders. The late Frigid cold snap she'd expected hadn't come to pass. At least not in the high-rise district. She thought it might have had something to do with the proximity to Yggdrasil, but she didn't dwell on it for long.

Volunteer groups worked in less than professional concert. Sure, they cleared out the rubble, even if it was more eventual than efficient. But their lack of coordination made it clear that they had been trained almost as well as they were being paid. Still, she couldn't fault them for the effort.

"Excuse me!" a throaty masculine voice called out in a tone that more demanded than commanded attention. MarLys took her time turning around. "What are you doing here?"

The head contractor was a man nearing sixty who wore his age all over himself. His hands were covered in calluses, his cheeks in salt and pepper stubble, his forehead in scowl lines. A beer gut strained his dress shirt which, paired with his necktie, clashed with his blue jeans and work boots. MarLys guessed that his white hardhat hid a hairline that was receding with no sign of slowing.

"Taking applications," MarLys called back, waving her portfolio.

The portly contractor grumbled and sneered. Behind him, KalChi shook her head at MarLys.

"Who are you?" he demanded, "Who are you with?"

"Sorry. Misunderstood," MarLys answered. The contractor folded his arms. "I'm MarLys from the Ministry of Human Resources. I'm here to see if any volunteers are interested in Ministry work."

The contractor grunted and looked aside. MarLys followed his line of sight to a man holding a single sheet of paper. She had met him a few days prior to coordinate their work in the high-rise district. But it had been so brief, and he had been so disinterested, that she forgot his name. She watched him out of the corner of her eye.

"And you?" the contractor asked him.

"Audit," the man called back, taking a long drag off his cigarette.

"You need to give me more than that."

"Actually," the man said, pausing for one more drag, "I don't." He approached the contractor. "But since you asked so nicely, I'll tell you anyway," the man continued, stopping at a considerable distance, "My name is PavRal. I'm with the Ministry of Defense. And I'm making observations to be analyzed for potential threats. Good enough?"

The contractor regarded PavRal for a hard moment, culminating in a dismissive grunt. PavRal gave him an exaggerated half-salute, half-wave. The two turned away from one another.

Both of their answers were cover stories, of course. Perhaps ironically, though, PavRal's cover was MarLys's actual reason for being there. Problem was, threat analysis was too suspicious a reason for someone from Human Resources to be there. At the same time, someone from Defense pushing for certain volunteers to be sent away was comparably odd. MarLys's applications were genuine though, serving as an out for the volunteers on PavRal's list.

"I know who you are," PavRal told her.

"Yeah," she exhaled, "I just told him. Good auditing." They weren't to discuss their actual assignments while on site, even with each other.

A smile isolated itself to the bottom half of his face. "Just like you to exploit a technicality," he said. The corner of MarLys's mouth flicked out a sneer. "I mean, I know what you are."

"And what's that?" MarLys asked, taking a couple of lingering steps toward him, "A dyke? A Hybrid-fucker?" She stopped and shrugged. "Good job there, cauliflower. You really pulled me out of the closet."

"Funny," PavRal muttered, "Not what I meant. You and I come from the…" He mimed adjusting a necktie. "… same background."

"Ex-courier?" MarLys asked. PavRal nodded. "I've put that behind me."

"Yes, of course. That makes sense, what with your…" PavRal agreed, rolling his hand, "… you know. Story."

MarLys flattened her mouth and nodded, taking the conversation as being over. She watched the contractor's crew as they rushed about with recording instruments she couldn't hope to identify. One crewmember in particular caught her attention. This one kept her head down like she was allergic to eye contact as she planted various single-colored flags throughout the wreckage. As clueless as MarLys was about the instruments, she was that much more so about the color coding of the flags.

"I envy you, by the way," PavRal blurted out. MarLys turned her head, "Things ending up like they have for you."

"Come again?"

"A lot of us left Black Tie when their illicit dealings were brought to our attention," he clarified, "You're the first to be offered protection."

"Maybe because I was the first to offer dirt," MarLys suggested, "The rest of you had to have it pointed out to you."

"Perhaps," PavRal said, shrugging half-heartedly, "Point is, you landed yourself a sweet gig."

"Now you're just selling yourself short," MarLys insisted, "We're both personal assistants to Ministry executives. The only difference is a single rank."

"Yes, well, SenRas is a bigger deal than EshCal," PavRal said, "As I'm sure you know."

"That's subjective."

"Forty years isn't."

"No, I suppose not," MarLys said. PavRal's angle had come together, and she was going to see it through. "Tenure aside, I'd be happy to work for either of them."

"I suppose so," PavRal knuckled under. He looked MarLys over in a way that she was sure was meant to put her off. "So, where do you keep yours?"

"Excuse me?" she baited, "My what?"

"Your bug," he rasped, "Where do you keep your wire?"

"Oh sweetie," she said, "You could search me until it gets awkward for you, and you still wouldn't find it."

"That good, huh?" he said, folding his arms, "Well, I guess you'd have to be to work for SenRas."

MarLys returned the isolated smile. "Whatever helps you sleep at night, cauliflower."

"Khirsan!" MalVek bellowed.

He folded his arms behind his back as he considered the array of portal generators mounted upon the wall. Narrowing his eyes, he peered into the layers of portals, a composite of fractured imagery somehow beyond even his own comprehension.

"My Lord?" Khirsan answered from the doorway.

"The homunculi are standing by, correct?" MalVek asked, continuing to gaze into the stacked portals.

"As per your orders, My Lord," Khirsan said, bowing.

MalVek turned to face him. "Ready an examination room for one. Tell it that Jevana will come shortly."

"I'll see to it right away, My Lord," Khirsan said, "Do you have a certain one in mind?"

"No, choose as you wish."

As Khirsan exited into the hall, MalVek raised his gloved hand and, closing one eye, aligned it with one of the portal generators. With a flick of his finger, he moved the power switch, turning off the device from two meters away. He repeated with the others, growing more comfortable with the effort, until only one remained.

"Come forth, Jevana," he called into the last portal image.

Jevana hopped out of the fractal pool of light in the wall, smoothly falling to one knee as she landed. As she rose to her feet, she wrenched her hat from her head and pulled her ponytail loose.

"Your timing is impeccable, My Lord," she said, unzipping her coveralls, "I had just finished planting the beacons."

"I know."

"Then, I suppose you also know that PavRal has been compromised?"

"I know he speaks too much for his own good," MalVek corrected as he deactivated the last generator. "Compromised is too strong a word, however. His hubris may yet be of use toward the exodus."

"Of course, My Lord. I apologize," Jevana said, bowing as she stepped out of her coveralls. She shook the mats and folds out of her scrubs. "What would you have me do now?"

"Khirsan is readying an examination room and a homunculus for you as I speak," MalVek said, "You are to perform a spinal tap and an occipital biopsy on the homunculus."

"Oh, what fun," Jevana snickered, "And what am I to do with Khirsan?"

"Nothing," MalVek muttered, "For now. He still has his uses."

Jevana grazed her fingernails along MalVek's shoulder as she brushed past him on her way to the door. "Hmm. I suppose he does."

Once she was out of earshot, MalVek turned the generators back on one by one in faster succession than he'd turned them off. He stared into the composite of liquid fractals, trying to isolate a single layer.

"What is the purpose of this?" boomed a voice from the doorway. MalVek didn't bother with acknowledgments. "The homunculi are crucial to your end of the arrangement. So to what end are you having surgery performed on them?" Footsteps approached, stopping two strides from his back. "And what further business do you have on Heniokhos Boulevard?"

That got MalVek's attention. He spun to face Mortvill, finding him well out of arm's reach. Were he judging right, an assertion he only doubted for his current eye strain, he was within reach of The Harvester's sword.

"You can see clearly through these?" The General asked.

"Well enough to discern a familiar location," The Harvester said, "I should suppose no better than you." His mask shifted. "That is what you wish to gain from this procedure."

"Yes," The General nodded, "Why do you wear that thing when we are alone? I know your face."

"Personal preference," The Harvester insisted, "Supposing you succeed, what do you hope to accomplish next?"

"Eliminating liabilities," The General answered. "While I have you here," he segued, "I need your input on something."

"Oh? What might that be?"

"It was too ambitious to try to replicate Epesol with pedestrian metals."

"Only a fool would think that was even plausible."

"I've come to realize that not even the craftsmanship of the Quircois could compensate for inadequate materials," The General continued, ignoring the insult, "That said, could one use Galanite in place of Hephaeseum?"

"So, even you do not know of another vein of Hephaeseum?" The Harvester observed, "You may just be able to comprehend the molecular discrepancies between the two. That said, with the talents of the Quircois, it may be possible to substitute Hephaeseum with Galanite. Or any ethermetal for that matter, though the task becomes increasingly difficult the more distant their origins from one another."

"Would Gaibhneum be easier?"

"Yes, but how would you acquire it?"

"Fair point," The General considered, rubbing his chin, "Galanite is more accessible. Less interference in Kirts than Quarun."

"You might try Vulcalt," The Harvester suggested, "had you not ordered the homunculi to kill The Politician."

"They only attacked because he had become a liability," The General deflected, "Besides, I have other contacts in Tanelen."

"Ones with access to Vulcalt?" The Harvester challenged. The General dodged eye contact. "Well, I will say that The Politician's soul was delicious," he continued, "And should you stray too far from or, Goddess forbid, renege on our arrangement, I'm sure I'll find yours equally so."

The Harvester took his leave of The General's research hall without waiting for a response. MalVek watched him with a mask of stoicism, which turned to a grimace at the empty space once The Harvester had rounded the doorframe.

He turned his attention to a luminous green map of Ouristihra. Perhaps a thousand dots speckled the map. An anomaly in the shadows between Berininite proper and the annex island caught his eye. It was a cluster of dulled dots of light.

With a swipe of his hand, the cluster scrambled west-northwest. After perhaps a minute, it came aglow in red. He swiped his hand downward, then nudged to the right, and the specks moved more slowly east-southeast.

The cluster flickered brightly. Violently. The dots of light huddled close, as though they were all trying to occupy the same space. And as they drew perhaps closer than humanly possible, the specks faded to black. MalVek flicked his finger, and the display returned to the present.

"Damn that Berininite invalid," he grumbled, "How could he not have seen this?" He paced in long purposeful strides. "A group activation absent any of our chambers. An excess of our ambitions! And I missed it because of that damnable fool," he spat, "Sinkua did him a mercy, killing him before I could get my hands on him."

In the corner of his eye, he saw Jevana appear in the doorframe, holding a pair of large syringes. He waved her into the room, and she held eye contact with something close to arrogance as she crossed the research hall.

"The samples are ready, My Lord," Jevana said, bowing her head as she held out the two syringes.

"Splendid!" MalVek remarked.

He swiped them from her and uncapped one of them. He pulled up the back of his shirt and jammed the needle into his spine. Jevana chewed on the corner of her bottom lip as she watched him inject the clear, unassuming liquid.

MalVek tossed the empty syringe aside and uncapped the second needle. Jevana bit her lip with greater earnest as the first syringe shattered, metal and all, against the wall. MalVek aligned the second needle with the base of his skull and injected the grayish pink substance into his brainstem.

"Those should take effect shortly," he said as he crumbled the second syringe in his fist, "Stay and bear witness."

"Thank you, My Lord," Jevana professed, "Anything to be of service."

One by one, MalVek remotely reactivated the portal generators on the wall. The first was as clear as ever. Two, he could distinguish with no effort. At the third and fourth, he began to notice the effort, but it was still minimal. Far better than before. They appeared as a single composite image, but now, not only could he distinguish them more easily, he could determine their relative positions in real space.

But at five, that all began to break down. He deactivated the set.

"We can allow it more time."

Chapter 29

Galo climbed out of the passenger's side of the pickup truck as the driver set the parking brake. He circled to the back of the bed and waited. The blinds in the living room window split for a moment.

"So, where do you want to put this?" the driver asked as he opened the tailgate and dropped the loading ramp, "Can't get it through the front door, I don't think. Garage, maybe?"

"Lawn's fine, thank you," Galo insisted.

"So, it's a lawn ornament, then? Guess it makes…"

"Galo!"

Nikasu ran from the front door, tramped across the lawn, and leapt at Galo. He caught her, spun her around, and set her down between himself and the driver.

"I'm glad you're here," he said, kissing her on the cheek. He kept his hand on Nikasu's shoulder as he addressed the driver. "She can help us unload the statue."

"Oh. Okay," the driver nodded, his eyebrow flinching, "Spotter'd be nice, yeah."

"Do you mind?" Galo asked. Nikasu shook her head. "Okay, come on up."

The three of them climbed up into the bed of the truck. Galo and the driver positioned themselves on either side of the statue, crouched and put their arms around it. Nikasu stood facing the cabin and put her hands against its back.

The driver's eyes widened as they lifted the thing with greater ease than he had expected. With the help of Nikasu's subtle manipulation, they worked it down the ramp and over to the middle of the front lawn.

"Thanks for everything, sir," Galo said, shaking the driver's hand, "By the way, it just occurred to me that I never caught your name."

"Huh? Oh yeah. I know who you are, so I didn't think to introduce myself," the driver said, "My name is MelDas."

Nikasu gave a small wave. "Nikasu."

MelDas nodded to her, then to Galo. He climbed back into his truck and drove away.

Galo turned to Nikasu. "So, who's here?"

"Odin and BeiLou are home," Nikasu said, "Vielle's visiting. Where's Sinkua?"

"I sent him to see Doctor Ophalin. He had an especially bad episode," he explained. She cast her eyes down and shifted her weight. "Sorry, I assumed Malia had told you."

"She did," Nikasu said. She paused and shook her head. "Actually, no. Dad and Vielle told me where she was taking him. I just thought he'd be done in time for you to pick him up."

Galo nodded. "Out with it," he said, "What's bothering you?"

"Lot of things," Nikasu muttered, "It's just… The Nemesis Ion Cloud comes out tonight. I thought we'd all be here for it."

"I'd like that, too," Galo said, pulled her into a hug, "But this was a medical emergency. But just remember that if there's any way for him to be here, he'll find it."

"I know, but…" she said, her voice trailing off.

"… But?"

"I just…" Nikasu sighed, "I want to wait until Sinkua's here. But I want to tell you. But I'm not ready to talk about it. But I need to. And…" She squeezed her eyes shut and shook her head. "I don't know what to do."

Galo brushed her hair back from her face and cupped his hand over her cheek. She sighed and leaned into it, closing her eyes. Galo shut his eyes as well, and the sightless vision of her melted into his mind's eye. Only this time, notions of blackness stained her presence.

"I understand," he whispered as he opened his eyes.

"Thank you," she exhaled, opening her eyes as well, "Vielle saved me. She used Yggdrasil to stop it."

"So, we were right about the roots?"

"I think so."

Galo took in a deep breath and released it slowly. His body trembled with a discomforting blend of relief and dread.

"So, this is Arestor, huh?" Nikasu asked, clearly ready to change the subject.

"What's left of him, anyway."

"He's dead, isn't he?" she deduced, "That's what you meant when you said you'd explain later."

"Essentially, but it's more complicated than that," Galo said, "Sinkua gave me the rundown before he left with Malia. Arestor is dead, but he hasn't completely reached the second life. Some of his tsora is trapped in this statue. It's been leaking out and, he said, unraveling as it does."

"Oh shit!" Nikasu gasped, rubbing the statue's pockmarked arm, "Can't we do for him?"

"Phoenix said to bring him to Odin."

"I'll go get him."

Nikasu headed back up the front walk, nearly bumping into Vielle at the front door. They had a brief exchange, well beyond Galo's hearing, and continued on their ways. Vielle sidled up to Galo in front of the statue.

"Bit of an ugly brute, isn't he?" she asked, looking up at Arestor. She turned to Galo. "Statue's a mess, too."

Galo laughed with sarcastic emphasis. "He's dead, but he's trapped in there," he explained, not wanting to repeat the whole story, "Nikasu's bringing Odin out here to help."

"Yeah, she said she was going to get him," Vielle said, "It's too bad. He looks like he could put up a hell of a fight."

"Sure does," Galo agreed, his voice trailing off. He stopped and blinked, turning to face Vielle. "So, I understand you and Yggdrasil stopped a mutual episode between Sinkua and Nikasu."

"We did," she said, "And honestly, I have no idea how Sinkua does it."

"Which part?"

"Blacks out and only sleeps for a few hours. I slept for a day and a half."

Galo laughed genuinely this time, fading into a droning sigh. "I hate what this portends," he said, his voice gone somber, "Both of them having those episodes."

"Taking care of one has been hard enough," Vielle commiserated, "And this means either of them could activate the afflicted."

"I think so, too. So, whichever one of them The Avatars find more pliable," Galo said, "they'll consider the other to be disposable."

"Yeah," Vielle said, casting her eyes down, "It's not like Laboratory 1341 where they needed you alive." She looked up, meeting his eyes. "And this time, they know the threat I represent."

"Right," Galo choked out, dreading the thought and embarrassed that it hadn't quite occurred to him.

Nikasu announced her return from the front step. Odin followed close behind with his spear strapped to his back. BeiLou came a few steps behind him.

Galo stepped into Odin's path and took a deep breath as he braced to explain Arestor's circumstances. As he gesticulated, Odin put his finger on Galo's knuckles and nudged Galo's hand down to his side.

"Save your breath, child," he insisted, "I will see for myself."

Galo stepped aside, and Odin stood before the sea-worn statue. He unholstered his spear and pressed the tip against Arestor's chest, closing his eye as he just punctured the copper. Sparks sputtered from his body and spear alike as he muttered, presumably in Fjarthursk. Odin withdrew the weapon down to his side and stepped back.

"I am indeed the only one left who can help him," Odin assessed, "And though I agreed infrequently with his principles, he is deserving of this mercy."

Odin took several steps back from the statue. He reached forward with all but his index and pinky fingers curled into a fist. Turning his head a bit, he centered his line of sight along his outstretched arm.

With his other hand, he raised his spear to his shoulder. Electrical sparks coursed along his arm and his spear. In a single inhumanly swift motion, he pulled back his extended arm and brought his spear-arm forward, shaking the front lawn with his momentum.

The air thrummed as the spear plunged through it with such force that it seemed it could shake apart the very molecules. Bursts of lightning streaked behind the spear in every color in the visible spectrum, reaching within a few hairs' breadths of Odin's outstretched hand.

The rainbow lightning faded into the deepest crimson as the spear punctured Arestor's chest. Statue and spear quaked together as the lightning fed itself into them. As the last of it vanished, the spear exploded forth and through the statue with the deafening percussion of a sonic boom.

The spear erupted out of Arestor's back, carrying his luminous shape, formed largely of frayed and loosely woven strands of earthen light. Tightly wound strands in his shoulders loosened as his face turned skyward. The spear skewered a tree three lawns down the road, the entire head and a handful of handle coming out of the other side of the trunk.

A vortex opened in the space in front of the tree, coursing with a synergetic mingling of darkness and light. The vortex enveloped the woven light form of Arestor and closed around him.

Odin hunched over, panting from the exertion. "Stripping the soul as that is a strain not strictly necessary," he said, excusing his sudden fatigue, "But scarcely could I ask any of you to carry his body to the vortex after you have brought him so far."

EshCal crossed Phylus's office as he gestured to the seat across from his desk. She tucked a small stack of papers under her arm as she pulled the chair out.

"EshCal. Always a pleasure," Phylus welcomed, "What brings you here?"

"What do you make of MarLys?" EshCal asked.

"Professionally or personally?"

"Both."

"She's a good person and, from what I've heard, generally a good worker. Earns her paycheck at the very least," Phylus said, "What is this about?"

EshCal laid the papers on the table, keeping her hand atop them. "You know PavRal?"

"Your assistant?" he asked. EshCal nodded. "Yes. Why?"

"Look at this," she said, sliding the papers to him, "It's the transcript of a conversation he had with MarLys."

"Were either of them aware they were being recorded?" Phylus asked. EshCal shook her head. "Well, this sounds pretty incriminating on his part." He slipped on his reading glasses. "Although he kept it vague enough that he could weasel out of it if he goes on trial."

"I noticed that," EshCal said, "If I didn't know better, I might think he knew that I'd planted a bug on him."

"If you didn't know better?"

"SenRas and I played this very close to the chest."

"I see," Phylus nodded, "It might be that he's just cautious." He returned the papers as he finished reading. "This is about her tenure with Black Tie, right?"

"I expected that would be obvious to you," EshCal said, setting the papers on her lap. "But yes, I realize there's nothing else incriminating here, but if what PavRal is implying is true…"

"Yes, the lack of evidence itself may be taken to be incriminating," Phylus realized, "Not that it would hold up in court."

"Of course not."

"But if Black Tie bided their time with SenRas for this long, they would only assign someone that careful to him."

"Well, if nothing else, it looks like The Avatars are using Black Tie to collect intel on deserters."

"And we have every reason to believe SenRas's old employer was a recruitment group," Phylus added, "How compromised do you think you are?"

"Scarcely," EshCal said, "I hired PavRal because I was suspicious of Black Tie, even before MarLys came into your daughter's life. I've kept him at arm's length."

Phylus's desk phone interrupted him. He gestured for her to stay.

"ArcNosian Ministry of Foreign Affairs," he greeted, "Prime Minister Phylus speaking."

"Phylus," the caller said in a thick Tanelenese accent, "Are you alone?"

He signaled for EshCal to keep silent. "Yes," he insisted, "Who am I speaking with?"

"My name is General Sbaglien. I'm with the Tanelenese Military," Sbaglien answered, "I have sensitive business to discuss with you."

"Sbaglien?" Phylus asked, "I don't believe we've met."

"My apologies, sir. We've been in the same room but did not speak," Sbaglien explained, "And frankly, you have my apologies for what transpired after."

"I see," Phylus said, nodding in realization, "So, what's troubling you?"

"You spoke with Noble Doyen Joren following the Ouristihran Union Assembly," Sbaglien opened, "Did he give you any indication as to his travel itinerary?"

"No, I'm afraid not," Phylus said, "I assume you haven't heard from him since then?"

"I have not," Sbaglien said, clearing his throat. "Would you... mind if I spoke candidly, sir?"

"I'd go so far as to encourage it," Phylus insisted, "What's on your mind?"

"Joren has spent a considerable amount of personal resources investigating your disappearance," Sbaglien explained, "Even since you've returned."

"I never knew," Phylus said, "When you see him again, tell him I appreciate his concern."

"Well, I'm worried that there might be a connection between that and his extended absence," Sbaglien said, "Do you remember where they took you?"

"You think somebody took him there," Phylus deduced, "Unfortunately, I can't remember anything to narrow down the location."

"I feared that might be the case," Sbaglien sighed, "But I thought it would be best to ask, anyway."

"Sorry I couldn't be of more help," Phylus said, "But if I do come up with something, can I call you back at this number?"

"I'd appreciate it if you did."

As Phylus ended the call, EshCal gestured inquisitively.

"MalVek got Joren," he said, "In the same sense that he got me."

"Shit," EshCal muttered, "So. MarLys?"

"I trust her," Phylus said, "Although, there is one thing that's bugging me."

"Cauliflower?"

"Yeah. Why did she call him that?"

"We don't know," EshCal said, "We think maybe it's an inside joke between her and Vielle."

"Not one that I'm aware of," Phylus said, "New slang, maybe?"

"Not that we've heard."

Phylus's personal phone rang. He muttered an expletive at the interruption as he took his portable phone from his pocket.

"Hello?"

EshCal braced herself to rise from her seat.

"Phylus?" the caller answered, "It's Malia. What are you doing this evening?"

Phylus gestured for EshCal to leave.

Murmurs bled through as Spril knocked on the door. He entwined his fingers behind his head and turned toward the ceiling, closing his eyes. Breathing deeply, he focused on keeping the murmurs as nondescript noise. Yrlis laid her hand over the small of his back, giving his senses something else to zero in on.

The door opened, and Spril released a long exhale as he opened his eyes. He looked down to find Chekov, his unwitting mother-in-law, standing with her mouth agape and her hand still clutching the doorknob.

"Hi…?" she puzzled, her voice trailing off. She shook her head as though to re-organize her thoughts. "I'm sorry. I assumed you were ensuring we'd never see each other again. So, this is rather…"

"… Unexpected?" Spril suggested.

"Yes. That," Chekov said, "So, what brings you back this way? I suppose Phy-lus told you where to find me."

"He did," Spril nodded, "And I'm here because I've reconsidered."

"Is that so?" Chekov challenged, folding her arms, "What changed your mind?"

"Well, just to be clear, I still loathe your meddling and insist you've caused more problems than you've solved."

"So, we're still a bunch of… What did you call us? Thunder cunts?"

"To your cores," Spril said, "But I realized it wouldn't be fair to take that out on all the people expecting me in the future."

"Well, I'm glad you're looking at this rationally," she said, stepping aside and waving them into the hotel suite, "I'll admit that things haven't gone as planned, but…"

"Did MalVek have any part in creating me?" Spril interrupted.

"None," she assured. She turned to Yrlis. "What are your thoughts on all of this?"

"I've come to terms with it," Yrlis said, "But I insist on helping with the activation process."

"Is that so?" Chekov asked.

"Every step of the way," Yrlis emphasized, "If he's going to lose his capacity for love, I want to hold his hand for the last time it means something to him."

"It was one of her two conditions for letting me go," Spril said.

"And the other?"

"Say hello to your new son-in-law."

Chekov tilted her head, looking back and forth between Spril and Yrlis. "I don't see the point," she said, "He's leaving soon, and you've vowed yourselves to each other for life?"

"I'd been assuming we'd get married since the end of the ArcNosian Civil War," Yrlis said, "And nothing but our own choices would stop me from seeing that through. Not that I'd expect you to understand. But I don't need you to either."

"Fair enough," Chekov shrugged, "Vielle gave him a greater capacity for emotional bonds than we had thought possible. So, maybe he'll still love you after the activation."

"Is The Omnimath here?" Spril asked, "I'd like to give him this news myself."

"He never returned," Chekov said, "And neither has NalSet since he went to find Sinkua and Farim in Quarun."

"Son of a bitch," Spril sighed, "So, you're the only one left from the future?"

"So it would appear," Chekov said, "Too many of us are in the wind or compromised to work as a functional organization anymore. But Farim has been cooperating with me on Dourias's diagrams. She also brought along an assistant medical examiner named Uro."

"Well, if Farim thinks he's worth working with, then good for you," Spril said, "I'm sorry to hear your team hasn't worked out. Honestly."

"Thank you," Chekov said, leading them deeper into the suite, "SenRas and EshCal are keeping their distance. But we have more or less reconciled with Malia. Dourias is back on his feet. And Gabdur is here. Elemeno is next door with Farim and Uro."

"Well, it sounds like you've held The Coalition together pretty well," Yrlis said, "I know it's not up to your original vision, being a subsidiary of the Task Force, but well…"

"The important thing is that we've gained Spril's cooperation," Chekov said, "I'm insisting that the others scatter and continue to work with the Task Force after we leave." As they entered the living room, she directed them to the empty couch. Malia and Dourias sat on the other, each more surprised than the other to see Spril. "Take a seat," she said, "I'll go get everyone else."

Chekov continued to the door at the back of the living room, only to have it open just before she reached it. A young man that Spril didn't recognize, Uro he presumed, popped his head in from the adjoining suite.

"Malia!" he called over, "Phone call for you."

Sinkua paced the room with his hands folded behind his back. Biological diagrams lined the walls, illustrating human organ systems in simplified color-coded forms. In the corner stood a bookshelf that was all but too small for its contents. Sinkua glanced over the titles on the spines, not daring to pull them loose for fear of toppling the bookshelf as they were so densely packed.

Nearly an entire shelf was dedicated to books by Chieftain Sage Gijin. Judging by the faded lettering, Sinkua assumed they were from before Takmet occupied his body. At the end stood one book by Chieftain Heir Gabdur. Yrlis and Chekov both had books on the shelf, the mother fewer than the daughter. Quantity proved meaningless though, as just trying to read the titles of Chekov's books hurt his head.

Sinkua chuckled to himself when he saw a rather dense book by Ophalin on the top shelf. Sure, staging his own book in his exam room was more than a tad braggadocious, but Sinkua couldn't blame him for it.

The rumble of caster wheels echoed in the hall, swelling toward the exam room. He watched the door with an eyebrow cocked, expecting to see an intern zoom by with a coding patient. Probably one who was just improperly connected to their monitors, seeing as nobody else sounded like they were in a hurry.

Instead, a hand grabbed the doorframe, and Ophalin swung around into the exam room, riding a scooter.

"Sinkua!" he remarked, "Been a while."

"Couple months since I saw you in ArcNos," Sinkua said, "Been hard to get out here for a proper appointment since I moved out of Ferya though."

"That's what I meant," Ophalin said, folding his scooter and leaning it against the wall, "I think this is your first time at my new practice."

"Yeah, I admit it confused me when the cab driver passed the hospital."

"Yeah? So, what do you think?"

"I like it," Sinkua said, "The overpacked bookshelf is a nice touch."

"I thought so, too," Ophalin said. He gestured to the top shelf. "You figure prominently in that one, by the way."

Sinkua nodded and hummed, unsure how to respond. Presumptuous or not, it seemed obvious that he would be in at least one of Ophalin's medical books. But he couldn't exactly be proud of the fact, given the circumstances. Then again, maybe it would be useful to the comparably afflicted.

"So, let's get to business," Ophalin said, "Tell me more about what happened."

"How much do you know?" Sinkua asked.

"I heard you had a bad episode."

"Well… Yes. I guess you could say that."

"Hmm. Bad how?"

"It, ah…" Sinkua pondered, "It came on easier than usual. Most times, I can hold it back for a while."

"Don't you normally have help with that?" Ophalin asked, "A friend will talk you through it, serving as a mental anchor, correct?"

"Well yes, it's easier that way," Sinkua admitted, "But I can do some on my own."

"And this particular episode?"

"I don't think anyone could have anchored me."

"I hate to bring this up, but…"

"I hate to say it," Sinkua interrupted, "but I don't think even Eytea could've done it."

"Interesting," Ophalin remarked, his eyebrows flying up his forehead, "Do you remember anything from during the episode?"

"Absolutely nothing."

"That is bad. Don't you normally retain some memories?"

"They're vague, but I can usually piece together what happened," Sinkua said, "But this time, I don't even know how I went from one end of the deck to the other."

"Like your blacked-out memories from your time in isolation?"

"Similar, yes. But not exactly the same."

Ophalin hummed and nodded as he wrote in his notepad. "What was different?"

"Mostly my sense of time."

"Explain?"

"Well, when I woke up on the boat, I had no idea how much time had passed. I thought I had been out for a few days," Sinkua said, "But on the island, I know how much time I lost."

"You didn't realize until later that you'd lost time on the island though, right?" Ophalin asked. Sinkua half nodded, half shrugged. "Perhaps, it had more to do with how long it was going on for. Chronic versus acute."

Sinkua chewed on the notion. He knew the time he had lost plus what he remembered added up to about four and a half years on the island. But that didn't mean he knew how much time he lost in any particular blackout. He nodded with dawning comprehension.

"Stronger onset, more pronounced memory loss," Ophalin reiterated, "Anything else I should know?"

"There…" Sinkua began, trailing off as his confidence in his explanation dwindled, "… never mind."

"No, not 'never mind.' Whatever happened, I need to know about it," Ophalin insisted, "In the strictest confidence, I assure you."

"I'm not worried about legal ramifications," Sinkua muttered, which was mostly true. Avatar prisons would do worse to him than government ones. "There was one other thing, but I don't think it would do you any good to hear about it."

"I realize how ironic it is for me to say this to you," Ophalin said, "But you'd be surprised. Out with it."

"There was, um…" Sinkua said, pausing to organize his thoughts, "There was a pile of dead bodies behind the bow." He glanced at Ophalin and saw that he was about to speak. "But there were ones who I remembered seeing die before my episode, and that wasn't where they fell."

"So, somebody moved the bodies?" Ophalin suggested, "Could you have done it while you were blacked out?"

"My body was too sore to tell," Sinkua pondered, "But I don't think I did. They looked like they'd walked there and collapsed."

"After they'd died?" Ophalin asked, as skeptical as Sinkua feared he would be. Sinkua nodded. "Well, I'm not sure what to make of that right off hand. But if I think of anything, I'll let you know." He wrote a couple more things in his notepad and set it on the counter. "Have you been taking your medicine?"

"Um…" Sinkua hesitated, "Not exactly." Annoyance crashed into Ophalin's features, but Sinkua cut him off. "To be fair, I thought I'd been cured. It's a longer and weirder story involving a magic tree and my doppelganger, but it made sense at the time. Now, I realize it was stupid."

Ophalin's mouth clapped shut. He mumbled and shrugged. "Well enough, then," he said, "But you're back to taking it as prescribed?" Sinkua nodded. "Great. Hopefully, this will be a onetime occurrence."

"Hopefully," Sinkua agreed, "By the way, I heard Yrlis sent you some notes about my case. Something about a genome map? Has anything become of that?"

"Yes, actually," Ophalin said, "Well, not so much as to get excited about just yet. We've run up against a dead end."

"How so?"

"I've figured out how to tailor a cure to your genome," Ophalin said, "but only on paper. Now, hypothetically, the fruits of the Sisyphus Fir might contain the necessary bonding agents."

"If you could get your hands on a mature one?"

"If Yrlis's theory is correct, yes."

"Well," Sinkua pondered, "I lived under Yggdrasil for two weeks, and there were all sorts of fruits growing from the roots. Maybe it can grow Sisyphus fruits to maturity, too."

"Interesting," Ophalin said, "But we can't just dig around in the roots waiting for one to turn up." He leaned back on the counter, his hands back at his sides and fingers drumming on the countertop. "I have an idea," he announced, pushing off of the counter, "Wait here. I need to ask one of my nurses something. She's into gardening, so it's more that she might have an idea. Anyway, I'll be right back."

Ophalin unfolded his scooter and rode out of the room. Sinkua returned to browsing the bookshelf, biding his time by reading titles he could barely comprehend, if at all. This sort of thing had never been his strong point. He understood as much as he needed to discuss his condition with Ophalin and Yrlis, and that was enough for him.

A few minutes later, Ophalin came whipping around the doorframe yet again.

"We're going to try grifting!" he announced.

Sinkua cocked his head.

"Grafting!" came a laughing voice from down the hall.

Ophalin's mouth narrowed. He looked down the hall, then back into the exam room. "Grafting," he corrected, "That makes a lot more sense. We're going to try grafting."

"And that will grow a Sisyphus fruit from Yggdrasil?"

"Theoretically."

"Well, I'll take a theory over knowing nothing any day," Sinkua said, "So, how do we do this?"

"Go to the nurses' station," Ophalin said, "Etrula will give you a list of what she needs. I'll look into it as well, but two sets of eyes and all of that."

"Got it," Sinkua nodded. He exchanged a firm handshake with Ophalin. "Thanks for everything."

"It's what I'm here for," Ophalin said, "Keeping taking your meds in the meantime."

Sinkua headed for the nurses' station, exchanging brief pleasantries with staff along the way. As he reached the station, he found a woman sitting at the computer, writing in a notepad, with half a dozen other people bustling about behind the elongated horseshoe desk.

"Hey!" the woman at the computer greeted, glancing up from her notepad, "What can I help you with?"

"I'm, ah…" Sinkua said, losing his words with so many strangers watching him. He'd become familiar with Ophalin's staff, but his private practice came with some new faces. "Ophalin said I need to talk to Etrula. I'm Sinkua. We're going to graft something?"

The nurse stretched her lanyard to show him her badge. "I'm Etrula," she said, letting the badge snap back against her chest, "So, you're Sinkua, huh? Heard a lot about you. Read a lot, actually." She stood up to hand him the list. "What I'm getting at is that your case is a big part of why I applied here. So, it's nice to meet you. And help you."

"Hey, thanks. I'm glad for the help," Sinkua said, taking the list.

He stepped aside as he looked it over. Mostly, she needed various cuts of Sisyphus Fir. And she was quite adamant that the Glaucus Fir, despite their aesthetic, would not do in a pinch. In the corner of his awareness, he heard the news on the lobby television discussing a rare cosmic event.

Sinkua pocketed the list and turned toward the television. The lunar blackout would come that night. The broadcaster said nothing of the Nemesis Ion Cloud, though. No surprise there.

"You into star-gazing?" Etrula asked, hunkered down on her forearms over the desk. "I remember watching the last one when I was in high school. With my boyfriend. Might be my husband if he hadn't been such a bummer blowfish about it. But I'm sure you don't want to hear about that."

"I need to get back to ArcNos," Sinkua muttered, "Shit."

"Oh, I don't think that's going to be possible," Etrula said, "Can your date meet you halfway? You'll have to find a new viewing spot, but…"

"It's not a date. It's my sister," Sinkua corrected, "Do you have an ArcNosian phone directory?"

"Not specifically," Etrula said. She crouched behind the desk and emerged with a large book. "But we do have an international one."

"Business listings?"

She crouched a second time and returned with another book. "Yep!"

Sinkua thanked her and took the directory to an empty seat. He turned first to the ArcNosian section, then within that, to the hotel listings. Now, he just needed to recall the name that Malia had told him.

Nikasu peered between the blinds. Nightfall had long since come, and the street beyond the lawn still lay silent. She sighed and plopped down on the couch, staring up at the ceiling.

"He would've been here if he could," Vielle said, sitting beside her, "Sinkua wouldn't deliberately skip out on any of us. It probably just took longer than they thought to get in to see Doctor Ophalin."

"I know. It's just..." Nikasu said, letting the words linger. She sighed and shook her head.

"Sweetie," BeiLou beckoned in as gentle a voice as she could manage. Nikasu glared across the living room at her. "Sorry. Sorry," BeiLou backpedaled, "This night only comes once every twenty-eight years. I know you were hoping more of your family would be here, but you can't keep waiting. We need Epelun and Nemesis."

"Epelun is the greater boon," Odin said, his eye shut and face toward the ceiling, "It is only necessary to call upon Nemesis in order to find Epelun."

"Great," Nikasu muttered, "No pressure or anything."

"Hey, whatever happens, we'll make it work," Vielle assured, "Either, neither, or both, we'll manage."

"The time for pleasantries has long expired," Odin scolded, "Since dusk, have I kept the sky clear for you. Take yourself to the rooftop and call out to Nemesis that he might bring to you Epelun."

Nikasu looked to Odin weakly. She hadn't asked him to do such a thing, nor had he mentioned it. He had been like this for hours, staring at the ceiling through his one good set of eyelids. Not realizing what he had been doing, she felt foolish and somehow like she had been taking him for granted.

"Look, none of us can comprehend how much it'll help if you can do this," Vielle said, "Except Odin, but whatever." She chuckled and placed her hand on Nikasu's shoulder. "I realize that's a lot of pressure, but you need to try."

"Naught ensures failure but enduring hesitance," Odin said.

"Nobody will think less of you if you try and fail," BeiLou added.

Nikasu huffed and grumbled. The more they assured her otherwise, the clearer it was that they were, in fact, pressuring her. They wouldn't have felt the need to point it out so aggressively if they hadn't been putting forth that impression.

The front door swung open, and she rose to meet whoever was on the other side.

"The ladder is in place," Galo announced. Upstairs, Luvros fluttered and swung in its cage. "I should check on her," Galo said, looking past Nikasu as she came to him. He looked down at her and asked, "Are you ready?"

She embraced him and buried her face in his chest. He put one arm around her back and stroked her hair with his other hand.

Everyone else, despite any good intentions, could only tell her how to feel. What to think. When to act. None of them thought to consider her outlook.

Sure, Odin's keeping the sky clear was a significant feat. Even considering the yet unknown extent of his power, it was surely a greater undertaking than leaning a ladder against the house. But Galo hadn't made it about himself.

She smeared her eyes on his shirt and beamed up at him. She cupped his chin and stretched up as she pulled him down, meeting halfway to kiss him.

"I'm ready."

Nikasu pulled her coat off the rack and swung it around her shoulders. She checked the pocket for the disc and breezed past Galo as she buttoned up. As the door shut behind her, the chill of both the night and anticipation washed over her.

She found the ladder propped against the side of the house with the base wedged into the grass and mud and the bottom meter frozen against the ground. It rattled as she climbed it, but she withheld the urge to lighten her body. Anything to save her strength for the task ahead.

Straddling the apex of the roof, Nikasu held the disc as she gazed into the dappled night sky. She had presumed that the Nemesis Ion Cloud would be easy to spot, that it would be a singular anomaly. What she hadn't banked on was that so many stars would become so much more visible, much less visible at all, without the moons. She turned the disc as she panned it across the sky, looking through it with one eye closed.

In a moment of realization, Nikasu lowered the disc and folded her hands behind her back. Instead of trying to find that exact pattern, now she searched for the black circles where the moons would have been.

She found them with only slight use of her light amplification. And once she did, the cluster of lights in the middle looked almost embarrassingly obvious. Nevertheless, she held the disc out before herself. The rest of the sky, the dense blackness and brilliant dapples between, fell into a blur as she shifted the disc into alignment.

A spot of light filled each of the holes, glinting off the imperfections around the edges. Nikasu gazed through, conjuring her milystis just shy of manifestation. She tightened her focus on those lights, individually and as a collective. She projected her feelings of rising milystis into the lights.

The essence of radiance, in every sense but visual, rushed toward her from the Nemesis Ion Cloud and the disc simultaneously. It was as though it came from beyond the moons but never been beyond arm's reach. A sensation of milystis washed over her, feeling so much like her own and yet so much more.

Palpable blackness washed the lights out of the holes, gradually consuming the entire disc. Nikasu lowered her hand and let the disc fall to her side as she beheld what had come to her from the depths of the night sky.

Its wings reached the center of the house across the street and the front lawn on the other side of the house behind them. Its torso stretched three stories upward, while its tail grazed the grass two floors down.

The dragon's scales were silverish black with highlights of the same dark purple as Nikasu's eyes. The leathery flesh of its sloping batlike wings were the same color. In fact, beyond a point at the end of one wing, it had no sharp angles on its body, the whole of it composed of smooth flowing arcs.

It held strong eye contact with Nikasu as it spoke to her. Though since it was in what she presumed to be Harkzanian, she understood none of it. She said so in as few words as possible, emphasizing her point with gestures. The dragon lowered its head, nearly knocking her off the roof with his disappointed sigh.

"Nikasu!" she shouted, pointing to herself.

"Ni… Ka… Su…" the dragon sounded out. He perched on the edge of the roof and curled in one wing. "Nemesis."

"Yes!" Nikasu delighted. She pointed to her eyes now. "Hybrid. Yours."

"Hy… brid. Yvret," Nemesis said, "Khosmaetherean. Desou. Yours."

"Khosmae… therean," Nikasu repeated, "Etherworlder. Mine."

"Hybrid… Mine. Yvret. Demou."

"I think we're beginning to understand one another."

Nemesis closed his eyes and nodded. His body shrank so smoothly that Nikasu thought for a moment that he was receding toward the horizon. But that one angular appendage remained the same size. As he reduced to slightly larger than her, he motioned for her to turn around.

Nikasu did so, and Nemesis rested his head atop hers. She closed her eyes and exhaled, trying to relax and trust him.

She shuddered as Nemesis laid his wings along her arms, holding her wrists with his claws. He lifted her arms, holding them outward. His scales felt simultaneously wet and dry, a somewhat reptilian sense of moisture without the actual presence of it.

The sensation ran down her head and along her cheeks. As it encircled her arms, she looked down to find that Nemesis was effectively melding his wing arms around her arms. In fact, his entire form was flattening and contouring around her body. To stay at her side, Nemesis shaped himself into armor for Nikasu.

As he squeezed her wrist, she closed her hand around that one pointed appendage. It was the only part of him that hadn't molded around her. Even his wing flesh had retracted under her arms like window shades. The appendage flattened and took on a silverish hue. The part in her hand shaped into a more comfortable grip, the space between flattening into a cross guard.

"Is this…" Nikasu gasped, admiring the sword that had formed from Nemesis's finger, "Is this Epelun?"

"Epelun," Nemesis repeated, speaking directly into her mind, "Nhai."

"I assume that means yes."

Nikasu stepped to the edge of the roof, only for Nemesis to pull her back. She gestured to the ladder, lowering her head to show him. He shook his head and hers with it. This, she realized, would take some adapting.

He lifted her arms again, unfurling his wings. Nemesis walked her to the edge and, despite her linguistically barriered protests, threw them both from the rooftop.

Between the outstretched wings and the gentle coursing of milystis though, she didn't plummet. She had used her gravimancy to slow her freefall many times, but not like this. As she looked down, the ground approached at a smooth walking pace.

She twirled Epelun around her wrist as they lit upon the grass. Even with no milystic effort, it felt nearly weightless. Yet, she sensed that her milystis could move through it as though it was her own body. Precise, focused, and wasteless.

At Nemesis's silent beckoning, Nikasu brought her eyes aglow. As starlight compounded in her eyes, three silhouettes coalesced out of the shadows. A pair of green spots shimmered from the tallest one. Nikasu gasped and sprinted toward them.

"You made it!" she cried out.

Chapter 30

Nikasu bounded toward Sinkua. Malia and Phylus stood just behind him, watching from his flanks.

"How did you all even…?"

Nemesis reared back and sprang from her body, his momentum pushing her to her hands and knees. With a spherical burst of silverish black and purple light, he re-inflated to his naturally robust state. He lifted Sinkua by the throat and snarled something in Harkzanian.

Sinkua jammed his thumb and forefinger into the dragon's nostrils. Black smoke erupted from Nemesis's mouth, and he dropped Sinkua out of equal parts contempt and necessity.

"Nemesis!" Nikasu shouted, stabbing Epelun into the ground.

"Allow me to field this one," Odin insisted, stepping off the porch with Galo and Vielle standing at his back, "Stay your hands."

Nikasu grumbled and stuffed her hands in her pockets. Sinkua stepped aside.

"Could you translate for me while I explain that I'm not who he thinks?" Sinkua asked.

"No. I will explain what happened," Odin said, "After I acquired your bearings to Arestor, I continued reading to the end of the thirteenth book."

"Yeah? And?" Sinkua asked.

"BeiLou will explain to you," Odin said, "as I will to Nemesis." He extended his hand. "Leave Phoenix with me. Ask the same of Galo with Leviathan, if you would."

A flood of warmth washed through Sinkua's body, assuring him he would be well enough without Phoenix for a time. He unclasped his necklace and placed it in Odin's outstretched hand.

"Come on, Nikasu," he called over, "Odin's going to clear things up. Let's get inside."

"What was that all about?" Malia asked as Nikasu joined them.

"Big misunderstanding," Sinkua said, "Nemesis thinks Tsenukoa, the previous Phoenix Hybrid, was a traitor. And that I'm him."

"Why would he…?"

"It's a long story."

"Leave it alone, Malia," Phylus urged.

"Hey, sorry about that," Nikasu said, throwing her arms around Sinkua's midsection, "You okay?"

"Yeah, I'm fi…"

"Great!" Nikasu exclaimed, pushing back and holding him at arm's length, "How much did you see? Did it look awesome? I felt like it was awesome."

"I saw the whole thing!" Sinkua exclaimed, "That was incredible!"

"I know, right! I pulled a dragon out of the sky!"

"You got on the roof and called a space dragon," Phylus laughed.

"No wonder you started going gray so young," Malia teased, "Your girls are growing giant trees and pulling dragons out of the cosmos."

"I'm going gray? My girls?" Phylus said, emphasizing the pronouns.

"We all know they're more yours than mine," Malia said, her voice tightening. She brushed one of many silver strands behind her ear. "As for the other thing, I don't know what you're talking about."

"Are you two done?" Nikasu asked, "Because I wanna get back to how I just pulled a motherfucking dragon out of motherfucking space!"

"And he turned into motherfucking armor!" Sinkua added.

"Hey, bring the party over here!" Vielle called over.

"We should," Sinkua said. He turned to walk back to the front door. "Let's take this inside while the Etherworlders hash things out."

"Sounds good to me," Nikasu said, forgetting Epelun as she followed, "So, how did you all get here, anyway?"

"I called Malia from Ophalin's office and asked her to pick me up," Sinkua added.

"Then, Malia called me and invited me over to the hotel," Phylus said.

"And I brought us all here with my portal strip," Malia said.

"Oh, cool! Thank you so much," Nikasu professed.

"The whole thing was Sinkua's idea," Malia said.

"Of course, it was," Sinkua said. He patted Galo's shoulder as they reached the stoop. "Hey brother," he said, "Odin wants an Etherworlder meeting."

Galo pulled the Serpent Bracer from his arm. "I'll see you guys inside," he said as he stepped down, "Great work, Nikasu. That was amazing."

"Explain why you are fraternizing with that traitor!" Nemesis demanded in his native Harkzanian.

"I do no such thing," Odin answered in Fjarthursk. He cast the Serpent Bracer onto the wet grass. "That man is no traitor."

"Had he his way, he would have surrendered Phoenix to Pandora," Nemesis snarled, "And those Lechuatzulan bastards who put her in that thing are little better."

"They derived the technique from the Quircois," Leviathan added in Mberhali, "Are they to blame as well?"

"That is another matter entirely."

"Put this on," Odin said, holding out the Phoenix medallion.

"Why?"

"She will corroborate," Odin said, "And for the sake of this conversation, you are to permit her to speak through you." Nemesis accepted the necklace with equal parts care and contempt. "First of all," Odin continued, "this Phoenix Hybrid does not remember any of his previous lives."

"Undoubtedly a side effect of that Lechuatzulan prison," Nemesis said.

A feminine voice issued from his open, unmoving mouth. "This may be true," Phoenix spoke through him, also in Harkzanian, "But do not hate my Hybrid or the gemologists. I permitted this to happen. Besides, the interior is quite spacious."

Nemesis shook his head and snarled as Phoenix fell silent.

"Why did you have yourself put into that ruby?" Leviathan asked, "Were you not satisfied with the security offered by the Quircois metallurgists?"

"They intended to bargain with Pandora," Odin said.

While they had been outside, the scent of dark hot chocolate had filled the kitchen and dining room. Phylus walked with Nikasu and Vielle to the living room. Meanwhile, Sinkua crossed into the kitchen and looked over BeiLou's shoulder into a pot on the stove.

"Odin said you needed to talk to me," he said.

"Oh, hey! You made it!" BeiLou remarked, stirring the pot, "And yes. Just let me finish this up. Actually, you know what? Um…" She stepped back and looked around. "Malia!" she called over, "Could you come finish this hot chocolate?"

"You're making hot chocolate at a time like this?" Sinkua asked, laughing under his breath.

"Hot chocolate needs no justification," BeiLou said as Malia passed between them, "Especially not dark chocolate. Now. Come on."

Sinkua waved Galo along as he came inside, and they followed BeiLou to the living room.

"How did everything go, Nikasu?" BeiLou asked, "Did you find Nemesis?"

"I did!" Nikasu remarked, "And everything was going great until he saw Sinkua."

"Yeah, Odin said the other day that Nemesis might, well, take issue with him," BeiLou said, "Is he taking care of it?"

Nikasu nodded.

"The others will be here shortly," Malia announced from the kitchen, "I asked them to give me a head start."

"Well, if you want to make enough cocoa for all of them, that's on you," BeiLou said as she settled into the recliner, "That's all I've got, and I'm not going out this late."

"So," Sinkua said, propping against the arm of the couch, "What did Tsenukoa write in the end of the last book?"

"Takmet's son Metkhal wrote that part," BeiLou said, "Tsenukoa left it with him before he went out to sea."

Malia joined them in the living room, carrying a tray of mugs.

"So, he was friends with the Chieftain Heir, too," Sinkua noted. He mouthed his gratitude to Malia as she handed him a mug.

"That must be how Grandpa ended up with your medallion," Galo provided, thanking Malia for the cocoa.

"It is," BeiLou confirmed, "Tsenukoa was going to use it to negotiate the terms of end-war with Pandora and Seriamus."

"It would never have worked!" Nemesis shouted, "He would sacrifice Phoenix for nothing."

"Her return is what they've been after since this whole ordeal began," Leviathan argued, "Regardless of what came of the other terms, he still would have fulfilled the prime obligation."

"He is ignorant," Nemesis spat, "Zeus ordered Phoenix's return. Pandora's aggression is a matter all its own."

"You hold too fast to your grudges," Odin insisted, "None among us can know if Pandora would have withdrawn once Phoenix had been returned. All we know is that we were wrong about your predecessor. He sought a bloodless resolution."

"A few seconds in our world, and he would…"

Nemesis's eyes rolled back, and his mouth lolled open. Phoenix's voice emerged, interrupting him through his own mouth.

"There would be a brief window of opportunity for me to break away," she said, "before I was obliterated along with him."

Nemesis shook his head and grunted.

"Very well," he said, "I concede his intentions were good, if perhaps reckless and misguided."

"I hoped you would come around," Odin said, "We cannot afford to lose another ally."

"How fare our numbers?"

"You stand among them."

"What were the terms?" Sinkua asked.

"Pandora would open a path to the Etherworld for Phoenix and Tsenukoa," BeiLou explained, "After a short time there, Tsenukoa would be… obliterated on a spiritual level."

"Wh-… What would happen to Phoenix?" Sinkua asked, swallowing hard.

"She would break away and return home."

"And Pandora?"

"She and her acolytes would find another sanctuary in our universe," BeiLou said, "Never to associate with us again."

"The four of us are all that remain?" Nemesis bellowed.

"We and Yggdrasil," Leviathan said, "Even the Trifecta has fallen."

"Impossible. I saw Yggdrasil fall before I withdrew to the cosmos."

"It would appear that someone has gone back and saved it," Odin said, "My presence is evidence enough of its return, should you find the quite sizeable roots along these lawns to be insufficient."

Nemesis considered the notion. Indeed, the only rational explanation for Odin's return was if Yggdrasil had returned. And the only rational explanation was for history to have been altered. That meant just one thing.

"… Bahamut has returned as well?"

"No, my friend," Odin said, "This was an achievement of human technology."

"Impossible!" Nemesis barked, "Bahamut's powers are irreplicable by humans."

"Learn quickly the futility of calling something impossible when it has clearly occurred," Odin warned, "Future-worlders walk among them. Humans from five centuries in the future harnessed the power to bend time and used it to come back to this era."

"Why now?"

"Because this is when Pandora would cross The Veil and bring this world to ruin."

"So, if the treaty had panned out, we wouldn't be dealing with this right now," Nikasu said, more thinking out loud than informing, "What stopped him?"

"The Trifecta," Galo said, "Takmet, Pahres, and Arestor. They created The Veil around Pandora and were turned to copper in the process."

"Metkhal wrote about that," BeiLou confirmed, "Tsenukoa entrusted his book and the Phoenix Ruby to the Chieftain Bloodline and went out to sea in search of other civilizations."

"Other civilizations?" Sinkua puzzled, "You mean beyond Ouristihra?"

"The sea had been rising for months with no sign of stopping," BeiLou said, "Tsenukoa set out to find places that hadn't been affected, because he was afraid that the whole continent would end up underwater."

"And that's when Masnethege became known as the Sacred City," Galo exhaled in realization, "Grandpa told me it was because it was the oldest standing civilization. I just never realized that…"

"All the others were destroyed," BeiLou provided, "Aside from a few scattered camps, all the survivors gathered in Masnethege."

"Well, before everyone else gets here, the four of us have something private to discuss," Vielle said, gesturing to the other Hybrids.

Gabdur stood with his arms folded behind his back as he peered into the cage atop the bureau. The bird inside turned toward him, tilting its head. Gabdur clicked his tongue at the purple-winged pigeon.

"The rest of you go on ahead," he said, "I'll be down shortly."

The rest of his entourage continued to the stairs without a further word. The bird cooed at Gabdur, indicating some degree of familiarity. Gabdur had mixed feelings about the bird's circumstances. On the one hand, her grand potential had been reduced to her being a house pet. On the other, what could have been a life of constant danger was now one of comfort.

Gabdur chuckled to himself as he listened to the commotion on the stairs. Four more sets of footsteps became entangled with the seven in his entourage. Those four came to the bedroom door soon after.

"What did you name her?" he asked.

"Phoenix said I should call her Luvros," Sinkua said, coming up beside him, "Thanks for her by the way."

"No sweat," Gabdur said, "Could you all give me a moment alone with Galo?" He turned to Galo. "If you have a moment, that is."

"Well…" Galo trailed off, looking to Vielle and Nikasu.

"Stay and talk with him," Vielle said, "We'll catch you up later."

"Could you bring Luvros back to my room when you're done?" Sinkua asked.

Galo nodded, and the others returned to the hall and continued on. Gabdur closed the bedroom door behind them and took a seat in the desk chair.

"I'm glad to see you made it back safely," he said, "What did you find out?"

"Arestor was… unviable," Galo said, "Odin sent him into the second life."

"That's not what I meant," Gabdur said, "But I am sorry to hear that."

"I don't know what you're getting at," Galo said, folding his arms.

"You've had the same look that Dad used to get when he was working an angle," Gabdur explained, "So, let me ask you again. What did you find out?"

"You knew I was plotting something, and you didn't say anything?"

"I knew I had to let it pan out."

"Well, it's all panned out now," Galo sighed, sitting at the end of the bed, "Ebralgi wasn't working alone."

"As The Geneticist, or…?"

"Ever," Galo asserted, "He's had an accomplice all along."

Gabdur leaned forward. "Who?"

"I had hoped the humans might grow wise in my absence," Nemesis lamented, "but they are just as arrogant as ever. If we could not stop Pandora, what difference could come from a few humans so disconnected from this era?"

"We do not know what transpired in the prior timeline," Odin said, "but their efforts have at least led to the restoration of Yggdrasil."

"They claim their leader lived through this time," Leviathan added, "He was the leader of The Avatars of Fate, who I believe are the current incarnation of The Stewards of Disarray. I do not know how this could be true, but if it is, he had a change of heart after Pandora escaped."

"Has enough time passed for another Tiamat Hybrid to have been born?" Nemesis asked, "For that matter, could another be born?"

"They claim he lived during our war as well," Phoenix interjected through Nemesis's gaping mouth, "I wouldn't have believed it either had I not seen them create a perfect image of Seriamus."

"Impo-..." Nemesis began to protest, shaking his head, "Preposterous. He was burned for his treachery. And even had he not been, he could not reasonably be so long-lived."

"I theorize that we have been mistaken in our understanding of Tiamat's relationship with her Hybrid," Odin explained, "Perhaps, Tiamat imparts the whole of prior memories upon each one."

Sinkua sat at the foot of his bed, far to one side. He had only been using one half of it, leaving the other empty for long enough for the sheets to have gone cold. There was no accounting for how he moved in his sleep, but he fell into it and arose from it on that side. Yet he couldn't bring himself to replace this bed with one better suited to one person. That other side was Eytea's, and it always would be.

This was different, though. They never had sides when they sat on the bed. Yet, here he was, afraid to let anyone, even himself, occupy her side in any capacity. All he could make of it was that he was even less ready to move on than the spit of credit he gave himself.

He sighed and looked over at Vielle and Nikasu. They spoke in mumbles and emphatic gestures, one sitting in his desk chair and the other leaning on the dresser.

"Well?" he asked, "What did you need to talk about?"

Nikasu mouthed something to Vielle, then spun to face Sinkua.

"I had an episode while you were gone," she spat quickly enough to sound like a single word. She took a deep breath and paced herself as she continued. "I didn't know that could happen. But it did."

Sinkua's mouth fell open. He stared at his sister, unblinking and dumbfounded. Suddenly, his subconscious pinings and ruminations over his dead fiancée seemed inconsequential.

"H-... H-how..." he exhaled, "How did this...? I mean... How did I...? How did we...?"

"How did we not see it coming?" Nikasu offered. Sinkua nodded. "I know I'm not as familiar with your episodes as our friends," she continued, "but I just assumed that your condition came from a reaction between your blood and the serums they made from mine. I didn't think it was something that I was carrying."

"When you were in captivity," Sinkua said, pulling off his bandana and plowing his fingers through his hair, "did you ever have any episodes? Any blackouts?"

Nikasu shook her head. "Not that I'm aware of."

Sinkua locked his fingers behind his head and looked down. "And since none of us have seen you have one, even with how much you've been through, I guess none of us considered you could have them." He looked up to face her, still slumping. "I'm sorry."

Nikasu smiled weakly and nodded, her eyes meeting his only briefly. Sinkua turned to Vielle.

"You seem anxious," he said, "Do you have something going on, too?"

"Well…" Vielle began, pursing her lips in contemplation. "I knew about her episode before anyone told me," she said, "And that you had one at the same time."

"… How?"

"I felt them," Vielle said, "through Yggdrasil."

"We have some kind of episode entanglement?" Sinkua puzzled, his eyes darting to Nikasu before returning to Vielle, "Did you have one, too?"

"No," she assured him, "Just the worst migraine ever and some kind of panic attack. Which still sucks, but I don't think it's quite as bad." She moved to the desk and held Nikasu's shoulder. "But Nikasu's came out of nowhere. We think yours triggered it."

"Well, mine didn't come out of nowhere," Sinkua said, "Which means we were right about Yggdrasil, and Nikasu is afflicted as well."

"On top of being an activator," Vielle added, "At least through an actuation chamber. I've been giving it some thought, and I believe she's the only afflicted who can do that. Given that it all, well, came from her blood."

"I turned people into monsters," Nikasu muttered, her voice muffled as she hugged her knees and buried her face, "And now I'm turning into one, too."

Sinkua gave Vielle an inquisitive glance.

"She grew mantis claws and chitin," she explained, "It fell off when I disrupted the connection."

Sinkua eyes flared, knuckles whitened, and teeth gritted. Any one thing that The Geneticist had done to her was worth killing over. But this went beyond that. He had ensured that, no matter how far she ran, she could never truly escape Yahsek.

That went beyond being worth killing over.

"It's okay," Sinkua said with a calm he'd scarcely known. A smile of equal parts confidence and resignation filled his face, "I can fix this."

A cacophony of footfalls in the stairwell permeated the sound of running water. Phylus glanced over his shoulder as he kept scrubbing cocoa-stained mugs. He nodded to Elemeno as she came around into the dining room.

"Welcome!" he called over the jetting water, "You just missed hot cocoa. Take it up with Malia."

The rest of them filed out of the stairwell after her, with Phylus giving only passing acknowledgment to each of them. But he turned sharply as an unfamiliar voice caught his attention.

"I can run out and get drinks for everyone," someone offered, "If you need me to, I mean."

Phylus glared at the young man for a hard moment, failing to place him as scalding water ran over his hand. Phylus shook his head and returned to his washing. In the corner of his eye, he watched Dourias hobble up alongside him and place a hand on his shoulder.

"How are you doing, Patriarch?" Dourias asked with a sly grin, "It is so good to see you again, my friend."

"Stressed if I'm being honest," Phylus said, jamming the sponge into a mug, "Just fine if I'm being polite." He rinsed the mug and set it in the dish drainer. "Who's that new guy, by the way?"

"Uro," Dourias said, "You met him last time we were all here."

"Huh. Really?" Phylus asked, casting a quick glance toward the living room, "Either that boy's too forgettable for his own good, or I'm too old for mine."

"To be fair, he didn't say much," Dourias added, "But Farim trusts him, so I should say he's good enough people."

Phylus turned off the water. He turned and leaned against the counter as he dried his hands.

Uro sat among the others like they were long friends. Farim trusted him, and she was often a good judge of people. But she had also trusted MalVek, so maybe she wasn't the best authority on that sort of thing. Then again, all of them had trusted MalVek.

"By the way, speaking of the hyperspace prison," Phylus said, balancing his voice between conversational and loud enough for eavesdropping. He gave Dourias the faintest wink. "I've been having some interesting side effects."

"Oh?" Dourias said, "From the prison or the goggles?" He chuckled to himself. "Or perhaps the food?"

"Might have to do with what I drank," Phylus remarked, nudging him with his elbow, "But no, seriously, I've been seeing hyperspace access points. Soft spots. Spatial abrasions. Whatever you'd like to call them. And when I see them, I can use them."

"Really?" Dourias asked, folding his arms and tilting his head a bit, "When you look inside, what do you see? Does it look like where they kept us?"

"Anything I put in goes straight through and pops out somewhere else," Phylus said, "I don't see anything in between."

"Interesting," Dourias said, rubbing his chin, "So they're like spontaneous free-floating portals?"

"Maybe not spontaneous," Phylus said, "From what I can tell, they appear when I'm especially calm."

"Would you be willing to stop by to give some samples?" Dourias asked, "I should say the worst of it would be a spinal tap."

"You don't intend to weaponized this, do you? Or force it on anyone?"

"Goodness, no! I'm thinking of search and rescue applications."

"Then I'm in," Phylus said, "I'll tell Malia when I've made a hole in my calendar."

"Seriously?" Gabdur recoiled, "But he's an idiot."

"The whole thing was an act," Galo said, turning his hands up in capitulation, "I was just as fooled as you were. Everyone was."

"Yeah," Gabdur exhaled, shaking his head, "Even his own family." He rubbed his chin. "Well, his sisters and their parents, anyway."

"Um... About that."

Gabdur's head snapped up. He ground his palm heel against the seat, digging his fingernails into the upholstery. "Don't tell me her sister was in on it, too."

"No, it was, um…" Galo trailed off, hesitating as he sorted his thoughts into something relatively painless. The effort, however, went unfulfilled. "Look, I'm just going to rip the bandage off," he said, "Zheal seduced you for political gain."

"Wh-… What?" Gabdur stammered, his mouth agape, "My marriage was… what? Just a means to an end?"

"Originally," Galo clarified, "The three of them were out to end our family's political authority."

"And what was Zheal's goal?" Gabdur asked, "Earn my trust, let Ebralgi kill me, then lobby to inherit my office?" His eyes widened. "Oh shit," he gasped, dragging his fingers through his hair, "The poison was meant for me."

"Borret said she was out to prove you were unfit to lead, at which point, they would push to have you removed from office," Galo explained. He looked his father square in the eyes. "But eventually, she honestly fell in love with you," he said, "I don't know if she abandoned the mission, but Ebralgi…"

"… decided she was a liability," Gabdur realized, casting his eyes down, "Where is Borret now?"

"Bottom of the Southland Sea," Galo said. Gabdur looked up with raised eyebrows. "He was going to kill himself, but Sinkua talked him down. But he only did it so he could shoot him instead."

Gabdur blinked hard. "Sinkua… actually shot somebody?"

Galo nodded. "Said he should have known he was a piece of shit and pulled the trigger."

"It's a shame," Gabdur said, "My mother was an only child. When I fell for a woman with siblings, I thought it would be great for our son to have aunts, uncles, and cousins."

"Might have been nice," Galo said with a half shrug and a wistful crooked grin, "But it isn't your fault that it didn't pan out."

"I guess not…" Gabdur sighed, "So, Borret's suicide attempt. I assume there was more to it than just the plot and cover coming undone."

"They were contracted with The Avatars of Fate. His end of the deal was to collect data for them," Galo explained, "By the way, he said there's no such position as The Investigator. They're a network of passive collectors.

"Anyway, now that I've dissolved our family's authority, The Avatars' end of the deal has been fulfilled. He decided to come clean and end his own life before they could come after him. He was afraid they'd force him into servitude on some island."

Gabdur leaned back with wide eyes and sighed loudly. Galo huffed and nodded emphatically.

"Did he give any indication as to which island he was referring to?" Gabdur asked, "It couldn't be the annex, could it?"

"It wouldn't be the first time they ran an operation there," Galo said, "But wouldn't it be the first time they returned to an abandoned facility?"

"As far as I'm aware, yes," Gabdur said, "So, what about Nalygen? Did she have any part in Ebralgi's plot?"

"Borret said she didn't even know about it."

"And you believe him?" Gabdur asked, "Have you spoken to her?"

"I'd like to, but it doesn't matter what I believe," Galo shrugged, "Either way, it's best that we stay out of each other's lives."

"Yeah, I suppose you're right," Gabdur said. He turned his ear toward the door. "It sounds like they're done with their talk. Take Luvros to Sinkua's room, then let's join the others downstairs."

Chapter 31

Sinkua followed Nikasu and Vielle down the stairs, with Galo and Gabdur following close behind. The front door opened as they reached the bottom of the stairs.

Odin entered first, handing Epelun to Nikasu with an admonishing glare. Leviathan followed, slithering up to Galo's forearm, where she reverted to her copper form. Nemesis stopped before Sinkua, reaching for his shoulder with the fingers on the end of his wing.

"I… apo… logize…" Nemesis sounded out, "I… have… mis… un… derstood."

The dragon lifted the Phoenix medallion from his own neck and placed it around Sinkua's. That familiar warmth filled every aspect of Sinkua's being as the gemstone and plate settled against his sternum. He gave Odin a quizzical glance.

"Phoenix taught him how to say that," Odin clarified, "All has been made clear."

"Same here," Sinkua said, "How do I tell him everything is okay?"

Phoenix fed the words into his thoughts, and he sounded them out. The smile Nemesis gave almost looked like a threat, if not for how he tried to show his teeth without curling his lips over his gums. He was, Sinkua realized, mimicking human gestures.

The four Hybrids and Gabdur all found seats in the already crowded living room. Odin and Nemesis posted in opposite corners of the exterior wall.

"So, Nikasu," Chekov opened, "I see you retrieved Epelun and Nemesis. Congratulations."

"Yep. And thank you," Nikasu said, "So, are you here to show us how to raise Drakougeneospa?"

"Actually, among other things, I'm here to ask you to wait a couple more days," Chekov said, "We've been preparing your neighbors to evacuate, but we need more time."

Nikasu gave Sinkua a wide-eyed stare. He returned the overwhelmed expression and shrugged. They both shook their heads, realizing in tandem how terribly they may have underestimated the vastness of the House of the Dragon Family.

"That's fine," Sinkua cut in, giving his sister time to find her composure, "So, what else did you come here for?"

"It concerns your sister, actually," Chekov said, "Nikasu, I understand you had an episode. Is that right?"

Nikasu looked askew with narrow eyes and her downturned mouth agape. She cast an offended glare back and forth between Phylus and BeiLou. Phylus mouthed an apology.

"Yeah," she said, turning back to Chekov.

"I need you to tell me as much as you can about it."

Nikasu looked back to Phylus.

"I told Malia that you had an episode and fainted," he assured her, "The details are your business."

"Well, I um…" Nikasu managed, closing her eyes as she cleared her throat.

"We have a couple of hypotheses about the diagrams," Dourias cut in, "Every bit of information will help."

Sinkua placed his hand on her shoulder and spoke to her in hushed tones. "Do you need to step outside and let Vielle and me explain?" he offered, "Galo can go with you. We'll catch you up later."

Nikasu cupped her hand over his, smiled, and shook her head. "I need to do this."

She called over to Nemesis and patted her own shoulders. Her dragon Etherworlder swooped between the furniture and came to crest on her shoulders. He shaped himself around her torso, returning to his armor form.

"The onset was spontaneous. No apparent trigger," Nikasu explained, holding steady eye contact with both Chekov and Dourias, "I lost control of myself, but I could still see everything that I was doing. I choke-lifted BeiLou at least a meter off the ground. When I was doing that, I noticed my arm was covered in chitin. That's the last thing I remember before Odin knocked me out."

"Well…" Dourias began, "One of our hypotheses concerning a seemingly crucial element of the diagrams is that it's a map of, in a manner of speaking, gravitational hot spots. But if you're having episodes, then…"

"Hey, let me stop you there," Vielle cut in, "The four of us are probably on the same train of thought as you two. So, I'll spare you the pussyfooting and spell out what we know." She paused to make sure both of them and the rest of The Coalition were listening. "Sinkua had an episode over the Southland Sea. It was strong enough to reach an Yggdrasil root in the seabed, where it traveled up here and triggered Nikasu's episode. That turned into some kind of horrible feedback loop, which went through me, giving me the biggest bitch of a migraine, but I was able to cut the connection."

Astonished and concerned eyes turned her way as the previously unaware all listened with greater earnest.

"We haven't figured out the purpose of this affliction, but everyone who has it is networked. It seems to be that Sinkua is the activator, and I'm the distributor. But it's more that they're using Yggdrasil, which I might not be necessary for," she continued, "Nikasu can apparently be either, but distribution might only work in an actuation chamber. And we don't know the range on those."

"That means that one of you," Galo interjected, "is disposable to MalVek and The Avatars. And so am I, as I have no role in whatever they're scheming."

"Does that mesh with your hypotheses?" Vielle asked.

"It does," Dourias said, grinning, "Our second hypothesis about the asset I mentioned is that it's a map of Yggdrasil's roots."

A square ray of fluorescent light was all that illuminated the room, with a soft electric hum accompanying it from just beyond its penumbra. A seated figure drummed out muted staccato rhythms, teasing a shadow over the table behind herself.

A sound came from outside. MarLys stopped and held her breath, listening. Silence. Another false alarm. She set back to her task, her eyes scanning the monitor as she played rhythms of espionage along the keyboard.

As cool as she played it, PavRal's words had stricken deep. But before she could make her move, she needed to know who her allies were. At least as important, she needed to know what enemies she might make in the process.

PavRal's mistaken assumption must have been an act. Obviously, he was just establishing a cover for the real spy. He couldn't have thought that she was still secretly working for Black Tie.

Or worse, he did, and SenRas would come to the same conclusion.

MarLys typed more aggressively as that thought crossed her mind. She combed through employee records of the Ministry of Covert Affairs. Or Human Resources. The two names had become interchangeable within that open-air office.

She paused on one particular record as the name caught her attention. MerSul. It stood out for how much he didn't stand out. The Ministry of Covert Affairs staffed just shy of thirty people, and MarLys had learned every name and face in ever greater earnest in her short tenure as SenRas's personal assistant. MerSul, however, was still vague.

MarLys remembered crossing theories with him when SenRas recapped their intel on The Avatars' rank and file. But she couldn't recall anything else he had said since. Either he was doing the bare minimum to keep his job, or he had taken care to get her onto his radar without revealing himself.

She was well aware of the narcissism and paranoia of such thoughts, but after PavRal tried to pin her as a mole, she wasn't going to let decorum interfere with her research. Besides, it wasn't just that he hadn't said anything memorable to her. She couldn't remember him having taken part in any Ministry discussions since that day.

If he wasn't the real spy, he was a formidable misdirection. In fact, that seemed more likely. MerSul was keeping her busy while the real mole gathered intel. She had, after all, pulled the thread to unravel Black Tie Delivery.

MerSul hadn't worked for Black Tie, but one of his employers did catch her attention. She felt like she should know it, but her thoughts fell just short of placing it. Dapper Rabbit. It sounded like the sort of bar that ran blackout curtains along the back of the foyer.

The security panel chimed, calling her attention to every noise outside the door. She had been so engrossed in her research that she hadn't heard anyone approaching. But she heard it all too clearly now. The sniffling of late Frigid congestion. The clearing throat of old age. The scuffing of dress shoes. The swishing of blended wool.

She turned off the monitor and tucked under the table where she unplugged the computer. But as suddenly as the sounds had arisen, they fell again. Not behind her concentration, but behind another sound.

A phone hummed.

"Odin, I think you said there's an Yggdrasil mapping system in Drakougene-ospa," Vielle said, "Can it map other things?"

"Yes. It can map many things," Odin said, "Provided milystis associated with that thing."

"It's made of the same stuff as Epelun and Epesol, isn't it?" Sinkua asked, "Some sort of milystic reactive metal?"

"It is indeed composed of Hephaeseum," Odin said, "As well as the mineral Hephaestite. Like most things crafted from these substances, it was made by the Quircois and the Lechuatzulans."

"I'm sorry," Uro interjected, "Did you say Quircois?"

"Yes," Odin said with a seeking stare, "Do you know of them?"

"I know we need to find him before MalVek does," Uro said, "He's trying to replicate Epesol, and he needs to find Quircois to do it."

"So much is faulty in that statement that I am unsure where to begin."

"Hold on, where the fuck is this coming from?" Farim admonished, "Where did you hear about this?"

"I've been receiving messages from someone at Hillside," Uro said, "I think it's Uncle Caylence."

"And you didn't think to mention this before now?" Farim scolded.

"This is the first time anything he's told me has been relevant," Uro defended, "Besides, since when have I been required to share every little thing? Do you need to know my blood type, too? Should I tell you about the herpes I…"

"Hey. Dumbass," Farim cut off, "Remember how you said you keep your mouth shut because it gets you in trouble? Do that now. And just so we're clear, yes, we do need to know about your intel and sources. Your blood and balls are your own business."

"I would have assumed that without saying," Gabdur added.

"Well, it would be impossible for anyone, even MalVek, to replicate Epesol," Odin assured, "The last cache of Hephaeseum is in Drakougeneospa, and no other ethermetal will suffice in its place. Further, Quircois is not the name of an individual. It is a nationality that once occupied what you know as Kirts. Their smiths held renown for their ability to work ethermetals to their greatest potential. As did the Lechuatzulans of what is now Lenguardia with etherstones."

"Tsenukoa contracted a team of Lechuatzulans to create this ruby," Phoenix projected into Sinkua's mind.

"Well, now that we know who's behind these relics, let's get back to the diagrams," Sinkua urged, "Doctor Ophalin has a lead on curing my condition. That would make Nikasu the only activator."

"But that would make you disposable," BeiLou said.

"One of us has to be," Sinkua said, gesturing to Nikasu, Vielle, and himself, "And I'd rather we say for ourselves than try to figure out who MalVek would pick. Besides, Galo and I have more experience watching each other's backs than anyone else."

"Well, I appreciate it," Vielle said, "Proving that I can disrupt distribution wasn't the smartest move on my part."

"The only use they ever had for me was activating the Mechanical Crypt, and even there, they had a backup plan," Galo said, "I've been disposable since the Heniokhos Disaster. Eytea, on the other hand, was probably always more of a threat than an asset. If any of us realized it sooner, she and I could have protected each other." He turned to Sinkua. "I'm sorry, brother."

"Thank you, but it's not your fault," Sinkua said.

"So, how soon can Ophalin cure you?" Elemeno asked.

"First, one of his nurses needs some Sisyphus cuttings," Sinkua said, "She gave me a list."

"I transferred my research grant to his practice when I sent him the genome map," Yrlis said, "They should be able to request them from the Arboreal Society of Tanelen."

Sinkua shrugged. "Nobody mentioned it."

"Give me the list," Farim interjected, "Uro and I will get them for you. I just need until next week to make arrangements." While Sinkua dug in his pocket, she glanced aside at Phylus. "I owe you one, the way I see it."

EshCal yanked the pull-chain, and warm lamplight enveloped her desk. She pushed her chair back into the shadows as she dug in her pocket.

She reached down to unlock the third drawer with a key scarcely bigger than her fingertip. She could hear it before she saw it, the rumble of dense glass telling that PavRal had fulfilled her request.

She lifted the bottle into the light and held it at arm's length. Sighing at the small print and her aging senses, she opened the shallow drawer just beneath the desk-top and plucked out her reading glasses.

Now able to read the small print, she found that PavRal had chosen a fifth of Ivarian rum. Good stuff all the same, but she wondered how he found it to be suited to the occasion. The closest tie she had to Ivaria was through Spril, and that was a distant childhood memory. And he hadn't played any part in the reconstruction agreement. If this was about her succeeding him, that was just an unnecessary salting of his wounds.

Salt.

EshCal scrutinized the bottleneck. The tamper-proof seal had been punctured. She reached for her desk phone.

"By the way," Gabdur said, "Galo brought some crucial information to my attention." He gestured to his son. "Galo?"

"When I discovered who had been siphoning intel to Ebralgi, I learned that The Avatars have a network of passive data collectors," Galo explained, "Anyone they can blackmail into wearing a wire." He turned to Malia. "There's never been any such position as The Investigator."

"Well, if I knew I was coming here to get my wounds salted, I'd have stopped for rum and limes," Malia said. Galo turned his hands up capitulatorily. "Sorry," Malia chuckled, shaking her head, "I know MalVek played me for years. Now, I have a better idea of how far it went."

"Yes, but you're missing the broader picture," Gabdur said, "We've been under the impression that MalVek collects intel with his frequency interceptors. But he actually has a network of passive spies feeding him information."

"We should assume he does both," Dourias said.

"He has access to frequency interceptor technology," Chekov added, "I watched NalSet build and test it with him."

"He has likely repurposed it to receive transmissions from his collector network," Dourias said, "Which would mean that an EMP blast ought to dismantle his intelligence foundation."

"Assuming any of us can get that close to him," Uro added. He shrank back as Dourias, along with Gabdur, Chekov, and Farim, turned to look at him.

"That goes without saying," Farim said, "But you've got a good point. We can't hinge any plans on pulling that off."

Silence settled into the room. Whether or not he realized it, Uro had encapsulated their entire situation with MalVek in just a few words. They could learn another of his capabilities every day from now until the Swelter, and it wouldn't do them any good if they couldn't get near him.

"Well, I guess I'd better be out with it before this silence gives birth," Spril said, launching to his feet almost too quickly to follow, "In light of recent developments, I've decided to cooperate with The Coalition."

SenRas listened by the door. Somebody was inside, but no matter how he concentrated, he couldn't tell anything beyond that. Whoever it was, they were taking special care to keep their breathing shallow.

If not for the electronic humming, he wouldn't have even known they were using a computer. They must have been using a keyboard pad, which meant they had to be one of his own. Not because nobody else would think to use one, but because only his staff would know where they were kept with the confidence to find them in silence.

Although he had his guesses, there was only one way to be sure. He swiped his card.

A sharp breath and a scuffing of plastic on tile answered the electronic chime. Lips smacked and breathing grew pronounced. Blended fabrics swished over each other. The electronic hum abruptly stopped.

But as SenRas reached for the door handle, his phone hummed in his pocket. He sighed and stepped back as he answered.

"Hello?"

"I have a question for you."

"Yes?"

"Do you know of any tasteless alcohol-soluble poisons?"

"Several. Why?"

"What about an antidote?"

"Well, there's no catch-all. What else do you know about it?"

"It's probably activated by salt."

"Well, that narrows it down but not much."

"Would an emetic help?"

"Most likely. Does this concern what I think it concerns?"

"It does."

"Well, on such short notice, an emetic is your best choice."

"I was hoping for better news than that."

"I'm sorry. Good luck."

The call ended, and SenRas returned his phone to his pocket. He took one last look at the door before he walked away.

MarLys could make her escape once she felt sure he had left.

"So…" Vielle chirped, her eyes cast downward, "… What made you change your mind?"

"It was…" Spril trailed off, pondering his words. He looked aside, exchanging warm glances with Yrlis. "… a talk with a colleague. I realized that even if I disagree with The Coalition Originals' methods so far, I shouldn't punish the people in their era." Yrlis whispered something to him and excused herself. She crossed the room as he continued. "It'll suck having to leave you all behind, but I have to do it. And I would have just snuck off after we dealt with Pandora instead of putting this on all of you like this, but once I start my treatments, I don't know how much longer I'll be… you know. Emotionally available."

Yrlis tucked in next to Vielle. She nudged her with her hip, and Vielle scooted aside to let her sit between herself and the arm of the couch. Yrlis put an arm around her.

"Hey, so I know me and you have had our ups and downs," Yrlis whispered, "But when he goes, do you think we could lean on each other when we're bummed out?"

Vielle glanced aside and cracked the tiniest of smiles. "Yeah," she managed, "I think that would be nice."

"I was hoping you'd say that," Yrlis beamed, "Sister-in-law."

"You guys got married!?" she exclaimed. The newlyweds both nodded. "When? Where? Was this before or after your decision to leave? Sorry. That came out meaner than I meant it to. Which was none. But… Yeah! What!?"

"We did it after I made my decision," Spril said, "It was one of Yrlis's conditions for coping with me leaving. That and taking part in administering my treatments."

"And you did it while you were still, as you put it, emotionally available," Galo realized, "What did you mean by that, anyway?"

"Just what it sounds like. If I become The Weapon, I might lose my emotional capacity," Spril explained, "It was a key feature in their genetic design. In fact, I wasn't even supposed to be able to form lasting personal bonds." He looked at Vielle. "But somebody changed that."

"M-… Me?" Vielle asked. Spril nodded. "How? I didn't… try to do anything."

"I don't know, but you did," Spril said, shrugging.

"Chekov mentioned that Pahres was incredibly charismatic," Sinkua said, "Supernaturally, I think."

"Preternaturally," Chekov corrected.

"Yggdrasil Hybrids are unifiers," Odin added, "They have naturally magnetic personalities with a great propensity for charisma."

"Well, if I'm not going to be the cold and calculating leader they're expecting," Spril said, "maybe I should lean into it and take lessons from you on how to be more charismatic."

"Oh, I think you're plenty charismatic," Vielle said, "And I'm sure you'll be fine even after your treatments. I mean, look at what you've done with ArcNos's reputation in just six years."

"Hey, that's right," Sinkua spoke up, "What's going to happen with your job?"

"EshCal will take his position," Phylus said, "Which leaves her spot open for nominees."

"I'm already on my way out," Spril said, "I extended my psych leave until a therapist approves me to return to work."

"Hey, I'm about to start classes to get my therapist's license," Vielle said.

"Well, you can practice on me. If I'm being honest, I'm not that interested in returning to work," Spril said, "I'm letting this serve as a transitional period for EshCal. Any therapy sessions will be for my own good."

"Well shit," Sinkua bemused. Spril gave him a quizzical look. "I was going to ask her for some sword training. But now it sounds like she'll be too busy."

"I'm… sorry?" Spril replied, more asking than stating, "You're actually seeking out melee weapon lessons?" Sinkua nodded. "That's not like you. What brought this on?"

"Buncha iola store pirates lopped off my backside and presented it under a cloche," Sinkua snarked, "You know. The usual reasons."

"Finally got your ass kicked, huh?" Spril snickered.

"I'd rather not talk about it," Sinkua insisted.

"It's fine. I'm just playing with you," Spril said, "But all this extra work could mean she'll need another assistant. If you work for her, she can give you pointers while you work."

"Wouldn't your assistant transfer to her?"

"He got reassigned during my first leave."

"Oh," was all Sinkua could say now. He leaned back as he considered the suggestion. "Yeah. I think I'll do it. That's probably the best way to reach her. And I could do with a job again."

"Yes, I was wondering about that," Phylus said, "How have you been paying for all of this?"

"CreSam and I paid off the house a long time ago," BeiLou interjected.

"Eytea and I had some money saved up," Sinkua said, "I've been frugal, but it's getting a bit, well, scant."

"Did she have life insurance?" Farim asked, "Sorry if that's a sore subject."

"It's fine," Sinkua insisted, "We both did. And we were each other's beneficiaries. I'm just... trying not to touch that money."

Sinkua felt eyes settle upon him. He found Vielle giving the saddest and warmest smile. Someone else, however, spoke first.

"We all understand, but that isn't what she'd want," Elemeno said, "Let her take care of you."

"Property taxes are due soon," BeiLou added, "Even if you started working for EshCal tomorrow, I don't think you'd earn enough in time."

"Eat the sandwich," Elemeno said, "son-in-law."

A grumble burbled out of the pile of blankets, stirred by a fading memory of a distant stimulus. The ticking of a clock filled the dark room. Long breaths segued into a rolling snore.

The phone rang again.

A pale arm shot out from under blankets. It pawed at the nightstand, knocking over a bottle of antacid tablets and threatening to take a glass of water with it. Eventually, it found the receiver and nearly dropped the base onto the floor as it pulled it under the blankets.

"H'llo?!"

"General Sbaglien?" the caller answered, her Southland accent prodding at his cognizance.

"... Speaking," Sbaglien grumbled.

"Sir!" she affirmed, "I formally request that you turn on your video cast. I wish to show you something."

"Inre... Colonel," he pleaded, "I want you to ask yourself something." He let his words linger. "Are you sure this can't wait until morning?"

"General Sbaglien," Colonel Inre urged, "I can't be sure someone else won't find this by then, and I don't intend to stay all night."

"Are you refusing to comply with an order, Colonel?"

"Sir?" Inre asked, "You never gave an order."

Sbaglien, still prostrate and blanketed, reflected in silence. Wakefulness was finally accepting him, and now he wondered what he had said to Inre. She had said something about a video cast. That much he was sure about. And apparently, he never gave an order, but he didn't know why she pointed that out.

He threw off the blankets and sat up.

"How long will this take?" he asked, "I was in the middle of something important."

"Sir, you were sleeping."

"As I said."

"Shouldn't be more than a moment," Inre assured, "Though I don't know how long it will take to, well, take it all in."

Sbaglien hummed absently as he walked to the living room. He had nothing to say but couldn't have the Colonel thinking he had gone back to sleep.

In the living room, he unrolled a projector screen in the middle of a vast empty wall. He pointed his phone at it and pushed a few buttons. A soft white glow filled the screen, while an icon in the corner indicated that it awaited a source.

"Okay, Colonel," he said, "I'm set."

"Okay, give me a sec," Inre said, her voice trailing off. Her face appeared on the screen a moment later. "There. Can you see me?"

"You did something different with your eyebrows," Sbaglien noted, "If this is why you dragged me out of bed, I'm going to rip them off and staple them to your upper lip."

"I did, and thank you for noticing," Inre said, "But no, sir, that's not why I called. I'm in the building where Prime Minister Phylus was being held."

"Any leads on the Noble Doyen?"

"See for yourself, sir."

The display blurred as Inre whipped the camera around. As she stopped, the image snapped into focus. Sbaglien narrowed his eyes, trying to understand what he was seeing.

It looked like pieces of a poorly designed mannequin. Smooth cuts and distinct angles occurred nowhere near any major joints. There were no visible fasteners. To wit, it would be impossible to assemble such a mannequin.

Except, he suddenly realized, it wasn't a mannequin.

"By the ether," Sbaglien gasped, "Is that...?"

Inre's hand entered the frame. She cupped the back of two-thirds of a head and turned it to face the camera. Most of Joren's lifeless face looked back at Sbaglien.

"By the ether!" he exclaimed, "What happened to him?"

"I'm still trying to figure that out, sir," Inre said, "Nobody else is here. They likely cleared out shortly after they did this to our Noble Doyen."

"That's a reasonable assumption," Sbaglien said, "Have you found any surveillance systems?"

"Not yet, sir."

"Keep looking. Bring me as much as you can carry and destroy the rest," he insisted, "That's an order."

"Understood, sir," Inre said, "There's just one more thing you need to be aware of."

"Yes, Colonel?"

"We're, ah... We're dealing with cannibals here."

Chapter 32

MarLys sat at her desk, separated from the rows of tables used by the rest of the Ministry. She looked out over the workforce now and again, somewhat longingly.

Sure, she was still their colleague, but the separation had her feeling socially isolated. Friends formed tighter bonds over their work, while she grew more obscure in her position.

Beyond that, she stole noting glances at two people in particular. The first was the man whose computer she had used the night before, making sure he didn't find anything out of place. The other was MerSul.

The door buzzer chimed. SenRas called out from his private micro-office, the only isolated structure aside from the bathroom.

"MarLys!" he called, "Get that, would you?"

Her desk phone rang as she rose to her feet. She stopped in mid-thrust to check on it. The caller identifier said it was from reception. Figuring she was calling about the visitor who just arrived, she hit the ignore call button.

MerSul also rose from his seat. She paused and gave him a quizzical look. The buzzer chimed again. He nodded aside toward the printer. MarLys continued to the door to welcome the guest.

"Hello. Welcome to the Ministry of Human…" she said, trailing off as she saw Sinkua. Her eyes came alight as she remarked, "Oh shit!"

Sinkua laughed boisterously. "Is that any way to talk to your girl-friend's half sister's half brother?"

"Oh, of course not. You're practically family," she said, casting a glare with an arched eyebrow.

Sinkua's face tightened as he turned his eyes downward. He cleared his throat and braved to make eye contact. MarLys's glare was unwavering.

That was until they both cracked into chuckles issuing forth in fits and puffs. She waved him in, and they slapped each other five from the side, which turned into a handshake and shoulder bump punctuated with hooked fingertips.

"Well, I'm glad to see you in a good mood," MarLys said, "So, what brings you up here? Business or social?"

"I'm here about a job," Sinkua said, "I'm applying to be EshCal's assistant. The receptionist told me to go through HR."

MarLys took only a second to process the implications. PavRal, though measured in his words, had basically confided in her that he had never been on the level. It seemed Sinkua had some insight on this matter, but with MerSul still a variable, she couldn't ask any probing questions in his presence.

"I see. Well, I'd be glad to help," MarLys said, masking her anxiousness with casual professionalism, "I'll just need to…"

A loud pop came from across the office, punctuated by someone shouting, "Fuck!"

MarLys and Sinkua looked aside. MerSul turned away from the printer with black ink splattered across the left half of his shirt.

"That guy gonna be okay?" Sinkua asked.

"He'll be fine," MarLys said, brushing the back of his hand as she breezed past him, "Walk with me. I want to introduce you."

She led Sinkua to the printer where MerSul stood clutching a fistful of screen wipes.

"Hey, don't sweat it. This is on me," she assured him, "I wanted you to meet my friend, anyway." She gestured to Sinkua. "This is Sinkua. He used to work in Foreign Affairs," she said, "Sinkua, this is MerSul. The guy you've been hearing about."

"Oh yeah?" MerSul prodded, the corner of his mouth flicking up as he offered Sinkua his hand, "What's she been saying about me?"

MarLys realized in that infinite split second between her introduction and MerSul's questions that she hadn't given Sinkua any indication of her angle. Or that she was even working one. But fortune sided with her, as he picked up on it and carried it perhaps better than she had planned.

"Not much to me. I catch most of it second hand," Sinkua bluffed, "Her girlfriend and I go back a ways. Both Subtransit Resistance vets. Sometimes, MarLys's work stories about you make her girlfriend wonders if she should be jealous."

"Really now?" MerSul said, his mouth curling into an arrogant grin. He looked aside at MarLys, who had begun cleaning the printer table. "She got a reason to be jealous?"

Sinkua prodded MerSul's chest. MerSul's attention snapped back to him with a scowl.

"I'd say not," Sinkua said, "Your tits are too small for her liking."

Somehow, MerSul's expression turned even more unamused. MarLys snickered not entirely to herself as MerSul pushed past them and headed back to his workstation.

"Nice one," she said, nudging Sinkua with her elbow, "Now, could you give me a hand with this? I'll get your papers sorted once we take care of this."

"Um. Sure," Sinkua said, shrugging, "No problem."

"Thanks, bud," MarLys said, handing him a few wipes, "And Vielle does have quite the scones for such a small plate, doesn't she?"

"Never thought about it," Sinkua said, taking to the mess.

"Good boy," MarLys said, reaching up to rub the top of his head. She pulled a pack of gum from her pocket. "Want a piece?"

Sinkua accepted the offer, and MarLys took one for herself as well.

EshCal unlocked the third drawer of her desk and withdrew the bottle of Ivarian rum. She placed it on top of the desk and leaned down, staring through the honey-colored liquor. Plucking at PavRal's nerves would be as simple as acknowledging the tampering, but it wouldn't prove his guilt.

She nudged the bottle into a streak of sunlight. She narrowed her eyes, scrutinizing the light passing through the rum. A cloud of discoloration swirled in the beam of light.

She pulled the bottle back out of the light and reached for the intercom.

"PavRal."

"Yes, High Minister?"

"Come to my office."

She centered her seat behind her desk, sat up straight, and locked her fingers, settling her fists atop her desk. PavRal came through the door shortly after.

"PavRal. Come in," she said, "Take a seat."

"Uh… Sure," PavRal rasped. He crossed the vast office and sat down. "Can I ask what this is about?"

"Well, I don't have my Prime Minister to share this lovely Ivarian rum with," she said, "So, I thought you and I could take a few shots together." She pushed the bottle to the middle of the desk, just beyond the sunbeam, and took a pair of shot glasses out of her desk. "After all, you helped make this happen."

"Well, I…" PavRal stammered. He chuckled nervously, struggling to keep eye contact. "I don't know how I helped, but I guess I could stay for a drink."

"Great!" EshCal exclaimed, clapping her hands loud enough to make him flinch, "Let's get day buzzed." She turned the bottle, putting the break in the seal in her line of sight. "Whoa…" she gasped, yanking the bottle back, "What's this?"

PavRal scooted closer and leaned in. "What's what?" he asked.

EshCal turned the bottle and tapped the neck. "This," she said, "There's a break in the seal." She looked at PavRal with an expression in the overlap between accusation, anxiety, and confusion. "It looks like it's been punctured."

PavRal swallowed hard and slouched back. "I'm sure it's nothing," he said, folding his arms.

"Yes. You're probably right," EshCal said, "Now, fetch the salt from the cabinet."

PavRal crossed EshCal's office to the corner hutch, while EshCal nudged the bottle into the patch of sunlight. She scowled at him as he returned, sending tremors through his facade of composure. The saltshaker rattled as he set it down.

"Something got you worked up, boy?" EshCal asked, "Is that cloud making you uneasy?"

"No, I just…" PavRal stammered, lowering himself into the chair, "I need a smoke."

EshCal grimaced and snickered. With her eyes fixed on him, she salted the rims, opened the bottle, and poured two shots. The anomalous cloud stretched and broke off into both shots. She pulled one to herself and slid the other to PavRal.

"Drink."

She raised her glass and watched as he mirrored. The faintest glimmer of an arrogant smile swept over his face as she brought her shot near her lips.

She had him.

EshCal threw back her shot. PavRal began to chuckle. Under his breath at first. Then louder. Bolder.

"You idiot," PavRal derided, "Did you really think I'd call your bluff?"

EshCal looked at him flatly. "Did you really think I only had a bluff to work with?"

She set her shot glass down and reached into the third drawer again. She took out a bottle of emetics and popped a pill. PavRal snickered, but for once, EshCal wasn't sure if it was out of arrogance or amusement at her foresight.

"So," he said, "How'd you figure it out?"

"I've suspected for months," EshCal said, her voice thready as her throat tightened. She turned and retched on the floor, returning to the conversation as though nothing untoward had occurred. "Now, I have enough evidence to have you locked up for treason."

"How did you...?" PavRal asked. His lips tightened into a sneer. "You're bluffing again. You don't have shit. You can't prove anything was wrong with your rum. Or that I had anything to do with it."

"Drink, then," EshCal ordered. PavRal's expression flattened and shoulders tensed. "Tell you what," she said, "I'll let you decide how this goes down."

"...What are my options?"

"Drink and confess, and I'll get you a commuted sentence."

"And if I don't?"

"If you don't drink, you have two choices," she said, "Either you come along peacefully while I bring my evidence before the federal court, where you will confess everything and accept the extent of your sentencing."

"...Or?"

"You face me in single combat for the opportunity to disappear into witness protection."

PavRal's hand trembled so hard that he sloshed the rum from his shot glass. He gritted his teeth, and his mouth curled down into a scowl. He launched from the seat and whipped his half-empty shot glass at her. EshCal tilted her head and let it breeze past.

PavRal swiped the open bottle, sloshing rum over his hand, and swung at her head. EshCal sprang from her seat, swiped the bottle with one hand, and grabbed his wrist with the other. She pressed his hand on the desk, pinning it with her index and middle fingers. Shoulders rippling with refined musculature, she slammed the bottle down within millimeters of his hand, spraying him and herself with dense glass shrapnel and a cascade of rum.

PavRal's eyes widened and twitched, as his thoughts caught up with all she had done in the space of a second. Every muscle in his arm tensed as he tried to withdraw his hand. EshCal, her face stern and calculating, kept his hand pinned with no evidence of exertion.

"Did you really think," EshCal derided, "that single combat was a viable option?" She leaned across the desk, putting her cheek within a hair's breadth of his. Her voice became smoky. "You were doomed to fail from the day I hired you," she said, cracking his metacarpals, "Now. Choose again."

"Okay, you've got all your papers, including your letter of re-hire," MarLys said, standing in the doorway, "Is there anything else that you need? Do you remember how to get there?"

"Yeah, well enough. So, I think that'll do it," Sinkua said, "Thanks a bunch."

"Any time, buddy," she grinned, clearing her throat. She gave him another enthusiastic handshake, keeping a whisper floating between them as they pulled close. "Keep your ears open."

"Are you in danger?"

"I don't know yet. Just..."

"I'll keep a lookout," he assured, "Pull back."

"Hey, and if you need anything else," she said, speaking at normal volume as they separated, "you know where to find me."

"Of course. Thank you," he said, "See you around, MarLys."

As he walked away, MarLys coughed into her hand. She wiped her hand on the doorframe, excusing herself to nobody in particular. As she headed back to her desk, the door fell shut behind her.

At least it appeared so from any of the workstations.

EshCal returned the saltshaker to the corner hutch and shut the door. The shot glasses, she set in the sink, but the more she thought about it, the better she thought of discarding them. Too bad, she thought. They had been a gift from Prime Duke Norum.

She took her mobile phone out of her pocket and tried to turn it on. It failed for the third time since PavRal left.

She flinched more than she cared to admit when an unexpected knock came at the door. PavRal was no longer a problem, but she couldn't shake her worry of accomplices. Even though she had suspected him for months, it had taken him that long to slip up.

Her stomach turned and face tightened as she walked to the door. She composed herself and opened it.

"Oh! Sinkua," she greeted, "Are you on my agenda for today?"

"No, sorry, this all came up suddenly," Sinkua said. He held up a small stack of papers. "I thought reception was going to call about me."

"I haven't heard anything," EshCal said. She stepped aside and waved him in. "But come on in. Tell me why you're here."

Sinkua entered and offered the papers to her.

"I'm here for a job," he said, "I'd like to work as your assistant."

EshCal's head snapped up from the papers. She could guess that he had gotten the idea from Spril. The question was exactly how much either of them knew, if anything.

"That's a rather specific position," she said, folding the papers and lowering them to her side. She cleared her throat and winced. "Quite a change from your last one, too. What brought this on?"

"I need a job. Property taxes are due soon," Sinkua said, "Spril told me yesterday that you could use another assistant, seeing as you're doing his job on top of your own."

EshCal regarded him for a moment, meanwhile scrutinizing how deeply the coincidence ran and how much was actually a coincidence.

"So, that's why he said you should come to me?" she asked, gesturing to the seat that PavRal had recently sat in, "Because I might need a new assistant?"

"Well, I..." Sinkua said, trailing off. He sniffed loudly. "Why does it smell like booze in here?"

"Because somebody spilled booze in here," she said matter-of-factly, "You see, I actually had to fire my assistant today. Just a few minutes ago, in fact. I tried to let him off easy with a parting drink, but he didn't take the news well."

Sinkua cocked his head and narrowed his eyes.

"You see why this is weird," she continued, gesturing to him emphatically, "I never told Spril I was having trouble with my assistant or the workload." She leaned over the desk, nostrils curling at the lingering smell of rum.

"So, what's the story? There are countless openings in the Ministry of Defense more suited to your experience. And even if he knew I was having trouble, he wouldn't be so obvious."

"I do need a job, and he did think you'd need a second assistant," Sinkua said, unbothered by the smell and her proximity, "But it first came up because I need sword training."

"Oh!" she said, leaning back into a more relaxed posture, "What sort of blade have you gotten yourself?"

"Broadsword," he said, "Big son of a bitch. About as long as Vielle is tall."

EshCal snickered at the description. "Well, I don't know how much I can help with that," she said, "I specialize in fencing swords."

"That's fine. I can actually handle it like one."

She pulled back and regarded him out of the corner of her eyes. Even outside of his episodes, she knew he was capable of alarming strength. He might have even been able to best her, reluctant as she was to admit it.

"Well, Sinkua, this has all certainly piqued my curiosity. So, I'll tell you what," she said, "If you have a working mobile phone that you don't mind parting with for a few minutes, we can work something out after I'm done with it."

He reached in his pocket and offered her a cheap burner phone. She managed a smile as she accepted it. The things usually lasted three months tops, but it had one over on hers in that it actually worked at the moment.

She dialed and turned her chair to put her back to him.

"Thank you for calling Dapper Rabbit," came the greeting, "What can we do to serve you today?"

"Hi, this is EshCal," she said, "Is Hibiscus available?"

"Oh, hello EshCal!" the receptionist chimed, "Yes, just a moment."

As the line fell to white noise, she turned and flashed Sinkua a smile. He returned the gesture, appearing deliberately distant. She turned back to the bookshelf behind her desk as the line became active again.

"Hey there, EshCal," Hibiscus greeted, her rich alto voice flowing melodiously even through the cheap earpiece, "What can I do for you, sweetie? You interested in a special rendezvous?"

"I'm just calling to tell you we got him."

"Oh? Him who?"

"Come on, Hibiscus," EshCal said, "PavRal."

"I know, I know," Hibiscus said, chirping the tiniest giggle, "I just like to tease you sometimes."

"I thought you only did that on the clock," EshCal laughed, "But anyway, I thought I'd see if you'd like to get drinks soon. This was a team effort, after all."

"Just drinks, huh?" Hibiscus asked, "Well, you are on our flat rate plan, so if that's what you want. Let me just check my calendar."

"No, off the clock," EshCal said, "As friends."

"Oh, um…" Hibiscus said, her voice trailing off, "I… try not to get attached to my clients like that."

"If it would make it less awkward, I could invite MerSul to join us," EshCal offered. She heard the chair behind her shift.

"Who?"

"MerSul. He's been helping on the side."

"Great. I'm glad for his help," Hibiscus said, "You just mentioned him like I already know him."

"Oh, did you two never meet there?" EshCal asked. The silence all but shouted Hibiscus's mounting confusion. "He used to work at Dapper Rabbit."

"No, he didn't."

"Are you sure? That's the whole reason I recommended him to SenRas."

"EshCal, I've been here from the start," Hibiscus said, "We've never had anyone by that name."

A series of heavy footfalls faded toward the door. EshCal turned around to find Sinkua tearing around the doorframe. She cleared her throat and winced.

"Are you okay?" Hibiscus asked.

"It's, ah..." EshCal said, "It appears to be under control."

MarLys looked toward the door as it opened. SenRas stuck his head out of his micro-office and called out to MerSul.

She turned back to her work, glancing aside at MerSul as he passed. He flicked his eyebrows up, like they had some inside joke that only he knew about.

He didn't know everything. In fact, he didn't know much. But he could piece together enough. MarLys was in danger. And MerSul was behind it.

Sinkua all but knocked his chair over as he tore out of EshCal's office, the stench of rum and something more acidic still lingering in his nostrils. He couldn't quite place that secondary smell, but he told himself that it didn't matter. For now, the most important thing was recalling the fastest way back to the Ministry of Human Resources.

MarLys focused on the conversation behind SenRas's micro-office door. She grabbed at bits and pieces, a word here and there, but nothing cohesive. But if she concentrated any harder, she'd risk losing discretion, and she didn't know if MerSul had any accomplices in their Ministry.

Nor did she know if he was actually up to anything. So far, she only had her suspicions. And given that she had, in fact, come from Black Tie, he surely had his own about her.

SenRas emerged again. "MarLys," he called over, "Step in here, please."

Sinkua barreled through the halls, bobbing and weaving around personnel and equipment. His pulse quickened and grew irregular while his throat tightened and burbled. He gritted his teeth and clenched his eyes shut, dodging from memory for a few seconds.

"Phoenix!" he shouted within his thoughts.

"I'm ready, Sinkua," she answered, "You fear for her life."

"Yes, but..." he thought, "I need you to hold off this episode."

"Had I the power to disrupt them, I would have been doing it all along."

As he came to an intersection, something in the corner of his eye gave Sinkua pause. An EMT came up the hall, pushing an empty wheelchair.

"Sinkua?" Phoenix beckoned, "What do you need me to do?"

"Talk to me," Sinkua thought, fixating on the EMT, "Calmly."

As Phoenix spoke nothing in particular into his mind, Sinkua watched the EMT bank the corner hard enough to tilt the wheelchair. He exhaled his tension as Human Resources was in the opposite direction. But as he took the turn himself, he realized something else.

The second smell finally made sense. He turned and called to the EMT, who only slowed to half speed as he looked over his shoulder.

"Defense?" Sinkua called over.

"Yeah!" the EMT shouted back.

"Faster," Sinkua said, pointing back around the corner he'd just come from.

That was all he could do for EshCal, and as the EMT followed his advice, he told himself that it would have to be enough.

MarLys looked back and forth between SenRas and MerSul as she entered the micro-office, guarded but trying to hide it. She knew it did no good with SenRas, but he wasn't her concern.

"What's this about?" she asked, immediately regretting that she had spoken first.

"Well, as you taught us, Black Tie Delivery has been used to facilitate communications among The Avatars of Fate and their sympathizers," SenRas began, staying seated, "Truthfully, we've suspected them for years, but you gave us undeniable proof."

"Right," MarLys said, nodding once. She flicked a glance toward MerSul. "What does he have to do with that?"

"Well, young lady, it's nothing personal, but we had to consider the possibility that your leak was a counter-intelligence ruse."

"Well, color me more offended than surprised," MarLys said, "But that doesn't answer my question, sir." She looked straight at MerSul. "What do you have to do with this? What's Dapper Rabbit?"

MerSul laughed jovially. "It's an escort service," he said, "Now, do you see why it was so curious that your girlfriend thought she should be jealous of me?"

"I guess so," MarLys snickered, looking him over, "So… I guess Dapper Rabbit and Black Tie have history, then?"

"We've been using former Dapper Rabbit escorts to keep tabs on former Black Tie couriers in Ministry jobs," SenRas said, "to put it succinctly. We have given quite a few current escorts considerable insurance in exchange for contributing to investigations as well."

"And I suppose MerSul has been keeping tabs on me?" MarLys asked.

"I planted a subdermal bug in the back of your left hand," SenRas said, "He coordinated with R&D on its development. And now, it's helped us take down PavRal."

She recalled her conversation with PavRal in the high-rise district. He had insisted that she was wearing a bug to siphon Ministry intel back to Black Tie, and she had dared him to search her.

She wanted to accost them for using her, in fact exploiting and endangering her, with neither her knowledge nor consent. But this wasn't the time. Besides, SenRas was acting with good intentions. As long as she was true to her word as a Black Tie deserter, he wouldn't have put her in more danger than she could handle.

"What's the verdict, then?" she asked.

"I'm happy to report that we've found you true to your word," MerSul said, "And I apologize for the deception. It's nice to come clean and finally truly meet you, MarLys."

As he brought his right hand up for a handshake, MarLys, being left-handed, brought up her left. They both paused as they brushed fingertips. MerSul chuckled as he showed his left hand, still stained with ink from the printer incident.

MarLys steeled herself as she offered her right hand instead. The broken cartridge had been a deliberate gambit. He had backed her into a corner, and he was giving her nothing.

All she could do was step on the trap.

Sinkua banked the corner in a furious sprint as Phoenix continued to pour out pleasantries. With the entrance to the Ministry of Human Resources just ahead, it struck Sinkua that he would need to be let inside. Assuming, that was, that his grandfather hadn't somehow programmed his handprint into the biometric scanner. But just as he thought to pitch his medallion at the door, with profuse apologies to Phoenix, something else caught his eye.

A strangely wide sliver of light shone from the doorframe. MarLys's angle became clearer, specifically the chewing gum and sore throat. Even with his singular focus as he charged the door, he couldn't help but be impressed by her cleverness.

He reminded himself to pay her just such a compliment after they dealt with MerSul. Whatever that man was plotting, MarLys would leave there alive if Sinkua had any say in the matter.

MerSul clamped down on MarLys's hand. It all happened too fast for her eyes to process. Too fast for SenRas to react to, even.

A long needle sprang from under MerSul's cuff, puncturing the underside of MarLys's wrist next to the radial pulse. A surge of electricity shot up her right arm, arcing across her chest and down her left arm.

MarLys convulsed violently as the voltage mounted. Her chest tightened as her heart palpitated. Her left hand burned as the same arm clenched and tingled. The stenches of burning flesh, metal, and acid flooded her nostrils.

Her peripheral vision narrowed, blurring around the edges. MerSul, soon to be her final sight, held fast with unsettling stoicism.

The door latch popped as it separated from the wad of chewed gum, and Sinkua stumbled through. He found the entire Ministry on their feet, except SenRas, MarLys, and MerSul were glaringly absent.

A stuttered scream shredded through the closed door in the corner. He urged Phoenix into silence and charged at the door.

MarLys's vision plunged into blackness. The sound of her own screams grew distant. The acrid stench of burning flesh gave way to that of rotting.

She could smell herself dying.

The distant sound of something thumping on metal stirred her thoughts for unplaceable reasons. Her mind faded toward nothing, and all she could do was try not to dwell on the betrayal that brought her here. All despite her efforts to protect herself.

In that instant, she realized what that thump had portended.

A sound like a far-off depth charge rumbled her chest cavity. A tingling sensation, this one wholly external, swept over her convulsing skin. For a moment, she felt an incomparable respite as the shock abated.

Nonetheless, her back met the floor as she met with unconsciousness.

Sinkua drew back his blazing fist. MarLys's screams from beyond the door became thready. The threat of an episode bubbled up, and he leaned on residual thoughts of Phoenix's voice to keep from boiling over.

His fist plowed through the door like it was made of paper. But instead of finding MerSul's back as he had predicted, he found an arm, tense and pulsating.

The screaming abated as he grabbed it. But in that same instant, he started convulsing uncontrollably. The shock surged up his arm and across his shoulders.

He wanted to let go. Every part of him wanted to release that arm. But for all his convulsing, he lost control of his every muscle.

The shock took hold of his necklace, looping around the chain and circulating in the medallion. Phoenix was powerless against it. The current gathered in the middle of his chest, culminating in a thunderous pop that bounced the medallion nearly horizontal.

To his relief, the blast knocked him away from the arm. As his singed medallion fell back into place, Sinkua collapsed as well. Ceiling panels warped and blurred as the Ministry staff swarmed the micro-office.

Then everything went black.

A man in crystal-lensed goggles with a chrysalis in the back emerged in the middle of the dilapidated room. Blood trickled from the back of his neck. A second man, far his senior, clung to the crook of his arm. A figure of indeterminate gender clutched the second man's ankles, scrambling upright as more of itself came into view. Blood burbled from an open wound on the back of its neck.

Shortly after they had all emerged, the goggled man pried the genderless one's hands off of the elder. As the elder shuffled off to the corner of the room, the one in goggles assaulted the genderless one until it was left lying facedown again. He pushed it back to where they had emerged until its legs vanished as though swallowed by the very air around them.

He fiddled with the back of his goggles. The crystal lenses dulled. The genderless one went limp. He pulled it forward, showing that everything below its abdomen had effectively been erased.

Sbaglien pressed a button on the remote, and the display went black.

"Were you able to recover any more film from that room?" he asked as he set down the remote.

"Nothing, sir," Inre said, "Everything before that moment was blank, as though the cameras were running but not recording."

"Interesting," Sbaglien said, pulling at his chin.

"Yes, but I would say the more pressing matter is those goggles."

"You're absolutely right, Inre. Any thoughts on where he might have gotten them?"

"I think we can assume he took them from that other person," Inre insisted, "It looks like the reason he's bleeding is that those goggles are fastened into the back of his neck. That fellow that dragged himself out with them was bleeding in the same spot."

"Perhaps, you're right," Sbaglien said, folding his arms, "But I think it's clear what we're dealing with here."

"… Is it, sir?"

"Phylus has stock in the power that was used to kill the Noble Doyen."

The next thing he remembered was the smell of leather and metal. Sounds came next, indeterminate conversations accompanied by a rattling rhythm. He felt the sense of movement next, even though he was sure he was sitting down. He opened his eyes to a view of his own lap.

"What's going on?" Sinkua asked.

"I'm taking you to the infirmary," someone behind him said. The nurse pushing his wheelchair, he gathered. "How much do you remember?"

"I remember… being shocked," Sinkua managed. His head snapped up. "Where's MarLys?"

"Right, you were electrocuted, and you blacked out."

"But I'm fine now, and I need to find MarLys."

"You need to be checked for underlying injuries," the nurse argued, "You'll see MarLys at the infirmary."

"She was rushed ahead?" Sinkua asked, "What's wrong?"

"You know I can't get into details, mate," the nurse said, "But her hand was mangled. I'll be impressed if she gets function of it back, but there's no calling it for certain, mind you."

"Son of a bitch," Sinkua muttered, rubbing his temples, "Which hand?"

"Ahh, left."

"Shit."

"I take it she's left-handed."

"Yes, and it's my fault that she's losing use of it," Sinkua grumbled, "I was too slow."

"Hey. Mate," the nurse beckoned, "Folks in HR told me what happened. They said she'd been screaming for a few seconds when you punched through the door. They don't know how you knew, but they're glad you did."

"What's your point?" Sinkua asked, "If I'd gotten there ten seconds sooner, she'd be okay?"

"She was electrocuted through her right hand."

"Then, what happened to her left?"

"It arced through her chest and down into her left hand," the nurse said, "So sure, if you'd gotten there sooner, she might be fine. But if you'd been a few seconds later, she'd have had a heart attack, and you and I'd having a much different conversation."

"Whoa…" Sinkua gasped, his eyes wide and luminous. This wasn't the kind of close call he was accustomed to.

"You saved her life, mate," the nurse said, patting his shoulder, "Now, it's my job to make sure you don't give up your own."

Chapter 33

Uro drummed his fingers as he watched the urban scenery zip by through glass and trickling slush. This was his first time in Tanelen, and from here, it wasn't much to look at. Not compared to the rumors, at least. For all the talk of their incredible technology, it actually tended toward the mundane.

A sign of particular interest approached, but Farim didn't slow down.

"Um…" he spoke up, clearing his throat as neither of them had spoken in an hour, "The Arboreal Society? You just passed it."

"Sure did," Farim said.

"Okay…" Uro said, "Why?"

"Same reason I used an alias and paid cash for this rental," she said, "Where MalVek's concerned, you and I are both fugitives."

"You think he'd have lookouts at the Arboreal Society?"

"At least for anyone asking about the Sisyphus Fir, yeah."

"Hmm… Makes sense," Uro said, "So what's the plan, then? We're just gonna go to the park and get the clippings ourselves?"

"Pretty much, yeah."

"Isn't that illegal?"

"Pretty much, yeah."

"What about the request from Etrula?" Uro asked, "Or Yrlis's research grant?"

"First one's just scribbles on a sticky note," Farim pointed out, "And Yrlis's name will throw up red flags."

"On top of this being about the Sisyphus Fir," Uro realized, "We're just operating on the assumption that MalVek has ears everywhere, aren't we?"

"Pretty much, yeah."

After a few more blocks, the buildings dwindled into trees and vast fields encircled by sidewalks and dotted with streetlights. A sign indicated a public park. Farim pulled into the parking lot and stopped the car.

"They're still open," Uro noted, gesturing to the sign. He noticed houses just beyond the edge of the park, some with lights on in the windows. "Is this because we'll look suspicious if we come here after hours?"

"You got it," Farim said as they both got out of the car, "By the way, about these messages you've been getting."

"What about them?"

"How are you getting them?"

Uro pulled a burner phone from his pocket and held it over the roof of the car for her to see.

"This showed up at the front desk the day after we checked into that hotel," he said, "Unmarked. Guy in the lobby said he was asked to give it to me."

"What the shit?" Farim exclaimed, "You've been chatting on the phone with someone at Hillside? Do either of you realize how many people you could be endangering?"

"Whoa whoa whoa!" Uro recoiled, "For one thing, this phone can't make outgoing calls. I can't endanger anyone with it."

"Accepting the calls puts people in danger," Farim countered, "Mal-Vek can intercept or trace them."

"I don't think he can trace them," Uro argued. Farim folded her arms. "The caller ID shows a different number every time. And the messages are in a computer voice."

"ID spoofing and text to voice software," Farim said, unfolding her arms, "Not the most elegant solution, but it gets the job done."

"And if MalVek has to be in the path of the signal, it's easy to get around that if the informant knows about where he is," Uro added, "Just need to be west of him."

"Right, assuming that's how it works," Farim said, "And that the informant knows about his implant."

"Even if he doesn't know, I think Caylence would assume he shouldn't call if MalVek is between us," he said, "Just seems like common sense after all the other precautions."

"Let's hope so," she said as they walked into the park, "Come to think of it, I need to ask Dourias about your uncle."

"To see about enlisting him?"

Farim shook her head. "I think they might have met before."

A glass half-emptied of whiskey hit the table next to a skimmer hat. A woman's hand smacked the table while her other still clutched the glass.

"Wait, wait, wait a minute," Hibiscus urged, clearing her throat of whiskey belches, "He just got up and walked out on the interview?"

"Yes!" EshCal exclaimed more loudly than she intended. She took a sip of her whiskey. "Walked in without an appointment. Walked out without saying anything."

"Was it because of MerSul?" Hibiscus asked. Her eyes widened. "Does he know him? Are they plotting something?"

"I'm getting to that, dumbass," EshCal laughed, poking Hibiscus's forehead, "So, I called the infirmary, right? Because that shit in the rum."

"Right, right, right," Hibiscus said, nodding vigorously, "PavRal poisoned you. 'Cause he's a little bitch."

"Yes!" EshCal exclaimed, again a bit too excitedly, "So, they take me in. Give me some medicine. Bing bang boom. Groovy gravy, baby. And guess who I see on my way out?"

"… PavRal?"

"No. Had him arrested."

"MerSul?"

"Arrested."

"The…" Hibiscus slurred, trailing off in intoxicated befuddlement, "… guy from… the interview?"

"Sinkua," EshCal clarified, "And no."

"Well… Fuck you, I hate this game!" Hibiscus shouted, segueing into disjointed chuckling.

"It was MarLys, of course."

Hibiscus's entire face turned deeply askew. "… Who?"

EshCal thought over what she could piece together from past conversations. They had talked about PavRal, Black Tie, and, of course, Dapper Rabbit. But to memory, she hadn't mentioned MerSul before that phone call, so she could assume she hadn't mentioned MarLys either. It would've been safer to have assumed that five minutes ago, but there she was.

"Works in HR. MerSul was trying to make her take the fall for his spy work," EshCal explained, "Didn't work. Tried to kill her instead. Electrocuted her."

"Oh shit!" Hibiscus cried, smacking the table, "Was she okay? Is she okay?"

"Well, her sleeves were all burned and torn, and she had these weird squiggly scars all over her arms," EshCal said, "And her left hand was all... What's the word? Um... Fucked up."

"What happened to it?"

"I don't know. But guess what she told me!"

"No!"

"Okay!" EshCal said, "Sinkua ran in and saved her. Took the shock for her."

"Okay, okay, okay. Let me make sure I got this," Hibiscus slurred, "He walks in unscheduled. Runs off unannounced..." She trailed off, her train of thought no longer running on schedule. But she powered onward. "Because he... somehow... knew that... MarLys was in danger. And he saves her by... taking the hit... in her... place?"

"Um... Yes," EshCal said, downing the last of her whiskey, "Don't know how he knew, but I guess it's not important right now."

"You gonna hire him?"

"Kinda be a cunt move if I don't."

"You damn well better!" Hibiscus exclaimed, "That's the kind of man whose dick I'd suck without running the meter."

EshCal belted out peals of obnoxious laughter. She nudged Hibiscus's shoulder with her fist, wobbling both her and her chair. But her face turned aghast with an abrupt realization.

"Oh shit..." she muttered, "No. You can't do that."

"Only the first time," Hibiscus assured, waggling her eyebrows as she licked her upper lip.

"No, not that," EshCal said, holding as stern of an expression as she could manage, "Don't tell him that. He just lost his fiancée, and he..."

"Oh shit!"

"Don't sweat it. You didn't..."

"You mean I get to meet him?!"

"That's not what I meant, but..."

"But I could, right?"

"Well," EshCal pondered, "I have to return his phone. And I know where he lives."

"Let's go, then!"

"You have to offer to promise to not to suck to his dick," EshCal insisted, more emphatically than anyone half as sober could have done, "... Promise to not offer to... Yes. Don't."

"I promise nothing," Hibiscus said through a toothy grin as she plunged her skimmer hat down to nearly cover her eyes.

"Hibiscus!"

"Fine. Fine, fine..."

"Great!" EshCal shouted, "Now, go order us their finest cab."

"And after the cabernet, we go see Sinkua?"

"After the cabernet, we order a taxicab."

"Cab and a cab!"

EshCal watched as Hibiscus hobbled off to the bar. She downed the last of her whiskey, then checked her handbag. Sinkua's phone was still there. She was no closer to knowing why he only had Biroe and Malia in his contacts, but now, it seemed less suspicious and more just curious.

The head of Odin's spear plunged through the hardwood dining room floor as though it were soft butter wrapped in wet paper. He slid it along the grain and pried up half a dozen floorboards at once. Beneath, through the cobwebs and dead pests in the foundation, was indiscernible darkness.

A hand settled upon Sinkua's shoulder, calling his attention away. As he turned around, Elemeno thrust a small glass canister into his hands.

"I found this in the medicine cabinet," she said, "Epchen verent. Real good burn ointment." She poked his chest, just below the necklace. "Use it if your scars itch while you're down there."

"Lady Elemeno," Odin admonished, dislodging another slab of floorboards, "I must insist that you wait outside."

"I'll go when you go," Elemeno insisted. She turned to Nikasu. "Put some on your collarbone. It'll help you breathe better. You've been stuffy today."

"So, once we're down there," Sinkua said, turning his attention to Odin, "where do we find the apparatus?"

"Should knowledge and memory serve," Odin said, "it would be in plain sight."

"Drakougeneospa's security is historically unbreachable," Phoenix assured within his mind, "Only those of or welcomed by the Dragon Family can enter."

Odin shattered the crossbeams under his boot. "All is set," he announced, "Lady Elemeno. We depart."

Elemeno brushed a bit of dust off of Sinkua's shirt. She pulled his face down by the chin and kissed the middle of his cheek. She stepped over to Nikasu and, finding her a sight closer to her equal in height, kissed her on the forehead.

"Good luck, kids," she said, "I'll be cheering you on from the perimeter."

Sinkua watched them leave. Once Elemeno had shut the front door, he turned back to Nikasu. She stared into the pit with her eyes aglow in rich plum.

"How deep is it?" he asked.

"I can't see the bottom," she said, "It's at least thirty meters."

"Definitely couldn't jump it," Sinkua said, scratching his beard, "Do you think you could lower us in?"

"Maybe, but..." Nikasu pondered. She waved Nemesis over, and he swooped onto her shoulders, melting into his organic armor state. "Okay!" she exclaimed, "Now, I definitely can."

Sinkua tightened his sword harness and double checked that Epesol was locked in its sheath. Nikasu did likewise with Epelun, then climbed onto Sinkua's back.

Sinkua clutched both of Nikasu's hands in one of his own. The other, he held out and alight with milystic flames. Then, attached to his sister and two Etherworlders, he stepped through his dining room floor and into the abyss.

Shortly beyond the common foundation and infrastructure, he snagged glimpses of increasingly unfamiliar construction as they fell deeper beneath the house. He could only imagine what Nikasu could see of these antiquated and perhaps extinct architectural styles.

The arches, oculi, and other such tracery reminded him of the Radial Axiom Arena, save for some unspecifiable quality. So influential a place as this surely informed architecture for ages. But as long forgotten as Drakougeneospa was, even a place as old as Radial Axiom couldn't be any more closely derived than a handful of degrees.

Between the palpable air and the slow descent, it felt more like sinking into disconcertingly comfortable tar than plunging into an ancient abyss. In fact, it took him a moment to notice when they stopped falling. Dusty marble replaced the dense air that had enveloped them for what could have been one or several minutes.

Nikasu climbed off his back and paced around, staying within his milystic torchlight. "Damn," she exhaled, all but breathless, "Even I can barely see anything."

"There are sconces along the walls," Phoenix spoke into Sinkua's mind, "I'll lead you to them."

While Phoenix gave him the first bearing, he reached up his shirt and rubbed a glob of epchen verent on his electrical burn scars. He shut the canister and, without a word, thrust it into Nikasu's hand and wandered off.

"Hey!" she called out as the edge of his firelight moved beyond her, "Where are you going?"

"Oh, sorry," he said, realizing he'd forgotten that only he could hear Phoenix. He poured a tad more milystic effort into his hand torch, growing the flames and spreading their light. "Phoenix is leading me to some sconces."

"I'll come with you."

Phoenix guided Sinkua to the wall with Nikasu close behind, wearing Nemesis as a suit of armor. For the first time in thousands of years, residents by birthright occupied Drakougeneospa. But of the two who could truly appreciate the scale and gravitas, one couldn't manifest, and a linguistic barrier best measured in millennia hindered the other.

Phoenix spoke anecdotes from the glory years of Drakougeneospa, impressing their grandeur upon Sinkua as she guided him. He knew he could never appreciate it as much as if he recalled his past lives, but he put a concerted effort into honest admiration and reverence. But as he sparked the last sconce and turned to see the room bathed in rich firelight, the effort became unnecessary.

Hibiscus's head dipped and lolled, rolling back against the rear deck of the car. She crumpled the embroidered swan silhouette on her jacket with the back of her head. She stared at the ceiling of the taxi, trying to focus on something she couldn't quite discern. She rubbed her cheek, smearing her makeup and dragging it through her hair. A lump formed in her throat as tears collected on her upturned eyes. Spitting an expletive, she pounded the backrest with the side of her fist.

A thumb and forefinger gripped her chin and pulled her head down.

"You okay?" EshCal asked, her eyes unfocused and cheeks red.

Hibiscus snorted errant mucus deeper into her sinus cavity. "You…" she muttered, clearing her throat, "You weren't supposed to see me like this."

"Like what?" EshCal pried, "We've gotten drunk together before. You just got carried away."

"No. No! No," Hibiscus cried out, dislodging her sweat-stained underwire from the underside of her breasts, "That was always… I don't know… Controlled."

EshCal stared at her hard despite her glazed eyes. "... I don't get it."

"Of course, you don't," Hibiscus chuckled, letting the tears fall, "You're as stupid as you are strong."

"Now, what's that supposed to mean?"

"You! You talk like you've... fallen for me," Hibiscus sputtered, "But you didn't. You fell in love with a character. And you're stupid. You big... stupid... beastly bitch."

"Hey, now!" EshCal admonished, "I may a beastly bitch, but I don't think I'm stupid." She smacked her lips and cleared her throat. "Smidge on the short side, at that."

Hibiscus's palm clapped across her cheek before EshCal realize she'd even begun to move. "Get serious," Hibiscus scolded, "This is why I didn't want to see you outside of work. Clients can't meet the real us. And I really like having you as a client."

"... You do?" EshCal asked. Hibiscus nodded emphatically. "But... why?" EshCal rubbed her own shoulder. "Wait. Are you overcharging me?"

"What? No!" Hibiscus exclaimed, "It's because I never have to fake my orgasms with you."

"Oh..."

"Yeah. 'Oh,'" she mocked, "But now that you've seen what I'm really like..."

That same thumb and forefinger interrupted her again, and EshCal pulled her in to introduce their lips for what might as well have been the first time. They had met before, but never without pretense of masquerades and contracts. This was nothing more and nothing less than an inimitable fusion of strength and warmth massaging her own practiced yet unfulfilled lips.

"I like this version better," EshCal said.

"... Really?" Hibiscus asked. EshCal nodded. "Wow," she gasped, "Didn't see that coming."

"What can I say? I have a soft spot for honesty," EshCal shrugged, "In all its raw... unhindered... truthy goodness."

Hibiscus laughed and wiped the tears from her eyes and cheeks. "Well, if we're gonna keep hanging out like this, I can't keep you as a client."

"I figured as much."

"And we can't be friends with benefits either."

EshCal stared at her for as long as it took the cab to move two blocks. "Well, that sucks," she finally blurted, "Company policy?"

"Company policy," Hibiscus nodded, "Not sure how they'd enforce it, but I'd rather not take my chances."

"Fuck it," EshCal said, "You're my favorite Rabbit, but there are others I like fucking. Not as easy to find someone else I can cut loose with like this."

"Really?" Hibiscus asked, "There's nobody else? What about Spril and Yrlis?"

"Colleague and loose association," EshCal said, "You're not the only one living in a masquerade. I don't have friends. I have... connections... colleagues... co... not friends. It's all just... dirty baggage."

The glass partition slid open.

"Hey!" the driver called back, "Either of you live in this neighborhood?"

"No," Hibiscus said, casting a sympathetic glance at EshCal, "Why?"

"Then, this is as far as I can take you," the driver said, "Neighborhood's blocked off. Residents and invited guests only."

"How come?" EshCal asked.

"Beats me. Half of dispatch says construction, other half demolition," the driver said, "Either way, the ride ends here."

EshCal fished her wallet out of her back pocket and slapped the fare and a healthy tip into the driver's hand. She piled out of the cab with Hibiscus close behind, the two bracing on each other as the driver turned around and left.

"Hey, I was thinking," Hibiscus said as they headed toward the barricade, "Now that I'm losing you as a client…"

"… Yes?"

"Is it cool with you if I blow this guy?"

"That wasn't why you couldn't!"

"Oh. Right," Hibiscus nodded, "Was it because he's going to work for you?"

"It's because his fiancée was just murdered," EshCal reminded, "It'd be rude to hit on him."

"Ahh. Okay. That sounds familiar."

"So, does this mean you'll tell me your real name now?"

"Nope."

Sinkua knelt and ran his fingertips along the marble floor. It felt just like the handle of his dagger.

Standing in the center of the cloister, the apparatus stretched up just shy of the height of the torchlight. Penumbral light glinted off the ethermetals, dancing between the ancient arches high above.

In its vertical center floated a cube of brilliant ethermetallic rods with a smaller one in its center, conjoined to it by its vertices. Surrounding the angular formation were rings of various sizes and nigh countless interactions. As complex as this assortment was though, above and below, it was truly incalculable.

Sinkua's head craned upward and mouth hung open as he approached the apparatus.

"Wh… What is…?" he stammered.

"Give me to Nemesis," Phoenix ordered.

Sinkua took off his necklace and held it aside, leaving it dangling as he kept staring up at the apparatus. After what could just as well have been a moment as several minutes, Phoenix spoke again.

"Sinkua?" she beckoned, "You…"

He shook his head, climbing out of his pondering. "Nikasu!" he called over, "Phoenix needs Nemesis so she can talk to both of us."

Nikasu patted and pushed up on the front of her shoulders. Nemesis pulled off of her back, uncurling and filling out to his full depth. Nikasu took Sinkua's necklace and placed it around Nemesis's neck. The dragon's eyes rolled back, and Phoenix's voice emerged from his hanging mouth.

"What stands before you is Drakospekarda. The Heart of the House of Dragons," Phoenix announced, "If even one sconce is unlit, it is imperceptible and intangible."

"I don't…" Sinkua stammered, "I can't even imagine how that's possible."

"What do these rings do?" Nikasu asked.

"This is a mathematical and artistic representation of the three planes," Phoenix explained, "The Etherworld above. The Netherworld below. And the Omphaloworld in the middle. All as seen by an observer capable of perceiving one more dimension than is needed to traverse these worlds. Ten above. Six below. Four in the middle."

"Did the Etherworlders create the Omphaloworld?" Sinkua asked.

"In a manner of speaking, yes," Phoenix said, "That manner being that we engineered the seeds and left them to grow."

"What about the Netherworld?"

"That was an eventuality of an unfortunate complication. Our calculations went amiss and rent our growing universe in twain."

"Is that where the second life takes place?" Nikasu asked.

"Only for the worst of souls," she said, "They are rarely found worthy of returning after their sevenfold lifetimes."

"And those boxes in the middle?"

"That is a hypercube, a common Omphaloworlder approximation of four-dimensional space."

"But why is something so angular in the middle of all these rings?" Sinkua asked, "And right in the center, no less?"

"It represents the Dragon Family, serving as a reminder to themselves that they were but one pale aspect of a nigh incomprehensible multiverse," Phoenix explained, "It sits at the center, however, because they were still arrogant enough to think that the Dragons, and they by extension, were at the center of all things."

Sinkua took in a deep breath through his nose, held it a moment, and slowly released it through his mouth. Gazing up through overlapping holes, he pulled off his bandana and ran his fingers through his hair.

"So, how does this work?" Nikasu asked. She gestured to one of the many slotted podiums around the drum table on which the apparatus was mounted. "Do these have something to do with it?"

"Choose any two opposite each other," Phoenix said, "Insert Epesol and Epelun into them."

Sinkua put his bandana back on while Nikasu positioned herself behind one of the podiums. He circled to the other end and stood behind the podium directly across from her.

Overlapping ethereal harmonics of Hephaeseum running along reinforced leather rippled throughout the cloister as they pulled Epesol and Epelun from their sheaths. Then, Sinkua and Nikasu, last heirs of the Dragon Family, plunged their birthright swords into antipodal keyholes to Drakospekarda.

The two cubes of the hypercube rotated independently, the linking rods passing vertices in a way that suggested sentience. The rings rotated, flipped, and rolled across, through, and around each other. The Omphaloworld rolled inward as it expanded, achieving an elaborate form of stasis. The Etherworld churned ever outward until all rings were tangential. The Netherworld churned chaotically, growing and contracting but always falling just short of equilibrium.

As the rings settled and the echoes calmed, dozens upon dozens of panels formed in the once seamless walls. They flipped to reveal sword mounts along the entire circumference of the cloister at perfect intervals. Many had broadswords resembling Epesol and Epelun upon them. Several, however, stood empty.

"I suppose we're meant to hang up our swords now?" Sinkua asked.

"Yes, but it is imperative that you hang them upon the correct mounts," Phoenix said, "It is an additional security measure by which they whosoever activate The Heart further prove their identities."

"What happens if we get it wrong?" Nikasu asked.

"It would move you outside," Phoenix said, "In these circumstances, whether you would be above ground, I neither can nor wish to answer."

Sinkua waited while Phoenix and Nemesis led Nikasu to Epelun's wall mount. Once she had hung her birthright sword, Sinkua joined them to be guided to Epesol's mount. As he walked the perimeter of the cloister, he realized just how essential that guidance was. Without perhaps the closest of scrutiny, the mounts were indistinguishable from one another.

As he hung Epesol in its rightful place, the floor pressed upward.

Grass and topsoil rolled away as the foundation erupted out of the ground like brick bamboo. Spiderweb cracks expanded across the lawn, yawning into a network of chasms. The driveway shattered, airing the soil beneath for the first time in decades.

A few meters into the foundation, the structure expanded, pushing through the fragmented landscape. Crowns of ancient towers pierced the sediment and rent the chain-link fence.

The demolition and awakening overflowed into the neighbors' properties. Massive arrays of gears groaned as they erected spires and towers from their dormancy since time immemorial. Modern houses buckled and crumbled against the emerging forces of ancient architecture and mechanisms.

Columns and buttresses rose and locked into place. Discordant bridges and arcades rotated as they climbed, converging into a complex network of ambulatories linked by open walkways. Styles changed markedly from the center outward, but the transitions were seamless. It was as though the house had grown, rather than having been built upon.

When the ground calmed, Drakougeneospa towered over the remainder of the neighborhood. It spanned four square blocks and stretched nine stories at its tallest point, two at its shortest.

The modern house at its peak cracked and shed its siding like an architectural egg. From that shell of modern construction emerged a white marble cupola, adorned with frescos of dragons.

"Now," Phoenix announced as the quaking stopped, "Announce your welcomed guests to Drakospekarda. Sinkua! Lord of Drakougeneospa! Repeat after me, then state their names."

She recited the words in Harkzanian, slowly and deliberately. Sinkua repeated them with equal deliberation, fearing the consequences of misspeaking. After three strings of words, Nemesis removed the necklace and returned it to him.

"Name them," he beckoned.

Sinkua rattled off the names of every friend and trusted ally. Galo and Vielle, fellow Hybrids of course. Spril, a man who, like himself, had lived beyond his own death. Phylus, father figure to the Hybrids. Elemeno, who had become his matriarchal counterpart. Farim and Biroe, steadfast remnants of the Subtransit Resistance. Yrlis, the doctor who had realized the completion of the genome and found the dormant Hybrid Chromosome in all people. Malia, the double agent and mother to his sister in pursuit of redemption. BeiLou, who had risen from death to correct the errant ways of her husband. Gabdur, the medical engineer who had faked his own death and now fought The

Avatars in the open. Ophalin, the doctor who never sought to be involved but endeavored to cure him, nonetheless. SenRas and EshCal, ever striving for reconciliation. MarLys, the whistleblower who had risked her life to uncover an Avatar communication network. KalChi, the accountant who had helped expose the illicit funding of Laboratory 1341. Chekov and Dourias for the knowledge of The Coalition. Jex and Murdega for the connections. Uro for the benefit of the doubt. Luvros, in case animals also needed to explicitly be welcomed. Odin and Leviathan in case the same could be said of other Etherworlders. Sleipnir, that Odin's horse could have shelter.

He thought long for other names as he read off a list of his neighbors whose homes were expected to be leveled by Drakougeneospa. He wanted to welcome EshCal's friend whom he had overheard on the phone, but he doubted Hibiscus was her real name.

Nikasu repeated Phoenix's Harkzanian recitation and added one more name.

Eytea.

Sinkua turned sharply, his head askew and mouth slack. Nikasu approached him and angled her index finger against his sternum.

"Look at what we've done here," she urged, "I don't care what anyone says the rules are. If you want her back, there is not a damn thing that anyone in any world can say or do to stop you."

Chapter 34

Phylus knocked on the hotel room door and shoved his hands in his pockets. He gritted his teeth and closed his eyes, breathing through his nose. He opened his eyes and, much to his chagrin, saw a ripple in the corner of his eye.

Fortunately, it was only a rogue eyelash, but in his irritation, he all but spat on his own face as he puffed it away.

The whole thing was a vicious cycle. The idea of looking into his condition made him anxious, and that anxiousness manifested as visions of soft spots. Or at least it could, and the possibility alone was enough to make him anxious.

He couldn't smoke here either. Hotel regulations forbade it, and he had been trying to cut back, anyway. If he swallowed and exhaled just right, he could still taste traces of his last one on the back of his tongue. Since he had forgotten to get a coffee in the lobby, this would have to do.

The doorknob turned. Phylus unfolded himself from his introspection and composed himself into something further from the brink of a breakdown. Or at least a facade of it.

"Ahh, Phylus," Dourias greeted as the door creaked open, "So wonderful to see you, my friend."

"Same to you, Dourias," Phylus said, offering a handshake which transitioned into a one-armed hug, "All the better if you've got a cup of coffee to spare."

"Oh! I'm afraid we don't have a pot made at the moment," Dourias said, waving Phylus inside and closing the door behind him, "I can ask Malia to put one on. I don't know what it is, but hers does taste quite better than mine."

Phylus removed his coat and hung it on an empty hook. Dourias headed for the door to the adjoining room.

"Who's here, anyway?" Phylus asked.

"Aside from she and I?" Dourias began, "Just Gabdur. He'll be taking your samples."

He gestured for Phylus to wait a moment. Malia emerged from the other room and, at Dourias's behest, made for the coffeemaker in the kitchenette.

"Where's everyone else?" Phylus asked.

"Farim and Uro are still looking for samples," Malia said, "Chekov is at Drakou."

"And Elemeno?"

"Being the mother-in-law she didn't quite get to be."

Phylus's brow tightened. He turned to Dourias for an explanation.

"You haven't heard?"

"I know he was engaged to Eytea. But what does she mean by that?" he turned sharply to Malia, "What do you mean by that?"

"Sinkua was electrocuted when he applied for that job. He spent the afternoon in the hospital," she said, visibly taken aback, "How have you not heard about this?"

"I haven't been there since the raising the other day, and I watched that from my car," Phylus explained, "And Vielle and MarLys have been staying there, so I'm a bit out of the loop."

"Phylus," Malia urged, approaching him, "MarLys is in the hospital."

"Wait. What?!" Phylus recoiled. Patches of his vision blurred. He cast his eyes down. The blurs didn't move. His jaw tightened as he squeezed his eyes shut, focusing on silencing the thrumming of manifesting soft spots. "How soon can you have the coffee ready, Malia?" he asked, "Turns out, I need a fix worse than I thought."

Malia held his shoulder and kissed his cheek. "Just give me ten minutes, babe," she said, "Go sit down. Dourias will get you up to speed."

Phylus made his way to one of the couches. Dourias followed, sitting across from him on the other couch.

"The day after that meeting, MarLys was electrocuted by her co-worker, a double agent named MerSul," Dourias explained, "Sinkua ran in and grabbed her, and the current arced to him."

"Probably because of that necklace," Phylus said, exhaling a fraction of his tension, "But why is she still in the hospital? She didn't have, well, cardiac problems, did she?"

"No, Sinkua stopped that much," Dourias said. The aroma of coffee wafted from the kitchenette. "She had a bug in the back of her left hand. Keeping tabs to see if she was on the level, as they say," he continued, clearing his throat, "He shook her right hand, and the bug pulled the current across her chest and into her left. The bug shorted out and leaked battery acid into her left hand."

"Oh shit..."

"Indeed," Dourias nodded, "Last I heard, her best-case scenario is near total paralysis of the hand. Amputation is still in the cards."

"Fuck," Phylus exhaled, "Where was SenRas?"

"I assume he was too startled to react in time," Dourias said, "As I understand, it all happened in about seven seconds. And MarLys was under audit. He had never so much as suspected MerSul."

Phylus looked up as he heard mugs settling onto a tray. Malia returned from the kitchenette with three cups of coffee and the warmest smile he'd seen all week.

His encroaching bliss, however, was disrupted as a lingering blur in the air opened into a spatial abrasion. He cringed as Malia walked into it, but, as his stress had lapsed his judgment, she passed by it as though it didn't exist. Because to her, it didn't.

"You okay, hon?" she asked, bending to give him a deliberate glimpse down her shirt as she handed him his mug, "Heavy stuff, huh?"

Malia handed the second mug to Dourias, then took the last for herself as she bent down to set the tray on the table. She plopped down beside Phylus and leaned against him. He looked aside to find her looking up at him as she sipped her coffee. He took a long swig.

"I'm just glad they're both okay," he said, grinning as the soft spot vanished, "That could've turned out a lot worse than it did."

Malia nudged him. "Hey, wait a sec," she urged, "Something just happened to you. Your eyes got all... I don't know. It was like you were happy to see something, but you're just staring off at nothing."

"He had been seeing a spatial abrasion," Dourias deduced, "It disappeared sometime between when you sat down and when he had a bit of coffee."

"The cleavage might have helped, too," Phylus snickered.

"I thought you said those appeared when you were calm," Malia puzzled. She sat up and looked him over. "Phylus!" she gasped, mouth agape in happy astonishment, "Were you working a con?"

"Yeah. I'm not sure about Uro."

"But you trust him enough to send him off with Farim?" Dourias challenged.

"I trust Farim enough to deal with him if he pulls anything," Phylus clarified, "Now, what do you say we call Gabdur in here and get started?"

Uro emerged from the bathroom, trailed by soapy steam that smelled faintly of mildew. A matted white robe covered his torso, the garment looking to have lost any comforting texture some dozen clients ago.

"Give it thirty minutes," he said, "The water heater probably went out of date before we were born."

"You have a lot of experience with seedy motels?" Farim teased, clapping something against her hand.

Uro swallowed hard at the sight of a folded envelope in her hand. "Wh… What have you got there?" he stammered, "Where did you find that?"

"You tell me," Farim said, standing to get nearer to eye level, "I was going to do something nice and wash both our clothes, but then, this fell out of your pocket."

"Well, it's private," Uro said, snatching it from her, "It's for Doctor Ophalin only. Sinkua asked me to deliver it."

"And not tell anyone else that you have it?" Farim challenged, "Not even me?"

"Nope. So, when we get back, don't let on that you saw it," he said.

Farim shook her head and sighed. "I can't decide if you're really this naïve or just play it well."

"What the hell do you mean by that?"

"… You haven't noticed?"

"Obviously not, or I wouldn't be asking!"

"Half the group thinks you might be a spy," Farim countered, "The other half isn't exactly adamant that you're not."

Uro's expression went flat. He settled onto the corner of the bed, staring off at nothing in particular.

"What about you?" he managed after a stretch, "What do you think?"

"I haven't ruled out the possibility," she said. He looked to her with his mouth agape and eyes pained. "But I doubt it," she continued, "if that makes you feel any better."

"You expect me to feel better when you think I might be a spy?" he spat, "Obviously, you brought me along to judge me. If you say I'm not on the level, I'm out. And I don't know if you've noticed this, Farim, but I've got nowhere else to go!"

"I'm not judging you, Uro," Farim chided, "I'm keeping you busy while the rest of the group decides about you."

She plopped down on the other foot corner of the bed. Uro looked down at the envelope, then back to Farim.

"None of them put you up to this?"

"This was my idea," Farim assured.

"So, either you and Sinkua just happened to both use this time to test my loyalty, or…" Uro pondered, "No… That doesn't make sense."

"Once you know him better, it'll make perfect sense," Farim said, "He's not worried about your loyalty. He genuinely doesn't want me to know about the envelope."

"Okay, fill me in," Uro implored, "Why wouldn't he want you to know?"

"Because he knows I'll interfere," Farim said, snatching it and springing to her feet.

"What are you doing?"

"Interfering."

She ripped open the envelope and dropped it as she unfolded the letter in a fit of near-miss paper cuts. Her face contorted with shock and annoyance as her eyes danced down the page. Gritting her teeth with vaguely sympathetic anger, she slammed the letter against Uro's chest, only then realizing it was written on the back of a genome map.

"Get dressed," she barked, "We have to collect everything again."

"Why?" Uro asked, letting the letter fall as he gathered his clothes, "What's wrong with the batch we've got?"

"It's fine," Farim said as she tied her shoes, "But if we don't double it, that bearded jackass is going to get himself killed."

"What?!" Uro cried out, snatching up the letter with only one arm in his shirt. His eyes darted along the page. "I thought he was making himself disposable to protect her."

"Well, he has different plans."

"I don't get this guy! Does he think Galo can protect her better than making her untouchable?"

"He thinks curing her and letting himself die will fix everything," she said, "But we don't even know the point of spreading that disease. And if I let him let himself die, his fiancée's gonna kick my ass from beyond the grave."

"Wait. Can she actually…"

"I wouldn't put it past her!"

No less than two minutes later, they stepped out under the dusky sky, leaving a lamp and the television on. Farim locked the door.

"Actually," Uro said as they headed down the sidewalk, "It's just as well that we have to go back to the park."

"Hm? Why's that?"

"When I was in the shower, I remembered how to reach one of Caylence's old friends. He might be able to help us get back to ArcNos if the docks are too dicey."

"And you need a burner phone to call him."

"I was thinking of a payphone. Saw a few in the park."

"Hmm. Yeah, that also works," Farim said, her attention wandering along the cracked asphalt, "So, who's this friend?"

"Jax? I think?" Uro said, pulling Farim's attention to him, "He runs a bed-and-breakfast in Quarun. He and my uncle used to talk shop when I was in high school."

"Jex," Farim said, "And now I'm sure that Dourias knew Caylence."

Phylus settled into the armchair as Gabdur closed the door. He turned his hand up, bracing his elbow in his other hand. Meanwhile, Gabdur prepared the phlebotomy kit, proving remarkably capable despite his handicap.

Gabdur thumbed a cotton ball against the mouth of an iodine bottle. He clasped the bottle between his middle and ring fingers and flipped it over. After a moment, he turned the bottle upright and set it on the table. The wet cotton ball, he thrust toward Phylus.

"Rub this into the crook of your elbow."

Phylus took it and did as instructed. "Want me to cap that?" he asked.

"I've got it, thank you," Gabdur said, "Just work that iodine in. I'll be along in a moment."

Phylus kept rubbing the iodine into the crook of his elbow while Gabdur prepared the sampling syringes. Gabdur soon returned to his side, where he took the cotton ball and gave a couple of finishing swipes for good measure.

"By the way, I'm sorry I didn't get to bring this up the other day, but," Phylus said, trailing off as he searched for the right words and the courage to follow through, "I'm sorry about Galo."

"You mean about his uncle?" Gabdur asked, flicking the cotton ball into the trashcan, "I didn't know he'd told you, but…"

"Not that," Phylus said, shaking his head, "I mean he…"

His words faded into a decrescendo of regret as Gabdur's brow tightened with prying confusion. Phylus knew he had no business being the one to break Galo's news, and he'd missed his only chance to gloss over his mistake.

"He what?" Gabdur demanded.

"He never told you?"

"Apparently not."

"Of course not," Phylus exhaled, swallowing thickly, "I don't know the details, mind you, but he said…"

"It's about the cough, isn't it?" Gabdur interrupted.

"I think so, yeah."

"… What is it?"

"You're sure you want me to tell you?" Phylus asked, "I don't think it's my place."

"I may need to confront him to get it out of him."

"All he told me is that he's dying. He didn't say how."

Gabdur stepped back to the wall. He slid down and sat with his forearm across his knees and his face turned upward. His breathing became faint with a single deep breath coming every few seconds.

"That little shit," he grumbled, the corner of his mouth flicking up, "Stubborn as the rest of us."

"He blew you off when you asked about his cough, didn't he?" Phylus gleaned, joining him by the wall. Gabdur nodded and leaned into him. "He just didn't want to worry you. It wasn't personal."

"I know, but," Gabdur said, "when I had to leave, I thought maybe if he wasn't raised by me or my father, he wouldn't grow up to be so… well…"

"Self-destructively stubborn?" Phylus provided. Gabdur nodded. "Might be more of a cultural matter than a family issue."

"You're probably right."

"Sinkua's the same way, and from what I hear, he basically grew up in Masnethege."

"That's what they say," Gabdur said, "Both of them hate to show weakness. Or drag people into their problems."

"Not if they can help it."

"So, you really don't know…"

Phylus's phone rang in his pocket. He signaled for Gabdur to wait a moment. The caller identifier said it was being forwarded from his office phone. That was odd for this time of evening, but it wasn't unheard of.

"I really don't," he said aside to Gabdur. He returned his attention to the phone as he answered. "ArcNosian Ministry of Foreign Affairs. Prime Minister Phylus speaking."

"You need to be careful how you appear in public," came a female voice with a thick Southlander accent

"I'm sorry?" Phylus said, "Could you perhaps elaborate? And while we're at it, tell me who I'm speaking with? I'm afraid I can't place your voice, madam."

"Conspiring minds implicate you in an assassination," she said, "Mind how you present yourself, lest you become embroiled in complications."

"Excuse me, but am I to understand this to be a threat?"

"It is a warning."

"So, more a promise," Phylus asserted, "I should inform you that the ArcNosian Ministries do not take such matters lightly. Your number has been traced, and…"

"No. It has not," she insisted, "You misunderstand me. This is a warning, but I will not be party to anything that might befall you."

"Who is this?"

"A concerned observer."

She cut the line before Phylus could press her for more.

MarLys angled her left elbow on the tabletop, resting her stump atop an orange. She ran a blade along the rind, near the top. She set the knife aside and flicked her thumbnail across the cut.

Not deep enough.

She took up the knife again, this time pushing it deep enough to spritz citric acid on her right hand. Slowly and deliberately, she carved a notch in the rind. Easy enough, even if it took upwards of half a minute. But when she withdrew the knife, she flicked juice over the table and dislodged the fruit from under her stump.

Cradling the knife handle in the crook of her thumb, MarLys lunged at the rolling orange. Instead, she flung the knife at the wall. It ricocheted, and she yelped an expletive as she pushed back from the table. The knife bounced and tumbled over the edge, landing between her feet. The orange came right behind it.

"Everything okay in here?" a voice behind her asked, accompanied by a gentle knocking.

"Fine. Just fine," MarLys insisted, spinning her chair to face the nurse in the open doorway, "Just a little mishap with… well… everything."

"Well, just keep at it. It takes time, but you'll get the hang of it."

"How long does that take?"

"Everyone's different," the nurse said, "By the way, there's someone here to see you, if you'd like to take a break."

"Oh? Who is it?"

"Prime Minister SenRas."

MarLys's expression flattened. She bent down to pick up the orange and set it on the table. Holding that in place with her stump, she retrieved the knife from the floor. As she righted herself, she drew back her stump and plunged the knife through the orange, skewering it to the table.

"I guess I should talk to him," MarLys said at last, "Send him in, please."

The nurse withdrew from the doorway. MarLys returned her attention to the orange, plucking at the rind with her thumbnail. It was slow going, but the orange wasn't going anywhere. She was perhaps a quarter of the way through when a chair rolled toward her.

"What do you want?" she asked.

"What I want doesn't matter," SenRas said, "I'm here to reconcile. What that means is a matter of your discretion."

"You mean you're here to clear your conscience so you can sleep better," MarLys deflected, turning to face him, "Meanwhile, Madam Chode Hand takes half an hour to peel a fucking orange."

"I have no defense for that," SenRas said, "But surely you have questions you'd like answered."

"Just one," MarLys said as she pulled off a piece of rind as long as her thumb. "Why?"

"I assure you it wasn't personal," SenRas sighed, "My every instinct told me you…"

"Not that," MarLys interrupted, flicking the piece of rind, "I know why I was being investigated, and I know why you trusted MerSul."

"Then… What do you want to know?"

"Why did you let it happen?"

"It wasn't until he was electrocuting you that I realized I had been conned," he said, "I trusted him right up until that moment."

"I know," MarLys said, ripping a wedge from the half-peeled orange. She shoved it into her cheek. "So, why didn't you do anything then?" She spat a seed from the corner of her mouth. "I mean, for fuck's sake, SenRas! If Sinkua hadn't picked up the breadcrumbs that I left for him, you'd be airing your conscience at my funeral."

"For that, I owe you both my gratitude," SenRas said, "Both for saving your life and showing me my misplaced trust."

"That's great, but it doesn't answer my question."

"As much as I suspect you'll loathe it, the answer is simply that I didn't have a plan."

MarLys stared at him as she dislodged another wedge. She stuffed it in her mouth, her eyes never wavering as she chewed. She spat the seeds and swallowed the rest.

"What the fuck do you mean?" she blurted out at last, "You're the guy who took down two Avatars with a piece of chain and a dirty shirt. You're a legend among everyone who hates them. And you expect me to believe that you didn't help me because you didn't have a fucking plan!?"

"I entered both of those fights knowing and in control of the circumstances," SenRas countered, "The truth is, my real weapon is manipulation. I'm no less a victim of diminished faculties than anyone else my age. If I ever appear swift, it's only because I had the fortune of foresight."

MarLys folded her arms and looked him over. After a moment, she sighed and shook her head.

"I guess, sometimes I forget how old you are," she said, "Sorry."

"Don't apologize," he insisted, "That's how I mean to be seen."

"I'll keep your secret then," MarLys promised, picking off a third wedge, "And I guess if your mind is your real weapon, you'll need someone around to keep it sharp."

"Your job will wait for you when you finish physical therapy," SenRas said, "I've even arranged to have you fitted with the best available prosthetic. My treat."

"Were you trying to bribe me in case we couldn't reconcile?" MarLys asked as she began peeling the other half of the orange.

"No, I would do this for you regardless of whether you came back to work for me," he said, "Or forgave me for failing you."

"Is this favor transferrable?"

"I haven't considered that," SenRas said, "What do you have in mind?"

"I promised Vielle I'd pay her tuition to get her therapist's license," MarLys explained, "But I can't do that on disability pay, and they haven't said how long it'll take me to get back to work."

"Give me the number to the bursar's office," SenRas said, "I'll take care of it."

"Meaning what?"

"Meaning I'll pay her tuition, and you and I will discuss repayment deductions when you return to work."

"Oh…" she said, and that was all she could manage for a lingering moment. If he was more patient than the bursar's office and less greedy than the bank, this would work out to her favor. "Thank you."

"Don't mention it," SenRas said, "And seeing as you'll be repaying me for this, I'll still buy that prosthetic I promised you."

Gabdur ripped the printed sheet from the roll along its perforation. He held it at near arm's length, looking slightly down his nose as he read it. In a fit of nerves, he scratched his leg, crumpling the paper against it. Looking again, his brow tightened in equal parts disappointment and frustration.

"Your blood chromium levels are in the normal range, too," he said, turning to Phylus, "That's the last blood test."

"It's just as well," Phylus said, "I passed my seasonal quota of orange juice and protein crackers three draws ago."

Gabdur managed a rueful chuckle. "Well, the good news is that we've eliminated a lot of possibilities," he said, "The bad news is that the other tests will be considerably more painful."

"What do you have in mind?"

"Spinal taps and biopsies."

Phylus's mouth narrowed and eyebrows flew up. "What sort of biopsies?"

"Neural," Gabdur said, "Brain stem and visual cortex."

Phylus scratched the back of his neck. "How drunk do I get to be?"

"Hmm? I didn't think about that," Gabdur said, rubbing his chin, "You get weird about anything hard touching you back there, don't you?"

"You noticed that, huh?" Phylus asked, fidgeting with his shirt collar.

"Not until just now," Gabdur admitted, "But now that I think about it, I haven't seen you in a starched collar since you came back."

A knock came at the door. Gabdur gave Phylus an inquisitive look, only to have it reciprocated. Malia and Dourias had left for Drakougeneospa a while ago, and Chekov knew his reasons for staying behind.

Gabdur opened the door with no particular expectations, only to feel like the contents of his chest cavity dropped into his lower abdomen. Galo stood outside the hotel suite with Nikasu at his side. Gabdur swallowed hard.

"I guess there's no more putting it off, huh?" he asked.

"No more putting…?" Galo puzzled. His confusion softened into sorrow. "Phylus told you, didn't he?"

"Yeah," Gabdur rasped, "So, what is it? I won't gloat if it's the cough."

"I have cancer," Galo said, "Stage three. Lung. Inoperable."

"Son of a bitch."

Galo snickered and scratched his leg. "That's no way to talk about your late wife."

Gabdur squinted and drew in his lips as he smiled, trying not to laugh as he reached out and patted Galo's shoulder. "Well, it's clear enough that that's not what you came here about," he said, "What's going on?"

Galo ran his hand through Sleipnir's mane. The octopedal horse kicked and pranced in place, still reveling in his new home even days later. As Galo thought on it, he realized that Sleipnir's joy went beyond merely having shelter. He had been locked out of the Omphaloworld for millennia and returned to a world wholly alien from the one he left beyond. The musk of Drakougeneospa may have been his last sanctuary of familiarity.

"I bet Elemeno goes crazy over you, huh?" Galo asked, neither expecting nor receiving a vocal response, "All this hair and eight hooves to tend to. She lost one of her horses last year. Adopted that one's brother out more recently."

"Galo!" Sinkua called over, "We're waiting for you."

Galo apologized and gave Sleipnir one last pat. He then hurried over to join Sinkua, Vielle, and Nikasu before the panoramic pebble mosaic map of Ouristihra as it had been in antiquity. Odin stood aside, supervising. In the corner of his eye, Galo stole a glimpse of a smile.

"So, who's going first?" Galo asked, "Nikasu?"

"I'll go," Vielle offered, "She could do without the pressure."

Vielle stood at arm's length from the map and extended her hands toward it. She closed her eyes and slowed her breathing as she pressed her fingertips against the stone. Her shoulders trembled, and the shaking radiated down her torso and along her limbs. Dust danced off the map as the tiny stones rattled.

A cluster of pebbles emitted a pine green shimmer, which grew to a steady glow as it branched and spread. Glowing green lines branched nearly all over the map, eventually reaching beyond the most distant current landmasses. A circular patch in the Southland Sea remained untouched though, an anomaly which surely indicated The Veil.

Vielle opened her eyes and stepped back, wiping the sweat from the back of her neck. Sinkua offered his bandana to her. She thanked him and apologized before wiping her face with it.

"Why am I surprised that that worked?" she chuckled, looking over the map. Still catching her breath, she gestured to the pebble mural, adorned with a snaking network of emerald lines. "Well," she said, "There's Yggdrasil's root system. Who's got the diagram?"

"I still have it," Odin spoke up, unfolding the paper as he approached, "And that is technically not Yggdrasil's roots but the arboreal leylines."

"Which Yggdrasil follows, right?"

"Largely, yes."

"Then, I'm calling it close enough," Vielle said, snatching the diagram. She turned to Sinkua. "Here," she said, holding the diagram out to him, "You'd be able to tell better than anyone."

Sinkua stepped back from the mural and held the diagram at arm's length. He closed one eye and shifted his arm little by little. After a few moments, he sighed and lowered his arm.

"It's a near perfect match," he said.

"So, MalVek knew Yggdrasil would come back at least ten years ago?" Nikasu asked as Sinkua and Vielle swapped the diagram and his bandana, "That's just... How do we fight someone with that kind of foresight?"

"Maybe it isn't foresight," Sinkua suggested, "We don't know when Pahres started to change."

"Just that it was around the time when the Platinum Orchid first appeared," Vielle added, nodding along.

"Maybe Yggdrasil isn't necessary for any of this," Galo said.

"It is possible that you are correct," Odin said, "Any form of energy that can move through Yggdrasil may also move through the arboreal leylines. The only caveat is that it does not move as efficiently."

"In either case, MalVek could only be calling the shots once something becomes inevitable," Sinkua suggested, "It's not foresight. He's just hoarding knowledge."

"I wish I could believe that," Nikasu said, shaking her head, "But I've been behind their lines. I've heard things. Even before he outed himself as a traitor, I felt..." She trailed off, her eyes narrowing with deepening contemplation. "Wait," she exhaled, "When they had me in the actuation chamber, I heard one of the techs say 'attempted activation.' Why would he say 'attempted' if..."?

"He didn't know Yggdrasil could distribute the activation," Sinkua realized, "MalVek's playing The Avatars, too. He's got them believing their whole endgame was built around you being the distributor."

"And you being the activator," Nikasu added, "But since Vielle planted Yggdrasil... I wonder if that's what Yahsek meant by pitting us against each other."

"Stronger one is the activator. The other is afflicted," Sinkua said, "Possibly. Probably. It would mean MalVek was willing to share his real plan with him."

"He probably framed it as a rehashing when it looked like they couldn't stop Vielle from planting the Platinum Orchid," Galo suggested, faintly aware of his voice trailing off. "By the way, I need to go back down there," he said, pointing to the anomaly on the map, "Nikasu, could you join me?"

"You and I alone at sea for a few days?" Nikasu asked, "I think I can manage that."

"We need to bring Gabdur as well," Galo said, "But I'll make sure that you and I have some time alone." He turned to Sinkua and Vielle. "I'd ask you two, but you have work and school. Plus, well, someone needs to monitor things up here."

"I understand," Sinkua said, patting his shoulder, "This is about the weird currents, isn't it?"

Galo nodded. "Also, Borret said something about being pressed into servitude on an island," he added, "I have my doubts, but the only theory I have is that he was talking about the Masnethegean annex."

Chapter 35

At just over a week since the raising of Drakougeneospa, the bustle of other families moving in had gone on long enough to become ambient noise. Spril wandered about, keeping his mind adrift and nerves calm as he traced the intricate line work with his eyes. He sidestepped and pivoted around movers and new residents now and again, only ever watching them in his periphery.

He bumped fists with Sinkua as he came through with a man and three children in tow. As sure as Spril was that he didn't recognize the man, something about him stirred up thoughts of billiards and diluted Schauzen's Deluxe. Nothing worth pursuing, but it was a curiously particular thought.

"We're almost ready for you," Chekov called over, "Come in here, please."

Spril spun on his heel, letting his other foot float limply. He ambled toward the study with no particular haste and just as much hesitation. As he entered, he found Chekov and Yrlis working side by side over a table. They moved in concert beyond that of a master and her apprentice, but not quite at that of partners.

"Perfect timing!" Yrlis remarked, her voice lilting, "The serum is all set. Come over here, husband."

Spril crossed the study to join his wife and mother-in-law in front of an apothecary table. Since the last of The Coalition had begun moving into Drakougeneospa, Chekov had been repurposing it to suit their more bleeding-edge pursuits.

"By the way," Spril said, "When is Gabdur moving in here with the rest of you?"

"Farim and Uro need to come home first. But I should say he'll be a more regular presence here once he's concluded his testing with Phylus," Chekov said, "He doesn't want to risk contaminating his work in transit."

"That's what I was getting at," Spril clarified, "When is he going to be done with Phylus?"

"He said it could be a few days, depending on how many biopsies he needs," Chekov said, "So, I should say he'll be done soon."

"Galo and Nikasu went to see Gabdur," Yrlis provided, "They said it was about the leyline map."

"What about it?" Chekov beckoned.

"I didn't ask," Yrlis shrugged, "They were in a hurry."

"Well, I suppose we'll find out for ourselves when they come home," Chekov said, "I just hope he didn't check out of the suite."

"Farim and Uro don't know about the move, do they?" Spril asked.

Chekov shook her head. "And we can't risk sending a message," she said, "Now, give me your neck."

Bracing on the apothecary table, Spril crouched before Chekov and looked down to expose the back of his neck. A tinge of metal on keratin announced the tip of a needle nestling against the base of his skull.

A sensation like burning ice coursed along his neural membranes. Tingling static shocks flowed over his body, enveloping him in thrumming sensations. He ground his fingertips against the apothecary table, drawing blood as he cracked his fingernails.

Curiously, that was the only unreasonable sound that he picked up

The sensations faded, and he let his body come upright and eyes open with a long exhale. He looked around, gauging his senses. His vision felt sharper, but he knew that could have just been a side effect of emerging from the fog he'd just been in.

A hand settled on his shoulder, and he turned to see Yrlis reaching out to him. "How do you…?" she began to ask.

"How do…?" Chekov interrupted, speaking from behind him.

"I feel okay," he cut off, gesturing to Yrlis. He turned to Chekov. "I suppose you'd mix red and blue, then add white."

Chekov beamed. "How do you make lilac paint?" she finished, "It's already working."

"Does this mean I can control those psychic moments, now?" Spril asked. Chekov nodded. "What about the amplified senses?"

"This will help, but later treatments will do more for that."

"Well then," Spril said, "Let's see what I can do so far."

He put his hands in his pockets and faced the ceiling with his eyes closed. At first, all he could hear was the blood from his fingertips gathering in the bottom of his pockets. The sounds of Yrlis readying first aid for his injuries were more or less at a proper volume for her proximity. He couldn't be sure she wasn't being overly loud about it.

Other sounds trickled in. The warbling of air around two exterior doors as a mover stepped into one and straight out of the other. The bewildered cursing of said mover. The frustrated cursing of his partner. The crashing of dropped furniture. Sinkua scrambling to apologize and rectify.

A young feminine voice drifted in from just beyond the property. Two masculine Southlander voices accompanied it, along with Phylus's unmistakable fading rasp, all to the tune of the low hum of a hydroelectric car.

Spril opened his eyes.

"They're almost back," he said.

"Great!" Chekov said, clapping her hands together. Yrlis, meanwhile, just looked at him with her mouth agape. "Let's see how Dourias and BeiLou are coming along with dinner."

Sinkua led MelDas and his three adolescent sons through the maze of corridors and conjoined rooms. He largely felt lost, navigating mostly by intuition, though a few oft-trodden places were already becoming familiar. They had booked electricians and plumbers to come lay wires and pipes in the coming weeks, but so vast an estate would be a lengthy undertaking. For now, people worked by candelabras, upturned flashlights, and, most impressively, a network of reflective panels left by the last residents.

Such was it when he led these new residents past the apothecary study. Long-maneuvered sunlight reflected off a disc on the ceiling, bathing the table and much of the surrounding space in warm light. Chekov and Yrlis had their backs to the door. Further down the hall, he bumped fists with Spril as he passed.

"Wasn't that was the Prime Minister of Defense?" MelDas asked, "I mean… Well…"

"Spril. Yeah," Sinkua said, "Come on. Keep up before I forget the way."

"Before you…?" MelDas puzzled, "Sorry. It's just that I've played billiards with a man who looked just like him. But he had hair, so…"

"Namias?"

"Yeah. You know him, too?"

"That's Spril. It's a thing he does," Sinkua said, "Or did once. I didn't know he kept doing it." He turned to face them, walking backward. "Do you mean you've never met him as himself?"

MelDas shook his head. "How long have you guys been friends?"

"Six or seven years," Sinkua shrugged. He flashed a smile at the youngest child. "I assumed you recognized him because you worked for him."

"My wife is another Prime Minister," he clarified, "She's been, um…"

"I know," Sinkua cut off as he caught the youngest son holding curious eye contact, "Spril told me everything I need to know."

A couple more turns brought them to something of an efficiency apartment. It had one large bed and three smaller ones, a living area, a kitchenette, and a single bathroom. MelDas directed his sons inside, insisting he would be along shortly.

"What's your take?" MelDas asked as the door shut, still keeping his voice low, "Do you think she actually did it?"

"Do you think she could?" Sinkua deflected, "I don't know enough to judge."

"That's the most reasonable answer I've heard yet."

"Besides, Spril said you and your kids need a safe place to live. That's enough for me. Her life choices don't define the rest of you."

"Thank you. That means more than you might realize," MelDas said, "But out of curiosity, what would you do if she had done it?"

"Honestly? I don't need to do anything," Sinkua said, "That's not the sort of thing you should worry about, anyway."

"My wife may have been involved in the biggest terrorist attack of the past century. I hardly think I shouldn't worry."

"Exactly. If she was, that should be your biggest concern. Not what I do about it."

"And if she wasn't?"

"Make sure whoever set her up doesn't catch on that you've caught on," Sinkua said, "And help people here hunt them down."

"And after that, you'll have her released?"

"Or break her out if we have to."

"What if I stopped her from confessing?"

"Whether she did it or not," Sinkua said, "you have to trust she has her reasons for confessing."

"You're right," MelDas said, nodding anxiously, "She knows what she's doing. I just have to trust her."

A distant thrumming and a near simultaneous crash echoed through the hall. As he realized what had most likely happened, Sinkua scrambled through MelDas's family's room.

Looking down from the sixth story window, he found a mover standing by the back door. Sinkua shouted down an apology, then rushed back out of the efficiency apartment. Now going as much on memory as intuition, he made for any staircase he could find to get down to the ground level.

Rounding a corner, he nearly collided with an androgynously styled figure coming in the opposite direction. Mostly, that was, save for an intriguing tinge of femininity. She laid her hand flat against his chest to stop herself and let out a small gasping laugh.

"Sorry about that," Hibiscus said, withdrawing her hand.

"Don't sweat it," Sinkua said, "By the way, this is embarrassing, but ah…"

"Yes?" she asked.

"Do you know the fastest way to the back door from here?"

"Yeah, I can get you there," she laughed, "Can I ask you for something though?"

"You mean beyond letting you stay here?" Sinkua asked, "Well, you did earn your place. So, what do you want?"

"You've been working for my friend EshCal," Hibiscus began, "And there's no way she hasn't figured out that you know my real name, and she'll probably start grilling you for it soon. Assuming she hasn't already."

"I already told you I'd keep it a secret," Sinkua reminded, "I don't grasp your reasoning, but it's yours to keep."

Hibiscus smiled and squeezed his hand. "Thank you," she said, "I just wanted to be sure."

The aromas of wood smoke and roasted meat wafted through the dining hall. Most of The Coalition, two Hybrids, and assorted friends filed in through the various entrances. Odin cleared a path for BeiLou and Dourias, who came bearing a long platter upon which lay a whole roasted lamb.

Over the next several minutes, the two retrieved the remaining dishes from the kitchen. Once that was done, they all gathered at one end of a long dining table, the first to feast there in thousands of years. Until then, with all the work to be done, meals had all been taken when and where they were convenient to the individual.

"Got room for four more?" came a voice from the doorway as BeiLou began carving the lamb.

Spril turned sharply. Phylus and Nikasu stood at the fore, flanked by Galo and Gabdur.

"I thought I heard you coming," Spril remarked.

"Do I really walk that loud?" Phylus asked, "Or is my breathing still that rough?"

"No, I mean I…" Spril stammered, "…Sorry, it's hard to explain."

"We started activating him, and now he has a bit more control over his amplified senses," Chekov offered as she scooped out some potatoes. She looked to Gabdur as she returned the serving spoon to the dish. "While I'm thinking of it, you didn't check out of the hotel, did you?"

"No, I didn't," Gabdur assured, "I nearly did until I realized that Farim and Uro don't know that we've relocated."

"Somebody will need to sleep there so they don't cancel our booking," Chekov said, "I'll leave you and Malia to make the arrangements for yourselves."

"So, the treatments are working?" Phylus asked, to which Chekov nodded, "Well, that's good. We need some good news."

"Yes, ah…" Galo began.

"Every blood test was a bust," Gabdur cut off, "I'm beginning to doubt we can safely harvest and replicate Phylus's new ability."

"Well, that's no matter for now," BeiLou said, "Come in and eat. There's plenty for everyone and then some."

The four of them found seats among the cluster of diners. All four Hybrids were there now with all known living parents. Odin and Nemesis joined them as well, while Leviathan remained on Galo's arm. Phoenix, of course, stayed in her necklace. Then there were the many remnants and hold-outs of The Coalition. Together, they dug into roasted lamb, numerous steamed vegetables, and various types of bread.

"So, we found something interesting on that Hephaestite map," Vielle said, breaking several minutes of vocal silence.

"A match for the diagram, I presume?" Dourias pried.

"Nearly perfect with Yggdrasil's roots," Sinkua said.

Odin cleared his throat.

"Sorry. With the arboreal leylines," Sinkua interrupted, "Which the roots follow, so we can stop nitpicking about it?"

"Insolent little…" Odin mumbled.

"Enough!" Chekov shouted, pounding her fist on the table, "Dourias, what do you make of it?"

"Nothing I'm ready to assert quite yet," Dourias said, a half-chewed bite of lamb tucked in his cheek, "Though it is curious that he knew Yggdrasil would return so long before all that business with the Platinum Orchid."

"Maybe, maybe not," Galo said, "What we do know is that Sinkua and Nikasu can both be activators or afflicted, and Yggdrasil acts as a distribution system."

"We believe that wasn't in his original plan," Sinkua added, "Apparently, some of the lower operatives didn't know that Nikasu could work as an activator. We think it might mean she was going to be a distributor."

"Rather, MalVek told them as much," Dourias added, "After all, regardless of what he said of it, he did draw the arboreal leylines into his designs."

"Do you know when the Platinum Orchid appeared?" Vielle asked.

"Only that it was while I was imprisoned," Dourias said, "But Pahres did come into the service of The Avatars shortly before they took me."

"Well, Nikasu, Gabdur, and I have something to investigate something in the Southland Sea," Galo said, "It might help you figure out the rest of the diagram."

Dourias hummed and nodded. "What have you found?"

"There's a circular hole in the leyline map."

"That's The Veil," Chekov said.

"Yes, well, people are being forced into servitude on some island," Galo continued, "I have a hunch that it has something to do with The Veil."

"And that it's on the Masnethegean annex," Sinkua added.

"Right, so Gabdur, Nikasu, and I will depart tomorrow morning to investigate," Galo said, "We'll check in as soon as we know something useful."

"I'm sorry," Malia said, "I still can't get past MalVek and the leylines. I mean, how could he…?"

"I know you feel like you should've seen it coming," Vielle said, "But you're no more to blame for being deceived than the rest of us. He probably made sure you didn't know who Pahres really was."

"Your powers hadn't surfaced when he made those plans," Chekov said, "But he did know about your ears. In fact, it was his idea to keep you a secret from Mortvill. Just in case you were the Yggdrasil Hybrid. He was afraid you'd be sacrificed."

"Why else would I have these ears?" Vielle asked.

"You could have been a Dryad," Chekov said, "They're the Yggdrasil Hybrid's acolytes. There have been a few to pop up since the tree was destroyed."

"Well, if Dryads can access the arboreal leylines, that would explain how Mal-Vek knew they were an option," Nikasu cut in, "He built his plan around Vielle once they had Pahres under their command. But he told The Avatars that I was the center-piece since I was more of a sure thing."

"Wouldn't The Harvester and The Omnimath both have known if a Dryad could be born into our generation?" Sinkua asked.

"The likelihood of it, yes," Chekov clarified.

"That means he had to keep you a secret from both sides," he continued, gesturing to Vielle.

"Okay, let me be sure I follow," Elemeno said, all heads turning toward her as she hadn't so much as cleared her throat the whole time, "Ten years ago, MalVek knew that Vielle would have the power to tap into the arboreal leylines. So, he built a plan that involved either Sinkua or Nikasu activating people with similar infections and Vielle spreading it. But he couldn't tell anyone about Vielle, so he framed it as Sinkua activating people and Nikasu spreading it through the gravitational leylines."

"Which was an easy sell since they already had me," Nikasu said, "Nobody would have suspected he was hiding anything."

"Also, he either used Pahres as a scapegoat or he genuinely needed his knowledge of the arboreal leylines," Sinkua said, "But yes, that's about the size of it."

"And once these three look into that business in the Southland Sea," Elemeno continued, "we'll know what he hopes to accomplish? Or rather, how?"

"Yes, hopefully this investigation will bridge the gap between his methods and his goals," Dourias said, "Now that he's bared his true self, it's safe to say that he's bringing everything to a head."

"Somehow, there's a short jump between this disease and bringing Pandora across The Veil," Gabdur said, "So short that we'll feel stupid for having not seen it sooner."

"And before we set out," Galo said, "there's one more thing I need to tell everyone."

Galo paused as he waited for all the sidebar conversations to end. Once the dining hall had gone silent, he bared the secret he had kept from so many of them. He had lung cancer, and he would be dead within three years.

Nobody said anything. They just sat, staring awestricken and silent. The only active reaction came when Elemeno rose from her seat. She walked around behind his chair and, without speaking a word, wrapped her arms around his shoulders, leaning the side of her head against his.

Phylus paused in the doorway to Chairwoman TolRou's office, casting a glance over at her assistant. He didn't look nearly as happy to see him this time. Quite the opposite, in fact, as he kept his eyes focused past him. Between this and the call a few evenings ago, Phylus steeled himself against his mounting anxiety.

"Madam Chairwoman," he said, lowering his head as the assistant shut the door behind him, "You asked to see me?"

"Yes, take a seat, Phylus," TolRou answered, "Please, excuse me for not standing to greet you. My knee is acting up today."

"It's no bother."

Phylus crossed the vast office, trying to silence his blind anticipation. He knew he had next to nothing to speculate from, but his cynicism snowballed despite this. By the time he reached the chair across from TolRou's desk, his thoughts were flooded with the worst considerations. Knowing how irrational they were did nothing to assuage his fears.

TolRou sighed as he sat down. "Well, I'm sure you're aware of the news," she began.

"I'm...," Phylus pondered, "Could you be more specific, please?"

"The news about Noble Doyen Joren," TolRou clarified. She pulled a stack of printed photographs from a desk drawer. "He was found dead in the same building where you were held hostage. I believe you will find these especially curious." She slid the stack across the desk.

Phylus took one look at the first picture and returned the stack back. The cauterized severs were quite familiar indeed. "You think I had something to do with this?"

"No, but members of the Tanelenese media and anonymous informants are making the case for it."

"Well," Phylus said, folding his arms. He held back a wince as the ridge of his hand pressed the bruise in the crook of his elbow. All those blood draws had left a lingering mark. "You wouldn't have called me in here just to tell me you're building a case for my defense. So, what's your angle?"

"I am building a case for your defense, and frankly, I'm offended that you would think otherwise," TolRou said, "But in the interest of maintaining public relations, we can no longer have you serving as the Prime Minister of Foreign Affairs."

"It sounds like you're asking me to resign," Phylus said.

"The idea came up, but no," TolRou said, "Parliament took a vote. We're merely asking you to relinquish your title to your second in command."

"So, you're asking me to switch jobs with High Minister Calhosin?"

"Yes."

"And if I don't, I suppose I'll be ousted?"

"Only for the sake of public relations," TolRou reiterated, "We're also offering you the opportunity to save face. This was a closed-door vote. Everyone will think you did this of your own volition."

"Well, it sounds like I have no choice," Phylus said, immediately regretting his phrasing, "I'm sorry. I don't mean to suggest that you've coerced me. I honestly think this would be for the best while I'm under investigation."

"I understand. And thank you," TolRou said, "There's just some paperwork you'll need to fill out."

"That's fine," Phylus nodded, "By the way, I need to confirm what time the trial starts tomorrow. I left the card in my pocket and put it through the wash."

"That's no trouble. There's been a change to the docket as of last night," TolRou said, "A memo was left for you."

Sinkua traced practiced patterns with his combat boots, scratching bass notes along the dense carpet. With it held in one hand, he drew similarly flowing patterns in the air with Epesol, kept sheathed for safety. He and his broadsword moved with fluidity equally unbefitting to their bulk.

EshCal observed with one eye on her work. Now and again, she called out directions and corrections, but mostly, she let him move freely and acquaint himself with her teachings.

"Who do I have a meeting with after lunch tomorrow?" she asked, "Watch the angles on your footwork."

"The Chief of Police from the capitol of Ierodhes," Sinkua said, "Discussing security hardware. Not that you asked."

"Good," EshCal said, "What time yesterday did I meet with the new head of the Haprianite Coastal Patrol?"

"Eleven," Sinkua said, his breath catching as he stumbled, "It was about those munitions they just happened to find six years ago."

"What's Hibiscus's real name?" she shot off.

"She's your friend," Sinkua said, never stopping but stumbling more often than he'd liked, "Ask her yourself."

EshCal laughed ruefully. "Did she offer you anything to protect her anonymity?"

"Such as?"

"Nothing in particular. It's just…" she trailed off, "You named her as a permanent guest in Drakou, and you're still keeping her name a secret. That's quite generous, even for you."

"She helped me save MarLys," Sinkua said, "and protect my grandfather. I would've been an ass if I didn't invite her. And the anonymity is because she asked politely."

The corner of EshCal's mouth flicked up. "What time is the court case tomorrow?"

"That was cancelled."

"That's not what it says on my itinerary."

Puzzled, Sinkua propped the sheathed sword against the side of EshCal's desk and came around behind her. Reading the itinerary over her shoulder, he found it did indeed still include FerLyn's court hearing. He mulled it over for a moment until his weapon in the corner of his eye kicked up a bout of recollection.

He unsheathed Epesol and put it aside. Holding it upside down over her desk, he shook the sheath until a crinkled and skewered sheet of paper fell out.

"Some squirrelly bloke from Parliament brought that while you were on lunch," he said, "I put it in there so I wouldn't forget. Yes, I'm aware of the irony."

Once she had gathered the last of her effects into it, Chairwoman TolRou locked her briefcase. She rose from her seat and, smoothing out her blazer, made for the door. But as she arrived and reached for the light switch, she took pause at a knock at the door.

Assuring herself of the small pistol concealed in her blazer, she pressed the intercom button.

"Office hours are over for the evening," she asserted, "You'll need to come back in the morning."

"This is the only way," the visitor answered.

TolRou couldn't quite place the voice, a shortcoming that she chalked up to the sound quality of the intercom. "Who am I speaking with?"

"FerLyn."

TolRou pressed her hand to the scanner beside the door. The locks disengaged, and the door came ajar. She beckoned the disgraced Prime Minister of Domestic Affairs into her office and shut the door behind her.

"What is this concerning?" TolRou asked.

"I'm here to plead guilty," FerLyn said with her hands jammed in her pockets, "To confess. Whatever I need to say."

"Your trial isn't until the day after tomorrow," TolRou reminded, "There's no reason for you to give up."

"I'm not giving up," FerLyn argued, "I'm doing what I needed to do all along."

"So, you did sign off on those contracts?"

"Yes."

"May I ask why you pled no contest?" TolRou beckoned, "Off the record, mind you."

"You and I both know there's no such thing as off the record," FerLyn sighed, "I stalled because I got scared."

"But now?"

"I've made peace with my fate."

Calhosin pressed his hand against the door, pausing to compose his words. This new paradigm hadn't been in place long enough to adjust to the change.

Eventually, he opted for the simple approach. He parted the doors just enough to fit his head through and peered inside.

"Phylus!" he called out.

"Prime Minister Calhosin," Phylus answered from what had, until the change, been Calhosin's desk. "What can I do for you?"

"I have a request."

"You mean an assignment."

"Yes, that," Calhosin said, "Sorry, this is all still a bit much for me."

"I understand. It's weird for me, too," Phylus assured, "But I don't blame you for what happened. Take ownership of the office. It's yours."

"Okay," Calhosin nodded, "Well, next week, we're completing the transition of the high-rise district restoration."

"Sounds like cause for celebration," Phylus said, raising his coffee mug, "At least I hope it's not too soon to say."

"Actually, it sounds to me like a cause for diplomacy," Calhosin countered, "I want you there on behalf of the Ministry of Foreign Affairs."

"I don't think that would be a good idea," Phylus said, "Half of Tanelen thinks I was involved in Noble Doyen Joren's assassination."

"Which is why you need to be there."

"I'm sorry, but I need to keep my head down unless I'm specifically called upon."

"Well, consider this specifically calling upon you," Calhosin insisted, "Tanelen is sending an auditor. Your presence will show that you're still willing to work with them."

"Or it will come off as apathy and hubris," Phylus countered, "Hell, it's bad enough that I'm still working here, much less as the damn High Minister."

"Phylus!" Calhosin boomed, "This is a non-negotiable order. Attend the transition or face disciplinary action."

Phylus went silent and stern, his eyes shifting along Calhosin's face. The corner of his mouth flicked up.

"This isn't about diplomacy," he said, "Except on the surface."

"You're perceptive," Calhosin said, "Sorry I had to get loud with you."

"It's fine. Sorry I had to push back," Phylus shrugged, "You want me to check for soft spots, right?"

"Yes, I do," Calhosin nodded, "But you do need to coordinate with Tanelen's auditor as well."

"Of course. I'll be there."

"You'll be meeting with Colonel Inre."

Calhosin shook his hand and left his old office to return to his new one, previously Phylus's. That outburst had done less than he'd hoped to help him adapt. He knew he might have to force it, but if he kept deferring to Phylus, it could appear that he meant to use him as a scapegoat. Worse, it could come to feel right.

Back in the office of the Prime Minister, Calhosin settled into his desk chair. As he studied the papers on his desk, his phone rang. He answered with pensive breath.

A panorama of fractalized light panels covered a stretch of the wall. MalVek stood before it with arms folded behind his back. He scratched his forearm, the slight ridges of subdermal metallic fibers still itching.

The echo of soft footfalls spread to fill the doorframe like cotton mesh. Silence followed, laced with palpable tension and anticipation. MalVek narrowed his eyes at one of the panels, pulling the image into tighter focus.

"Come forth, Jevana," he ordered.

Jevana came around in front of him, off to the side but still well within his forward vision. She kept her wrists crossed and her head down.

"What do you ask of me, Lord MalVek?" she asked, casting her eyes up expectantly.

"There is a radio station with international broadcast capabilities twenty-six kilometers from here," MalVek said, "Establish a gate into the DJ booth before tomorrow afternoon."

"Yes, sir," Jevana said, bowing deeply, "By any means necessary?"

"Leave neither witness nor casualty."

"Am I to understand that this is not a hostile takeover, then?"

"No more hostile than what I've done here," MalVek insisted, "My followers do so of their own volition, do you not?"

"Of course, My Lord," Jevana retracted, biting her lower lip, "I meant no disrespect."

"Of course, you didn't," MalVek chided, "No, I only mean to… borrow their capabilities. With their cooperation, mind you." He returned his attention to the array of light panels, eyes darting madly as he searched. "They will help me snuff out this treachery," he said, "You are dismissed."

He stood statuesque as Jevana left his sanctum. With a flick of the wrist, he willed the door shut. He pressed his finger to the underside of his ear. The sound of pensive breathing soon followed.

"Get the rest in position," he said, "Make ready for the exodus."

Chapter 36

The apparatus rattled as the dense metal gate moved along its tracks. The guard patted the prisoner on the shoulder and waved her into the ten square meter cell.

"Get comfortable," she said, "This is your home for the next twenty-five years."

"That'll do just fine," FerLyn managed, "I'll try not to cause any trouble."

"I have to say, given the circumstances, you're taking this well," the guard said as she closed the cell, "I can't tell if I should pity you or fear you. And let me tell you, that's a scary sort of confusion."

"Do neither," FerLyn insisted, "I've just resigned myself to my fate is all." She sat on the foot of the bed and took off her shoes. "Besides," she continued, "I'm in the second safest place in ArcNos."

"Oh?" the guard asked, leaning on the bars, "Where's the first?"

"With my family."

As the shoreline disappeared, Uro pulled the oars out of the water. He shook off the sheen of frost and laid them at his feet. Linking his hands between his knees, he looked to Farim and let out a long, relieved sigh.

"International waters," he said, "Now we wait."

"Well, I have to hand it to you," Farim said, "If you are a spy, you're very committed to your cover."

"How do you figure?"

"If I kill you out here, there'd be a maelstrom of paperwork before I even smelled a courthouse," she explained, "Could be decades before I'm convicted."

"Almost makes you want to trust me, doesn't it?" Uro asked, flashing a smile.

"Almost," she said, grinning, "I'll let you know when I see who Jex sent for us."

Uro's expression flattened. "I never told you he was sending someone."

"You didn't have to," Farim said, "Jex hates sea travel."

"Uncle Caylence never mentioned that," Uro conceded, "Sorry."

"It's okay," Farim shrugged, "Jex is what they call a Keeper. Dourias taught them how to recognize each other, but insisted they only interact with each other when it's absolutely necessary."

"Makes sense," Uro nodded. He looked toward the horizon, trying to make out the shape of anything at all. "I don't know who Jex sent, by the way," he continued, "All he said was that he knows just the man for the job."

"Another Keeper," Farim said, "Jex is the only one I know by name. I spent some time at Country Living between when Dourias vanished and the inception of the Subtransit Resistance."

Several minutes or perhaps a few hours passed in relative silence, save for brief exchanges and trivial observations. The sea rolled under their boat, signaling either a shift in the tide or an approaching craft. They turned to see a sloop looming over their second-hand canoe.

An anchor came overboard, and a man walked out onto the bow, waving broadly.

"Ahoy, there!" he called down, "Is that a lovely couple in need of rescuing?"

"We're not a couple," Farim blurted out, shaking her head at her knee-jerk priorities, "But..."

"Oh? Guess I was mistaken," the man shrugged, "Sorry to have bothered you."

"But we are stranded!" Uro shouted as the man disappeared behind the rail.

"Well, why didn't you say so in the first place?" the man asked as he reemerged, "You kids heading anywhere in particular?"

"East," Farim said, "And slightly south."

"Of course east. Ain't much use in heading west," the man chided, "End up in the endless blue before long. All that's good for is dying. Especially if you're the sort that doesn't wanna be found." He folded his arms and leaned on the rail. "Course, how do we know folks what get themselves lost out there don't wanna be found? Seeing as we never find them to ask."

"Can you help us?" Uro asked.

"Of course, I can," the man said, "Long as you don't mind we wander here a bit longer. I'm actually looking for someone. Lucky for you, hey?"

"It sure is," Farim said, "I'd hate to miss my reservation at Country Living."

A cheeky smile spread across the man's face. "I thought you might be the ones I was sent for," he beamed, "What's your names, scrappers?"

"She's Farim. Maybe you've heard of her," Uro said, "I'm Uro. You probably haven't heard of me."

"Well, Farim and Uro, climb aboard," he said as he hoisted a rope ladder over the rail, "Captain Murdega, at your service."

Nikasu straddled the starboard rail with one foot on the deck and other hooked around a pole. She gazed out over the star-dappled Southland Sea, letting the light cycle in her eyes until the depth of night took on a look of twilight. A wall of dense trees along the horizon slowly sidled toward them.

It occurred to her that she had never returned to that island since her imprisonment. The very thought of the place tightened her gut and dried her mouth, and she found herself white-knuckling the rail. Her forearms throbbed with a pain not entirely attributable to her grip.

Before the fear of transforming could run any deeper, she felt a hand settle upon her back. Broad and thick with callouses, but assuring in its firmness. Practiced in its touch, as though long versed in the art of personal care.

She loosened her grip on the rail and leaned into the hand. Tilting her head back, she smiled up at Galo. There was no point in giving her stress any further audience. Or in dragging him into it. He had come here on a mission. So as long as she could keep them under control, she could keep her problems aside.

"What's on your mind?" she asked, turning to face him more comfortably.

"Can't sleep," Galo said, "Too much on my mind. Same with you?"

"Something like that," Nikasu said, "My, uh... My rhythms are weird. You know? I rarely saw the sky when they had me. Never had a clock either. Hell, I couldn't even read an analog until Sinkua taught me."

"I actually didn't know that about you," Galo admitted, propping up beside her, "Wow. I am really nailing this boyfriend thing."

"Best I've ever had," Nikasu said, nudging him with her elbow, "Besides, the last man I shared a room with was a homicidal narcissist. So, you're certainly a step up in that regard."

They shared a laugh, then drifted into shared silence. The rolling of the sea came to sound like snoring. After some stretch of time, his hand found her shoulder. She looked up at him expectantly.

"How much can you see?" he asked.

"I, ah..." Nikasu fumbled, "I'm only using my night vision a little."

"Oh. Well, can you use your night vision with a telescope?"

"Never tried, but I don't see why not."

"Great," Galo said, "Because I'd like you to do some recon." He unfastened the spyglass from his belt and offered it to her. "Only if you're up for it," he added, "I understand you have history, and well..."

Nikasu kissed the corner of his mouth. "It's okay," she said as she took the spyglass, "I'll do it."

"I didn't even think about that until after we'd left," he admitted, "Sorry."

Watching him sidelong, she lifted the spyglass toward her face. She glided one hand out to the end with a twisting motion as she extended it to its full length, flashing a wink cheesy enough to serve with crackers and wine. Galo sputtered out fits of laughter.

"I think we're the only thing making this bearable for each other," she said, smiling aside at him, "I can't imagine you'd want to come back here if you didn't have to."

Galo didn't quite have words for this. Not in the customary sense. His response, rather, was a grunt that Nikasu took to be unenthusiastic agreement.

Nikasu set her thoughts on the horizon of tropical foliage and the glimmer of starlight on the sea. The lunar cycles had already put the triad of moons at vastly different phases.

Silhouettes formed between the trees as the light cycled within her eyes. The figures moved with perfect rigor, their spacing uniform and static. She focused on cycling the light more efficiently, trying ultimately in vain to see colors.

"There are people working," she said, collapsing the spyglass and handing it back to him, "Probably slaves."

"What makes you say that?" he asked, "That they're slaves, I mean."

"They move like they're used to being shackled together," Nikasu explained, "But as far as I can tell, they're not."

"Or they're under very strict supervision," Galo sighed, "So, that's what Borret meant. They're under some kind of enthrallment."

"What do you suppose they're doing?"

"I'm not sure. But I have a theory," Galo said, "I'm going to bring the ship between the island and Arestor's drop site to the east."

"Then, I'll check again from there?"

"Then, we bear south."

Time and again, Biroe's eyes darted aside, his attention pulled by what some part of him thought was more pressing than the conversation before him. Whether out of ambition or accommodation didn't concern him, but KalChi had assumed control of the discussion. Biroe thanked the contractor for his time and excused himself.

The roughened pavement rattled his wheelchair, even despite the all-terrain tires and suspension he'd had installed. Even though the volunteer crews hadn't been able to repave much of anything, it wasn't nearly as bad as it had been when they started. For one thing, the pavement was rather continuous now.

OshMar looked past him as he approached. JeiRol gave away his misgivings as he took a less than subtle step aside. Biroe gave him nothing more than an acknowledging glance.

"OshMar," Biroe said, nodding without reciprocation, "How are you holding up?"

"What do you want?" OshMar muttered.

"Just to say that I'm sorry about what happened with FerLyn," Biroe said, "I know she…"

"You're sorry?!" OshMar balked, "You testified against her, and now you want to apologize?"

"I'm not sorry for what I did," Biroe shot back, "I'm sorry she let you down."

"Save your crocodile tears for someone stupid enough to fall for them."

"Look, I get that this is difficult for you. She was your friend. It's hard to accept…"

"She was my best friend," OshMar snapped, "And she's in jail because of you."

"No. She's in jail because she committed treason," Biroe said, his brow and voice flat, "Like I said, I'm sorry she let you down. Not I. She."

"Her sons have to grow up without their mother," OshMar continued, "Their kids might even grow up without their grandmother. Did you even think about that?"

"Well, maybe she should have thought of that," Biroe said, his voice low. He leaned in, and his eyes grew wide as he shouted, "Before. She. Committed. Trea! Son!"

"You're such an asshole," OshMar grumbled, "You don't understand a damn thing."

"I understand not to piss on reconciliation," Biroe said, "And how to be objective."

"Oh, do you now?" OshMar scoffed, tipping his chin toward KalChi.

"Don't even start with that," Biroe scolded, "I didn't make my girlfriend my High Minister. I started dating my High Minister."

"And I wonder why you promoted her in the first place."

"Just because you think with your twig and berries doesn't mean all of us do."

"You really are an idiot," OshMar said, shaking his head, "You and everyone else. Let me show you something."

OshMar pulled a thin gold chain from under the collar of his shirt. Hanging from it were two rings, one with an inlaid sapphire, the other topaz. He unclasped it and passed it to Biroe.

"Wedding rings?" Biroe asked.

"Yes. Mine and my wife's," OshMar said, "Her name was Tulira. Most beautiful Feryan you could've ever met. I lost her and our son Vashiro during the war."

"Shit," Biroe managed. He returned the necklace and rings to OshMar. "I'm sorry."

"So am I," OshMar said, stuffing his hands in his pockets, "I filled the void with FerLyn's family, and now that that's gone…"

"You don't have to explain," Biroe insisted, "I get it."

"... You do?"

"Sort of. I didn't lose my family, but I was robbed of the option."

OshMar looked him over. "The accident blanked your bullets?"

"I don't think that's actually a thing, but yes, so to speak," Biroe said, "So, what's stopping you from spending time with FerLyn's family?"

"I don't know where they're staying," OshMar said, "They're in a wit pro safe house."

A shout from behind pierced the conversation. Biroe's wheelchair rattled as he twisted in his seat to find KalChi on her knees. The contractor offered her his hand as Biroe turned his wheelchair around.

"Hey guys!" JeiRol called over.

He pointed aside toward one of the rubble mounds. Fist-sized chunks of debris danced atop the pile. The beacon light flickered rapidly. Bigger pieces rattled as the tremors amplified.

Biroe looked to KalChi again. She was back on her feet, but the contractor still had her hand in a white-knuckle grip. Biroe called out as he powered toward them.

The contractor tightened his grip as more beacons flickered and debris hovered.

Among all the conversations and vehicles, Phylus caught notice of a Southlander woman in a highly decorated Tanelenese military uniform. Perhaps a score of faint geometric shadows adorned her clothing. His eyes shot toward every anomalous hum as he approached her, though he made eye contact once he realized she heard him coming.

"You must be Colonel Inre," he said. Her black leather gloves squeaked as they shook hands. "Phylus. High Minister of Foreign Affairs."

"Yes, I suppose there aren't many Southlanders in the Tanelenese military," Inre mused, "And I'm familiar with your work. I'd just like to say your act of diplomacy won't go unnoticed."

"That's good to hear," Phylus said, "I was worried my coming here might come off as arrogance."

"I can see how, but I would have thought you had a guilty conscience if you didn't come," she said. She looked around, casting her gaze beyond his shoulders. "By the way, I was told I'd be meeting with Brigadier General Elite EshCal as well."

"Oh, the High Minister?" he asked, "Or Prime Minister, rather. She won't be joining us today."

"Well, I'm sorry to hear that. I was looking forward to meeting her," Inre said, "Can I ask why not?"

Phylus's phone rang in his pocket. "That's probably her now."

The car that pulled up was familiar, but it wasn't the one she was expecting. EshCal's expression flattened as the window came down to reveal Spril in the driver's seat. No surprise, seeing as it was his car.

"You're not Hibiscus," she said.

"And you're not a Schaudie," he snipped back, "We're all disappointments today."

"Why are..."

"She's busy," he interrupted, "Get in."

Confused and frustrated, she complied. She thought better than to bite the offering hand and make things any worse for herself.

"Well, thank you for coming, I suppose," she sighed as she buckled her seatbelt, "How's therapy going?"

"Great for both of us," Spril said, "I get things off my chest. Vielle gets hands-on practice."

"Hold on," EshCal said, "You're seeing your kid sister instead of a real therapist?"

"She'll be a real therapist in a couple of years. And she already has a framework of who I am," Spril argued, "Besides, I've decided to resign."

"Well, I'm sure you'll think I'm full of it, but I'm sad to see you go," EshCal said, "But I'm glad you're looking out for your health."

"That's not my first concern," Spril said, "By the way, why didn't you ride with the tow truck driver?"

EshCal gave him a sidelong glance. If he was bluffing, his face did nothing to betray it. She sighed and shook her head.

"Driver said there's a policy against it."

"Really? Never heard of that one."

"Neither had I," she said, "But he said that's how it's always been."

EshCal's eyes narrowed at the changes in scenery. She thought he might have been taking a route that she didn't recognize. But it soon struck her that the shadows, for the direction they should have been going in, were wrong.

"Where are you taking me?" she demanded, "We're supposed to be going to the high-rise district."

"We're going to your assistant's house."

"Why?" she asked, "He's supposed to be at work."

"He's still at the office where you left him. He has nothing to do with this," Spril said, "My adoptive father asked me to do this. And there are only two people I have a harder time refusing than him." He set his eyes straight ahead. "And you're neither of them. So don't bother."

"Okay," EshCal said, taking a deep breath, "What's going on here?"

"Phylus suspects that Uro…"

"Who?"

"New guy. Assistant medical examiner from Hillside Oncology," Spril said, "Anyway, Phylus thinks he might be a spy for MalVek. Maybe."

"And what does this have to do with keeping me from my job?"

"Calhosin's also…"

"Hey!" EshCal cut off, "Did Phylus sabotage my car."

"Yes. Anyway…"

"Son of a bitch!"

"I'll be sure he gets the message," Spril said, grunting as he took a corner a bit too hard, "Anyway! Calhosin's also under scrutiny. Unofficially. Keep your mouth shut. Between those two and Joren's assassination…"

"He thinks MalVek will make his move today at the high-rise district," EshCal realized, "Given my history, he was right to separate me."

"He just wanted some muscle on the outside."

"I thought he'd be worried that they'd scapegoat me."

"EshCal," Spril urged, "You're the only one of us who still gets hung up on your history with The Avatars."

"Well, I'm still going to give him an earful for manipulating me," she said as she pulled out her phone.

"Do that!" he insisted, "He could do with the stress."

"Everything's being billed to me. Sorry. Gotta go. Bye!"

Phylus disconnected before EshCal could speak more than a word, and she didn't so much speak it as shout it.

"What was that about?" Inre asked.

"I borrowed her car last night," Phylus said, "And I may have accidentally left the reservoirs bottomed out."

"Well, that's incon..."

Phylus shushed her mid-word. He felt her glaring at him, but his attention was all but everywhere else. Distant air thrummed, and Phylus ground his teeth as he failed to zero in on the source.

A rumbling bubbled up through the low end of audibility as a hissing trilled down from the high end. Together, they rattled and skewered his spine like a series of tremoring needles. Inre didn't seem to notice either sound.

The hissing swelled into a sharp whistle. No time for words, he gave Inre a hard shove, knocking them both away from each other.

A broken signpost zipped between them like an urban javelin, vanishing through a ripple in the air near a rubble heap. Phylus looked to Inre apologetically, but he found her wide-eyed and clearly no longer concerned with his sudden aggression.

"How did you...?" she stammered.

"Single dad," he said, "Not much I don't notice."

"Fair play to you," Inre said, still catching her breath, "What the hell was that?"

"I don't..."

A shout from far behind interrupted him. Quicker than he could react, Inre had her sidearm trained past his shoulder. He braved a look back.

Biroe threw his wheelchair motor into full throttle, lunging with an impatience he'd never known. Just ahead, but still beyond his reach, KalChi struggled against the contractor. A pair of hands jostled his seat.

"Kill the motor!" OshMar ordered.

OshMar hit a swift stride well before the sound of the motor faded. Biroe thought back to when he and KalChi fled from biomech spiders out of Epsilon Burger.

He perked up with a start as JeiRol swooped in from his periphery.

Phylus's surroundings came into ever sharper focus. Beacons flickered over rubble piles, and from those heaps rose large pieces of debris. In the middle of it, KalChi struggled against the contractor's grip on her hand. JeiRol closed in from one direction, Biroe with OshMar's help from another.

A gunshot rang out, and a bullet ripped through the contractor's forearm. He screamed as he threw KalChi to her knees and clutched his bleeding arm.

KalChi stumbled away, rubbing her hand. She looked back at him, pity seeping between her fear and confusion as tears filled his eyes.

A piece of concrete glanced off of her shoulder. She winced and spun around to see where it had come from. Fragments of wreckage hovered up from the mounds of rubble.

She saw Biroe and OshMar rushing toward her. From off to the side came Jei-Rol, looking urgent for how little they knew each other. She waved them off and crouched beside the contractor.

"I need to bandage you!" KalChi shouted over the tremors, "Do you have a knife?"

The contractor shook his head vigorously. KalChi spotted a knife handle jutting from his tool belt. She wrestled the utility knife from its holster and, with the contractor writhing against reason, cut into the seam of his sleeve.

Something slammed into her back, driving her forward and plunging the knife through the contractor's shoulder. A pair of arms clamped around her and pulled her to her feet. The contractor scrambled upright and retreated on shaky legs.

"JeiRol!" KalChi shouted, "What the hell are you doing?"

Inre scarcely ruffled her uniform as she produced a knife from her waistband. But as she extended her arm, ArcNos's High Minister of Foreign Affairs grabbed her wrist. She glared at him hard, blade still pinched between her thumb and forefinger.

"Are you trying to start a war?" Phylus growled.

It wasn't an accusation. More an admonishment. As her temper cleared, she realized he was right to stop her.

First it had been Joren. That had gone on since ArcNos was split in two. He had just begun to pull away when Sbaglien fell under their guiles, and it wasn't long before he was found dead. Quite thoroughly, at that. Thus, in JeiRol, she only saw an Avatar influence to be purged. That clouded everything else, including diplomacy.

"Fine," she said, angling the handle toward him, "Take it."

He released her wrist and took the knife. "Does this mean the other twenty are going to stay put as well?"

KalChi wrestled one arm free and threw her elbow into JeiRol's stomach with the entire weight of her upper body. The Prime Minister heaved as he released her. She whirled around and cuffed him across the temple.

"Answer me, asshole!" she shouted, clocking him across the other temple, "What the hell is your problem?"

JeiRol straightened up and spat bloody mucus, smiling with everything but his eyes.

OshMar and Biroe stopped a ways off as KalChi clobbered JeiRol. Among all the rattling and rumbling, all the bits of stone flying about, a cacophonous clattering filtered through it all. OshMar panned for the source.

Some thirty meters off, half a sign post rotated as it bounced end to end, drumming fragments of busted masonry and rebar. It stopped suddenly, hovering a meter off the ground and pointing through all four of them.

OshMar called out as he hoisted up the back of Biroe's wheelchair, dumping him onto the ground. He threw himself down beside him, and the post flew from its roost.

JeiRol clenched his teeth and snarled, "For the arising."

KalChi's eyes widened at those words. In that same instant, OshMar called out to them. She whirled about so fast that her eyes only registered smears of brown and gray.

She found Biroe prostrate before his upturned wheelchair with Osh-Mar next to him. A broken sign post screamed over them, heading straight for her. Sooner than she could take cover, JeiRol's fist bunched in the back of her shirt.

In a single fluid motion, Inre snatched her knife from Phylus and sent it flying. She called out as it left her hand, and JeiRol jerked his head aside with his hand tangled in KalChi's shirt. The blade snapped his head back as it sunk into the corner of his eye socket, scarcely scratching his eyeball.

Biroe cried out as the pole plunged into KalChi's abdomen and erupted from her back with a spray of blood. He scrambled along on his elbows with a shame deeper than he'd ever fathomed.

Her eyes were empty by the time he got to her. His hands trembled as he cupped her face, leaving ragged bloody handprints on her cheeks. The entire front half of his body had been saturated in her blood as he dragged himself through the growing puddle.

A foot glanced off his side. Biroe looked up to find JeiRol staggering with a knife sticking out of his eye. He glowered up at him, the man who had assured the death of the most important person in his life. The man who had reveled in it. The Avatar sympathizer. The traitor. The saboteur. The interloper.

The murderer.

Biroe yanked JeiRol's foot out from under him, flipping him onto his back. No sooner had JeiRol landed than Biroe was upon him with his knee in his groin and a hand clasping his throat. Blood burbled out as JeiRol pulled the knife from his eye socket, and he stabbed at Biroe.

Biroe grabbed JeiRol by the wrist just as the tip of the knife pinned his shirt to his sternum. His eyes hard and steely, Biroe pushed back and twisted until he heard bones crack. JeiRol yowled and dropped the knife. Biroe snatched it up and brought the blade down upon him.

"You motherfucker!" he shouted, repeatedly slamming the knife into JeiRol's chest. "Bleed like she did, you bastard. Bleed like she did!"

Phylus and Inre converged with OshMar, and the three crouched around Biroe. OshMar put his hand on Biroe's back as he continued stabbing JeiRol's long-dead body.

"Biroe? Biroe," he beckoned, "It's over. He's dead."

"We still need to figure out what's going on here," Inre urged, "The workers are…"

Biroe whirled on her and pointed the knife at her throat. "You could have stopped him!" he cried out, "Her blood is on your hands, too!"

He slammed the knife down, but Phylus grabbed his wrist, stopping the blade just shy of the back of Inre's hand. Phylus glared at him as he took the knife.

"You know she couldn't," Phylus scolded, "Look around you."

Biroe looked up and beyond their immediate surroundings. His eyes widened as they passed over each pile of clattering debris.

"Wh… What are those clouds?" he asked.

"Those clouds," Phylus said, "are what's going on here. OshMar. Inre. Grab my arm."

The two complied, and their eyes widened just as Biroe's had.

"What are they?" OshMar managed.

"I call them spatial abrasions. They lead into four-dimensional space. Hyperspace," Phylus explained, "Some are dead ends. Some go through."

"Like portals," Inre said, "Are they what…?"

"I've seen the security video," Phylus said, "These were used to kill Joren. That's why I've been implicated."

"You figured it out, huh?" Inre asked.

"That it was you on the phone? Yes," Phylus said, "I stole some goggles that let me see and interact with them. But, they've had some residual effects."

"Sounds annoying," OshMar empathized, "So, what's the plan?"

"You can only see and thus interact with the abrasions when we're touching," Phylus said, "And as mean a throw as you've got, Inre, it's useless with them."

"You can only send things through when you're touching them?"

"Exactly."

"I was thinking this debris was getting sucked in," OshMar said, "Guess not, then?"

"I don't think you're far off. I've never experienced a vacuum effect with these, so it must be that someone on the other side is causing it."

"You mean like telekinesis?" Biroe asked.

"Something like that," Phylus said.

"You go after him," Inre declared, "I'll keep these two safe."

"What should we do about the contractor?" OshMar asked.

"He's not important," Phylus said, "But if you can get your hands on him, take him in for questioning."

Still clutching Inre's throwing knife, Phylus powered forth along the trajectory of the broken sign post. Some twenty steps out, he scooped up the bloodied length of metal without breaking his stride.

Debris glanced off his body with ever greater impact and frequency. He gritted his teeth through it all, even as welts began to form. His singular focus was on the roiling sheet of fractalized light straight ahead.

Phylus narrowed his eyes, forcing some semblance of focus into the warbling image. A stout humanoid form took shape. He pulled the pole back to his shoulder and hit a roaring sprint.

With a potent cocktail of adrenaline and a colorful expletive, Phylus slammed the pole through the abrasion. His body jolted as it suddenly hit a full stop.

An overwhelming force yanked him off his feet and into the hole. He planted his feet to stop from being pulled all the way in. As he steadied himself, legs in ArcNos and upper body he knew not where, he came face to face with the man responsible.

"Hello, Patriarch," MalVek spat, "Has that harlot filled your head with thoughts of vengeance?"

"MalVek," Phylus sneered, "I figured you'd pull something today."

Phylus pulled back on the pole with both hands. It didn't budge. MalVek's one-handed grip showed no strain. Phylus noticed ridges around MalVek's arm and bits of frayed metal poking out.

"Well, you know I just love to exceed expectations," MalVek chimed. He squeezed harder, molding the pole to his grip.

"What have you done to yourself?" Phylus gasped, "You've become a monster."

"No more than the rest of you," MalVek said. His other arm shot out and grabbed Phylus's wrist. "Which reminds me!" he continued, "What say you we see what happens when you can't see these access points anymore."

Phylus looked around himself and noticed a contraption surrounding the abrasion that he was sticking out of. MalVek had created a machine to generate a network of them, a far more advanced version of the portal strip.

"Jevana!" MalVek called out.

A glassy-eyed woman in a button-up shirt joined them. Her face was heavy with the burden of a singular obsession and whatever she had been promised for it. She gave Phylus the coldest smile he'd ever seen hit a person's eyes as she undid the first two buttons and reached into her shirt.

Phylus's gut churned as Jevana came up with a pack of his favorite brand of cigarettes. MalVek wasn't going to turn off the apparatus. He was going to stop him from seeing them. Less pressing for now, this meant his own colleague had betrayed him.

Jevana's eyes pulled his in as she took a long drag off the cigarette. She took it just so steadily that the embers never faded, never fell, reducing it to a filter and a full-length cherry. All the worse for Phylus's composure, she wasn't short of breath.

He felt himself hardening as she cupped his chin. She pursed her lips against his and worked his mouth open. Warm chills washed over his body as she released the smoke into his mouth in as long and steady a stream as she had taken it in.

A sense of urgency pulled him from his lust. Phylus slammed his palm heel into Jevana's clavicle, knocking her away. He brought Inre's knife through and slammed it into MalVek's eyeball.

MalVek just chuckled and clenched his eye shut. Phylus pulled back on the knife, but it wouldn't budge.

"I must admit, I did not see that coming," MalVek said, "But you've piqued my curiosity. Could you still see in four dimensions if you can't properly see in three?"

MalVek pushed Phylus's hand back, taking the knife out of his head with it. Phylus struggled against him, trying to wriggle free. But he didn't turn the knife on him.

Instead, MalVek pushed his palm heel against Phylus's eye socket and closed his wounded eye. Phylus screamed as a sudden stabbing pain shot through the middle of his eye. Blood framed his obstructed line of sight. The stabbing sensation radiated to the edges of his eye socket. The crimson framing clouded and darkened. The stabbing became throbbing, and soon, he could see nothing. MalVek withdrew his hand.

When MalVek opened his wounded eye, it was once again whole. Phylus pawed at his own face, his screams compounding as he found an empty eye socket and blood smeared over half his face.

"Hmm. Well, I suppose it doesn't matter if you're on this side," MalVek mused, "Leave. I'm done with you."

MalVek palmed Phylus's face and pushed him back through to the high-rise district. Phylus couldn't see the soft spots anymore, which brought on a moment of gratitude that his face had been last to come through. He heard Inre call out to him, then surrendered himself to unconsciousness.

Chapter 37

Farim observed the contours and nuances of the lobby while she and Uro waited for service. Nurses and administrative staff kept busy with all manner of work. She thought Uro might know specifics, but she didn't find them of any consequence at the moment. Curiously, though, she couldn't recall having seen this building on her drive from the western ports to Elemeno's house.

"This guy must have moved after he saw Sinkua," Uro said in eerie serendipity, "Look at this place. There's no way he has time for walk-ins."

Farim chuckled to herself. "Not why I thought, but it isn't anything you would know about," she said, "This place isn't along the route from Elemeno's old place and the western docks."

Someone settled in Farim's periphery, sitting stationary aside from the rapid clacking of fingertips along a keyboard. Farim turned to face this furious typist.

"Can I help you?" the nurse asked, somehow sounding attentive without so much as glancing away from the monitor.

"We have a delivery for one of the nurses," Farim said.

"Etrula," Uro added, holding up the two bags.

The nurse pulled her badge out on its lanyard, continuing to type with one hand. "That's me," she remarked as the lanyard retracted, "Sinkua send you?"

"I take it you don't get many personal deliveries at the office?"

"Not in motel laundry bags," Etrula mused, finally pulling her attention away from the computer, "Give them here. Let me make sure you got everything."

Uro passed her one of the bags, and Etrula reached in and pulled out the checklist. As she rifled through the contents, she put a third check mark next to each item.

"Did you bring me two of everything?" she asked, gesturing to the second bag, "Thorough. I like that."

"Actually, we…" Farim said.

"So, how'd you two end up doing this for him?"

"He saved my life," Farim said, "More literally than you're probably thinking."

"Same," Uro said, "Not as literally or even directly."

"Oh, hey!" Etrula remarked, "Did he get to see the lunar blackout with his sister?"

"He made it home just in time," Farim said.

"Well, that's just wonderful. I'm not even going to ask how he pulled that off," Etrula said, "So, you were going to tell me why you got two of everything?"

"His sister has basically the same condition."

"Different strain," Uro cut in, "Similar condition."

"He wants Ophalin to synthesize two versions of the antidote," Farim continued, "He actually just wanted one for her, but I'm not about to let him get away with sacrificing himself."

"His fiancée would kick her ass," Uro said, "From beyond the grave, apparently."

"Well, as entertaining as I'm sure that would be, I won't have any butt-kicking poltergeists on my conscience," Etrula said, "I'll make sure Ophalin gets the message about Sinkua's sister. Do you have her contact information? She'll need to come in to have blood drawn."

"Her genome map is in the other bag," Uro said, "Sinkua wrote a note to Ophalin on the back. It explains everything."

Etrula motioned for him to put the second bag on the desk. As he complied, she reached in and pulled out the taped-up envelope.

"Is this it?" she asked. Uro nodded. "Great! Thank you. I'll forward all of this to Doctor Ophalin. Tell Sinkua we've started the grafting process."

Farim and Uro both thanked her, and they wove around bustling staff to the exit. As they returned to the rental car, she considered how he had handled the bags. It could have been a coincidence. After all, there were only two ways he could have done it.

"I noticed you gave her the bag without the letter first," she said, "I suppose you did that on purpose?"

"It was a last-second decision, but yes. Sinkua's condition has advanced further, so it needs to take priority," Uro said, "Nice to know you think I could be that clever."

"I was thinking practical. The plan they agreed on was to make Nikasu untouchable," Farim corrected, "But I'll give you clever, too."

As they settled into the rental car, Uro cleared his throat and spoke again. "Well..." he said, "Would it be clever to think that Murdega might forget we're here and leave without us?"

Farim shook her head. "That whole thing is an act."

"I don't know," Uro said, "I feel like there's some truth to it."

"Well, if he did strand us, we'll have to call someone to pick us up," Farim said, "I don't have the cash on hand for two ferry tickets."

"I've got my bank card," Uro said, "I understand why you don't want to use yours, but I don't think MalVek is searching for me that tenaciously."

"You certainly don't have the history that I do," Farim agreed, "Well, let's just hope you're wrong about Murdega and that it doesn't come to that."

Nikasu peered through the spyglass over the Southland Sea. She couldn't see any land on any horizon. Her eyes flared a brilliant shade of violet as she let the starlight cycle within them. A long shadow coalesced just beneath the water's surface. She followed it with the spyglass until it terminated into blocky angles.

"It's an underwater bridge," she said, lowering the spyglass, "It isn't finished."

"They mean to reach The Veil by foot," Gabdur asserted, scratching his leg, "I'll ask Chekov if she knows how they broke through in her history."

"While we're here, we should check on The Veil," Galo added, "I need to find out if they've interfered with it."

Nikasu turned to the crow's nest, where her Etherworlder was perched. "Nemesis!" she called up, "Erkasi maz?" She turned to Galo. "That means 'Are you coming along?' in Harkzanian," she said, "I think."

Nemesis answered in Harkzanian, but to Nikasu's chagrin, he quickly surpassed her capacity for the language. As she frantically signaled for him to slow down, Leviathan surfaced alongside the vessel. Water flowed off her body as she peered over the railing.

"He wants to know where you're asking him to go," she clarified, "But he and I would be wise to stay behind. The Veil is volatile to milystis."

"What about me and Galo?"

"You would be hurt, but your tsora and Omphaloworlder flesh will protect you," Leviathan said, "Etherworlders are pure milystis."

"Which means The Veil could destroy you," Galo said, "That's why even Pandora can't get out."

"Precisely," Leviathan said, "That you possess tsora of the Omphaloworld and milystis of the Etherworld is how your kind came to be called Hybrids."

"Well then," Galo said, turning to Gabdur, "Would you mind tending to the ship while Nikasu and I run recon?"

"I'll keep an eye on it," Gabdur said, "Don't do anything rash if you don't have to do."

Phylus drew more than a few sidelong glances as he crossed the lobby. Colleagues and co-workers gossiped in hushed tones as they gestured to him. He ignored them as he waited in line, an easy task since nobody approached him.

"Good morning, VirLet," he said, hunkering down on his elbows as he reached the reception desk, "I need to ask a favor."

"Morning, High Minister. Stylish piece of eyewear you got there," VirLet said, gesturing to his eyepatch, "What can I do for you?"

"Could page Prime Minister Calhosin down here?" Phylus said, "I'd like to talk to him before I head up."

"Right away, bloke," VirLet said, "Go on and stand aside, will you?"

Phylus paced the lobby with his head down and his hands folded behind his back. Eventually, Calhosin emerged from one of the elevators.

Phylus noticed him out of the corner of his eye but continued pacing as though he hadn't. The man carried a satchel. An odd sight, but Phylus assumed VirLet had caught him on his way to a meeting.

Phylus spun on Calhosin as he came within arm's reach. The new Prime Minister flinched and withdrew his outstretched arm.

"Phylus. Good to have you back," Calhosin said, "My condolences for your eye. What can I do for you?"

"What you can do is shut up and listen very closely to what I have to say so you understand every word," Phylus asserted, his voice low and gravelly, "I know you've been funneling intel to The Avatars of Fate. I know you brought this upon me." He pulled up his eyepatch, showing his sealed eyelids. "And if I look hard enough, I know I can implicate you in KalChi's murder."

Calhosin looked him over. "That's quite a laundry list of accusations," he said after a stretch.

"Quite a laundry list of crimes," Phylus countered, "So, do you know what I'm going to do about it?"

Calhosin cocked an eyebrow. The man had no sense of contrition. He was all but goading.

"Not a damn thing," Phylus said. Calhosin's eyebrows flew up. "Not at first. No. We're going to go about our lives as always." He paced around him, gesticulating with the hand on the side of his good eye. "And eventually, you'll start thinking I forgave and forgot. Then, you'll stop looking over your shoulder. And the day after that happens," he faced him bodily, angling his index finger against the bridge of Calhosin's nose, "I'm gonna pry your eyeball out with a spoon. Not for a black-market transplant. No, I'm gonna put that bitch on a chain and wear it around my neck."

Calhosin stepped back and lowered his head. This was the first glimmer of guilt in his body language, and it was unsettlingly paltry.

Phylus gritted his teeth. Surely, the only way someone could so flippantly face such accusations from someone of his standing was to be near MalVek's degree of sociopathy.

"It sounds like we need to speak outside," Calhosin said, gesturing with a satchel strap.

"Was that a threat?"

"Not as much as what you just said," Calhosin chuckled, "Points for creativity by the way." He showed his palms. "No, it's just obvious that you wanted witnesses in case I tried to fight you, but you also didn't want people eavesdropping," he clarified, "That'll be easier to accomplish outside than muttering in the lobby. Come on. I can see an empty bench from here."

Calhosin brushed past him, leaving Phylus with no choice but to follow. He sat on the bench he had pointed out and laid the satchel on his lap. Phylus sat beside him, dividing his attention between his face and the bag.

"Well, it's about time you figured it out," Calhosin said, speaking at full volume, "What tipped you off?"

"That's my business," Phylus said, "But what are you getting at?"

"I got myself mixed up with them. I've come to regret it."

"Then why not just confess?"

"It's not that simple. You should know that."

"Fine, but why did a High Minister have to die for you to come clean?"

"Why did hundreds of civilians have to die for EshCal to defect?" Calhosin countered, "But no, she's not the subject here. I digress. But I had no designs on KalChi. If I had any control over the situation, neither of you would have been hurt."

"Weak sentiment from the man who held the door open for both," Phylus said, "What are you hoping to gain here?"

"I'm in too deep," Calhosin said, "I need your help."

"I know people who can help you escape The Avatars of Fate, but I can't help you avoid the legal consequences."

"I wouldn't think of skirting due process," Calhosin said, "No, I deserve whatever comes my way from that bench. I didn't have an honorable ulterior motive. I was driven by greed alone."

"You're trying to undo whatever you've done for them," Phylus asserted, "That's why you had to get caught. They'd catch on if you confessed."

"Your mind's in the right place. Look at this," Calhosin said. From the satchel, he produced a metal disc a bit wider than his palm. "That's a new piece of Avatar tech," he said, "They call it a lily pad. It generates a spatial abrasion around the holder and moves them to a predetermined location."

"Lily pad. As in a jumping off point," Phylus said, rolling it in his hand. The exterior was smooth and deceptively bare, "They've combined The Coalition's portal strips with their own hyperspace goggles."

"But unlike the portal strips, these are programmed remotely," Calhosin said, "I need you to find a way to reprogram them."

"Well, my best shot at that, nobody's heard from in weeks," Phylus lamented, "I have a few other connections I can tap though. How much time do we have?"

"Until I'm sentenced. I have to take it in with me."

Phylus chewed on the implications. JeiRol's brazen actions at the high-rise district came to mind. Then came MerSul and PavRal's coordinated assault on EshCal and MarLys.

"PavRal and MerSul have lily pads, too," he asserted, "There's also one in JeiRol's office, isn't there?"

"Those three and several others," Calhosin confirmed, "They're using this wave of Task Force vigilantism to have sympathizers and activists get themselves arrested."

His use of the third person didn't escape Phylus's notice. "Who talked you into this?"

"I… don't remember his face," Calhosin said, lowering his eyes.

"Because he was wearing a mask?"

"No, it's just that when I try to remember, it's like…. Well, it's not like there's nothing there. It's just that it won't come together."

Phylus suppressed the urge to shudder at the implications. "How many need to be reprogrammed?" he asked.

"As many as possible," Calhosin said, "I realize it's a tall order, but I'm hoping there's a way to access the master controls through one of the lily pads."

"Tallest order I've heard in some time," Phylus said, "Do you know where they're programmed to take the prisoners?"

Calhosin shook his head. "Just that he calls it the exodus."

Biroe traced the vaulted ceiling with his eyes as he sat before the ArcNosian Parliament. The Representatives sat on an elevated bench with Chairwoman TolRou higher at the center.

He drew his eyes down as he suspected TolRou was nearly finished speaking. Admittedly, he had only been listening in passing for some time.

"Prime Minister Biroe," TolRou called, "how do you plea?"

"I'm willing to submit to a psychological evaluation," Biroe said, "I'll even undergo anger therapy, should Parliament deem it necessary. But I will not serve prison time for a fit of rage against a dead traitor."

"Traitor or not, JeiRol was entitled to due process," TolRou argued, "Even were he to have been sentenced to death, it would not have been your place to carry out the charges."

"JeiRol was as good as dead when I stabbed him," he insisted, "Tanelen's Colonel Inre threw a knife into his eye. He was bleeding out."

"Well, since your passion for classical architecture took precedence over the reading of your charges, I'll explain again," TolRou said, leveling her eyes at him, "The autopsy performed on Prime Minister JeiRol bore out that the cerebral trauma would not have proven fatal given expedient medical treatment. In lay terms, he was alive and could have gone on as such had you not attacked him. Ergo, you are being charged with manslaughter."

Biroe's throat tightened. He had killed once before, and it had taken years for him to come to terms with it. That soldier whose name he never learned and JeiRol were on the wrong side of history, enabling treason and effecting societal sabotage.

But this time, there was no rift between himself and his victim. There was no societal fracture, no speculations of war. He had killed a colleague. He had murdered. And there would be consequences.

"I... I didn't know," he stammered, "He killed KalChi, and I... I lost my composure... I didn't... I didn't mean to..."

"Parliament is sympathetic to your plight," TolRou said, "And you should know that these circumstances are not without precedence."

Biroe furrowed his brow. His first thought went to Malia's murder of LenSom, but those circumstances were starkly different. But no matter his efforts, he couldn't recall any other

"Are you talking about the death of the previous Chairman?" he asked, "Because that isn't much the same, but I can't think of a more similar case in recent history."

"I am," she nodded, "Parliament is aware of the dissimilarities. Thus, you might anticipate a commuted sentence but not a full dismissal of the charges."

The door opened as a knock came upon it. Chairwoman TolRou's head snapped up, her calm demeanor turning to a scowl.

"You are trespassing upon a federal hearing," she scolded, "Please, see yourself out."

"I'm sorry. I have an urgent message for the defendant from Prime Minister SenRas," MarLys said, peeking in from behind the door, "It'll just be a moment."

"Very well, then," TolRou sighed, "Speak your message."

"... Right here?"

"Yes. If it applies to the case, we all need to hear it."

"I'm not sure if it's relevant," MarLys hesitated, "I mean... It could be. I haven't..."

"Just give me the damn message!" Biroe shouted, jerking around in his seat. His chest tightened at the sight of the clasping hook affixed to her wrist. "Sorry. What is it?"

"SenRas wants to see you after your case. He might be able to help you," MarLys said. She looked up at TolRou. "Would that be possible, Chairwoman?"

"A pair of officers will escort him to your Ministry when we adjourn."

"Thank you," Biroe said, speaking to both of them. He turned to MarLys. "Wasn't he getting you a good prosthetic?"

"Temporary," MarLys said, "I gotta go. Good luck."

Sinkua rifled through the papers on his desk, turning his head incrementally more askew as he worked. He felt EshCal's eyes upon him and tried to put her out of his periphery without her realizing. But even as his neck tightened, he could still see her out of the corner of his eyes. He sighed and looked her way.

"If you need something, just ask," he implored, "That is what you pay me for."

"Sorry," EshCal said, leaning into her backrest, "It's personal, and we're not close like that."

"Fine, then let me restain your desk," he said, gesturing to the scattered spots of peeled staining, "and we'll go from there."

"Why are you so hung up on that? I told you, maintenance will get to it."

"Vielle says I use favors as a coping tool," Sinkua said, "But I should dial it back from free housing and resurrections sometimes."

"Well, I suppose that makes sense," EshCal said, spinning her seat to face him, "Okay. There's that funeral coming up. Private affair. I want to put you as my plus-one."

"You need someone looking out for trouble?" Sinkua speculated, "No, that's not it. You said it was personal."

"It crossed my mind," EshCal admitted, "But no, I need you there as moral support."

"I don't follow," Sinkua said, "Aren't you closer with the Generals and Brigadiers?"

"That's the problem," she said, "I have a reputation as a stone cold hardass."

"You don't want them to see you cry?"

"I don't want everyone who sees me cry to take it the wrong way," she clarified, "They'll all assume my tears are purely patriotic. I just need one person there who I know understands what I'm really feeling."

"You used to count on Spril for that, didn't you?" he asked. She nodded. "I'll be there," Sinkua promised, "I didn't know you and KalChi were that close though."

"Oh! You didn't hear?" she gasped.

"I've been a little preoccupied. Mainly with worrying."

"Yeah, I suppose you would have a lot on your mind right now," she reflected, "Well, this is going to be a group funeral."

The carnage hung thick in OshMar's memories as he drove back to the capital. KalChi's torso split open and Biroe stabbed JeiRol's lifeless body, over and over, until his mind's eye was stained red. Then, the crimson melted away, and the whole thing started over again.

The drive had long been familiar enough to fade into muscle memory. It was only as a voice came on the radio that he took notice of anything beyond his horrible introspection. Not because it came in the middle of a song, but because this deejay didn't work for the station he was listening to.

"What's happening, everybody? It's your old pal Dirty Frog," the deejay said, "Sorry to cut in on the jams for your drive home. I'll get you back to that in a moment. But first, I've got a breaking story about to burn through my desk."

OshMar turned up the volume.

"Matter of fact, I want to address you as your neighbor, your friend. A fellow Ouristihran and maybe even a fellow Quarunite. So, this is Poralmus speaking from here on," the deejay continued, "As you might have heard, FerLyn, ArcNos's Prime Minister of Domestic Affairs, was recently arrested on charges of treason. Well, this afternoon, she was found deceased in her cell. Her death is being ruled a suicide."

OshMar's mouth hung open. The carnage of the afternoon melted into visions of his best friend dead in a prison cell. A prison cell that she was sentenced to because of his hubris and failures.

"Now, I know we all have an opinion about her and the case," Poralmus continued, "But let's remember that her husband and their three sons are innocent in all of this. So, let's have some kind words for the loved ones who survived her. I'll open the phone lines in ten minutes. For now, back to the music."

The broadcast repeated, this time with Dirty Frog's introduction mumbled incoherently. And again after that, now with every word of FerLyn's death ringing crisp and clear while the rest was muffled. Again and again still, until it was all a warbling buzz punctuated with mentions of FerLyn's suicide. And it was all set to traces of ArcNosian electronica music.

A bridge manifested in his line of sight. Absent any conscious effort, he jerked the steering wheel to the side. The nose of the car caved in as it broke through the guard rail.

As the car broke the water's surface, he banged his forehead against the steering wheel, knocking himself out. Not even the muffled screams from behind could shake him. With the contractor tied up in the back seat and the driver blacked out at wheel, OshMar's car sank to the bottom of the river.

The sound came as though through a burlap sack of molasses. She pressed deeper into the polyester fabric and synthetic stuffing as the warbling pounding persisted. Incomprehensible voices joined it.

She turned, and light came through her eyelids. The pounding warped into clanging. The voices became more distinct. She opened her eyes and found her cellmate glaring urgently while a guard knocked on the bars with her tonfa.

"FerLyn!" her cellmate exclaimed, "We've been trying to wake you for least five minutes. She's got other places to be, lass."

"Sorry. Sorry," FerLyn muttered, looking to the guard, "What is it?"

"Morning news," she said, flashing up a newspaper, "There's a story I think you'd be better off learning in private."

The guard looked at the cellmate. FerLyn shook her head.

"She's fine," she insisted, "Go on."

The guard opened the paper and passed it through the bars. FerLyn accepted and took it to the foot of her bunk to read.

Her face morphed between shock and despair as the reality set in. The cause was officially undetermined, but she had her speculation. OshMar's body had washed up on a riverbank, and it began with his trying to protect her and her family.

"Thank you for letting me know like this," she managed as she returned the paper.

"As long as you're no trouble, it's no trouble," the guard said as she refolded the newspaper, "Sorry it happened though."

"I think I need some time alone," FerLyn said, "Could I maybe have breakfast in here today?"

"I'll see if we can swing that."

Not long after, FerLyn's cellmate went to the cafeteria for breakfast by herself. Same went at yard time, when FerLyn asked to stay inside to reflect.

But that time, the cellmate returned to find FerLyn hanging from the light fixture by her bedsheets. And throughout the entire examination process, nobody documented the bite marks on the inner side of the noose.

"So, the story is that FerLyn hung herself when she heard OshMar had drowned?"

"Officially, yes," EshCal said, giving him a knowing glance, "His death was ruled an accident."

"Well, that sounds like a load of bollocks," Sinkua derided, "I assume Covert Affairs is already looking into it."

"I haven't asked, but I'm assuming they are," EshCal said, "Lot of people are saying they heard FerLyn's death announced on the radio the day before it happened."

"That could just be a hoax though."

"All at the same time and from the same station?"

"Well, that could be something."

"But nobody's been able to come up with a recording, and the deejay missing," EshCal continued, "And when they found OshMar's car, his radio wasn't tuned to that station."

"What news station was it on?"

"They're saying it came from a Quarunite acid rock station. The deejay went by Dirty Frog."

"Heard of him. Eytea was a fan," Sinkua said, "But why would he take part in this? He was never political."

"I'm sure that'll be the first thing Covert asks him when they find him," EshCal said, "But for now, can I count on you as my plus-one?"

"Yeah, of course," Sinkua said, nodding as he paced the office. He pulled off his bandana and dragged his fingers through his hair. "Son of a bitch," he muttered, "I have to tell her family."

"Oh, that's right. They're staying at Drakou, aren't they?" EshCal gasped, "Well, not to sound callous, but if you need a menial task to do while you think it over, I could do with having my desk restained."

"What color do you want?" Sinkua asked, "Same as now?"

"Actually, I'd like to change it to cherry seta," EshCal said, "Get it imported if you have to."

Sinkua stopped a few steps from the door as someone knocked. EshCal pressed the button under her desk, and Biroe entered with his hands behind his back and a police escort.

"Biroe," Sinkua nodded, "I take it your case didn't go well."

"Not really," Biroe said, "I have a favor to ask. Could you to come with me to the morgue?"

Sinkua nodded. "I'll see what I can do."

A streak of crimson along the horizon brought a tinge of visibility to the first stars of the night sky. Galo's head dipped, and his hair in his eyes startled him awake. He had little sense of time, but the encroaching dusk told him they had been walking for hours. And that was just since they'd reached the end of the bridge.

Nikasu clung to his arm, keeping their centers of gravity low. Galo, meanwhile, froze the water before them. He suffered frequent coughing fits, which were almost always punctuated by his hocking black mucus into the sea. His secret was out, and he no longer had to be subtle about that. Though from the pitying look in Nikasu's eyes, he knew she'd rather not see it.

"Do you see anything?" he asked.

"Nothing I'd think was The Veil," she said, her eyes shimmering. She looked behind them. "I can't see the end of the bridge anymore."

"Do you think this might have been a trap?"

"Pretty elaborate trap."

They shuffled forth a while longer, gaining little ground and sharing even fewer words. Nikasu cleared her throat.

"If we were," she continued, "Hypothetically, I mean. How fast could Leviathan get to us?"

"Fast enough," Galo said, the salty air throwing him strait into a coughing fit.

Powering through the mouthfuls of dark phlegm, he stepped out onto slush formed from a lackluster milystic effort. Nikasu pulled him back and anchored him. They sat together while he caught his breath.

"Fresh water freezes easier than sea water, right?" she asked as she got to her feet.

"By two degrees, yes," Galo said, "Why?"

"Well, if I'm thinking right..."

As she trailed off, she unsheathed Epelun and dipped the tip in the water. The ripples flattened, and the faintest purple shimmer carved a path through the reflected fading starlight. The scattered slurry began to converge, to coalesce.

Galo pushed himself to his feet. "How are you doing that?"

"Salt is denser than water," Nikasu explained, "I figured if I ramped up the gravity, the salt would separate out."

"And make the rest of the water easier to freeze," he realized, "That's pretty damn cool. Are you okay to keep this up?"

"Yes, but only because I have Epelun," she said, "No way I could do this and balance us on my own. No matter how many angry pep talks my brother gives me."

"He does have a certain way of motivating people," he agreed, "Always has."

"You don't have some crushes on him, do you?" Nikasu snickered.

"That's not how that term works, and no," Galo laughed, "It turns out I was wrong about being bisexual. Or if I am, what was happening has nothing to do with it."

"Hmm. So, what was it, then?"

"My grandfather had a certain clairvoyance. I've inherited it."

"So, you can see tsora and milystis?"

"I can only see tsora with skin contact," Galo explained, "But I can see milystis remotely. I don't think I can see it or sense it as far away as he could though."

"I guess you figured it out when you and Sinkua were down here?" Nikasu asked, "I just know that, when I had my episode, I left a huge dent in the ground because my milystis spiked."

Galo nodded. "I saw his milystis change in my mind's eye," he said, "It turned pitch black."

They walked with the tips of their weapons in the water, the conversation turning decidedly more idle. At one point, Galo recounted how Gijin had given him the glaive, saying some people called it the sword of the sea. Nikasu implored him to ask Leviathan if it had a special name in Mberhali.

As the sky turned orange and pink, the air grew heavy, and his vision blurred. Galo stumbled into a crouch, nearly falling into the water. Looking aside, he found Nikasu had stumbled as well. Whatever had afflicted him was taking her, too.

She gritted her teeth and forced herself to her feet with more than a few grunts and stumbles. Wobbling like a marionette, she pulled on his arm, beckoning him to stand. He grasped her arm and pulled back as she nearly staggered off the bridge, then pulled himself to stand.

"I think we found The Veil," he managed, pulling both of them back from the end of the bridge, "Can you see anything?"

"Colors. Very… swirly and… vague," she muddled, "You know how it looks when light hits a puddle with oil on it? It's sort of like that, but in the air."

"If I could focus, I'm sure I could get a vision of it," Galo said, "From what we've heard about it, it sounds quasi-milystic."

"Not made of milystis, but something close to it?"

"Possibly, yes. How are you taking this so well, anyway?"

"It reminds me of being drunk," she said, "The Geneticist sometimes experimented on me with alcohol."

"Fucker," Galo muttered, "Well, let's head back. I'll call for Leviathan when we're a safe distance from The Veil."

"Should we ask her and Nemesis to destroy the bridge?"

"As fun as that would be, I don't think we should. We don't want MalVek knowing we've been down here," he reasoned, "Assuming we haven't somehow tipped him off already."

"Or," Nikasu said emphatically, "We goad him out into the open, and maybe I get to cut a bitch?"

Galo laughed. "Maybe we will," he said, willing the ice bridge to melt behind them as they walked, "Leviathan certainly has a taste for destroying Avatar constructs."

The mortician scanned the serial numbers along the wall, checking them against the manila folder in his hand. Biroe sat aside, flanked by his police escorts. Sinkua stood further off, mentally preparing himself.

He had only performed one deliberate resurrection. The other was accidental and had been done with Yggdrasil's help. On top of that, he and KalChi had never been close. Their only common ground was that he was acquainted with her boyfriend. Sinkua realized he would need to empathize with Biroe's concern for her to pull this off.

"Here we are," the mortician announced as he unlocked the drawer, "Don't know why you brought this scruffy bloke here. Just staring at the floor like an absolute tosser. But let's be about it, then."

Sinkua looked up and furrowed his brow at him. One of Biroe's police escorts brought him alongside the drawer as the mortician pulled it out. The other stayed aside. Sinkua waited a moment, then walked up to the other side of the drawer.

His stomach churned as she came into view. Something had gored through her midsection. Sinew and severed arteries lined the gaping wound. A pair of cracked vertebra jutted into the top and bottom.

Sinkua's hand trembled as he brought it to her shoulder. He closed his eyes, but before Phoenix could speak, visions of Eytea newly slaughtered flashed through his mind. When he opened his eyes, for a split second, he saw her face melded with KalChi's.

His thoughts became consumed by his every failure and his powerlessness against the one death he most wished to undo. This self-loathing hallucination entrenched him so deeply, in fact, that he wasn't sure if the sheets under KalChi's body were actually purple.

"Boy looks like he's never seen a dead body," the mortician derided, chuckling at himself, "What'd you bring him here for, anyway?"

"The sheets," Sinkua grumbled, leveling his eyes at Biroe, "What color are they?"

Biroe was somewhere between too puzzled at the question and too engrossed in the sight of KalChi's dead body to answer.

"They're purple," the second escort offered, "Odd question to be sure, but there it is."

Sinkua nodded vigorously, coughing out something like gratitude through the bloody phlegm in his throat. His temple throbbed and vision narrowed. He clutched the edge of the slab, feeling the metal dent against his fingertips. He turned sharply and threw a bullet of a punch square at the center of the mortician's face.

The mortician staggered back, cursing and clutching his nose with blood seeping between his fingers. Sinkua half-swaggered half-staggered toward him in slow deliberate strides.

"What's with you, man?" the mortician cried out, "Was it the jabs? I was just having a bit of sport with you, yeah? Yeah?"

"Don't act like you didn't know, you fucking cunt," Sinkua growled.

He threw another punch, this one aimed at the chest. The mortician's sternum cracked, and he collapsed onto his backside. Sinkua forced himself to pull away and turn back to the slab.

"I can't," he choked out.

"Don't do this to me," Biroe muttered.

"It's too…"

"You can't just get my hopes up," Biroe snarled, "then come down here…"

"She's…"

"… start throwing punches…"

"It's too much…"

"… and refuse to help her!"

Sinkua braced his forearms on the edge of the slab as his knees buckled.

"I can't do it," he choked through a throat full of blood, "It's… She's…"

"Then what good are you?" Biroe snarled, "Just because she didn't take to you like that nomadic whore."

Temple throbbing and blood running from the corner of his mouth, Sinkua flung the slab back into the wall. He took two steps forward, then planted his foot in the middle of Biroe's chest. He clenched his fists, breathing raggedly as he glared down at the prostrate man with his single leg draped over the edge of his upturned wheelchair.

"You fucking asshole," Biroe grumbled, his voice tightening. He looked to the police escort nearest to him. "A hand up?"

Sinkua collapsed to his hands and knees, coughing up blood. The other officer crouched beside him, just out of arm's reach.

"Soon as you've sorted yourself out," he said, "I'm afraid I have to take you into custody."

Chapter 38

"Prisoner 161-80-819?"

"Do I have a visitor?"

"Your bail has been posted in the amount of thirteen hundred twenty iolas."

"I'm free to go, then?"

"Yes, but you're also to be suspended without pay for twenty-one days."

"Calendar or business?"

"Calendar. Fifteen business days. You'll also need to complete at least fifty-five hours of community service during that time."

"Do you know who paid my bail?"

"I'm afraid not. Someone from Foreign Affairs dropped it off."

Farim and Uro sat across from each other in a sparsely appointed midship cabin. The room bobbed and dipped against the storm, despite their roughly central position. The rumble of thunder and waves reverberated through the walls.

"I may be way off base here," Uro said, looking up as though trying to see through to the deck, "but I think his belligerence is all an act. No way somebody that drunk could navigate through this storm."

"We'll make a proper detective of you yet," Farim said.

"By the way, once this immediate threat with MalVek is taken care of," he said, "do you think you'd like to…"

"Don't finish that sentence," she cut in, "Don't ask me out. It'll just make things weird."

Uro gave her a puzzled stare. "I was going to ask to keep working together," he corrected, "I'd like to keep learning with someone who treats me like a partner."

"Oh…" Farim managed, "Well, I mean… I wouldn't quite call you a partner, but…"

"Closer than Uncle Caylence does."

"That much was obvious."

"Besides, you've got that whole forbidden love ordeal with Sinkua."

"No, we don't," Farim sighed, rolling her eyes, "I just don't see you that way."

"You don't?" Uro asked. He shook his head and added, "I mean, you don't have anything going on with Sinkua?"

"That hug and kiss was just a cover," she explained, "I needed to tell him about Jevana."

"I know," Uro said, grabbing the table as the room dipped hard, "I meant how you act around him."

"There's nothing there."

"Well, I wouldn't blame you if there was," he shrugged, "Man's a bit of an ass, but his sort of intensity could be fun for a few rounds."

Farim looked him over and chuckled under her breath. "Well, I don't think you're his type," she said, "But for the sake of pretending I didn't make this awkward, I'd like to keep working with you, too."

The door opened, and a shipmate popped his head in. "Storm's getting worse," he said, "Captain says to secure the furniture, then get on the bilge pumps."

Raindrops battered the deck, creating a sheen of mist over vessel and sea alike. Galo steered while Gabdur worked the sails and Nikasu watched the horizon from the crow's nest. Leviathan swam below the hull, calming the stormy waters around the ship. Nemesis flew just ahead, flattening the shroud of mist so Nikasu could better navigate.

"Land! Due north-northwest!" Nikasu called down.

"Ivaria is just ahead!" Gabdur relayed to Galo.

Over the next hour, the coast of Ivaria came more clearly into view. The five of them stuck to their duties, with Gabdur voicing numerous elaborate curses for their fortunes. The rain had only been the latest matter, and Leviathan and Galo were both too occupied to redirect it.

The dock workers who greeted them seemed unbothered by the rain as they cast their ropes at the ship. Gabdur rolled up the sails while Nikasu climbed down from the crow's nest. Nemesis returned to the ship, where he assumed his armor form upon Nikasu's back. Leviathan spiraled out of the sea in a milystic waterspout, shrinking to coil around Galo's forearm.

"Looks like your motor gave out!" a portsman called over the battering rain, "You'll need to wait until this rain clears before we can work on it!"

Galo pulled his hair back and rang it out. "Sorry, could you say that again?"

"I said you'll need…"

"Don't tell me you don't know who this is," a second portsman interrupted, "I think we can fix his ship in this rain."

"He's a civilian now, ain't he?" the first one rebutted, "Might have yourself a right point, had he not given up his birthright."

"Not that, you bumbling knob," the second chided, "He's one of them what helped Murdega get us the rights to these very ships."

"Slipped my mind, must admit," the first remarked, looking Galo over, "Say, where's your friend with the eyes like your girlfriend's got?"

"Sinkua's in ArcNos," Galo said, "You two know Murdega?"

"Course. Work with him," the second portsman said, "You looking for him?"

"My first mate needs to speak with him," Galo said.

"Afraid that can't happen anytime soon. Man's in the Northland Sea," the first said, "Worst of this's up that way."

Galo consulted with Leviathan and learned that she couldn't help without interfering with tidal patterns too drastically. He turned to Gabdur. "As much as I'm loath to accept it, it looks like we'll have to leave Farim and Uro to handle themselves."

"It's possible that he's up there looking for them," Gabdur said, "Though I don't know how they would have gotten in touch with him."

"We should all be so lucky," Galo said. He looked to the two portsmen. "How long will it take to fix the engine?"

"Can't say until we get a look at it. Oughtn't be more than half a worknight."

"In that case, let me see what I can do about this rain."

Somber string quartet melodies laced the warmed air as it circulated throughout the room. Handwoven chains of laurels and ivy lined the mahogany wall panels. Chairwoman TolRou stood at the head of the room with three large framed portraits at her back. Assortments of blue and gold ivy flowers adorned the frames. The entire room thrummed with soft conversations and careful footfalls.

EshCal looked about as TolRou spoke of KalChi's work and personal life. She had heard the rumors, had even seen him in handcuffs, but she still held out for another explanation. Now, there was no use for denial. Biroe would miss his girlfriend's funeral because of a crime of passion he'd committed on her behalf.

Her eyes warm and heavy, she drifted her hand aside. Another found it, warm and rough, and gave hers a firm squeeze. She turned to Sinkua, who kept his face forward and shoulders relaxed. He flashed her a smile as she exhaled her gratitude.

Phylus sidled up to Sinkua and patted his shoulder. He mouthed an apologetic platitude to EshCal.

"How's your scar?" Sinkua asked.

"Itches sometimes," Phylus said, "Did Inre figure anything out?"

Sinkua shook his head. "No luck with R&D?"

"Not enough time," Phylus said, "SenRas was looking into other sources. I don't know that anything came of it."

"Damn," Sinkua sighed, perhaps too loudly as the High Minister of Education glowered at him. He mouthed an apology before returning his attention to Phylus. "We might be too late. I heard Calhosin's sentence started this morning."

"It did as far as I know," Phylus said under his breath, "Hey, what's SouSol's problem?"

"She thinks I'm a bad role model because I didn't go to college."

EshCal chuckled and nudged him with her elbow. He barely moved. "Well, whatever the exodus is," she said, "tonight would be tactically ideal. A lot of powerful people are out of the way."

Swallowing hard, Phylus looked about as though some indeterminate thing was suddenly out of place. "Do either of you feel that?" he asked.

Sinkua shook his head. "Can you still see soft spots?"

"No, but…" Phylus trailed off, raising a finger.

"Same feeling you got at Heniokhos?" EshCal whispered.

Phylus nodded, his eye wide with fear.

The professor had gone on lecturing for well over an hour. Most of the class, Vielle included, had kept their attention through it all. There only being ten students meant they had no crowd to vanish into if they slacked off. Despite this, two of them let their attention meander out the window.

"Just a friendly reminder that this a therapy licensure class," the professor said, "If you're that fascinated by this storm, perhaps you'd be better suited to a meteorology program."

"Not that, sir," one of them protested.

"Well, whatever it is, keep your eyes forward. For both our sakes."

"Something's going on downtown," the other said, "At the capitol building."

The professor sighed and rolled his eyes. "I know I'll regret this, but…"

"Vielle!" the first called out, "Doesn't your girlfriend work there?"

"Yes, but she's…" Vielle trailed off, eyes widening as realization settled in. She rose from her desk and crossed the room to the window.

"She's what?" the first window-watcher pried, "Off for the night?"

Vielle nodded absently. Off in the distance, the capitol building shimmered in a dreadfully familiar way. "I'm sorry," she exhaled, her voice thready, "I need to go."

People screamed and scrambled as holes burst out of the walls in rapid succession. Fragments of drywall and framing shot across the room, breaking against backs and glancing off shoulders. Phylus rushed the stage and grabbed the microphone that TolRou had dropped.

"We need to evacuate!" he announced, "Do not use the elevators. I repeat, do not use the elevators!"

Nearly everyone converged on the double doors. Phylus hopped off stage, ducking debris and forcing his breathing to stay even. His throat caught as a desperate voice cried out over the commotion.

"The door is stuck!" TolRou yelled.

"Move!" Sinkua bellowed.

He stepped back, rolled his neck, and shook out his arms. He swept his hand up, washing pale green flames over the door. In his periphery, he glimpsed MarLys looking past him with wide, fearful eyes.

Sinkua barreled forth, forceful blinks flashing incrementally paler green fire upon the door.

MarLys rushed past him in the opposite direction.

The crowd cleared a wider path with his every pyromantic blink.

She fell to her knees, enduring carpet burns as she slid under a flying length of corner framing.

His keraunographic scars itched as his medallion bounced against his chest.

She raised her clasping tool, her own keraunographic scars pulsating as her arm tensed.

He threw a shoulder forward and rammed a hole through the double doors, launching the latch and lock mechanism at the opposite wall.

She snagged the wood on a perpendicular trajectory and, with a surge of adrenaline, launched herself upright and slammed the framing against the floor.

They looked to one another with mirrored posture, both clutching their dominant shoulder. Sinkua shoved open what was left of the doors. While everyone else scrambled out, SenRas approached MarLys.

"Do you still have the hair tie that Vielle gave you?"

"Purse," she said, still catching her breath.

"Get to the ground with it as quick as you can," he ordered, "Get help from Drakou."

"I think I can make it down the fire escape if I hurry."

"Well, don't dawdle," SenRas insisted, "And thank you for covering him."

She gave her heart a double pat. "I owed him."

Accelerated by a precision sequence of Yggdrasil's roots pressing under her feet, Vielle broke ahead of the crowd in the final stretch of the hall. Just before the door, she whipped around and called back to her professor and classmates.

"Alert the first responders!" she shouted, launching the door open with a reverse kick.

She ran out into the storm, cupping her hands over her ears to filter out the sounds of rainfall and thunder. She closed her eyes and listened, but the noise of the storm washed out the voices. Murky water splashed up to her knees as she ran to her motorcycle in loping stomps.

Vielle sped out of the parking lot with fans of water spraying high enough to obscure her from either side. Yggdrasil aided her balance and momentum against her constant hydroplaning. The rapid splattering of thick raindrops echoed inside her helmet. And through it all, a faint voice began to emerge.

MarLys cracked the window with her hook hand, enduring slices and nicks as she punched out loose glass fragments. She stepped out onto the balcony, then threw her hair into a quick ponytail with a hair tie from her purse. Rain mixed with blood from her fresh cuts, striping her arms red and pink.

She threw herself onto the first ladder, finding virtually no purchase on the rain-slick rungs. Instead, she hooked her prosthetic over the top rung and let herself drop, controlling her fall by catching herself on each rung in rapid succession. A clanging cacophony resonated throughout the entire fire escape apparatus as she devoured the distance between the assembly hall and the sidewalk.

MarLys gave the last ladder two kicks, but it didn't drop. She took a deep breath, the balcony shaking violently, and vaulted over the rail. Her knees popped as she hit the sidewalk, dropping into a deep crouch.

She took off for a nearby surface root in long, flatfooted strides. As she ran, she called out to Vielle, beckoning her to bring anyone she could from Drakougeneospa.

Water flew from Vielle's body and bike as she rode into the parking garage. She pulled hard to one side, fishtailing under the security bar. She whipped a milystic vine around a pillar, righting herself and reinforcing the cracked stone as she flung herself around the corner.

The floor shifted and skewed as she rode deeper into the underground parking structure. Cars tilted up onto their sides, tumbling over each other and into the walls. As she dodged raining concrete and rebar, Vielle summoned the roots of Yggdrasil from below the structure to reinforce the support pillars.

Screams resonated throughout the scrambling mass as pieces of architecture caromed off heads and plowed through torsos. They cried out as they collapsed, both the dead and the dying, their final words swallowed by commotion.

Sinkua took point, scorching offending projectiles with sapphire flames. Phylus and EshCal flanked him, calling out warnings and guidance to those following. SenRas, knowing the capitol building most intimately, plotted their route as he anticipated hazards.

The entrance to the stairwell to the lobby was jammed too tightly for Sinkua and EshCal to contend with. Not with the constant looming threat of careening infrastructure. His pyromancy was of little use, what with the door being metallic. SenRas directed them on an alternate route, not to the lobby, but to the parking structure under the building.

Sinkua hit the scorched double doors without slowing, blasting them from their hinges at the expense of his shoulder. Large lengths of the driving paths had collapsed, cutting off a direct path to the exit. They had to assume that if they went down far enough, they could find their way across and climb back up.

Lengths of vine threaded the cracks in the pillars and floors. MarLys had done it. Vielle had come in time, and further help would follow.

Vielle's vision blurred. Her balance faltered. Still, she pressed on, willing roots and milystic vines through the decaying structure.

At the bottom of the parking garage, she dismounted and let her bike fall with the motor still running. The structure was still tremoring, but it was somewhat, in a word, contained. As she sat to catch her breath, a rippling of light in the corner of her eye pulled her attention.

EshCal broke ahead at the sight of a motorcycle upended between two overturned cars. She leapt and twisted with a celerity born from decades of training. With a powerful thrust, she slammed her feet into the upturned motorcycle, knocking it loose and opening a path.

She slowed to a slight limping jog, holding her knee. Sinkua swooped in alongside her and put his arm around her shoulder, pushing her along at his pace. By the next turn, she suppressed the pain enough to run on her own.

Soon after they started making their way upward, the top of the ramp gave out, and a van came tumbling down at them. Sinkua shouted the others back. With her injury, EshCal couldn't get out of the way fast enough, and Sinkua couldn't pull her clear with his aching shoulder.

They stood together and braced for impact.

Galo stood on the dock with his arms outstretched and hands upturned, willing the rain to bend around an area larger than his ship. Murdega's associates worked hurriedly, often glancing up at the redirected rain.

Galo's stomach tightened. His vision blurred. He cleared his throat, but the strain persisted. The sense of disassociated tangibility becoming intangible washed over him. Visions became too dampened to hear, sounds too occluded to see.

The rain collapsed in a torrent as he collapsed to his hands and knees. He vomited over the side of the dock. Nikasu rushed to him and knelt beside him. Gabdur hunkered down at his other side.

"What happened?" Nikasu asked, "What's wrong?"

"Rest," Gabdur beckoned, "You've been at it for hours."

Galo shook his head, his face sticky with tears and rain. "Something terrible has happened."

The tumbling van slammed into their hands, their arms recoiling and joints popping. The two held their ground, arms trembling as they strained to hold the vehicle back. EshCal's knee gave out for a split second, letting her end of the van slide back. Sinkua eased his end back to level it as she regained herself.

Sinkua darted his eyes aside, dancing them through the waiting crowd of survivors. There was no path around the van, and nobody was in any shape to help. He stole fleeting glimpses of their body language, creating composites of their attitudes and intentions.

He brought his eyes forward as he and EshCal pushed against the van. It kept sliding, though they slowed it to a grueling crawl. Sinkua's throat tingled with the taste of iron.

"We've been set up," he said, keeping his voice low.

"Was afraid of that," EshCal muttered.

"Van's packed," Sinkua said, "Traitors among us."

"Who?"

"SouSol. Others will protect her."

"Right. When we're pushed to the wall, we jump," she ordered, "You take point. I'll circle around."

"Got it," he said, spitting blood aside, "Watch your knee."

"And you watch your shoulder," she said, "Oh, and Sinkua?"

"Yeah?"

"Sorry I talked you out of bringing Epesol."

His shoulder throbbed as they let the van slide further down the ramp. He noticed EshCal shifting her weight to favor her unhurt knee. Holding back no longer took any effort, as they were both struggling to hold their footing.

His vision began to blur, and a vein in his temple throbbed. The taste of iron bubbled to up fill his mouth. He spat bloody phlegm aside, muttering expletives as he endeavored to steady his breathing.

He looked over at SenRas and, with a hard blink, cast a spark at his grandfather's feet, grabbing his attention. Through eye movements and subtle nods, he had him get Phylus's attention and warned them both to watch for saboteurs among them.

His heels hit the wall. His arms drew back, elbows bending deeper as the weighted van pressed on. At the sound of EshCal's fingers tapping the van, he braced to jump.

"One," she exhaled, voice low with strain and clandestinity.

His shoulder popped as he shifted his weight toward the outside.

"Two."

His breathing labored, he spat bloody mucus. It tasted of bile. The van groaned up the ramp.

"Three!"

Sinkua and EshCal lunged away from the van in tandem. He slipped on blood and mucus, banging his sore shoulder against the wall. The van crashed into the wall with a sickening crunch and an agonized scream.

Blood filled his mouth. His breathing grew labored. Horrid screams kept resonating from the other side of the van.

With a plasmatic bellow, he pounded his fiery fists against the grill. Someone important was on the other side, suffering. He grasped the dented grill and under the bumper, pulling back on the overturned vehicle. The van groaned, drawing up more screams from the other side.

Rapid footfalls pulled at his attention. A mass of warped voices churned behind him. He couldn't make sense of any of them.

Grasping lucidity, he spun about just as a length of rebar caromed off of his head. Blood-laced vomit erupted from his throat. He swiped at the air, but the assailant struck him across the opposite temple, hard enough to pop his neck.

Sinkua collapsed facedown in a pool of blood and vomit. As his vision went black, the screaming became clear. EshCal had been pinned down.

And then there was nothing.

A silhouette occluded the panel of fractalized light. Vielle clutched her chest as she limped toward it, straining to see it more clearly. As the light faded, it came into sharper focus. Mortvill approached, his body language giving away no more than his blank metallic mask. A sword hilt peeked over his shoulder.

"What are you doing here?" Vielle demanded, standing as tall as possible.

"Vielle. Legendary Hybrid of the Etherworlder Construct Yggdrasil," Mortvill announced, approaching on long deliberate strides, "You have reached the extent of your utility." He reached over his shoulder and gripped a sword handle. "Thus, I grant you rest."

"So," Vielle snarled, manifesting a pair of thorny whips with a flick of her wrists, "You're that one."

He pulled the sword from the holster on his back. Vielle's eyes widened at the sight of it. Mortvill brandished a broadsword with one hand, treating the thing like a dirk.

"Wh... Who... Who....?" she stammered, gritting her teeth, "... Show me your face."

Mortvill paused, lowering the sword to his side. He seemed to consider the request, as far as she could tell. After a moment, he bowed his head.

"Very well. I will grant you a final request."

Mortvill removed the mask to reveal a middle-aged face deep with wisdom and pain far beyond its years. But he had those eyes. Abyssal pools of darkness lined with penumbral auras. His were just like theirs, only deeper and black.

Vielle tightened her grip on her whips. Fatigue dissolved in a cloud of adrenaline and fury.

"You mother..."

With a surge of milystis, she extended her whips and curled the thorns.

"... fucking..."

She drew back both whips and charged at him.

"... traitor!"

Vielle slashed at Mortvill in a crisscross motion, scores of thorns ripping through the air. But nothing else. By the time she realized he had moved, his blade had nicked her femoral artery.

She collapsed, screaming and sobbing.

"Wh... Why?"

"To put you in your place."

Lying facedown in a growing pool of blood, Vielle reached for The Harvester as he vanished into the rippling panel of light. Blurry afterimages of dots of light crowded her eyes as the portal dissolved. Swelling darkness encroached on her peripheral vision.

Sounds became deep and distant, the hum of her motorcycle becoming a prolonged groan. MarLys's voice came into her mind as though through a long tunnel. She no longer understood words. All that remained of her grasp on language was a vague sense of emotions. MarLys was pleading, desperate, and confused.

Vielle dragged her fingers through her blood. As her thoughts withered, she scribbled a simple message. She reached out to Yggdrasil with the last of her cognition, hoping that somebody would find her message.

But as she collapsed, her hand smeared through the blood. Her last words corrupted, life abandoned Vielle.

Chapter 39

Calhosin sat at the foot of his cot, rapidly drumming his foot on the concrete floor. He pulled his lily pad from a pocket he had stitched inside his jumpsuit, rolling it in his hand.

Phylus had returned it with an assurance that he had the matter under control. Calhosin hadn't put much faith in that promise. Not that he could protest, though. His lily pad had remained inactive.

From down the way, he could hear PavRal and MerSul talking. He couldn't pick out any details of their conversation, but it assured him that the other lily pads hadn't been activated either.

Distant shouts cascaded down the corridor in the wake of metallic rattling. Calhosin's lily pad trembled in his hand. He returned it to his makeshift pocket and pushed himself to his feet.

Light poured from the device, diffusing through the fabric of his jumpsuit. The glow swelled and enveloped his body, cocooning him in palpable luminescence. It contracted into the shape of his body, and he felt himself being pulled in imperceptible directions. It felt as though the lily pad was trying to pull him perpendicular to all three dimensions, straining him through the very fabric of the space.

Electrical webbing manifested all around him. It unfolded into a wall directly in his path, knocking him back into perceptible three-dimensional space. He looked around to find scores of fellow convicts sitting along the perimeter of the prison yard, each looking more puzzled than the last and just as drenched as the next.

Calhosin and several others wandered the muddy yard, a disrupted gathering awash in confusion. The luminous haloes around the security lights abruptly stopped just above the top of the perimeter wall. Curious obelisks were affixed to several of the fence posts. As he approached one for a better look, a figure in a hooded raincoat emerged through the gate, silhouetted by a pair of spotlights which were also abruptly cut off.

"Well, if Sbaglien didn't want my head in a cloche already, he'll damn sure be after it now," she announced, "But I'm sorry, The Scout won't be taking any of you."

SenRas staggered back as the van and his grandson hit the wall in near unison. EshCal screamed from the other side. SenRas stood bewildered and helpless as Sinkua pulled on the van, managing only to draw out ever more dreadful screams from EshCal. A hand on his shoulder pushed him aside, and SouSol rushed past him, wielding a length of rebar.

SenRas called out to Phylus and pointed emphatically toward the other end of the van. Phylus scrambled to help EshCal, while SenRas gave chase.

SenRas closed in but was still out of reach as SouSol brained his grandson with the rebar. She swung a second time as Sinkua turned around. SenRas dug in his pocket with one hand as he reached for SouSol's shoulder with the other. She whipped around as SenRas brought up the contents of his pocket. His manriki met hard with the underside of her jaw, snapping her head back.

She jabbed him in the abdomen with the end of the rebar, doubling him over. SenRas leaned aside to goad her into hubris. As she swung for his face, he pulled the manriki taut, snagging the rebar. SenRas twisted and pulled SouSol's forearm behind her back, disarming and incapacitating her.

He spun her about and pinned her to the wall, only to notice that Sinkua had vanished during their scuffle. Numerous survivors charged up the decaying ramp, their voices compounding into a frantic snarl. Up at the head, SenRas spotted a pair of combat boots dragging the ground.

SenRas bashed SouSol's face against the wall, then whirled her around to cast her prostrate on the mucky concrete. Joints creaking and muscles aching, he ran into the swarm of survivors. He pushed and wedged his way past people as he moved up the ramp, closing in on Sinkua's captors.

But he broke through to the front only in time to see a portal closing behind them. The Prime Minister of Education stood crying out with his arm outstretched. NeiRos staggered back, screaming as he fell onto his backside. SenRas hurried to his side.

"NeiRos!" SenRas pleaded, "Did you see where they went?"

"My… My hand…"

"What about your…?" SenRas trailed off as he looked down to find NeiRos's came to a cauterized halt midway down the forearm. "Bloody shit," he muttered, "We'll get you help soon. Now, did you see where they took him?"

NeiRos shook his head, clenching his teeth. SenRas spat an expletive and called down to Phylus.

"How is she?" he asked.

Phylus lifted his eyepatch and scratched his scar. "Her legs are pinned below the knees."

"Fuck!"

"I'm still alive!" EshCal slurred, "Sinkua. Where?"

"Captured," SenRas said. He eyed the crowd, picking out half a dozen who looked particularly strong. "You six, on the van."

As they complied, SenRas nudged two more people, directing them to join Phylus at EshCal's side. He looked aside at NeiRos.

"Your second in command is problematic," he said.

SenRas then bid him to wait as he hurried to EshCal's side. The remaining survivors circled NeiRos, shielding him.

The six that SenRas had assigned to the task dragged the weighted van away from the wall. He and Phylus pulled EshCal free. Her shins and feet had been crushed, and bloody bone fragments and shredded tissue dangled from the wounds. SenRas and Phylus each took her by a shoulder, interlocking their each of their other hands behind her head. The other two survivors took her by the thighs. They hoisted her to chest level and started up the ramp.

"Okay, boys," EshCal slurred, "What's the plan?"

"Run!" SenRas barked at the waiting ring of survivors.

"Excellent. Put me down, and we'll set to."

"EshCal," Phylus beckoned, "your legs have been crushed."

"Have they?" she puzzled, "So that's why I can't feel them. Well, if it's all the same to you, I don't think I can be awake for this."

EshCal's body became deadweight as she blacked out, but her bearers kept her steady. They joined the last survivors, confident that all but one of the saboteurs had fled with Sinkua. As a cooperative unit, they made their way toward to street level.

NeiRos elected to leave SouSol behind, lying in a smattering of blood and phlegm.

MarLys rushed around to the parking structure entrance, where she found roughly thirty survivors emerging. Nearly half the crowd from the funeral was gone, and those remaining were looking dismal. Her stomach folded over on itself as EshCal and NeiRos were escorted past her. One of the survivors took SenRas's place in carrying EshCal, and SenRas came to MarLys's side.

"Where is everyone?" he urged.

"I don't know," MarLys shrugged, "She sent first responders instead."

"That'll do."

Phylus came back around the corner, having left EshCal with the medical workers in front of the capitol building. "Where's Vielle?" he asked.

"I thought she went down and found you," MarLys said.

"No, we saw vines in the pillars and thought she was out here with you."

"I never saw..."

MarLys's mouth hung open. Her eyes trailed up the side of the building, and she gestured for SenRas and Phylus to look as well.

Trails of brilliant green motes spiraled up the height of the building. Woven vines followed close behind, tightening as they settled into their positions.

"She did it!" MarLys exclaimed, "I don't know where she is, but she did it."

Phylus grabbed her by the arm and sprinted back to the parking structure. A few levels down, she saw a van against the wall with sickening amounts of blood on either side. SouSol lay beside it, struggling to come up onto her hands and knees. Before MarLys could so much as think what to ask, Phylus kicked SouSol in the side of the head and kept running.

"Hey, hold on!" MarLys beckoned, "Did Sinkua come out with you?"

"No," Phylus said, "Turncoats took him."

"Son of a bitch!"

"Sorry. We'll talk when we find Vielle."

On the bottom level, they found her motorcycle, overturned and still running. The stench of blood hit so thick that the very air felt wet. They rushed through the dimness toward the source of the smell.

MarLys's legs weakened and stomach twisted at the sight of what remained of her. Phylus dropped to his knees beside Vielle's clothes in a pool of blood. MarLys crouched beside him, jaw trembling as she tried to process what could have happened.

"So... much blood..." she stammered, "How does...? How...? Why would...? Who?"

"You..." Phylus snarled with tears in his eyes, "This is your fault!"

The back of his hand clapped hard against her temple. As her head snapped aside, he blindsided her with a sloppy haymaker. MarLys narrowly stopped herself from falling into Vielle's blood.

Eyes watering, she sniffed and cleared her throat. As she wiped the tears from her face, she noticed something in the blood around one of Vielle's sleeves.

"There's a message here," she gasped.

"Don't you try to weasel your way out," Phylus grumbled, "You pulled her into this!"

Footsteps rounded the corner. "No, she didn't," SenRas interjected, "MarLys's message never reached her."

"How could you possibly know that?" Phylus demanded.

"She was supposed to bring help," MarLys choked out.

"What do you call the medics up there?" Phylus protested.

"Help, but..." MarLys stammered, "Anyone who saw this place shaking could've called them if their phone worked."

"I told her to get help from Drakou," SenRas said, "Do you really think nobody was available?"

"Then how did...?"

"She must have been able see the capitol building from her classroom," MarLys gasped as she realized this herself.

"Of course. She called for medics and came of her own volition," Phylus said, his eyes cast down, "I'm sorry."

"It's fine. I understand why you felt the way you did," MarLys said, "Do either of you have a camera? It looks like she left a message, but she fell across it."

SenRas and Phylus looked at each other, then both shook their heads.

"Do you have a pen?" SenRas asked.

"I have an eyeliner pen," MarLys said, "But what are you going to write on?"

"Use my arm," Phylus insisted, rolling up his sleeve.

While SenRas sketched what remained of Vielle's final message, they all shared what they of their circumstances. EshCal and NeiRos were both being taken to a hospital. Given how compromised they had just found the Ministries were, SenRas insisted on sending them to a non-Ministry facility. Other survivors who had suffered injuries were being treated on sight, theirs being comparatively minor.

What was to be done about SouSol was a question with no good answers. If they left her behind, they risked her running off with intel. Killing her could have made her a martyr. Sparing her could have been exploited.

"I'll take her," Phylus said, "I can sit on her until we figure something out."

"Don't trouble yourself with that," SenRas insisted, "It's a fine enough idea, but I ought to be the one to do it."

"He would be better at squeezing information out of her," MarLys said.

"I just thought you might be too busy with all the new investigations that just cropped up," Phylus said. He looked down at his arm, checking SenRas's progress in copying Vielle's smeared message. "It's funny, isn't it?" he continued, chuckling through welling tears, "I've just lost my daughter. I have to tell her mother and her sister that she's gone. I also have to tell that sister that her brother was kidnapped. And here I am, concerned with whether you'll have time to keep an eye on a turncoat."

"Well, don't trouble yourself," SenRas said, "I'll be taking some time off considering recent events. Particularly, my failings."

"Are you thinking of retiring?" Phylus asked.

"I passed retirement age during CreSam's rise," SenRas said, "I think I've only held out this long because I feel that I still have unfinished business."

"I know people who would say you've done more than enough," Phylus said, "But it's your decision."

"Yes, well," SenRas sighed, "If my mind is going, I have no more weapons in this fight."

Calhosin wiped the rain from his face in a fruitless attempt to clear the glare of the security lights. "Sbaglien has no skin in this fight," he said, "Now, you're clearly well-resourced, but there are people here who won't hesitate to go through you."

Hands aloft, he approached the intruder. Before he could see her face though, a faint swishing plunged a knife into the ground where he was about to step. He stopped, flashed a smile, and took a step back.

"I'm sure they could, but it wouldn't do them any good," the intruder said, "I'm their only way out of here."

By this time, the prisoners had long been gathering behind Calhosin.

"Well, from the looks of you, it won't take much to convince you," MerSul said, licking his gums, "Now, how that comes about depends on who you deal with."

"Fuck that," PavRal snarled, "Who do you think you are, cauliflower?" Calhosin looked back at him, shaking his head. "Do you have any idea what you're interfering with?"

"More than you know what you've gotten yourselves into," the intruder said, "You were all being conscripted into a war."

"We know," Calhosin said, "We're launching a revolution. As much as I loathe it, war gets the fastest results."

"A war between Tanelen and ArcNos?"

Calhosin faltered, but he played it cool and folded his arms, looking over her silhouette for some identifying shape. He found nothing in the bulky raincoat but betrayed just as much of his ignorance.

"Well, if you expect us to take your word," he said, "you should at least show us your face."

The intruder took a full step forward and pulled back the hood on her raincoat. "For those of you who might not recognize me," she said, "I am Colonel Inre from Tanelen."

"You killed JeiRol," PavRal shouted over the rain, "Why should we trust you?"

The hum of a motor and a muddy sloshing permeated the sound of rain. "She didn't kill him," Biroe said, "I did. That's why I'm in here."

"I don't think you want to admit to that," MerSul said, much of the crowd turning with him to face Biroe, "That would place you squarely against us."

"Have your little revolution. They come and go faster than lunar blackouts," Biroe shrugged, "Whatever it takes to put Sinkua in his place."

"Sinkua?" MerSul scoffed, "Fuck that guy. He stopped me from dropping that whistleblower bitch in Covert Affairs. What'd he do to you?"

"He refused to resurrect KalChi," Biroe grumbled. He rubbed his sternum. "Gave me a nice souvenir just for asking."

"Tall bloke with a red bandana?" PavRal asked, to which Biroe nodded, "I hate the bastard, too. News to me, hearing he can resurrect folks, but he ain't exactly obligated to do it. You need to come better than that if you want in on this after what you did to JeiRol."

"Get it through your fuckwitted skulls!" Inre shouted, "There is no revolution. There is a war between ArcNos and Tanelen."

"You already said that," PavRal said, "Never said why we should trust you though."

"She's bluffing," MerSul called, "The power shift in Tanelen has left them vulnerable. They won't go to war with us."

"Not nearly as vulnerable as the bunch of you have made ArcNos," Inre said, "Yes, a war would hurt Tanelen, but it would devastate ArcNos."

"Whatever it takes to clear out the traitors and plutocrats," Calhosin shrugged, "They cast out imperial rule only to build a new empire on top of it. And while those toy soldiers were playing house in the Subtransit, I was in Masnethege because the Chieftain Sage's advisors were threatening war on his behalf, and he didn't have the sense to talk them down."

"I was part of EshCal's counter-mutiny," PavRal added, "She gunned down my brother's ship before I could talk to him."

"ArcNos's secrets are controlled by CreSam's closest advisor, who also let The Avatars into ArcNos in the first place," MerSul said, "The only way to clear the corruption is to wipe the whole slate and start fresh."

"So, you see?" Calhosin said, "Your threats of devastation aren't threats at all."

"You can have your revolution soon enough," Inre promised, "But on your own terms. Not any laid about by The Avatars of Fate."

"I disagree with their convoluted sense of accountability, but even you must admit there's much to be said of their technocratic philosophy," Calhosin said, "We intend to take advantage of that."

"Noble Doyen Joren had similar intentions," Inre said, "They assassinated him for questioning their doctrines."

"That won't happen to us," MerSul boasted, "We outnumber them."

"No, you don't, and it wouldn't matter if you did," Inre scolded, "Everyone, shut up and listen. The exodus wouldn't kick off the revolution they promised you. You would have been sacrificial catalysts in a Northlands war. So yes, ArcNos would get a clean slate, but you'd have no say in what becomes of it."

Calhosin looked her over. "Well, if Sbaglien is among The Named, as you've suggested…"

"He's The Scout."

"Right. Well, he would find a way to declare war with or without us."

"But, if she's in here, he's lost a tactical advantage," PavRal suggested.

"What are you talking about?" MerSul scoffed, "He just says we took her hostage, and he has a perfectly valid reason to declare war."

"I'm not talking about justification, you thundering knob flicker," PavRal snipped, "I mean what I said. He's got less of an advantage without her. I think maybe we give her the benefit of the doubt and cooperate."

"Hey, both of you do me a favor, and stop trying to speak for me," Inre scolded, "I want Sbaglien to threaten war and show his true affiliations. It'll make things that much easier when I assassinate him. That way, we both get our revolution without The Avatars' meddling."

"I'm afraid I don't follow your logic, then," Calhosin admitted, "Why have you trapped yourself in here with us?"

"This barrier can only be breached from the outside," Inre said, "Not even a radio signal can get out. Only one other person has a key, and neither The Avatars nor your people on the outside have any chance of discovering who he is. Meaning that when Sbaglien tracks me here, none of you can be implicated in anything he does. And when he tries to force me to permit the exodus…" She whipped a knife at the barrier. It glanced off with a brilliant flash, and she swiped it from the air as it spun back to her. "… Well, Biroe knows what I'm capable of."

"In that case," Calhosin said, swallowing hard to mask a subtle wink, "what can we do to prove our cooperation?"

"Show me to the ironworks," Inre said, slicking back her rain-soaked hair as she returned the gesture, "After I have a word with the guards, we'll make scrap of your lily pads."

Hibiscus sat in the corner with an open magazine overturned on her lap. She watched as EshCal hoisted herself over a pair of parallel bars. A nurse fastened detachable prosthetics to EshCal's stumps, then ducked under the bars. She would use these for physical therapy while a set fitted to her were being cast.

"So, I stopped by Drakou a couple weeks ago," Hibiscus said as EshCal lowered her temporary feet onto the floor, "I thought I'd see how Spril and Yrlis are doing. And ask Sinkua how he's taking to working for you."

"I thought you lived there now," EshCal said, muttering an expletive as she stumbled, "How is that baldheaded weirdo though?"

"I have a room there, but I still have my condo for now," Hibiscus clarified, "He's doing good. Their marriage is getting on just fine. Especially given the circumstances." She paused, not immediately realizing that she was staring. "Sinkua was at work, though."

"Well, he's still learning, but he was doing just fine up until he got suspended. He's attentive and eager to help," EshCal said, "After what happened at the funeral, I might offer him a raise. Well, if he's willing to come back once he finds his way home."

Hibiscus shot an inquiring glance toward the nurse. EshCal furrowed her brow and nodded.

"Any idea where they took him?"

"No, but I'm not the smartest person who wants him found."

"It probably has something to do with the exodus."

"Almost definitely, which should mean he's almost definitely still alive."

Hibiscus began pacing the room. She noticed the nurse watching her obliquely. At first, she thought he was suspicious of her, but she soon realized he was checking her out, possibly thinking to ask about her rates. She was wearing a Dapper Rabbit top, after all.

"So, did they stop the exodus?" she asked.

"Until we hear from Colonel Inre, we can't know if there even was an exodus to stop," EshCal said, "But if nobody's heard from her since before the funeral, I suppose that means there's a safeguard in place."

"I haven't been to the house since then," Hibiscus said, "So, Phylus left it to her?"

"He told me before the funeral that she had an idea of how to stymy it, but she admitted it was pretty speculative," EshCal explained, "I didn't ask him for details. All I know is, if it worked, nobody could get in touch with her for a while."

Hibiscus hummed as she sauntered to the end of the bars. EshCal needed motivation, having stumbled nearly every step. Hibiscus grasped the ends of the bars and arched her back, groaning as she stretched.

"Yes, it's quite troubling when people can't… reach the people who need them," she teased, "But I guess in this case, it's a good thing."

"Yes," EshCal said, eyes lingering as she found her balance, "Yes, these certainly are counterintuitive circumstances."

Hibiscus grinned wickedly, standing with her back exaggeratedly straight. She looked aside at the nurse, finding him trying not to stare. She flashed him a wink and the call-me hand gesture before returning her attention to EshCal.

Her eyes flew open wide as she found EshCal standing well within arm's reach. Either the motivation had been particularly effective, or EshCal had used her arms to move down the bars. She looked to the nurse for answers.

But as she did, calloused fingertips brushed across her protruding breasts. She yelped and pulled back, laughing as she cast an accusing glare on EshCal.

"Keep your hands to yourself," she said, folding her arms over her chest.

"Sorry, I must have misread you," EshCal said, grinning wryly, "Myriela."

Hibiscus's eyes widened. Her mouth hung open. EshCal gestured to her top. She looked down to find her visitor's badge had been flipped around. Hibiscus, or rather Myriela, laughed and shook her head.

"You know, I thought about giving a fake name, but then I thought I shouldn't mess with their records." She turned and propped her butt on one of the bars. "But it also means your new boyfriend can't book me if he heard my real name."

"I didn't hear shit!" the nurse said.

"You won't get in trouble, will you?" EshCal asked, leaning on the opposite bar.

"Now you think about that?" Myriela laughed, "No. It's okay. You found out on your own. Just don't use it when I'm trawling for clients."

"I'll try. It's a beautiful name, by the way," EshCal said, "Sounds Kirtsian."

"Well, my father is Lenguardian, and my mother is from Quarun," Myriela said, "So, I suppose if you split the difference…"

EshCal rolled her eyes and laughed. "Of course, it wouldn't be Kirtsian," she said, "The last natural-born citizen must be older than me, and that, you are not."

Myriela nodded. "From what I hear, they've got more commuters than residents," she said, "It's some tax loophole the factory owners are exploiting."

Phylus sparked his fifth or eighth cigarette since he'd left the capitol building. He held it between his lips as he shielded it and the lighter from the rain with his other hand. His hands trembled so much that he lit the middle of the paper and nearly burned his palm.

Just like the others, the first taste folded his stomach in on itself. He didn't deserve such a treat as Ierodhesan tobacco. But to deny himself would have been to find comfort in escaping his shame. So, he indulged in his spite as the rain reduced it to smoldering.

The rain obscured his tears as he ambled along, feet scarcely leaving the pavement. His eyes fixated on nothing in particular. Faint voices milled around him, coaxing him into some vague awareness of people offering concern. Empty platitudes cast for a feel-good story they could pat themselves on the back with.

He took a while to realize the rain had stopped. The ground had also smoothed, and it felt like midday. At the sound of a muffled voice, he realized he had wandered indoors. He crumpled his smoldering cigarette and pitched it in the rubbish bin.

The voice faded as he wandered. The floor turned soft, and the walls closed in with regularly intervaled doors. Once or twice that he was aware of, he pulled out another cigarette, only to drop it as he recalled his whereabouts.

He stopped before a door. There was nothing special about it, but it stirred a sense of importance. He lobbed his fist against it and waited.

With a clacking and a fiddling, the door came open. Malia stood before him, looking just as puzzled as she did aghast. He hated himself for what he had to do. Hated his subconscience for pulling him here.

His mouth fell open.

The words fell out.

That evening, their daughter had been killed.

MarLys narrowed her eyes as she applied the concealer. Her stomach twinged at the familiarity, conjuring up something almost resembling pity. Even after the countless winding kilometers to baffle her internal compass, after the hours waited for scabbing to set in, MarLys still couldn't wholly numb herself to this woman's injuries. Not even when she reminded herself what she had done and seen to.

"Looks like he got you good," MarLys said as she leaned back to check her work, "But it's nothing I haven't seen before."

"Which one?" SouSol asked, her eyes darting aside accusingly.

"Which one, what?" MarLys asked, "I don't mean I've seen this from either of them. It's just that…"

"Which one got me good?" SouSol cut in, "Your boss when he sucker punched me, or Phylus when he literally kicked me while I was down."

"Don't know which is whose, so both, I guess," MarLys shrugged. She gestured to SouSol's swollen eye. "But I meant I've done this to myself."

"I've heard my fill of your stories about Chairman LenSom," SouSol derided, "Perish the thought of regaling me."

MarLys inspected her work one more time. She closed the makeup kit and stuffed it back in her purse. Before she shut her bag, though, she took out her Yggdrasil hair tie and put her hair back up.

"… That's it, then?" SouSol asked.

"You know my story," MarLys shrugged, "I hate telling it. So yeah. That's it."

"There is," came SenRas's voice from the dining room as he crossed the threshold, "one story I would just love to hear from you."

SouSol crossed her legs and put one hand on her knee. "Oh, I'm not sure I could tell any of them in a way you'd comprehend," she said, "But perhaps, you're, well, clever enough to follow along."

SenRas flashed a smile that only grazed his eyes. "Where was my grandson taken?"

"Who?"

"Of course you'd say that," SenRas muttered, "What is the exodus?"

"Have you consulted a dictionary?" SouSol derided, "Honestly, if this is the best you can do, it's no wonder MerSul loathes you."

"So, MerSul is part of it," MarLys piped up, "Who else?"

"Please," SouSol said, "I gave you nothing more with that than SenRas did by calling Sinkua his grandson."

"Fair enough," MarLys said, "Did you know you were endangering Vielle's life when you attacked Sinkua?"

"Again. Who?" SouSol snarked, "Yes, I heard about your girlfriend dying in the parking garage. Tragic stuff, but I had nothing to do with it. How could I?"

"You obviously work for The Avatars of Fate," SenRas said, "They deal in probabilistic foresight. Yes, I know a big word. Contain your shock."

"Actually," MarLys said, "I think she works for MalVek."

"Really now?" SenRas said, looking past SouSol, "I thought they were one and the same."

"MalVek is something more," MarLys insisted, "He deals more in the improbable and irrational."

"The word you're looking for is chaos," SouSol grated, "Lord MalVek deals in chaos."

Uro felt the ship lurch from within their midships cabin. The round clanging of bells permeated the walls through the fading hiss of rainfall.

"We're almost back on land," Uro said, smiling as his eyes followed the noises in the ceiling.

"Finally," Farim sighed.

"So, are you going to tell the others I'm on the level?"

"I'll put in a good word for you," she said, "That's all I can do."

Uro smiled weakly. "Thanks."

"Of course, I don't know how much good it will do after I talked you into going back on your word to him," Farim pondered, "And you can't say you coerced me. He'd never believe you got one over on me."

"You can convince him it was for the best," Uro said, "He'll listen to you."

"Well, we did get two of..." she said, trailing off as Uro's burner phone rang, "... everything. Answer it."

Uro did so, listening to the mechanical hum for a moment. Assured that there wasn't a person on the other end, he spoke a generic greeting to trigger the voice activated system.

"Retrieve a writing implement and paper," came a computerized voice, "Press one when you are ready to proceed."

Without a word, he crossed the cabin to find a pencil and notepad in a desk drawer. He ripped off the first sheet and set it on the desk. He pressed one.

"The following information can be repeated only once. Listen carefully and transcribe it perfectly. This data will be destroyed upon termination of this call. Press one when you are ready to proceed."

Uro set the phone to speaker, put it down, and pressed one. After a second, the voice launched into a string of numbers. Uro following along with pencil and paper.

At the end, it prompted him for the option to repeat the string. He accepted the offer, reading along under his breath with the pencil tip hovering over the paper. As he found no errors, he disconnected and put everything away.

"Any ideas?" he asked as he turned to face Farim.

"Nothing at the moment," Farim shrugged. She held out her pocket notepad, showing she had also taken the numbers down. "I'll think it over on the cab ride back."

"That worries me that you don't even have a hunch," Uro said, pacing, "Something must have happened while we were away."

Galo shambled down the ramp, slouching with heavy arms and shallow breath. Gabdur and Nikasu flanked him, each holding a shoulder. He felt Leviathan's thoughts within his own, her fleeting presence pulling fragments of notions to the surface.

"I'm sorry," she said, "I'm limited by the depth of your clairvoyance. No measure of your consciousness pinpointed the source."

Even in his mind, he could only manage a grunt of acknowledgment. He had been carrying this emotive sickness since nightfall. Now, with sunlight threatening the darkness, it had left him so weak as to be all but incapable of self-care.

"You're looking a bit sallow there, friend," a portsman at the bottom of the ramp said, "Look to have been in that storm a touch too long."

"Something a bit like that," Gabdur said, "He just needs something to settle his stomach."

"We got seasickness pills in the lobby," the portsman said, "Recommend you take them prior, but after'll do you, too."

"Thank you, we'll look into it."

Gabdur returned his attention to Galo, speaking under his breath to keep the conversation relatively private.

"We need to stop by the hotel first," he said, "We'll pick up Malia and take her with us to Drakougeneospa."

"Maybe Chekov or Dourias can figure out what's bothering you," Nikasu said to Galo.

"Feels like I'm dying," Galo muttered, "I wonder if Uro could figure out how it happened."

"Don't talk like that," Nikasu accosted, "Please."

Phylus looked to Malia as someone knocked on the door. She nodded without looking up from her mug of tea. Clutching the hotel robe around himself, he shuffled to answer the door.

Farim flinched at the sight of him. For a moment, he thought it was because she hadn't expected him. But when Uro reacted similarly, he remembered they didn't know about the eyepatch. Or a lot else, for that matter.

"Dude," Farim remarked, "What the hell happened to your eye?"

"There was an incident," Phylus said, "I got in an accident and… lost it."

"Do you think he's not telling us something?" Uro asked Farim.

"Yeah," she said, "What aren't you telling us?"

"Anything that I'd have to repeat later," he said, "A lot happened while you were gone."

"Why would you have to repeat any of it?" Farim asked.

"Galo left with Nikasu and Gabdur a few days after you," Phylus said, "And I'm still trying to make sense of everything myself."

"Well…" Uro said, "Can we come in and sit down while you figure it out?"

Phylus nodded and stepped aside. As he closed the door behind them, he made eye contact with Malia. He shook his head at her inquisitive stare, and she bolstered her composure as best she could manage.

"So, what'd they leave for?" Farim asked.

"Galo wanted to investigate something in the Southland Sea. His uncle, not Ebralgi, had mentioned forced labor," Phylus recounted. He looked to Uro. "By the way, sorry about giving you the runaround. I had to be sure."

"What are you talking about?" Uro asked, "Sinkua gave me that letter."

"What are you talking about?" Phylus deflected, "I gave you and someone else conflicting intel to see if one of you was a spy."

"It's true," Malia piped up, smiling across the top of her mug, "Did the double agent in me damn proud."

"Farim, I thought you picked up on that," Phylus said, "I thought that was why you took him with you."

Farim shook her head. "I picked up on your suspicion, but it's not like I could've gotten specifics about your plan," she said, "I was just keeping him out of the way while the rest of you made up your minds."

"Well, I trust him. The other guy acted on the intel."

"I trust him, too," she said, "Now…"

"Thank you!" Uro remarked, apologizing as Farim glared at him.

"Who was the other guy?" Farim asked.

"Matter for later," Phylus deflected, "What was in Sinkua's letter?"

"Nikasu's genome map and instructions for his doctor to make the treatment for her instead," Uro recounted, "Sinkua told me not to tell anyone except his doctor."

"What was he testing?" Phylus said, "Whether orders or morals are more important to you?"

"I don't think he was testing him. I think he really didn't want anyone to interfere," Farim said, "But, I found the letter, and of course, I interfered. We doubled the order and asked a nurse to make sure both got made."

"So, what has Sinkua been up to?" Uro asked, "I need to tell him that Farim got his letter from me."

"He and Nikasu raised the house under their house. Drakougene-ospa. Bigger than you can imagine. Bunch of their neighbors live there, seeing as it destroyed their houses," Phylus said, "He also got a job as EshCal's personal assistant, and she started training him in sword fighting."

"There were some informants outed in the Ministries," Malia added, "EshCal's now former assistant and some guy in Covert Affairs."

"They also figured out that part of Dourias's diagrams matches up with Yggdrasil's roots," Phylus said, "There's a map in one of the basements of Drakou that reacts to milystis. It's also what led Galo on his investigation. The map had a hole in the Southland Sea."

"Around where they found Arestor?" Uro pressed.

"Not far off."

"Well, I spoke with Gabdur shortly before you two came along," Malia said, "They should be here soon."

Over the next hour or so, Phylus recounted FerLyn's arrest but not her death. He told how Spril had promised to protect her but not how he fulfilled that promise. They had already heard about Joren's death and Sbaglien's temporary succession, but Phylus told how he was part of the investigation into Joren's assassination. That segued into how Gabdur hadn't been able to pinpoint the biological root of his soft spot visions, and how he no longer had them since he lost his depth perception. He also clarified that stress had actually triggered them.

When Galo and the others arrived, Phylus found him looking as defeated as he had felt since last night. Without words, he pulled the young man into the sort of hug that Gabdur couldn't give. Not for his missing an arm, but because for all their reconciliation, their bond only ran as deep as genetics.

"What happened?" Galo asked as Nikasu walked into Malia's arms, "I felt something. Can't shake it."

"He says it's clairvoyance, like his grandfather had," Gabdur said, "The one he knew. Not the one that raised me."

"We'll talk about it at Drakou, okay?" Phylus said, to which Galo nodded. He turned to Malia, keeping one hand on Galo's shoulder. "Honey, call SenRas. Tell him and MarLys that we're going to the house soon."

"So, besides feeling sick toward the end," Farim said to Galo, "how was the rest of your trip?"

"Informative," Gabdur said, "But it's also best saved for the house."

"Fair enough," she said, "Phylus just caught us up on what happened between when we left and when you left."

"Oh?" Gabdur remarked, turning to Phylus, "And since?"

Phylus sighed "Get comfortable."

As they settled in, Phylus recounted most of what had transpired in that time. He told how Calhosin had been an Avatar informant turned contrite. He told what little they knew about the exodus. He talked about how Inre had come as an emissary, gathering intel to prevent a Northland war and prove his innocence. He told that she had taken sanctuary in ArcNos, as she suspected Sbaglien was out to kill or frame her.

In recounting the attack on the high-rise district, he explained MalVek's latest tech as best he could. The branching soft spot generator. The telekinesis. The wound transfer which he had lost his eye to. He told how Inre had tried to save KalChi from JeiRol, only for both ArcNosians to end up dead. He explained that Biroe had been arrested for unwittingly killing JeiRol. He told how OshMar and FerLyn had officially committed suicide but the timing and nature had been suspect.

Galo wondered aloud if what he felt was the sum of all those deaths. Phylus entertained the possibility. Malia returned from her phone call soon after, and they made ready to return to Drakougeneospa.

All that remained was to tell them what had happened at the funeral.

SenRas leaned back, looking SouSol over as he weighed her lingering words. His tongue dragged across his teeth, pushing his lips into a sneer.

"Chaos, you say?" he asked, his tongue smacking off of his teeth, "Does that mean you arbitrarily contend any effort to establish order?"

"Sounds stupid," MarLys blurted, "No wonder your operations are a mess. You're opposed to cohesion on principle."

SouSol smiled bleakly at MarLys. "We don't need to resist order," she said, "Disorder is the ultimate eventuality."

"You speak of entropy, yes?" SenRas asked.

"Naturally," SouSol said, "All systems become more entropic as time passes. Thus, the universe favors those who can thrive under discord."

"Do you mean to say that you're more evolved than us?"

"Not more evolved," SouSol said, clicking her tongue, "Better adapted, because we've chosen to be."

"Oh, come off it!" MarLys guffawed, "I cut off MerSul's plans with a vague message and a wad of gum. Better adapted, my ass."

"Each of you who opposed us is now an amputee," SouSol scolded, "Do not presume to have outsmarted any of us."

"My, my," MarLys goaded, "How predictable."

A cold smile swept across SouSol's face. "You're trying to anger me. It isn't going to work," she said, "You know about the exodus. That means you know they were all arrested on purpose."

"My, my," MarLys doubled down, "How logical."

"Keep humoring yourself, child," SouSol chided, "The exodus is inevitable. Every attempt to infiltrate it has been thwarted."

"Actually," SenRas said, leaning forward, "That's not entirely true."

"What are you getting at?" SouSol asked.

"Inre," he said, "To wit, she has at least disrupted it."

"Impossible," SouSol argued, "The lily pads are uncrackable."

"Well, I admit that I'm working off something of an assumption," SenRas said, "I heard that, if she succeeded, we wouldn't see or hear from her for a while."

"Where is she?"

"At the prison, I suppose."

"You both report to General Sbaglien, don't you?" MarLys asked, "I wonder who'd look worse for her success. Him for being sabotaged or you for letting it happen? Either way, this does not bode well for you."

SouSol turned to face SenRas. "Release me," she demanded, "I insist on investigating this claim."

SenRas gestured to the front door. "It locks from the inside. You could have left at any time."

SouSol lunged out of her seat. Her eyes darted between them as she backed up toward the door. With vacant faces, they watched her hesitate by the door. As they betrayed nothing of a bluff, she threw the door open.

Framed pictures rattled on the walls as she slammed the door behind herself. MarLys chuckled as she got to her feet.

"Guess you've still got it, huh?" she chided.

"Better than we let her think, anyway," SenRas said. The phone rang. "That must be Malia."

Chapter 40

Cars coming and going from Drakougeneospa at all hours had never been a cause for concern. Not with how many families lived there. But three arriving like a procession at any hour was cause for curiosity.

"That's probably Phylus, for one," Spril said, setting his cards down. He looked to BeiLou. "Come on. Sinkua and SenRas might be with them."

"Oh, I sure as hell hope so," BeiLou sighed, slapping her cards down, "I just want to know if I'm allowed to be mad at them for not calling all night." She looked to Dourias inquisitively.

"Oh, no thank you," Dourias said, "My bones still ache from that storm. Besides, if Farim is back, she'll appreciate having an easy time finding me for once."

"I'll keep an eye on them," Elemeno offered with a sly wink, "Make sure they don't look at your cards."

"Buttmunch probably already knows what the rest of us have," Yrlis chided, grinning at Spril. He narrowed his eyes at her, and she laughed. "Just go downstairs."

Spril kept one ear tuned to the front lot as he and BeiLou headed down the marble and wrought iron staircases. For all its idiosyncrasies and inconsistencies, he had come to learn the inside of this place rather well enough that he didn't need his full attention to navigate it. But not, it seemed, well enough to count the voices out front at the same time.

"You can sort of read people's minds, right?" BeiLou asked.

"Only if it's something they're probably about to say," Spril said, "Why do you ask?"

BeiLou looked at him expectantly.

"It's not a parlor trick, BeiLou," Spril said, rolling his eyes, "Just tell me."

"Sorry. I just wanted to experience it first hand," BeiLou said, "Well anyway, have you ever picked anything up off of MeiLom or SenRas? You know? Feeling weird about calling me their mom or their daughter?"

"No. Why would they?"

"Well, SenRas and I barely knew each other, for one," she said, "And Sinkua, well, I had him when I was twenty-two. Now, he's twenty-six, and I'm only thirty-two."

"Why should that matter?" he countered, "I call Phylus my father, and he's only ten years older than me."

BeiLou smiled at him with something close to pity. "What about your biological father?"

"I... don't remember him," Spril said, "I haven't thought about my biological parents in over twenty years."

"You buried them," she said, shaking her head as soon as the words came out, "Figuratively, I mean. Sorry. I heard how they died." She paused to catch her breath. "I just mean you disconnected yourself from the tragedy. MeiLom did the same. He only moved back to his childhood home because he had nowhere else to go, and he decorated it so nothing was where CreSam and I had it. He even changed his name to distance himself."

"You're partly right about the name, but that's about it," Spril argued, "He came back to make better memories. And so Nikasu could grow up in what should have been her childhood home. And he redecorated to forget watching you die and living alone with CreSam. Not to forget either of you. Especially not you. No matter the age gap, you're still his mother."

"I hid my involvement to protect him from CreSam's dealings," BeiLou sighed as they rounded the end of the spiral staircase into the main vestibule, "I can't imagine him calling me mom without remembering me as a coward."

"There's actually a very simple explanation," he insisted. She cocked an eyebrow, more confused than inquisitive. His expression flattened. "You didn't ask why I remember my childhood with Phylus but not my childhood with my biological parents," he realized, "Did you?"

"No," she said, "I thought about it, but I figured it was because he raised you into adulthood."

"I'm sure that's part of it," Spril said, "Sorry. I guess my foresight still needs tuning."

"Don't sweat it," BeiLou shrugged, "You were saying."

"Right. Well, it's how they engineered me," Spril said, "I wasn't supposed to be able to form meaningful bonds. But then Phylus became a permanent fixture in my life." He paused as he grabbed a door handle. "And before long, Vielle came into the family."

The double doors opened as Phylus reached for the handle, yanking him out of his introspection. He was vaguely aware of Nikasu and less so of Galo being similarly startled. He sighed and shook his head. He called himself The Hybrids' father figure, and here he had news that would devastate these two but couldn't spare a thought for their feelings.

"Why's everyone so glum?" BeiLou asked, "Get in here."

Phylus waved everyone past him, entering last. He turned to Spril as he and BeiLou closed the doors behind him.

"Is everyone else here?" he asked.

"Everyone but Vielle and Sinkua," Spril said, "I assume they're right behind you?"

"Um…" Phylus stalled, unable to find the words despite all his years as a diplomat, "Let's go catch up. We've all got a lot to talk about."

Spril looked him up and down. Phylus had no idea how much he gleaned or if he was reading him. But Spril just flattened his expression and nodded. Phylus had resigned himself to having to discuss Vielle's death again all too soon, but the fewer times he had to do it, the better.

Back up in the rumpus room, handshakes and hugs were exchanged all around as the newly arrived relieved themselves of their luggage. Farim and Uro had traveled light, as had the southbound crew. Thus, much of it was the last of the gear from the hotel suite, most of which was Gabdur's medical equipment.

"It is so wonderful to see you again," Dourias said, holding Farim at arm's length as they withdrew from a clutching hug, "I am most glad the storm did not take you." He slapped Uro on the shoulder. "And you as well," he beamed, "Awfully good to see you are well."

"Thank you, sir," Uro exhaled, bowing his head, "Um, I was wondering, sir, if you could tell me something."

"I will do my best," Dourias said, "Ask away, my boy."

"Did you know a man named Caylence?"

"Caylence?" Dourias repeated, "Yes, he was once what we call a Keeper. But he had long retired at the time of my… incident." He looked Uro up and down. "Why do you ask?"

"He's my uncle."

"Oh! Why hadn't you mentioned this sooner? We might not have been so wary of you."

"I didn't know he knew anyone here."

"And what is Caylence doing these days, hm?"

"He's a medical examiner at Hillside Oncology. I worked as his assistant," Uro said, "Which means he's been behind enemy lines since I left with Farim."

"Oh, that is most dreadful," Dourias said, "But if anyone there were better prepared than he for such an ordeal, I would be most fascinated to meet them."

"Speaking of doctors," Farim said, "Where's Sinkua? We have some news for him."

"Also, where's Vielle?" Nikasu asked. She looked to Spril. "Have you seen her?"

Spril shook his head.

"I'm gonna need everybody to sit down," Phylus sighed, "And please, for the sake of… everything… don't interrupt me. Okay?"

He took the moments that it took everyone to settle in to gather his thoughts. It wasn't enough, and at that point, he knew it never would be. He took a deep breath and powered forth.

"For any of you who haven't heard, the capitol building came under attack during last night's funeral. I couldn't see any soft spots on account of my eye, but it played out just like MalVek's attack on the high-rise district," he explained, "MarLys went outside and used her Yggdrasil hair tie to call Vielle for help. Vielle was supposed to call here and get anyone who was available to meet her there.

"She never got the call. But she came anyway. We believe she saw the building shaking from her classroom window," he continued, running his hand through his already sweaty hair, "We… Fuck." Tears welled in his eyes as he swallowed a lump in his throat. "After the attack ended, we… We found her at the bottom of… Dammit!" The tears overflowed, caking sticky salt in his stubble.

"F… Found her?" Nikasu asked.

"What was… left of her," Phylus managed, "Her clothes and… a… pool of blood. Too much… so much blood."

"How much?" Spril asked, his voice forced steady, "How much blood, Phylus?"

"More than anybody could have survived," SenRas provided, "We believe she died quickly. In that, we can take solace."

"No," Phylus refused, "We take solace in that she saved all of us. Yggdrasil's roots now hold the infrastructure together."

"Where was Sinkua?" Nikasu asked, clinging to Galo, "He could have protected her."

"Where the hell was Odin?" Galo snarled, "If he's sworn to protect Yggdrasil, he should be sworn to protect her by extension."

"He should be sworn to protect all of you," BeiLou insisted, "But he's in the same place he's been since you left. Bottom basement, digging out the shaft to the Hephaeseum mine."

"Sinkua and EshCal fell into a trap. Neither he nor Vielle knew what was happening to the other," Phylus said, reining in the conversation, "EshCal lost both legs just below the knees. They captured Sinkua."

BeiLou rose to approach him. "And what," she asked, "did you do to stop them?"

Phylus struggled to meet her steely gaze. "Far less than I wish I had," he confessed, "The whole thing just... I have no excuses." He threw his hands up. "For fuck's sake. NeiRos! Prime Minister of Education. Never knew your son. Lost half his arm trying to save him. Portal closed on him."

"So, that's it, then? I've lost my husband and my son to The Avatars of Fate?" BeiLou rasped, her voice trembling, "Because The Coalition, the Task Force, or whatever name any of you have come up with couldn't protect them?"

Nikasu looked up from the tears she had been feeding into Galo's shirt. "That's not true."

"Don't defend them," BeiLou scolded, "You of all people should know better."

"That's enough, BeiLou," Malia countered.

"Think what you want," Nikasu said, "But my brother is still alive." She looked up at Galo. "You can sense him, right?"

"I can't control it that well," Galo said, shaking his head, "But... How do you figure?"

"Because Vielle is dead," Nikasu said, wincing at the sound of it, "Remember, only one of the three of us can be disposable."

"One activator and one distributor," Galo realized, "They have to keep Sinkua alive."

"And when we find him, he can bring Vielle back!"

"Don't get your hopes up," Chekov said, "Odin said he can't revive other Hybrids."

"Fuck that one-eyed cunt and the rules he rode in here with," Nikasu snapped, "Sinkua will find a way to bring back Eytea, and she'll bring Vielle with her."

"This is assuming that whoever attacked Vielle was coordinating with MalVek," SenRas said, "Sinkua was the target. Vielle was a matter of opportunity. As much as I hate to think it, we must consider the possibility that they were both killed."

"Well..." Gabdur sighed, "If that's what's become of it... At least MalVek's plans fell apart."

"Do we know who killed her?" Galo asked.

"No, but she tried to leave a message," SenRas said, "Phylus?"

Phylus signaled Malia, who produced a sheet of paper from her pocket. She handed it to Galo.

"SenRas drew that on Phylus's arm before he came to the hotel," she explained.

Galo looked over the scribblings for a moment, then passed it to Spril.

"Vielle wrote that in her blood," Phylus said, "But her hand smeared through it."

"We can't quite tell what it says," Malia added.

"I... think I can guess," Chekov said, her lips tight with anxiety, "Something to the effect of... Mortvill is a Dragon Hybrid?"

All heads snapped toward her. Even Gabdur for all his time with The Coalition and Dourias for all his insight hadn't been aware of this.

"He's one of us?!" Galo barked.

"He can just walk in here any time he wants?" Nikasu cried out, "He's a fucking Dragon Hybrid, and he's hunting me and my brother?!"

"Sinkua didn't have his sword when he came for me," Farim rasped with sick realization, "But he had it when we left. Someone there got their hands on it. Mortvill was trying to raise the house on his own."

"That means we know which one of them survived," Chekov said, choking on the words, "The Omnimath went after The Harvester when MalVek took Nikasu. It would seem that… only The Harvester left there alive." She held her head in her hands. "I've lost everyone that I came here with."

"All the more important that I go back with you, then," Spril said, "Just as soon as I've avenged Vielle."

"Who's his Etherworlder?" Nikasu asked, "I thought there was just our five and Pandora. Or is it Pandora? Oh shit! Is she a Dragon!?"

"No, she isn't. And technically, what you said is true," Chekov said, "Mortvill was bound to Tiamat, Etherworlder of the dead and dying. But Pandora consumed her. Mortvill pledged Tiamat and his servitude to her in a bargain for his life. Pandora let him keep his powers and Epemort, the Sword of the Dead, so that he could serve her for much longer, and better, at that. But Tiamat now only exists as part of Pandora's milystis."

"Idiot," Galo muttered.

"The Omnimath would have agreed with you."

"So, MalVek captured Sinkua, and The Harvester killed Vielle," Spril said, gritting his teeth, "He's obviously using Sinkua as bait."

"Which obviously we're going to take," Nikasu interjected.

"Obviously," Spril said, "But if he doesn't know The Harvester killed Vielle, he could have killed Sinkua to eliminate the resurrection factor."

"Or perhaps as a power move against The Harvester," SenRas suggested, "These are two domineering and manipulative personalities. They will not share a throne."

"But," Uro piped up, "He didn't kill him."

"Come again?" Spril asked.

"Sinkua's alive," Uro said, "We know he is."

"On what evidence, young man?" SenRas asked, "We have circumstances to the affirmative and contrary."

"Because we're indoors," Uro said, furrowing his brow, "Phylus. You explained it when we were waiting for the cabs."

Phylus cocked his head in reflection. They had discussed how the house worked, but distress scattered his thoughts.

"That's right!" Farim remarked, "Sinkua had to tell the house that we're welcome here. If he were dead, we'd all be outside."

"Drakospekarda," Phylus gasped, "Son of a bitch. How did none of us see that?"

"I'm not as close to all of this as the rest of you are," Uro said.

"Uro!" Farim exclaimed, "The numbers!"

"What about…?" Uro pondered, "You think that has something to do with this?"

"You said it means something happened while we were gone," she reasoned, "This is a whole lot of something."

"What are these numbers?" Malia asked.

"Caylence has been leaking intel to me," Uro said, producing the paper from his pocket.

"His methods are secure," Farim assured.

"As I would expect from Caylence," Dourias said, "Go on, then."

"Just before we docked, I got a call with a list of numbers," Uro explained, extending the paper toward Malia's outstretched hand, "Maybe they'll tell us more about what happened to Sinkua."

"Actually," Malia said as she settled back, "Spril, I think you…"

Spril swiped the paper from behind her seat. She jumped and turned at his abrupt presence.

"I deciphered the last coded message," Spril explained, "When you asked about the numbers, I figured that would occur to you, too."

"Well," Dourias said, his breath heavy, "we actually know what Mal-Vek means to do with Sinkua. Not precisely how, mind you, but we know his intentions."

Sinkua felt something cold pressing across his limbs. The ground felt unnatural. Artificial. It wasn't quite a floor, though. Concepts floated just beyond comprehension. He also felt, though he couldn't explain it, sideways.

The memory of pain radiated from the side of his head. Peripheral redness encroached on the darkness in his mind's eye. The coldness tingled. He became aware of every hair on his arms as they stood at attention.

His eyes shot open as electricity surged through his body. With a stuttered bellow, he convulsed and writhed against his bindings. His circumstances became clear, but he still had no sense of the time between the parking structure and now.

His eyes focused on MalVek, who looked up at him with a remote in his hand. Sinkua realized he had been strapped to a gurney and turned upright. Sinkua flicked his wrist, but the flame he conjured circled just beyond the clamps and dissipated. MalVek's smile barely touched his eyes.

"Were you aware that the ArcNosian authorities made an oversight when they disposed of The Scout's body?" he asked, "Well, I suppose with what you knew at the time…"

"What are you…?" Sinkua puzzled, trying and failing twice more to produce flames, "His resurrection chip was destroyed. And what does that have to do with this? Are you using me to create another one?"

"Just like you," MalVek scoffed, "Clever in your own stupid way. But ultimately wrong."

"Then…?"

"He had a second power. Though to your credit, or rather lack of discredit, even The Geneticist was blinded by what you call the resurrection chip," MalVek said, "His body diverted milystic attacks. Now, where do you suppose he learned how to do that?"

Sinkua's eyes widened with realization. "The Weapon," he gasped, "That's how Spril fought off Ozzera's biomechs."

"There we are. I knew you'd find your way there," MalVek said, "Of course, your feather-backed girlfriend would have figured it out as soon as she learned about The Weapon."

"Keep her name out of your mouth," Sinkua snarled, willing a concentration of milystis into his hand.

"She also would have realized after one failure that you can't overpower it. Same as you can't punch through a monopolar force field," MalVek goaded, "I did warn EshCal that that girl was too clever. I'm not sure which is more tragic. That Eytea had to die for that cleverness. Or that EshCal had to be discarded for proving unfit to follow me."

Sinkua wrenched against the gurney. The bindings creaked and dug into his flesh. The taste of iron rose into the back of his throat. He wrenched again, this time breaking the bindings on his arm off of the cot. He reached across himself to free his other arm.

"Lie down," MalVek scolded, his voice reverberating.

Sinkua complied without a thought, flattening against the gurney with both arms at his sides. On some level, he knew it was irrational, but he couldn't shake the fear that trying to move his unbound arm would be unbearably painful.

"I also borrowed something for myself from The Weapon," MalVek said, "The Politician made a fascinating test pilot."

"Is that also where you learned how to steal body parts?" Sinkua taunted, "Yeah. I know about the eye. And somehow or another, I'm returning it to Phylus."

"As much of a nuisance as that bastard has been," MalVek snarled, "a single eye is far from the worst of fair recompense."

"Tell me something," Sinkua said, "Do you have any talents of your own? Or do you just steal them from people who are better than you?"

MalVek mashed a button on the remote. Sinkua coughed and sputtered bloody smoke as he convulsed through a second wave of electricity. His eyes rolled back in his head.

An impact like a steel bludgeon collided with his sternum. As the wind left his lungs, his convulsing stopped. He toppled backward, gurney and all, and tumbled across the room until a wall stopped him.

He didn't hear any footsteps through all the clattering, but the moment he stopped, he found MalVek standing over him.

"I had hoped to lure Nikasu here," MalVek said, "that she might watch you become The Beast and you watch her become enthralled to it."

"Vielle would stop it," Sinkua coughed, "Always will."

"I wouldn't be so sure," MalVek said, "But now, there's no reason we can't do a few dry runs in the meantime." He drew his photonic weapon generator, manifesting his hammer with the push of a button. "So, let's be on with it."

Spril excused himself to work on the number cypher. Uro offered to help, but Spril insisted he stay and listen to Dourias.

"Do you already know what he's going to say?" Uro asked.

"No, but it'll be easier for me if Yrlis fills me in later," Spril said, "It's too…" He trailed off and gestured broadly. "… loud in here."

"Now then. Dourias," Gabdur beckoned as Spril left, "Are we to understand that you've decoded your tattoos?"

"You are indeed," Dourias boasted, "Now…"

"Any thoughts on the exodus?" Phylus cut in, "Sorry."

"Quite fine, my friend, but I'm afraid not," Dourias said, "Now, with all we had deciphered before, we didn't know how it could culminate in reawakening Pandora. The arising, as they call it. This is where the soft spots and the Eyes of the Dragon come into play. At a certain point in the episode, the activator becomes both enthralled and enthralling. He or she zeroes in on a singular obsession and forces this same thought upon all in the activation network. That obsession is to reach a particular destination, and they will be quick to remove any and all interference."

"The bodies on my ship," Galo said, "After Sinkua's milystis went dark, they were all gathered by the bow."

Dourias nodded. "Now, we can assume that the destination is The Veil," he continued, "Which...?" He gestured to Galo.

"We found it," Galo said, "It's... toxic to milystis."

"MalVek has thralls working in Berinin," Nikasu added, "They're building an underwater bridge to it."

"But how are they going to get there?" Gabdur asked, "I can't imagine they'll just mill about on a boat."

"As I said, soft spots and Eyes of the Dragon," Dourias reminded, "MalVek has established a series of soft spots around Ouristihra, which the activated will pass through with the help of homunculi equipped with the Eyes of the Dragon."

"The last soft spot should be near the start of the bridge," Galo added, "It isn't much, but we at least have that to work off of, should it go that far."

"Yes, but if they reach The Veil, they will throw themselves at it," Dourias said, "The activation will cause tsora to react much in the same way as milystis."

"They're going to sacrifice themselves," Nikasu gasped.

Dourias nodded somberly. "And The Veil will come apart."

"If Sinkua is wearing his necklace, Phoenix will be destroyed," Galo added, "Etherworlders are pure milystis."

"Back when The Omnimath was The Harvester, he had a similar but less ambitious plan," Chekov said, "He meant to throw Sinkua at The Veil to break it and present Phoenix to Pandora as appeasement. But Phoenix was destroyed, just like you said. MalVek built his plan off of his knowledge of that failure."

"So... my brother's going to kill himself and his Etherworlder...?" Nikasu choked out, swallowing hard, "Where or... how will I be when this is happening?"

"We are uncertain on that front," Dourias said, "When Vielle acted as the distributor, she retained some control of her mental faculties. So, you may be able to join the fight in keeping them from The Veil."

"Or in stopping the activation!" Nikasu said, perking up, "Just like Vielle did!"

"Yes, quite," Dourias agreed, "Or because you could have been the activator and are afflicted, you may be activated yourself."

"Oh. Right," Nikasu said, her shoulders slumping.

Uro put his hand up sheepishly.

"You don't have to raise your hand, my boy," Dourias sighed, "Just speak up."

"Okay, um... Question about the Eyes of the Dragon," Uro said, lowering his hand, "What do they do? Do they let people see soft spots?"

"Essentially, yes," Dourias said, "They allow four-dimensional vision and travel."

"They're the goggles I stole to escape the hyperspace prison," Phylus added, "I was having residual effects until this happened." He gestured to his eyepatch.

"That's what I was getting at," Uro said, "If you wore them again, could you get your depth perception back?"

"That's, um... That's a good question," Phylus said, "They probably could. And I'm sure Gabdur and Chekov could make it so they don't have to be drilled into my head..."

"…. But?"

"But we don't have them anymore," he went on, "Inre reverse engineered the hardware in her attempt to stop the exodus."

"Wait, how did that work?" Farim asked, "You never said she had anything to do with it."

"I had to wait until we were somewhere secure," Phylus reasoned, "With some equipment from NalSet's workshop and the added work power of some of our residents, she built forcefield generators with Eyes of the Dragon circuitry in the guts."

"She made forcefields that even blocked portals?" Farim realized, her mouth agape, "I... That's incredible."

"Well, she said that the idea was speculative at best. But it seems to have worked. I tried to call her, but it disconnects the instant she picks up," Phylus said, "My signal can get in, but hers can't get out."

"But then, how is she going to get out?" Uro asked, "Or wait! That's her leverage with the prisoners, isn't it?"

"Exactly," Phylus said, "She's one of two people who knows how to deactivate the generators."

"Who's the other?"

"That would be me, young man," Elemeno said, startling most as she hadn't spoken this entire time.

"Nobody suspects her," Yrlis said, "Nobody sees her coming."

The door opened, and Spril poked his head in from the next room.

"You're already done?" Farim asked, her mouth agape.

"Slapdash code. Not hard to crack," he shrugged, then turned his attention to Yrlis, "Come fill me in?"

"Sure thing, hon," Yrlis said as she bounced from her seat. She turned to address the assemblage. "I'll be back in a few."

"So will I," Spril added, "We'll go over the entry plan when I do."

"You already…" Malia began.

"Working on it," Spril said, tapping the side of his head.

"But you need…" Gabdur added.

"I need to know MalVek's full plan," Spril interrupted. He shut his eyes and shook his head. "Sorry. I need to stop doing that. We'll be back in a few."

A palpable heat filled the room, rippling the air and bearing down as though it had its own mass. The smell it coaxed from metal felt as though it could galvanize the lungs. Tonight, conductive metals gave an acrid quality to the odors of the ironworks.

Donning thick elbow-length gloves, Inre pulled one such acrid ember from the furnace with tongs as long as her arm. The disc glowed orange with chartreuse veins. Inre fixed her gas-masked stare on MerSul as she set the smoldering lily pad on the anvil, nodding in a gesture of both acknowledgment and command.

MerSul reached aside with a beckoning motion, and PavRal slapped a sledgehammer handle into his palm. He raised the hammer above his head and released a cathartic bellow as he crashed it down upon his smoldering lily pad. The middle flattened, and the edges bulged and cracked in a brilliant display of emerald sparks.

"Well, you all look to be having a wonderful time here," came a far Northland voice.

MerSul yelped and staggered, nearly dropping the sledge on his own feet. He composed himself and turned to face the door with everyone else. Fractalized light dissipated behind two figures.

"Hello, Sbaglien," Inre said, projecting her voice through her mask, "I'm disappointed. I thought you'd find me before morning."

"My..." Sbaglien began, looking to the woman at his side, "... escort informed me you've stopped the exodus. I had to see for myself." His eyes panned the ironworks. "Looks to me like there wasn't much to see, this being your grand gambit."

"Oh, I'd say you don't know the half of it."

Sbaglien bared the tips of his teeth as he smiled. "Nor do you, whelp," he flicked his glance aside, "What say you, SouSol?"

In the dim lobby of the bed-and-breakfast, Jex poured himself a mug of decaffeinated coffee, leaving a bit of space at the top. From a safe behind the counter, he took a flask of Ierodhesan whiskey.

He turned off the last light on the ground floor as he sipped his nightcap. With a swipe of his access card, he took a sandwich from the vending machine. Spinach and tomato with smoked salmon.

Jex headed upstairs to wind down the night in front of the television. Only, a knock at the door had other plans for him. He headed back down and looked out the window.

Spril, the one he now knew to be The Weapon, stood at the fore. To his left stood Chekov, ever faithful to the mission, and Dourias looking too much like his own father. Standing to Spril's right had to have been Yrlis by how she grasped his hand.

Back a ways, he recognized Malia from past visits and Nikasu by her eyes. Phylus, he knew by reputation and proximity to them.

Within half an arm's reach of Nikasu was The Last Chieftain Sage, standing with shoulders wide in a guarding stance. Aleepo and Picuarus, rather Gabdur and Elemeno, flanked Galo.

Farther aside was the very image of a woman who had visited twenty years ago, but she'd scarcely aged. By all reason, she couldn't have been BeiLou, yet she stood with familial proximity to SenRas.

The lines in SenRas face were thick with the fatigue of a life spent running. MarLys stood ready, familiar only his knowledge of her prosthetic hand.

Aside from Malia's stood Farim with who he deduced to be Uro.

Notably absent were the man who would either be The Beast or The Warrior and the Yggdrasil Hybrid. Sinkua and Vielle. And the posture of those who'd come spoke plenty toward the reasons.

Jex walked to the phone as Spril knocked again. He dialed and waited.

"Hello?"

"Murdega?"

"Speaking."

"This is Jex."

"What is it now?"

"I may need your services again. Stand by."

Chapter 41

Gentle rain fell from the night sky, all but starless for the dense cloud cover. Six days since heavy storms racked the entire continent, and flash storms still cropped up like rumbling aftershocks. Fading penumbrae radiated from darkened streetlights. A flicker of heat lightning bared the silhouette of a broad man with a gas mask hanging off the back of his head.

Galo intertwined his thoughts with Leviathan's. They coordinated his actions and her involvement down to the finest muscle movements. He lowered and secured his gas mask. Galo thumped his chest.

And he ran.

Some dozen people huddled in the gazebo to keep out of the rain. Nobody spoke. Nobody made eye contact. Each of them just fixated on their own thoughts and cigarette.

With a crack of thunder, the lights in the parking lot and along the side of the building went out. The battery-powered lamp clipped to the ceiling of the gazebo made a beacon of the smoke break structure.

"Guess we better head back," another worker grumbled as he shuffled out of the gazebo.

The rest of them followed, and Elemeno melted into the crowd.

Light hovered over the exposed circuit panel, following the screwdriver in Yrlis's hand. Farim held the light steady, careful not to look directly at the open panel. Nikasu perched atop the streetlamp, watching from the obscurity of relative darkness.

Lightning flashed. Yrlis snapped the wire with her screwdriver, and a cascade of darkness swept across the property and beyond.

Enrobed in Nemesis, Nikasu jumped down and lit upon the wet grass. She pressed her fingers to her upper sternum.

"Side Team Beta success," she said, "Standing by."

Threads strained as Elemeno shoved her hands deeper into her pockets. The pattering of rain masked the jangling of her fingers combing through dozens of tiny metal beads.

She lifted a hand to prop the door as she reached the rear entrance, only to cast her eyes up and find a man at least as tall as her son-in-law holding it open. She gave him a flat smile and a nod as she returned that hand to her pocket.

He winked at her.

The seams of her pockets popped, and the beads trickled out. They scattered to the walls, continuing to roll as though guided by unseen forces. If not for the commotion of the facility, she may have heard the collective thrumming of infrared frequencies.

MarLys watched from atop a tree branch as the rear entrance closed. She swung to the underside of the branch and propped her feet against the trunk. She kicked off and released the branch, springing out to land clear of the surface roots.

She leaned in and slapped the trunk. The butt of a rifle emerged from the foliage. MarLys accepted it and stepped back. Phylus shuffled down the trunk.

Phylus nodded toward the rear entrance. As they walked, MarLys pressed on her sternum.

"Rear Team. She's in," she said, "Waiting to follow."

Flanked by Malia and SenRas, Murdega stepped off the dock and onto the beach. He patted a portsman on the shoulder and nodded to the illuminated frame behind the aft of his ship. The portsman reached into his tool belt as he swaggered toward the frame. Fractal light and electricity crackled off the treated wood even as he set into dismantling it.

Murdega pressed his hand to his sternum as the three of them trekked inland under the humid warmth of the Southland Spring night.

"Relay Team proceeding on foot," he reported, "Silent until landing."

Spril sat with his eyes shut and his hands over his mouth. His wire could only transmit. Chekov had insisted on it. Or rather, she had begun to, but he saw her reasoning and spoke first.

With his eyes closed and breath steady, he could just make out each of their voices. Save for the Relay Team, of course.

BeiLou and Uro had been the only candidates for his team. Uro had skills that were needed elsewhere. That and he talked too much when he had something to say. If he wasn't seeking validation, he was agitating arguments.

Spril shook his head at his own wandering thoughts. He heard a faint metallic cascade beyond the rain.

"They're in place," he exhaled, opening his eyes, "We move soon."

BeiLou nodded. "Who do you think we'll see in there?"

Spril gave her a sidelong glance, pondering her many potential voices as they echoed back from two seconds in the future. "Between The Beast and The Warrior?"

BeiLou reached down her shirt, fiddling with her wire. "I've heard he gets pretty scary when he goes on a blackout rage," she said, "But I don't think that's The Beast that Gabdur talked about at the bed-and-breakfast. Not after what happened to Nikasu."

"Do you think...?" Spril said, trailing off into an epiphany, "How long has he been using the morningstar?"

"...I don't know. He must have picked it up after I died," BeiLou said, "Eytea never let on that she knew him without it. Where..."

"Side Team Alpha," he announced as he activated his wire, "When did the target acquire his signature weapon?"

Jex pulled his finger away from his ear as he turned to Chekov.

"They've docked," he said, "Continuing on foot."

Chekov nodded. "Keep it off the waves," she said, "I'll relay the coordinates."

Uro looked back and forth between Gabdur and Galo. Gabdur shook his head. Gas mask hanging off the back of his head, Galo pressed a finger to his sternum.

"Just shy of fifteen."

Dourias's eyes danced along the monitor as geometric assets fizzled into existence. Individuals and the composite shifted and rotated with every motion of his gloved hand. He had only been listening to the conversation at the periphery of his attention, his focus occupied with the map compilation software. The abrupt sound of Chekov's voice, however, snagged his awareness in earnest.

"NalSet planted it," she said, "He never said why."

"Whose idea was it?" came Spril's voice through their earpieces.

"His own," Chekov said, "Where are…?"

"I'm calling for backup," Spril interrupted, "Sorry. I have a theory."

"We'll check in when we know more," BeiLou added, "Side Team Alpha standing by and investigating."

Myriela and EshCal looked aside from the end of the balance bars at the sound of EshCal's phone ringing in her overnight bag. They turned back to one another, sharing heavy expectations through silent eye contact.

"Bring me that, please," EshCal said, her voice thready with anxiety.

By the time she had said it, though, the nurse was halfway to them with her still-ringing phone in hand. He passed it to EshCal, who answered while balancing most of her weight on one hand.

"Ministry of Defense. Prime Minister EshCal speaking."

"Please tell me you're not in the office right now."

"No, Spril," EshCal exhaled, tension dissolving from her shoulders, "I'm in the hospital. How are things?"

"Complicated," Spril said, "Listen, I know you can't help directly, but I need something delivered from Drakou."

"And you can't get there yourself," EshCal deduced, more stating than asking, "And I'm the only person whose number you have who's also welcome there."

"Yes, everyone's busy. Can you help?"

"Where are you?"

"I've got Relay on the line," someone said from aside. EshCal couldn't place the voice.

"Who is…?" EshCal began to ask.

"Complicated," Spril doubled down. He spoke aside. "Good. Give me a minute."

"Fine. I'm sure you have a good reason to keep quiet on the details," EshCal conceded, "Will Hibiscus do?"

"Will I do for what?" Hibiscus asked.

"Spril needs a favor," EshCal said, "Delivery from Drakou."

"Give it here."

Dourias clapped once as the monitor beeped. Chekov and Jex turned sharply and glared at him. He smiled meekly as he mouthed an apology, then put his finger to his chest again.

"Cover Team. Map data complete," Dourias said, "Uploading to your heads-ups."

"Gonna be pretty rudimentary," Jex added, "Never got to field test this tech."

Gabdur, Uro, and Galo all pulled their gas masks over their faces. As they tightened the straps, a green wireframe map of the facility fizzled into one lens of each of their goggles.

Gabdur watched as Galo's posture shifted from pensive to eager. He pressed the wire on his chest.

"Roll out in three…"

Lightning flickered.

"Two…"

Galo took off running.

Elemeno paused at a vending machine next to the lobby. After a moment's consideration, she bought a can of cranberry rutabaga juice, reasoning it to be the heaviest flavor. As she squatted to take it, she slipped a metal ball from her pocket. The clunk masked the clang, and she walked to the stairwell as the ball rolled into the lobby. The door shut behind her, and she stopped for a drink to the sound of steady hissing and compounding panicked coughing.

Roughly his own height shy of the door, Galo leapt and tucked his legs up. He twisted his body and, with Leviathan's aid, aligned his feet in perfect symmetry with the doors. He let all conscious effort fall blank as his deeper thoughts pulled everything into place. Every bone, every muscle, every impulse floated into perfect timing.

This was revenge. This was reclamation. And for him, it began with this moment.

His coiled body released its potential energy down his legs. Both feet slammed against the door, fracturing it and cracking the frame. As he followed through, the hinges snapped apart. The broken door flew out of the frame, sailing into the lobby.

Galo landed in a crouch and stayed there. He split his focus between the map in his lens and the people stumbling and coughing under the spreading cloud of white smoke. The bomb beside the circular reception desk sputtered as it neared the end of its capacity.

A hand grabbed Galo's shoulder as he got back to his feet. Uro moved past him and hopped the reception desk. Gabdur made for the stairwell with a second mask bound to his forearm. Galo stood with his glaive upright and sheathed in thick leather, just in case.

SouSol advanced from Sbaglien's flank, her presence seeming to push him aside. Inre sneered as she dragged her tongue across her teeth.

"Give her some credit, would you?" SouSol insisted, "I'm sure they explained it in a way that even a mongrel such as she could understand."

"Excuse me!?" Inre recoiled.

Her hand snapped up, pressing two fingers against SouSol's clavicle. But no sooner had she made contact than Sbaglien snatched her fingers and bent them back toward her wrist. She gritted her teeth, refusing to let him hear her scream.

"Actually, she explained it to us," PavRal said, muscling his way into the middle of them, "She says we're being exploited to start a war between Tanelen and ArcNos."

"And you believe her?" SouSol asked, "It's tragic, really. NeiRos's failures are so chronic, we often lose sight of the acute."

"I do," PavRal asserted, "Maybe your sanctimony works on Parliament, but I don't buy it. You came here with the de facto Noble Doyen. You both have a stake in the exodus."

"I came in search of my second in command," Sbaglien insisted, "I was given to understand that she was taken hostage."

"And I joined him as an act of diplomacy," SouSol added, glancing aside at Calhosin, "Seeing as Foreign Affairs has been so mired in scandal."

"You see? My presence is only to undo her interference," Sbaglien said, gesturing to Inre, "She's taken the lot of you hostage, yet her subordinates and supporters are livid at her alleged imprisonment. So, return her to me, and you can all go on with this exodus that she spoke of."

"These men are no more hostages than I am," Inre said, "But I'm the one who decides when we leave, and it's all or none."

"I'd expect such braggadocio from a mongrel," SouSol scoffed, "What say you we see what the guards think of this?"

"We have an understanding with them," Calhosin interjected, "Unlike in the women's prison. Maybe you should have staged the exodus there."

SouSol and Sbaglien turned to him sharply. Sbaglien's mouth warped into a scowl that dominated his entire face.

"Don't you dare…"

"The opinions of outsiders are as inconsequential as those of mongrels," SouSol cut off, disregarding Sbaglien's mounting ire, "My only concern is with the advancement of true-blooded ArcNosians."

"Nearly half of Parliament is foreign-born or foreign-parented," PavRal said, "Same with the Prime and High Ministers."

"So, you already see the problem. There may yet be hope for you," SouSol said, "We must teach the true history of ArcNos. From Kirts shouldering us with their economic crisis to the Ouristihran Union conspiring for our eradication."

"And yet, your grand plans for indoctrination fall to the mercy of a mongrel and an outsider," Inre said, sweeping her arms out in a mocking gesture, "Nobody leaves without my permission."

SouSol looked her over. "You already said that," she scoffed, "You're bluffing."

"She trapped us all here," MerSul said, shaking his head, "Whole place is lined with forcefield towers. Ones that can't even be portaled through."

SouSol turned to Inre, her eyes wide with calculating fury. Her fingers twitched. Her eyes darted aside. Inre narrowed her own as SouSol's settled on the anvil. SouSol lunged.

But as soon as she set her hand on the tongs, PavRal grabbed her wrist. The smoking remains of MerSul's lily pad bounced off the anvil and hit the floor.

"Let her go," MerSul bellowed.

"Haven't you been listening?" PavRal snarled, squeezing SouSol's wrist.

"Haven't you?" MerSul countered, "She has a point. They're holding us back."

"No. No, I want a revolution, but…." PavRal stammered, "But not like this."

"If you won't stand down, I'll have no choice but to brand you an impediment to diplomacy," Sbaglien said, "Should you still not…"

His expression flattened all but for his widened eyes and further paling face.

"Speaking of branding," Biroe said, his gloved hand disappearing behind Sbaglien's back, from which rose swirling smoke, "I should tell you, I've killed quicker over less. So, don't, as they say, fuck with me. Okay?"

"Kill me here, and you'll have a war on your conscience."

"Wouldn't be my first."

Sbaglien kicked Biroe in the chest, taking blisters to his back as he up-turned the disgraced accountant in his wheelchair. SouSol twisted out of Pav-Ral's faltering grasp, and she and MerSul flanked Sbaglien.

"Anything I do to either of you will be framed in the preservation of diplomacy," Inre said, eyeing Sbaglien and SouSol as she advanced with Calhosin and PavRal at her sides. "But dead or alive, your empire falls with the barrier towers."

The computer interface wasn't quite the same as any Uro had encoun-tered in his job, but he found it intuitive enough that he took to it quickly. He soon became so entrenched in his work, that it was only when he heard a voice that he remembered to blink.

"You doing okay?" Farim asked.

"Yeah," Uro said, "Sorry. Zoned out."

"Got my mask. Thank you," Elemeno added, "Looking for good search points."

"Good. Good."

Uro settled back into his work, focusing so far past his goggles that his eyes no longer processed the map. Soon, he found and accessed the secu-rity system.

"Are you almost done?" Nikasu asked, "Side Team Beta is itching to fuck someone up."

"Someone in particular or just in general?" Uro asked.

"Someone in particular," Nikasu said, "Anyone else, depends how bad they interfere."

"Lethal force is a last resort," Spril scolded.

"I know," Nikasu said, eyes rolling in her voice, "Like I said."

A message scrawled across the computer screen. Uro squatted under the desk to unplug the machine, then sliced the cord with his pocketknife.

"Forward Team is in," he announced, "Security systems are down. Can't do anything about manual locks from here."

Leaning next to the door, Phylus detached the gun magazine and stuffed it in his pocket. MarLys worked her hook into the crack between the door and the frame. Phylus inserted a new magazine and turned to face the door.

"Almost got it?" he asked.

MarLys pulled down until she struck deadbolt, cranking her shoulder as she wrenched the hook against it. The mechanism creaked, and the door shifted.

"Alpha is in," BeiLou said through their earpieces.

"Step back," Phylus ordered, "Put your mask on."

"Gonna do this the loud way?" MarLys asked as she complied.

"It s that or be too late to help."

Phylus pressed the gun barrel against the deadbolt keyhole and pulled the trigger twice. The first caused a dull thud. With the second came a thunderous pop, and the lock split into a perfectly round hole. He stepped back and shouldered his gun. As he put his gas mask on, he realized the map was over his eyepatch.

"I'll need you to be my navigator," he said.

MarLys nodded as she fished the excess debris out of the hole. She pulled out the last fragment of deadbolt and opened the door. She put a finger to her chest.

"Rear Team is in."

Spril slung his backpack around to his front and unzipped it. As he rifled about in his pack, he cocked his ear at the distant sound of bending metal. He pulled out a handheld resonant disrupter and let the backpack fall.

BeiLou gathered up the pack as he affixed the disrupter to the door. She fished out a belt and shoulder strap adorned with small metal balls. He struck the door with the tuning fork and activated the mounted disrupter.

"Beta is in," came Nikasu's voice.

The door rippled like stricken gelatin. Spril plunged his quarterstaff through and swirling it to create an opening. Once the hole was wide enough, he sheathed his staff and deactivated and detached the disrupter.

BeiLou stuffed the disrupter in the backpack and handed it back to Spril. She plucked one of the balls from her shoulder strap, pressed a button, and lobbed it through the hole. She and Spril secured their gas masks, and they followed shortly behind the gas grenade as she announced their entrance.

Nikasu jammed the tip of Epelun into the keyhole and closed her eyes. As she channeled her milystis through the blade, Nemesis murmured within her mind in Harkzanian peppered with broken Ouristihran.

A cacophonous kachunking rattled her focus. She opened her eyes to find the door had accordioned. She yanked her sword out of the keyhole and kicked the mangled door out of the frame. Then, followed by Yrlis and Farim, who held a cloth-wrapped wrench the size of her forearm and a fiberglass boat oar respectively, Nikasu walked through the vacated doorframe.

"Beta is in," she said as they fastened their masks.

White smoke licked Galo's and Uro's backs as they entered the stairwell. Elemeno and Gabdur greeted them with approving nods.

"Have you found anything yet?" Uro asked, "Nothing stands out to me."

Elemeno raised one finger. "Okay, I'm seeing three locations for the actuation chamber," she announced, "It should be a small room at the end of a long hall. Everyone see them?"

Affirmatives mutters trickled through the earpieces.

"Great!" Elemeno remarked, "Spril, how should we go about this?"

"You four head up top and take the northwest quadrant," Spril ordered, "Beta, southeast chamber. Rear, head to the west central chamber. Alpha will meet you on the way."

With Epelun in its sheath, Nikasu took point as Side Team Beta charged up the hall. She swept her arm, and Nemesis peeled away and corkscrewed at the door at the end of the hall. The fluidic Etherworlder buckled the plated window, expanding in the opening to rend the door into dozens of fragments.

Nikasu, Farim, and Yrlis scrambled over the wreckage, only to shuffle to a halt around Nemesis. The dragon snarled and hissed, grumbling in far more Harkzanian than Nikasu could translate. But she understood well enough.

Glass-eyed operatives converged on them in focused yet lumbering motions, their goal singular but their capacity limited. They clutched factory tools and office equipment as though they were weapons. Some had stripped themselves of shirts or pants, holding them ready to smother or strangle.

"Have they been activated?" Yrlis asked, "I thought they'd be... worse, I guess?"

"The activated are hyper aggressive," MarLys supplied, "You wouldn't have time to wonder."

"They're under MalVek's influence," Nikasu said, "Thralls, like Galo and I saw in the Southlands."

Nemesis lunged into the crowd, knocking the nearest few onto their backs. The prostrate thralls answered with a wave of shrieks that swept back through the crowd. They scrambled upright and swiped at Nemesis with limbs jittering and flailing.

"In a jam here," Farim announced, "How's everyone else?"

Answers of no particular consequence trickled in as she squeezed a device on the handle of her oar. Electricity crackled between two prongs on the plate, and she followed Nikasu and Yrlis into the throng.

Nikasu flowed through the crowd, bashing thralls with the flat of her sheathed sword. With her other hand, she alternated between buckling their joints under their own weight and making them too light to walk strait. Stomach acid burbled in her throat, reminding her of the strain of such erratic use of her powers.

Yrlis moved with comparatively clumsy purpose and focus. Her wrench gave an extra half meter to her already impressive reach, her being only a few centimeters shorter than Spril. She had never thought much of the combat applications of her neuroanatomical knowledge, but zeroing in on the perfect points to target felt more like instinct than deliberation.

Farim swept her oar up to bash a thrall on the underside of the chin. The impact snapped his head back, and the electrified posts set him convulsing as he collapsed. His mouth foamed as his eyes rolled back in his head, and he stopped moving.

"How's the shock oar working?" Jex asked.

"Too strong for this," Farim said, deactivating the posts, "Accidentally killed one. Sorry."

"Dang. I was worried about that," Jex lamented, "I'll make it adjustable."

"Concept works though," Farim said, cracking another thrall with the broadside of the oar, "Keeping it off, unless..."

She trailed off as a length of pole at the end of a coiled cord shot out of the back of the crowd. A length of the cord wrapped around a thrall's neck, and the pole wrapped around to slide between the coils. The cord became taut, choking the thrall and slamming him to the floor.

The cord unraveled and retracted. It emerged twice more in less ambitious strikes, bashing thralls across the temple. A tall figure emerged, his eyes wild with an overwrought amalgam of relief, impatience, hopelessness, and fury.

"You're with the woman out back, aren't you?" he asked as his segmented staff came back together, "Don't worry. I'm on your side."

"Yeah, thanks. But who are you?" Nikasu asked, keeping him in the corner of her eye as she warded off thralls.

"Khirsan," he said, "Uro might have mentioned me."

"Khirsan!" Uro exclaimed, "Ask him if he knows where they took Sinkua."

"He didn't, but he clearly knows you," Farim said, "Help us clear out, and I can let you talk to him."

"That's why I'm here."

Rapid footfalls filled the stairwell as the Forward Team plus Elemeno ascended toward the top floor. Galo took the lead, gripping his sheathed glaive in one hand and using the other to whip around banisters.

"Uro, you know, with your friend Khirsan being here," Elemeno said, trailing off.

"He must have been working with Caylence," Uro remarked, "They resisted his control."

"It looks that way," Elemeno agreed, clearing her throat, "But I was going to say he probably sent you those messages."

"Maybe. Probably," Uro said, his voice quickening, "Khirsan must be working…"

"Careful what you say," Chekov cut in, "We can't guarantee that he can't tap these lines."

"It's okay. I know what you're thinking, Uro," Elemeno said, "We might have more allies than we thought thanks to you."

"Elemeno," Phylus scolded, "Stop it."

"I'm sorry," Elemeno said, "Point made. We're done."

"I mean stop sheltering him," Phylus said, "Enough of us are thinking it."

"Well, I just don't think this is the time," Elemeno said, "And honestly, I think I have more of a sense for that than you do."

"Did you forget what just happened?" MarLys added.

"No, I haven't, but…"

"Or about me?" Spril added.

"Well, that's different…"

"What are you guys talking about?" Uro asked, his voice faltering.

"Uro," Phylus sighed, "If Khirsan is looking for you, he probably did send those messages, which means your uncle is probably dead."

"What? That's ridiculous," Uro deflected, "Caylence is just lying low. I'm sure he's back at Hillside."

"Well… That's not unreasonable," MarLys added, "I hope you're right, but you need to be ready for the possibility that you're not. Okay?"

"I'll keep it in mind," Uro grumbled, "I just…"

Galo rushed ahead as he rounded onto the topmost staircase. He rammed the door open with his shoulder and barreled through.

"We've got a more immediate problem," Gabdur remarked, "Galo just vanished."

The mingled stenches of his own fluids overwhelmed him as the blood rushed to Sinkua's head, startling him awake. MalVek had tied his bandana over his nose and mouth, and his only sense of how much time had passed was the fact that his secretions had dried into the fabric.

His gurney was overturned, and he hung from the underside by straps around his wrists and ankles. A trough of cold water sat below, and he strained to keep the back of his head against the gurney. MalVek stood over him, stomping the frame at irregular intervals and impacts.

Sinkua panted raggedly as his head was thrown forward. His one good eye grew wide, his other swollen and blood-crusted, as his nose and chin broke the water's surface. Saturation spread through the bandana, adding a mildew odor to the stench of dried secretions.

As he pulled himself up, muscles cramped and quivering, MalVek bludgeoned the back of his head through the canvas. Sinkua writhed as his face slammed into the water. Flecks of dry blood floated from his wounded eye.

Blood laced with the last acid his stomach could spare scraped its way up his throat and splattered against the bandana as the room rolled end over end. The drenched bandana had plastered against his face, making it difficult to breathe. He winced at the stinging fluorescent lights.

MalVek stood over him, head cocked and staring at nothing in particular. He narrowed his eyes, seeming to listen to something beyond Sinkua's faltering senses.

"Well, it took them nearly a week to find you, but your friends are finally here," MalVek said, his face smearing into a grimace, "Let's see what sort of fun we can have with them."

"What're you…" Sinkua choked out.

"Jevana!" MalVek shouted.

Seconds or minutes later, the face of the woman who had killed Farim came into view. She smiled down at him, sickly sweet considering his pain and vulnerability.

"Hey there, Scruffles," Jevana said, her smile touching her eyes with a measure of wrongness, "Remember me?" She turned to MalVek. "What do you need from me?" she asked, "Oh! Are we going to finish the Flush Protocol?"

"Not yet," MalVek said with a voice like hot tar, "Keep him busy while I tend to the control center." He pulled the bandana under Sinkua's chin, staring at him as he continued speaking to Jevana. "But take care not to activate him yet."

Chapter 42

"Empires?" SouSol scoffed, "Paltry things. No, child, we deal in nothing less than legacies."

"Do you really think you have the stomach for conquest?" Sbaglien asked, "Recall that it was my tutelage that brought you this far."

As he spoke, he produced a photonic emission weapon from his belt. When he activated it, half of its length separated into a series of metal rings, spaced by narrowing lengths of solid light.

"What the hell is that?" PavRal gasped.

"The future of warfare, boy."

Scarcely more than his hand moved as Sbaglien cracked the photonic whip down the middle of PavRal's body. Rather, he would have, but Inre pivoted behind PavRal and spun him aside. Searing tile fragments flew up as Sbaglien missed his mark faster than he realized what had happened.

Inre produced a dagger from under her clothes and whipped it at Sbaglien. In that same instance, he turned at her as he realized she had interfered. He leaned to dodge, and the blade stuck hilt-deep into the boiler.

MerSul caught PavRal by the shirt and lobbed a haymaker, apologizing all the while. PavRal buried his fist into MerSul's stomach, drawing out an agonized cry that nearly drowned out his reciprocating apology.

But despite their contrition, those two blows were the last push to collapse the exodus prisoners into a mass brawl. With no particular sense or direction, they knocked and shoved each other into walls and equipment. The boiler cooked the stenches of secretions emanating from the melee.

SouSol looked Calhosin over with a derisive sneer. "You think I'll dirty my hands with you, outsider?"

"I think you're allergic to doing your own dirty work," Calhosin said, swaggering toward her, "But it's in my nature to accommodate."

He crouched to grab the tongs off the floor. SouSol called out to Sbaglien, only to be ignored.

Sbaglien cracked his whip horizontally, leaving a trail of sparks punctuated with a blinding pop. Inre squinted as she leaned aside, propping her upper body weight on her hand. As the light faded, she sprang upright with two daggers between her fingers.

The first, she flung wide and to the right, goading Sbaglien to bob to the left. The second, she flipped into her other hand and stabbed at Sbaglien as he came into its path.

Calhosin cracked SouSol across the temple with the hot tongs, eliciting a shrill cry as her sweaty skin sizzled. He kicked her in the abdomen, staggering her back. He grabbed her by the shirt collar and whipped her around to put her back to the anvil.

"I tried so hard to minimize the damages once I came to my senses," he said, cupping her chin, "FerLyn's death was inevitable. But OshMar's wasn't. Nor was KalChi's. Biroe didn't have to end up here." He pushed her back, bending her over the anvil. "But do you know what's been eating at me most of all?"

A barrier of light manifested around Sbaglien's face and throat. For all their momentum, Inre's knife chipped at the tip and cracked a few centimeters down the middle. It flipped back and tumbled over her wrist as her fist continued forth and blistered on the photonic shield.

Inre stared with her mouth agape and trembling. Sbaglien grimaced and ripped open his shirt with fingers bathed in hardened light, revealing a vest adorned with a grid of photonic emission weapon power cores. It didn't look like an official Avatar device, but it had clearly achieved the desired effect.

"You're not The Scout, are you?"

With one last lunge, Calhosin forced SouSol prostrate atop the anvil. He leaned over her and angled the tongs against her eye socket.

"Phylus lost an eye," he said, "because of people that you keep working with."

"He lost an eye because of his own stupidity," SouSol spat, writhing against the lingering heat of the tongs, "Bloody outsider was long overdue for his comeuppance. As are you."

Her scream was nearly as sickening as the popping and cracking as Calhosin jammed the tongs down the sides of her eyeball. SouSol squirmed and cried out as he squeezed and twisted, drawing blood and ocular fluid out of her socket.

"Scout. Politician. General. Hunter," Sbaglien said, lobbing a luminous backhanded punch, "I act as whatever I must."

Inre ducked the punch, her body atremble. "You mean to be the new..."

"I mean to discard the childish notion of The Named."

Calhosin wrenched back on the tongs. SouSol cried out in prolonged agony as the last vein snapped, taking the optic nerve with it. For all the accumulated tension, the tongs snapped out of Calhosin's grip, flinging SouSol's severed eyeball across the ironworks.

"My only concern is with the advancement of true-blooded ArcNosians."

Everyone stopped at the sound of her voice, herself included. On a television hanging from the corner of the ceiling, a video of the moments before their brawl had started playing. It went black just after Sbaglien kicked Biroe and was immediately followed by Biroe's voice over the PA system.

"I'm guessing by now you've all made a damn mess of everything," he said, "Well, the guards are ready to transmit this and any other relevant security data to everybody you wouldn't want seeing it."

Inre smirked. "He told you not to fuck with him," she said as she produced a small remote from one of her dagger compartments, "You really should've listened."

But before she could dial, Sbaglien's hand snapped out with the streak of hardened light, snatching the remote. He clenched his fist, destroying the remote and thus any anticipation of escape. Inre had no way of knowing when the other keyholder would deem it necessary to act.

"Do you have any idea what you've done?"

Stomach acid and flecks of partially digested food speckled Nikasu's goggles as she quadrupled a thrall's gravity in the space of a blink. She spun away as she glimpsed a wrench in her periphery, smearing the vomit from her lenses as Yrlis bludgeoned the thrall.

"Galo!" she shouted, "Are you still here?"

She bobbed under the grabbing hands of two other thralls. As they stumbled, she held her sheathed sword flat against one's abdomen. She depleted the thrall's gravity, pulled back, and knocked her back with a flat thrust. She lunged back against the other, pushing him into the path of Farim's fiberglass oar.

"I think so," Galo answered, "No idea where."

"You can't tell from your heads-up?" Yrlis asked, "No personal indicator, so I guess not."

"The maps are useless," Farim said, doubling a thrall over with a blow to the gut, "Spril, let us know if you find a pattern."

"Copy," Spril answered a moment later.

No sooner had he acknowledged her than he let out an ear-splitting, agonized cry. A voice like hot tar filled the room, coming from everywhere and nowhere all at once.

"Well, if anyone were to find a pattern, it would be him," MalVek postulated, "Not that there is a pattern. But that wouldn't stop The Weapon."

"Dourias!" Farim called out, "How vulnerable are these lines?"

"My apologies," Jex answered, "Those were my doing."

"I don't need to tap your communications. I can hear everything in this building," MalVek scoffed, "And to think I thought to commend you for realizing Galo was not an isolated incident."

Spril huddled on the floor with his arms locked around his head, biceps clamping his ears. He winced through his teeth, eyes clenched painfully tight. Fingertips brushed his shoulder like rusty railroad spikes.

"Spril. You can fight this," BeiLou exhaled in a distant shout, "Don't let him overwhelm you."

"It's too loud," he choked, his breath tasting like wet iron, "Everything's too… everything."

"Dampen your senses," she said, "Stop trying to hear everything."

"But if I don't…" he grasped, "They'll… I can't just leave…"

"I'll be your ears," she offered, "Okay?"

He nodded and steadied his breathing, casting off the sounds of the other teams. As the sum of noise became tolerable, he cleared his throat and rose on shaky legs.

"Fantastic," BeiLou beamed, "Couldn't have either of us leaving each other alone. So, what's the plan from here?"

"Somehow, he's booby trapped the building with invisible portals," Spril said, "I don't know how, but…"

"So nice of you to join the rest of the class," MalVek taunted, "Go on, then. But…?"

"MalVek, I'm gonna have to ask you to eat a whole bunch of dicks," Spril said. He returned his attention to BeiLou, lowering his voice. "Throw one of..."

"I can still hear you."

Spril sighed and rolled his eyes. He tapped his chest and pointed to BeiLou. He mimed holding something, then throwing it. He moved one finger in a long arc, but he interrupted himself with a swipe of his hand, which he followed with a halting motion. He repeated the arc, this time completing it, and made a walking motion with two fingers. Once more, he mimed holding something, then made circles with his index finger.

BeiLou nodded hard as she plucked a gas bomb from her shoulder strap. She hit the button and whipped it down the hall. Its flight was unhindered, and its smoke spewed and billowed without anomaly.

Spril took the lead as they continued down the hall. He took care to keep his footfalls out of lockstep with hers, overriding years of ingrained behavior. But as they passed her gas bomb, the sound of his footsteps fell into solitude.

"Well, I should still be able to find my way around," MarLys said, "Courier work has given me a good internal compass."

"Can you tell where we end up if we get gated?" Phylus asked.

"If we're in the west side of the building, at least."

"Oh, MarLys," came that voice like liquid asphalt, "You have a guest joining you shortly. Give her a property greeting, would you?" His tenor became reverberant. "Show her how that hook feels on her neck."

MarLys and Phylus looked to each other and swallowed hard.

"Spril just..." BeiLou said as she appeared next to them, "Nope. I'm the one who got moved."

MarLys's upper body trembled at the sound of her voice. She grasped her hook tightly enough to threaten breaking skin.

"What's going on?" BeiLou asked, her voice shaky, "Spril is out of earshot, and I've got a situation here."

"What's the issue?" Galo asked.

Before she could answer, MarLys threw herself at her, swiping at her neck with a wretched shriek. Phylus's hand snapped out and grabbed MarLys by the back of the shirt, yanking her back against him. MarLys writhed and gnashed as she swiped at the space between herself and BeiLou.

"Run!" Phylus barked.

"Elemeno," MalVek called, his voice resonating throughout the stairwell, "Or shall I call you Picuarus?"

"What do you want, MalVek?" Elemeno challenged.

"Hmph. Not surprised I knew about your alias. You might have endured The Era of Chaos," MalVek mused, "But have you thought about the lives you compromised when you broke Nikasu out? Your triggering of the Flush Protocol activated dozens with neither goal nor guidance."

"They became monsters," Elemeno argued, her fingers trembling, "We had no choice but to..."

"Nevertheless, it was your doing," MalVek interrupted, "You entered the actuation chamber despite your supervisor's orders to the contrary. Isn't that right, Teyaku?"

"My doing hadn't a damn thing to do with what you did to them!" Elemeno shouted, "You designed the gun. You crafted the bullets. You pulled the trigger. Don't cop it off on me because I lived near the iron mine, you thimble-witted crumblecock!"

A dragging silence set in. Elemeno looked to Gabdur and Uro with wide yet obstructed eyes as she caught her breath. She mouthed to them how good it had felt, though she knew they couldn't see her mouth.

"Well, the blame is no matter," MalVek said, his voice turning vibrational as he continued, "Since you lot won't leave that stairwell, Elemeno, see how long that rail can withstand your weight against it."

Wholly atremble, Elemeno threw her body against the railing. She looked to the two men in silent pleading as she leaned her stocky frame into it. They lunged at her, each hooking one of her arms with their own.

"Uro," MalVek drolled, "Help her along."

Uro rasped and heaved as his body leaned forward, driving Elemeno that much harder into the rail. They looked to one another, exchanging thready apologies through teary eyes.

"What are you going…" Uro choked out.

"That will come in time," MalVek interrupted, "As for you, Gabdur."

Gabdur ignored him as he focused on prying Uro and Elemeno from the rail. "Walk away."

With a twisting backhand swing, Khirsan bound a thrall's arm with his segmented staff. The last one standing, one pull dislocated his shoulder, and a second slammed him into the floor.

"We're clear for now," Khirsan said, retracting his staff, "Can I talk to Uro now? And maybe see your faces?"

"That seems fair. Just let me…" Farim said, trailing off as she wrestled off her gas mask and dislodged her earpiece, "… There we are."

"Well, this is surreal," Khirsan mused, "Thank you for helping Uro, by the way."

"It's… less trouble than I thought, really," Farim said as Yrlis and Nikasu lifted their masks, "He's…"

"Not that you're in any position to speak with him," MalVek announced, "Or rather… Well, you get the idea."

"What have you done with Uro?" Khirsan demanded, "I've done everything you…"

"I haven't done anything with him," MalVek deflected, "But since you insist on proving your loyalty, look to the youngest among them. She's the one with purple eyes. Do you see her?"

Khirsan's body stiffened, and no matter how he strained otherwise, his face pivoted toward Nikasu. "Y… Yes."

"Good. Now. See that sword on her back? I'd like you to take it from her."

Despite the contrary tension in every muscle, Khirsan shambled toward Nikasu. The violet-eyed Hybrid scrambled back, cornering herself. Farim and Yrlis both grabbed him, only to be dragged along by the combination of his size and his disregard for all but his quarry.

"Don't fight it, Nikasu," MalVek insisted, "In fact, see that those two can never interfere again."

Nikasu shrieked as she charged at the tangle of Farim, Yrlis, and Khirsan. But in the instant she set forth, a shadowy smear of silver and amethyst blindsided her from the other end of the room. Nemesis wrapped himself around her, Epelun and all, and pinned her to the floor.

"Interesting," MalVek mused, "But I wonder, Nemesis, where your loyalties lie. And how far they go. But for now, Farim, Yrlis, your only desire is to find a pattern in the portals."

Chekov flung open the glove compartment and rifled through it. Papers and hand tools fell into her lap. Her breathing growing ragged, she swept them aside and reached under the seat.

Vaguely aware of Dourias's voice, Chekov yanked the storage bin out with enough force to scatter half its contents. She rooted through a pile with each hand, huffing and wincing at each passing second of failure.

She found the two things she needed, one from the discarded heap, the other still in the bin. Tucking them under her arm, she rammed the door open and stumbled out of the van.

Muttering denials through her tightening throat, she wrestled with the tool's controls as she tramped across the parking lot. A voice trailed behind her, but she kept moving.

The tip of the pen warmed quickly enough that the rain soon sizzled on contact. Cries from her earpiece compounded beyond the point of ignoring. She threw herself at the wall, rolling against it.

"Chekov!" Dourias shouted.

She jumped and looked up, mouth agape and atremble, but she gave him no further regard. His presence was meaningless. Without a word, she reached down her shirt and ripped off her wire, then plucked out her earpiece. Hands trembling, she unraveled a length from the spool and suspended it over the smoldering pen tip. She craned her neck and flung her hair aside.

"What are you doing?" Dourias cried out.

Chekov jumped again as he grabbed her wrist. She held eye contact, forcing herself to acknowledge him.

"I have to go," she choked out, "I'm sorry. I have to go."

"Go where?" Dourias urged.

"I have to get him," Chekov stammered, pulling away, "I have to get him out. I have to go."

"Who? Sinkua?" Dourias asked, "They're in there getting him."

"No. They're in there dying, and it's my fault," Chekov said, lifting the spool to her ear, "Not Sinkua."

"Spril?"

"Yes. We have to go."

"Chekov?" Dourias gasped, "What are you saying?"

"I'm sorry. I can't fix this," Chekov said, eyes wide on an otherwise stern face, "We have to go."

"You keep saying that, but I…"

"Dourias," she beckoned, "I'm sorry. But you know I didn't come her to save your world."

Dourias sighed and nodded. "You came to fix yours."

"Yeah," Chekov exhaled, cupping his cheek, "I'm sorry for everything that went wrong. I've been trying to fix it, but…"

Dourias shook his head as he clasped his hand over hers. "I understand," he said, "Retreat with The Weapon. We're among friends who can finish things here."

"Thank you, dear," Chekov said, kissing his fingertips, "You know what to tell our daughter."

"I'll think of something," he choked out.

"I know you will," she smiled, "NalSet's temporal shifter is back at Drakougeneospa. Make sure he makes it home if you find him."

"When."

She nodded.

Dourias turned and walked away, the rainfall obscuring him. Chekov craned her neck and lifted the pen and spool once again. She ground her teeth, stifling the urge to scream as hot solder dripped into her ear canal.

Spril expanded his senses in brief and irregular intervals. Galo could handle himself well enough, but Spril held himself accountable for BeiLou's safety. But the screams of his companions and a fear of MalVek's new power kept shoving him back into sensory isolation.

Accepting that Phylus had taken on the duty of safeguarding Sinkua's mother, Spril shallowed his breathing and scaled back his senses to the bare functional minimum. Perhaps, with a shred of luck, MalVek had lost sight of him when BeiLou moved.

He drifted upright, careful not to bear down abruptly. There was no saving them. All he could do for his companions was go after MalVek. Rid them of him. Somehow.

Erratic footsteps approached from behind as a voice called out. He turned to see Chekov scrambling through the dissipating gas, clutching her shirt over her nose and mouth.

Spril pulled off his mask and held his breath. He swiftly closed the distance between them and shoved the mask over her head as he caught her by an arm. Bloody discharge trickled from her ears with the stench of hot metal.

He walked her to a clearing as she trembled and babbled through the breathing filter. Once they were beyond the lingering gas, he wrestled the mask off and tucked it under his arm.

"What have you done to yourself?" he asked.

She shook her head, eyes wide with insurmountable fear. "We have to go," she insisted.

Spril tilted his head for a better look at her ears. He couldn't see the source of the discharge, but she had apparently rendered herself hard of hearing. He had no way of telling if it was permanent, but she clearly thought it was worth the risk.

He shook his head in a mix of opposition and confusion. He probed her thoughts, but what he picked up was too erratic to tell where she was going with any of it. The only sensible conclusion was that she'd come to take him back to their home time.

"I'm sorry, but…"

Light enveloped her faster than she could react, her expression never changing within that split second. She vanished with it, leaving an afterimage in the approximate shape of her silhouette.

Spril pressed his wire. "Hey, I don't know if I'm reaching any of you," he said, "but keep a lookout for Chekov. She's…"

"She's safe," MalVek announced, "She is no longer here, but…"

"Where did you take her?" Spril shouted, "Is she…"

"I have no further business with the hyperspace prison," MalVek interrupted. His voice became reverberant. "Do not fret. Seek out your friends. Perhaps, you can give them something like hope."

Spril walked away with his mask tucked under his arms. He narrowed his eyes, grasping for some sign of approaching soft spots. But warnings were as scarce as the abrasions themselves, as neither came his way.

It occurred to him that he was moving of his own volition, not because MalVek had told him to. He was just returning to what he had been doing before Chekov showed up. He was willing to believe that she was in the here and now, just not in range of their comms. But he couldn't help but worry.

This meant that MalVek had no power over him. It seemed his power was akin to Ozzera's control of the biomechs. Something quasi-milystic that Spril could deflect.

If he was right, he could free his friends from MalVek's enthrallment. And after that, the other thralls. In that moment, MalVek's true weakness occurred to him.

It wasn't that he had overlooked his immunity. It wasn't that he was limited by the nature of Faux-Hybrids. It wasn't even his arrogance.

For all his power, MalVek was still bound by logic.

Yrlis and Farim rarely blinked as they walked in lockstep with their eyes fixed straight ahead. They mumbled rapidly to one another, exchanging observations. Now and again, their surroundings folded and unfolded into something similar yet incongruous.

At the sight of a bald man with a gas mask under his arm, a thread of longing pulled at Yrlis's thoughts. She gritted her teeth as she and Farim kept muttering to one another.

"Have either of you seen BeiLou?" he asked with a voice as familiar as a distant memory.

He raised his hands to his shoulders as he passed between them. His fingertips grazed their cheeks, and the smog within her mind dissipated.

"Keep up the act," he whispered as he put on his gas mask.

Yrlis looked to Farim. Lucidity had returned to her eyes. As deep a corner as they'd been backed into, hope still had something to say about it. And it spoke in the voice of her husband.

BeiLou's footfalls clapped in rapid succession, compounding echoes in the long corridor. Eyes wide and breath ragged, her head swiveled in constant observation of her surroundings. Through a combination of adrenaline and repetition, the abruptly changing walls no longer disconcerted her.

The fact that a hook-handed young woman with murderous compulsion pursued her also took precedence over the oddity of spontaneous teleportation.

A door opened at the end of the hall. BeiLou shuffled to a halt as thralls poured out, armed and glassy eyed. She looked down the adjoining hall. Light and shadow peeled back to reveal MarLys with her left arm convulsing.

BeiLou ripped a gas bomb off her strap and hurled into the outpouring of thralls. She charged into the crowd, bobbing and dodging to scatter their individual focuses.

The gas was quick to stupefy them to where, even collectively, they presented little more than an idle threat. But their mass could insulate her, possibly even keep her out of MarLys's sight long enough for her to give up the hunt.

BeiLou grumbled an expletive as MarLys tore around the corner and charged with no apparent regard for the horde of lumbering bodies. As BeiLou turned to run, she heard another set of footsteps. These sounded more in control. Focused. Urgent. She looked back just in time to see Phylus drop MarLys with a haymaker to the back of her head.

Phylus tipped his chin toward something behind her. BeiLou looked back to find Spril amongst thralls with dim sparks of lucidity in their eyes. He stumbled as they staggered into him, his staff sheathed and arms limp.

She and Phylus hurried to his aid, pulling collapsing thralls away from him. He patted them both on the shoulder, mask pulling up as he flashed a smile.

Puzzled by both his gesture and his calmness, they watched him walk deeper into the hall. He knelt beside MarLys. Her weight shifted as Spril cupped his hand against her cheek.

Spril came upright and kept walking. BeiLou and Phylus looked to each other in silent calculation. Whatever Spril had done wasn't a matter for discussion. Not with MalVek's all-consuming ears.

Without words, they went and sat at MarLys's side.

Galo paused as the narrow hall abruptly expanded into a rather vast room. Sparse speckles and smears of blood decorated the floor. The place smelled of bile and blood iron. Toward the back was a gurney with a trough of water underneath and an unfamiliar woman hunched over a man upon it.

She came upright, revealing that the man's pants were around his knees. Galo gasped as Sinkua's borderline catatonic face came into view. The woman turned around and swiped a dollop of red and white liquid from her cheek and sucked it off her finger.

"Well, hey there. You must be here for Scruffles," she said, "Or maybe you want to beg for a place at Lord MalVek's side."

"Who the fuck are…" Galo snarled.

"Oh, but if that's the case, you should know that I'm his favorite," she said. She thrust her thumb over her shoulder. "His too, apparently."

Light rippled and peeled away to reveal MalVek. Galo recoiled at the sight of metal and lengths of wire woven throughout his flesh.

"Clothe the catalyst and be gone with him, Jevana," MalVek said, "I've made the necessary arrangements."

Galo watched his friend's face as Jevana pulled Sinkua's pants up. His eyes were unfocused, but his expression tightened at a dense popping as Jevana lurched upward. Galo winced sympathetically. Jevana giggled at her further brutalization of Sinkua's genitals.

"Should I expect you to join us, My Lord?" Jevana asked.

"No," MalVek said, his eyes fixed on Galo, "I have everything I was after."

Sinkua wrenched against his bindings as Jevana pulled the gurney. A vein is his temple pulsated. Ephemeral brick red flames swept over him, casting long shallow shadows and flicking up wisps of ebony smoke.

"Get back here!" Galo bellowed.

Jevana stopped and looked back. Galo swept his arm, launching a flurry of spiral icicles. Jevana looked on with empty eyes, unmoved by the coming assault. Unmoved because it moved for her.

"Toodles, Bubbles," Jevana chimed as the icicles dissolved.

"Who… are you?" Galo choked out.

He cast off his bafflement and drew his glaive. In three healthy strides, he devoured the space between them, discarding his sheath and pulling the blade back over his shoulder.

"Stay your arm, Galo!" MalVek reverberated.

Without a thought, Galo halted and lowered his glaive.

"You son of a bitch," he grumbled as Jevana left with Sinkua.

"Letting you go with him doesn't factor into my plan," MalVek said, "In fact, the only use I have for you is admittedly petty vengeance."

"I best you twice in single combat, and you resort to tying my arms down?" Galo scoffed, "You certainly have a hollow notion of victory."

"Oh, don't get the wrong idea. You will fight me at your full capacity," MalVek said, activating his photonic warhammer, "Because I only brought you here to waste your time."

Chapter 43

The fog dissolved from Khirsan's mind as the shape of his quarry vanished under the dragon's flesh. He shook his head, shoulders slumping as the tension left them. He stepped back and cleared his throat.

"Sorry, I didn't know he could do that," he muttered, "Can you manage yourself?"

Nikasu lifted her head, perhaps with Nemesis's help, and took stock of her surroundings. Her body rolled upright like a string puppet as Nemesis drew her onto her feet. She mumbled under her breath, convening with her Etherworlder beyond Khirsan's hearing.

"Mental functions have normalized with the targets beyond my perception," Nikasu said, her violet eyes unfocused.

"I…" Khirsan puzzled, "Yeah. Same."

"Sorry. Everything is cloudy," Nikasu said, "I'm okay now. Do you know where Farim and Yrlis went?"

"No, but we need to move regardless," Khirsan said, "These people might wake up soon, and I need to find Uro."

"Last I heard, he was in a stairwell connecting to the lobby," Nikasu recounted, "They were looking for a room in the northwest quadrant."

"I can get us there," Khirsan said, beginning to walk. He paused and looked back to find Nikasu standing still. "Are you coming with me, or are you going to watch over them?"

"Why is it so urgent for you to see Uro?" Nikasu pried, "He never mentioned you."

Khirsan swallowed hard, casting his eyes down. "I witnessed his uncle's murder," he sighed, "I need to tell him in person. I also have something for him from Caylence."

"We all sort of thought he had died," Nikasu said, coming to his side, "You were sending those messages, then?"

Khirsan nodded. "I can't take all the credit," he said, "I was working from notes in Caylence's office. I don't know if he was insightful or just paranoid, but he had safeguards planned out in case he or his nephew were ever in mortal danger."

"Well, whatever he was, we might not have had a chance to save my brother without him. When we're done here, I'd like to go visit his grave to offer my respects."

"He… doesn't have a grave," Khirsan said, "But as soon as I can, I'll take you to his office."

"I'm sorry to hear that," Nikasu said. She lowered her voice to a whisper. "So, can I ask what you brought?"

"It's called Project Cerulean," he whispered, "Caylence was working with other doctors, off the books, to develop… I don't know what to call it. It's like what happened to the people here, but worse."

"Activation," Nikasu supplied, "And this vaccine worked?"

"Sort of. Caylence died before they finished it," Khirsan said, "The other morgue staff continued his work, but they couldn't track down any of his contacts. They did what they could from his notes."

"How much do you have?"

"I took a shot and brought one with me," he said, patting a pouch strapped to his leg, "There's more at Hillside. This is all I had time to get."

"I have a portal strip," she whispered, "We'll find Uro, and the three of us will go back for the rest. Can we synthesize more from there?"

"Possibly, but I don't know," he said, "But I hope you understand this isn't a sure thing. It didn't even protect me from his hypnosis."

"I know," Nikasu said, "But right now, even good intentions are worth investing hope in."

His flesh metal crackled as MalVek hurled his hammer with a thunderous bellow. Galo leaned aside, catching himself on his hand, and raised his glaive. Just before impact, MalVek grimaced and thrust his hand. The metal crackled again, and the hammer accelerated.

The photonic hammer's momentum dragged Galo's glaive against his grip, pulling him up off of his feet. He released his weapon to let it fly off with the hammer. Galo twisted in the air to come down on his back, rolling from pelvis to shoulders, and launched onto his feet.

In the space of that technique, MalVek had moved behind where the gurney had been. Galo's arm hair stood on end with coursing milystis as he barreled forth. But by the time he took two steps, MalVek had devoured and defecated the distance between them.

Galo's face contorted as the ex-Coalitionist buried his craggy fist in his abdomen. He headbutted MalVek between the eyes and pushed him back out of arm's reach.

MalVek grasped at the air. Galo flung a blade of ice with the sweeping motion that flowed into a dodging pivot. Blood trickled from MalVek's hand as the ice sliced it open and melted into the wound. And it squirted between his knuckles as his photonic hammer clapped back into his grip.

Galo dropped to one knee as the hammer flew over him and pounded his fist against the floor. His knuckles screamed as the polished concrete shattered. A stream of milystis coursed through the floor and coalesced before Mal-Vek, erupting into a column of ice.

Galo bounded back, keeping his eyes on the ice column. He crouched to recover his glaive, only to stagger as he found MalVek at his side. He glared at the crackling woven metal, wondering about its functions and limits.

MalVek grabbed his hand with his wounded one. Galo's eyes widened as his palm stung and burned. Wrench as he did, he was merciless against MalVek's unbothered grasp. When this monster of a man finally permitted him use of his own hand, Galo pulled back to find his palm ripped open, while MalVek's was unscathed.

Galo cracked the flat of his glaive against the handle of MalVek's hammer, dragging the tip of the blade across MalVek's knuckles. With Mal-Vek's grip weakened for a split second, Galo knocked the weapon from his hand and across the actuation chamber. Galo threw his glaive in the opposite direction, the blade sticking in the wall.

"You want fisticuffs?" he shouted, pitching the Serpent Bracer, "I've got everything you need right here."

Spril closed his eyes and quieted his breathing. With some focus, he enhanced only his sense of smell. From beyond the hall came the salty odors of tears and sweat. The stink of cracked grout mingled with them.

The smells grew stronger. A pair of shouts became audible even with his hearing unenhanced. Spril hastened his stride.

Uro white-knuckled the railing as he struggled against the urge to lurch forward. With his weight bearing on her, Elemeno ground her upper back against the rail. Uro's sweaty hands slid outward, collapsing his body even harder against hers.

Grout scattered as bolts popped out of their mounts. Uro and Elemeno cried out as the feet of the railing uprooted from the concrete.

Bile ran from the corner of Sinkua's mouth as his gurney flipped upright. His neck tensed as a sharp fingernail grazed his cheek. His breathing and pulse erratic, he cast his eyes down and aside.

"You…" he grumbled at the sight of Jevana, "What are you doing with me?"

"Sorry, Scruffles. Fun time is over," Jevana chimed, patting his groin, "Back to orders from Lord MalVek. But I do have a present for you." She turned her back to him. "Well, another one," she said, chuckling as she faced him again, "Here. This belongs to you."

The taste of burnt blood filled Sinkua's mouth as Jevana presented a sheathed broadsword. She revealed a few centimeters, and his skin thrummed as his milystis and the Hephaeseum called out to one another. Threads snapped and singed as he strained against his bindings. Shallow flames swept along his body.

"Where did you…" he grunted, "You don't have the right to hold that."

"Oh, but Lord Harvester asked me to give it to you," she said, "But really, you're in no place to tell me what rights I have." She unclipped his bindings with a few flicks of her wrist. "You are just a tool, after all," she said, thrusting Epesol into his hands, "Now. Through the portal we go."

"I'll let you have that one," MalVek said.

As his words resonated, he moved around Galo so quickly that he all but vanished from his sight. Galo only became aware that he had moved when his elbow collided with his spine. Galo's back arched as he ground his teeth, and he staggered forward.

As he came down, he cross stepped and pivoted to clip MalVek across the back of the head with his heel. As MalVek shifted his stance to face him, Galo brought his foot down and lunged to stomp kick the side of MalVek's knee.

MalVek grimaced as he popped his knee back into alignment. He threw a backhanded punch at Galo's jaw. The Southlander Hybrid ducked the blow, and MalVek thrust a knee at his chin.

Galo moved with the momentum, bending into a back handspring. Upon landing, he swept his arm to launch a wave of water speckled with a flurry of icicles. Occluded from his opponent, he clutched his chest as he struggled to catch his breath.

MalVek charged through the rushing ice and water. With Galo breathless and startled, he devoured the space between them and buried his fist in his abdomen. Galo dug his heels in, but MalVek's momentum drove him across the floor.

Galo pivoted out of MalVek's path and behind him. MalVek spun about with his fist plowing the air with thunderous momentum. Galo ducked and bludgeoned MalVek's chin with his palm heel. He palmed MalVek's face and erupted scalding water from his hand.

MalVek grabbed Galo's arm and hurled him over his shoulder. Galo slid across the floor and bashed his head against the wall near where the gurney had been.

Galo glimpsed his glaive in the opposite corner. Prostrate, he manifested a column of ice under the water trough. The water scattered as the trough flipped. Galo clenched his fist, spreading it into smaller drops with his milystic will. He wrenched his arm back, turning them into a volley of sleet and scalding water and launched them with a sweep of his arm.

Galo ran close behind the volley, while MalVek braced himself against every slash and singe. As Galo passed his periphery, MalVek knocked him off course with a sharp strike to the side of the head.

They turned to face one another as they bounded back toward opposite walls. Flesh metal crackling, MalVek moved more than half the width of the room in the time it took Galo to cover three strides.

"I concur," MalVek snarled, "That is enough!"

He reached aside with his hand open. Electricity arced amongst the metal in his arm. His silenced photonic weapon generator rattled and leapt toward him.

Galo erupted a column of ice beneath his glaive, launching it toward himself.

Spril threw the stairwell door open and grabbed the back of Uro's shirt. He locked eyes with Elemeno as she looked to him with overwhelming fear and urgency in her eyes. His grip on Uro strained as the young man pushed harder against Elemeno. Spril pulled Uro back and lurched forward to clasp his hand over Elemeno's shoulder.

"I've got you," he exhaled, gritting his teeth, "I've got you."

The air and light between the staircases stirred.

Light fractalized and folded, collapsing into darkness that rippled much like the depths of Yggdrasil. Sinkua tamped down the taste of smoke and bile in the back of his throat. As the negative liquid fractals disintegrated, mottled light filled his eyes.

Looking up the stairwell, he found the cloudy image of someone being bent back over the top rail. His senses rushed back, drawn in by urgency of realization.

"Get your hands off her!" he shouted, white-knuckling Epesol.

Sheets of low, shadowy flames swept over his skin. Bile haunted his throat yet again.

"Sinkua!" Spril called down, "We need you to…"

"See?" Jevana said from just beyond his peripheral vision, "Just a tool."

Sinkua stared up at the three of them, Elemeno at the mercy of Spril and Uro. He was unsure what Spril had said to him. Unsure if he had spoken at all, for that matter. Wisps of black smoke and bile vapor floated on every exhalation.

The snapping of the last bolts rattle Spril's eardrums like the familiar sound of a bullet exploding against his skull. He winced at the trauma just long enough to realize too late that his grip had faltered.

His mouth fell agape as his eyes shot open wide. He knocked Uro aside as he reached for Elemeno. His fingertips grazed hers, but the pair failed to take hold of one another.

"It's not his fault," Elemeno said, eyes pleading as she fell back, "Tell him."

An alphanumeric string trailed through Spril's mind. It curled in on itself and took up residence there, glimmering in the corner of every thought.

Elemeno hit the floor with a loud, sickening crack. Her broken body lay at the center of a radial spray of blood, bone chips, and organ fragments. Spril watched in unsettling detail as the last traces of life left her eyes, forever to be haunted by the knowledge that she had lived even a second in such a condition.

At her side, Sinkua appeared catatonic. So damaged had he been by whatever trauma he had endured here that he fell past fury and straight into silent bewilderment. Into shock.

A plume of black smoke erupted from Sinkua's facial orifices with a stench of acidic fumes. It rolled down his body like scorched smog. Shallow brick red flames rippled along his flesh, casting long low shadows.

Emptiness blindsided and devoured Spril's thoughts. It wasn't shock that Sinkua had fallen into. It was something more and something less all at once. It was burning coldness. Calculated, apathetic rage. Urgency scorched his path, necessitating destruction that he neither craved nor abhorred. He only hungered for it to fulfill a need, but that need was indiscriminate.

The sheath to Epesol turned to ash in his hands. Drenched in shallow flames and long shadows, his entire body smoldered like brimstone. Liquid silver trickled off his neck and shoulders. His ruby fused against his chest. His once brilliant green eyes faded into shades of pine.

A gurgling bellow called Spril's attention aside. He scrambled back to the wall at the sight of what was becoming of Uro. Curled up and writhing, his cheeks and jaw seemed to melt toward his collarbone. The skin around his lips stretched as his mouth grew too tall to contain. His lips peeled back, revealing teeth that had grown to a length well beyond reasonable utility.

Halfway down the stairwell, another door crashed open. As Spril looked toward the noise, he found Sinkua and that woman had vanished. Only Elemeno's body remained, and that string coiled through his thoughts once again.

The Harvester stood with his hands folded behind his back, staring up at the wall. The glowing green map of Ouristihra served as the only light in the room. Muffled screams seeped through the walls.

A cluster of red lights flickered into existence in their vicinity on the map. His eyes traced predictions and patterns along memorized leylines as more red pinpoints came alight further and further out. He brought his finger to his ear.

"Scatter them."

"Of course."

His mask pulled back as he smiled.

"I've almost found you," he said, "Just a little longer."

A wall of darkness crashed over Nikasu, straining through her like a toxic mesh. The pressure pulled her down with a knee-jerk milystic spike that splintered the floor. Chunky blood fell from her lips as she coughed.

"Are... Are you activating?" Khirsan gasped.

She could hear calculation in his voice. She anchored her thoughts to that concept, holding on to something she had observed with her own mind. A shadow stretched over her.

"Don't," she rasped.

"But..." Khirsan stammered, taking the shadow with him as he stepped back, "If you activate, then..."

"Different," Nikasu choked out, "Doubt works."

Nikasu kept her head down, staring at the cracks in the floor. Though she felt a sense of strength rising within her, her forearms remained unchanged in her periphery. The spiderweb cracks grew with no discernible effort. Her thoughts on his voice remained clear.

"Don't need," she continued.

Her entire body tightened. Each muscle, her jaw, her throat, her toes and fists, everything down to her ponytail clenched. A chorus of blood-curdling screams swelled from beyond the corridor. Nevertheless, her body remained unchanged.

"Find Uro," Nikasu said as she forced herself upright, "Go outside."

Khirsan offered his hand. "What about...?" he asked, gesturing with the syringe as he put it back in the pouch.

"People outside help," she said, unsheathing Epelun, "Go. I cover."

"I can't let you deal with that on your own," Khirsan argued as the screams compounded. He snapped his segmented staff from its harness. "We'll fight our way out together."

"No!" Nikasu shouted. She pointed down the hall. "I activate. I deactivate."

"I... What?" he puzzled, "You can deactivate them?"

Nikasu nodded emphatically. She swayed his body as she thrust her finger against his chest. From this angle, she realized he was actually taller than her brother. She used this thought as another anchor.

"No you, maybe no antidote," she said, "Go."

BeiLou whipped an orb into a tangled, shambling mass of the activated. A plume of yellow smoke spewed from the orb as it settled amidst the dehumanized monstrosities. At her back, Phylus rent cartilage and tissue with sharpshooting precision belying his lost depth perception. MarLys lay between them, scarcely stirring.

As the snarling masses quieted somewhat, a humming from the walls became audible. She brought her hand to her chest.

"Anyone else hear that?" she asked.

"Hear what?" Yrlis called back, "How can you even hear anything over these things?"

"Where the hell are those coordinates!?" Farim shouted, punctuating with a sickening smack.

"There's a grinding," BeiLou said, "I can't tell where it's coming from."

"I hear it, t..." Phylus said.

His voice didn't so much trail off as vanish. Looking back, BeiLou saw that he had as well.

"I just lost Phylus," she announced.

"There are machines in the walls," Gabdur said, "Like in the Mechanical Crypt."

"Mobile portals," Farim said, "Of course."

"Run if you hear them coming," Gabdur added.

BeiLou watched MarLys gradually vanish as a humming drew closer. In the other direction, the activated closed in despite the sallow smoke melting flesh from sinew.

"Guys?" she exhaled, "I'm trapped."

Wood fibers strained in his grip as Galo snatched his glaive out of the air. He whirled around, redirecting its momentum, and hurled it to puncture MalVek's airborne weapon.

Galo's glaive and MalVek's photonic generator tumbled under perpendicular forces. Sparks erupted from MalVek's flesh metal as he curled his knuckles. The weapons hung in place, wobbling between pulling toward him and continuing on their natural path.

The handle broke off the glaive and flew toward MalVek. The blade resumed its trajectory, skewering the photonic generator onto the wall.

"Ogunite," he grumbled, "I should have known."

Galo clutched his chest as he reached toward his blade.

"But you didn't," MalVek added. He picked up the glaive handle. "You have no idea what you're doing. As always."

Disfigured sightless visions cropped up throughout Galo's mind's eye. MalVek crossed the room in slow strides with the rough end of the glaive handle dragging the floor.

"You sense them, don't you?" MalVek goaded. He brought his finger to his ear. "Scatter them."

Spril watched as a tall man in a security uniform erupted through the door, nearly crashing into the rail. The man recoiled at the sight of Elemeno below.

"Who are you?" Spril called down.

"Khirsan," the man answered, the briefest eye contact impressing every shred of anxiety and misgiving upon Spril's thoughts, "I'm looking for Uro."

Spril introduced himself. "He's up here, but…"

"I know."

Khirsan bounded up the flights of stairs, his build allowing him to take three or four stairs in a stride. As he emerged onto the top landing, he pulled a syringe from a pouch strapped to his leg.

"Keep hold of yourself, Uro," Khirsan said as he knelt beside what had become of him. He looked up at Spril. "You need to get out of here, man."

Spril looked him over. All he knew was that this man knew Uro and appeared to have come to help. Spril looked at the gnarled disfigurement of Uro, then over the rail at Elemeno's body. As skeptical as he was, he had no time to pry.

Spril shuffled down the stairs as Khirsan plunged the syringe into Uro's jugular. He whipped around each bend, anchoring himself on the banister. As he neared the bottom, he hopped the banister and caught himself on the next one down. This way, he took the final floors in a handful of seconds.

Elemeno's body twitched at his feet. As the alphanumeric string threaded through his thoughts again, he finally realized its relevance. He apologized as he crouched beside her and rooted through her pockets. He pulled back as her mangled thigh spasmed against his hand, but he came up with a small remote.

A distant grinding pulled his attention upward. He sensed nothing of Uro or Khirsan beyond a lingering scent. He shouted up to them. No answer. Narrowing his eyes, he saw a faint rippling across the width of the stairwell. It crept downward, narrowing between the flights and expanding as it passed them.

He had heard Gabdur and Farim deduce that there were mobile portal generators in the walls. But he hadn't considered that they could be oriented vertically. Nor had he found a pattern in them. He also didn't know if Khirsan had saved Uro.

He looked back and forth between the exit door and the rippling light. The mobile portals were hunting his friends. One by one, they were being cornered, and their lines went dead. If he wanted answers, wanted to fight back, perhaps the only way was to stop running.

Spril ascended the stairs.

Malia stood before the Chieftain Sage hut, looking out over the village. SenRas and Murdega stood at her sides, watching and listening.

"Doesn't look like anyone's here," Murdega said, "Do you think they all got taken?"

"Hopefully they had already relocated," Malia said.

"There's no point in hoping," SenRas said as he walked away, "We need to keep moving."

"Keep a weather eye," Murdega said as he followed, "No telling what we're up against from here."

Malia looked to the grassy flap, then to the derelict village. She winced and swallowed hard, hesitant to move in either direction. Go inside, and she'd relive the memory of giving up her daughter. Walk away, and she'd leave the point where she last truly felt like a mother.

Malia closed her eyes and took a deep breath. "Right," she said, opening her eyes as she followed them, "No point in hoping."

Throngs of activated agents shambled in from the end of the hall. Nikasu angled Epelun forward as she flowed into a defensive posture. If she could keep them in this building, maybe The Veil would stay standing.

Her hip twitched, and her foot shifted. She looked down at her legs, expecting to find chitin stretching her jeans. Nemesis murmured something in Harkzanian within her mind. It was beyond her grasp of the language, but she understood enough to glean his intentions. Where she might fall short, he would guide her movements.

Beyond being largely bipedal, the activated could scarcely be recognized as human in origin. Bones jutted out where they had outgrown their flesh, stretching as often as they punctured. Eyes expanded and compounded, or they sunk into recesses. Lips curled back to expose gnarled teeth or stretched into hooked bills.

"Word on lethal force?" she asked, wincing against the palpable urge to activate, "Really hoping yes."

From her earpiece, she heard faint mutterings and sounds of combat. But nobody answered. She swallowed hard.

"Gonna go yes."

Nikasu charged with a vicious battle cry, drawing Epelun down to her side. She pivoted and ducked a slashing forearm claw, gliding her blade along a scaly abdomen. Kneeling, Nikasu thrust her sword up through another torso. Brackish blood churned from the wound as she ripped Epelun back. She sprang upright and skewered the forehead of a third activated agent.

Her thoughts grew cloudy as she exerted milystis through the blade, collapsing the activated into a heap of itself. Nemesis peeled away and corkscrewed into a streak of amethyst and dark silver, buckling joints in his wake. He left a vision behind in her thoughts, a message that transcended the language threshold.

She halted her milystic effort, and her mind became clear. Nemesis would fight on the milystic front, she on the physical. To use her powers was to tempt activation.

A sudden light from the direction of the building pulled at Jex's attention. As emergency lights had gone on and off throughout the evening, he only gave it a passing glance. But as he realized what he had seen, he put the window down to look in greater earnest.

The front door wasn't just open. It had ceased to exist along with the frame and much of the surrounding masonry. Scores of monstrosities poured from the structural wound, led by a human woman and a homunculus with crystal goggles. Just behind them was a burning silhouette, the only humanoid shape among the beasts.

Sinkua had been activated.

The homunculus reached behind its head, and the crystal lenses came alight. It grabbed Sinkua's hand and put it on its shoulder. In a wave of compliance, the rest followed until they were all connected to the homunculus. They continued forward, vanishing just beyond where they had stopped.

Much of their clothing had been shredded in the course of transformation. But toward the back, Jex noticed one with far different fabric scraps than the rest. Different and, he realized, familiar. Dourias had also activated. He pressed the button to his comm.

"Jex. Cover Team," he said, "Is anybody still in there?"

Myriela stood in the hall, puzzling over the open hall closet door. Nobody ever left it open because it blocked the adjacent door. She had a different purpose here though, so she slunk around the closet door, leaving it open for someone else to ponder, and slipped into Sinkua's bedroom.

As she did, it occurred to her that she had never so much as looked into this room. With what she knew of his past and had promised EshCal, it felt somewhat taboo. It had all been drunken banter, but the fact still stood that she had joked about offering sexual favors to a man who had just witnessed his fiancee's murder. And now she was lurking about in his bedroom.

One half of the bed was almost perfectly made up, the other disheveled by restlessness. He still slept like he had someone beside him, and from the creases in the otherwise immaculate side, he still reached for that someone in his sleep.

Her phone rang, and she composed herself as she answered. "Hello?"

"SenRas speaking. I have your coordinates."

Myriela grabbed a mostly used notepad off the top of the dresser. "Go ahead."

She took down each number as it was read to her. Once she read them back, SenRas disconnected without another word. She drew in a deep breath and set to searching for the items that Spril had requested.

The morningstar was easy enough to find. That was hanging in the closet, still dirty with oil and urban detritus from the high-rise district. The dagger, however, eluded her for so long that she ended up triple-checking places immediately after double-checking them.

A coo and a rattling caught her ear. She looked up to see a purple-winged pigeon bobbing in its cage.

"Hey there, Luvros," Myriela said, "Do you know where Sinkua's dagger is?"

The bird cooed and bobbed her head as she nipped at the cage door.

"You wanna keep me company while I look?" Myriela asked, "Well, I guess there's no harm in it."

She closed the bedroom door and opened the cage. Luvros fluttered out and settled on the desk. Myriela kept one eye on the bird as she continued searching.

After a few minutes, Luvros swooped under the dresser, cooing all the while. It was when the bird fell silent that alarmed Myriela.

Myriela looked under the dresser, only to find a large hole carved out of the wall. Concluding Luvros must have escaped through it, Myriela stood to pull the dresser aside, then lay down for a better look into the hole. Sure enough, the excavation had torn the bottom of it clean through to the outside.

Peering through the hole, she saw Luvros walking on some piece of architecture that she couldn't name. Just aside from her was a dagger with a white marble handle.

Nikasu angled her sword forward as she shifted her stance. She steadied her breath, acclimating to her static weight. She had grown so accustomed to fluctuating her personal gravity as she moved that maintaining that milystic flow had become a passive effort. Now, while Nemesis caved activated beasts in on themselves, Nikasu worked to suppress that flow.

Jex's voice came through her earpiece, asking who remained inside.

"I think it's just me," she said, "And Nemesis."

"The…" Jex hesitated, "What became of the others?"

"Disappeared," Nikasu said, pivoting under a talon.

"Moving portals, yes?" he affirmed, "I certainly hope that's all it was. Sinkua just left, and well…"

"Activated?" she asked.

"Buck naked and looked like brimstone," Jex said, "I'm surprised you're still normal."

"I'm managing," Nikasu grunted, skewering a monstrosity, "I don't know how, but it never fully set in."

"Well, I'm glad for it," he said, his voice fluctuating and threaded with the noises of rummaging, "Dourias was also activated. He's bringing up the rear on this portal launch party."

"Dammit. Have you seen Khirsan?" she asked, cleaving an arm, "Uro's friend."

"No, I…" he said, trailing off, "SenRas is on the line. Patching."

Gnarled fingers and grabbed at Nikasu as she bobbed and pivoted deeper into the shambling mass of the activated. She skewered them as they came within reach, but they were still closing in. With her slightest acknowledgment, SenRas rattled off the coordinates as she wrenched for the elbow room to free Epelun from a leathery abdomen.

"He needs clothes," Nikasu said after she repeated back the coordinates, "Jex says he's naked and burning."

"He burned his own clothes off, didn't he?" SenRas asked, clearing stifling a chuckle, "Sorry. I shouldn't laugh at that. I'll have it taken care of. Signing..."

"Hey! Real quick. Have you heard of Project Cerulean?" Nikasu interrupted, "Uro's friend mentioned it. Might be useful."

"Sorry, no," SenRas said, "I'll ask Malia and Murdega though."

"I'll check Chekov and Dourias's notes out here," Jex offered, "Ending the call."

The line went silent. Nikasu looked beyond her fray.

"Nemesis!" she cried out, "Tsero prorsmo!"

Now that Nikasu knew her destination, Nemesis spiraled his body and bored into the wall like an ebony and amethyst drill. Seconds later, he burst out, shredding the wall as he expanded within it.

Nemesis spread his wings and enveloped most of the activated around Nikasu. He spun with them in his grasp, his body crackling with gravimantic energy. Opening his wings, he cast their crushed bodies at his feet. He turned to face Nikasu, glaring down at the remaining activated with the back of his head against the ceiling.

"Go," he bellowed, "I cover."

"Tha akouthiset?" Nikasu asked.

Nemesis nodded. "I will follow."

Hibiscus choked up her grip on the sledgehammer. She reared back, then drove it into the drywall. As she stepped back, MelDas stepped in for a turn.

"Thanks for helping with this," Hibiscus said, swinging again, "I know it's a weird request."

"Not the weirdest I've taken part in," MelDas shrugged, grunting as he took another swing, "Not a by a long shot."

Hibiscus's phone rang, and she excused herself to answer it.

"Hey, sorry about the delay," she opened, "There's been some... complications."

"Is it anything you can't handle?" SenRas asked.

"No, it's just..." Hibiscus said, trailing off as she realized how long it would take to explain, "Never mind. What do you need?"

"Sinkua's naked and on fire."

"Straight to the point, I see," she chuckled, "Don't worry. I'll take care of it."

"Step aside, MalVek," Galo commanded, his outstretched arm tensing.

"Oh, I'm afraid you won't be coming to anybody's rescue," MalVek goaded.

"No, I'd just rather kill you to your face," Galo said, "But if you leave me no choice!"

Every mote of scattered moisture rose to waist level. MalVek's eyes widened. Galo jerked his elbow back and clenched his fist tight enough to threaten bleeding.

MalVek whipped around to see the glaive blade streaking toward him as his skewered generator hit the floor. He pulled aside, but the Ogunite blade ripped across his side, dragging bloody sinew and kidney tissue.

The hovering water converged on Galo in the wake of the bloodstained blade. He reached out with his other hand and clamped the blade, pivoting back with the momentum as the milystic water coalesced over his body.

Galo lay his Ogunite blade atop his forearm, sealing it with a coating of ice. Snapping his elbows back to his sides, he froze the water motes into crystalline armor. MalVek sneered at him, eyes twitching.

"You've cast your candle upon the bonfire, boy," he derided, "You can't sustain this for long."

Galo gorged himself on the space between them with swiftness belying his bulky armor. He clipped MalVek's temple with his heel and followed with a slash across MalVek's abdomen. MalVek staggered as lengths of flesh metal snapped in two, and Galo planted his foot in the middle of his bleeding abdomen.

MalVek dropped the broken glaive handle and stumbled back, blood dripping from his head and belly. He shuffled back toward the wall, wincing and flinching at every celeritous blow that Galo threw his way.

Galo ground his teeth, suppressing the rising urge for a coughing fit. He danced about in his crystal armor, overwhelming MalVek with whipping kicks and Ogunite slashes. But with his back to the wall, MalVek reached up and snatched Galo's foot, stopping it cold.

The mad traitor clutched the Leviathan Hybrid by the ankle. Flesh metal crackling, MalVek lifted until Galo's other foot slid out from underneath him.

"Enough of you!" he bellowed, hurling Galo across the actuation chamber.

Galo landed just past the middle of the room and slid to the wall. His throat tasted like sickness and blood.

"You churlish brat," MalVek snarled, his photonic generator jumping into his outstretched hand, "I have endured your humiliations for too long!"

"Then perhaps," Galo grunted, pushing himself to his feet, "you should stop being such a fucking embarrassment."

Palpable heat emanated from MalVek as he manifested a photonic hammer of a far grander scale than his usual arming. The handle reached well over two meters, while the head was roughly the size of Galo in his crystal armor. MalVek spun the hammer around his head, scorch-carving a wide channel out of the wall behind himself.

"You have always failed to comprehend the scope of matters you meddle with," MalVek seethed, "Fitting that you would be destroyed by powers beyond your ken."

Sparks spewed from his embedded shards of metal as MalVek ripped across the actuation chamber. Only, he fell short, as Galo only needed to take a quarter of the distance for himself to stop him.

MalVek reached out to push him back, but with his feet frozen in place, Galo gouged his blade into MalVek's gut with their combined momentum. All but the boots of his crystal armor softened to a malleable slush. He twisted the blade through MalVek's spine and ground his fist against the wound, as his armor melted.

Blood ran from the corners of MalVek's mouth. His mammoth hammer hit the floor, boring a hole through to the level below in the time it took it to dissolve.

Galo's melted armor coalesced around his shoulder. Cramming his fist into the wound, the milystic water jetted down his arm as his knuckles met entrails. Scales rippled into the surface as horns sprouted from the end of the stream.

Leviathan took shape, her mouth agape with scores of serrated teeth. She chomped at MalVek's midsection, chewing through his abdomen. She left his torso and legs connected by little more than two strips of flesh and obliques. She devoured flesh, organs, and bones indiscriminately, pulverizing it all in her gaping maw. Expanding to fill the wound she had bored, she coiled around MalVek's body.

Galo's mouth fell open, spilling blood and dead lung tissue. His arms dropped to his side as he fell against MalVek's shoulder. Exhausted, he allowed his eyes to close.

Chapter 44

Nikasu mounted her portal strip to the hole Nemesis had made in the wall. She dialed frantically, shaky fingers trying to keep up with her mouth as she rattled off the coordinates again and again. All the while, her eyes kept flicking back to the fighting.

One of the activated beasts broke away and lunged at her. Gnarled teeth and keratin gnashed at her as she dove through the amorphous portal.

She tumbled out into tropical greenery, and the sound of gnashing followed. She whipped around to find that abomination trying to pursue her as the fractalized image of Nemesis pulled it back. Nikasu cleaved the creature's head at the jawline and reached for the portal strip.

In a fleeting moment of miscommunication, Nemesis skewered the beast with his tail, collapsing the hole in the wall with the follow-through. Plaster and drywall tumbled out of the collapsing portal around the creature's forelimb and bisected head.

As she caught her breath, Nikasu looked up to see one branch from each of the two trees tied together. The Relay Team had probably meant for her or Nemesis to sever it on arrival. She muttered an expletive at Nemesis having been left behind, hoping he would find his way there soon. Or at all.

A rustling pulled at her attention.

"Hoy there, Nikasu," Murdega said with a nonchalant salute, "Right glad to see you made it as you and not some other sort."

"Murdega. Thank you. I don't..." Nikasu said, trailing off as she looked around, "Where are the others?"

"We're here, dear," came Malia's voice from behind the portal trees.

Nikasu turned to see her and SenRas approaching. Neither had made much noise when they emerged from the tropical brush, one a bit less than the other. She had her guess, as much as it mattered.

"Hey, Mom," Nikasu said, flashing a tired smile, "SenRas."

"The start of the bridge is at the opposite corner of the island, and crossing the dig site appears to be out of the question," SenRas said, "So, we'd best start working our way around."

"I'd best, you mean," Nikasu insisted, "If any of us are going to get through to Sinkua, it'll be me. The rest of you would just be endangering yourselves."

"Those thralls keep looking this way whenever we crest the hell," Malia said, "They're not activated, and they don't seem aggressive. But they look ready to fight if we get too close."

"In that case," Nikasu pondered, leaning on Epelun, "I guess I shouldn't leave you alone, in case they do activate."

SenRas patted her on the shoulder as he walked past her. As Malia came up alongside her, Nikasu turned to follow.

"I'll set to scouting nearby open waters," Murdega said, "I'll buzz if I find anything of concern."

Yrlis winced as brilliance rattled her senses. The light faded as her pupils adjusted, and her surroundings became clear.

She stood at the outer edge of a parking lot under a streetlight that was attached to a telephone pole. She looked back to see dissipating fractalized light in the frame formed by that and the adjacent pole and the cable between them. Sighing with resignation, she looked out over the parking lot to see where she had landed.

This place gripped her thoughts with a vague sense of familiarity. It had fallen into disuse though, leaving no literal signs for her to work from.

"Do you remember this place?" Chekov asked, abruptly announcing herself.

Yrlis's throat lurched. Something about that question tightened the hold of familiarity, pulled her closer to it. Chekov spoke again before she could answer.

"You were just shy of eleven."

"It's where you arranged for me to meet Spril," Yrlis said, "And where you created Vielle." She began to pace the parking lot. "And I'd turned eleven the month before."

Chekov sighed. "Can you honestly say you're upset with me for either of those?"

"No. I came to love them both of my own volition," Yrlis said, "But tell me something." She turned to face her, only to recoil hard enough to derail her own train of thought. "What the hell happened to your ears?"

"I went in for Spril," Chekov confessed, "I was running away."

"And this was the only way you could think of to protect yourself?" Yrlis asked, raising her voice out of courtesy, "How much can you hear?"

Chekov shrugged. "Maybe a quarter?"

"You soldered your ears shut, and it wouldn't even have worked?"

"Rub it in a little harder. I think you missed a spot," Chekov scolded. She sighed and shook her head. "Sorry. What did you want to know?"

"Hm?" Yrlis pondered, searching her thoughts, "Oh right. Did you know what would happen to them?"

"Spril? Yes, of course," Chekov said, "But I had no way of knowing that The Harvester would be as adamant as he was in pursuing Vielle. The Omnimath certainly never indicated it."

"But you did know…?"

"That Malia was a Carrier? Yes," Chekov interrupted, "But Phylus isn't, and neither of them are descended from the Dragon Family. With only one Carrier parent, their baby could only have been a human or a Dryad."

"And you tried for the latter," Yrlis gleaned.

"Of course!" Chekov said, throwing her hands up in resignation, "We were cultivating the greatest weapon this world has ever had on its side. The least we could do was leave behind as many defenses as we could when we take him for ourselves."

"I'll just have to live with that, I guess," Yrlis sighed, "Catch."

She lobbed her wrench to Chekov, who jumped back to let it fall at her feet.

"What are you doing?" Chekov asked, slinking down to grab the wrench.

"MalVek sent us here. He can send things after us. You need to arm yourself."

"But what about you? What are you going to do?"

"I'm a veteran of the Subtransit Resistance. Makeshift gear is my bread and butter and my jam," Yrlis said, grabbing and bracing her foot against a handicap parking sign, "So, I'm going to survive the night, thank my husband ever so thoroughly for strangling MalVek, and then send him off very happy to have known me."

"You're taking this well," Chekov said, "all things considered."

"I've come to terms with having to watch Spril walk out of my life," Yrlis said, wrenching back on the sign, "Your world needs him more than I do. Especially if you're going back like that. And maybe alone."

"And your world needs people to keep Vielle's memory alive."

Jagged churning lights pierced the gaps between Spril's eyelashes, alerting him to every bit of ash and blood they had collected. Reverberant shrieking rattled his inner ear. The stenches of searing flesh and fearful sweat compounded, though the former took on a less tragic and more savory undertone.

He slowly opened his eyes as the lights dimmed and noises calmed. Dining room patrons had huddled back against the walls of the restaurant. Kitchen staff looked on dumbfounded, while the teenager at the register had the security pistol pointed at the middle of the dining room.

Spril followed the barrel to find Uro thrashing under Khirsan's knee and forearm. Bloody vomit had puddled under his cheek, but his face was reverting to its natural shape. Still, his eyes dilated and contracted erratically as he spat and gnashed his teeth.

"The antidote isn't finished," Khirsan said, meeting Spril's pensive gaze, "but it's functional. Is this his first time?"

"That I know of," Spril said, signaling to everyone that they had matters under control, "What's this antidote?"

"Okay. Hopefully, that means this stuff still has a good chance of working," Khirsan sighed. He looked up and cleared his throat. "It protects against activation, as Nikasu called it."

"That's why you didn't change," Spril realized, "This comes from Hillside?"

"Caylence was the only person I know who was working on it," Khirsan said, "They all communicated with tracking pigeons and coded messages. They called it Project Cerulean."

Spril knelt beside them. "Why cerulean?"

"Because it's blue?" Khirsan shrugged, "The important thing is that there's more at Hillside. Nikasu was going to escort Uro and I there to retrieve it," he said, "Do you know where we are?"

"Epsilon Burger," Spril said, "We're in ArcNos."

"Dammit!" Khirsan growled, "Do you have one of those portal thingies?"

Spril shook his head, his thoughts drifting from the conversation as he scrutinized the room. The door and windows were the most obvious. The chairs were movable and thus probably out of the question. The tables were bolted down, though.

"What's on your mind?" Khirsan pried.

"Something's going to follow us," Spril said, "Lot of somethings, probably. I'm scoping entry points."

"We're going to fight them here?" Khirsan asked, "We can't risk that collateral damage. Besides, we don't…"

"We aren't fighting anyone," Spril interrupted, leaning into the pronouns, "You are leading an evacuation the instant the next portal opens, regardless of Uro's condition."

"What about you?"

"I'm going to the capitol prison."

"I trust you have your reasons," Khirsan said, "But what about Project Cerulean?"

"That's still your promise to make good on."

The drill groaned as the battery ran dry. Jex cursed at whoever had forgotten to charge it, but it held out just long enough to finish the job. He jostled the passenger's side door, ensuring that it had been unhinged.

Across the parking lot, the line of activated marched into a portal visible only to them and only by their collective touch, culminating on the homunculus in crystal goggles.

Jex dropped the drill in the box at his feet and took out the only two spider mines they had thought to pack. Holding the unhinged door in place, he affixed the mines to the left and right sides.

A bestial bellow erupted from the building, shattering windows as the entire thing rattled. The chain of activated took pause at the sound.

Jex lay across the seats, propped up on his elbows. He drew his legs back and kicked both mines simultaneously. They blasted through the unhinged door and launched it across the parking lot.

As it flew, Jex realized his timing had been slightly off. It would break the chain, but it wouldn't hit Dourias. He dug through the box, looking for a fast idea and the means to execute it.

The busted door slammed into and toppled two activated, breaking the last dozen off of the chain. The rest proceeded with no regard for them.

Jex mounted a portal strip in the doorway and began to dial. He pounded the car horn, drawing the attention of the abandoned activated. With Dourias among them, they turned their fury toward Jex.

He trained a shotgun on the shambling mass. Each shot took one down, and each one dropped rose the ire of the others. They soon ran at him, gnashing and snarling.

When only Dourias remained, Jex struck the last keystroke on the portal strip. As Dourias pounced, he vanished through the sheet of fractalized light.

Jex strapped the shotgun to his back. He got out of the van on the driver's side and circled around to follow Dourias through the portal.

They hadn't had any coordinates for Hillside Oncology in their database, but he had found a set within a short drive. Now, Jex only needed to knock out his old recruiter and convince someone to allow the bestial old man into their car.

Nikasu hunkered down on the sand, staring out over the sea at a low angle. Light cycled behind her amethyst eyes, bringing greater clarity despite the scarce stars and sparse moonlight.

"They rebuilt the bridge," she said, sighing with unsurprised disdain as she took off her shoes and lobbed them aside, "No idea how far they got."

"Leviathan destroyed it a bit over a week ago, didn't she?" SenRas asked.

"I can't imagine they've gotten very far," Malia added.

"Which means they can't break The Veil."

"Yeah, but..." Nikasu said, trailing off as wrestled off her sweaty socks and flung them toward her shoes. "They're going to walk down that bridge either way."

"And drown," Malia sighed, "If the bridge doesn't reach past standing depth, it might be possible to save them, but..."

Breakers wrapped around Nikasu's ankles. She looked down and watched as sea foam swept far up over dry sand. Fast for a tide to rise, she thought.

"But their deaths won't doom the rest of us," SenRas said, his face cast down, "And yes, I am aware that that includes my grandson." He lifted his head to address Nikasu directly. "Understand that I am not numb. I know it will hurt to watch my grandson die. To watch you watch your brother die," he told her, "But I have accepted that I could outlive him. At least this way, he'll be dying to protect the world."

"If I have any say in it, none of them have to die tonight," Nikasu said, still watching the sea foam, "I'm the distributor. Whatever I did to keep from activating, I should be able to reverse theirs, too."

"I suppose that's a hope worth holding on to," Malia said, "I know SenRas and I argue a lot, but we've, well... We've both got your back."

Nikasu snickered, lifting her head just enough to look aside at her. "I love you, too."

"Sea looks awfully spiteful all a sudden," Murdega said through her earpiece, "Anything weird on your beach?"

"Tide just rose pretty fast," Nikasu said, "But I don't think it's unusually high."

"Can we get in touch with Galo?" SenRas suggested, "He might be able to sense Sinkua and whoever's following him. Give us an idea of their numbers and proximity."

"Jex called for a headcount just before I left," Nikasu recalled, "Nobody said anything. I think he got thrown out with everyone else."

"I'll put out some feelers," Malia said, wrangling her mobile phone from her pocket, "Maybe someone's seen him."

"... too," Phylus said, his gaze flitting as his surroundings had changed mid-blink, "now that... you mention it."

He turned around, scratching the back of his head. His eye twitched hard enough to tug at the corner of his mouth. He recognized where he had landed, but he had never seen it so late. Or so empty.

Most of all, though, he had never been whisked there in the middle of a sentence. His first thought was that he needed a cigarette. As much as that shamed him, his second thought made him sick. His reason for trying to quit was gone.

A groaning at his feet pawed at his attention. He hunkered down next to MarLys and jostled her by her shoulder. She stirred and shifted as though settling into a bed. He gave a sad smile at her misplaced comfort.

"Wake up," he beckoned, "MarLys. Come on."

"Hrmph?" she grunted, "What's going on?"

"I had to knock you out," he said, "I'm sorry."

"'S fine," she mumbled, "Is BeiLou okay?"

"Yeah, last I saw," he sighed, "So, you remember that?"

MarLys nodded weakly. "I want to tell her I'm sorry." She lifted her head and looked around. "Where are we?"

"Ouristihran Union building," Phylus said, "Union Parliament's across the street."

MarLys's head turned sharply to face him. "How long was I out?"

"Just a few minutes," Phylus assured her as he came upright, "MalVek had moving portal strips in the walls."

"Crafty bastard," she muttered, getting to her feet by Phylus's outstretched hand, "Where's BeiLou? I feel like I remember hearing her voice."

"You were between BeiLou and me, but I haven't seen her here," he said. He fiddled with his comm. "No signal. Figures."

"You know, the intelligence agent in me wants to say there's a reason he sent you and me here," MarLys said, "It seems like too much trouble to separate us from her."

"I had the same thought," Phylus said, "Unfortunately, the diplomat in me is useless here." He turned to face her. "What about the courier in you?" he asked, "What's she saying?"

MarLys swallowed hard. "She's looking for the fastest way out of here."

"Hello?"

She stopped and listened. All that came to her was her own echo.

"Anyone?"

Still the same. Her echo was fixed straight ahead.

"Phylus?"

He didn't answer. Nobody did. She jabbed at her comm. Nothing.

She checked her shoulder strap to find she was still just as armed as a moment ago. With that small assurance, BeiLou began to walk, dragging her fingertips along the wall in search of a light switch.

Gabdur stood in the penumbra of an old streetlamp, staring down at the foliage around his feet. He scratched the side of his leg. No sooner had he said to run from the noise than the noise had outrun him.

"He sent you here too, huh?" someone asked.

He looked up, breaking his own introspection. Farim stood by the next streetlamp, outside its light. He nodded and hunkered down.

"Does this flower patch look smaller to you?" he asked.

"Sorry, I didn't make a note of it," Farim said as she approached, "Why?"

Gabdur rubbed his thumb over the snipped end of a flower stem. He picked up a loose blue rose petal. As he got back to his feet, he presented it to her.

"These were cut recently," he said, "I didn't notice it before."

Farim accepted the petal. "Can you tell how recently?"

"Not from here," Gabdur said. He cast his gaze over the field and adjacent parking lot. "No sign of Jex either."

"I'm worried about Dourias," Farim said as she began pacing, "They're probably both still back there."

"There should be some portal strips inside," Gabdur said, nodding toward the building, "We'll go back and get them and my son out of there."

"Sinkua was probably activated when MalVek scattered us," Farim said, "Once we find Galo, he and I will go after him. You bring Dourias and Jex back here."

Gabdur shook his head. "I'm following you once they're safe."

Galo opened his eyes, jumping at the feeling of torrential rain washing over him. Rather, he jumped within his mind. His body didn't move. Seawater lapped at his feet. He looked up and out toward the horizon through no will of his own.

"I don't know what you expect to find out there," he said. His mouth movements felt wrong, and this wasn't his voice.

"Answers," came another voice, "There must be a way to reconcile this."

"And what do you suppose?" Galo's other voice asked, "That you'll have a divine vision in the middle of the sea?"

"Metkhal," his friend urged, "You know there's more to it than that."

"Those visions are memories of your past lives, Tsenukoa!" Metkhal scolded while Galo listened from his internal vantage point, "If they were prophecies, you wouldn't have tried to make peace with Pandora."

Tsenukoa shook his head. "You don't know that," he said, "But this is all beyond the point. I know they're memories." Steam billowed between his fingers as he swept the rain from his face. "There are other civilizations out there. Ones that the Etherworlders have not influenced."

Metkhal sighed. "You're impossible," he chuckled, "You're absurd. You're ridiculous. And you won't change your mind."

"Of course, I won't," Tsenukoa said, grinning back, "We occupy such a small area of this planet. Surely, humanity has sprung up elsewhere. And if they've been in contact with the Etherworlders…?"

"They would only make contact if they needed something from us," Metkhal concluded.

Tsenukoa placed his hand on Metkhal's shoulder. Galo's consciousness rushed forward as a strangely sharp sightless vision manifested. These names were familiar, but just out of reach.

"You'll see that my books remain safe, yes?" Tsenukoa asked.

"Of course, my friend," Metkhal said, holding Tsenukoa's shoulder, "The ruby as well."

"Thank you," Tsenukoa said. He withdrew his hand away and held both behind his back. "And if you could…" He dragged his foot through the knee-deep water. "That is, if you see Kanet…"

"You'll tell him when you get back," Metkhal insisted, "I'll keep Gungnir safe for him."

Tsenukoa laughed despite the choking in his voice. "You doubt that I'll find anything, but you're confident that I'll make it back despite this?" he challenged, broadly gesturing toward the rising ocean, "My friend, I think you might be the impossible one."

"It's an impossible time we live in," Metkhal said, pulling him into a hug. Galo's sightless vision flared. "How better to adapt than to be impossible ourselves?"

"Well wishes, friend," Tsenukoa said, "I'd best be going before the sea becomes impossible as well."

"Before it swallows all those other islands out there?" Metkhal said, smirking.

"Masnethege may be the last bastion," Tsenukoa nodded, "But I won't return until I know for sure."

"I'll hold this place for you to return to," Metkhal said, "Famujokoa will always be welcome in Mberhan."

The ground lurched. The horizon bowed inward. Neither of them reacted. Galo realized only he was aware of it. His consciousness buried in this ancient mind, he scrambled for release.

"I am so sorry," came a ubiquitous voice.

Metkhal and Tsenukoa continued bantering while Galo grew increasingly unaware of their words. Natural and ambient sounds became dull and hollow. What words he heard became unrecognizable.

"This was all I could do."

A blackness beyond night encroached upon the edge of the sky. It was an absence of everything. Light. Matter. Awareness. He couldn't look down, but at the thought, he had a vision of a similar darkness spreading inward along the ground.

"I have failed all of you."

A horrid shrieking rattled all that remained beyond the blackness, from the surrounding ocean to the minutiae within his mind. A wretched crunching and crashing enveloped the very concept of his awareness as the void consumed everything else.

"Farewell, my dear friend."

Galo floated in nothingness.

Scattered raindrops pitted the sand. Red streaks lined the eastern horizon, casting the faintest of long shadows up the beach. Nikasu took two steps up the beach, away from the yet still rising tide.

Tension snaked through her chest and abdomen. Her jaw clenched, and her forearms tightened. She trudged further from the shore, propping up on her toes to see over the hill.

Malia turned toward her from the crest of the hill. SenRas kept his back to her and squared his shoulders.

"They're here!" Malia said through her earpiece.

Mottled light speckled the sand alongside Nikasu. As they dissipated, they seemed to coalesce into a dim shadow.

"He must not cross this point."

Nikasu's childhood rushed back at the sound of that voice. The tension in her body melted into a sense of weakness and insecurity. She had only ever heard it with Ebralgi's. The Geneticist's. Father's.

She trembled as she turned to face him. Her arms hung heavily, and she kept her head cast down despite her will to the contrary. Her stomach lurched as she caught that mask in the corner of her eye.

"Wh… What are you…?"

"Forget what The Geneticist, Ozzera, and Yahsek taught you," he commanded, "Are you in any shape to fight?"

Her composure trickled back. It wasn't the encouragement but his beckoning. This man she had thought unmovable was nothing more than that. A man. And he needed her. She gritted her teeth.

"How dare you stand beside me!" she shouted, "After everything you've done? How dare you!"

The Harvester winced. "You speak of the Yggdrasil Hybrid."

"She had a name. Has a name!" Nikasu scolded, "It's Vielle."

"I am well aware, child…"

"And you'll repeat it with your last breath, you shitdusting traitor!"

Nikasu grabbed Epelun, but The Harvester faced her bodily and pressed two fingers on the base of her throat, holding her at arm's length.

"Yes, I took your sister's life. For that, you have my sympathy," he lectured, "But for the act itself, I will not apologize, as one does not express sorrow for acts of necessity."

"Necessity?" Nikasu scoffed, coughing as she pulled back, "According to who? You and your Avatars of Fate?"

"These matters are beyond my design," The Harvester said, "The Veil must fall, and with it or by my hand, so too must your brother. But we must spare Phoenix."

"I don't know what you're after with Phoenix," Nikasu said, tightening her hold on Epelun, "But I won't just stand here and let you kill my brother."

"You insolent child!" The Harvester scolded, "Think you I would delight in slaying one of the last of our kind? I have endeavored to circumvent this, but Sinkua must perish. I do this without the slightest malice."

"If that's how you feel," Nikasu said, unsheathing Epelun. She pressed her comm. "Mom. SenRas. Hold the hill."

"I will find neither pride nor necessity in taking your life," The Harvester sighed as he slid Epemort out of its scabbard, "Know that should you persist in impeding me, you enter death in vain."

Galo opened his eyes to see the broken floor of the actuation chamber. His vision was blurry and tinged with red. He blinked a few times, but he was too delirious to tell if it helped. Blackness encroached on his periphery.

He lobbed his gaze about, head dipping and focus withering. Crimson spatters covered the fractured walls and dripped from the cracked ceiling.

"By the..." Galo gasped, choking on the taste of blood in his throat, "By the ether..."

"Back with us, boy?" a warbly voice asked. It sounded like MalVek, but that was impossible. Galo had watched him die. "You went catatonic," the voice continued, "Where'd the old sea snake send you, hm?"

"Le... vi..."

Galo's head slumped to find Leviathan strewn across the floor. Something had clamped her so tightly it had broken her in half, leaving the severed ends pinched and mangled.

Galo's throat lurched. He put a hand to his stomach, only to grasp at air. Looking down further, his last threads of rationality unraveled as he found a frayed hole where his stomach and a bit of his chest should have been. Sticky blood covered his legs and pooled around his feet.

It wasn't possible. He had gored a hole through MalVek. Leviathan had disemboweled him and consumed a third of his torso. The memory was so vivid. That vision, whatever it had been, was already vague in all but concept, but he could mentally recreate his fight with perfect clarity.

He had watched MalVek die.

And yet, here Galo stood, pleading with whatever powers might answer to wake him from this nightmare. To put him back together. To dissolve this illusion.

"Oh, I know you must be feeling empty inside," that voice said.

Galo looked up, his eyes focusing all too perfectly. And there he was. MalVek. Whole and vigorous.

Galo dropped to his knees. MalVek crouched to look him in the eyes, his lips curling into a wry smirk.

"But she's just beside herself with grief!"

Galo hit the floor to the sound of MalVek's maniacal laughter. As darkness encroached from imperceptible directions, that cackling persisted until it was the only thing he could sense.

And then Galo was no more.

Chapter 45

Malia pressed her fingers to her sternum. "Murdega?" she beckoned.

She paused and held her breath, watching the oncoming wall of the activated stretch and deepen. There was no answer. What that meant for Murdega, she couldn't say. Her immediate concern was that he couldn't come or send anyone to their aid.

"How the hell does she expect us to hold against this?" she sighed, "There's no way we're prepared for this."

"And what more should we have done to prepare?" SenRas asked, "We are armed, undamaged, and ambulatory." He unsheathed his spatha as he wrapped his manriki around his other hand. "Given the conditions of our friends, that is more than sufficient."

Malia sighed and nodded. She drew twin pistols from her hip holsters and trained them on the expanding wall with her fingers off the triggers. Under her breath, she cursed MalVek for having tainted her trust in the photonic weapons. Otherwise, only her own stamina would dictate when she took action, and even that wouldn't make much difference.

The Berininite thralls stood toward the southern horizon. They appeared to not move, aside from occasionally looking westward. The bottom half of their faces were wrapped in dark blue fabric with what, from her distance, looked like a bird silhouette emblazoned on some of them.

Thick black smoke billowed over the opposite hill. A silhouette brushed with shallow flames followed. It came to stand at the center of the outpour, where it stared out over the valley.

A thunderous bellow rolled forth, picking up the cries and roars of the hundreds of activated along the way. The accumulation of noise rattled Malia's chest cavity. She roped in her composure and retrained her pistols, and the activated came storming down the hill.

"Hold your ground," SenRas said, "I'll advance if necessary."

The front of the wall hit the valley. Malia popped off a staggered pair of shots, hitting two activated in the leg. Both still tried to run, only to topple and trip another half dozen between them.

A muffled gunshot came from the south. Four more followed in rapid succession. Streaks of deep blue spattered across the upper torsos of five of the activated. As the rest advanced, those five collapsed onto their hands and knees. Malia shifted her aim away from them.

"Southward," she said, "What do you see?"

"The thralls have guns," SenRas reported, "I'm beginning to think they're not thralls."

"They've been..." Malia puzzled, trailing off as the implications settled in. She glanced aside toward the Berininites. One man made brief eye contact and tapped his temple. Malia flashed a grin. "Of course."

"Of course?"

"Sanus was infected," Malia said, shooting at the north end of the wall, "Nenbard developed a suppressant."

"Ahh, yes. MarLys reported as much," SenRas recalled, "This must be the Project Cerulean Nikasu asked about."

The first activated to have been shot returned to a more human shape, trembling and mostly naked. The activated gave them no regard as they advanced.

Shots from the south and subsequent blue streaks rapidly compounded. But even at their peak, they were only a shove against the wave of hundreds. Malia dug her feet in and shot faster, not waiting to see if one pair hit their marks before they fired the next.

The foremost of the activated reached the deepest part of the valley. Malia focused on them, aiming for the legs. Blue shots from the Berininite sentinels painted the necks and chests of the encumbered masses.

As he reached the depth of the valley, the brimstone silhouette of Sinkua hastened through the crowd. Streaks of indigo evaporated in his proximity.

"I know this is a bad time," SenRas said, "But do you recall what one smells when having a stroke?"

"Burnt toast, but I think that's a myth," Malia said, "Why?"

"Doubly a relief, then," he sighed, "I've caught a whiff of burning sage."

A flash of red and a guttural scream erupted from near the front of the wall. The brimstone shell of Sinkua lowered Epesol as he advanced, unbothered by the man falling in two at his side. The deceased, his humanity restored, had been split from left shoulder to right hip.

Malia's throat tightened. She dropped a dozen activated around him, hoping to slow him without wounding him or drawing his ire.

Then, she felt his eyes upon her.

Nikasu cast her focus around The Harvester. A ring of wet sand surrounding him tightened with a vague threat of vitrification. He angled Epemort to place its tip near Epelun, blade but not hand crossing the gravimantic threshold.

"Still you persist?" he asked.

Nikasu gave a beckoning gesture. The Harvester advanced, but the threshold closed in. He stumbled into a crouch under his own amplified weight.

She slashed upward. He straightened up and leaned back, and the tip of her sword etched a line up the center of his mask. A shifting in its fit signaled a scrutinizing expression.

"The Geneticist was right about you," The Harvester said, holding his lower back as he righted himself, "All three of them feared how strong…"

"I know," Nikasu interrupted, "And you have no idea how right they were."

One side of The Harvester's mask flicked upward. He lunged low with his blade forward at an awkward angle. Nikasu once again cast her milystic will toward him, but her focus yielded nothing as they collided with his blade.

Breath betrayed her as his palm heel crashed into her solar plexus. He lifted his hand as she staggered back. She came upright to see tendrils of purple fog swirling around his fingers.

He clenched his fist, and the fog tendrils sprang at her, seeping into her skin. They clutched at the depths of her being, pressure bearing on the very notion of her vital organs.

"Take this as a sign of my respect," he said, stumbling her with a sharp jerk, "My seeking a swift victory is an acknowledgment of your strength."

Nikasu's throat burned as neck muscles tightened. Tension pulsated through her forearms. Her vision went blurry with flickers of heightened clarity. These, she realized, came in synchronicity with the pulsating tension.

She lunged through the assault on her vitality, chitin shrapnel falling from her forearm as she reciprocated the blow to the solar plexus. The Harvester winced and stumbled, and Nikasu forced him to his knees with a surge of milystis.

She focused beyond him as she slashed at a wide angle. He grunted as he pulled back yet again, only this time to be caught in a wave of gravimantic milystis. Her blade narrowly missed his eye as it sliced from his cheekbone to the opposite end of his hairline.

The lower portion of his mask hit the sand, revealing a jet black eye with a penumbral aura. He sighed and cast off the rest of it.

"As you appear to have suspected," he said, "How did you figure it out?"

"Vielle left a message," Nikasu said, staring into those abyssal eyes, "And MalVek left at least one loose end in The Coalition."

"Both eventualities that I did not account for," The Harvester sighed, grazing his face with his fingertips, "Have you been told that I entered Drakougeneospa?"

"You did what?!"

Nikasu's eyes flared as she thrust her palm heel at him, dropped him to his hands and knees with an erupting mass of purple milystis. She lunged with Epelun across her torso, but she slashed only the vacant air where The Harvester had just been.

Nikasu stiffened as she felt the tip of a sword angled against the back of her neck.

"You know quite well that to set foot there is equally my birthright as yours," The Harvester said, "More to the point, I might give you reason to re-think your stance here."

Nikasu shifted her body weight. The blade followed. He had her at a disadvantage, and she saw no clear way out.

"… Speak," she demanded.

"I came to retrieve Epesol for Sinkua."

"Why would you…?"

"Necessity," The Harvester interrupted, "The most urgent matter is the mortal threat he poses to us both as we are."

Nikasu chewed on the implications. Sinkua had been activated beyond any episodes she had seen. Her own threat of activation was still taxing whatever reserve of willpower was holding it back. Adrenaline and the three cups of coffee she'd had at Country Living were running thin.

Nikasu sighed and lowered her head. She turned Epelun downward and plunged it into the sand.

"You have a point," she said, "The way things are now, he would kill us both."

"I am glad you understand," he said, "Our wisest course of action…"

In a single swift motion, Nikasu ripped Epelun from the sand and sliced The Harvester's face, mirroring the mark she'd left upon unmasking him.

"So, I'll change the way things are," she asserted, "I can talk Sinkua down from his episodes."

"You foolish…!"

"I'm holding off my own activation," she continued, despite his interruption, "Once you're out of my way, I can help him do the same."

"Suppose you can't," The Harvester challenged as he began to circle her, "Suppose we both perish here. What then, child?"

"The bridge to The Veil is incomplete," Nikasu said, her throat tightening, "If we die, Sinkua advances and drowns."

"You would sacrifice the last of the Dragon Family to preserve The Veil?"

Nikasu nodded.

"Noble," The Harvester said, "But I'll not stand for it."

He lunged and slashed, nearly catching her off guard. She bent back as she raised Epelun, catching his blade against her own. Chitin fragments emerged and crumbled from her forearms as she struggled against him.

A sudden heat washed over her just before a ball of flames crashed and dissolved against their blades, forcing them apart.

Uro opened his eyes to a heap of fabric, wet with drool. He lifted his head and looked around, blinking away the fatigue. He was sitting in a restaurant booth. He rubbed the back of his head as he tried to piece together the events that could have taken him from a terrorist facility to a burger joint.

"How do you feel?" someone asked.

Uro looked toward the voice to find Khirsan sitting across the table from him. He shut his eyes and shook his head. That just complicated things further.

"What are you…" Uro muttered, "I mean… How?"

"Project Cerulean," Khirsan said, sipping his drink, "I'll fill you in on the details as you come around."

"I…" Uro stammered. His head swiveled, compensating for his narrow periphery, and he found another cup. He mumbled his gratitude and took a sip. "I started to activate?"

Khirsan nodded.

"But… you didn't?"

Khirsan shook his head.

"I thought…" Uro cough, "I thought we were all doped with the substance. Do you mean…?"

"Like I said," Khirsan reiterated, "Project Cerulean."

"That thing Seirakh and Uncle were working on?" Uro asked, "They got it to work?"

"More or less," Khirsan said, "Functional prototype. Very limited samples."

"But it was enough to protect you," Uro pointed out, "And to save me." He laughed as wakefulness came on with a sense of hope. "Khirsan! This is our ace in the hole!"

"Damn right, my guy," Khirsan beamed, leaning back with his drink, "Problem is, we're in ArcNos, and what we need is in Quarun."

"And the activated are on course for the Southlands," Uro sighed, looking down at the table as he mulled through his thoughts.

"Yeah, it's a conundrum," Khirsan nodded, "Spril said to evacuate this place when something comes after us. Even if I have to drag you."

"He's that sure that they're still chasing us?"

Khirsan nodded. "But since we have time, we need to figure out how we can get more units of Project Cerulean."

"Well, I might he able to get my hands on a portal strip," Uro said, "We can find one back at Drakougeneospa. The House of Dragons."

"Great," Khirsan said, "Close by?"

"Hour or so by train," Uro said, "But… come to think of it, maybe we shouldn't. MalVek's probably targeting it."

"A place called The House of Dragons can't protect itself?"

"Well, it's… complicated," Uro said, "But there might be another way."

"Something MalVek wouldn't go after?" Khirsan asked.

Uro nodded. "I've seen your sister around," he said.

"Oh yeah?" Khirsan said, "How's she doing?"

"She's, um… She's good. I think. I haven't spoken with her. Just seen her in and out of Drakou," Uro explained, "Anyway, she has a, um, friend."

"In her line of work, I'm sure she has a lot of um-friends."

Uro glared at him, but his expression softened as Khirsan flashed a grin. "Right," he sighed, "Well, this particular friend might have a portal strip."

"And this friend is less vulnerable than Drakou?"

"MalVek probably thinks she's dead, and even if he doesn't, I don't think he knows where to find her."

"So, where do we find her?"

"Hospital," Uro said, "Downtown in the capitol."

"Soon as you feel right, you should go there yourself," Khirsan said, "I'll stay and direct the evacuation. Do you have your cell?"

"What? No, I…" Uro stammered, "We shouldn't split up. That's what MalVek wants."

"We need to get to Hillside, but we also need to help evacuate this place."

"Then let's just…"

"We have two jobs to do and not enough time to both do both," Khirsan asserted, "You know this area better than me. You should go to the hospital."

"With your background, EshCal is more likely to listen to you," Uro argued, "She doesn't even know me."

"I'm sure you can manage it. Besides, MalVek is more interested in finding me than you."

"Well then, if you go, maybe he'll just send something after you and spare all these other people."

"No, it's better if I can contain it instead of leading it around town."

Uro sighed. "Well, I guess you have a point. I do know where the hospital is. And you are better with threat containment."

Khirsan smirked. "I do have some experience in that regard."

"But since you mentioned it, why would he want to find you?"

"He may or may not have caught on that I may or may not have sabotaged one of his projects."

Hibiscus leaned out of the hole in the wall, searching the ancient architecture for that dagger as her eyes adjusted to the darkness. When it came into focus, she reached her hand back and made a beckoning motion. A moment later, a wooden handle wrapped in a chain hit her hand. She brought it around, holding Sinkua's morningstar out the side of the top floor of Drakougeneospa, and let it drop.

"Do you know how you're going to get to them?" MelDas asked, "I mean after the portal."

"Walk?" Hibiscus shrugged. The morningstar knocked the dagger from its perch, and both tumbled to the ground. "Why?"

"These coordinates," MelDas said, "They're quite a ways from the southern coast."

"Well, it's not like I can take my car through."

"No, but my oldest has a dirt bike you could borrow."

"I wouldn't call it borrowing," she said, "I can't promise I'll bring it back in one piece."

"Given the circumstances, I don't think that's a big deal," he insisted, "I don't follow everything that's been happening, but there are worse things than a wrecked bike at stake here."

"Well, yes, but…" Hibiscus said, "It's just that your kids have been through so much. Are you sure he won't mind?"

"He's my son," MelDas said, "If he minds, I'll see to it that he doesn't."

"Okay," Hibiscus laughed, "Meet me outside with it. And thank you."

"I should warn you, the headlight has been finicky."

Malia scrambled back as Sinkua reached the base of the hill. Foliage ignited in an arm's width radius. The other activated cleared a path with no discernible acknowledgment. They struck down those restored by the Berininite sentinels with thoughtless efficiency.

Malia emptied and reloaded clips faster than she could register if and where each shot had landed. Her aim faltered in her rising panic, but she kept the barrels pointed toward the lower half of the mass of activated who had yet to move aside for the brimstone silhouette.

His eyes never left her. He grabbed a restored by the back of the neck and tossed him aside. He kicked over an activated and burned it as he walked along its back. Malia's next shot only threw up sand and ash. Her next two went wide.

She wiped the sweat from her eyes and sent another bullet into his fiery wake as he cleaved an activated. She realized then that she was no longer aiming at the activated. Part of her was trying to take him down directly, while her morality fought against her ruthless pragmatism.

The choking heat pressed into her before he was halfway up the hill. Malia's hands trembled the closer Sinkua came, shots scattering around him. As he crested the hill, layers of sweat plastered her clothes down. Unbearably hot, her pistols fell from her hands.

He stood over her, black smoke billowing from his naked brimstone body. His shadowed emerald eyes were both dense with fury and devoid of awareness.

Sinkua raised his sword across his shoulder. Malia shielded her face with her forearms, cowering and pleading. But a dull thud and a sizzling interrupted her fear.

She opened her eyes to see SenRas standing between them with his manriki pulled taut and Epesol bearing down on it. His fingers sizzled as the ambient heat fried his flesh through the chain links. SenRas twisted the manriki, slightly redirecting the blade before it sliced his manriki in two.

SenRas successively popped Sinkua between the eyes with both severed ends of his manriki. Sinkua hammered SenRas's temple with the side of his fist, scorching his flesh and sending him tumbling along the crest of the hill.

SenRas hurled his spatha, and Malia caught it and, in the same motion, batted Epesol off course from her own neck. Sinkua showed no emotion as he advanced. Malia shuffled backward, costing the spatha ever more of its structural integrity with each attack she deflected.

Sinkua bent the spatha blade with Epesol and tore it from Malia's grasp. Malia scrambled back and lost her footing, rolling backward to end up on her elbows and knees. She pushed herself up just in time to see the tip of Epesol roaring toward her. She closed her eyes and ground her teeth, bracing for the inevitable.

A pair of leathery hands grabbed her by the shoulders and flipped her up onto her back. Prostrate, she opened her eyes and saw SenRas standing over her.

Epesol erupted through his sternum in a spray of blood and scorched bone fragments. His eyes went blank. Blood trickled from his mouth as he coughed. He looked down at Malia and gave a weak smile.

"Was only a matter of time," he said.

Blood spewed from the wound as Epesol retracted. SenRas collapsed, dead before his body settled on the smoky ground. And all Malia could do was scramble aside as Sinkua and the swarm of activated advanced on the beach.

Calhosin leaned on the crossbar of his cell gate, looking down the corridor. SouSol paced with Sbaglien and MerSul in tow and guards posted at regular intervals. Not all of them had had an understanding with the exodus inmates, and even some who had were browbeaten into submission by Sbaglien and SouSol.

Across and down the way, he spotted Inre in her cell. She was also watching their jailers survey their quarry. He gave a subtle nod.

"Whatever you're plotting, let me get clear of the fallout first," Biroe said behind him, "I've had enough of getting knocked on my back for one lifetime."

Calhosin looked over his shoulder. "You know, what happened with Sinkua and KalChi…"

"If you're going to tell me to get over it, don't bother," Biroe interrupted, "I'm not done seething about it."

"Do I look like your therapist?" Calhosin scolded, "I was going to say I'm sort of to blame."

A short squeaking of ungreased axles brought Biroe to his side.

"What are you talking about?" Biroe asked, glowering up at him, "How could you possibly have…"

"I set it up," Calhosin said, "I knew Sinkua's power to revive the dead would eventually occur to you. So, I bribed the medical examiner to use purple sheets and insult Sinkua if he had the chance. I needed him to snap, but I didn't want him to take his anger out on you. Unfortunately, that meant he couldn't revive Kal…"

His words halted as pressure bore down on his kidney. He looked down to see Biroe clutching him by the oblique, grinding his well-exercised fingers against his flesh.

"Why?" Biroe snarled, "You killed my hope. You made me hate a broken man. Why!?"

Calhosin grabbed Biroe's wrist and tried to wrench his hand away. "To pr… protect us."

Biroe released him. "What do you mean?"

"I knew what we were getting into," Calhosin said, rubbing his side, "The exodus. Not those two taking over. I just thought it would be good to have a Hybrid on our side. Sinkua was the most opportune."

Biroe sighed and lowered his head. "You could have told me," he insisted, "I would have gone along with it."

"No, you wouldn't," Calhosin said as he resumed watching SouSol pace, "Most people couldn't have."

"In that case, could you stop involving me in your schemes?" Biroe insisted, "Being collateral damage once is enough."

"You'll be fine," Calhosin said, clearing his throat, "I'll keep an eye on you."

He made eye contact with Inre and winked at her just as SouSol passed through his line of sight. Her necktie eyepatch wrinkled as she glared at him.

Calhosin pointed to his eyes with his index and middle fingers, then to hers, except he lowered his middle finger. SouSol stormed over to his cell and swatted the gate with the tonfa she had confiscated. Calhosin suppressed the urge to flinch.

"You might think you have nothing left to lose, outsider," she scolded, "But I promise you there are much worse things in store for you and your friends if this little insubordination keeps up."

"Oh, do you promise?" Calhosin goaded, "Well, I hope you can keep that promise. Because I promised my friends they'd all get to take a swing at you."

"You think you're so clever," SouSol challenged, "Your rebellion fell apart with a single gesture. I could just as easily…"

"That is unadvisable, madam," Sbaglien interrupted, "He means to exploit your anger."

"Business as usual for you, General Sbaglien," Inre said, "Cozying up half a step behind your superior. You have most of the authority, but they insulate you from most of the consequences. Second in command, in name only."

"Ramble to your contentment, dear Colonel," Sbaglien deflected with melodious whimsy, "You won't have my anger to exploit."

"Why not?" Inre asked, "Because this High Minister won't permit it?"

"Both of you think the same way," Calhosin added, "Which works fine for an individual. But two people like that working together?"

"It'll never work," Inre said, "Will it, Noble Doyen?"

A fifth voice, emotionless and unfamiliar, joined them. "I would say your failure is quite clear."

Calhosin and Inre tried to look down the hall. He couldn't see anything from his vantage point and guessed she couldn't either. Whoever it was, Sbaglien feared them far more than the irreverence of SouSol's sneer suggested.

A perfectly androgynous figure passed through Calhosin's view, giving him no regard. Much to her lividness, it gave SouSol the same lack of regard even as it stopped just short of colliding with her. Its focus lay solely on Sbaglien.

"Explain your failure," it said.

"I have not failed," Sbaglien said, "Every subject of the exodus has been gathered. I even threw in a few extras."

"They were the result of happenstance," it said, "Lord MalVek thanks you for the gifts, but this is not the predetermined location."

"I admit we've been delayed. There were complications."

"By failing to work through those complications, you have failed in your mission."

"They put up more of a fight than expected," Sbaglien said. He gestured to Calhosin and Inre. "Those two destroyed the lily pads and trapped us here."

"Don't act so arrogant either," SouSol said, "because now, you're trapped, too."

The homunculus palmed her face, never moving its eyes from Sbaglien. With a wrenching of its arm, blood and bone fragments erupted from SouSol's neck as the top of her head touched her shoulder. The homunculus released her, and she collapsed in a heap of herself.

"Cattle does not speak."

Nikasu stepped back from The Harvester and lowered Epelun. She looked inland with her eyes aglow, and her throat tightened as she saw what had become of her brother. He advanced with purpose but not haste as a swarm of malformed creatures crested the hill behind him.

"What will you do?" The Harvester asked, "Do you intend to continue fighting me? If you believe you can stop me, you are short on time to do so."

Nikasu looked to The Harvester. She couldn't fathom what he intended to do with Phoenix, but it was a far less urgent matter than his intention to destroy The Veil.

She looked back to the brimstone shell of her brother. Sinkua's eyes were faint at this distance, but she felt she saw something within them. The faintest spark told of the whisper of the man trapped within.

He hadn't been molded into The Beast. The Beast had been molded around him.

She sheathed Epelun and swung the scabbard onto her back.

"I'm going to talk to him," she said, "You gambled your soul away with Tiamat. His is still his own."

She ignored The Harvester's glare as she walked inland. She knew he wanted to launch at her for those words, but she also knew that he wouldn't while he was so emotionally compromised.

Shots from behind the hill spattered blue on the necks of the activated behind Sinkua. Nobody involved in the extraction operation had mentioned blue paintballs. Project Cerulean came to mind, which meant that either the Berininites had escaped enthrallment or Khirsan and Uro had already acquired more samples. All the better, those hit by the blue shots stopped and reverted to their human shape. It was clearly Project Cerulean, and it worked.

The remaining swarm halted as Sinkua stopped on the side of the hill. A volley of shots depleted their numbers with streaks of blue. But Sinkua stood indifferent, his nearly empty eyes locked with Nikasu's.

Nikasu stepped forward with her hands out at her sides. But as she called out to him, he released a primal roar and charged down the hill. Several masked Berininites crested the hill to hold back the activated.

Nikasu swung her scabbard around to her front, only to overshoot and put it back at her side. She unclasped it and dropped it in the rapidly drying grass. Her attention shifted between Epelun as she scrambled to unsheathe it and Sinkua as he devoured the space between them. He drew Epesol across himself within the last few steps.

With a streak of black and violet, The Harvester manifested between them and batted Epesol aside. Nikasu clenched her fist and pulled The Harvester down with a bombardment of gravimantic milystis. He swept Epemort along the dried grass, and Nikasu rolled back beyond its reach.

Flames erupted on The Harvester's shoulder, but the flat of his blade swiftly doused them. Nikasu sprang to her feet and slashed at him, but he leaned forward just enough to keep the tip off his back. Sinkua took a swing that threatened to cleave chest from belly, but The Harvester pivoted under it and slashed at Nikasu.

Nikasu sidestepped the blade and pinned it down with the tip of Epelun. She stomped on the flat of Epemort as she flooded his arm with milystis, forcing the weapon from his hand. Sinkua raised Epesol overhead. Nikasu grabbed The Harvester's arm and pulled him facedown and out of the way.

"Sinkua, wait!" she cried out.

Epesol roared down, flames erupting as it missed its mark. Sinkua advanced with no regard for The Harvester as he stepped on his back. Nikasu couldn't comprehend why she had saved The Harvester, but she tried not to dwell on it. The worst she figured was that she wanted him alive to stop Sinkua if she couldn't. She put herself in Sinkua's path.

"Listen to me," she insisted, "This isn't you. You're going to be okay. You need to stop and think."

He lifted Epesol across his shoulder.

"Remember what they did to you," Nikasu rasped as she shuffled back.

The Phoenix ruby pulsated as shallow roiling flames manifested on his blade.

"Stop doing what MalVek wants," she pleaded, "You're better than this!"

He slashed at her torso, but his back arched, redirecting the blade over her head. Eyes wide, she stepped back and aside to find The Harvester behind him with his fist jammed against his spine.

Sinkua swept his arm as he whipped around, hurling a volley of aerial flames. The Harvester caught them on the flat of Epemort, dousing the milystic flames with his incompatible Hephaeseum. He staggered, but he kept his eyes on Sinkua's shoulders.

As she watched their swords collide in a burst of embers and ebony, Nikasu realized The Harvester had diverted Sinkua from his goal. Perhaps, without it in his line of sight, he'd be more willing to listen. But as she moved into his periphery, she felt a wave of milystis wash over her from above.

She looked up to see fading streaks of purple and silver smeared across the sky. The ground vibrated with a dense thud, and Nikasu spun around to find Nemesis behind her, standing as tall as when he first came down from his ion cloud.

"We must go," he implored.

"Deboro!" she cried out, "… Naboro… vothiso!"

"Speak Ouristihran. Faster," Nemesis said, "Help for him coming. We need to be… ah…"

"Somewhere else?" Nikasu said.

"Yes. For now," he said, lowering his head, "If Veil and Sinkua fall, you must be ready."

"I understand," she sighed, straddling his neck, "Spril's plan worked?"

"Someone comes with things he asked."

Sparks crackled in MalVek's flesh metal as he panned the vast wall monitor. Yellow dots speckled the green-lined map of Ouristihra. In the Southlands, red dots clustered so tightly as to be uncountable. The cluster had been moving and growing for some time, but now it churned and hesitated. One, far brighter than the rest, stood beyond them, also halted.

"Everyone is in position," he said, "We depart shortly."

"Yes, My Lord," Jevana said, "The Harvester has dispatched as well."

"As instructed," MalVek said, his eyes never leaving the screen, "It would appear he's succeeded in delaying our curmudgeonly friend."

"My Lord? I don't understand. Do you want him to stop him?"

"I want what he wants. To destroy The Veil and save Phoenix."

"But…" she said, her eyes narrowing, "… You have something else in mind for her."

"Seriamus is unworthy of that power," MalVek scowled, "As she is now, Pandora is scarcely better."

"Well, I'm worried The Harvester will fail us. What will we do then?"

"Until my designs on you as the new host have panned out, there is no us, and your opinion is of no concern to me," he said, "Phoenix is a garnish. A pleasant and welcome addition, but ultimately not mandatory. That is why I am more deserving than they. I do not so covet it that I would compromise to lessers."

"Of course, My Lord," Jevana said, "None above you."

"And before you think to mention it," MalVek continued, "I know what The Harvester did before he left."

Dirt bike tires chewed mud and foliage and sprayed them over Myriela's pants. She squinted against the harsh humid wind, the visor being too dark with the headlight flickering. Luvros fluttered behind her shoulder.

She felt heavy as a shadow swept over her, but she chalked it up to nerves. The clamor of battle carried over from just beyond the hill. She picked up an unplaceable floral and herbal smell, which came to smell increasingly burnt. Sinkua must have been close by.

Myriela fishtailed hard enough to nearly topple the bike as she came upon the madness in the valley. Nightmarish creatures thrashed about, showing no particular intelligence beyond a certain fatal compulsion. Humans in various states of tattered undress scrambled amongst them, bewildered of anything but the need to escape.

Curiously, they all looked to have spatters of blue on their necks and chests. A couple score Berininites proved to be responsible. They kept their guns trained on the hundreds of creatures as they spread to keep them surrounded.

As she drove beyond the valley, Myriela came upon two men clashing swords in rapid succession. One of them looked to be on fire, much as she had been told he would.

Myriela took the morningstar from the saddlebag behind the seat. Luvros fell back, hovering a couple meters behind her. She leaned into the throttle as far as it would go, then kept leaning. She called out his name and let his morningstar fly.

With equal parts practice and prediction, Spril whipped and wove the borrowed motorcycle through the predawn traffic. Gritting his teeth, he reduced the glare of headlights on the visor to pinpoints. The inside smelled like cigarettes, arguably the owner's favorite brand. He noted to himself to get the man a pack for his help.

He had to assume that something had gone wrong if Inre still had the barrier up. MalVek must have noticed when the exodus was interrupted. So, with headlights and taillights zipping along his periphery, he weighed potential entry and attack plans against the contents of his pack.

He had the resonant disrupter for whatever it was worth. He also had assorted spare gas bombs for BeiLou's shoulder strap. Now, if only he had asked her what each one did. As it was, using them would be a matter of intuition and luck. Mostly luck.

But he did have his quarterstaff, as always. With the remote in his pocket and the code memorized, that would have to do.

The last thing he could recall was a woman lying broken at his feet. Since then had been something less than nothingness. An antithesis of presence wherein time wasn't even a concept. Now, after what could just as well have been seconds as weeks, some weapon lay at his feet on scorched soil.

Nothing else existed. Whatever the world might have been, it was now isolated to this small space. There was this weapon. This burnt soil. And his remaining sense of self. Compulsion drove him to pick up the weapon.

The side of his neck twitched, reminding him of his own presence beyond the conceptual. The weapon felt comfortable in his hand. Familiar. He swayed his arm, assuring himself that those too were his own.

The end of the weapon seemed like an entirely alien presence. It just floated, going where it wanted with no deference for his thoughts.

He winced and lurched away as it jabbed his hip and rolled along his pelvis. The chain jumped as he flicked his wrist, as though it might coax the ball to be agreeable. But as it swayed back, it glanced off his hip again.

He gritted his teeth. The side of his neck twitched and locked up. Over and again, he tried to control this ball, but it never failed to eventually turn against him.

There was no forcing it into submission. In this microcosm of a world, this weapon existed only to betray him. It was the instrument of his self-destruction.

His eyes twitched. A taste like the smell of the chain filled his mouth. His body grew cold. But for a moment, it felt right.

He hacked furiously, spraying crimson across the scorched mud. That same redness trickled over his chin and down his neck as a bestial roar erupted from his throat.

His focus became impossibly clear. He could see every fragment of soil, every ash mote in the air. He could see them as they were and as they could be, individually and collectively. Gazing into the chain, he found that same feeling in the links.

But words for all of this eluded him. Everything was bound by an underlying sense of hatred. But that hatred had a purpose. A need to protect something.

There were things beyond this microcosm. Something he was compelled to destroy. And something for which he sought retribution.

"Who are you?"

The very existence of spoken language expanded his world. He gritted his teeth as he tightened his grip on his morningstar.

"I'm not the one you should be worried about."

His breathing grew ragged and erratic. A third voice called out from within. Oddly feminine, despite his assumptions. It spoke gibberish, but he found it comforting somehow. Heat swept down each arm, feeling purposeful as it coalesced in his hands.

"Sinkua!"

That broke into his sense of language. More than that, it reached his sense of himself. He forced his mind to form words.

"That's... my name?"

His inner voice was masculine. The feminine voice was something else inside himself. Somehow, that didn't worry him. It belonged there. It shared his space as its own unique entity, guiding and enhancing him.

"I've been trying to reach you for hours," the feminine voice said, "It's good to have you back, Sinkua."

"Where... was I?" he asked, recalling Phoenix as he comprehended his own name.

"We'll hash that out later. For now, look straight ahead."

That wet metallic taste rose again at the sight of what stood before him. The sword in the man's hand made him realize that he held a strikingly similar one. His face was freshly scarred. He had eyes like burnt ebony. And he looked appalled to see him.

"Do you know who that is?"

"Yeah. Leader of The Avatars of Fate."

"He goes by The Harvester."

"There's something strange about him. He feels... powerful."

"He's centuries old. Inhumanly agile. Preserved by multitudes of souls."

"Do you remember my plan with the minotaur?"

"Yes, you were going to free Arestor."

"We're going to try that."

Chapter 46

Sinkua rushed The Harvester, flames spewing from the tip of Epesol as he carved a line in the burnt soil. He swung his morningstar overhead and jerked his arm to slam it down from its peak. The Harvester deflected it with the flat of his blade.

Sinkua swept Epesol upward, creating a shielding fan of flames. The Harvester sidestepped it swiftly enough to billow the smoke. He sliced through the flames, dissolving them with his blade's incompatibility, and shifted back in front of Sinkua to throw a cannonball of a punch at his chest.

Sinkua pivoted and delivered a barefoot kick to the underside of The Harvester's ribcage. The Harvester staggered and pivoted back, slashing at Sinkua's outstretched leg.

As the blade came up, Sinkua brought his leg down past it. He stepped in and turned, bringing his other foot up as it came ablaze in brilliant viridian. His flames erupted but dissolved as his foot crashed against the flat of The Harvester's blade. But his own brute force jerked The Harvester's arm aside and threatened to rip the sword from his hand.

Smoked erupted from the ground as Sinkua stomped his doused foot. He swung his morningstar wide, but The Harvester leaned back to let the spikes whisk past his face. With two flicks of his wrist, Sinkua popped the ball up, then slammed it down. Only, The Harvester tilted his head at the first and twisted his torso at the second.

It only existed for a split second, but Sinkua had created his opening. Scorching energy radiated from chest, channeled down his leg, and concentrated in his foot. He stepped in and, with a bestial roar from the depths of his lungs, crashed his blazing foot into the underside of The Harvester's ribcage.

The first blow had only been to sensitize the area. But this follow-up went beyond exploiting that soreness. He splintered three of The Harvester's ribs and left a blister in the approximate shape of his foot.

As The Harvester doubled over, another feeling tugged at Sinkua. He no longer saw the shoes that he recalled having on when that broken older woman was at his feet. Glancing down at himself, he found he was bare down to his feet. The only thing quite as puzzling as waking up nude from functional catatonia was that he also had a ruby embedded in his chest. Phoenix reminded him that it was her home, but that didn't explain how or why it was fused with his skin.

Sinkua closed his eyes and steadied his breathing. Memories of his life before the blackout trickled back. And as they did, his episode was forced to an end.

"I ought to have slain you while you were entranced," The Harvester muttered.

"How long have I been like this?" Sinkua asked.

"Since you set out for this place. But how did you come back from that?"

"I don't know. But I think I should cover up before we go on."

"Well, perhaps this insolent woman who brought you that abominable weapon also thought to bring you clean undergarments."

Sinkua extended Epesol toward him and pivoted. Purple wings blurred toward the edges of his forward vision. Beyond them, he spotted a woman in a skimmer cap straddling a bike. He blinked hard and shook his head.

Luvros fluttered around to hover by his shoulder. Hibiscus, her real name surfacing from buried memories, pulled an armful of clothing from the saddlebag. Sinkua looked to The Harvester, who rolled his eyes and waved him over to her.

As he came to her side, he found she had indeed brought him a pair of underwear. Beyond that, she brought a pair of once black jeans, now gray and softened with wear. There were his combat boots and the back strap for his morningstar. But instead of a shirt, she had brought a long jacket.

His jaw tightened as he clutched this last garment. Memories of blood and shattered asphalt filled his thoughts. But behind them came an incomparable flavor of happiness. It was one of Eytea's dusters.

"Myriela?" he beckoned as he dressed himself, "What's going on? How and why are you even here?"

"I'm not up to speed on everything," she confessed, "Spril thought your morningstar might help you with... whatever that was. And SenRas said you burned your clothes off."

"Thank you but..." he stammered, "How did you get dragged into this? We just met."

"After you were abducted, everyone who could went looking for you. Spril called EshCal and asked if she could send someone," she explained, "I took a portal strip from Chekov's room and this dirt bike from MelDas's oldest son."

Sinkua's mouth fell open. "Everybody?" He let out a long exhale as she nodded. "Shit," he sighed, "How's EshCal? I remember hearing her scream, but..."

"She lost her legs just below the knees," Myriela said, "It's slow, but she's getting on with prosthetics and physical rehab."

"Son of a bitch." He paced as he wrestled his arms into the duster. "I should've seen it coming."

"By all means, keep chatting away," The Harvester goaded.

"Oh, come on," she scoffed, "She's the freaking Prime Minister of Defense, Brigadier General Elite, or whatever they're calling her now."

"I would prefer to grant you the honor of a fighting death," The Harvester continued.

"If she didn't see it coming, her secretary shouldn't beat himself up," Myriela said, "Even if he did figure out that shit with MarLys. How did you do that, anyway?"

"I, uh... She'll tell you later," Sinkua said, securing his dagger to his waist.

"Oh! That reminds me," she said, gesturing to the dagger holster, "I found a sword sheath in the other bedroom. Don't know whose it is, but I thought you might need it."

"It's CreSam's. And yes, thank you," he said, taking it from the side of the bike, "But... I do still have one more favor to ask."

"But know well that I will stab you through the back, should necessity dictate it!" The Harvester bellowed.

"I promised EshCal I'd restain her desk, but I don't know when or if I'll get to it," Sinkua said, gritting his teeth as he rolled his shoulders to loosen the sleeves. "I need you to make sure it gets done."

"I..." Myriela trailed off into a sigh and shook her head, "Never let anyone say you don't keep a promise. What color?"

"Cherry seta," he said, "There's a can on its way to her office."

Her eyes widened. Sinkua realized she was looking beyond him as he heard rapid footfalls crunching the scorched soil. He shoved her away with a hand to her sternum as he took up his morningstar with the other. Sinkua whipped around and swung his morningstar into the diminishing space between himself and The Harvester.

The chain wrapped around The Harvester's sword, spikes chipping against the flat of the blade. Sinkua yanked back, setting The Harvester stumbling forward, and buried his foot in his abdomen. The Harvester's grip faltered, but he tightened his hold at the base of the handle as he regained his footing.

He turned the blade with a flick of the wrist, threatening the chain of Sinkua's morningstar as he slid it free. Sinkua lunged under the blade, swiping at his legs with Epesol, but The Harvester deflected and pinned it with a downward thrust.

Sinkua stomp-kicked The Harvester's elbow and pulled Epesol out from under the other sword. He swung his morningstar at The Harvester's head. As The Harvester ducked the spiked ball, Sinkua snapped it downward and thrust his knee up at The Harvester's downturned face.

Flames erupted from Sinkua's knee and enveloped The Harvester's head upon impact. His head whipped back, compounding the momentum as the ball collided with the back of his head. The spikes failed to penetrate bone, but the impact dropped him to his hands and knees.

"That sword," Sinkua said, "It's made of Hephaeseum, isn't it?"

"Yes. You and I are both of the Dragon Family. That must be obvious even to you," The Harvester goaded, "This is Epemort, known in Ouristihran as the Sword of the Dead. I was bound to Tiamat."

Sinkua angled the tip of Epesol to the back of his head. "Was?"

"I pledged her to Pandora to gain her favor."

"You're a traitor of every degree," Sinkua snarled, hand trembling as he pressed his sword into flesh, "The only way you're worthy of touching one of our relics is to die by it."

"You said as much several centuries ago, when you were called Tetsen Drukoa."

Sinkua tightened his jaw against the curiosity of having had two names, assuming it to be the same as if he went by MeiLom Sinkua.

"Now that I've aligned with Tetsen's vision, still you call me a traitor," The Harvester snickered, "Ironic."

"You're talking about surrendering Phoenix in exchange for Pandora's withdrawal?"

"I am. Though you must die to destroy The Veil, if I am..."

His head snapped back as Sinkua's fiery boot collided with his face, and The Harvester rolled up onto his back. Sinkua stood over him and planted a foot on his chest.

"Well, it's been a few lifetimes since then. I've come to realize it was a stupid plan," Sinkua goaded, "You should have stuck to your principles."

The Harvester yanked Sinkua's leg, sending him stumbling aside. Sinkua snapped his morningstar at The Harvester's hand, snagging the flesh between his fingers. The Harvester rolled up onto his feet and slashed Epemort against the dirt.

"You arrogant bastard!" he bellowed, "Phoenix can only be returned unbound to you. Thus I can only offer it between your death and rebirth."

"I have zero capacity to trust you," Sinkua chided, coursing milystis along Epesol, "When I return Phoenix to the Etherworld, it won't be through Pandora, and it won't be through you!"

He slashed the air, releasing the milystis as a fiery crescent. Sinkua ran behind it and, as it dissolved, pivoted around Epemort. He brought his foot up as he came around and clipped The Harvester on the back of the head.

The Harvester slashed at the underside of his foot. Sinkua bellowed an expletive and clashed his morningstar against Epemort. He lunged and slammed his palm heel against The Harvester's sternum.

The Harvester grabbed his arm and twisted it up behind Sinkua's back with nearly imperceptible celerity. Sinkua writhed against him, but The Harvester launched him across the ground with a kick to the back. Sinkua grabbed at the ground as he rolled, but he only stopped as he collided with a rocky upcropping.

"You never said he had superhuman strength," he thought toward Phoenix.

"Sorry, I didn't know until now," Phoenix defended, "But I don't think it's persistent. Look."

Sinkua watched The Harvester's shoulders slump and shudder as he walked. The exertion, incredible as it was, had clearly taxed him.

"Can you see any of the souls he's consumed?" Sinkua thought, using the rock to pull himself to his feet.

"Not effectively," Phoenix said, "Numbers, motion, and distance are all hindering me."

"Well then," Sinkua thought, slapping the rock, "Let's tease a few more feats of strength out of him."

Sinkua barreled forth, flames erupting with every footfall. He pulled both Epesol and his morningstar back, arms and weapons coursing with milystis. The Harvester rolled his shoulders and charged in kind, Epemort drawn back in a mirroring position.

The Harvester slashed first. Sinkua pivoted under the blade, anchoring himself with Epesol angled against the dirt. He came around behind The Harvester and buried his foot in the small of his back.

The Harvester turned on him with another bout of superhuman celerity. Black and purple tendrils billowed from his fingertips. Sinkua pushed back from Epesol, his throat constricting from the proximity of the necromantic milystic. He pulled his dagger from under the duster and slashed the underside of The Harvester's forearm.

The Harvester drove Epemort at his throat. Sinkua ducked the attack and drove his dagger into The Harvester's abdomen. Leaving it there, he snatched up his swaying sword.

"What are you doing?" Phoenix scolded, "Remember what Takmet told you!"

"He's what drives me to fight!"

Black and purple tendrils rose from his body as The Harvester ripped out the dagger and whipped it into the dirt. Sinkua glimpsed a fresh welt on The Harvester's hand as he brought it aglow in violet and ebony. Ripples of light manifested in the air and began to converge on him.

"Ambient fragments of the dead are everywhere," he boomed, strands of flesh stitching his wounds shut, "Play at battle to your heart's content, but know that you cannot overpower me."

Sinkua let his guard down just long enough for The Harvester to plow his fist against his chest, just below the Phoenix Ruby. Sinkua collapsed backward, tumbling in uncountable reverse somersaults. Eventually, he settled facedown, snickering into the dirt and ash.

He pushed himself to his feet and swaggered toward The Harvester in long, swaying strides.

"Ambient fragments, huh?" Sinkua goaded, "Well, that's a fancy way of saying you're scared of me. I mean, you have all these souls, but you… what? Already used them? Don't want to? Can't?"

"Still your tongue, lest I drag it from your throat, you insolent whelp."

"And you're a festering cod testicle. As I was saying!" Sinkua continued, "Clearly, I've frightened you, and it isn't fair that I'm more heavily armed than you. So, let's even things out."

Sinkua sheathed Epesol and pitched it aside. He whirled his morningstar, bringing the spiked head aglow with red-hot milystis as he built momentum. With a ring of flames roaring alongside him, he charged at The Harvester.

The Harvester sidestepped his barreling assault with imperceptible swiftness. Before Sinkua realized where he had ended up, a foot cracked his ribs and sent him rolling across the ground again.

He repeated this half a dozen times, charging with his morningstar ablaze only to get knocked down and away, often into a rocky upcropping. Black and purple smoke enveloped The Harvester's body. Sinkua's breathing grew ragged. His jaw clenched. The vein along his temple throbbed. The taste of blood wafted up from his throat. Phoenix talked to him about nothing in particular.

He charged at The Harvester one last time. The flames enveloping his spinning morningstar flashed into a blinding aquamarine glow.

Sinkua clenched his fist, and a fireburst just below the ground launched Epesol. He hurled his morningstar at The Harvester and snatched his sword from the cloud of dust and smoke without breaking his stride.

The Harvester rushed him, winding back for a kick to the sternum. Instead, Sinkua jumped and slammed his feet into The Harvester's ribcage. The force of impact and his own redirected momentum sent The Harvester staggering back several meters.

Sinkua hurled Epesol like a javelin, finding its mark in The Harvester's chest. It bisected his sternum as it plunged into his chest and split his upper spine as it erupted out of his back in a spray of blood and blackish purple milystic tendrils.

Sinkua charged behind it, grabbing the handle and The Harvester's shoulder as he caught up. He ran with them, driving his impaled opponent with greater force than The Harvester could square himself against.

With a thunderous bellow, Sinkua slammed The Harvester into a rocky up-cropping and skewered him to it with Epesol. A swell of milystic heat sealed the cracked stone around the blade.

"What do you think you're going to do?" The Harvester challenged as Sinkua stepped back, "Pandora is indestructible, and only two people can reason with her. I'm one. The other isn't you."

Sinkua extended his hand and closed his eyes. "Okay," he thought through a long exhale, "Can you get something now?"

"Yes, I think so."

"Good. I assumed getting Epesol near him was the next best thing to getting you closer."

"You could approximate it as an extension of my mind," Phoenix answered, "Now, let me concentrate."

"Or do you think you can leave me here to die?" The Harvester asked.

"The thought crossed my mind," Sinkua said, "But I know it wouldn't work, so shut up before you even start."

"Then what do you think you can do, boy?" The Harvester goaded, "Veil or not, so long as Pandora and Seriamus exist here, this world will never know peace. Should MalVek destroy The Veil, he will use them to usher in The Era of Chaos. Only through my intervention can The Veil fall and what remains of Ouristihra not be sundered by Chaos."

"I've got one!" Phoenix announced.

"I'm going to destroy all four of you," Sinkua said, opening his eyes, "And for no other reason than convenience, I'm starting with you."

He clenched his fist and pulled back. Ripples of light manifested in the air between them, stretching toward Sinkua. A gaping pain ate through his abdomen, as though it was being ripped apart from the inside.

A figure formed of woven blue light occupied Sinkua's mind's eye. It radiated a sense of bonding, of belonging. But just beyond that came an encroaching feeling of dread and finality. It passed in a split second. But the vision and feeling burned itself into his memories exactly as Eytea's death had.

Sinkua charged at The Harvester with fits and patches of shallow flames roiling over his flesh. Blinding flashes of white fire erupted with every crash of his boots against the soil. Phoenix continued pulling souls, the pain of each death amplifying Sinkua's fury.

Sinkua swiped his morningstar from just before The Harvester's feet and cracked it across the traitorous Tiamat Hybrid's face, shredding flesh and uprooting teeth.

"You motherfucker!" Sinkua roared. He bashed the morningstar against the other side. "How dare you take Galo's soul!"

Sinkua mounted the rocky upcropping and pummeled The Harvester's face, neck, and collarbone with fiery fists.

"Who else is in there!?" he bellowed, "Eytea? Gijin? Elemeno?"

He sprang off and engulfed his morningstar in blinding white fire. Bones cracked and sinew melted with every strike.

"Let!" He bashed a shoulder into the socket.

"Them!" A blow to the collarbone shattered it.

"Out!!!" A strike to the throat splayed it open.

Ripples of light passed through Sinkua and dissolved behind him. None felt familiar. Few felt whole. But his rage never subsided.

Three more strikes between the impacted shoulder and the shattered collarbone reduced the area to scorched bone fragments and mangled flesh. He grabbed The Harvester's arm, cooking his skin in his grasp, and ripped it off with a bestial roar.

Sinkua brutalized The Harvester's neck with a morningstar blow to the jugular. A mirroring strike to the other side shredded and scorched the last bits of healthy flesh. He threw down his morningstar.

Sinkua wrapped his hand around the exposed length of spinal column, glaring into The Harvester's pale and tremoring face as his searing grasp liquefied cartilage and fused nerves to bone. As the mass became frail and brittle, he loosened his grip.

"Hear me!" Sinkua bellowed, "I am Lord Sinkua of Drakougeneospa. Empowered by Harkzanian nobility. Named by Mberhali honor. Armed by Quircois ingenuity. Fortified by Lechuatzulan craftwork. For your crimes of treason, I cast you out. Mortvill! You are hereby banished from House and Family alike!"

Stone turned to dust as his knuckles carved a gulley along the rocky upcropping. And as he followed through with his wrecking ball punch, he fragmented the jaw and top vertebra, knocking the rest of The Harvester's skull away as his flesh eroded.

Sinkua staggered back and doubled over, his breathing heavy and ragged. But the taste of blood didn't rise from his throat. In fact, what had been there subsided. The roiling flames calmed. And tears filled his eyes.

He dropped to his elbows and knees, sobbing into the ashy soil.

"I am so sorry, my friend," Phoenix consoled, "I could not identify him among the masses. Otherwise, I…"

"We both know that's a lie."

"Sinkua, we…"

"But thank you for that," Sinkua continued, "I… would've broken down if I knew."

"There's still work to do," Phoenix said, "Once you're ready."

"Nikasu is here, isn't she?"

"She and Nemesis, yes. Among others. Will you tell her?"

"When it's opportune."

Sinkua got to his feet, dusting off his elbows and knees. He pulled Epesol from The Harvester's already desiccated chest and slid it into the sheath. He recovered his dagger and tucked it inside the duster. He gathered up his morningstar and bound the chain. With his old weapon down at his side, he shuffled away from the sounds of the ocean.

He looked about but saw no sign of Myriela, save for one set of tire tracks. Either he was missing the second, or she had ridden back along the first. He would have doubted neither. He picked up a pair of handheld scythes from near the tracks, though with the enduring blur in his mind, their relevance was slow to coalesce. He tucked them into the back of his belt.

Sinkua scooped up The Harvester's severed head as he came upon it. What little flesh remained was gray and clung to the skull. Teeth rattled out, and bits of skin flaked off in his hand. The eyes had already decayed.

Just ahead, he saw an older woman kneeling at the top of the hill. He couldn't identify her beyond her not being Myriela. She looked to be in distress. Either she was already involved and something had gone wrong, or she got involved, which was something wrong in and of itself. In short, nothing worse could come of his helping. So he hoped.

As he neared the crest of the hill, he saw someone else just beyond her. A figure lay covered in blood. He gasped, and the woman jumped and turned at the sound of it.

"Sinkua?" she asked, her voice thready.

"Malia?" he returned, continuing up the hill, "She didn't say you…"

He trailed off as he looked to the body lying before her. His mouth hung agape, chin trembling, as his gaze settled upon that face. The face of his grandfather. Lifeless yet resigned. Not without regrets. Just accepting.

Sinkua knelt beside SenRas's dead body. Much of the blood was still wet. He brushed his fingers over his grandfather's shirt until he found a wound. His throat caught as he traced it with his fingertip. It was tall and narrow.

"He... He did it to protect me," Malia stammered.

"From me?" Sinkua asked.

"No! No," she insisted, holding his tricep, "Not from you. From what had happened to you."

"I don't see how that's any better," he spat, drawing his dagger, "My best friend was killed trying to rescue me. My mother-in-law was killed to activate me. And what I became killed my grandfather."

"Wh-what are you going to do with that?"

"Who else was there?" He peeled the blood-saturated shirt away from SenRas's chest.

"I don't..."

"Who else!?"

Malia swallowed hard as Sinkua pierced the shirt. "It wasn't because you were taken," she said, "But we... lost Vielle."

Sinkua ground his teeth. But the taste of blood didn't bubble up. His temple didn't throb. His rage had burned out. Only sorrow remained. He withdrew the dagger from SenRas's shirt.

"How did it happen?"

"She was at the bottom of the parking garage."

"SenRas and MarLys worked together to call her for help. I remember seeing vines. They were keeping the place from collapsing."

"She was supposed to call for reinforcements," she said, "Help, I mean. Not... structural."

"And what? You weren't fast enough?" he asked. He wanted to scold her. To blame her. But he understood that flavor of regret all too well.

Malia shook her head. "She never called," she said, "We think she saw the building shaking and came of her own accord."

"Sounds like her," he sighed, "How did she die, then? Overexertion."

Malia shook her head again, lips tightening as she swallowed hard. "The Harvester found her, bled her out," she said, her voice trembling, "She tried to leave a message in her blood. She said he's..."

"A Dragon Hybrid. I know," he interrupted, "In that case, you should have this." He set the skull by her bent knee.

"Whose is this?"

"His."

Her eyes came alight, misting with incalculable emotion. "You mean you've...?"

He nodded. "The Harvester is dead," Sinkua said, "by my hand."

She wrapped an arm around his neck and leaned into him. "Thank you."

Beyond SenRas's body, he found scrambling masses of subhuman creatures in the valley. Masked figures with guns surrounded them from the hillsides. Especially curious, it looked like the beasts bled dark blue where they'd been shot.

"What's going on down there?" he asked, "Are those activated people?"

"Yeah," she said, pulling back, "They followed you here. You were all going to walk into The Veil. All of you would have died, including Phoenix. And The Veil would have been broken."

"Across the sea?"

"There was a bridge, slightly submerged," Malia clarified, "Leviathan destroyed it. So, you weren't going to walk to The Veil so much as, well…"

"Right," Sinkua nodded, "But I thought they would stop and revert when I did." He turned to her sharply as realization struck. "Where's Nikasu?"

"She's in the valley with Nemesis," she said, "They're holding them down while the Berininites, well, fix them."

Creatures and humans alike struggled to so much as shuffle their feet. In the middle stood Nikasu, adorned in silver and purple dragon scales. The few creatures who mustered the resilience to lash at her, she swatted away with her sheathed sword.

These were few, however, and they became all the fewer as the masked Berininites gunned them down. He realized the creatures didn't bleed blue. Rather, the shots themselves were full of viscous blue liquid. It didn't look like anything that Galo or Ophalin had created for his condition. Nor would he have guessed it came from the Sisyphus Fir. But somehow, it was reversing their activations.

"What exactly is that stuff?"

"Nikasu said Uro's friend mentioned Project Cerulean. That's apparently it," Malia said, "SenRas and I figured it's connected to the suppressant that Nenbard made for Sanus."

Sinkua turned his head to face her. "Did it not work on me?"

"They tried, but you were too hot." She pinched the bridge of her nose. "I mean actual heat from your body, of course. Not, you know…"

"No, I get it," he assured, "It evaporated?"

Malia nodded. She sat with her legs crossed. One hand palmed The Harvester's skull, the other rested on SenRas's shoulder. "I think it works by inhaling the vapors."

"I'm getting the same idea," Sinkua agreed, "Maybe if it had evaporated closer to me."

He got back to his feet, sheathed his dagger, and began walking along the crest of the hill. He'd barely gone three steps before Malia called to him.

"Where are you going?"

"To get shot," he said, "MalVek's probably still alive. So are Seriamus and Pandora, especially if he has his way."

Malia nodded and waved him off. He turned to walk the crest again, but this time, he stopped within the first three strides.

"Oh! I wanted to ask you," he said as he turned back around, "Did you see Hibiscus?"

"EshCal's hooker friend?"

"Escort. But yes. Her."

"No. Why?"

"She brought me my weapons and these clothes," Sinkua said, "I wanted to thank her and make sure she's okay."

"She probably steered wide of this area," Malia said, "Ether knows I would have if I'd had the option."

"You and SenRas stood guard to stop me from crashing The Veil. Or drowning myself," he assessed. She exhaled her affirmation. Sinkua smiled and lowered his head. "Thank you," he said, "So listen. I'm sure MalVek knows I'm here. And when he realizes The Veil is still standing, he's going to come after me."

"I understand," Malia said, "I'll clear everyone out once I talk to Nikasu. Should I take her with me, or...?"

"That's up to her."

Walking the crest, he expected the usual stenches of mass combat. Gun smoke and machine oil. Trampled and burnt grass. Blood and sweat. Instead, it conjured vague memories of the overindulgent dinner parties that CreSam once or twice hosted for colleagues and superiors. There was a faintly floral undertone with a savory overtone.

One of the masked Berininites did a double take as he came into her periphery. She shouldered her gun and approached him, head cocked and eyes narrowed. He stopped and let her come to him. She stopped just before arm's reach and pulled down her avian-adorned mask.

"I'm glad to see you're normal, but you've got some nerve walking over here like this," Nalygen said, "What's going on in your head, boy?"

"Sorry. I'm trying to keep my distance from, well, that," Sinkua said, gesturing to the valley, "But I..." He trailed off as a nagging memory pulled at his thoughts. "Actually, I need to apologize to you. About..."

"About my brother," she cut off, "I know. You killed him and dumped him in the sea."

Sinkua's expression flattened as he nodded. "Yeah. I guess I did," he sighed, "Look, I know you two were close. I mean, you lost so much other family, and I get that. But..."

"Make your point."

"Do you..." Sinkua stopped to consider his words, "Do you know what he did? With The Avatars?"

"Of course, I know!" Nalygen scolded, "We all wanted the Chieftain Bloodline out of power. Ebralgi was just the most aggressive about it. And before you ask, no, I didn't know he'd poisoned my addax stew."

A man beyond her shoulder looked their way, avoiding prolonging the brief eye contact that he made with Sinkua.

"So, you also know The Avatars of Fate employed Borret as a data collector?"

"Yes. And I know his being an idiot was all an act," she said, "I gave Zheal the idea to pass on to him. Said he'd been in an accident shortly before she started drawing Gabdur's advances.".

"That way, the Chieftains would feel like they could speak freely in front of him," Sinkua realized, "And after they were unseated, at least one of you would have clean hands."

"About time you thought something through like you used to do," Nalygen derided.

The man looked over again. Sinkua gestured to him.

"Do I know that guy?"

Nalygen glanced back, and the man shifted his head slightly to the side. She turned back.

"No," she said, "Now, I want to make it clear that the only one of us who wanted any of them dead was Ebralgi. The rest of us liked them as people. Point of fact, I made my addax stew using Gijin's research to fight the damage that Ebralgi had done."

"I'm sorry," Sinkua nodded, "I know neither of you could openly discuss it, but I wish I'd known somehow. Instead, Borret ambushed Galo's ship when..."

"That doesn't give you the right," Nalygen interrupted, "His life was not yours to judge."

"Honestly, I only learned about his work with The Avatars later," he said, "His crew attacked me to try to activate me."

"That. Doesn't. Give you. The right."

"I'm not making excuses. I'm just… confessing," he clarified, "I was so out of it that I didn't recognize him. Once I did, I realized he'd been tenuously connected to my mother's death. That was…"

"That doesn't…"

"I know it doesn't give me the right," Sinkua cut back in, "I just need to come clean. If you want to hate me, I can live with that."

"I can't hate you after everything else you did for us," Nalygen said, "But while you will always be an ally to Berinin, you are no friend of mine."

Sinkua drew in a deep breath and exhaled longly as he stuffed his hands in the duster's pockets. "Well, friend or not, I need a favor that's bigger than either of us."

"It had better be bearings to the pier," she said, "You might reactivate at this proximity."

"I need everyone else off the island. MalVek's going to come here looking for me, and he'll kill anyone between us," Sinkua said, "Whatever's in those bullets, I need you to…"

With a pop and a crack, his head snapped back. Blue droplets speckled the bottom of his periphery. The floral and savory smells became pungent.

"There. You're protected," Nalygen asserted, "Now, keep your distance."

"Thank you," he said, "But I still need to talk to my sister."

He dug his heels into the soil as he shuffled sideways down the hill. Blue capsules whizzed by, striking the dwindling number of the activated. Those who had regained their humanity wandered in varying states of lucidity and undress, the most conscious guiding the rest to the nearest hill.

Sinkua looked up as lightning struck the northern horizon. The color was slightly wrong. He furrowed his brow and listened. Thunder rolled unusually slowly. As the sky quieted, he returned his attention to the valley.

He found Nikasu looking back at him. She had the blue substance splattered over her collarbone. Nemesis separated from her shoulders and returned to form. While he knocked the activated about, Nikasu huddled over and hurried through the crowd.

"Brother!" she exclaimed as she emerged upon the hillside, "Looks like you found out about Project Cerulean."

"Yeah, Malia said that's probably what this stuff is. Some kind of… activation suppressant?"

"I didn't ask, but probably. Nemesis just swooped me in, and I said 'Hit me!' And you know, when a girl wears a dragon, you don't ask questions," she rambled, laughing through her panting, "Uro's friend Khirsan told me about it. He was a…"

"We've met," Sinkua cut off, "Sorry, I need to catch you up, and I don't know how long we have."

"You think MalVek's coming after us."

"Just me."

"Maybe, maybe not," Nikasu shrugged, "Either way, I'm staying."

"I thought so," Sinkua said, "Anyway, I killed The Harvester."

"Oh, shit yeah! How'd you pull that off?" she asked, "Sorry, I don't mean like… It's just that I've never seen anyone move that fast."

"Phoenix told me he feeds off the souls of the dead."

"Yeah, he had the power of Tiamat."

"Right," Sinkua nodded, "Well, we revived a bunch of those souls. I don't think they'll come back to life, but it shook them loose so they could find their way to the afterlife."

"And he just... what? Decayed?"

"Basically."

His throat tightened at the detail he withheld. Lightning struck again, this one noticeably closer than the last. Unnerving as it was, he reveled in the diversion from his shaken composure.

"Are SenRas and my mom still here?" she asked as the thunder settled.

"Yes, but um..." Sinkua hesitated against the lump in his throat. He was holding on to too many secrets. "I gave The Harvester's skull to Malia. As for SenRas, well, I..."

Nikasu looked up to meet his downturned eyes. Though he didn't know what his face was broadcasting, it apparently said enough. Nikasu put her arm around his neck and leaned her forehead against his chest.

"I'm sorry," she exhaled, "It wasn't your fault."

"I'm trying to tell myself that," he sighed, "So, once this mess is cleared up..."

They both winced as lightning struck the northern coast, thunder clapping with scarcely a delay. At this proximity, it had a purplish hue.

"Malia's going to lead everyone off the island except you and me," Sinkua said, "Also Phoenix and..."

Lightning crashed again, still drawing closer. Thunder came more in a series of discrete percussive strikes than a steady rumble.

"... Nemesis, of course."

"What about whoever brought you your clothes?" she asked, "Are they still here?"

"Hibiscus," he said, "I think she already left."

"Well, she wasn't my first guess."

"Oh! But she also left these behind," Sinkua said, drawing the scythes from behind his back, "It just occurred to me that these are yours. Not sure where she got the idea."

"EshCal trained me with these," Nikasu said as she took her twin scythes, "She must have suggested..."

Fuchsia lightning struck the middle of the valley, spraying cerulean sparks tinged with green over the collapsing horde. Sinkua and Nikasu spat expletives as they shielded their eyes against the enduring shimmering. A towering silhouette flickered into coherence.

Sinkua grimaced as the light faded, and he proceeded down the hill. The Berininites stopped shooting. The restored righted themselves well before the activated, but looking upon what had caused that brilliant crash rattled any regained composure.

Odin sat resplendently atop Sleipnir at the center of the crater. Gripping his spear, he cast his monocular gaze over the horde as they stared back in wonder. Shoulders squared and expression flat, Sinkua walked straight at him with none of their reverence.

"I need to speak with you, Odin!"

"And I you, Sinkua."

A path manifested at Odin's unspoken will. Sinkua didn't slow in his approach, and when Odin came within reach, he grabbed the Etherworlder by the ankle and threw his weight into pulling down. Odin toppled from his mount, but he caught and righted himself with his spear before his body settled on the trampled foliage.

"What the hell is wrong with you!?"

They had both shouted the same question at each other, and now they stood glaring at each other. Odin ground his teeth.

"Where have you been?" Sinkua snarled, "MalVek nearly destroyed the capitol building to abduct me. The Harvester killed Vielle to get her out of the way. People who shouldn't be involved came to rescue me. All those people got turned into monsters because of me. And I don't know how many people we killed on our way to throw ourselves at The Veil." He jabbed his finger against Odin's chest. "Now, where the fuck were you!?"

"You insolent bastard," Odin grumbled, pushing Sinkua's hand away with his fingertip, "I was reopening the mines beneath Husefamidraget."

Sinkua clutched his scalp, digging his fingers into the newly bare skin. "Why would you…?" he grumbled, "How is that more important than protecting The Veil?"

"The Omphaloworld faces threats which beget the return of Quircois and Lechuatzulan craftwork," Odin explained, "As to The Veil, the only mandate is that you and Phoenix be alive upon its collapse."

"If you mean for me to bargain Phoenix away like The Harvester did," Sinkua said, gripping Epesol, "I'll take your head just as I did his."

"I have no such intention," Odin deflected, "But speak you true? You overpowered the Tiamat Hybrid?"

"Epemort is near the beach with most of his bones. Malia has his skull."

"So, he meant for you to offer Phoenix to Pandora for a cease to conflict?" he considered, "Curious. Tetsen Drukoa had similar intentions, and The Harvester's predecessor stood in opposition."

"I'm aware of the irony," Sinkua said, "But that wasn't his predecessor. They're the same person."

"I beg your pardon?"

"The Tiamat Hybrid has been feeding on souls to keep himself alive since back when those books were written," he explained, "Phoenix said he's several centuries old. She and I resurrected several of the stolen souls to pull them out of his body."

"It would seem Chekov spoke true of The Harvester's lifespan," Odin said, "I had theorized that Tiamat passed knowledge along her line of Hybrids, but I defer to Phoenix's judgment. Further, if speak you true of your technique, I offer my respect for your resolve."

"Thank you," Sinkua said, clearing his throat, "So, what's your plan?"

"When Tetsen had Phoenix stored within that ruby, he protected her from Pandora's Box," Odin explained, "That is what enables Pandora to assimilate the powers of deceased Etherworlders and their Hybrids."

"Like the swords?" Sinkua asked.

"The ruby is on so much greater a magnitude that the Lechuatzulans only succeeded in crafting the one," Odin clarified, "Without it, Pandora could kill and assimilate Phoenix, but you would retain a fraction of your powers through Epesol. Much in the same as The Harvester did with Epemort after he surrendered Tiamat."

"So, she can't take Phoenix by force," Sinkua reasoned, "Which means she won't kill either of us."

"So we ought to reason."

"Meaning you do want me to bargain with her."

"Pandora is too absorbed with the notion of absolute power to allow you to die," Odin assured, "Phoenix is her only option for the power to restore the deceased."

"Yeah well, I don't know what you got on my professional life from Eytea's memories," Sinkua said, "But my career as a diplomat was spectacularly not that stellar. And that was with humans. Not an Etherworlder-eating genocidal Goddess of Chaos. And what about the language barrier? It's not like she'll pop out conversational in Ouristihran."

"No, but it ought not take her more than a few minutes."

"It took you a few days to sort of speak it!"

"She has certain advantages of perception," Odin said, "But I only need you to occupy her for a spell."

"How long and to what end?" Sinkua asked.

"I deciphered the last pieces of Dourias's diagram. Your friends had thought them superfluous, but they contain MalVek's intentions for the homunculi," Odin explained, "They are transference golems. Powers born of either of our worlds may be cultivated within them and thus transferred into a permanent host. See you where this leads?"

"I think so," Sinkua said, "But damn, I hope I'm wrong."

"I doubt you are."

"MalVek is going to divide her power among the homunculi and take it for himself?"

Odin nodded. "He means to unseat her and become the God of Chaos."

"She'll sense the homunculi when The Veil falls," Sinkua reasoned, "And he thinks she'll be tempted by the chance to extend her reach before she picks up on his treachery. But would she fall for that?"

"She has long been farther disconnected from this world than I had been," Odin said, "And powerful as he is, MalVek is of no historical consequence between our worlds and is thus beyond her suspicion."

"So, if she falls for it," Sinkua considered, "do you think I'm strong enough to kill her while her power is separated across several bodies?"

"We ought not assume that her full strength will be the sum of the possessed homunculi and what she retains," Odin reasoned, "But it will narrow your disadvantage such that you will at least find it easier to convince her to depart in peace."

"She'll realize the Omphaloworld has become too much of a threat," Sinkua said, "So, she'll either agree to leave without Phoenix…"

"So I predict."

"… Or, she'll destroy the world and Phoenix along with it."

"That is a slight possibility but one, nonetheless."

"There's also a chance that MalVek becomes the God of Chaos," Sinkua added, "And with her being more than the sum of the parts, we could end up with both a God and Goddess of Chaos."

"We should be so fortunate!" Odin remarked, "They would never co-exist."

Sinkua cocked a brow. "Let me make sure I have this right," he said, "I'm going to tempt Pandora with Phoenix, maybe negotiate like Tetsen Drukoa would have done. She's going to use MalVek's homunculi to spread her powers. While she's weakened, I'll have an easier time fighting or bargaining with her. But even if I fail, I will have distracted her while MalVek becomes the God of Chaos. Then, they'll fight to the death, and we'll kill the survivor while they're weakened from the fight."

"You understand correctly," Odin nodded.

"That plan is batshit ridiculous," Sinkua said, "But our best alternative is to just keep guarding The Veil."

"It faces too many threats not to destroy it on our own terms."

"Agreed. There's one more thing I need to do before we set off," he said, "Fill Nikasu in, then meet me by the beach."

Sinkua wove around people struggling to their feet as he made his way back to the hillside. Some of them reached out to him for a hand up, and he barely broke stride as he gave it. Nikasu came down the hill to meet him halfway.

"What's going on?" she asked, "Where has he been?"

"He was opening the mines below the house," he said, "MalVek is going to use the homunculi to leech Pandora's powers and become the God of Chaos. This is the first I'm hearing about those, but Odin says they're transference golems."

"Oh, bastards!" Nikasu remarked, "So, what's our plan? He can't destroy The Veil now, I don't think. So, do we find everyone and all go after him?"

"Odin's going to fill you in on the details," Sinkua said, "But I need you to stay here while he takes me to destroy The Veil."

"How is he…?" Nikasu pondered, "No! No, I'm not leaving you to face Pandora alone."

"Don't think of it like that. Think of it as watching my back in case MalVek comes here looking for me."

"Is that before or after he becomes the God of Chaos?"

"It's shortly before he becomes a dead bastard," Sinkua said, "But if I can trust you to square up on the potential God of Chaos, you can trust me against the Goddess of Chaos."

"I don't know which I hate more. How impossible you are or how that's one of the most endearing things about you."

"Yeah, well, I don't know how far stubbornness will take me here." He nodded toward Nalygen. "And I don't think she'll cooperate with Malia either."

"You need me to make sure they evacuate?"

"I told her everyone needs to be gone before MalVek shows up, but I doubt she listened."

"I'll see to it," Nikasu said, holding his shoulder, "You go deal with Pandora and Seriamus. I'll deal with MalVek."

"You make it sound so simple."

"Whatever it takes to not get pants-shitting scared. But can you ask my mom something for me?"

"Name it."

"Ask if she can go back and fetch Galo," she requested, "Everyone else got scattered, but I think he's still there."

Sinkua's throat tightened, but he kept his face neutral and breathing steady. "I'll see what she says."

Just the thought of his name illuminated the vision of his milystis. His stomach tightened, feeling as though it were being pulled apart. This, he realized, must have been the pain of Galo's death. And for trying to cheat the system, for trying to resurrect a fellow Hybrid, this would be his punishment.

A distantly familiar coldness enveloped him. As he walked the crest of the hill, memories of facing the firing squad without the Phoenix Ruby coalesced. He realized what that feeling portended.

"Phoenix…" he muttered under his breath, "I think… you should check on Leviathan."

"I'm afraid you're right," she said, "I've been reaching out since I sensed Galo within The Harvester. There is no sign of her."

"… Shit."

Sorrow was giving way to resignation. Not to defeat. No, he would fight all the same. All the harder, even. But his power of resurrection had come to mean accepting the inevitability of death all over again. He had just begun to come to terms with that for Eytea, and now the milystic vision of Galo re-doubled the frequent reminders that he would never have them back. His only reprieve with Vielle's death was that he carried neither witness memories nor milystic visions.

Nikasu was the last person alive who could understand his pain. And though she witnessed Eytea and surely knew about Vielle, he couldn't tell her about Galo. In fact, Odin's gambit made it even more crucial that she didn't know until she faced MalVek.

He wasn't too proud to admit that she was better than him at weaponizing negative emotions. She'd had more practice, what with her gravimancy having been cultivated under the suppression of self-loathing. If she could focus the pain of losing Galo on MalVek, especially knowing he had been the one to kill him, she could break him in ways that he could never re-cover from.

As loath as he was to think it, that might have been Nikasu's only ad-vantage over MalVek. The man had slain a Hybrid and Etherworlder duo, likely in tandem. The only thing either of them had that Galo didn't was weaponizable rage.

Sinkua knelt beside SenRas's body and unsheathed his dagger.

"What did Nikasu say?" Malia asked.

"She's going to help you evacuate everyone, but she's staying here in case MalVek shows up," he said, slipping the knife into the hole he'd previ-ously made in SenRas's shirt, "Odin is taking me across The Veil to face Seri-amus and Pandora."

"How are you going…?"

"I don't know. But she wants you to find Galo."

"But didn't you say…" She trailed off as Sinkua stopped to look up at her. She closed her eyes and nodded. "Bold move," she said as he resumed cut-ting, "Are you sure it's safe?"

"No." He bared most of SenRas's torso as he peeled away the fabric. "But we're not exactly spoiled for options."

Sinkua got back to his feet and continued toward the beach. As he walked, he squeezed and stretched the corners of the bloody cloth. He laid it over his bare scalp, wrapping it just above his browline, and tied it in the back.

Odin and Sleipnir were already at the beach when he arrived.

"Okay," Sinkua said, "Let's go."

Odin offered his hand. "Very well, then," he said, "Climb up."

Chapter 47

Seafoam spattered and planks rattled under Sleipnir's galloping. Odin clutched the reins, his focus fixed straight ahead. Sinkua clutched the saddle as he watched the choppy waters.

His face tightened as he recalled the last time he'd been on horseback. It had been when he, Galo, and Eytea went to the docks in Ferya, just after his diagnosis. Even when he lived in Ferya, he had never gotten back in the saddle.

His stomach turned and throat lurched. Ripples in the sea blurred together. He needed to think about something else, but only one other thing came to mind.

"You know, Odin, I ah…" he hesitated, "I found out that Galo died. The Harvester took his soul."

"That should not be possible for him to have consumed his soul, but I sense that you speak genuinely," Odin said, keeping forward, "Death is part of the cycle, but it is tragic to lose those dear to us."

"I think the hardest part was that I couldn't tell Nikasu," Sinkua said, "Not that I couldn't bring myself to. I need her in the dark for now."

"Wise," Odin nodded, "Know you if he had the glory of dying in battle?"

"He went down fighting. That much, I'm sure of."

"You felt it when you drew upon his milystis?"

"Yeah. He'd been deeply wounded," Sinkua said, shuddering, "We also think Leviathan's dead. Phoenix can't find her."

"That explains these waters and is most unfortunate," Odin proclaimed in a seamless blend of pragmatism and mourning, "You suppose true of Galo's passing, then. Further, MalVek and The Harvester are more formidable than even I had perceived."

"Yeah, well, if my math is…"

The choppiness in the water deepened just ahead, where there loomed a deep shadow. Sinkua flared his eyes and focused. As the translucency of the sea became clear, he inhaled sharply.

"Odin!" he shouted, "The bridge is incomplete!"

Odin chuckled. "The bridge is a formality," he remarked, "Recall you how Sleipnir traversed down the roots of Yggdrasil in your pursuit?"

Before Sinkua could so much as reflect on that night, Sleipnir crossed the end of the bridge. But his hooves only sank into the water as much as they would in firm mud. Odin thumped Sleipnir's shoulder appreciatively.

"The Veil is just ahead, old friend!" he exclaimed, "May your honor be never forgotten."

The Southland Sea rattled under Sleipnir's hooves. The water grew more violent, lapping up the massive equine's legs to lash at its riders' shins.

Looking back, Sinkua found he could no longer see the coast. Whatever became of Nikasu or himself, he was too far out to help or be helped. Returning his attention forward, he saw a ripple in the distant air.

"We draw near The Veil," Odin announced, "Secure your weapons."

Sinkua watched the ripple as he tightened and double checked his straps and sheaths. That single ripple multiplied and spread like an iridescent infestation.

He hadn't asked Odin how he planned to break through The Veil. He just supposed he would use his spear, same as he had done to release Arestor from his copper prison. But as the iridescence stretched toward his periphery, Odin kept his spear on his back. In a sickening epiphany, the purpose of his last words to Sleipnir became clear.

"Odin, you can't!" Sinkua protested, "We've already lost too much!"

"This is as it must be," Odin insisted, "Your concern is merited, but let it not cloud your judgment." He turned and set his hand on Sinkua's shoulder. "Besides, Sleipnir volunteered for this," he asserted, "Just as you agreed to your role."

Sinkua writhed as Odin took the duster in his fist and flailed as he pitched him over the water. He hit the water hard, tumbling through the churning. Gasping and heaving, he wrestled his bearings back into his grasp.

"Bastard," he muttered, "You absolute bastard."

Odin sprang from Sleipnir's back, and the horse continued with no visible concern for itself. The iridescence of The Veil lashed out in shimmering tendrils, piercing Sleipnir's flesh. Luminescence seeped from the cracks that formed around the punctures. More iridescent strands wrapped around his body, causing his flesh to smear like half-dried metallic paint.

As Sleipnir disintegrated, the tendrils pulsated with an eldritch hunger. Odin stopped falling. Sinkua pitched a ball of fire, but it dissolved long before it even reached the visible part of The Veil. He dove to swim after him.

By the time he emerged, though, he was hardly any nearer. Hardly enough to matter anyway. The Veil already had Odin. In a final protest, the thunderous Etherworlder pulled his spear from his back and hurled it at the shimmering infestation with a bestial bellow.

The spear vanished through The Veil, and soon, Odin was gone as well.

But where it had seized him and Sleipnir, the tendrils of iridescence had vanished. A seashore appeared through a hole in the air. The presence of The Veil became clear.

Sinkua swam toward it as the hole widened, fragments of iridescence falling away like malformed glass. The breaks stretched toward opposing horizons as he reached standing depth.

And as he stood upon the beach, unknown to the world for thousands of years, he looked up to a midday sky with stationary clouds. Cracks spread through it, and shimmering fragments rained down to reveal a stormy pred-awn sky.

The Veil had been destroyed, and Sinkua stood beside Odin's spear with mementos and ancient memories to face what waited beyond.

The truck lurched to a sudden halt, nearly dropping Jex in his crouching position. He braced himself and adjusted the balled-up coat from under Dourias's head. The transformation had been subsiding, but Jex still took care to keep him less than conscious.

The back window of the cabin opened, and the driver called back to them.

"Radio says there's a wreck up ahead," she said, "Can you see anything?"

Jex stood and looked out over the gridlock traffic. Four blocks ahead, a figure of unremarkable stature stood in the middle of the intersection. Nobody tried to go around them or urge them to move. In fact, some of those nearest even tried to back up into the surrounding traffic jams.

Shortly beyond that figure was a car halfway on the sidewalk with its front bumper folded around a utility pole. Just past that, half a car, split lengthwise, lay open end up. The driver emerged with his right side caked in blood and his clothes shredded.

"Someone's in the intersection," Jex said, "A car got split in two. I can only see one half. Driver's alive."

"Well, isn't that just a son of a bitch," the driver spat, "This got something to do with your snarly friend?"

Jex sighed. "I'm afraid so," he said, "Would you like me to take him on foot?"

"No, they might not see you walk off," she said, "How many shots you got left in that gun?"

"Just one, I'm afraid."

"That won't do," the driver said, "Sorry, but I don't know you well enough to suppose you can take them down in one shot."

"I wouldn't suppose it either."

"Soon as I can squeeze out of here, you get their attention, and we'll lure them out."

"Okay," Jex said, "But as soon as we're clear, let us off and get as far from here as you can."

"On the off chance that I can't outrun it," the driver said, "I've got a compound bow in the tool chest."

Farim upturned a box, spilling its contents across and off the counter. Gabdur jumped and shot a flat glare from the doorway. Farim mouthed an apology as she began rifling through the scattered paraphernalia.

She separated the photonic emission weapons easily enough. Unfortunately, when they were deactivated, they all looked more or less identical. And there were quite a few of them just in this box.

"Hey, so about these photon weapons," she said, "Was The Coalition planning to arm the whole Subtransit Resistance with these?"

"It was considered," Gabdur said, squinting at the display on the portal strip, "But Mortvill was too untrusting to let it happen."

"Untrusting of us or the construction on these things?" Under a certain angle of light, she found a basic engraving of a scimitar on one of them. "I mean, I'd get it if he didn't trust me with one of these things. I shot NalSet's knee off."

"Both but I think more the latter," he said, "And yes, you do have a reputation for being, well… extreme at times."

"… But?"

Gabdur laughed under his breath. "But your heart and mind have always been in the right place."

"Hence the training wheels?" Farim asked, gesturing to the fiberglass oar.

"Just making sure you can still handle yourself," Gabdur said. He slapped the doorframe and got to his feet. "Got it!"

"Same!" she announced, holding out the generator marked with a fauchard, "Do you think we have time to find something like an oar for me?"

"Oh, you have more time than you realize," a third voice said, "Neither of you will be going anywhere."

At the top of the stairs stood a figure of perfect androgyny and stoicism.

"Homunculus," Farim grumbled, "What do you want?"

"What I want is of no consequence," it said, "Lord MalVek has assigned me to keep you here for as long as necessary."

"So, he admits we're a threat?" Gabdur asked.

"A nuisance," the homunculus corrected, "He is more concerned with where you have come than with who you are."

"He's afraid of the photon weapons," Farim said as it descended the stairs, "And somehow, they don't respond to you, do they?"

The homunculus met her glare as flatly as ever.

"Phylus overpowered two of you with a lunch tray," she continued, grabbing one of the generators, "What makes him think you can subdue us when we have a box of photon weapons?"

"Because I have seized control of this establishment's security system."

Farim gave Gabdur a concerned and urging look.

"Remote controlled portals in every window and door," he explained, "They were decommissioned because of instability and the potential for sabotage."

"Lord MalVek has programmed them into a complex series of loops," the homunculus explained, "He and I are the only ones capable of deactivating it."

Farim cursed and pitched the generator back into the pile. "What does he want, then?"

"To keep you from leaving here," the homunculus said, "And for me to stay for the duration."

Fractured antique rooftops crested the horizon as Sinkua walked away from the ocean. The unfamiliar flora only looked to be a few weeks overgrown. Indeed, this entire island had been suspended in time, neither aging nor decaying from the moment The Trifecta erected The Veil.

As the rooftops came into clearer view, he saw how they told of what had become of this place before its temporal suspension. They weren't worn down by the disuse of abandonment. They were scorched and melted. They were shorn through. They were pocked to crumbling. They were chewed, crushed, and eroded.

"Was this city like this before The Veil?" Sinkua mumbled.

"Bealstilla fell long before that day," Phoenix answered, her voice thready, "It was Pandora's first conquest and was long contested by two camps seeking to memorialize it. One in their memory. The other in her honor."

The air grew acrid as the shadows of absent objects cast over the quaking ground. Black lightning erupted from the soil, hinting at a towering silhouette. Flora froze and shattered. The shards spiraled around the smoke left by the dark lightning. The smoke coalesced into swarms of insects. Dark lighting erupted once more, projecting the smoke bugs into the ice flora to burst into miniscule plasma flares.

The fading lights zipped around in increasingly rapid rings. They closed in on each other with every revolution, though they never collided. As they came in tighter, the towering silhouette became more distinct.

As the figure's colors bled through the melting flares, Sinkua realized it was exactly as he recalled. There stood the basis of the titan he had faced in the Radial Axiom Arena. This one, the true Seriamus, was clearly possessed of powers that none among The Avatars could have imitated in their wireframe model. But it boded well that Sinkua had exceeded it in brute force for even a moment.

Seriamus looked down at Sinkua and took a single step toward him. Sinkua maintained a stern expression. Seriamus thumped the business end of his hammer against the ground and lowered himself to one knee.

"Tetsen Drukoa," he exhaled, his voice weaving between familiar and predatory. He continued speaking in a dialect unlike any of the ancient languages that Sinkua was aware of. Consonants clustered in ways that shouldn't have been possible for human tongues, and syllables overlapped as vowels folded back on themselves.

"He wants to know if you're ready to honor the bargain," Phoenix clarified, "If you are, they won't hold the interruption against you or the Omphaloworld."

"I'm only speaking to Pandora," Sinkua asserted, meeting Seriamus's black and crimson gaze, "And I don't trust his promise on its face. Or his face, for that matter."

Seriamus spoke further, his ire unclear as to whether it came from this strange new language or this strange new incarnation of Tetsen Drukoa. Sinkua didn't know much about him, but he was quite sure he didn't go about in combat boots, a bloody head wrap, and a women's duster with the bottom half of his face painted blue.

"He says you can speak to Pandora once you agree to give me to her," Phoenix said, "He's obscuring her presence until you do."

"Bit of an obvious deception," Sinkua thought, "He knows he can't take you by force, right?"

"They both do. There's any number of angles at play here."

"And I play into any number of them no matter what I do."

"Yes. Or don't do."

"How bad are the angles that I play into if I skin him to patch some of these roofs?"

"Probably no worse than any other. After all, he's no longer a problem if he's dead."

Sinkua dug his boots into the dirt. "I don't understand you, you malformed fuckbasket," he called up, "Stand down and bring me your Etherworlder."

His grinding teeth rattled the air and sent tremors through Sinkua's body as Seriamus leaned down to a disconcerting proximity. The space from his eyes to his chin was that of Sinkua's eyes to his navel, perhaps pelvis.

Sinkua flicked open the bindings as he unholstered his morningstar and cracked the flaming head across Seriamus's lower lip. Seriamus reared back and shook the ground with his bellow.

Sinkua leapt back as Seriamus swung his hammer hard enough to thin the air. As Sinkua narrowly dodged, the titan hefted the maul overhead. Sinkua stared up at it, hovering a good seven eight meters above him, and he coursed milystis through his morningstar until it radiated faintly red.

Seriamus brought the hammer crashing down, and Sinkua stood defiantly until it was too late to redirect it. He bounded aside, snapping his morningstar out with flames bursting from the spiked ball. But as the hammer cratered the ground, a cloud of black leeches erupted around it. Sinkua's milystic fire caught the leeches instead of the hammer, and they scattered into the ancient flora.

As the flaming bloodsuckers scorched the foliage, Seriamus pulled his hammer back and thrust his empty hand forward. Wind roared from his palm, throwing up frozen and ashen detritus. Sinkua dug his feet in against the tempest. He slammed Epesol into the ground, white-knuckling the handle and pommel.

Seriamus lunged and bellowed, shaking the ground around Sinkua's feet. The soil around Epesol grayed and hardened, while that under Sinkua's feet scattered into fine sand. The air rushing around him tightened, clamping nearly to the point of choking.

Sinkua's grip failed, and he tumbled backward with the tempest. He rolled and bounced for countless meters, wincing with every strike against the ground. As the wind eased up, he dragged himself to a halt, gasping for breath. When he pushed himself upright, he came to face a flying mass of leeches suspended in something sickly green.

Seriamus swept his hand, and the leeches shattered into a mass of sinew and blood. Sinkua threw his hand up, erupting a pillar of flames beneath it. But the roiling blood and sludge stretched into a sickly flying serpent and whipped around the column of fire. Sinkua charged the field, snapping up scattered fires around the sludge snake.

The snake whipped around him, but he kept running. The scrambling leeches began to burn out, dotting the scorched foliage with wriggling embers. Sinkua dove as Epesol nearly came within reach.

The sludge snake snapped across his body, scattering its composition over his torso. He staggered back, skin bubbling and welting. No sooner had the sludge settled than the hammer flew at him again.

A metallic taste wafted up from Sinkua's tightening throat. The vein along his temple throbbed. But as he felt his muscles tighten, Project Cerulean kept him grounded. Each knuckle popped in rapid succession as he clenched his fist. With a furious roar, he threw a fiery punch at Seriamus's hammer, halting it dead in its path.

Black lightning erupted around Sinkua as he moved in to obstruct the hammer more bodily. He dug his feet in as he kept one hand on the head and grabbed the handle with the other. Holes opened in the surrounding ground, the soil hardening in the shape of toothy masses.

Seriamus lifted his hammer with Sinkua hanging from it. He brought the Phoenix Hybrid to eye level and spoke in that nauseating dialect. Sinkua still understood none of it, but his throat burned with a powerful need to vomit. Seriamus snapped his hammer out, flinging Sinkua from it. Sinkua ripped a fistful of scorched fibers from the handle, crushing them in his grasp as he rolled to a halt.

"He says you've forfeited the arrangement," Phoenix supplied.

"Never wanted it," Sinkua grunted, pushing himself to his feet, "But I figured."

Sinkua bound his morningstar and charged again as the wriggling embers coalesced. The ground rose to consume him, but he shouldered through the dirt and kept running. Seriamus flung a volley of frozen daggers. Sinkua rolled under them, scarcely losing momentum as he came upright.

Seriamus stomped the ground, spreading a spiderwebbing network of thick black lines. Sinkua measured his steps more on instinct than calculation as he bounded along the narrowing spaces between them. A tar-like substance reached up, stretching into long points. It grabbed at him and lashed at Epesol.

With a furious war cry, an aura of lapping flames encompassed Sinkua's body. The tar shrieked as it sizzled and snapped back from his body. As he came within the last few bounds of Epesol, he put one hand over the Phoenix Ruby and extended the other.

Shallow flames danced over his skin as the blade glowed crimson. The stone it was embedded in blackened with faint orange lines channeling along the surface. A shadow stretched and loomed as he drew his morningstar. Hurling it like a javelin, he fractured the ground near his sword.

An invisible battering ram bludgeoned him, but Sinkua powered through the raw kinetic energy. He slid into a crouch alongside Epesol, one hand taking the handle while the other struck the flat of the blade. The sword plowed out of the heated rocks, throwing shards of brimstone at Seriamus. As the titan staggered, Sinkua whipped Epesol crosswise, flinging hot slag and partially melted stone.

Brimstone cracks formed under his every footfall as Sinkua devoured the space between himself and the Pandora Hybrid. But Seriamus relaxed his hammer arm, holding his other hand aloft instead. With a swirl of pastel light from Seriamus's fingertips, Sinkua came to an abrupt and dizzying halt.

A disorienting darkness flashed around Spril, and the street came to feel disassociated from itself. Coming through the next intersection, he confirmed that this wasn't the street he had been riding along.

Spril turned to get back on a route to the prison, but another dark flash repositioned and reoriented him. He stopped and dismounted to survey his surroundings, keeping as many of the sparse other people in his periphery as he could.

None of them vanished. Nobody appeared from nothing. Chekov had mentioned psychosis, so it was possible that it had begun to manifest despite his submitting to treatments. But he checked his watch and found that only moments had passed since the first flash. He wasn't blacking out and losing time.

Spril dampened all other external stimuli senses to fortify his vision. He looked along the faces of the surrounding buildings. The edge of one was ever so slightly blurry. He zeroed in on that point, and the blur deepened and spread.

With a disorienting snap, his senses rebalanced, and the anomalous patch normalized. Someone was sending him through spatial abrasions, even though he couldn't see them, and somehow, he was the only one affected.

"Channeling through the ground?" he mumbled, thinking aloud.

The feasibility of it wasn't up for debate. It was happening. But as to how, he reasoned it would be best achieved with a group of homunculi working in tandem. But the more homunculi were involved, the less discreet they could be. He thus reached two equally most likely possibilities. Either this was the work of one powerful yet vulnerable homunculus, or MalVek had come after him himself.

"There's a bus terminal just past this hill," Phylus said, shoulders hunched under the sparse but heavy raindrops, "We'll take one to the docks and figure out our next move."

"Do they run this late?" MarLys asked, jogging to match his urgent strides.

"Infrequent, but yeah."

The rainfall nestled itself into the verbal silence. No sooner had they closed in on the bus terminal than MarLys thought to break that silence.

"Hey, since we're going to be waiting for a while," she began, swallowing pensively, "If you want to talk about what happened, I…"

"Not yet," Phylus sighed, "But you'll be the first to know when I'm ready."

"… Really?" MarLys asked, "I would have thought…"

With a flash of darkness across Phylus's line of sight, MarLys's voice vanished. The terminal and the sidewalk went with it and were replaced by a wide stoop and a stone facade. Phylus was back at the Ouristihran Union building.

Muttering an expletive, he turned to head down the stairs. But he'd only taken three steps when a thrumming and a yelp pulled his attention back. MarLys now stood atop the stoop.

"What the shit?" she exclaimed, "He booby trapped the bus terminal?"

"Looks that way," he said, rejoining her.

Both their heads snapped aside at a rustling from the hedge row.

"Someone's coming," Phylus whispered, reaching for his rifle, "Homunculus, I'd bet."

"I think it's afraid of you," MarLys suggested. She looked down at her dented hook and sighed. "I should've insisted on a weapon."

The sound of rummaging ended with a cry of delight, and a beam of light shone across the room. Chekov slammed the drawer shut and waved the flashlight toward Yrlis.

"Come on. The generator's downstairs," she beckoned, "Leave the sign here."

"You know," Yrlis said, leaning the sign against the wall, "This is why I keep physical copies of everything. Power outages are always a problem, even when sabotage isn't."

"Well, if it's any consolation, I do that with everything else," Chekov said as she banged on the door handle with the wrench, "But it was safer to keep Vielle's records only on this computer."

"Safe from insider sabotage, even?"

"Yes, unless the saboteur can read minds. I encrypted it with no outside input. I'm the only one who knows how to access these files."

An echoing thunk drew Yrlis's attention back up the hall. A series of sharper clunks followed, punctuated by another thunk.

"What's wrong?" Chekov asked.

"I think someone just locked us in here," Yrlis said, "Go work on the generator. I'll go get the sign and stand guard."

Air and light rippled, peeling away with long shadows to reveal two figures with their fingers entwined. One was a person of perfect neutrality. Genderless. Emotionless. Nondescript save for the blue crystals embedded in its eye sockets. The other was Jevana, all but baring fangs with her predatory smirk.

Nikasu looked to them as though she had been expecting them and had grown bored with waiting. The homunculus betrayed no emotion, but Jevana almost winced at the lack of reaction.

Jevana released the homunculus's hand, and the air and light folded around the stoic being. Nikasu whipped a scythe at the homunculus, burying the blade between its eye sockets. The visible part of it turned bloody and singed at the divide, and that portion of its body collapsed.

"One down," Nikasu said. She snapped her fingers, and Nemesis sprang onto her shoulders. "One conniving little bitch tart to go."

Jevana scoffed and smirked. "You think killing one homunculus will hurt Lord MalVek? They're tools. Just like you and Scruffles."

"I think they're worth more than your pride will let you let on," Nikasu said, approaching in slow deliberate strides, "Well, his pride. You're just following his lead. I get it. You think the safest place is in his shadow. I was like that. But then, somebody comes along and tough-loves the truth into you." She stopped and leaned in. "And you realize that all along, the only thing the shadow controlled was your self-perception."

"You really are something else," Jevana chuckled, pushing Nikasu away with two fingers to her clavicle, "You loopy bitch. Lord MalVek can make more homunculi whenever he wants. He's got dozens of candidates."

Nikasu gasped. "The exodus?"

"About time you figured that out," Jevana scoffed, "As for your trapped in shadows bullshit, I've chosen my place knowing full well what he's after."

"You're okay with him becoming the God of Chaos?" Nikasu asked, setting her hand on the pommel of Epelun.

"Chaos is entropy, and the entropy is the eventuality of everything," Jevana proclaimed, "When he makes me his Hybrid, I'll be the only person in this world anywhere near the shadow of his equal."

"Well, thanks for the intel," Nikasu said, moving her grip to the hilt, "But if that's how you feel…"

Nikasu sprang forth as she whipped Epelun and its scabbard in opposite directions. Jevana stood her ground as she pulled her hand across herself, making a zipper motion with her thumb and first two fingers.

Epelun grew heavy, too much so for Nikasu's adrenaline to manage. The sword glanced off her shoulder on its way to the ground, bruising her even through Nemesis's protection.

Nikasu took a step back. "What… the shit… are you?"

"I don't know if anyone told you about The Scout," Jevana said, crouching to retrieve the scythe from the homunculus's forehead, "Don't care honestly. But let's just say I'm an upgrade."

Nikasu drew her second scythe and pointed it at Jevana. The Chaos Hybrid-in-Potentia twirled the first scythe around her wrist with the deftness of years of practice.

"I heard how the first Scout died," Nikasu said, "I don't need powers to deal with you."

Sinkua blinked away the excess light to find himself standing in an expanse of ash. He surveyed his surroundings. The broken rooftops of Bealstilla still lined the distance. But in the immediate, there was only ash.

He remembered Seriamus. He remembered running. And he remembered a flash of light. Everything between then and now was blacked out, though. And it felt as though he could have lost hours. Putting his hand to his chest, he found the Phoenix Ruby was hot to the touch.

"What happened?" he asked.

She didn't answer. He internalized the words. Phoenix remained silent. Sinkua sighed, turned around, and began walking back to the beach.

As he made his way through the ancient foliage, a faint burning smell teased his nostrils. He attributed it to whatever he and Phoenix had done in the ashen clearing and pressed on. But what he couldn't reconcile were the shadows that flashed across his mind's eye whenever he blinked.

As he came within earshot of the sea, he heard his name called from aside. He turned to see Nikasu running up from the beach. The tension left his shoulders as he stopped to let her come to him.

Nikasu looked him over. "Hey, are you okay? You look pretty rough."

"Yeah, I'm uh..." Sinkua blinked, wincing as the shadow flashed more strongly than ever. "... I'm good. How are things on your end?"

"Probably not good," Nikasu sighed, "I couldn't find either of them over here. What about you? You look like you've been in a fight."

"I... um... found Seriamus. Pandora's Hybrid."

"No shit? And you came back here for my help?"

"No, I..."

"Well, where is the bastard?" Nikasu asked, "Pandora might've slipped out when The Veil fell, but let's deal with him first."

"No, it's okay," Sinkua insisted, "We already dealt with him. Phoenix must've gone berserk. All that's left of him is a blanket of ashes."

"No shit!?" Nikasu exclaimed, throwing her arms around him, "Well, let's go back to the beach and figure out how to get off this island so we can go after Pandora."

As they walked alongside each other, thoughts of Galo pulled at the back of Sinkua's throat. He still couldn't tell her. Not yet. Even with The Harvester and Seriamus dead, there was still too much left to do.

But if the past was any indication, this was the sort of secret that would only get worse the longer he kept it. He nudged her as the end of a polearm emerged from behind a dune.

"Nikasu, there's something I..."

He stopped as the entirety of the polearm, save for the spearhead in the sand, came into view. As did an axe blade. This wasn't Odin's spear. It was Eytea's halberd. He turned to face her.

"Something you...?" she beckoned, looking him over, "Are you okay, brother?"

Without a word, Sinkua clapped his knuckles across Nikasu's jaw.

Uro tapped on the security glass. His other hand clutched his coat against the residual chills of the rain he'd just come in from. Nobody answered, even though he could see the back of their head just a couple meters away. He tapped harder, and by how they shifted to square the back of their chair with the window, they ignored him harder.

Uro jabbed the call button, and the receptionist rolled his eyes so hard he could all but hear them as he turned around. Uro tightened his lips against the urge to mouth off as the receptionist wheeled his seat to the window.

"Yeah, I see you," he scolded through the speaker, "Ambulatory. All your limbs. No abnormal excretions. Sign in and wait."

"I'm not here as a patient," Uro said, "I'm actually..."

The receptionist rapped his fingers on the glass, indicating a schedule affixed to it in vinyl characters. "Visiting hours aren't for another three hours."

Uro leaned his palm heels on the counter and stared at his feet as he spoke. "What if I told you I'm here to see Brigadier General Elite EshCal?"

"Then you must think I'm as stupid as you are if you think I'd wake her up without a gaggle of orderlies."

"It's a matter of life and death," Uro insisted, "on a bigger scale than I have the patience to explain to you."

"If it's that serious, I'm sure she already knows," the receptionist deflected.

Uro's eyes met the receptionist's. "What about her short list?"

The receptionist cocked a brow. "Her what?"

"Every overnight patient gives a list of people who can come see them any time."

"Sorry, bloke," the receptionist said, "That's just a rumor."

Uro produced his ID badge from his wallet and slapped it on the counter. "That's just what we're trained to say," Uro deflected, "Keeps people from guessing their way in."

The receptionist's eyes widened as he looked at the badge. He turned off the speaker and opened the panel in the security glass. "Hillside?" he asked, "You sure you're not here as a patient?"

"Yes. Why?"

"You been on a leave of absence?" the receptionist prodded, "Place was condemned weeks ago. Chemical leak or something. People from there keep coming up sick ever since."

Uro shook his head. Khirsan hadn't mentioned any of this. "Disciplinary leave," he lied, "This is the first I'm hearing about this though. I haven't been following the news from home lately, you know."

"I'd say not," the receptionist nodded, "Well look, you're right about the short list. But hers is only three people, and I can see from here that two of them certainly aren't you. So, unless you're this third one, I can't do anything for you."

Uro knew one of them was probably Myriela. But beyond her dalliances with his friend's elder sister, what he knew about EshCal only scratched the surface of her professional life. Spril was a logical candidate, and he had been in the news enough that anyone in ArcNos could point him out. But the only other name he knew to be associated with her usually wasn't the sort that made the short list. But given the circumstances, just maybe.

"My name is Sinkua," Uro said, "I'm her secretary."

The receptionist looked him over. "Good enough for me."

Nikasu slashed as Jevana advanced, but Jevana pivoted under the blade and responded with a backhand swing. Nikasu hooked the blade with her own and twisted Jevana's arm behind her back. Jevana spun out of the hold and kneed Nikasu in the abdomen. But Nikasu grabbed her knee and headbutted the bridge of her nose.

The two slashed and dodged, parried and pivoted, over the homunculus's body for several minutes with neither taking the advantage for more than a split second. Nikasu broke the pattern by dropping her scythe and stepping into an attack. She yanked Jevana by the wrist and slammed her palm into her opponent's throat. With a split-second milystic boost, Nikasu choke slammed Jevana onto the dead homunculus.

Jevana glared into her as she twisted Nikasu's wrist hard enough to pull her off balance. Jevana rolled on top of her, pinned her by the throat, and pounded the bridge of her nose.

"You wanna square up?" Nikasu choked, snorting back the trickling blood, "You'd better know how to fight like an animal."

Nikasu hocked blood and mucus over Jevana's eyes. She hammer-punched both temples, then jammed her thumbs into Jevana's eyes as she pressed on her temples. With Jevana disoriented, Nikasu reclaimed her stolen scythe, then pushed Jevana off and grabbed the one she'd just dropped. She pinned Jevana with a knee on her sternum and crossed the scythe blades over her neck.

"Where's MalVek?" Nikasu grumbled, "Why did he only send you and a homunculus?"

"What's wrong?" Jevana chuckled, "Are you upset that he didn't come after you himself?" She wiped the blood and mucus from her eyes. "Look, I'm only saying this because you can't do anything about it. And because I love the look of false hope in your eyes. But he's tending to the exodus."

Nikasu pressed into Jevana's sternum. "Extracting powers from the homunculi?"

"So, you know his intentions," Jevana said, "And you know his means. If there hadn't been so many minds working at it, I might be impressed. Which of your friends figured it out?"

As Nikasu tensed with aggravation, Jevana plowed her knee into her crotch. Nikasu lost her balance, hands sliding off the scythes, and Jevana pushed her off.

"Now that I've answered your question," Jevana said, "tell me where Scruffles is."

Nikasu chortled. "Why? Are you scared of him?"

"Not at all. I was sent to check on him when the migration stopped here."

"Odin took him to The Veil," Nikasu said, "He sacrificed himself to keep Phoenix from both Pandora and MalVek. Odin ought to be fighting Pandora right now."

Jevana flashed a cold smile. "I don't buy it. You'd be a lot more torn up."

"It doesn't matter what you believe," Nikasu shrugged, "He wouldn't have given Phoenix to either of them."

"Of course he wouldn't. Anyone can see how fucking stubborn he is," Jevana remarked, "So, don't you think Lord MalVek would have accounted for that?"

"It can't be taken by force," Nikasu said, "That includes coercion."

"Well, that's debatable. But it doesn't matter. As long as he dies within the next few days, we'll have Phoenix at our fingertips."

Nikasu's eyes widened "What are you...?"

"Now, as much as I'd love to kill you and be done with it," Jevana taunted, "I'm really looking forward to watching the hope in Auntie Nikasu's eyes die."

Nikasu grimaced against Sinkua's fist as her body blackened into a silhouette. It shattered into a swarm of rudimentary bugs with wings too large for their bodies. As they scattered and circled around Sinkua, the sky burned away to reveal another behind it. The sea smeared and jolted. The axe blade of Eytea's halberd shimmered and vanished.

Sinkua touched the Phoenix Ruby. It was only as warm as usual. "Can you hear me now?"

"I always could," Phoenix said, "But you couldn't hear me. That's why…"

A bestial shriek rattled Sinkua's ears hard enough to drown out Phoenix's voice. He turned and staggered at the sight of an ember worm towering over him. Black bugs flitted about, melting into and erupting from its body.

Sinkua trembled as the worm bellowed down at him, opening its mouth wider than his body. As it bore down on him, Sinkua plunged Epesol into its mouth and through the back of its head. He wrenched the blade one way, then the other, cleaving the top half of the worm's head from the rest of its body.

But as the worm hit the ground, its severed body part flowed back into place. Sinkua stomped it, scattering the embers, but those recoalesced as well. The reformed ember worm bludgeoned Sinkua with the back of its head. Prostrate, he glared up at its eyeless face as it loomed over him.

"Get back to Seriamus!" Phoenix insisted, "He's sustaining it."

Sinkua rolled away and launched to his feet as the worm came down, hitting a full sprint within a couple of strides. The worm gave chase, but for all its durability, its bulk and blindness made it slow.

"You were saying?" Sinkua thought as he widened the distance between himself and the ember worm.

"That's why I showed you those visions," Phoenix continued.

"You mean the shadows?"

"They were your memories from before the flash."

"And Eytea's halberd?"

"Not me," she said, "Seriamus created an illusion from your memories and perceptions. You still think of Odin's spear as Eytea's halberd."

"How can we be sure we're not in another illusion?" Sinkua asked.

"My ruby appears to protect me and our connection from this power," Phoenix reasoned, "Though I know not how he acquired it."

"That's unsettling, but we'll figure it out later," Sinkua said, "For now, how far back can you show me memories from?"

"I can convey memories from any time we've been bound to one another."

"Every incarnation?"

"Yes."

"Does that include muscle memory?"

"To my recollection, you're the first incarnation to ask. Why?"

Sinkua's eyes flared as Seriamus emerged over the horizon. He grasped the handle of Epesol. His rising fury tightened into a sharp focus, and his muscles relaxed. Phoenix understood.

Khirsan glanced at the clock as he flicked a meager bite onto the tip of his fork. He'd been picking at his salad for well over an hour, and he'd yet to hear from Uro.

He and nearly everyone else looked to the door as it chimed and opened. Those who had witnessed their portaled arrival had mostly cleared out, but those remaining maintained a palpable tension.

The new guest panned the room with empty eyes. Khirsan turned back to his salad before it noticed him. He took a few long gulps of his drink while they placed their order. As they found a seat, Khirsan approached the counter with his empty cup.

"Hey bud, could I get a refill?" he asked. As the cashier took his cup, Khirsan flicked his eyes aside and lowered his voice. "That's the one."

Khirsan let his gaze wander in practiced nonchalance while he waited. As he panned the dining room, he nearly took a pause that would have betrayed his suspicions. The homunculus was staring straight at him.

Sinkua sidestepped Seriamus's hammer as it came crashing down. Three more bounds, and he leapt and drew his dagger in midair. He plunged the blade under Seriamus's kneecap and vaulted up to the Hybrid giant's torso. As he hung from a mass of abdominal, Sinkua drew Epesol from its borrowed scabbard.

Seriamus knocked him away with a fist as big as his torso. Sinkua rolled as he landed and came upright as Seriamus reared back. The Pandora Hybrid lunged at him, bellowing loudly enough to rattle the flora and stones.

Sinkua's bones ached. His skin stung. He shielded his face with his forearms. Strands of blood rippled through his periphery.

Memories of another life flickered through his mind's eye, coalescing knowledge beyond his own. He uncrossed his forearms and brought his palms together, then separated them with his hands cupped. A disc of flames manifested, and he willed the heat forward against the sound waves.

Sinkua dug his boots in as Seriamus bellowed louder. Sweat smeared Sinkua's face and neck. The taste of blood filled his throat. He slid backward, but his heat shield held.

Seriamus lifted his head and pulled his hammer across his shoulder. Sinkua looked up at him with distant eyes. The hammer roared at him from high and aside.

Sinkua dove into a somersault, unclipping the bindings on his morningstar as he came upright. He swung and wrapped the chain around the handle of the hammer. With a solid pull, he halted the beastly weapon.

"Stronger now," Seriamus snarled, "Strong to break illusion. Strong to stop hammer."

Sinkua glared up at him with his eyes flared. This monster had learned in minutes what had taken Odin nearly two weeks. Sinkua grimaced, maintaining the facade of being unimpressed and unintimidated.

"Shut your whore mouth," he muttered as smoke rippled from the morningstar chain, "You'll never be worthy of Phoenix. And flattery will get you nowhere."

"More tenacious than last I saw you, Tetsen Drukoa," Seriamus sounded out, his mouth straining around each syllable, "Do you would well serving Goddess Pandora."

"That is no longer my name."

"Call yourself what now?"

"You'll die before you learn it."

Seriamus snarled and yanked his hammer upward. But Sinkua pulled down in the same instant, snapping the handle in an eruption of splinters and ash. Seriamus thrust the severed handle down. Sinkua drew Epesol as he dodged, batting the handle with the flat of his blade.

Seriamus punched the ground as he fell forward. Sinkua leapt onto the fist, vaulted to Seriamus's torso, and swung around behind his shoulders. He stretched his morningstar chain across Seriamus's throat. The chain reddened as he pulled back, melting Seriamus's flesh around the links.

Seriamus bucked and twisted, throwing Sinkua from his back. The morningstar remained embedded in his neck. Sinkua slashed the first set of knuckles that came his way. The next, he spun away from and stabbed Epesol into the side of the fist. The smell of burning plants grew strong.

"The worm nears," Phoenix implored, "End this quickly."

Seriamus recovered his broken weapon, taking one end in each hand. Sinkua danced around every swing, slashing and stabbing them as he dodged within the narrowest of margins. He moved with something beyond instinct, taking no conscious effort and yet ascending the limitations of cognizance. This he knew to be a product of the collective of his previous incarnations.

Black lightning burst from the jagged end of the broken handle. Sinkua poised Epesol before himself, and the shock dissipated against the Hephaeseum blade.

Seriamus plunged the makeshift spear at him. Sinkua sidestepped and batted it with the flat of Epesol. He took hold of the handle and ripped it from Seriamus's hand.

Sinkua sprang aside and pounded his dagger the rest of the way into Seriamus's knee, handle and all. As the giant snarled in his own absurd language, Sinkua spun about and hurled the crude spear through the ember worm. When he came around, Seriamus had fallen onto his forearms.

Sinkua bounded onto the back of Seriamus's shoulders. He pulled the handle of his morningstar across the back of Seriamus's neck, then stabbed Epesol through until the tip emerged through a chain link.

Sinkua held the hilt of Epesol in one hand and his morningstar chain in the other. He wrenched to the side, but the entangled weapons scarcely moved. He pulled harder, muscles threatening to rupture under the seemingly futile exertion.

"Sinkua! The worm!" Phoenix implored, "Hurry!"

He looked out to see the ember worm within a stone's throw and devouring the remaining distance. Visions of Nikasu flickered in its place.

This thing had taken his sister's likeness to get near him. To kill him. And had Seriamus's illusion not faltered, it would have slain him with his believing it was by her hand. It sullied her image. Poisoned her name. Exploited her like MalVek and The Geneticist before it.

Sinkua's temple throbbed. Blood filled his throat. Shallow flames swept over his skin despite Project Cerulean.

But this rage was focused. He felt as though he could make out the shape of every sinew, every tissue, and every vein in Seriamus's neck. All the way down to the bone.

Seriamus threw himself upright. Sinkua dug his boots into his back and tightened his grip on the entangled weapons. He twisted his entire body with the force of a focused episode. Epesol carved through Seriamus's neck in a path of scorched flesh. But Seriamus bucked hard, throwing Sinkua from his back.

Sinkua tumbled across the ground, rolling up to his feet only when he sensed he was beyond Seriamus's reach. When he looked up, he found the Pandora Hybrid still clung to life despite the meager hold his head had on the rest of his body.

Flames erupted from under Sinkua's feet as he charged at the lumbering giant. Whether by Seriamus's faltering life or Sinkua's heightened focus, Seriamus's swatting felt ungainly. Sinkua ducked under his legs and spun to a halt as he grabbed the business half of the broken hammer.

The ember worm gaped its smoldering maw at him. He lifted the hammer overhead and sent it flying. It pounded the air as it spun end over end and met its mark against the side of Seriamus's face.

The remaining strands of flesh and sinew ripped away. Seriamus's head fell from his shoulders. His body tumbled and crashed. The ember worm scattered.

Sinkua collapsed to his hands and knees as the pain of every exertion settled in. The shallow flames vanished, as did the throbbing in his temple and the taste of blood. He dragged himself to Seriamus's body and fished out each of his weapons.

"Couldn't you keep that up a little longer?" he muttered, "I still have to… Pandora…"

"Focusing through your episodes has always been more your own doing than you realize," Phoenix clarified, "But it would seem Project Cerulean afforded you additional control over this heightened episode."

"You think between that and your voice, I could handle myself with it in full effect?"

"Entirely in your brimstone form?"

"Yeah. I'm gonna need it against Pandora," Sinkua said, "I don't think Nikasu will get here soon enough to help."

"I'll do what I can," Phoenix promised, "But so soon after your other experiments, I fear that it will exceed you."

"Aunt…? You're not…? No," Nikasu stammered as she staggered back and aside, "How could you…? No! He wouldn't!"

"Oh now, it is too soon to say. What kind of nurse would I be if I said I was pregnant just a few hours after getting some bareback?" Jevana said, "But yes, he would, and he did. In fact, he was very willing once got over his misgivings."

Nikasu's mouth hung agape. "But… Eytea…"

"Now, he's run off to face Pandora alone like the foolhardy jackass that he is," Jevana continued, "And when he gets himself killed, the child he left in me will become the new Phoenix Hybrid."

"Sure," Nikasu muttered, "Assuming you get pregnant."

"It's not a perfect plan, but I've given myself every advantage," Jevana said, "Besides, even if I'm not, watching you grasp at…"

"No," Nikasu cut in, "I mean assuming you live long enough to conceive."

Laughter erupted from Jevana's throat. "You really think you can kill me while I'm carrying…"

"It's not even implanted yet, you morally defunct shit-spigot!"

Nikasu hurled a scythe at Jevana. Nemesis sprang from Nikasu's shoulders and shot past it. Jevana backhanded the air, and a percussive wave slammed into Nemesis. But though it staggered him, he powered through to kick her with both feet. The scythe passed under him on an unbroken trajectory for Jevana's chest.

But Jevana vanished in a thunderous flash of crackling light and rippling shadows. Nemesis righted himself and faced Nikasu, focusing beyond her. Nikasu turned around to find Jevana several meters behind her, clinging to MalVek's arm.

"This is where we part ways for a time," MalVek implored, "We all have greater priorities for which none of us gain by staying here."

"No, my morning is wide open to waste a kidnapper and a rapist," Nikasu said, "Sinkua can handle himself in the meantime."

"Of course. And where is he right now?" MalVek asked, "Did he leave you here to face me alone?"

"Don't try to lie to him," Jevana interjected, "You're horrible at it."

"Odin took him to the island on Sleipnir."

"He is in Bealstilla?" MalVek asked.

"If that's what's on the other side of The Veil, then yeah."

The corner of MalVek's mouth flicked up. "What of The Harvester?"

"Dead," Nikasu stated, "Sinkua killed him."

MalVek turned to Jevana. "We must go," he said, "The final phase will soon go into motion."

"Hold on!"

"Nikasu, I am sparing your life that you might aid your brother," MalVek said, "See that you do not squander it."

"I know what you're planning," Nikasu announced, "You're using the homunculi to take Pandora's powers and become the God of Chaos."

"Entropy is the ultimate eventuality. By my hands or Pandora's, this world will succumb to chaos," MalVek said, "If by mine, I can only guarantee your life and safety if you desist in pursuing us."

"Sounds like you want us to kill her for you," Nikasu goaded, "Or are you afraid that you couldn't stand up to her after I'm done with you?"

"Your tenacity is why I have chosen to let you live in my world, but my patience with it has its limits," MalVek cautioned, "Conquest is inevitable. Do not squander the favor of the autarch you know."

Electrical arcs flickered amongst his flesh metal. Air and light folded around himself and Jevana, and when the ripples calmed, they were gone. Nikasu grabbed her scythes, then recovered Epelun and faced Nemesis as she returned it to its scabbard.

"Take me to Bealstilla."

Sinkua kept a tight grip on the hilt of his sword as he walked toward the ruins of Bealstilla. He cast his eyes all about, never letting them settle on a single point for more than a split second. He trusted Phoenix to assess hazards, as he looked far too briefly to do it himself.

He paused as wind churned through the tree line just ahead. Tiny spots of grass flattened to the sound of metallic buzzing. Dull scattered hums soon compounded and expanded into a mind-rattling cacophony. The noise amplified and tightened as thousands of bugs coalesced, trampling the grass with their wingbeats.

Black lightning arced between bugs, tethering them as they rose around one another. Pairs connected into chains. Chains joined into clusters. Clusters folded into indescribable shapes.

With no discernible pattern, the bugs burst into brackish green sludge. The stench irritated his welts as the sludge filled the gaps in the net of black lightning. It multiplied as it drooled over the roiling form.

Wind shrieked around it, scattering the sludge. The grass blackened as the sickly substance rained down on it, and the wind shattered and scattered it.

The ground quaked as the form settled upon it. Cracks spread in a spiderweb pattern, conjuring up a seeping of lava. This pyroclastic flow collected around the figure, flowing up to cover its surface.

Colors and textures bled together to tease the limits of human comprehension. Scorching heat enveloped Sinkua as biting cold penetrated into his very bones. The urge to run off screaming took a stranglehold while any thoughts other than fighting became incomprehensible.

Distinct curves and angles settled into the form as ashen gnats flitted around it. Something vaguely humanoid took shape, save for the look of melting like hot taffy. Spots of iridescence flickered where the gnats crashed into it until the whole thing shimmered.

Colors settled. Textures swept over it. A face became distinct where one ought to have been. In the space of a few seconds, where there had been nobody, a being who thrummed with incomprehensibility stood before Sinkua and Phoenix.

Her clothes both clung to and billowed from her body. Deep black hair with streaks of stony gray and brilliant silver hung to her knees. The slightest movement of her head caused her eyes to shimmer through a detailed gradient from blood red to tar black.

Reptilian scales covered her throat and the bottom half of her face. Her fingers were far longer than her palms and had five or six knuckles each. And when she opened her mouth to speak, her teeth were too numerous to sit comfortably within it.

"Tetsen Drukoa," she rasped, beckoning him closer.

Every shred of reason as well as Phoenix screamed at him not to listen. But through no will of his own, his feet shuffled forth. Arms limp at his sides, Sinkua stood before Pandora.

She reached up and cupped his chin, drumming her fingertips on his temple and hairline. Incomprehensible words burbled from her throat in what he could only conclude to be the same language that Seriamus had spoken.

"This is poison," he responded, indicating the substance on his chin, "Do you understand me?"

Pandora released him and stepped back. She closed her eyes and faced skyward. Sinkua went for Epesol, but as touched the hilt, Pandora flicked her wrist, compelling him to withdraw his hand.

"Are you working on a way around this?" Sinkua thought.

"I'm trying," Phoenix answered, "The depth of her compulsion pales all others."

Pandora opened her eyes and faced Sinkua. "How long have I been here?"

"The Trifecta sealed you here about five thousand years ago."

Pandora's attention flitted about, jumping through a dozen points by the time he finished answering her question. She cocked her ear and narrowed her eyes.

"This world speaks only one language," she observed, cheeks stretching with a gnarled smile, "And its only constant is its inconsistency. How lovely. It's as though every Omphaloworlder tongue has coalesced into a tribute to me."

"You always were such a narcissist," Sinkua said, "I was stupid to think a few millennia in isolation would change you."

"Do you really remember feeling that way? Or did Phoenix convince you of such?" Pandora asked, "Such a long time to hold a curse so close. It must now be only moments between your death and rebirth." She dragged her fingertip along his jawline. "What do you call this body?"

"…Sinkua."

"Curious," she said, smiling with all but her eyes, "Similar to the name given to you by Takmet of the Mberhali."

"He also gave me this name," Sinkua said, "Pahres's ploy to betray The Trifecta backfired. Takmet saw the Hybrids return from extinction and laid the groundwork for us to deal with the threats that would come with it."

"As would be his wont," Pandora said, "Now, he gets to spend tens of thousands of years gathering a wealth of experiences and observations in the afterlife. But for all your efforts and losses, what will you receive? A moment to reconcile with your loved ones before you're dragged back into this world. Does it not boil your blood, Tsenukoa?"

"Sinkua," he corrected, "And what each of us gets has no bearing on the other."

"Perhaps not. But don't you wish you were granted the same standard as everyone else? Do you not wish to have more time with your Eytea?"

"Nobody gave you permission to speak her name," Sinkua snarled, "And of course I do. But it can't happen."

"Oh, but it can. Just make good on the promise you made to me back then," Pandora said, running her fingers along his shoulder, "I'll even ignore the fact that you killed my pet. He did draw upon you before he'd broken the language barrier, after all."

"I'm afraid that's not going to happen," Sinkua asserted, brushing her hand aside, "Not the way you think. The only way you're leaving the Omphaloworld with Phoenix is to escort us both to the Etherworld."

"Yes, at which time, I will depart in peace to seek other conquests."

"Without Phoenix."

"That is not as we agreed," Pandora growled, "Your freedom and this world's peace were your price for this power."

"This power has never been for sale."

"Tsenukoa felt differently. In fact, he was quite eager to make the exchange. Perhaps, he felt more strongly about his special someone than you do about yours."

"None of me have ever, would ever, or will ever offer Phoenix to you," Sinkua said, his eyes aglow as they locked with hers, "Not Sinkua. Not MeiLom. Not Tsenukoa. Not Tetsen Drukoa." He lowered himself to her eye level. "Not even whoever I was when you razed Bealstilla because I wouldn't let you have your way."

"You lie!" Pandora shouted, the tree line trembling, "Tetsen swore the power of Phoenix to me!"

"Maybe he lied," Sinkua shrugged, "Maybe we both lied. Maybe you're remembering wrong. Point is, you're not getting her."

"No… No. No! I would not have been fooled for so long," Pandora grumbled, coiling her fingers into bulky fists, "It's you. You're the liar. How dare you try to deceive the Goddess of Chaos!"

"And how dare you threaten the Phoenix Hybrid," Sinkua spat back, "What are you going to do? Kill me? Take Phoenix by force?"

Pandora ground her teeth, and it sounded like broken glass being trampled against gravel. "My power may not be absolute," she snarled, "But think it not beyond me to compel you to surrender her willingly."

"My will with her transcends my body and the brain that comes with it," he said, "Not even you could change my mind fast enough."

"I've waited thousands of years atop thirteen human generations. The time I need is but paltry in comparison."

"I guess you forgot. Probably because you didn't understand me yet," Sinkua said. He tapped his lower lip. "This is poison," he reiterated, "I'll be incapacitated in a few minutes. Dead within the hour."

"Then I will wait until your new host to be old enough to surrender Phoenix of its own accord."

"Sure, it would be just like you to resort to taking her from a child," Sinkua pondered, "But that child will be the son of my sister and Takmet's descendent. If I die here, he'll be born under two compulsory Hybrid inheritances. And she'll raise him to be more powerful and stubborn than any of his predecessors on either side."

"A Dual Hybrid does sound most curious," Pandora said, grazing the tip of her tongue over her teeth, "But there are ways to compel a person beyond reordering their thoughts. Ways that would break even someone as stubborn as you."

"What are you…?"

Pandora swept her arms out as she floated above Sinkua's reach. Numerous iridescent orbs erupted through her flesh, spattering the ground with tar-like blood. Her wounds mended themselves as the dirt sizzled. The orbs spun in self-conflicting directions as they expanded.

"I hear your friends in the wind," Pandora boomed, "And a most loyal acolyte has granted me the means by which to pursue them all at once."

"You wouldn't!" Sinkua protested.

With bone-rattling thunder, the orbs screamed over horizon within the space of a blink. Pandora slowly descended.

"Remain here to fight my core, and they will all perish. Give chase, and you might save somebody," she continued, "The only way to save everyone is to surrender Phoenix to me. To persist in your folly would be to doom them all."

"I've got worse deaths on my hands already," Sinkua said, drawing Epesol, "I can live with theirs until the poison kills me."

Chapter 48

A northbound flash swept across Nikasu's peripheral vision. She looked to the horizon just in time to see specks of light disappearing across it.

"Were those...?" she asked, "Did they come from Bealstilla?"

Nemesis grunted in acknowledgment. "Pandora shares her power."

"Odin isn't back," Nikasu pondered, rubbing the back of her head, "Comms are still out. I can't send anyone after MalVek."

"We continue to Bealstilla," he said, "As you insisted."

"That was before I knew how close he was to his goal," she said, "We can't leave him alone with his new powers."

Nemesis kept flying as he looked over his shoulder to face her. "Do not doubt yourself," he said, "Our options are unfavorable, but Bealstilla is the best of them. Your brother overexerts himself."

"Right," Nikasu sighed, nodding vigorously, "Right. You're right. We know where Pandora is. Odin is probably looking for MalVek."

"If that is how you feel," Pandora said as she descended, "then I'll suffer you no further."

The air cracked as she swept her arm, throwing a tight arc of howling wind. Sinkua pivoted aside as the air blade sheared his lapels. A thrust of her palm bludgeoned him with air, staggering him.

With a blink, Pandora pulled the ground up around Sinkua's legs. His eyes widened as he writhed in vain against the earthen restraints. Pandora clasped her hands together, fingers curling to meet their own palm heel.

As she pulled them apart, a beast of a weapon manifested. It was formed of brimstone which seeped green sludge as much as pyroclasm. The pole ran at least their combined heights, and the head, a battle axe coupled with a warhammer, was at least as big as Sinkua and that much denser.

Pandora brandished the hulking thing with a single hand as she drifted backward on a cushion of air. She landed and drew back the toxic brimstone weapon, turning to put the hammer head at the front of a forehand swing.

"Seriamus would have wanted it this way," she said.

And she swung for the head.

Windows and windshields buckled and fragmented in the wake of the orb of light as it shot up the street. The driver swung her legs up onto the dashboard and knocked her windshield out of the frame with two solid double kicks.

"Oh, that looks bad," she said, craning her neck.

"I don't suppo..."

Thunder washed out Jex's voice as the orb collided with the homunculus. It rose into the air as the light sunk into and spread throughout its body. The light faded, and the homunculus lit upon the pavement.

"If these motherbuggers would keep moving!" the driver shouted, pounding the horn.

When they heard the homunculus was pursuing one of her stowaways, the drivers around her had managed a wide enough berth that she had turned her truck almost sideways. But now she sat twice as vulnerable across two lanes of traffic.

A churning black and green mass collided with the front of a nearby car, folding the bumper inward. Leeches exploded from the point of impact, wriggling into the gridlock and out of sight. The driver of that car had been knocked unconscious.

A second mass of leeches and sludge crushed the engine compartment and upended the vehicle. Jex's driver exploited the tragedy and turned through the opening.

Yet another toxic volley cracked the hood of yet another car. People abandoned their vehicles to flee on foot, only to scream as they were set upon by what must have been hundreds of leeches blanketing that stretch of road.

Jex pounded the roof. The driver glanced back to see him with the tool chest open.

"It's all the way at the bottom," she said as she continued reorienting the truck, "Haven't used it in a while."

Masses of toxic leeches kept crashing into gridlocked cars. Jex opened the box and pulled out anything that wasn't a bow or arrows with no caution beyond not hurting Dourias. The transformation had largely reverted, but his pulse remained vigorous.

Noxious fumes pounded him as he came up with the driver's compound bow. He turned his back to the cabin to face the rear of another vehicle. The driver had found just enough of a path to force her way through.

Jex brought the compound bow up to his chest. He drew back and centered the homunculus's head in the sight. And he let the arrow fly.

Sinkua snapped his morningstar out, coiling the chain around the handle of the toxic brimstone weapon. Jerking down with both hands, he redirected it to his confines within the last split second. Released, he left his morningstar to charge with Epesol drawn.

Pandora retracted her weapon, swinging at him from alternating sides. But Sinkua avoided every one of them with the compounded instincts of numerous lifetimes. He hurled a churning mass of fire from his free hand, moving his dagger under his sleeve while he was obscured.

The fire splashed over Pandora in a billowing sheet of smoke. She stepped through, unscathed beyond some dull smoldering at the edges of her clothes. She gripped her weapon by its head.

Finally exerting some apparent effort, Pandora squeezed the dual head. The entirety of it shattered. But before the fragments even began to fall, they reordered themselves into black lightning of similar shape.

Sinkua held the flat of Epesol forward as Pandora reshaped the black lightning into a massive orb. She sent it his way with a flick of her wrist, and he charged forward.

Th orb crashed into him, tightening and agitating every muscle in his body at once. Epesol had offered no protection. The scars on his chest throbbed as he fell to his hands and knees. His dagger fell from his sleeve, bouncing beyond his reach.

"You pitiful bastard," Pandora snarled, "Did you think your ruse would hold up?"

Sinkua coughed and trembled as he forced himself back to his feet. He looked at her, struggling to focus. Choking on his inability to form words, he just shook his head.

Yrlis entered the front hall just in time to see a shimmering homunculus light upon the foyer floor. The homunculus locked her in eye contact. With a clench of its fist, the front door peeled apart into strips of metal.

Yrlis spat an expletive and ran further down the hall. The echoes of stripping construction pursued her as she scrambled around the corner and into the maintenance office.

She grabbed the uprooted sign and spun around to face the noises. An animate entanglement of metal and masonry filled the width of the doorframe. The thing clacked its malformed feet, looking like some arachnid that evolution had had the mercy and sense not to conjure up.

She screamed as she ran at it and wedged the edge of the sign deep into its thorax. It buckled and collapsed, and Yrlis pulled the sign out, bounded over it, and rushed down the hall.

More animate entanglements took shape from the rippings. Their being too numerous and replaceable, Yrlis kept her weapon at her side and just kept running.

As she neared the lobby, Yrlis glimpsed the homunculus in the corner of her eye. It stood just behind the window between the lobby and the front hall. It struck the window, shattering the entire security glass pane.

Yrlis recoiled as glass shards sprayed across her body. When she opened her eyes, she saw countless golems taking shape from the stripped walls and furniture. The homunculus stood at the center now, its eyes as empty as they were mad.

Her skin tingled in bits and patches. The lights kicked on, scattering glints all around her. As her eyes adjusted, she found herself surrounded by clumps of glass shards in the shape of locusts. Glass dust flew from every wingbeat as they zipped down the hall.

"Mom! Run!" Yrlis shouted as she gave chase.

Pandora reared back and unleashed a mind-rending scream. Threads of the duster unraveled and fell to pieces as the sonic barrage wrapped around him. Strands of flesh twisted and coiled as they peeled away.

Sinkua strained to lift his hands, but his joints were too stiff from the shock. Now, merely standing was a struggle, but the scream had such a stranglehold on him that it kept him upright.

"Ph… Phoenix…" he choked out.

The Phoenix Ruby glowed brilliantly. The light spread in front of him with distinct edges. Soon, new cuts no longer formed. Just past the edge of the heat barrier, the air rippled with the continued audio onslaught.

Sinkua slashed Epesol, launching the shield at Pandora. It went up in a towering conflagration as it crashed into her.

Pandora sprang through the flames with black smoke billowing from her reddened skin. Sinkua sliced her tricep as she reached for him, but she was undeterred. The ground sizzled as her blood dripped on it.

She palmed his face, enveloping his head with her spidery fingers. Her momentum knocked him off his feet, and she held him aloft by his head. With a vicious shriek, she flung him into a hurricane gale, leaving Epesol behind.

The nurse flicked side-eye at Uro as they walked. This one was far quieter but much less receptive of his claimed identity than the one in the lobby. She had made this known by saying nothing except that he looked nothing like what she had heard.

She stopped at a door and knocked.

"Madam Minister? You have a visitor."

Fabrics rustled. Someone coughed. A throat cleared.

"Now?" EshCal grumbled, "Why the…?" She sighed. "Who is it?"

The nurse glared emphatically at Uro. He swallowed hard, and she rolled her eyes.

"He says he's Sinkua."

The bed creaked.

"Send him in."

The nurse opened the door and muttered to herself as she walked away.

Uro could feel EshCal's seething eyes upon him as he stepped into the room. Too afraid to make eye contact, he began stammering through words before he had even closed the door.

"Madam Brigadier General Elite, I…"

"Who in the hell are you?" EshCal demanded. She narrowed her eyes as she looked him over. "Wait. I've seen you at Drakou."

"I'm sorry for the deception," Uro said, approaching the bed, "And yes. My name is Uro. Farim brought me in after…"

"I've heard the story," she interrupted, "Where's Sinkua?"

"I don't know," he said, "I blacked out, and we got scattered. But MalVek needs him, so he's probably still alive."

"That'll have to do," she sighed, "Now, what are you doing here?"

"A bunch of us have a condition like his," Uro said, "We're all linked."

"That's what you meant by blacking out."

Uro nodded. "There's a functional antidote at Hillside. I need to recover the formula and remaining samples."

"And how am I supposed to help with that?"

EshCal threw back her bedsheet. Uro winced and recoiled at the sight of her, the reality being far worse than he had imagined. Her legs stopped just below the knees, tapering off into a stitched-up mess of tattered flesh. Speckles of blood stained the sheets.

"I need your portal strip," Uro said, struggling to look at any part of her as her legs were always in his periphery.

"Why mine?" she demanded, "Why didn't you…?"

"You were closer than Drakou," Uro said, "And MalVek doesn't know where you are."

Her expression flattened. "Reasonable," she conceded, "But I can't help you."

"Is it… because you don't have it with you?"

"I do, but I can't lend it to you."

Uro tangled his hand in his hair. "Look, I don't care what kind of policy you're under. This super-fucking-cedes it!" he snarled, "This is an order from Spril himself. So, either help me or so help me, I'll put everything you own on the top shelf, you impossible pile of stumps."

"You pretended to be Sinkua. Do you understand the weight of that lie? The last time I saw him, my personal assistant, he was being assaulted and abducted, and I couldn't do anything about it. Did you even think about my end of the exchange when the nurse announced that he'd come to see me, only for some whiny bossy bumblefuck to walk in?"

"But…"

"And now, I'm supposed to believe that Spril trusted you alone with this task?" EshCal continued, "Why don't you invoke the third name on my list? That's sure to change my mind!"

"Actually, I…" Uro trailed off into a sigh, "The sarcasm was uncalled for."

"So's your attitude," EshCal said, "Look, I can't add this hospital to the portal network."

"How could you…?"

"I said no."

Uro grumbled as he paced the room, desperation taking hold as he considered his increasingly limited options.

"Where is it?" he demanded.

"Why?"

Uro rushed across the room and pinned her by the throat. "Where is it!?"

EshCal twisted his wrist with her thumb and two fingers, propping herself up with her other hand as she bent him over.

"I gave you my answer," she said, "And that's all you're leaving here with."

Uro struggled uselessly against her. "Fine. Fine!"

EshCal released him, and he pulled back, rubbing his shoulder.

"You need to leave," she said.

"Yeah," he grumbled, "Tell Myriela I said hello next time you fuck her."

Sinkua's shoulder jammed into the socket as it hit the ground. He bounced and rolled for several meters, flailing as the wind carried him. As he settled by the roots of an ancient tree, the ground began to vibrate.

He sank as he came up to his hands and knees, the vibrations drawing him in. He tried to come up to his feet, but his legs refused to stay under him. Sweat pooled, and his breathing grew ragged.

The tree line flashed before him with a harsh thrum. But just as quickly, it vanished back toward the horizon, leaving Pandora in its place. She stood unaffected by the trembling soil, watching with eyes that betrayed nothing.

"This has become quite like a game for me, you know," she said, "I have more time than the world to grow stronger, while you keep starting over with nothing but fleeting glimpses of old memories. It's funny the way so many of you have thought it wise or even honorable to fight me."

Sinkua had sunken to his chest, but he still writhed against his earthen binds. He hocked a salvo of mucus and blood at Pandora only to have it fall short. She sneered, and he yowled as the ground hardened around him.

"But this one has failed to amuse me," she continued, clenching her fist to further tighten his confines.

"I knew…" he choked out, "… couldn't… fool you… long."

A screaming streak of silver and amethyst blindsided her with claws gnashing wildly. Nemesis deposited Nikasu before Sinkua as he swooped around to shield them from Pandora.

Nikasu set Sinkua's morningstar down and lay her hands on the stone.

"Sorry it took so long," Nikasu said, "Odin didn't come back for me."

"He died," Sinkua said, wriggling against his confines, "Wasn't his plan."

"Damn," she muttered, "Hold still. I'll get you out."

"Pandora," Nemesis snarled, "Your existence is anathema to all."

"So. You survived," Pandora sneered, "Let's see what I can do about that."

Spril's feet grew numb as a warbling scream spiked his hearing. He looked toward the source and saw a ball of light, twisting and whipping with meshing colors. The smell of rain vanished and his mouth dried as he focused on it.

The thing thrummed with energy, palpable even at a distance of two blocks. Then three. Four. Five and onward. Soon, a silhouette atop a ten-story building came into sharp focus.

"How the...?" Spril muttered, "From there?"

As little time as he had to consider the homunculus's capabilities, he had even less once the orb struck. He watched through heightened vision as the light lifted and coursed through its body. The thing looked straight at him as it settled upon the rooftop, as though it could see him just as clearly.

Spril's senses snapped back to normalcy. As his sight of it pulled back, the homunculus stepped out from the edge of the rooftop.

It plummeted the full ten stories in a static standing position and hit the concrete with no effort to absorb its landing. Instead, the ground took the impact as an entire sidewalk panel shattered. Shockwaves rippled, setting street signs trembling.

More shockwaves came with its every step. As they compounded around Spril, he felt something he hadn't felt in over twenty years. And with that came a fear he'd not experienced in just as long.

His eyes widened and mouth trembled. He hunkered down on the quaking asphalt, incapable of willing his body to do anything else. Hugging his knees to his chest, he mumbled to himself.

"Ma... Pa... Ma... Pa... Ma... Pa..."

The homunculus closed in with each step threatening ever nearer vehicles and structures.

Nemesis blurred forth and grabbed at Pandora with his hind legs. Pandora became a blackish scaly blur as she rushed his charge. His claws snapped shut, but she slipped through and grabbed him by the throat.

Nemesis's body became slack as Pandora crushed his neck. As blood trickled from his mouth, she windmilled her arm, flinging him end over end and pulverizing the ground with his body. She lifted his head high, most of his sizeable form slumped beside her, and hurled him into a wind stream.

But as she took off after him, she suddenly couldn't move her legs. A pale halo radiated from the ground.

"He trapped you while you were showing off," Nikasu said, brandishing her scythes.

"Where is Tetsen?" she snarled, hair coiling as though each lock was independently prehensile.

She whipped about and caught the chain of Sinkua's morningstar, the spiked ball bouncing off her forearm without breaking the skin. In the same instant, her hair snapped back and seized Nikasu by her arms and neck.

"There you are, child," she exhaled, "Have I changed your mind yet?"

Sinkua strained against her mockingly minimal effort. The chain reddened at his will, but the mounting heat failed to so much as annoy Pandora. With an ear-splitting bellow, he unleashed a surge of milystis strong enough to explode white flames from the links.

Pandora snapped back, more out of startlement than pain. Nikasu wriggled one wrist just loose enough to cut herself free, robbing Pandora of numerous keratin whips. Sinkua landed a cannonball of a flaming punch to her mouth. And with a blur of silver and purple, Nemesis blindsided her with a drill of slashing claws.

Khirsan's head throbbed as he suddenly felt like he was falling. As he regained his composure, the air thrummed with a vague sense of unfamiliarity.

Screams from outside pulled every eye to the window just as a bloodied man slammed against it. He drew back and struck again, this time with a pair of blades erupting through his chest.

The window fragmented with two sprays of red mist as the dead body collapsed through with a creature of chitin and alloy on his back. Its underbelly glowed red. Patrons recoiled, screamed, and scattered. Several ran for the door, but more such abominations piled in and block the exit. The cashier ducked behind the counter, while the rest of the staff fled into the back, calling anyone in earshot to follow.

Khirsan stood his ground and drew his segmented staff. The creature on the man's back turned its head in his direction. Khirsan ran at it, keeping its focus on him.

He swung at the creature as it pounced. Its light went out upon impact, just before it shattered. The thing fell lifeless, just as more piled in behind it.

They scrambled about, becoming consumed by their own madness as countless masses of them spontaneously shorted out. Khirsan watched them circling as he loosened the staff segments.

A shot rang out and carved through an underbelly light. Khirsan looked back to the counter. The cashier had a pistol trained on the door.

"I've seen these," he said, swallowing hard, "Must be a Hybrid in here."

Pandora's jaw extended as she stretched her mouth around Sinkua's outstretched fist. She chomped down, spraying blood as dozens of teeth rent flesh and pocked bones.

Still holding his fist in her mouth, Pandora hurled an iridescent black orb at Nemesis as he leaned into a stop. Nikasu called out a warning, but the blast vanished.

Sinkua set his other fist ablaze and drove it at Pandora's stomach. But his fist vanished through undisturbed light and air.

The blast reappeared behind Nikasu, launching her forward as it slammed into her back. She crashed into Pandora, pushing her mouth further down Sinkua's arm. At the same time, Sinkua's own fist emerged behind his own back and knocking himself even deeper into Pandora's toothy grasp.

Nemesis zipped around Pandora, wrapped his wings around Nikasu, and kept flying. Pandora managed a vicious smile around a mouthful of forearm. Sinkua's blood ran from the corners of her mouth, and he went pale as he struggled to free himself.

She released his arm, revealing a tattered mess of bloodied flesh with spots of bone laid bare.

"Perhaps, if my word that I am pursuing your friends will not sway you," Pandora said, "watching as I hunt your sister will make you more pliable."

"You'll have to go through me," Sinkua snarled.

"And how do you think you'll stop me? Punch me? Hold up your sword? Throw fire at me?" Pandora taunted, "You're out of your depth, child."

"Whatever you need to tell yourself," Sinkua snickered, "I've always got at least one more trick up my sleeve."

"Oh?" she scoffed, "And what…"

"The one where I annoy you until you make a mistake."

He swept his arm out, flinging dozens of rivulets of blood at her face. Before that hand stopped, he snapped his morningstar out and jerked it into a sudden backhand swing.

Pandora made no effort to avoid the spiked ball. Instead, it glanced off with more apparent damage to the weapon than to her body. She chuckled as she drifted back beyond his reach.

"Well, since you're so insistent that I stay," she said, covering her face with her hands, "I can humor you while still pursuing your sister and her bastard dragon."

She swept her hands apart to reveal a face reduced to only a nose. She ran her fingers through her hair, coiling it around them. At the ends, she yanked out several locks of hair. They hovered and flitted about. Some had eyeballs at the end, the hairs looking like veins or optic nerves. The rest curled into the shape of overly toothy mouths.

With a snap of her fingers, they scattered toward the coastline, Bealstilla, and every horizon in between. Her eyes and mouth reemerged as though they'd only been hiding.

In a snap assumption that Nemesis had gone to ground in the fallen town, Sinkua beat out a hard sprint to Bealstilla. Pandora had found his weakness. Protecting Nikasu took precedence.

"C… Cattle?" Sbaglien stammered as he scrambled away from Sou-Sol's dead body, "They were promised a revolution. I was promised a revolution!"

"And to a revolution shall you all contribute," the homunculus said, stepping over SouSol to maintain their proximity, "The cattle will be divided into four classes. Food, servants, sentries…"

Sbaglien swallowed hard. "And the last?"

"Those lucky few will become homunculi," it said, "Transference golems for Lord MalVek's master plan."

Gates rattled as prisoners wrenched the bars. They squeezed their arms through, trying to reach around and finagle with their locks. Imprisoned guards checked their pockets, grasping at the hope that their captors had overlooked a key.

"This isn't what we signed on for!" PavRal shouted, "Nobody said a damn thing about a master plan!"

"It is beyond you," the homunculus said. It lowered its voice to speak only to Sbaglien. "Stand aside."

"And if I don't?" Sbaglien asked, "Suppose I stand right the fuck in your way? What class does that put me in?"

"This is your eventuality," it said, "But it is not your time."

The homunculus lifted Sbaglien by his bottom jaw and flung him aside, bouncing him off a gate. A whirling orb of light came roaring down the corridor.

Gates and walls bowed and buckled in its wake. MerSul dove aside but was knocked into the wall and collapsed. The homunculus took the impact, levitating as the light flowed throughout its body.

Sbaglien helped MerSul to his feet, never taking his eyes off the homunculus.

"A homunculus, then? That's what he wants from me?" Sbaglien hissed, "Well, you can tell that lying…"

"No longer."

Hands snapped up to shield ears as the homunculus released a thunderous bellow that shook dust and paint flakes from the walls and bars. Sbaglien and MerSul cried out as they squeezed their arms around their heads. The crack in the walls deepened and spread. The very air trembled against the decibel assault.

Their eyes went blank, their arms slack. The homunculus relented. Sbaglien and MerSul collapsed in two heaps of flesh with hardly any bone structure between them.

It was several minutes more before the echoes fell silent.

Flames erupted around Sinkua's every footfall, scorching the antique flora and hardening the soil to brimstone. Hair-tailed eyeballs zipped in and out of his path, stealing glances at him from numerous angles.

He took a crack at one, puncturing the eyeball and shredding the tail. As the remains fell, a second swooped in and flew straight at Sinkua. The pupil expanded to overtake first the iris, then the entire sclera.

It contracted as an iridescent black beam fired from the flying eyeball. Sinkua ducked it, never breaking his stride, and it left a small crater behind him. He swatted it down before it could fire again.

A mouth came at him from the side, trembling his flesh with its shrieking. But a stream of fire from his hand quickly silenced it. The ground rumbled, the sound growing louder and nearer.

He closed in on the tree line. Hair-tailed eyeballs and flying mouths swooped around him, bombarding him with dark iridescent blasts and shredding screams. And he burned and batted them away.

Just before the trees, he spotted first Epesol, then his dagger. He scooped each one up, carrying the sword but sheathing the dagger under the duster. He strapped his morningstar to his back as he ran.

The ground swelled as he crossed into the small stretch of trees. Everything trembled. Splits ran through stones and ground. Narrow peaks sprouted around him, uprooting and toppling trees.

As he came into the clearing, the seisms continued past Sinkua, branching and multiplying. With Nemesis hovering at her side, Nikasu stood panting in the ruined plaza of Bealstilla.

And in a flash of dark, Pandora manifested between him and them.

Splinters and embers sprayed into the cabin as the orb of light blasted through the wall. Its wake bowed the front desk and knocked the contents to the floor as it thrummed across the room. The orb swerved and flew up the stairs to crash into the homunculus.

"This looks bad," Farim said, transfixed on the glowing levitating homunculus as she pawed at the scattered photon weapon generators, "Can we fight it? Or…?"

"I don't…" Gabdur pondered, eyes wide with panicked analysis, "No. Not here. We draw it out."

He angled his head toward the new hole. Farim blinked hard in understanding. Gabdur signaled for her to wait until he'd gone before she followed, then scrambled to the hole. He propped his hand on the edge and vaulted through.

But as Farim rounded the front desk, a crash and an expletive from a guest room told her his plan had failed. The homunculus lowered itself, emitting a faint glow as it hovered a centimeter off the floor. It descended the stairs.

"Such fortunate happenstance," it said, "I came to monitor you in this prison of portals and became the conduit for this power."

With a flick of its finger, the register vanished into an ephemeral smear of colored light and rematerialized in the air. It slammed into Farim's chest, knocking her onto her backside. Only as she fell did she hear the bang and jangle of the register erupting into flight.

Gabdur rushed around the corner and down the stairs. But a slight lifting of the homunculus's hand caused the staircase to stretch upward, bringing the bottom level with the top.

Gabdur produced a photon emission weapon and activated it as he leapt from the distorting staircase. He hurled the photonic fauchard straight at the homunculus.

The empowered homunculus gestured with its thumb and forefinger, and the fauchard vanished just as the register had, also flying straight at Farim. Only this time, she saw it coming. She pivoted out of the way and snatched it as it passed, spinning full circle with the momentum.

Farim paced sideways with the homunculus mirroring her, the two circling one another. Gabdur got to his feet and mirrored her as well, stepping lightly.

The homunculus's spatial warping powers appeared to work by line of sight. So, if he and Farim could maintain their alignments, one of them could get the drop. But they'd only have one shot, and even if he could get to the other photon weapons, they activated too loudly.

The spider mine in his coat would have to do.

Sinkua shouted Nikasu's name as he carved the ground with the tip of Epesol. Sweeping it up created a wave of flames taller than himself and nearly as wide. Pandora lifted her hand just before the flames obscured her, and Sinkua twitched his fingers on his ruined arm.

The wave of fire flattened against Pandora's hand. Her chuckling seeped through the fading roar as the wall of fire shattered and dissipated.

"You should have known better," she derided.

Sinkua spun around and slashed at the air, blood flailing from his arm. Lips, teeth, hair, and ocular fluid rained from his sword's trajectory. He came full circle, eyes aglow to see through the smoke.

"I did."

Pandora turned to put Sinkua and Nikasu at opposite ends of her periphery. Nikasu donned her Nemesis armor with the dragon's wings spread. She clutched Epelun with her scythes lying at either side, well out of reach. Facial detritus rained around her as she stared Pandora down.

Pandora curled her fingers at her. Nikasu's eyes widened as she and Nemesis vanished into a smear of light. The very space between where they were and where they ended up warbled as they reappeared. In a glimpse of eye contact with Sinkua, Nikasu dropped Epelun.

Sinkua set his tattered forearm on fire as he charged at Pandora. He side-stepped Nikasu and Nemesis as they were launched at him. He grabbed Epelun with his bad hand, milystic flames shying back toward his elbow. Passing it to his other hand, he hurled it as far as he could in Nikasu's general direction.

Pandora manifested an ice halberd with a flick of her forearm. Black lightning erupted from the spear tip as she thrust it at him.

Shallow flames danced over Sinkua's skin as he threw Epesol and dropped into a roll. Intense air pressure from the milystic bolt knocked him flat as he passed under it. But he swiftly righted himself, grabbed Epesol, and kept running.

Blade ablaze, he melted a large segment of Pandora's ice halberd and shattered the rest. But before Epesol could find flesh, Sinkua cried out as the very space between himself and some indeterminant elsewhere gather all at once against his bad arm.

His vision smeared, and his skin stung as he flew and tumbled. He white-knuckled his sword, jaw clenched and unblinking as he grasped at his bearings. He thrust Epesol at the ground.

The sword found its mark, carving a gully as he kept flying for a few more meters. He regained his footing, hold his sword to stay upright. Everything around him tilted and skewed, and he couldn't tell if it was Pandora's doing or just the dizziness.

Off in the distance, Nikasu and Nemesis rushed Pandora. The Goddess of Chaos flicked her fingers again, but Nemesis lunged aside and flung Nikasu in the opposite direction, leaving only dust to Pandora's spatial assault.

They engaged her from opposite sides, charging and retreating to tease out and dodge her attacks. Sinkua beat out rapid stomping footfalls to devour the distance between him from them.

Shallow flames formed around the scars outlining the Phoenix Ruby. They spread to envelop his torso, then continued down his limbs. His focus grew painfully sharp. Glowing red smoke billowed from his throat.

Phoenix's voice wove through his mind, saying nothing in particular. The smell of Project Cerulean thickened as the shallow flames gathered over his face. He grazed his fingers over his collarbone as he ran.

It didn't burn his skin. Nor did it strip him of his cognizance. Project Cerulean hadn't cured him. It couldn't even serve as a suppressant against his heightened episodes. Instead, it did something far more useful for the circumstances.

It gave him control.

Corpses in varying states of decomposition shambled across the parking lot. They wandered the streets and sidewalks, grabbing panicked morning commuters. People long dead, now reduced to skeletons, latched onto pedestrians with bony digits.

Phylus stood barefoot on the stoop, toes curled over the edge, with his rifle trained on the foremost corpse. He shot at the thigh, shredding rotten sinew and splintering bone. The zombie collapsed but kept pulling itself along with its hands.

But it was slower and hindered those around it. Phylus fired two more shots, collapsing another two zombies. Others stumbled over them, making them that much easier of targets.

Nonetheless, they advanced. Shooting the head had proven ineffective, given that many of them had little or no brain matter, anyway.

"MarLys!" Phylus shouted, "Where did that light end up?"

"It's… right…" MarLys stammered, "It's on your eight. Seven. Nine. Dammit! It's moving too fast!"

"How far?"

"I can't…"

"Dammit, MarLys!" Phylus bellowed, "You're my second eye!"

Screams from the streets swelled into a macabre crescendo. The stench of fresh blood intensified to mingle with that of rotting flesh. Gunshots rang out as people fought back. But the screams and stink of blood scarcely subsided.

Armored vehicles slowed alongside the parking lot, only to pass it up. They circled out of Phylus's periphery. He muttered under his breath as he kept dropping zombies.

"Clip!" he called as the trigger clicked.

"Last one," MarLys said, slapping it into his hand.

"Fuck," he muttered. He surveyed the crowd of zombies. They'd slowed significantly. More people fought back. But they were nowhere near stopping. "Where's the light?" he asked, "Roughly."

"Between my nine and yours," MarLys said, "Half to three-quarters kilometer."

"Go inside. Barricade the door," Phylus ordered, "Arm yourself."

"Why? What are you planning to do?"

"I'm going out for a closer shot."

"I thought you needed me to be your second eye," MarLys spat.

"I get my depth back when I'm stressed," Phylus deflected, "Now, go inside."

"But you can't shoot right when you're stressed," she said, "Give me the gun. I'll do it."

"You can't shoot at all!"

"Then teach me."

"What?!" he recoiled, striking down yet another zombie, "We don't have…"

"Yes, we do!" MarLys insisted, "I'm sick of people getting hurt protecting me. Show me how to protect myself!"

Sinkua stomped out the distance on a path to skew the line between Nikasu and Nemesis. He sprang from a few meters out, propelled by the firestorm under his feet. Holding Epesol aloft, he twisted his body and tucked his legs in. Just before he came within Pandora's reach, he threw both feet forward.

They found their mark, blindsiding Pandora with a drop kick that punctuated half a kilometer of ferocity and fire. He toppled and tumbled her with the impact. He slashed the air as he came upright, casting a wave of dark blue fire at her prostrate body as Nikasu and Nemesis converged on her.

Pandora floated upward beyond the flames. She turned her body upright, standing two meters above the ground. The air churned around her as black lightning crackled. Prehensile locks coiling and whipping, she brought her hand to her shoulder.

With a sweep of her hand, her hair stretched into points and screamed down at Nikasu and Nemesis. Sinkua pulled the wave back, cocooning them in milystic blue fire. The dagger locks scorched and frayed against it.

The cocoon contracted into a perfect sphere. Sinkua clenched his fist, erupting it under Pandora's feet. As Pandora staggered from the blast, Nikasu's arm, enveloped in Nemesis's flesh, snapped through the smoke and grabbed her by the ankle, slamming her into the ground. Nemesis drifted them back as Sinkua closed in.

Pandora launched to her feet with a burst of black and green smoke. She thrust both hands, propelling volleys of leeches from her fingertips. Nemesis spread his wings, casting them aside and pulling Nikasu skyward. Sinkua hurled a fiery arc with a swipe of Epesol, reducing the leeches to ash.

Nikasu angled Epelun down at Pandora, coalescing silverish purple milystis in the tip. Sinkua rushed through the falling ashes and slashed at Pandora's scaly throat. She lunged aside only to find her legs would barely move. She caught Epesol on her forearm, the blade cutting through her skin only to stop dead against her dense muscle tissue.

She thrust her other hand upward, casting an icy tempest that tossed and sliced at Nemesis and Nikasu. Sinkua tried to withdraw Epesol, but Pandora's forearm muscle gripped it too tightly. She reached for the Phoenix Ruby with black and purple smoke billowing from her fingertips.

Nikasu hit the ground cocooned by Nemesis. They tumbled together and came up well behind Pandora's back. Sinkua crashed the bottom of his boot with Pandora's sternum in a plume of fire and smoke. She staggered back, releasing Epesol.

Nikasu and Nemesis hovered at ankle elevation as they charged into her. Nikasu slashed at her back, but Pandora whipped around and swatted the flat of the blade with the back of her hand. Nikasu spun with the deflection, pivoting around to her side where Nemesis swiped at Pandora with his wing claws.

But Pandora wrapped those claws in her spidery fingers. Nemesis writhed in vain as she crushed his claws in her tightening clutches. Nikasu slashed at her, but she kept out of reach. Nemesis tried to dislodge from Nikasu, but a firm pull from Pandora held them together.

Black blood spattered over them in a burst of smoke and cyan fire. The smoke scattered, revealing a blade protruding from Pandora's chest. She released Nemesis, sputtering and drooling blood. Sinkua ripped Epesol out of her, his brimstone body spewing flames as he spun around and slashed at her neck.

Pandora whipped about, her eyes steely as she clamped the blade between her thumb and forefinger. Sinkua wrenched Epesol with both hands, but Pandora was unflinching as she stared him down. The edges of her wound threaded around each other, stitching itself shut.

The back of Pandora's tunic shredded as black and green tentacles erupted from her shoulder blades. They coiled around Nikasu's and Nemesis's limbs and throat, holding them aloft and at bay. Nemesis swiped at the tentacles with his damaged wings, but they wriggled and coiled to stay out of reach.

Patches of Sinkua's shallow flames flickered away. His shoulders grew heavy, his vision blurry. Pandora ripped Epesol out of his hands, and the flames dissipated with a prolonged sizzle. She flung the blade well beyond his reach.

Purple light erupted from Nikasu's coated hands. Her scythes popped off the ground and sailed toward her. Nemesis snatched them in his wings and passed them to Nikasu. With a twist of both wrists, she cut him and herself free.

As Pandora spun to face them, Sinkua snapped out his morningstar, wrapping the chain around her neck. He jerked back, pulling her away from Nikasu, who sliced her abdomen with countering backhanded swipes.

Sinkua let the chain fall and palm-heeled Pandora's collarbone to drive her to the ground. He stomped her chest as he dangled the spiked ball over her face. He wound back, focusing on the area between her temple and her jugular.

Pandora's mouth gaped inhumanly wide, and swarms upon swarms of silver locusts shot from her throat. Sinkua writhed and swatted at them as they picked at his flesh. But they flew off after just a taste, scattering above to blot out the dawn sky.

Nikasu dove at Pandora as she sprang to her feet. Nemesis wrapped Pandora in his wings, pushing the tattered remnants of his claws into her shoulders. A silverish purple glow coursed down Nemesis's wings as they enveloped Pandora and spun with her. Nikasu pressed the tip of Epelun into Pandora's chest, intensifying the glow.

Pandora planted her feet and grabbed Nikasu by the lower jaw, halting their spin. The purple glow dissolved. Her puncture sealed itself, pushing Epelun out of her body.

"Away with you!"

Pandora hurled them aside and returned her attention to Sinkua. She lifted her hand, willing the ball and chain upward. He pulled back, but it only answered her, bobbing and twitching with every flick of her fingers. Weary and clumsy, a slash at her throat once again ended with her catching the blade.

"I am merciful," she said, "One last chance to give Phoenix willingly."

Sinkua considered the dagger. She had seen that coming before though. Catching her by surprise with that was out of the question. Besides, there was one last thing to do before he lined it with her blood. Something both for which he fought and which drove him to fight. He only hoped he hadn't sullied the blade when he stabbed The Harvester.

He gave only a grunt in response.

Pandora closed her hand and snapped it open. The chain links snapped apart, suspending in the air for a second before she let them and the spiked ball fall. She stripped him of Epesol and flung it far.

"As theirs is on your hands," she said, lifting him by his lower jaw, "So too shall they have your blood."

She hurled him in nearly the same trajectory as Nikasu. But for how far he bounced, wincing at every collision with the ground, they ended up a considerable distance apart.

Mounds of soil swelled and ruptured. Pocked bones and desiccated flesh reached through the holes. Corpses and skeletons clawed to the surface, unarmed but numerous.

Nikasu called Sinkua's name. As he looked to her, she threw her scythes to him. He gathered them up and took a split second to assess their weight and balance before the undead were upon them.

Paired with their Etherworlders, brother and sister, last by blood of Drakougeneospa and last of the Hybrids, slashed into the unrelenting wall of reanimated corpses. Their lifeless eyes and empty sockets looked upon Sinkua with distant familiarity and far stronger spite.

But despite their frailty, they didn't stay down for long. And not only were their numbers too great, more emerged so continuously that it began to seem Pandora had a truly unending supply of them at her call.

Nikasu's knees hit the ground. She coughed and spat up blood as Nemesis struggled to keep hold of her. Sinkua collapsed next. The undead swarmed them and hoisted their bodies upright.

Sinkua looked to Nikasu. He exhaled an apology, then mouthed a plea for her trust. He turned to face Pandora.

"Pandora!" he shouted, "I surrender!"

Chapter 49

Jex aligned his next shot as the truck rumbled down the road. He stole a glance at the quiver by his feet. It was down to four arrows.

His attention snapped up at the sound of an erupting mass of toxic leeches. He shot on knee-jerk reflexes, rupturing the mass and scattering its contents.

As the brackish mist cleared, the shimmering homunculus narrowed the gap. It moved on all fours, limbs flailing as it horked up more wriggling sludge.

"Hurry up with that!" the driver called back.

"I'm working on it, miss," Jex grumbled, nocking the next arrow.

"You…" Dourias muttered.

Startled, Jex misfired, leaving just three shots. He looked down to see Dourias conscious and reverted, staring up at the early dawn sky.

"You fixed me?" Dourias asked.

Jex nodded as he nocked another arrow and tucked the next one between his fingers. One shot left if these missed.

"Why are…" Dourias strained, "… Quarun? How?"

Jex shredded a volley of leech sludge with the first arrow, quickly following with the arrow between his fingers. It glanced off the homunculus's head, slowing it.

"Hillside Oncology."

"They killed Farim," Dourias muttered, "Sinkua. Uro. Helped."

"Uro left allies there," Jex said, lining up his last shot, "They have a cure."

"Oh… Good."

Jex tightened his focus, casting out everything but himself, the bow and arrow, and the homunculus. He shallowed his breathing, timing the movements with the sound of his own pulse. He released the arrow.

And it skewered the homunculus's head.

The skeletons collapsed into heaps of bones. The zombies dropped and crumbled.

"What treachery is this, Tetsen?" Pandora asked as she approached.

"No treachery," Sinkua said, keeping his hands over his head, "Giving you this power is better than the alternative."

"What alternative do you speak of?"

"The acolyte you sensed," he said, "He's trying to unseat you and become the God of Chaos."

Pandora belted out a bone-shaking laugh. "Preposterous!"

"Keep your promise, and you can have Phoenix," Sinkua said, "Rid us and yourself of your usurper and cease hostilities against our world."

"My promise was to depart in peace, and to that will I bind," she swore, "But I have no obligation to protect you from the acolyte."

"I'm in no position to negotiate," he conceded, "We have a deal."

Pandora approached more urgently now, beckoning him to stand and come closer. Sinkua shook his head. He drew his dagger and pointed to Nikasu with the handle.

"Nikasu will bring you the dagger," he insisted, "You know I'd never risk her life trying to trick you."

Chekov tore around the corner, anchoring herself on the wall. Yrlis trailed a few steps behind, batting at infrastructure golems with the uprooted parking sign. The homunculus pursued at a distance, too deeply surrounded for Yrlis to engage it directly.

"Come on! It's straight ahead!" Chekov shouted.

Yrlis shouldered the sign and focused on running, quickly overtaking her mother. They scrambled into the office with considerable distance on the golems.

Yrlis went to close and lock the door, but Chekov pulled her away and applied her portal strip to the frame. She punched in the coordinates, then joined Yrlis at the desk as blue fractalized light filled the doorway.

They divided their efforts between searching computer files and searching the desk, ignoring the sounds of the incoming golems. But they quickly found themselves backed up to the wall as the foremost passed through the light and into the room.

Chekov cowered while Yrlis fought them off. The mother kept gathering Vielle's files while the daughter swatted glass and drywall golems with a parking sign. Yrlis called out for an explanation, but Chekov said she was just as confused.

Yrlis engaged the homunculus as it entered the office. Chekov charged in behind her.

But she didn't attack the homunculus. Chekov spun Yrlis by the shoulders, tucking a folded paper into her daughter's shirt pocket.

"You're my favorite creation," she whispered, kissing her between the eyes.

And she shoved her through the portal.

Yrlis watched from the other side as the golems swarmed her mother. Chekov pulled a metal rod out of her coat, and Yrlis screamed as she plunged it into the base of her skull.

Glass bugs swarmed her as she punched buttons on the rod. An electrical mesh formed around her, shattering and melting the bugs. Colorful flames filled the gaps. The whole thing pulled tight against her body. Golems snapped at her, burning themselves on her cocoon.

Her back arched as she rose off the ground. Fire and arcs surged into a blur of colors. It halted for a second, leaving her silently hovering.

A sphere of light erupted from her body, scorching and pulverizing golems. It stretched to the walls as it flattened, rending the rest and the homunculus.

When the light faded, Chekov was gone.

Sinkua offered his dagger to Nikasu with firm but apologetic eyes. Nikasu grabbed his wrist and pulled him nearer.

"Don't," she pleaded, "You can't do this."

"I have to," he said, returning her scythes, "We're barely holding on. We have to cut MalVek off before he gets this strong."

"But we are holding on," Nikasu said, "And Galo will be here soon."

"Nikasu…"

"You know him!" she cut off, "He's on his way right now."

"Nikasu," Sinkua implored, "When all of you were rescuing me…" He trailed off, clearing his throat. "MalVek and The Harvester got to him."

Nikasu's eyes welled up. Her chin trembled. "You mean he's…?"

"I dislodged his soul from The Harvester," he said, "Leviathan is gone, too."

"H… How? How could…?" she stammered, "No. He couldn't have."

"I don't know if this will comfort you as much as it did me," he said, "But I think it took both of them to take him down."

"It doesn't," Nikasu said, stymying a chuckle against her tears, "But Leviathan? Did The Harvester…?"

Sinkua passed his dagger to his free hand. He brushed her cheekbones, wiping away her tears with the back of his hand and the flat of his dagger. He pulled her hand against the Phoenix Ruby.

Phoenix's thoughts coursed through Nemesis and trickled into Nikasu's mind. She looked up at Sinkua with wide eyes and put her other arm around him. He put both arms around her, sandwiching her hand between them. She leaned her forehead against his shoulder.

With teary eyes, Nikasu accepted the dagger.

Uro paid the cabby before the car came to a full stop. The driver began to ask about the mansion, but Uro climbed out and slammed the door.

Uro grumbled to himself as he stormed across the lawn. The sun was nearly up. It had been so long since they had been scattered, he would surely be too late no matter how soon he got the formula and samples. And regardless of who else wouldn't cooperate, he alone would be held to blame.

Not that that was anything new. It was just like Jevana without the intimacy.

He threw open the front door, closed his eyes, took a deep breath, and stepped through. The air thrummed and thudded, and when he opened his eyes, he stood in the back yard.

He blurted an expletive. Someone called to him, and a middle-aged man ran up to greet him.

"Uro, right?" he said, offering a handshake, "MelDas. I don't think we've…"

"We have," Uro interrupted, accepting the handshake halfheartedly, "Briefly."

"Seems we have a problem."

"No shit," Uro said, "I need a portal strip so I can get back to Quarun, and I've been in a hurry for a few hours. So, I'm damn sure too late now, but…"

"Whoa whoa, calm down there," MelDas said, "I'm sure I can get you a portal strip."

"You can?" Uro asked, "So, you can get inside?"

"Oh, no, I'm afraid not. Nobody can."

"Then why…?"

"Am I the only one here?" MelDas supplied, "Everyone else went out. My kids are with my sister. I stayed behind in case anyone came home."

"Then where are you going to get a portal strip?"

"FerLyn," MelDas said, "She didn't talk much about her professional life, but I figure she must have those kinds of connections."

Uro pinched the bridge of his nose. "You think," he grumbled, "we can visit your wife in prison and ask her for a portal strip?"

"Well, I know it won't be as quick as you'd like."

"It won't happen at all, because she's dead, you jackass," Uro said, "Your wife hung herself. Nobody told you because they thought they were protecting you."

"What...?" MelDas stammered, "That can't be right. She would never."

"She did," Uro said, "Pretty sure she was having an affair, too. She and OshMar had a double suicide pact."

"Well, I don't..." MelDas said, hunkering down in the grass, "I can't... First the house... Then... No. OshMar was my friend. But now..."

"Look, you wanna blubber and be useless, that's on you," Uro chided, "I'll take the long way to Quarun." He shoved his hands in his pockets and walked away, heading around to the front of Drakougeneospa. "Like I should've been doing all along."

Pandora smiled at Nikasu with piercing eyes as she accepted the dagger. She brushed past her, dragging her fingertip along the girl's cheek.

"We'll be done here soon," she whispered.

When she reached Sinkua, she pulled his folded arms apart. But as she went in with the dagger, he nudged it aside.

"Not like that," he said, maliceless and steady, "If it was that simple, I wouldn't carry that around with me."

"I suppose not," Pandora said, retracting the dagger, "What do I do, then?"

"We've agreed to our terms. Now we need a blood bond," Sinkua explained, "Lift the dagger and let me hold it with you."

Pandora did as instructed, interlocking her fingers with his. Though hers encircled his entire hand and came around to her own wrist.

"Good," Sinkua said, measuring his eye contact with her, "Now, we each draw blood. A drop is enough, so don't overdo it."

"Sinkua, dear, I know better than to kill you when I'm this close to my prize."

"And I know better than to think I could kill you with this dagger."

They nodded to each other, then each nicked the back of their other hand with the dagger. Red and black bloods mingled into a single rivulet.

"Now, we pierce the Phoenix Ruby together," Sinkua said, "and she'll become bound to you."

Together, Sinkua and Pandora plunged the dagger into the center of the four-pointed ruby star. Pyromantic milystis spewed from the punctured Phoenix Ruby, churning around the two of them. Sinkua's body grew cold. His vision blurred. His shoulders slumped. Cracks spread from the edges of the hole, reaching for the tips of the star.

Pandora tightened her grip as she tipped his chin up, locking him in eye contact. After a lingering stare, she pulled him in and whispered in his ear.

"But you'd gladly risk your own, wouldn't you?"

Spril clenched his eyes shut. His last memories of his birth parents swarmed his thoughts. That old house, giant in the eyes of a child, crumbled around him. But for all his fear and the distortion of time, he only ran up and down the hall. He never moved beyond his parents' bedroom. He was trapped in a cycle of failure.

Through what little effort he could exert, he focused on his parents telling him to leave. This wasn't a chance at redemption. He couldn't change his past. He couldn't have known then what he knew now. He was trapped by his desire to assert new knowledge on an old memory.

He walked away, just as it had actually happened. Soon, he was pounding on the front door, and Phylus dragged him out.

The memory blurred through several months. Phylus taught him things that his parents didn't get the chance to. He met Yrlis. He held Vielle for the first time. And through it all, he held on to thoughts of his parents. Not their deaths, but their lives.

He hadn't forgotten them. He had just buried the memory of failure and loss so deeply that they went with it.

Spril opened his eyes. The ground felt silent, but trembling windows on nearby buildings said otherwise. He got to his feet and beat out a fierce sprint toward the shimmering homunculus.

Fresh cracks swept under his feet as buildings blurred past. The wind whipped and pounded against his face. The homunculus stomped, shredding the pavement with shockwaves.

But Spril powered through, weight and center of gravity shifting with the tremors. One block away, he drew his quarterstaff and brought it to his shoulder.

He didn't slow until he was three steps past the shimmering homunculus. The end of his quarterstaff went into its mouth and erupted under the base of its skull. Spril dragged it out of the street and drove into the side of the building it had jumped from.

Spril pulled his quarterstaff from the dead homunculus and looked back to where he had left the motorcycle.

Sinkua struggled in vain against Pandora's strength as she punctured his sternum. His bones creaked as she clamped harder.

But in a streak of silver and violet, Nemesis took hold of her, all but manifesting upon her. The gravimantic dragon wrenched against her, keeping her from driving the blade deeper but failing to pull her back.

Pandora whirled on him in a nigh imperceptible blur. Nemesis slashed against her momentum, cleaving her hand behind the wrist. Scarcely flinching at the loss, she snatched him by the throat with her other hand and hurled him up and away.

She clenched her fist, and Nemesis suspended in the air. As she slowly opened her hand, his colors blurred and smeared toward opposite horizons in ephemeral flickers. Soon, his body itself flickered as well until it became a pale fleeting glimmer.

Pandora flattened her hand. The blurs of color snapped away from his body and regained their shapes at opposite ends of the streak. Each with one half of Nemesis's body.

Nikasu cried out in anguish at the death of her Etherworlder. Her Khosmaetherean. And again when her brother's blood splattered over Pandora's back as he drove the dagger into his own chest.

Khirsan whipped at the biomechs with his segmented staff. Other patrons, the particularly brave or reckless, joined in with whatever they could arm themselves with. The cashier spent his bullets sparingly, aiming only at those well away from other people.

But they kept piling in. Stranger still, they endured surely fatal impacts about as often as they spontaneously shorted out.

Khirsan's focus faltered as someone entered with alarming calmness and grabbed an empty tray from above the garbage can. Still fighting off the encroaching hordes, Khirsan called out to the man, but he didn't answer.

Instead, the man walked to an empty booth, pulled the tray to his shoulder, and threw his entire torso into one solid swing.

The biomechs vanished along with the damage they had done. Slumped over the table under the newcomer's tray lay a faintly glowing homunculus.

Khirsan waved the cashier into the dining room as he approached the newcomer.

"How did you..."

He turned around and shook his head. Fixating on Khirsan's face, he signaled for him to speak.

"How did you know?" Khirsan asked, "Why weren't you affected?"

"I'm deaf," the man sounded out, "He was too calm."

"Wow. Thank you," Khirsan said, making sure the man could see his mouth, "You knew that thing was doing it just from that?"

"I guessed," he said, "And he looked like an asshole."

The deaf man and Khirsan shared a brief laugh.

"You should go," Khirsan insisted, "You don't want to deal with the guy who set this up."

The deaf man gave him a firm handshake, then helped himself to a cup of ice water on his way out the door.

Khirsan turned to the cashier and beckoned for the gun. The cashier shook his head.

"You can't just kill a man for..."

"That isn't a man," Khirsan interrupted, "It's not even human. It's an unfeeling and unthinking instrument of war. No conscience. Mock sentience."

"Maybe we should try..."

"To reason with them? To save them?" Khirsan chided, "I admire your compassion, but it's misplaced. They don't have the capacity to want anything else."

The cashier began to mount a third protest. Khirsan snatched the pistol from his inattentive hand. He pressed the barrel to the back of the homunculus's head and pulled the trigger.

The shimmer faded. Khirsan slapped the gun back into the cashier's hand, and he left to pick up Uro's trail.

Blood trickled from the crooked wound as Sinkua staggered back. Milystis poured out more aggressively, pulling back to encompass only himself. It grew thicker, glowed brighter.

Pandora grabbed at him, but the milystis solidified into a shield of light. She reared back and snarled at him.

Brilliant crimson milystis cocooned Sinkua in solid light. The chrysalis elevated, lifting him with it. Ruby fragments crumbled from his chest and melted into the milystis as they fell past his feet. Pandora rose to meet him, but a concussive blast from his shell knocked her to the ground.

Avian legs sprouted from the bottom of the chrysalis. The top assumed the shape of a beaked dragon's head. Wings reached out from the sides, stretching beyond the edges of the plaza. The draconic mass with Sinkua floating in the center rippled into textures of scales and feathers.

Sinkua turned his head to face Nikasu. Phoenix's head moved in unison. He reached out his hand, and Phoenix curled a wing to Nikasu's side. As he spoke, his voice channeled down the fiery wing to reach her.

"Hold... your... ground."

Sinkua and Phoenix tucked in their limbs, swelling the light to blinding intensity, and opened with a deafening bellow and shriek.

Milystis and fire swept across and beyond the ruined plaza of Bealstilla. Sinkua's body charred and hardened into brimstone and ash. Cracks wove through his flesh. Fragments of him crumbled away and cast off through the milystic conflagration. Layer by layer, his body disintegrated into scorched detritus.

The milystic glow faded. But Bealstilla still burned. And Sinkua's ashes fell upon the city.

A distant hum echoed down the hall. Calhosin rattled his bars and called to the homunculus.

"You need someone to take his place, right?" he said, nodding to Sbaglien's remains, "Take me. Leave everyone else out of it."

The homunculus regarded him coldly as it walked to his cell. "You are unworthy, cattle."

"Calhosin!" PavRal called out, "What are you doing?"

The homunculus turned to face PavRal. "You might do."

Calhosin grabbed the homunculus and slammed it back against the bars. The homunculus whirled on him and unleashed a thunderous bellow. Calhosin spun behind the wall as the gate buckled and collapsed.

He rushed across the hall, while Biroe and the guard accompanying them retreated. Calhosin rattled PavRal's gate, goading the homunculus to shout it down. As Calhosin ran to Inre's cell, the homunculus caught PavRal by the throat and hurled him into the back of his cell. A faint clacking joined the distant hum.

The homunculus caught up to Calhosin. He scrambled out of the way as it shouted, but Inre didn't fare as well. The crumpled gate launched out of the frame and glanced off her shoulder before breaking the back wall. Inre vanished through the hole.

Calhosin clamped his hands around the homunculus's throat. The homunculus wrenched his hands off and jabbed him in the solar plexus, doubling him over.

PavRal ran at the homunculus from behind. But he approached too noisily, and the homunculus whirled to palm his face and shoved him at the wall. The clacking hastened as it grew louder.

"Your arrogance," the homunculus rasped at Calhosin, "renders you unworthy of even being food." It rolled its neck and swallowed. "Die as the traitor did," it said, its voice clear and robust, "Purposeless."

Spril tore into the hall on an electric motorcycle, clapping his quarterstaff against the floor. The shimmering homunculus bellowed at him, rippling the walls and ceiling. He hurled his quarterstaff, but the churning air suspended it and reduced it to splinters. Spril braked and leaned into a fishtail, sliding under the destructive sound waves.

The bellowing stopped as a blade erupted from the homunculus's neck. Another followed between its eyes. As it collapsed, Inre stood behind it at the end of the hall, hand extended.

They exchanged introductions as she approached. Spril relayed news of Elemeno's death, explaining that she had entrusted him with the remote and code. The barrier was down.

Being that she wasn't a prisoner, Spril offered Inre a ride out on the borrowed motorcycle. He promised the rest that he would appeal to Chairwoman TolRou to have them relocated.

The air thrummed far behind them, but the hum of the motor and tires on concrete drowned it out.

Nikasu slowly pushed herself upright as the flames subsided. Soot caked her sweaty skin, but she was unharmed. Tears smeared through the ash on her cheeks.

Her Etherworlder was gone. Phoenix was gone. Her brother was gone. What remained of Bealstilla had been razed. But Pandora had been obliterated. The only thing left to do was to destroy MalVek.

She was the last Hybrid, Yggdrasil the last Etherworlder. But with only a fraction of Pandora's powers in his arsenal, she felt they just might stand a chance.

Her throat swelled and heart sank as a silhouette manifested in the dissipating smoke. Wriggling tentacles sprouted from the shape. Nikasu's arms tensed.

The smoke cleared, and there stood Pandora, nude and covered in ashes and char marks. She sauntered across the plaza ruins with black and green tentacles writhing from her back. A new hand grew from the thick black blood falling from her wrist.

Nikasu collapsed to her hands and knees. Ashy rivulets of sweat and tears fell from her face. Her breathing grew ragged. Her muscles tightened beyond pain and into adrenalized numbness.

Black and purple oil seeped through her pores and hardened into chitin. Her eye sockets stretched, eyeballs expanding to fill them. Her pupils compounded. Her chitinous limbs extended, forearm plates stretching into blades. The ground beneath her hands and knees sank under the mounting concentration of gravimantic milystis.

Curved iridescent blades sprouted from Pandora's hands. Nikasu peeled a scythe out of her chitin and whipped it at Pandora with devastating force.

Pandora pointed a blade at it. The air thrummed, and the scythe collapsed. She dashed at Nikasu, carving a gully with her milystis as she hovered just above the ground.

Nikasu drew her second scythe and caught Pandora's first iridescent blur of a slash on it. Her legs became heavy, knees locking and feet digging into the ground. She tried to counteract Pandora's gravimantic force, but her bones strained as Pandora amplified her output.

Nikasu ground her teeth as Pandora bobbed and shifted around her, despite her milystic efforts to hold her in place. Immobilized from the waist down, she twisted her mantis-like torso to follow her. Nikasu deflected Pandora's screaming slashes with the benefits of accelerated perception and numerous vantage points.

But her vision clouded with every inhuman effort. Pandora scarcely bothered to parry or dodge, as even with her amplified strength, Nikasu's scythe and claws barely scathed her skin.

Pandora grabbed her by the throat. Nikasu dropped her scythe as her body lightened abruptly enough to nauseate her. She swept her leg across Pandora's ankles, nicking flesh and pulling her feet out from under her. Pandora hovered on a downdraft, though, and she flung Nikasu away. Sky and ground from some two dozen angles spiraled by as Nikasu tumbled through the air.

She landed facedown. As she looked up, she saw Pandora straight ahead and approaching in no particular hurry. In one direction lay Epelun. In another, closer but more in Pandora's path, was one of her scythes. Her second was behind Pandora. She couldn't see Epesol, last resort though it was.

The ground rumbled. Nikasu struggled to her feet. Her vision melted into shadows and smoke. Unarmed beyond her chitin and faltering activation, she watched as the blurring form of Pandora approached.

Nikasu silently stood her ground.

Gabdur closed in on the homunculus with every circling step. Farim twirled the photonic fauchard around her wrist.

Gabdur lunged with the spider mine, but its prongs only scraped the homunculus's side as it whirled around. With a flick of its index finger, Gabdur vanished and reappeared halfway across the lobby and from there sailed into the wall.

But in the time it took the homunculus to turn around, Farim cleaved its head with a single decisive swipe.

Gabdur groaned as he struggled to get back to his feet. Farim crossed the lobby to help. But both froze as a third voice filled the room.

"I should thank you," the voice said, "They're so much easier to harvest when their head isn't in the way."

Light and shadows unfolded, and MalVek and Jevana emerged.

Farim ran at them. Jevana turned to face her and clenched her fist. The photonic fauchard disintegrated as the generator bent around Farim's hand. Farim halted and stammered, shaking it off of her hand. Jevana smiled with empty eyes.

"Ferrokinesis," MalVek said, "Very useful for dealing with uppity interlopers."

He beckoned Jevana's attention and gestured to Gabdur. With a flick of her wrist, the spider mine flew from his hand and embedded in the wall.

MalVek crouched beside the beheaded homunculus and sank his teeth into the exposed spinal column. Pinkish fluid ran down his chin and the homunculus's back as he sucked out blood and spinal fluid.

MalVek came upright with the desiccated homunculus at his feet. Jevana hit the button on the spider mine, blasting a hole in the exterior wall. MalVek gave her a beckoning gesture, and she vanished and reappeared at his side. Sections of wall continued to break away, the hole spreading to connect with windows and the hole left by the orb.

Gabdur and Farim charged at them. But with a wave of MalVek's hand, shadows and light folded to envelop Jevana and himself. In a blink, they were gone. The fractalized light of an active portal filled the spreading hole.

Chitin chipped and melted off of Nikasu's skin. Her compound eyes reverted to their natural Hybrid state. Her body trembled as she tapped into milystic stores deeper than she had ever reached.

The rumbling in the ground drew closer. Nikasu lowered herself to one knee and wedged her fingers in the charred soil. She fixated on Epelun.

Pandora paused and traced Nikasu's gaze. She smirked and continued her tauntful sauntering.

But her next steps were heavy and strained by Nikasu's compounding milystic will. By the time Nikasu could barely hold her head up, Pandora could no longer muster the strength to lift her own legs.

Pandora flicked her elbows, and a pair of iridescent scimitars wrapped in black lightning spawned from her forearms. She threw both, and lightning arced between them as they wove around each other.

The air crackled as the rumbling crescendoed into a domineering thunder. A monstrous spear burst through Pandora's chest, spraying tar-like blood as it gored her torso.

Odin rode Sleipnir into the scorched plaza as his spear split the iridescent scimitars. The gaping hole in Pandora began to weave itself shut as she whirled on the resurrected Etherworlder duo. Odin seized her by the throat as his spear struck the ground far behind Nikasu.

A vortex opened at the strike point, a churning essence of darkness. Odin crushed Pandora's neck in his hand, and her body went limp.

Odin rode past Nikasu with no acknowledgment. He flung Pandora into the void where she began to unravel into strands of gleaming darkness. Odin recovered his spear and rode off toward the horizon.

The vortex closed. Pandora was no more. The Netherworld had consumed her.

Phylus shoved the rifle into MarLys's hand. "Do exactly as I tell you."

She braced the barrel on her claw hand and curled her natural hand over the trigger housing. With his guidance, she nestled the stock against the crook of her shoulder. She watched the distant homunculus through the sight, drifting to keep it centered.

Together, MarLys and Phylus gauged the wind by the rustling of leaves. She shifted her focus, tracking the homunculus off center to accommodate. She took a few deep steadying breaths.

At the end of a long exhale, at Phylus's direction, MarLys pulled the trigger. The shimmer faded, and the remaining silhouette collapsed.

The undead dropped where they stood. Shortly after, the armored vehicles filed into the parking lot. MarLys set the rifle down as she and Phylus sat together on the stoop.

Phylus's earpiece buzzed. MarLys's soon followed.

Nikasu collapsed into a heap of herself. She hugged her knees to her chest as tears smeared her ashy cheeks. The sound of Sleipnir's galloping vanished behind the distant roll of the ocean.

Her earpiece buzzed. She whimpered, stricken by a nauseating clash of hope and despair. Hand trembling, she managed to push the button.

"H-... Hello?"

"... Nikasu?"

She pushed herself somewhat upright. "Mister Murdega?"

"No need for formality," he said, "We lost touch, but it looks like we're coming back online now. Don't know how either happened, but..."

"Murdega?" Nikasu cut in, "Have you seen my mom?"

Malia's voice came through from a slight distance. "I'm right here, sweetie," she said, "Nalygen invited me to ride back to Berinin with her. But I found Murdega and went with him instead."

"What happened, Nikasu?" Murdega asked, "Where are you?"

"Galo got left behind when we got scattered," Nikasu said, swallowing hard. Her earpiece clicked. "MalVek and The Harvester killed him and Leviathan."

"Oh Nikasu," Malia gasped, her voice clear now, "I am so sorry."

"Wait to apologize," Nikasu insisted, "Odin and Sleipnir died to destroy The Veil. Sinkua killed Seriamus. Nemesis and I helped him and Phoenix fight Pandora. Pandora killed Nemesis. Sinkua and Phoenix sacrificed themselves. Burned down Bealstilla. Pandora survived. Odin and Sleipnir came back. Threw Pandora into the Netherworld."

"Oh…" Malia exhaled, "Oh wow. I am… I don't know. That's a lot to take in. Anything you need, you just tell me, okay."

"Could you just…" Nikasu said, choking back tears, "Could you come pick me up? I don't want to be here anymore."

"Where are you?" Murdega asked, "Where exactly was The Veil?"

"Show me true north, and I can get the bearings," Malia said, "Sit tight, Nikasu. We'll be there soon."

"Okay. Thank you," Nikasu said, "I'll make a signal fire."

"I'll stay on with you the whole time."

"Thanks, Mom," Nikasu said, "Have you heard from Dad?"

"Phylus? Not yet."

"Okay. I'm gonna try to reach him."

"That's a good idea," Malia said, "I'll work on everyone else."

Phylus and MarLys listened as the others checked in and reported. Meanwhile, federal leaders, Judges, and their drivers and guards filed out of their armored cars, puzzling at the scattered corpses. High Magistrate Orthean approached the stoop with his eyes narrowed and mouth agape.

"Prime Minister Phylus!" he remarked, as much relieved as startled, "What's going on here? Who's this with you?"

"And what happened to your eye?" Governess Premier Subralis interjected, "And her hand?"

"Well, I'll just say what we're all thinking," Grand Sultan Zelphius said, "How the fuck did all these dead bodies get here?"

Phylus stepped to the edge of the stoop to look over the gathered crowd. As unsettling reports accumulated in his earpiece, he came to wear a stern scowl.

"I would dare say," he began, "that none of us truly deserves to be here. That is not particularly to say that we are to blame for what happened. But we certainly are accountable. Here we stand, the greatest influences in Ouristihra, but by our failures in judgment have we enabled catastrophe.

The parking lot at Hillside Oncology was full when they pulled in. But the lights were out, and every tire they could see had gone flat.

Jex roused Dourias. No response. His heartbeat and radial pulses were silent. Jex struck the back window.

The driver parked and came around to the back of the truck. She urged Jex to wait with Dourias while she scouted for help. He asked that she open the window and keep the radio on. When she had opened her door, he heard a snippet of some other strange phenomenon on the radio. He needed to hear more.

As Jex sat and listened to what must have been other homunculus sightings, his earpiece buzzed.

"What we need to understand is that what we just experienced, the aftermath of which surrounds us, was not an isolated incident. As I speak, dozens of corroborated reports of similar events are being broadcast over numerous radio stations. Countless eye witnesses have reported strange balls of light flying in from the south and striking enigmatic figures. They were androgynous and apathetic, remarkable only in how perfectly neutral they appeared. These figures absorbed the light, and each became the epicenter of a supernatural event.

Yrlis sat before a doorframe in the middle of a gunmetal gray room. When the portal light dissipated, the frame rolled to a different spot along a network of meandering tracks embedded in the floor.

The room had no windows and no doors. There was a chair and a desk with a single drawer and a typewriter. Next to it was a filing cabinet. Inside the desk drawer, she found a single portal strip and two folders. One was labeled for The Weapon. The other for Dryads and the Yggdrasil Hybrid.

"Seisms far from fault lines. Tornadoes moving uphill. Deep freezes in the Southlands. Sudden wildfires in the Northlands. Black lightning from clear skies. Swaths of unidentifiable worms in green sludge. Mass hallucinations. Metal spontaneously bending and unraveling. Inorganic materials forming animate creatures. Buildings and other large objects vanishing through ripples of light. And, of course, the dead walking.

"Before this, there were several sightings of a growing migration of semi-humanoid creatures. They literally appeared out of nowhere and vanished just the same. While they ignored anyone not in their path, those who were, quite tragically, met grisly ends.

Uro sat in the back of a cab, watching the sunrise through the windshield. His new friends had weeded him out. The people they trusted didn't trust him. Drakougeneospa had shunned him. Certain that he was too late to make any difference, he wondered if it was worth retrieving Project Cerulean.

Or if it was worth proving himself.

"This is where we come to be accountable. Both these creatures and the glowing figures were weapons of those who masterminded these phenomena. But while the glowing figures were instruments, the creatures were victims forced into such states and thus into servitude.

The churning sounds closed in on Spril and Inre as they fled on the borrowed motorcycle. Inre looked back, spat an expletive, and shook Spril's shoulder.

Luminous liquid fractals unfolded through the interior walls of the prison. Spril stopped the bike to consider their options, wincing as the dull humming swelled to a deafening thunder. He rubbed the back of his neck, looking back and forth between the encroaching fractals and the remaining halls. His head bobbed, eyelids becoming heavy.

Inre pivoted in front of him and nudged him into the back seat, then kept driving for the exit.

"Piecemeal efforts of rebels and visionaries had nearly eradicated The Avatars of Fate. But when we were asked to finish the job, we answered with complacency at best, corroboration at worst. They were thus revitalized, stronger and more subversive than ever. And why did we allow this to happen? What did any of us stand to gain?

"The Avatars of Fate promise prosperity to their followers. But they offer it not to the destitute but to those already in positions of influence. Wealth and prestige for those with plenty. Yet, despite our bounties, many of us allow ourselves to be leashed by greed. They buy our silence and cooperation, and they seize our influence as they convince us that they bestowed it on us. And with this manipulation, they tell us who to fear.

Khirsan asked the hospital receptionist if Uro had signed in as a guest, but just like the last two, this one hadn't seen him. Though hope dwindled, he persisted in asking about EshCal.

She was a patient at this one, but even though he had come during visiting hours, there were only two guests who were permitted to see her. Her security had been cinched up since her most recent visitor.

Sinkua had tried to strangle her.

"Many here have gone on record as resenting and distrusting the Hybrids. They have been called unruly, inhuman, impunitous, and narcissistic. The Avatars convinced us that the Hybrids sought to conquer and supplant the very human society that they were born into. The society they fought to protect. See, while these phenomena arose from The Avatars enslaving Hybrids, those very Hybrids broke their chains and sought to destroy the source.

"In fact, three Hybrids gave their lives to this cause in the past week, leaving only one of them alive. And while only one Hybrid was my genetic kin, every one of them has been like a son or daughter to me. But I no longer have any resentment for any of you. Just as they fought for everyone unconditionally, I extend my hand for unity.

Convicts and guards walked the open prison halls with drifting eyes as liquid fractals spread over the walls and floors. MalVek had cast them into this boundless churning sea with a gesture. His companion had hoisted the dead homunculus across her shoulders, and the three had vanished.

And Spril and Inre had left them behind.

"It may have taken the Hybrids' unique capabilities to stop the source of this catastrophe. But it was human intellect and perseverance that overcame each phenomenon. And since a threat still looms with the new leader of The Avatars of Fate empowered by these events, it is our responsibility to unify and stop him.

"Now, I would never claim that I alone know or know at all how to stop him. All I know is that we must cooperate with one another with honesty and transparency. If those who have coordinated with The Avatars will sever your ties, I and the rest of us will forgive and work with you. But if you will not, even knowing what their machinations have wrought, know that a world that cannot survive you is a world that will not suffer you.

Gabdur ran his thumb along a seam in the floorboards. At a slight dip, he dug his thumbnail in and flipped up a tiny panel. He pushed the uncovered button, and a larger panel opened to reveal a staircase into a cellar. He beckoned Farim.

"Gather up anything that looks like it has anything to do with portal generation," Gabdur urged, "I'll deal with the vending machines."

Farim nodded and headed into the cellar. Gabdur, meanwhile, grabbed a weapon generator and made for the vending machines. He stared off into the distance.

The walls had been destroyed. Churning liquid fractals stretched to every horizon. And they were beginning to encroach on the floorboards.

"For the rest, I ask not that you line up behind me. I am not your leader. History should not remember my name through this better than any of yours. But what we do will resonate through the posterity that we will ensure. And so, I invite you to stand with me!

Nikasu sat in Murdega's dinghy, hugging her knees to her chest. She leaned against Malia as she listened to the other voices in her earpiece. She no longer found solace in sharing what happened in Bealstilla, and news from elsewhere scarcely fared better.

Dourias's heart couldn't endure the transformation. None of them had been able to reach Uro, Farim, or Gabdur. Without Uro, nobody could check in on Khirsan either. Calling Yrlis and Spril both turned up dead air, as did Chekov and BeiLou.

There had been no sightings of the activated since the Berininites stonewalled them with Project Cerulean. Radio stations still reported homunculus encounters though. Scattered among them were sightings of strange creatures, though they were more confused than hostile. And nobody could account for MalVek and Jevana.

In the space of a week, Nikasu had lost her sister, her boyfriend, her Etherworlder, and her brother. Pandora and Seriamus had been stopped, but a comparable threat still loomed. Despite their extensive planning, the mission to save Sinkua had been an absolute catastrophe.

Nikasu stared out across the sea.

"Stand with me if you want to break your chains of greed! Stand with me if the only hate you know is for the hateful! Stand with me if you serve all people whom you govern!

"Stand with me if you cannot stand the sight of what we have become."

Epilogue

"Have you made amends with your compatriots?"

"We are, well, functionally amicable. Why do you ask?"

"This one is different. I believe he may know."

"I certainly never told him. I would not have troubled him so."

"I know. But he had a certain burden in his eyes."

"Suppose you are correct. What do you expect to come of it?"

"If there is a way back, he will find it. Help him to the best of your abilities. All of you."

"I have said I always will, and I am a man of my word. But what can we expect of you?"

"I will assist in ways to which I am specifically suited."

"Well, as much as I cannot take miracles for granted, we will help him if he returns."

"Curious. Did you not tell me you are no longer loyal to people?"

"I said I only swear servitude to principles. My loyalty to people is bilateral."

"What about my brother?"

"I promised him justice. That, my friend, will come in time."

About the Author

Meticulous to the point of obsession and ambitious to the point of anxiety, E. A. Setser is a career author and publisher trapped in a wage laborer's body. He holds a degree in accounting, which has nothing to do with any job he's ever been hired for, but it probably helps with being the founder of Social Detriment Publishing. Maybe.

E.A. lives in Indiana with his wife Celia, their son Tavin, and their cats, Bast and Echo.

A Note From the Author

Thank you so much for taking the time to read this story. Developing it, as well as the series as a whole, has been a labor of love for years. So, it means a lot when somebody decides to try it, whether they're dipping a toe in or diving headlong.

Now, I'd just like to ask that you leave a review on Amazon. I do read reviews, at least for now, and take constructive feedback into consideration.

Oh, and tell your friends about it. Especially if you liked it. Which I'm assuming you at least sort of did if you read this far. Gosh, I hope you didn't hate this book and only put up with it because you were hoping it would turn out to be so bad that it's good. That would make this whole closing awkward.

Until the next one.

Erik (E. A.) Setser